GW01605939

THE JUDAICA IMPRINT
FOR THOUGHTFUL PEOPLE

the

network

A WORLDWIDE PLOT TO LAUNCH THE FOURTH REICH

A NOVEL BY

NACHMAN SELTZER

First edition – First impression / November 2008

This is a work of fiction. Names, characters, places, and incidents are either the product of the author's imagination or are used fictitiously. Any resemblance to actual persons, living or dead, or locales is entirely coincidental.

Published by **SHAAR PRESS**
Distributed by MESORAH PUBLICATIONS, LTD.
4401 Second Avenue / Brooklyn, N.Y 11232 / (718) 921-9000

Distributed in Israel by SIFRIATI / A. GITLER
6 Hayarkon Street / Bnei Brak 51127

Distributed in Europe by LEHMANNS
Unit E, Viking Business Park, Rolling Mill Road / Jarrow, Tyne and Wear, NE32 3DP/ England

Distributed in Australia and New Zealand by GOLDS WORLD OF JUDAICA
3-13 William Street / Balaclava, Melbourne 3183 / Victoria Australia

Distributed in South Africa by KOLLEL BOOKSHOP
Ivy Common / 105 William Road / Norwood 2192, Johannesburg, South Africa

ISBN 10: 1-4226-0871-9 / ISBN 13: 978-1-4226-0871-5

Printed in the United States of America by Noble Book Press
Custom bound by Sefercraft, Inc. / 4401 Second Avenue / Brooklyn N.Y. 11232

To Yael Miriam, Adina Shira, and Ari Bari

And to Mir Bus Number 66, whose chashuve riders allow me and my laptop the use of the front seat, each and every day.

"Being assured by the Germans that they have reformed, the world has dropped the whole subject of what made Hans and Fritz commit the greatest mass horror in the pages of history. The only practical way yet discovered by the world for curing its ills is to forget about them. And hope for the best.

"I think otherwise about the Germans. They have not reformed. They are resting."

Perfidy by Ben Hecht

Acknowledgments

To the *Ribono shel Olam*, for sending me the inspiration and patience to see my projects through.

To Miriam Zakon, who has been there from the beginning.

To Shmuel Blitz and the rest of the ArtScroll team, for the effort they put into this manuscript.

To Michelle Katz, whose comments and enthusiasm were much appreciated.

And to my wife, Aliza, who watched as it all developed, who confidently believed in me and whose loyalty and support are unwavering. You are the best.

into the room's frightened occupants. Having said his piece, he turned on his heel and exited the room. The women sprang into action. The children finished the food remaining on their plates, washed their hands, then donned their thick overcoats. They were led from the room into a large conservatory at the front of the building. Its giant windows presenting an unobstructed view of the raging river, which was still covered by an uncommonly thick fog.

As they stared through the frosted windows, the fog began to lift, granting them a clear view of the turbulent river adjacent to their shelter. Even as they looked, the water began to swirl even faster. They stared in fascination at the gray metal emerging swiftly from the river's depths. The water parted to reveal the submarine's periscope. Then they were able to see the conning tower as well. Shortly thereafter, the remainder of the submarine's deck became visible.

The hatch opened and a gangplank was laid across the narrow gap, thereby linking the giant "sea creature" and the pier. Von Renbach strode across, the confidence unmistakable in the broadness of the shoulders and the keen perception in his eyes. An officer of the *Kriegsmarine* stood in the U-boat's entrance. He was clad in the white dress uniform of the Navy befitting the commander of a German sub.

"*Korvettenkapitan* Hans Berger at your service," he said after the obligatory *Heil Hitlers* had been exchanged.

"Here are your orders from Berlin," Von Renbach replied. "As you can see, they are detailed and in need of study, but the gist of your mission is summarized on the first page."

He waited for the U-boat captain to scan the written words. "The children are awaiting your order to board ship," Von Renbach said after the captain had assimilated his orders, "and I myself will ensure that everything goes as planned."

Berger moved his hand in submission, and the women began shepherding their charges from the building, down the pier, across the shaky gangplank and into the U-boat. They walked unsteadily, expelling bursts of warm breath into the frigid air. Due to their exhaustion, as much as from the submarine's movement in the shifting waters, they had to concentrate on keeping their balance. Within 20 minutes, they were all below deck. They took no notice of the faraway shouts, as the sailors undid the ropes and the U-boat slid away from the pier to be swallowed up by the dark waters of the approaching Baltic Sea.

PART ONE

1 Reb Zack

Jerusalem, Israel
March 12, 2009

I have an intellectually challenging position. I am a *Shoel U'Meishiv*, and my job is to answer the questions of the boys in the yeshivah. Some of the boys are sharp thinkers who challenge me with their analytical minds. They are always seeking for that perfect question, that amazing *p'shat*, that brilliant *chakirah*. That keeps me on my toes, makes my job interesting and stimulating, and makes getting up in the morning worthwhile. They are the ones who greet me with a big smile when I walk into the *beis midrash* in the morning, come over and begin bombarding me with their thoughts even before I've gotten my Gemara opened on the *shtender*. But there are others of course.

They aren't in a rush to enter the *beis midrash*, and once there, they aren't in any rush to open their Gemaras and begin to learn. They would much prefer to get a cup of coffee and to stand around discussing the merits of caffeinated versus decaf coffee. For many of these youths, yeshivah is a place to survive, to plod through for a year or two before moving on to bigger and better things. And even though they are there and they might as well learn, many of them kind of drift through the year.

You might be surprised, but it's not that hard to do. Especially in the winter when the Jerusalem wind gusts can push you around, a *bachur* can be forgiven for wanting to curl up under his thick blanket and pretend that he never heard the alarm clock go off. But the thing is, these are the ones who make my job so rewarding. They are my real challenge. Of course I love seeing the overall change in the atmosphere around Chanukah time when the serious *bachurim* are beginning to put in the serious learning time. But all that is nothing compared to the satisfaction that I have when I see one of the less-motivated guys starting to show even the slightest interest. But I'm getting ahead of myself.

My name is Zecharia Bernstein; known to one and all as Reb Zack. I'm on the tallish side, with a somewhat muscular build. I have straight black hair and blue eyes, and I use contact lenses. I'm about seven years older than the average *bachur* in our yeshivah, which makes me kind of like an older brother and kind of a *mashgiach*. I serve as a go-between with the boys and the *hanhalah*, appreciated by both. The boys feel that I understand them since I'm not that much older then they are, and the administration knows they can trust me to implement policy while keeping everyone happy at the same time. It's not an easy job, but I love it and take it very seriously. I make sure to prepare the Gemara before coming to yeshivah, and make sure I have a comprehensive knowledge of the basic *rishonim* as well.

The yeshivah is a middle-of-the-road place. It caters to boys from regular backgrounds whose brothers are in the top yeshivos like Mir or Brisk. Our boys, for the most part, however, are not as motivated as their brothers. Whatever the reasons, our boys can be a challenge.

I've met many of their older brothers when they come over to see how their younger siblings are doing. It makes it easier to understand my boys, and why they turned out the way they did. They probably took one look at their older brothers, decided keeping up was going to be too much of a hassle and chose a lesser competitive path. So we ended up rated not at the top but definitely nowhere near the bottom and are very pleased with our status.

Once in a while we get the atypical *baal teshuvah* as well: the kind of guy who gets his foundation in *frumkeit* at Aish HaTorah or Ohr Sameach and then seeks to make himself a niche in the FFB world. Those guys are very motivated and learning with them is a pleasure. They can be a source of friction at times, as well, when they see the regular guys wasting time over a backgammon game and give them a *mussar shmuess*. But for the most part both groups get along pretty well.

I'm at the yeshivah for the major portion of the day, but the main part of my job takes place during night *seder*. That's when I get a chance to *chap* a *shmooze* with many of the boys. This is when I come to know their personalities, their likes and dislikes. I learn what makes them angry, what they find hard to forgive, how their parents treated them and why they chose our yeshivah. I see them come into the *beis midrash*, starched shirts and hair brushed, and I see myself not so long ago and I understand everything they're going through. I'm there usually four or five times a week and I love it. The other nights, I'm free to prepare my classes or to do whatever I need to do at home.

I sit at a table in the back of the *beis midrash*. My back is to the shelves of *sefarim* lining the walls, and I try to have a bottle of Coke handy at all times under the table. My table is old and worn and covered with scratches from the pens of countless *bachurim* who have sat there over the years. Here is where the sharp guys come, holding a *Koveitz Shiurim* in their hands, asking a *kasha* on the Rashba or the Meiri. Here is where we sit on those long Thursday nights putting together a *chabura* to be delivered the next morning. And here was where I came to meet Mordy.

You have to understand that Mordy looked to the entire world like a regular guy from a normal Flatbush or Far Rockaway home. Aside from the warm *shalom aleichem* that I give every new *bachur*, I hadn't really been that involved with him. Well put together in a pressed white shirt and dark dress pants, he could have been a poster boy for us. Dirty-blond hair with a cowlick that wouldn't quit, he stood at just under 6 feet. His face was a little tanned. He had been with us for a couple of semesters, and somehow we had passed each other by like two ships in the night. But I took a sudden intense look at Mordy during Minchah one day near the end of his fourth *z'man*, and suddenly realized that there was a lot going on beneath the placid surface he presented to the world. Something told me that here was a boy who warranted my attention.

There was something in the way he stood, something in the slight slump of his shoulders that gave away his loneliness, his insecurity. It was there for a second and then it was gone, and I was left wondering if I had imagined the whole thing. I walk around sometimes during night *seder* to get a sense of what everyone is up to, and that night I made sure to end up at his seat. He was sitting with his *chavrusa* and he was listening to him as he read the first Tosafos on the *daf*. I remember, it was the first *perek* of *Gittin* and his study partner was learning Tosafos at top speed when Mordy stopped him with a barrage of questions.

The partner had obviously underestimated Mordy and was unprepared for the unexpected onslaught. I intervened with an answer, but Mordy dealt with me quickly as well. We flipped open a couple of *sefarim* and began searching through the *mefarshim* to see if any addressed his question. After a 10-minute search, we found it in the *Maggid Mishnah*. This led into a lengthy discussion between the two of us (his *chavrusa* had since retired for the evening), and our voices rose higher and higher until we finally resolved the question to our mutual satisfaction.

We looked around, suddenly aware of the silence in what had been a very noisy room just a half-hour earlier. I introduced myself again to Mordy while offering him a cup of Coke at the same time. "I'm Reb Zack," I said jokingly (because he definitely knew who I was), while pouring from the tepid warm bottle. "What's your name again?"

"Mordy," he replied. "Mordy Kahane."

"Well," I continued, "nice to meet you, Reb Mordechai Kahane. Where did you learn before coming here?"

I was expecting him to say something like Long Beach or Torah Temimah after seeing the way he could learn, but it was nothing like that at all.

"I was at Yeshivas Moreh Derech," he said, naming a famous *baal teshuvah* yeshivah in Yerushalayim, "and before that I was at university." I could tell that he was bracing himself for a barrage of questions. So I decided to change course. Instead I sat him down by my scratched and beat-up table and told him about myself. I spoke to him about my family and told him about my wife and kids. I spoke about the yeshivos where I had learned, both in New Jersey as well as in Eretz Yisrael.

Slowly he began to relax. His shoulders lost their rigidness, and he drank some Coke. I opened the shopping bag nestled by my feet and took out a cake that had been intended for the upcoming Shabbos, and gave him a slice. We sat and spoke to each other, and it was a fascinating conversation. I mean, it's not that often that you come across someone this smart with so many well-grounded opinions. Usually boys his age were more the listening type. Not Mordy. He had something to add to everything I said, and his comments were on target.

I found myself inviting him for the Friday-night *seudah* even though my wife had already mentioned that we had too many guests for Shabbos lunch and she needed a break on Friday night. But this was something else. I knew she would agree once I explained the background a little bit. It was very late by the time we finished. I shook his hand warmly and told him that I would see him at davening the next morning. I watched him leave the *beis midrash*, the slight slump in his shoulders, the uncertainty in his gait and couldn't figure him out at all! Then I removed a notebook from my drawer and began writing my impressions of that day.

I put Mordy's name on the top of the second page. It was amazing how much information my brain had assimilated. I wrote and wrote, making observations and character-trait assessments. When I finally finished writing, I reviewed what I had written and became aware that I had written a full page about Mordy and only a line or two about everybody else. Then I closed up shop and went home. Avigail wasn't exactly thrilled when I confessed that I had invited a *bachur* for Friday-night dinner, but I told her when she would meet him she would understand. Then if she still didn't agree, I owed her a meal at any restaurant of her choice, barring the most expensive ones, of course.

"You owe me a night out, anyway," she retorted in that I'm-not-mollified-yet-but-I'm-getting-there tone of voice, but then she smiled and went back to braiding *challos*. What can I say? I have a great wife.

~

The learning at the yeshivah is divided into several groups. On Friday morning one *bachur* delivers a *chabura* for the benefit of the other members of his group. I serve as a rotating consultant wending my way from group to group, listening to this one and asking a question to the next. Most of the *chaburos* were operating along expected lines: The typical questions, the straightforward answers. But in the corner of the *beis midrash* there were fireworks going on. Mordy was delivering the *chabura* in his group, and the place was up in arms!

I made my way over to the group trying to get a handle on what they were discussing. Mordy was quoting the Kehillas Yaakov, something about a monkey being used as a messenger to deliver a *get*, and everyone was jumping on him. He handled it all with charm, with aplomb and answered them all one by one. It was amazing to watch him in action, and I told him so. Then I pointed out that he hadn't answered every last question, because there was a Maharsha who disagreed with his *p'shat*. He just smiled at me and said that it would be our secret.

I was becoming more and more impressed by Reb Mordy Kahane and by his intellect and acumen. I was really looking forward to hearing my wife's take on him as well. I was sure she would have some interesting observations. Patting him on the back, I called out, "See you later," and ran to purchase the chopped liver for Shabbos lunch.

Friday afternoon had the kind of dull grayness that comes before rain. The wind blew dust particles through the streets and the smell of mildew permeated the air. I walked to the *mikveh*, holding my bag of clothes in my hand, hoping to get back home before the storm hit. As I entered the steamy room, I was greeted by several of my *bachurim*, Mordy among them. There was a *mikveh* closer to the yeshivah, but the cleanliness of this one was a decided attraction.. As I was leaving, I noticed Mordy lingering at the exit.

"What's up, Mordy?" I asked placing my hand on his shoulder.

"Nothing much," he replied. Then gathering up his courage he asked, "Are you sure that tonight's good for you? You're not too busy or anything?"

"Mordy," I said, "relax; it's going to be great! Of course it's O.K.! My family is looking forward to meeting you. We'll walk back together from yeshivah after davening, okay?" He smiled but I wondered if he was really reassured. He left the building, and I watched his tall frame rounding the corner. A good-looking boy, just lacking a touch of self-confidence. Shrugging my shoulders, I turned and left the *mikveh*. It was starting to drizzle as I approached my house, and I ran the final distance, only just beating the downpour.

The remainder of the afternoon passed in that Friday mellow mood. The CD player was on, and sometimes the kids and I just drop everything that we're doing and dance around. Then I sample the food — supposedly to make sure that everything is the way it should be — you know, no sugar in place of salt or anything like that but really because I can't wait to taste it, it's that good. Then there's getting the kids' bath ready, then clearing the dining-room table and setting it with the candlesticks, putting on the *blech* and getting dressed for Shabbos. At last, it was time to leave for shul.

Avigail and the kids were dressed in their Shabbos finery as I wished them all a "Good Shabbos," and headed out into the rawness of the winter evening. The tapping of my shoes on the sidewalk reverberated through the hilly street. I stuck my hands deep into my pockets, and looked forward to returning home and not having to venture out again for a while.

The yeshivah windows were beacons of light in a dreary world. I could hear the sounds of learning emanating into the late afternoon. The closer I got, the louder they became. Then there was a *klap* on the *bimah* and I heard the *chazzan* begin *Kabbalas Shabbos*. I ran up the stairs while taking off my coat and flung open the doors to the *beis midrash*, buttoning my suit jacket at the same time. The room was packed. I strode up the aisle, taking my seat beside the *mashgiach*, giving a quick glance around as I did so. I gazed at the rows of *bachurim* before me. Row after row of earnest faces peering into their *siddurim*, some davening out loud, others murmuring quietly to themselves. My eyes scanned the rows, subconsciously searching for the boy who so intrigued me, but not finding him. I felt a gnawing discomfort, and I found it hard to have *kavannah* and daven the way that I knew I should.

Every time the doors opened I found my eyes straying in that direction, hoping that Mordy would be the one coming through. The *chazzan* began *Lechah Dodi*, and we all began to sing in unison, those in back harmonizing in three-part harmony. I began to feel the tension leave my body. I had done the best I could. If Mordy wasn't coming to davening, that was his business. He was a big boy and nobody would benefit by my taking an undue interest in every aspect of his life.

The *chazzan* began *Lo seivoshi* using the Kossovar *nigun*, and the *mispallelim* really got into it. It's our *mashgiach's* favorite. Sure enough, he left his seat and began to form a circle, motioning to the guys that he wanted to dance. We grabbed hands and began to dance in unity, singing the holy words of *bo'ee v'shalom*, feeling the warmth and camaraderie of yeshivah life.

Faster and faster the circle moved as the song raged on with a life of its own. The *mashgiach's* face shone with a special Shabbos glow. The song reached a crescendo, and everyone froze for a moment before returning to their places, as the joy and beauty of Shabbos filled the room. At that point, the doors opened slightly, and Mordy entered the room, mingling with the *bachurim* returning to their places. He reached his place, inconspicuously opened his siddur to the right place and joined in the davening for *Mizmor Shir*.

I wished I knew what was going through the mind of this very special *bachur* standing in front of me and davening, as if his very life depended on what he was saying. The *mashgiach* spoke about the *parashah*, expounding with his usual clarity and humor. Then there was Maariv, and before I knew it, the davening was over and it was time to go home.

Everyone filed past the *Rosh Yeshivah* and *mashgiach* to wish them a *Gut Shabbos*, and there was Mordy as well, still looking apprehensive, the freckles on his face evident despite his tan. He gave me a shy smile when our eyes met, and I nodded to him. The *Rosh Yeshivah* had a few questions for me, so it was 10 minutes before we were able to leave and head home.

It was a night of promise. There was a calm in the air, the feeling that comes after a storm. The street was littered with leaves, and I softly hummed as we strolled down the street. I told Mordy what I always like to say: that the joys of living in Eretz Yisrael included the closing of the streets to traffic on Shabbos. We could hear the singing of *Shalom Aleichem* beginning to filter down from the nearby buildings, so we quickened our pace.

Mordy followed me into the lobby of my building. We were home and the sounds of children playing were clearly heard. I knocked and we could hear the scramble of kids running to the door. I turned the knob and we walked inside to a Shabbos paradise.

The sight never ceases to amaze me although it is something I have experienced every Shabbos of my life: A snowy white tablecloth draped the dining-room table. A bouquet of flowers perched proudly on the sideboard. The smell of chicken soup and kugel wafted through the air reminding us that we should get started. My wife rose from the couch and headed to the kitchen for the grape juice. I looked at Mordy and saw something in his eyes, and I just knew that tonight was going to be great.

We sang *Shalom Aleichem* and *Eishes Chayil* and I made *Kiddush*. Mordy occupied the place of honor beside my son Yeshaya, who was behaving very maturely for a 2-year-old that evening. I *bentched* the kids and we washed. Even the *challos* tasted extra special. Everything that was happening was so amazing because I knew that Mordy was finding it just the way I had hoped he would.

We sang the *zemiros* that the kids knew and they joined in, their high-pitched voices blending alongside my own deeper tenor. I asked them the questions on the *parashah* that their teachers had sent home, and rewarded them accordingly when they knew the answers. We ate delicious food, sang some more and laughed for what seemed like hours.

Then it was time to put the kids to bed. They said goodnight to Mordy, and Avigail took them into their room for *Shema*. Yeshaya ran out to give Mordy one last "Good Shabbos" hug and eventually the children's room became still. The discarded toys on the living-room floor took on a forlorn look, and the house settled into the "Shabbos Mode."

With Mordy relaxed, happy and well fed, I was hoping that he would clue me in to what was going on in his life, or at the very least tell me his background. But for the moment, that was not forthcoming, and that was fine for now. We began to sing some *zemiros* in low voices. When Avigail came out of the children's room motioning that everyone was sleeping, she began serving dessert. Suddenly, a boom of thunder resounded in the distance, and the sound of rain sizzled outside the porch door. There was a tremendous crash and a sharp flare of lightning, and the lights flickered and went out. We were left sitting around the table, the sole illumination coming from the remaining oil in the candlesticks.

The room had shrunk to our immediate island. The bookcases, coffee table and couches were shrouded in mystery, and the kitchen a world of its own. We had entered into a tiny magical place with three people, and a table laden with the Shabbos best. Our faces took on the shadows of the candlelight and it became something special: a meal to remember. The singing was more heartfelt and the food tasted better. Mordy's eyes glistened in the pool of soft light, and he offered a *d'var Torah* to which we listened attentively.

With the children safely asleep in bed, Avigail was able to join our conversation. She began asking Mordy about himself, where he was from and similar questions. Under her soft-spoken prodding, he opened up, displaying a sense of humor I hadn't noticed before and which was sharp and on the mark. He responded to her genuine interest and soon found himself sharing more than he would normally have. He even began volunteering stories about his childhood and his years in school, and how he had been offered a scholarship to some of the most prestigious universities in America. He was relaxed, the slump in his shoulders no longer visible.

Suddenly, there was a knock on the door. I answered and found six *bachurim* from the yeshivah in sodden overcoats and hats dripping water, waiting outside, having decided to brave the inclement weather for one of their frequent Friday-night visits. I ushered them inside and they settled around the table. They began to sing: a sea of harmony in a comforting darkness, the serenity of the soul. We sang with no thoughts of impressing anyone, no ideas of outdoing the next one. It was pure heart music as I like to call it.

Divrei Torah followed, and a *l'chaim* with a good *schnaps* and oatmeal cookies. More singing followed. The night wore on, and as one of the cups of oil flickered and went out, the crackling sound of its final gasps was taken as a signal. The *bachurim* put on their coats and got ready to leave. I escorted them outside and sent them on their way, motioning for Mordy to come back in for a minute or two.

The rain was letting up as Avigail wrapped a piece of cake for him to take back to yeshivah. I helped him on with his overcoat and escorted him out of the dark, but warm home and into the lobby. We waited together for a momentary lull in the downpour.

"Reb Zack," he said.

"Yes, Mordy," I replied.

"Thank you for the meal. It was one of the most memorable meals I have ever experienced. You are one of the most amazing couples I have ever met. Thank you so much."

I held his hand between my own and told him that he could count on me if ever he needed anything. The rain showed little sign of letting up, so I gave him a light push in the direction of the street, and watched as he melded with the streams of water cascading down the deserted boulevard. Then I turned and reentered the apartment. With the last cup of oil extinguished, the house was draped in complete darkness, and it was time to say "Good Shabbos."

Sunday morning a tape was playing in the dorm when I went to gather the guys to go to the *beis midrash*. The *sugya* this morning was difficult, and as soon as one *bachur* had finished asking his questions, another would materialize in his place. Before I knew it, it was time for *shiur*. I looked around the rapidly emptying room with the feeling of satisfaction I have after a morning of hard learning. Then I opened my Mishnayos to begin my own learning *sedarim*, but something caught my eye. I looked up for a second and I saw Mordy sitting in his seat near the front of the room not doing anything, just staring into space. I figured that I wouldn't disturb him, but wait a while before going over to ask if everything was all right. So I did my daily quota of Mishnayos and

Mishnah Berurah. Seeing that he was still sitting there, I made my way over to him.

"Mordy," I said tentatively, and he jumped.

"Oh hi, Reb Zack," he said, but I could see his brow furrowed and the look in his eyes. There was something bothering this boy; something on his mind that was troubling him, not allowing him to learn. I wanted to help him, but the request had to come from him. It couldn't be something that I was foisting on him.

"I'm going to *shiur,*" he told me good-naturedly, doing his best to act as if everything was just fine. He rose, slipping a piece of paper in his pocket as he did so. I was able to see that it was a printout of an e-mail. Then removing his Gemara from the *shtender,* he left the *beis midrash,* giving me a little wave as he went through the door. He was older then the average *bachur* in the yeshivah and had been around. The move would have to come from him.

The day passed in a blur of learning, lunch at home and then back for second *seder.* I gave a brief *mussar chabura* at 6:30 and then there was Maariv and supper. I had a private *chavrusa* with one of the boys who wanted to finish a *masechta* on his own. Then there was night *seder* till 10:30, when the *beis medrash* slowly emptied, except for the *masmidim* who were settled in their corners with *sefarim* piled in front of them. I gathered my *sefarim* and took the empty Coke bottle from under my table and walked out the door.

The wind was whistling through the streets during my five-minute walk home. As I walked, I went over my day in technicolor, examining each event to see if it was handled in the right way. As I reached the end of the block, I stopped to glance inside the neighborhood park out of sheer habit, and saw a form hunched over on one of the benches, huddled into his windbreaker. I took a second look and saw that it was Mordy. He was wearing a black turtleneck, black sweatpants and sneakers, and looked as if he was unwinding after a run through the park.

I can be candid at times, and this was one of those times. I knew that he was having trouble initiating a conversation and that he needed me to set the ball rolling. The look on his face indicated that he really wanted to talk. "What's wrong, Mordy?" I asked.

He was quiet for 20 seconds then replied, "Who says anything is wrong?"

"It's written all over you," I told him. "Look, whatever it is, this is not your normal mode of behavior. You are a top *bachur* who knows how to learn, and you are most definitely not the type to sit all by your lonesome in some park on a cold winter night. So what's the deal? Does it have anything to do with the e-mail I saw you holding earlier?"

"Yes," he whispered.

"Do you want to tell me about it?" I asked.

"Not yet, Reb Zack, I'm not ready to talk, yet. I'm really confused and I don't know what to do. But I'm trying to think it through on my own, and I'm hoping to come to some sort of understanding, to a decision."

If I would have been better acquainted with Mordy, I might have known what to say to that. If he was saying that he needed time alone to sort things out, that seemed like a reasonable request, so who was I to keep on prying.

"O.K.," I said. "But Mordy, just remember there really is no reason for you to shoulder something painful all on your own. There is an entire staff of amazing people waiting and eager to help you: each one of them with years of hands-on experience in every type of problem."

"I know," he said. "You're one of them."

I don't usually blush, but even men have emotions, believe it or not. "Hey, don't mention it," I said. "That's what they pay me for."

He smiled at me.

I discussed my concerns with Avigail, who had all sorts of theories about the nature of Mordy's problem. I sat back, kicked off my shoes and listened as she went off on wings of fantasy involving the Mafia, a parent who was unwell or the lack of funds to pay for his learning in Israel.

"Come into the kitchen and have some ice cream," she said. "This will take your mind off your worries," and before long I was able, for a moment, to set aside all thoughts of suffering students, and just relax. Eventually I headed for bed. I went to sleep, hoping that the morrow would bring some insight into Mordy and his dilemma.

Morning dawned with a midwinter cheerfulness. All those gray days with cloudy skies and hours of rain, and then you get up in the morning and the sky is a cobalt blue and there's a freshness in the air. There is nothing quite like winter (or for that matter spring, summer and fall) in Yerushalayim.

I got to yeshivah earlier than usual and went directly to the *mashgiach's* office. There is a list on his desk with the names of all the students and where they had previously learned. I looked for Mordy's name, and there was all the relevant information including the rabbi who had recommended our yeshivah.

Without putting too much thought into it, I lifted the receiver and dialed the number of the *baal teshuvah* yeshivah that had been Mordy's home for about a year. The phone rang many times before it was answered. A voice whispered, "Good morning, Yeshivas Moreh Derech."

"Hello," I replied, "this is Rabbi Zecharia Bernstein from Kedushas Yisrael calling. I'd like to speak with Rabbi Meir Goodman. Is he in yet?"

The voice murmured that he would check, and dropped the receiver. I was treated to a minute's worth of receiver hitting wall, swinging back and striking again. I could hear the background morning noise of yeshivah life through the phone wires. After a three-minute wait, a deeper voice came on the line. "Good morning," it said, "this is Rabbi Goodman. How can I be of assistance?"

"Hi," I said, "this is Zecharia Bernstein from Kedushas Yisrael. I'm calling regarding a *bachur* named Mordy Kahane who studied at your institution for about a year."

"One second," he said. "Mordy Kahane ... Mordy Kahane ... the name does sound familiar. Right! I remember. He did learn here, but he left about two years ago."

"How can that be?" I objected. "Mordy came to my yeshivah about a year ago. I have his application in front of me, and it lists here that his last place of learning was your yeshivah. He most definitely does not note any significant lapse in his learning and Torah way of life!"

"I don't know what to tell you," he said. "This is the situation. Mordy did learn here, and I recall that he was much sharper than most. He was a serious and diligent student and had very fine *middos*. But he wasn't so happy here."

"Why not?" I asked him.

"Well," he said, trying to remember exactly why Mordy Kahane hadn't liked Moreh Derech. "It's really been a while, so you'll excuse me for not being 100 percent up to date with all this information. But to the best of my recollection, he wasn't so happy with the fact that it was a *baal teshuvah* yeshivah. He loved learning — don't get me wrong — but he wasn't a big fan of the pressure."

"What do you mean, 'pressure'?" I asked.

"Well, try to look at it from a *baal teshuvah's* point of view for a second. Most of them are guys in their mid-20's, guys who had been for the most part successful before arriving at the yeshivah. Some dropped out of college, others gave up careers that they had already established or were in the process of establishing. They are goal-oriented boys, and they give up a tremendous amount when they set it all aside and come study in Yerushalayim.

"So the thing is, they can get very serious about their learning. So if they see someone who isn't up to the level — someone who seems to be goofing off — they have a tendency to criticize and be intolerant. If I'm not mistaken that was something that Mordy didn't like. He himself was never on the receiving end of anyone's criticism since he was very serious about his learning. But the whole attitude bothered him, and I think he was looking for a more 'chilled-out' kind of place."

"I see," I said. "I guess that explains why he came to us. The only question remaining is where he was and what he was doing from the time he left you until he showed up at our door."

"Yes, that is an important question," Rabbi Goodman said. "I hope I was able to help you out, and if you have any more questions feel free to give me a call."

I assured him that I would do just that, and we hung up with mutual wishes of *hatzlachah* on all sides. I gently replaced the receiver in its cradle, leaned back in my chair and stared at the wall near the window. *Where had he been for all that time?* The *gedolim* pictures on the walls stared right back at me, with the Chazon Ish instructing me with his piercing look to find out what was going on here.

I left the office, the thoughts whirling around my brain and went down to the dorm to round up the guys for first *seder*. Most of the rooms were empty — a good sign — but there were one or two *bachurim* who still needed prodding. I came to the last room in the hall, and after knocking on the door, I walked in finding one guy in bed in an otherwise empty room. I pulled the *trissim* upward in one yanking motion letting in the sunlight and fresh air, waking up the guy who groaned and rolled over with his pillow covering his face.

"Rise and shine, Shuey," I said cheerfully. I pulled his pillow out from under his head and got him into a sitting position. I gave him a moment to orient himself, and as I stood there I glanced around the room studying the pictures that the guys had over their beds. Then I saw Mordy's bed with an incredible number of the most beautiful pictures hanging beside it. There were photos of sunrises and sunsets, and the most amazing shots of Shacharis on the beach at dawn, with the sun shining through the palm trees and the water sparkling in the morning shine.

There were candid shots of people laughing with cups held aloft. There were dancing dolphins in Eilat, desert hikes and there proudly displayed was a blown-up photo of Mordy, standing at ease in a desert. He was clad in shorts and T-shirt with a group of people gathered around him. He was explaining something and he looked completely in his element. He looked happy and tanned and full of life and fun. There was a row of freckles marching up and over the bridge of his nose and he was smiling. I found myself smiling back at the picture.

I told Shuey to find a *minyan,* daven and begin learning without wasting any more time, and then I went into the *beis midrash* and put in a good two hours of *sugya* time.

Toward the end of the *seder*, Mordy approached holding a *Ketzos* in his hand and we discussed his question and the *Nesivos's* answer. When we finished up, I asked him if we could go for a walk during lunch. He agreed and left to go to *shiur*. I remained at my desk and thought about the enigma that was Mordy. I wondered what information was waiting for me behind that *yeshivah* facade, and if I would be able to help him.

It was still sunny as we descended the five flights of stairs leading to the back door of the yeshivah and the nearby garden. We meandered in the direction of the park where the neighborhood kids hung out. It was still early and the park was deserted. We strolled along a path, and as we rounded the bend we were struck by an incredible view. The park was set on the edge of the mountain, and we could feel the wind rushing by our faces, pushing us so that we felt as if we were tottering on the brink of the mountainside. It was an exhilarating experience.

Mordy stood beside me taking in the view, and together we enjoyed the leaves swaying in the breeze. I turned to look at Mordy at the same moment that he turned toward me and we grinned at each other. I led him through the park where we sat down in the grass, picking at the stems, and I wondered where to start.

"So, Mordy," I said, "why don't you tell me a little bit more about yourself?"

"O.K.," he said. "I grew up in Ithaca, a medium-sized city in Upstate

New York. Ithaca is an attractive college town. There are many beautiful parks, and the sound of children playing is normal and welcomed.

"I was always known as one of the smartest kids in my class," Mordy continued, "and since my parents usually bought me the latest electronic equipment, I was very popular as well.

"Jews weren't much in the news back in Ithaca, New York. Nobody mentioned the Jews for good or for bad, and I grew up without any mention of religion in my home.

"All that changed the year that Brian walked into my life."

2

Mordy

Ithaca, New York
April 8, 1999

Baseball season in Ithaca is taken very seriously by the inhabitants. There are leagues for every age, and the spark of competition gives life an edge. Every game is packed with families rooting for their high-school slugger, little-league pitcher or hard-working father out on the turf enjoying his Sunday afternoon time off. In a town where so much significance and attention was given to sports, it was no wonder that little Matt Kahane became known at a relatively young age.

From the moment Matt walked onto the ball field, everyone could see that he had that special grace natural to sports stars: the easy swinging of hips, the powerful arm and the ability to maneuver in any position he played. He was particularly good at shortstop, but he performed with distinction in almost every other position as well. Matt, in short, was every coach's dream. He began playing ball at the earliest eligible age and soon became a familiar sight on the sod, swinging his bat and sending the ball soaring into the stands.

After tryouts in different positions, they eventually settled on shortstop where he consistently ran faster, caught better, jumped higher and broke every established town record for child baseball prodigies.

He hit more home runs than anyone his age ever had before him, and his coach was a happy man. Thus the years passed, with Matt not only growing older but becoming a better baseball player in the process.

Through it all, he maintained very decent grades in school, was clean cut and a friend to one and all. Parents pointed him out to their children as a role model, but this didn't stop them from wanting to be his friend. The stands in Ithaca were full when Matt was playing ball, especially when the visiting team was visitors from out of town. They never knew what to expect, and the local populace loved to watch the reaction to their little wonder boy.

Matt would step up to the plate, study the pitcher and knock the ball into the outfield. The players, not having expected anything close to what he had done, would be sent scrambling in the vague hope of catching up to the ball. Matt would race around the bases toward home where he would be picked up by his teammates in a display of camaraderie. Nothing in the world compared to the smell of the peanuts and hot dogs, the roar of the crowd and the feel of the freshly mowed grass.

That was the way it was, at least until the day Brian McHalten moved to Ithaca. Brian was just as good a player as Matt was, and he had strengths that Matt didn't possess. Half a year older, he was taller than Matt and a little heavier as well, and he could hit the ball further and even run almost as fast. All in all, they were pretty evenly matched, and for the first time, Matt found himself with competition. That in itself wouldn't have been so bad, but having Brian around was no fun at all. What began as small rivalries developed into something much more serious, and in no time at all everyone knew that Matt and Brian could not be together for longer than 10 minutes before the sparks began to fly.

That was all off the sports field. When they were playing ball however, all fighting was put on hold, until the game was over. Brian was the team's center fielder and Matt continued at shortstop. The year they were in eighth grade was the season that everything came apart. Life was becoming unbearable to Matt whenever Brian was around. He speculated that Brian was spreading all sorts of sordid tales behind his back. Wherever he went, he had the strangest feeling that the other kids were talking about him — never to his face of course — but he knew that it was true. He was still in a position of power in relation to Brian, since eight years of bonding with the same kids doesn't evaporate from one minute to the next. But it was only a matter of time.

He would never know exactly why Brian had made it his mission to turn his life into a horror of vicious whispers and malicious slander. But the fact was that he had done all that and much more, and the tide of friendships was slowly turning in Brian's favor. Then came the first round of the Little League play-offs, and life reverted to normal for a few weeks. But it was only on the surface. Matt felt it when he walked into the locker room after a workout, and the guys stopped talking all of a sudden. There was Brian sitting right in the middle of the room with a huge smile on his face and hate smoking from his eyes. He ignored it as best he could, but he knew that it was only a matter of time before they had a showdown. It was going to happen; the only question was when.

The games passed one after another. Their team, the Ithaca Tigers, was better than ever. The stands were packed, not a seat was empty. Entire families attended each game: fathers, mothers and extended families. The crowd roared in anticipation whenever one of their sluggers stepped up to the plate. The Tigers lived up to and surpassed all expectations, and the adoration of the town knew no limits for their young stars.

The Tigers emerged in first place and moved like a tidal wave into the final play-offs prior to the Little League World Series. They took the first and second games at home with rapid force deploying a blitzkrieg of energy. Game three was lost at a park an hour away, as was game four. And so it went until they were gathered for the final deciding game of the series in the Tigers' home park: the grass cut short like a crew cut, the stands full of so many people cheering for their amazing athletes.

The game began with the opposing team up at bat. "Stan the man" Corkly was on the mound sending the visitors his best curveballs and knuckleballs, which he had perfected over the season and which were lethal examples of speed and talent. The opposing team, clueless in how to counter a style they had rarely encountered, struck out in a matter of a few short minutes. The Tigers trotted home amidst the shrieks of delight emanating from behind the stands.

But the opposing team hadn't come this far in the play-offs without knowing how to play. They, too, had a very good pitcher, and he had his own style which would take the Tigers time to get used to; time that they didn't have. They managed to score two runs in the first inning, were then retired and were held scoreless for the next four innings. The visitors came back at them with a vengeance and fury, and pulled forward to pass them until they were leading by three runs after seven innings.

The Tigers were beginning to get nervous, and the sounds from the crowd were reminiscent of Yankee Stadium under pressure. The umpire had come very close to being assaulted on three separate occasions. Both teams had sweat streaming down their backs and from their scalps.

The Tigers took the field and held the other team with bases loaded and one out. The next player popped up to center, and Brian picked the ball out of the sky as if he was catching a piece of cake, then threw it to the pitcher. The player on third broke for home, and there was action galore, as the pitcher raced for home tossing the ball to the catcher at the final moment. The runner was tagged out as he slid into home plate, the dust rising in a cloud of glory unconquered.

Once again the Tigers were up at bat, and this time they were able to rally with two runs and a sacrifice, leaving players on second and third. Then Brian was up, and he sent one flying into left field. It was caught but the man on third tagged up and headed home, scoring easily, tying the score once again. The next player struck out, and the team trudged wearily out to the field once again. It was the ninth inning. They would have to hold them and then score a few using their final chance.

Somehow "Stan the man" let one go by that was much too easy, and the batter socked it right down the middle sending it deep into right field. Ricky raced backward and picked up the ball on its second bounce, pulling back his hand and throwing it to second base, where the runner stopped and waited, his chest heaving with exertion. The game had gotten infinitely more exciting, and they were actually holding their breath. The next player struck out, as if "Stan the man" was trying to make amends. But then wiry Tim Seeber stepped up and sent one straight at Matt, who dove for the ball which went straight through his legs. It was picked up by Brian, who sent it to third where it was caught and the runner was stopped.

The team looked with murderous eyes at the huddled form of Matt, who knew that he'd never live this one down. The next hit was a calculated shot straight down the first-base line, sending the man on third home. By the end of the inning, the visitors were ahead by two. Matt knew that he had nailed his coffin shut unless he compensated by hitting something worthwhile. And he had every chance in the book to do just that.

The first man up led with a single, which was followed by a pop-up to right, which was followed by yet another single. The next batter delivered a stunning shot over the shortstop's head sending the man on third home. That made it men on first and second, and the Tigers down by one run, when the next man struck out. Matt's turn came. He trotted to home plate with a sinking feeling in his stomach. As he passed Brian sitting between two of the biggest boys on the team, he heard something which turned his legs into jelly.

"Don't mess up, Jewboy, you hear me! Mess up and you'll know what pain is all about!" These lines were spoken through closed lips, but the all boys sitting there nodded and he knew — he finally knew — what it was they had been talking about all those times he had come into the locker room and they had suddenly become quiet. He was a Jew, whatever that was, and they had just threatened him as so many gentiles had threatened his ancestors before him. He didn't know how he knew that, but it was suddenly crystal clear to him that he was in serious danger.

His legs trembled and almost gave out as he faced the pitcher and tried to concentrate, to feel the power he always felt when up at bat. But the power had deserted him, and he stood there with the strength of a little baby. The pitch came and he swung, but the ball zipped passed him leaving an illusionary gust of wind in its place. The second pitch came and he let it go. It was a ball and he breathed a very heartfelt breath of sheer relief. Why was he feeling this way? These boys were his friends! They had attended kindergarten together, played at one another's homes, celebrated their birthday parties through so many years! Maybe he was exaggerating the whole thing, but deep down he knew that it wasn't so. They were going to get him; it was just a matter of time.

The next pitch came and he took it. The bat tipped the ball into foul territory. Again the ball came at him in a cloud of terror, and it went foul again. The groan of dismay from the crowd as they realized what had happened was loud with anger and electric with dangerous currents. He stared at the ball in the pitcher's hand, watched as it was released, saw it come closer and closer, focused on it like it was a message from heaven. Again it went foul. Sweat was running down his scalp and into his eyes, stinging them with the salty liquid. He wiped his hands on his pants and waited for the next pitch. He swung. The ball hit the bat and rocketed straight into the pitcher's outstretched glove to the shouts of delight of the victorious team and the cries of disappointment of what felt like the whole world.

Broken, he made his way back to the dugout, the weight of the world on his shoulders, a cry of fear sitting unspoken deep in his throat. As he passed the group of his teammates in the dugout, each made a cutting motion across his throat. And even as he accepted the handshakes of the members of his team and the victorious visitors, he knew what it meant to be afraid.

The next few days passed in a haze of self-inflicted punishment. On the one hand, he was constantly kicking himself as to how he had bungled a supreme opportunity. Of all people, for him to have let his team down! The star of the stadium, the coolest operator, under pressure had thrown in the towel, had disappointed an entire town. On the other hand, he knew why it had happened. The fear alone had been sufficient to make him lose it, to convince him that he wasn't good enough to do what he was supposed to do, something which he knew that he could do. Instead of having his team back him up, he had had the knowledge that there was an entire fifth column hoping he would fail, gloating in his discomfort, secure in their feelings of hate even though his future meant the end of the dream of going to Williamsport, Pennsylvania for the Little League World Series. He knew that come what may, they would get him; that he was in their sight.

So he watched his step and looked out for himself as best as he could. He kept to the sidelines and took care to stay in the immediate vicinity of any available teacher that he could see. He arrived at different times, varying his schedule to keep them off his back. As soon as the bell signifying dismissal had rung, he was on his feet, jacket already on, book bag clutched in his right hand, eyes focused firmly on the door and freedom. He would race down through the halls in the direction of the entrance, dodging passing students and the custodian's carts. Upon clearing the big double doors he'd look both ways as if he were crossing the street and then sprint across the school's gigantic yard until he passed the monkey bars and swings, passed the basketball and racquetball courts and was out through the gate and then homeward.

His eyes would flash intently as he assessed the situation, sending a message to his brain informing him whether he was safe or not. He would run, oh how he ran! Like the wind on a blustery day. His cowlick stood upright as he ran headfirst into the wind and his book bag would bump against him with every step that he took. He did his best to put himself into the mind-set of the enemy, trying to imagine what he would do if he was the one attempting to corner someone on the run. He came to the conclusion that they would be waiting for him at some point on his way out of the schoolyard. There was no alternative, he would have to outthink and outguess them.

A few days went by with snide comments and clumsy attempts at shoving him and his food tray in the lunchroom, with crude messages scrawled on his locker. He had the feeling that there wasn't a soul who was sympathetic to his horrible situation. But through it all he remained vigilant and focused. He had tried telling his parents about what he was up against. They took it seriously but were powerless to act against the subtle form of harassment.

"You know what the principal would say to me if I called him up and told him what your classmates have been doing to you," his father had told him. "He'd say that there wasn't sufficient proof for anything to be done and that he'd keep a sharp lookout. But the truth is," continued his dad, "he probably wouldn't do anything of the sort since he himself is a huge ball fan, and was very unhappy with the fact that the team lost. I don't think that telling him in this case would do much good at all."

So they hadn't behaved like little kids who were running to the teacher for protection. He had taken it like a man. But his father did make up to meet him after school. For an entire week he was waiting for his son at the gate in his blue reefer jacket and corduroy pants, his six-foot bulk instilling a welcoming confidence in the badly shaken child.

With a week having gone by peacefully and uneventfully, his father felt that things had reverted back to normal, and that it was no longer imperative for him to put in a daily appearance. But Matt knew that the danger had not been averted, that they were only biding their time for the perfect moment to attack. At that point, they would stream out of the woodwork and there would be nowhere to run. He knew this in the uncanny way that he knew many things, for he sensed the malignancy and destruction that was waiting at his doorstep.

It happened two weeks later.

He exited the building and headed in the direction of home, through the playground and toward the street. There was an alcove next to the red-brick building forming a space in which the boys hung out and which they considered their clubhouse. The farther back into the alcove one went the darker and more obscured it became. Matt usually made sure to give it a wide berth, afraid of what might be waiting there.

He moved along at a quick clip, skirting the playground equipment, but then saw something that made him hesitate. There at the gate stood one of Brian's trusted lieutenants, a boy that Matt knew would have little trouble hurting him, who wouldn't think twice about causing him pain. The sight of the boy standing guard at the fence caused Matt to double back, to move in the direction of the alcove almost without knowing what he was doing. He was about five feet away when two boys came running out of the alcove heading straight toward him. He started to run to the gate and away from the alcove, but the brute from the fence had turned toward the playground and was moving up to block off any retreat he might have had in mind.

The moment of truth had arrived. It was now or never. He broke into a run, evading the two boys and moving in the direction of the monkey bars. But now there were another two boys closing in on him from between the monkey bars, turning the whole operation into a well-planned ambush. Anywhere he turned they were coming straight at him with ferocity on their faces and mayhem in their hearts. There was one remaining option and he ran for it. He doubled back in the direction of the giant sandbox located on the far side of the playground, racing with all his might as the animals converged into one big pack of wolves intent on devouring the innocent and lonely lamb.

They were all together, running after him, screaming and cursing, the anti-Semitic slurs coasting along in the wind like 10,000 swords of steel, their blades sending out rays of emotional pain, cutting to the core of his heart. He hastened past the swings, and jumped over the seesaw. He sped through a crowd of young girls, who were intently involved in a game of hopscotch, pebbles flying in all directions, girls screeching in dismay as the crowd of boys pursued him, their mob mentality openly displayed for all to see.

They were baying like hounds, frothing at the mouth, and he was running for his life. He was panting from the exertion, the insides of his chest feeling like it was on fire, and all the while they were drawing closer, their shouts reverberating through the air, echoing strongly as if magnified by a hundred microphones. He was an Olympic runner and his goal was in sight. There was the sandbox: a colossal wood-enclosed structure filled to the brim with sand and toys.

At the end of the sandbox stood a huge "thing" (for lack of a better word) that could not be described as anything in particular. It was a large climbing-activity-structure thing, and that was the way it was known, as in "Want to meet me at the thing?" Some called it "the wooden thing," but to the majority of the student body it was known as "the thing." "The thing" stood very high and wide. It was comprised of several levels, and included a variety of different activities one could enjoy while in its wooden embrace. There were poles to slide down while pretending you were a fireman, and wooden slats held in place by chains which rattled as you ran across their length during cops and robbers.

He reached the sandbox and jumped the little metal fence sinking into the sand as he did so. Ignoring the sand seeping into his sneakers, he raced across the box reaching the base of "the thing" in record time. Clutching the ladder's handles, he began to haul himself upward three rungs at a time, moving with accuracy in the direction of the uppermost floor. The pack down below had reached the sandbox and would begin climbing after him in a matter of moments. He reached the top level and flipped himself over the side before standing up and running across the surface to the far side. There was a slide there that led down to an otherwise inaccessible level.

Here he paused for a moment to catch his breath and stood poised at the top of the pole waiting for them to come. He could hear them ascending the ladder, the aggression needing an outlet, their fists waiting to strike him and then there they were; the first of the gang reached the top of "the thing," and they paused for a moment to regroup and assess the situation. They looked around from slide to slide finally seeing him waiting for them. With a roar, they took up the chase and he hurtled down the slide, hit the level underneath and then lowered himself to the level under that, using the floor to brace himself.

He was now two levels beneath them, and they were beginning to slide down as he grabbed the overhanging branch of a tree which grew alongside "the thing." The tree grew on the other side of the wall that separated the playground from Ithaca's nonsectarian only cemetery. Using the branch, he swung from the level he was standing on to the wall, where he stopped, balanced and looked back for a second to see where the enemy was. Eight feet below and spread out like a poster board, lay the cemetery.

He could see the graves interspersed by foliage and greenery, the paths leading to them perfectly manicured and well tended by a team of the most expert groundskeepers. He glanced back and saw the first of the pack lowering themselves from level two to level three, and watched as one of them lost his grip and plunged headfirst to the sandbox where he landed amidst a cloud of sand, dust and newly broken toys.

There was no time to waste. Silently he begged forgiveness from the deceased for what he was about to do. He then grabbed the branch and jumped off the wall, swinging gracefully through the air and landing with a thud on the roof of a stone gazebo housing the patriarch of Ithaca, one of its pioneer citizens. He startled a number of birds who took off in mad flight, but other than that the landing had proceeded as expected. He let the branch go, silently thanking the tree that had made it all possible and watched as the branch swung back into place. He then let himself down from the roof of the gazebo, jumped the final four feet and broke into a run in the direction of the cemetery's gate and freedom.

The gang watching from level three was struck dumb by his impudent move, and were fearful of copying his brilliant maneuver. Leaving them there, he turned his back and began walking away. But there was something nagging at his mind, something that was not right about the scene he had just witnessed. He searched his mind for what it was, but it continued to elude him, dancing right there beyond his grasp. He made his solitary way through row after row of tombstones and stone mausoleums eventually reaching the broader road on which the cars drove and gardeners traveled around on their golf carts. He turned to the right and began the long trek to the exit.

And then just as he had almost reached the exit, he knew what it was that had been bothering him. His brain had seen that someone was missing from the chase, someone important, an integral member who hadn't been after him, because he had outguessed and outmaneuvered him. And a second later he saw that he was right, as Brian McHalten detached himself from behind one of the many trees bordering the side of the road and sauntered toward him, the look of the winner on his face.

"So," he began, as his wavy black hair and dark green eyes made him as charismatic as ever, "you thought you got away? Do you think that I'm stupid? As soon as I saw you heading toward 'the thing,' I knew that this would be your ultimate destination. And the truth is," here Brian paused for emphasis, "the truth is what better place than a cemetery for me to beat you up, for me to show you the difference between Jew and Gentile."

As Brian gloated, Matt kept his eyes on the bigger boy waiting for the chance, for the moment he would make a mistake. He painted an unimpressed look on his face and stared Brian down, while knowing exactly how much danger he was in. On second thought, however, the true danger was when Brian was with his gang. Now he was alone, for the time being, and by himself he wasn't that frightening. Still, Matt didn't want to fight him, had no interest in proving anything to the bully, so he began to talk to him trying to stall for time.

"Would you mind explaining why you have a problem with me?" he said. "I never met you before this year, and I never had any problems with anyone in my class or school before you came along. So why don't you take a moment to explain where all this animosity is coming from!"

"You really want to know," said Brian, "I'll tell you. I have no problem explaining why I hate your guts! From the first day when I walked into the classroom and saw you, I knew that you were a Jew. It was written all over your face in neon lights. Jew! Jew! Jew! All it took was a little investigation on my part and I was able to find out that I was right on the mark. You are Jewish, and I hate you just because you're a Jew!" Brian's face had gone from its normally pale whiteness to a beet red, and he was so infused with hatred, he was sputtering with indignation and rage.

"My parents despise the Jews. My grandparents froth at the mouth at the mere mention of anything having to do with the Jews! Everyone I know can't stand them and makes fun of the Jews! The Jews run this country. They are the deciding force behind the economy. Half of the country's foreign policy is generated based on what the Jewish people want and need and their powerful lobby on Capitol Hill! And it was because of the Jews that my grandfather lost his job!"

"What are you talking about?" Matt asked in disbelief, not knowing how to react to the deranged boy in front of him.

"When my grandfather moved to America from Ireland, he was a young boy with no support and no friends or family. To pay for his food, he took a job in a factory that was owned by a Jewish man. The man exploited his workers making them work 14-hour days, and he paid them pennies. One day Grandpa got sick," Brian went on speaking softly, almost to himself. "He was so sick that he couldn't get out of bed. Throughout the day he tossed and turned all alone in the dirty and disgusting room that he called home, crying out for someone to help him, for someone to ease the pain. But nobody came. Nobody cared.

"For three days he lay in bed, feverish and delirious, imagining his parents in Ireland, talking to the walls, becoming so weak that he almost died from severe lack of water and food. He finally lost consciousness, and when he awoke, he crawled out of bed, climbed down the steep flight of tenement stairs and just about fell into the restaurant adjacent to his building. The owner, an Italian man, took pity on him and gave him some food and water, let him lie down on a bench in the back of the store and helped him return to himself. It took a week to regain his strength, and another few days until he was able to walk and even contemplate returning to the factory. But he knew that he had to go back. He desperately needed that job to earn a living, meager as it was. He had been a hard worker, had always come on time, had been the epitome of reliability. So he returned.

"He walked into the owner's office, hat in hand, to request his job back. He explained that he had gotten sick, that he had been so sick that he had just laid in bed waiting to die and that by some miracle he had been able to pull himself out of the apartment and into the restaurant. He asked the boss for a second chance, begged him, in fact. He promised him that he wouldn't be sorry, that he would work harder than anyone in the whole place. And you know what he did?" Brian asked a white-faced Matt. "The fat Jewish owner got out of his chair, walked over to the cowering little boy in front of him, picked him up by his collar and threw him out of the factory! And do you want to know what his name was?" Brian screamed at a much-shaken Matt. "The owner's name was Kahane! How's that for a coincidence?!"

Matt knew that there was nothing left to do but run. So he ran. He ran as if his life depended on it, using all the remaining energy that he possessed to put distance between himself and the madman who was pursuing him. Then the sky changed. Just like that, it went from a brilliant blue to a downcast gray. Huge clouds began moving into place for a tremendous thunderstorm. They were dark and angry looking, and to Matt, glancing up at them as he ran, they looked positively menacing. It was going to pour. Still, Brian chased him.

The first drops fell. They were not the typically smallish drops one associates with the beginning of a rainfall. These were large drops, and they were hitting the pavement with little smacks as they splattered every which way. His shirt was already wet, and his hair was starting to lie flat on his head. Still, he ran up one row of graves and down another, through a well-tended grove of gnarled oaks planted precisely in a row and past the monuments and sculptures, the mausoleums and gazebos.

His hair was totally plastered to his head by now. His shirt and pants were soaking wet, rain pelting on his body slowing him down with its weight. His sneakers were sodden and sopping, water squelching out of them with every step he took.

Finally, he couldn't take it anymore. He hadn't done anything wrong! Why did he have to run? Was it his fault that some horrible Jewish boss who shared his last name had mistreated Brian's grandfather!?

He turned around in a split-second decision. As thunder crashed all around him and the trees swayed alarmingly from side to side sending a shower of leaves downward in every direction, as the lightning flashed across the acrid sky and evening overtook the day, he turned around. He let Brian catch up to him, waited for that perfect moment and belted him one right in the face! He followed the first one up with another one to the stomach and waited for Brian to fall.

But Brian didn't fall! He steadied himself, and with amazing fortitude, grabbed a fallen branch and went after Matt bellowing like a wounded bear, screaming and crying as the leaves brushed his face and night began to settle over the graveyard. And then they fought. Brian was bigger and angrier, but Matt was full of indignation at what the other boy had done to him. Their emotions just about evened things out. They rolled in the dirt pummeling one another with their fists, scratching each other's arms, head butting and kicking. At one point Matt seized a handful of Brian's hair and pulled. They separated and stood up facing each other and still Brian wouldn't quit. Bleeding and hurt, he charged at Matt one more time, and this time Matt simply sidestepped him and Brian fell to the ground.

Matt ran away, through the rain, knowing that there was nothing more that could happen to him; that he was wetter than he had ever been and the rain couldn't harm him. He ran through the downpour, liberated and in bondage simultaneously. He knew that Brian was chasing him through the darkness of the graveyard, but he had reached the point of no longer caring. He ran like a demon past grave after grave, seeing the letters carved in granite and marble with the rain streaming down, and he sobbed from sheer exhaustion and the exhilaration of no longer being afraid.

The cemetery's gates came into view. Tall and forbidding, the metal fence — sharp and pointed at the tops — was waiting to impale anyone trying to climb over. He went under, just squeezed himself between the bottom of the fence and the ground, scraping his elbows and face as he did so, but at last emerging from the graveyard to the street outside. The street lamps were illuminating the empty road that stretched off seemingly into infinity, and he wept like he had never wept before.

A pair of headlights came at him from the distance, and the closer they came, the more he was sure that they were his. They stopped close by, and the door opened up on the driver's side and his father stepped out. A look of disbelief crossed his face as he witnessed his son's sorry state. He did not say a word. He just walked over to his son and hugged him close to his chest, disregarding the mud, blood and rain which were soiling his wool suit, their tears mingling together, streaming off them to fall to the ground. Matt had no idea how long they stood there.

They finally broke apart and his father supported him to the car. The radio was playing as if all was normal in the world, as if the last two hours had never taken place, as if he had dreamed up the whole thing. But his wet and bloodied clothing and swollen battered face bore testimony that it had truly taken place. He knew then that he would never forget what had happened that night for as long as he lived.

3
Dietrich Eberhart

Hamburg, Germany
January 13, 2009

The nightclub was bursting at the seams. The area by the bar was packed shoulder to shoulder, four rows deep. Bartenders worked nonstop, passing out drinks as if this was the last drop of alcohol on the face of the planet. Club Salute on a Saturday night was the place to be. The band was playing an eclectic mix of jazz and trance music that had a tinge of the military to it. The crowd was trendy and young, but there was something about them, something in the look in their eyes that hinted at people who weren't just hanging out for a drink. They were there for something more than that.

The front of the club faced a busy street, sandwiched between a department store and a restaurant. There was a constant surge of traffic as the patrons pulled up in their Audis and BMWs, handed the keys to the attendants and went into the club. Club Salute catered to the upper-class echelon of German society, but many of the artsy set enjoyed hanging out there as well. The management didn't encourage them, but didn't send them on their way either. They were good for window dressing. If they suspected or understood why they were tolerated at Club Salute, they made no mention of it, only continued to come and soak up the atmosphere. This was the new Germany after all. Everyone was friends, everyone was into business and it was all about making money. Idealism was a thing of the past.

The rear of the club opened into a narrow alleyway, with sufficient room for one car at a time. Right now, that one car was a silver-toned BMW convertible with its top down. Two bodyguards got out of the car first. After ascertaining that everything was as it should be, they gave the driver a nod. He turned off the ignition, swung open his door and pressed a few buttons on his keypad. There was a series of shrill beeps, and the car settled down to wait for its master's return.

The man was tall with broad shoulders and light blond hair that was cut in a short, almost military style. His nose was straight and his jaw square. His eyes were his most prominent feature. They changed color with his mood. When happy, they were a marine blue. When upset, they became a stormy gray, and they were pitch black when he was frustrated. Eyes are the window to the soul, and these eyes showed this soul's utter complexity with every mood swing. He was happy now, or at least confident that things were going according to plan, as evidenced in the blueness of his eyes and in the striding gait of his walk. With confidence — shoulders thrown back – he tapped the wall panel adjacent to the steel door, the green light came on and they were buzzed inside the club.

He entered and was immediately greeted with deferential nods by the security men seated in front of a computer console. The alleyway, the street in front of the club and the inside of the building were all completely monitored 24/7. They were not taking any chances, certainly not with the current situation. The future of Germany was at stake, and they couldn't afford mess-ups! The security men were all graduates of the finest combat units in the German army, and they were the top of the line, sharp eyed and well-oiled fighting machines. But even the toughest German soldier quaked in his boots when he met the boss. He might have been young in years, but his leadership qualities were outstanding, and he had been acknowledged as their leader by everyone with a vested interest in the cause.

The Eberhart family was as influential as any ruling clique in modern-day Germany. They had been growing steadily more powerful before the war, and had emerged from World War II as the de facto leaders of postwar

Europe. They had a hand in real estate, and owned a significant portion of the German media: television channels, radio stations, newspapers and magazines of all types. Always desiring to keep ahead of the game, they had invested heavily in most of the prime Internet providers, and were a controlling factor in what was presented on World Wide Web.

But their main business was the sale of weapons. They manufactured missiles, and had a major share in much of the high-tech toys that sought to replace the need for humans on the battlefields. They were brokers as well, ready to mediate a contract between two parties from across the world.

The scion of the family — the heir apparent — was Dietrich Eberhart. The young Eberhart had finished first in his class in high school, and received a full scholarship to the Sorbonne in Paris, where he had graduated in the top five percentile as well. He had the agile mind of the international businessman, without any morals to accompany it.

He walked down the long sterile hallway, stopping at the glass elevator. His bodyguards accompanied him, and they rode to the next level, where his office afforded a bird's-eye view of the entire club, allowing him to see what was happening everywhere at all times.

He entered his office and headed to his desk. As always, the surface was chillingly neat. Any papers he had left remained precisely where he had left them. He took a seat behind the black chrome desk, sinking into the swivel chair, and pressed a series of buttons on the console beside his desk.

"Yes," came the disembodied voice through the speaker.

"Is everything ready for tonight's meeting?" he asked the voice.

"Yes, Herr Eberhart," came the timid reply.

"Good," he said and clicked off.

He called down to the restaurant for a dinner of blood sausage and German potato salad, and washed it down with a thick ice-cold lager. The bodyguards sat on a pair of suede couches in the corner of the office, and flipped through some of the magazines that were piled on a sharp-edged bronze-and-glass coffee table. Satisfied that everything was the way that he wanted, Eberhart turned on the monitors on the wall opposite his desk to see what was happening in the bar below. He clicked the mouse, and the screen moved to another room — a private room for members only — where the meeting was slated to take place.

He focused on the decor. He nodded to himself satisfied. They had done his will and he was pleased. The meeting wasn't going to start for another hour, and he yawned. The Eberhart real-estate company had recently acquired an upscale high-tech company on London's Canary Wharf, which meant that currently he was traveling a lot more than he preferred. Even with a private jet, constant flying was taxing. But tonight's meeting/rally was a mixture of pleasure and responsibility: pleasure, because it was a cause that he truly believed in; and responsibility, because the Eberhart family took their obligations to Germany seriously. This was part of their campaign for the "new Germany," one which they intended to carry out until the end.

If only his father was alive today to see what the movement had become! He would have been so proud. They had gone from being a movement of haunted people, meek individuals who were forced to hide their opinions from those around them for fear of being arrested. Not any longer. Today, more and more young people were joining the movement, identifying with their ideals and convictions. There were so many people in the Germany of today who believed that some of those policies that had once been law were not so misplaced after all. Foreigners were a curse, Jews were a curse, Russian immigrants were a blight on society, and the Muslims, forget about it! They were taking over Europe! When the movement reasserted control over their country, the practice of Islam in Germany would be forbidden. But all that was still to come. Right now, they were standing on the threshold of the future. They were strong and their power was growing. Every year, their popularity increased as more people realized that they were speaking the truth about the world.

Dietrich stood up and went to the big one-way window that overlooked the dance floor below. The club was becoming more congested as the night wore on. But most of the liberal set had left, and a more serious, businesslike group of people were chatting animatedly with one another. Some were dancing; others stood or sat sipping their drinks. They would begin in one half-hour. The doormen were by now only allowing entrance to those who arrived with invitations, and even those people who were already in the club would not be allowed into the private room where the rally would take place without proof that they were supposed to be there.

No. The ones attending tonight's rally were those who had demonstrated their belief in the cause, who had supported the cause with their time and money. These were the people who had been invited and welcomed here tonight. The majority of the people milling about the club were children or grandchildren of the original party members; people who remembered their fathers and grandfathers in uniform. People who could recall a time when they were proud of their country, and who identified with that feeling and wished for it to return.

Eberhart glanced at his watch and felt the familiar stirring of excitement before he had to address a crowd. A shot of adrenalin rushed through him, and he didn't feel the slightest bit of fatigue even though he hadn't slept more then two hours in the past 24 hours. He ran his fingers through his short cropped hair, and slipped on his suit jacket. He tightened the knot of his tie. If one looked closely at his tie, it was possible to discern a swastika discreetly woven into the design. It wasn't blatant, but it was there, just like the neo-Nazi Party of the Germany of today; not very obvious, not overly conspicuous, but very much a part of the German society of the new millennium. And who knew, perhaps they would be able to continue where they had been forced to stop last time.

It was coming down to the wire, and the time for action was fast approaching. If they waited much longer, all their efforts would have been for naught. Down below, people headed toward the side of the room where the double doors had been opened, disclosing an auditorium with a stage, podium and microphone all set up and ready for him. It was time. He watched the people streaming into the large room. Here and there, someone was stopped by the security forces and asked for his invitation. Anyone who couldn't produce the necessary invitation was asked to leave. Eberhart exited his office and took the elevator to the ground floor, using a hallway that led to a door at the rear of the auditorium. He sat on a leather couch and waited for his security personnel to inform him that all those assembled were seated.

Five minutes later, his bodyguard motioned that it was time. Dietrich Eberhart rose in one fluid motion and strode to the door. He entered the auditorium with a flourish, heading to the stage, standing tall and confident, his broad shoulders cutting a figure that made the people in the hall crane their necks to see him. He was their hero. Most of the people in this room wanted the days of glory to return. Dietrich was making their dream a reality. He took the stairs two at a time and within seconds was standing at the podium. It was the way he did everything, quickly, decisively and perfectly. If you would have asked him, he would have replied that it was the German way. He removed a speech from his pocket and smoothed the papers on the lectern without taking his eyes from the audience for a moment. He held them without blinking, and they stared back, mesmerized by the power of his gaze, by the potent look in his eye. Finally, he picked up the speech, refolded it and returned it to his pocket. He had decided to speak from the heart.

"My friends," he began, "I look around me at this gathering, and I see how far we have come. On every front and from every angle, we have succeeded in surpassing the dreams of our fathers. They left us a country in ruins and we have rebuilt it to its former glory. Look around you," he shouted, raising his arm and pointing toward the distance, "in every direction, great citadels have arisen; towers of finance and culture and art, reminiscent of the Germany of old. We have overcome the fetters with which we were bound by the rest of the world and are once again on the ascent." His deep voice resonated throughout the auditorium. "We are airborne, my friends! Like the eagles soaring high above. Like the finest pilots of the German air force. And now there can be no stopping us."

A gigantic screen lit up above Eberhart's head, and his eyes glittered in the neon lights. "Let us recall our past with wonder, and dream of an even greater future to come."

The screen came alive with the rallies of the past. *Der Fuhrer* standing on the podium at Nuremberg, arm outstretched in the Nazi salute. The sound came on through the speakers, coarse and high pitched, Hitler's voice sending a tingle up the spine of everyone in the hall. This was *Der Fuhrer*: the man who had led their grandparents into the battlefields of Europe and the deserts of North Africa; the man who had nearly conquered Russia. He raved and ranted, he hissed and spewed forth sewage and hate, and the people in the hall loved it. When Hitler called for a salute, they rose en masse and saluted along with the crowds at the Nuremberg rally. They were united in heart, spirit and mind. They were Nazis.

Eberhart turned to them and roared: "Are you ready for the great takeover?"

They were not sure to what he was referring, but they cheered enthusiastically. He was above himself now, swept away in his own rhetoric, and the people sensed that he was giving them groundbreaking news tonight.

"My friends," he spoke softly now. He was mesmerizing and the assembled watched him spellbound.

"You miss the past, don't you? You wish that you had had the opportunity to have lived and experienced the life that our grandparents had even if it was far too brief, don't you?! Well, then, so be it. You will have that life again! Germany is going to rise and conquer once again. We have the power. But in a much more sophisticated style this time. We can subjugate the world without going to war, without risking millions of our best and most talented youth on the battlefields of the world. I'm talking raw power of the most impressive kind." He paused.

The people gazing at him held their breaths. "This time we are going all the way. Soon, you will know what I'm talking about. When that time arrives, and our power is returned to us, then, the future government of Germany sits before me. The future ambassadors and governors, the future leaders of the Reichstag, the future thinkers and policy makers of the greatest nation on earth are seated right here in this hall. Could I ask for more? Could *Der Fuhrer* have asked for more?" The hall exploded in an outpouring of support for the man who had led Germany to its lowest abyss in history while the screens came alive once again, and Hitler was screaming about the Thousand-Year Reich.

"Yes," yelled Eberhart over the noise of Hitler's fanatical ranting and the crowd's adoration, "this time it will be the way you wanted it, *Mein Fuhrer.*Adolph. This time we will succeed." And then they were simply out of control, because they understood that it was a matter of time before the world as they knew it would cease to exist, and a new and glorious future would take its place.

Denver, Colorado
January 27, 2009

Denver, Colorado is a beautiful capital city in the Rocky Mountains. Physical fitness aficionados stream there from throughout America to enjoy the many hiking trails that meander their way through the mountain range. It is home to some of the most spectacular scenery in the world, a place where the evergreens grow tall and sturdy and the air is redolent with nature's pungency. The city itself is fairly cosmopolitan with the laid-back attitude attributed to the Midwest. The calm is only disrupted when the Broncos charge toward the Super Bowl, with the city overcome by a deluge of purple and orange. Denver is Middle America at its best.

Danny Taylor owned a bar on the outskirts of the city not far from the giant area that had been appropriated by the electric company many years before. The bar was known as Danny's Den, and was a favorite watering hole for many of the electric company's workers. They frequented the bar at the end of a long day mending cables and untangling crossed wires. The bar also sported a restaurant which served spicy chili and apple pie packed so full that it shared the city's nickname: mile high. The men came as much for Danny himself as for the food and drink.

Danny, you see, was the heart and soul of the place. He opened the joint in the morning and locked its doors at night. He was quick with a joke, and could mix the most obscure, little-known drinks in a matter of moments. He was a large man, weighing in at 270 pounds, with sandy-colored hair, light brown eyes and a broad grin. He was in his 60's and still strong as an ox. The men would gather in the early evenings, sitting on the round stools, joking with one another, catching a meal or shooting a game of pool. There were a row of telephones at the back of the long and narrow room that were designated for public use, and one phone near the front of the room beside the bar that was off limits to the patrons. There was a jukebox in the corner, which was always playing something — usually Country and Western — and the atmosphere was one of hearty goodwill, Denver style. That was what made the whole scenario that much more bizarre.

Monday evening about an hour before closing time, the phone at the bar rang. It rang three times before anyone heard it, the noise in the bar being what it was. One of the men sitting at the bar finally answered the phone and asked who it was. As they were talking, Danny returned to the room. The customer casually told Danny that there was a man on the other end of the line who wanted to know if they were serving T-bone steaks that night. Danny picked up the phone and replied that they were all out. Then abandoning the bar in the middle of the busiest hour of the evening, he motioned to his employees that he was going out. He exited the bar in the direction of the stairs leading to the upper area of the building, where his living quarters were located.

Five minutes later, he was out the door and getting into his brand-new Land Rover. He turned on the ignition and, spraying gravel all over the parking lot, sped out of the lot in the direction of the highway. From there it had been a five-minute drive to the huge complex used by the electric company. It was from here that the electric company supplied electricity to half the city as well as a vast number of small towns, hiking grounds and mining stations all across the Rockies.

At 11 o'clock that night, Danny Taylor drove at a very fast clip directly toward the electrical site. He drove up to the guardhouse and paused while the surprised guard emerged to see who it was seeking entrance. The man knew Danny as did all the workers, and he managed a smile and a greeting before Danny blew him away with the shotgun he had kept hidden from view. Then wasting no time, he shot through the barrier and into the compound, heading for the gigantic electrical grid. He crashed through the gate that surrounded the many rows of metal pipes, grids and tall cylinders. Then fun-filled, wholesome Danny Taylor got out of his car, and began pouring gasoline around the base of the electrical grid, making sure that the area was thoroughly saturated.

He positioned the Land Rover in the direction of the exit, and threw a lit match onto the gasoline, while gunning the engine at the same time. He didn't look back as the match caught, as the sheet of flames shot upward all over the installation or as the lights over half the city flickered then began dying out. He rode to a secret camping spot prepared years earlier, and parked his car under a large outcropping of stone where it was well hidden and out of sight. He sat there watching the horizon, as the night passed and dawn slowly broke over the Rocky Mountains, heralding a touch of daylight to a city with no artificial lighting.

4

Jason Leonard Frost

Vatican City, Rome, Italy
December 5, 2008

The old men moved with the silence of the grave. It was time to make a decision. Bedecked from head to toe in crimson robes, 165 cardinals of the Catholic Church had gathered from across the world for the ancient ceremony of *Il Conclave*. It was they who shared the responsibility for choosing the man who would rule over a billion Catholics. The cardinals of the august committee exchanged looks of increasing agitation as one by one they entered the chamber where *Il Conclave* would take place. It had been thus named by men of the cloth who were long gone, but although the origin of the chamber might remain shrouded in mystery, what transpired in the octagonal chamber of chiseled stone was by far more mysterious. The walls of the chamber had been painted with frescoes in the most brilliant of colors by some of the most talented artists who had ever lived.

It was here that the powerful College of Cardinals gathered when they were called upon to make a momentous decision. It was to this chamber that the men in red came, when the church was faced with a crisis that threatened to destroy them. It was from here that the proclamations emerged, the ideas and concepts that would impact the entire Catholic world. The men who had assembled in the chamber that evening were mainly old and wrinkled, yet resonated with a power so intense, so sinister that it brought the Middle Ages to mind. They had come from around the world, although the majority were European: from Italy, France, Spain and Poland.

As soon as the cardinals were safely inside the chamber, the Swiss Guard would lock the doors and blacken the windows, ensuring that no signals or messages were sent to the outside world. They would be kept in seclusion until they had successfully elected the next pope.

Cardinal Stephen Venuci spoke first. Senior among his brethren, his opinion was far more influential than was appropriate among the council.

"It is fifteen days since the pontiff died," he said, a fair amount of sadness evident in his voice. Whether it was genuine or not, it served the purpose.

The man seated at his right — his face a mask of wrinkles, his left hand paralyzed by a mild stroke he had suffered at an early age — sat contemplatively and stroked the 5-o'clock shadow that he sported. A stifling silence settled on the room like a smothering woolen blanket in summertime. The curtains had been drawn. The room was dimly lit, and the contrast to the brilliant sunlight of the outside world was startling.

"It is time for the deliberations to begin," Venuci said slowly, ponderously. "Each man seated here will set forth his recommendation for the man he feels will be the most suited to be our future papal leader."

A babble of voices filled the room — elderly voices — each one straining to be heard above his neighbor. Venuci raised his arms for silence. Slowly the cardinals quieted down, waiting to hear what he was going to say.

"My brethren," he said, speaking with passion, every word that he uttered quivering in the air before settling on the heavy wooden table in front of them. "My brothers," he said again, "let us be wise and do our utmost to arrive at the proper conclusions. We have a short amount of time to decide which man from our esteemed group is most worthy of the role. Let us get through the deliberations now and put them behind us. We are all familiar with the candidates. Please take your time, and remember, the future lies in your hands. Choose wisely!"

The room became deathly still. Paper and pens were passed around. The men sat in their ruby-colored robes and scribbled names on the paper before them. They filled their water glasses from the pitchers that had been brought in prior to the room being sealed, and wiped the perspiration on their brows. It was tedious work, with no room allowed for error. They would be choosing the man who would be ruling over one billion people! He would be in charge of billions of dollars' worth of real estate, and the overseer of orphanages, monasteries and a host of churches. He had to be honest, media savvy and a master performer. It wasn't at all like the old days when the pope was secreted in the cloisters.

The pontiff of today was seen on TV and was a familiar figure in many countries. Consequently, the decision was a much more difficult one to make. The choice would have to be made between five men. Each had served for years in the church, proving his dedication, time and again. Each had evidenced extraordinary leadership skills over the last few decades. Each had the distinguished stature of a man capable of leading an entire world of people into the future. They were the cream of the crop, the jewels of the church, the prophets of Rome.

Geraldo Munzioni was the cardinal of Florence. Fernandez Mendoza was the cardinal of Toledo and the most respected churchman in Spain. Wladyslaw Mzlyzvesty was the cardinal of Warsaw. Jason Leonard Frost was the cardinal of New York. Venuci was the fifth man of their group, celebrated perhaps, but not of the same caliber, and that was a fact. They would have to set humbleness aside when it came to momentous decisions such as these.

The chamber hosted a mélange of aromas, none of them savory: the strong smell of sweat, and the waxy smell of the burning candles, as minuscule wisps of smoke soared upward coming to rest directly under the ceiling, smothering the atmosphere. There was a smell of hope, of fear for the future and the smell of apprehension. It was time to take a vote. One by one the assembled cast their votes into the designated chalice. One by one they verified that they were voting one time only, and then they returned to their seats, their faces masks of discretion.

The voting was finally over. The counting could begin. One by one, the votes were counted, the results tallied on a piece of parchment. It took quite a while, but eventually, the tally was completed and the results were finalized. Everyone could plainly see who the next pontiff would be. Joyous looks illuminated the faces of one and all. The doubts were over, the festivities could begin; a new reign, a new empire was now ready to emerge.

The bullets were burned and the white smoke — indicative that their new pope was chosen — emerged from the chimney accompanied by the ringing of the bells.

The doors of the chamber could finally be opened, letting in some fresh air, cleaning out the tepid odor from their midst. The cardinals filed out as quickly as their elderly legs would carry them. They were full of decorum and pride as befitting the task that had been entrusted to them. They gathered on or near the veranda, gazing down on the huge plaza, packed with people who had come from all over the world for this moment. They reveled in the exquisite joy that they assumed was felt by the very heavens themselves.

The chosen man radiated happiness, his life's dream come true. Having replaced his cardinal's attire for the pristine white robes of the papacy, his face glowed. He was dispensing blessings like they were candies. The crowd was devouring his presence, was desirous of his words. He would have to speak. He made his slow and ponderous way to the podium, and was assisted up the short flight of stairs. Looking at the packed square in front of him, at the glow of the cameras on his face, at the adoration of the millions of people, the newly elected pope, former cardinal of Toledo, Fernandez Mendoza smiled and began to speak, the media beaming his words around the world. All rejoiced. All except one.

The evening wore on and on. The crowd was ecstatic. There was no earthly way that he would be able to maneuver himself away. With heart pounding in anger and frustration, he waited for the ceremony to be over, for all the believers to go home. Tears welled up in the corners of his eyes, and he swallowed the lump in his throat. He should have been the one elected! He should have been the one up there on the podium giving an inspiring speech to millions of avid listeners! He was the most fitting by far, and yet, here he was, standing among the most elite members of the church and not up on the stage where he truly belonged.

The evening was beginning its descent. The night felt golden, full of expectation. The stars shone brightly, challenging them individually and collectively with their brilliance. The people began to leave. Here and there someone fainted as a result of having stood outside for too long. The show was over. Soon he would be able to leave, to be out of sight of all his colleagues, the cardinals of the Church, who looked at him with sympathy, but who in reality didn't vote him in because of who he was. And who was he really? Even he wasn't sure.

He went down the Via Sistina, turning right on the Via Urbana, walking without thinking, like a man possessed, until he reached the Via del Colosseo, the street where his hotel was located. He peered into one of the storefronts that he passed and took a moment to glare at his reflection. He stood tall and broad with a shock of white hair that contrasted with his dark suit. His eyes held a melancholy, a sense of loss, of brooding in their depths, but there was nothing he could do about that. Losing was part of life, but that didn't stop him from hating them. He smiled at his reflection, but there was fire in his eyes, and the look that he saw in his reflection frightened him. Turning on his heel, he pushed opened the revolving doors and entered the ancient building.

The concierge was beside him in an instant.

"Good evening, Eminence," he said bowing slightly, the very picture of deference.

He inclined his head with a smile that bespoke serenity and holiness.

"Can I be of service in any way?" the concierge asked.

"I would like a light dinner in my room, please," he replied. "Some onion soup, a small pasta, half a bottle of your best red wine."

"Certainly, Eminence," the concierge said amiably. "It will be ready before you turn around."

He wished the man good night and crossed the lobby, past the potted plants and overstuffed coaches, under the numerous arches and shadowy alcoves and entered the elevator. He was swiftly deposited outside his door, and was enjoying an excellent dinner shortly after that. When he had finished the last drop of wine, he lit a cigar and, opening the glass doors leading to the balcony, breathed in a deep breath of night air. Far below, the festivities were still going on with abandon. The holy city was far from sleep. He wiped his brow and felt a tremor pass through his hand. For the first time in a very long time, Cardinal Jason Leonard Frost of New York State, didn't know what to do with himself.

∽∽

He left Rome on the first available flight. He flew first class, which wasn't unusual for a cardinal, and slept most of the way. His sleep was a troubled one, and he cried out from time to time causing a passing stewardess to shake him awake.

"Sir," she called out, "you're having a nightmare. Wake up, sir."

Shaking off the cobwebs, he looked around at the other passengers, and realized that they were all staring at the distinguished-looking man with curiosity. He thanked the young woman for waking him, and asked her for an aspirin and water. Then he drank two cups of water and tried to go back to sleep. He couldn't. He felt absolutely terrible. He felt wronged and castigated, although there was no earthly reason for him to feel that way. The cardinals had voted, and everything had been aboveboard, so there was no reason for him to feel this way. Yet, if he examined the whole scenario, he knew that he was the logical choice for pope.

He was far better liked than the Spaniard, far more articulate and learned. He was better educated, he was more pious. He was far more intelligent as well. He even carried himself with the demeanor of a pope. What had happened? Why was he here on the plane heading back to New York instead of celebrating his new position in the Vatican right now? Deep down, however, his mind told him that he knew the answer. And if he knew the answer, then there was no reason in the world that the church wouldn't know it as well. It had to do with his penchant for purchasing rare paintings of European art. That in itself wasn't such a strange hobby. Many upper-level churchmen had collections of some sort. Some collected rare coins, others stamps. There was even one bishop from South Africa who collected vintage automobiles. No, that wasn't the strange part.

What was strange about his hobby was the type of paintings that they were. The scenes on the paintings were usually Jewish themes straight out of the mists of time: scenes from the *shtetls* of Eastern Europe, little children seated around a pot-bellied stove, learning from crumbling texts under the stern gaze of a gray-bearded man, the pallid faces of yesteryear. It appeared like a fairy tale and maybe it was, but who could tell just by peering into a painting? He couldn't help it. Anytime he passed an art gallery, anytime he was in a place known for its artwork, his antenna went up and he was on the alert.

The climax had been when he had taken a sabbatical to the Holy Land a few years before. He had thought that he would be overcome by all the places considered holy and historical to Christianity. But that hadn't happened in the least. Instead of traveling to Upper Nazareth in the Galilee or to the shrines all over East Jerusalem, he had discovered that he had zero interest in them. In fact, on the few times that he had been persuaded to take part in an expedition, he had found himself bored beyond belief with all the "holiness." Instead, all he wanted to do was to take in the Jewish aspects of Jerusalem, the mysticism of the ancient city of Tzfat, the beauty of the sun setting behind the Tomb of the Patriarchs.

He roamed the country from north to south all adrift, like a lost board awash at sea, searching, but not fully aware of what he was searching for. He was truly at peace, however, when he discovered the world of Jewish art. He browsed for hours in the musty quiet of the tiny galleries, the scent of oil paint filling the air like the fragrance of time. There were so many galleries with high-quality art. The artist quarter in Tzfat alone held numerous alleyways with twisted paths filled with tapestries and paintings, and he was able to lose himself for hours, for days in their midst. And that was when he had discovered his passion with a vengeance. He'd always felt drawn to Jewish art. But now, the images filled his mind with their pull, and he began to collect them seriously.

He had himself driven to the old city of Jaffa where he spent a number of days just browsing. He went around the country drinking in the sights, both on and off the canvases, and he was overwhelmed by what he saw, by the treasures that he had uncovered. He pulled out his leather wallet, removed his credit card and swiped away. He had all his newfound treasures shipped to New York where he had them proudly displayed on his walls to their maximum advantage.

For some reason he hadn't found it strange that he, a cardinal in the Catholic Church, should be displaying such overtly Jewish art. But while it seemed like the most natural thing in the world for him to be doing this, it didn't quite seem that way to many others in the church. There were whispers he ignored, even while they grew in substance and sound. He simply didn't care what they thought. It was *his* home after all, and if it offended them, they didn't have to visit. To him the matter was closed. To many others, however, it obviously had been anything but.

A short while later, he had taken a trip to Europe, and once there, he was summoned to Rome to meet with his superiors. He recalled the meeting as if it were yesterday. He had entered the halls of that most powerful of complexes, past the Swiss Guards, past the sculptures and fountains, and down the endless corridors; past the Vatican library containing thousands of priceless manuscripts and past the archives, replete with thousands, maybe millions of documents relating to the generations of church business around the world. Religious art, statues and mosaics covered the walls. Without a word he followed the young priest, who was escorting him, until they reached a winding staircase which they ascended higher and higher until he was dizzy and short of breath. When they reached a door made of the thickest wood, the priest knocked and they entered.

The four walls of the chamber were covered with maps of the world. There were pins on many of the spots in different colors and the ceiling was a realistic portrayal of heaven. It was absolutely breathtaking and he was properly awed. But the gathering at the table took his breath away a lot more than the ceiling display.

There were several individuals seated around the table hosted by a cardinal with a florid face which bore the scars of youthful acne. He was fierce, and he bristled with unlimited power. It was whispered that this was the man who was the real power behind the pope. He was the man who was hosting the meeting, and Cardinal Jason Leonard Frost wondered for the first time what he had done to merit being in such majestic company. The answer wasn't long in coming.

He was shown to his seat at the foot of the ornate table. The armchairs were as ancient as the Vatican, and would have fetched a fortune on the open market. He tried to find a comfortable position in the chair, but gave it up as a losing proposition. Nobody wanted to move, to disturb the silence, to bring undue attention to themselves. This was the secret church, the stealth behind the open facade. This was fire, and if you weren't careful, you were apt to be burned.

"Fernandez Mendoza," the priest thundered in the direction of the Spaniard who had been sitting so complacently mere seconds before. Mendoza jumped in his place.

"Yes," he managed to coax out.

"Mendoza, tell me," continued the man with a contemptuous drawl, "do you feel that gambling is an activity worthy of somebody in your august position?"

Cardinal Mendoza's face flushed. It was obvious that he was wondering how on earth this was relevant.

"So," went on the priest remorselessly. "Did you perhaps feel that we in the church would not find it boorish — downright indecent even — that one of our organization's highest-ranking members could be found most regularly at the velvet-covered gaming tables in Monte Carlo? Did you think that this wouldn't disturb us?

"And you," he said turning to Cardinal Munzioni, "a cardinal from

Florence, what about you? Drinking like a pig on wheels and ending up drunk in a fountain in the middle of your hometown! The absolute disgrace, the shame, the horror! Is this the best that the church has to offer nowadays?" Frost was sweating heavily, awaiting his turn, sure that any second now they would be hounding him as well. It came.

"Cardinal Frost," said the voice in a clipped and distant manner. "What on earth possesses a cardinal in the Catholic Church to travel to the Holy Land and to return with such inappropriate artwork?" It was clear that the church had been ruthless in its investigations of the men who were slated to hold the highest offices. Nobody wanted to be told in future years that they had made a horrendous mistake by placing someone in the position to be elected to one of the highest offices in the world, only to discover that the person who they had previously considered to be a man with an impeccable record was in reality a drunkard or a gambler, or worst of all, a Jew lover, heaven forbid! The audience gasped.

"It is merely artwork," Frost managed to blurt out.

"Nothing is merely anything," replied the priest. "Every single thing that you men do means something to us here at the Vatican. Don't you realize, gentlemen, that you are being groomed for the top slots? Don't you have any brains at all? Do you want people to be able to boast that they bested the pope in a game of poker?" He expected them to put aside their little foibles and desires, and to behave like the leaders they were.

The meeting ended on a tense note. Frost was seething inside, and he wasn't even sure why. He tried to analyze his feelings on the ride back to his hotel, and failed abysmally to arrive at any solid conclusions. More than the church's involvement in his private life bothered him; he wanted to know why he of all people felt the need to purchase all this Jewish artwork in the first place. It wasn't as if he had any Jewish connections, or cared about the Jewish people or the nation of Israel in any way. He was a cardinal in the Catholic Church! So why did he persist on harming himself? He searched his heart, and didn't know what to answer. But his very being rebelled at the thought of having to remove the artwork from his walls.

The paintings in his living and dining rooms were removed, while those in the study and library — rooms he kept mostly for his own use — remained. They were replaced by old masters, pleasing to everyone, and he hoped that his gesture would appease the puppeteers from Rome.

In the meanwhile, however, he arrived at some conclusions. It was time for him to check out his past; for him to understand where he had come from, what horrors lay behind closed doors, what monsters hid in the essence of his soul. He had to find himself before it was too late. For that he would have to take a trip back into his past, to discover who he had been. He would keep a low profile, but he would begin his investigation without antagonizing anyone. Because this was something he needed to do before it was too late.

Ithaca, New York
December 10, 2008

Cardinal Frost had always been a solitary person, and hadn't minded the loneliness that was part and parcel of the life he led. He had acquired a number of close friends over the course of his life, and had enjoyed deep and lasting relationships with them. Sometimes it was the people who had nothing to do with the life you led who had the ability to understand you better then anyone else. They possessed the distance that was needed. There were other members of the church that he had befriended over the years. They held each other in high esteem, and enjoyed discussing events of mutual interest. But for the most part, the bishops and cardinals that he was acquainted with were not those to whom he would go to for advice. He had other friends who would be able to suggest a course of action.

Jason Leonard Frost had been a cardinal of the archdiocese of New York for several years. He was headquartered in New York City and that is where he conducted all church business. Prior to his appointment he had been the Bishop of Ithaca and it was there that he felt most at home. In lieu of this he had continued to maintain his old residence in Ithaca and it was to there that he fled whenever his presence was not needed for official church duties. Here he could relax, shrug the onerous burden of responsibility from his shoulders and melt into the general populace with few the wiser as to his official status. And it was here he headed after he had been denied his rightful role as *Il Papa.* He left word with his staff that he was taking an unscheduled bring leave of absence to take care of personal matters.

The next morning dawned balmy and springlike. He had taken a sleeping pill and he had slept deeply without dreaming. He felt refreshed; if not emotionally, at least physically. He left his collar at home, and donned a tan corduroy jacket. He wore a pair of comfortable twill trousers and looked like a retired citizen going about his business. As he strolled down the street, he could smell the fragrance of the flowers that the town gardeners planted on every available surface. It was a glorious morning. The sun shone brightly and Frost felt alive and full of vitality for the first time in quite a while. He stopped at a coffee shop along the way and purchased a cappuccino and a cherry Danish. Carrying his breakfast, he continued down the street nodding hellos to strangers he passed on the way and receiving them in return.

Eventually, he reached the park in the center of town, and he turned off onto the path that ran parallel to the bicycle track. Avid bikers listened to music and ignored the world as they cycled. This was a peaceful island; an oasis in the midst of the city's busy schedule. Soon Frost reached the section of the park that had been designated for more sedentary people who were less inclined to do much strenuous activity. Here were a number of Ping-Pong tables and specially designed tables where the older generation played chess. This was where he had met Al, a Caribbean native, about five years before.

Frost enjoyed a challenging game of chess with a worthy adversary. He'd throw himself into the game, becoming absorbed in a way that boded no good for his opponents. When he played, his concentration was absolute, and he was very good. He had devoted many a night to studying the game and the famous moves of chess champions around the world. So when he felt like it, Frost would demolish his opponents without batting an eyelash. But there were other regulars in the park who were good enough to hold their own against him. Those were the games that stretched on and on.

He entered the chess-table enclosure and scanned the area for Al, finally finding him at the farthest corner engrossed in a thick book, oblivious to the world, as the wind gently tousled his curly black hair. From time to time, Al would reach for the cup of coffee that was on the table beside him and take a delicate sip from the slowly cooling brew. He was about 60 years old, and had lived a rough life, putting in long hours at work, but he never complained. He just smiled mysteriously and his eyes would light up, and when Al smiled, the world smiled with him.

Frost studied his friend from afar. He saw a still-powerful, rugged man, whose hair was beginning to be streaked with gray. Frost approached the bench and, sitting down, removed his breakfast from the brown bag and began to eat.

"About time you got here," Al observed from under bushy eyebrows.

"I've been here for a while," Frost replied, "but I saw that you were too busy reading for me to disturb you. So I just stood and watched you, and then I realized that if I just stood and kept watch, I could be standing here all day. So I overcame my aversion to disturbing my good friend, Al, and here I am. Danish?" he offered, extending a piece in Al's general direction.

"I think I will," Al accepted.

"Glorious day today, huh?" Al managed through a mouthful of cherry Danish.

"Top of the line, top of the line," Frost replied. They sat together in companionable silence, and ate and drank without speaking. This was one of the reasons that Frost liked Al so much. Al didn't feel that people always had to talk. He was content to gaze at a sunset, to appreciate the world's beauty in silent contemplation.

"Game of chess?" Al finally asked.

"I'm game," Frost said. They set up the pieces on the table and chose for white. Frost won and the game got underway. But he wasn't concentrating. That became supremely clear the moment Al made a tentative try at Kasparov's famous opening move, and Frost didn't block it effectively. It was obvious that something was on his mind.

Midway into the game, Al leaned back on the bench and said, "O.K., Jason, out with it. You're not concentrating; you're just not yourself today. Want to tell me what's going on?" Frost leaned back as well and studied his friend's face. Al was concerned and Frost was touched.

"I'll tell you, Al," Frost began. "It's not really something that I can put my finger on. It's just that for a while now, I've been having questions and doubts about who I am. I mean, I know who I am. I've been a fine, upstanding member of the Catholic Church for almost my entire life. I'm a cardinal, a man of the cloth, and, on the surface at least, successful. But look, Al," Frost said, and he was almost in tears, "I just returned from Rome and the whole pope-choosing ceremony, and you and I both know that if there was any candidate that deserved to be the next pope, it was Jason Leonard Frost. But surprise, surprise, Cardinal Frost wasn't chosen! Why was that? I don't understand! I was the best man for the job, with the right seniority. So what was it? Why did they pick the man from Spain? He's a good guy and everything, but he's not pope material, and they had to know that. I feel like I was stabbed in the back!!

"I gave my best years; scratch that! I gave my entire life for the church, and when it came time for payback, when it came time for me to take my rightful place at its head, I was suddenly declared a pariah! My question is: Why?! There has got to be a reason things happened this way!" He stopped for a second, thinking.

"I'll tell you something else. I don't even know who I really am! I don't know where I'm truly from, in what part of the world my parents were raised. How can I expect to take over something as deeply rooted in history as the church, when I myself have such a glaring void in the same area that the church so excels in? I should have tried harder to get to the bottom of who I am! Instead of investigating, I've subdued the questions inside me, hoping they would all go away, and now I'm suffering all the more for it!"

Al listened quietly as always, contemplating that which he had heard, consolidating the whole picture. He had learned how to listen during his many years on the police force. The best weapon an officer could own was his ability to listen and assimilate all information that came his way, because the sooner he had the general picture in his mind, the closer he was to putting the whole thing together.

"Jason," Al said at last when his friend had finished pouring out his heart to him.

"Yes," Frost mumbled.

"Jason," Al said again. "This is what I think. Right now, you have a major authority problem. You don't understand or agree with the decisions that have been made in Rome. For some reason, you are also finding that you know next to nothing about your background. While somewhere in the depths of your subconscious you realize that you know a tremendous amount, the key to making that information available is just not there. It's missing, and until you discover that key, there is no way for you to unearth the mystery of who Cardinal Jason Frost really is!" Frost was nodding his head while his friend was speaking.

"You're right for wanting to know about your past. You're probably correct in guessing that your past got in the way when it came the time to choose a new pope, because the past can do that very easily. But you'll only know if your suspicions are accurate if you actually go out there and search and sift through all those years that you don't know about: the missing years. Only then do I think you have a chance to discover who you really are and why your life turned out the way it did." Frost was in complete agreement with everything Al was saying.

"I see that we're eye to eye with one another," Al said, "so here's what I suggest."

"Talk to me," Frost said. "Spit it out."

"I'm thinking that it's time for me and you to take a little trip to wherever the archives are located."

"Archives?" broke in Frost.

"Yes, Jason," Al continued. "If you want to know where you are from and who your parents were, well then, that's going to mean a trip to the church archives, where they keep that kind of information. We go down there, pay them a visit, get the information that we need and then you are on the road to discovering who you are. Sounds good, doesn't it?!"

"Sounds great, actually," Frost replied.

"O.K.," said Al, "well, then, where are those archives located?"

"Well, there are many archives," Frost said. "Some are at the church's main archive center in Manhattan. There are many other archive centers where they keep more sensitive information: Connecticut, Boston ... There's a lot of places."

"Well, at least we have a starting point," Al said.

"We?" Frost wondered aloud.

"We," said Al confidently. "Let me ask you this, buddy. Just because you're a cardinal, does that mean that you have unlimited access to any file that you might conceivably want to look at?"

"No, probably not," Frost replied.

"Well, then," said Al, "it's time to get out the old uniform from the closet and dust off the badge. Business calls. We're going to find out everything we can about the man known as Jason Leonard Frost. Where did you grow up?"

"In an obscure Catholic orphanage in Oyster Bay on Long Island. But do you really think, Al, that you can find out this information that I haven't been able to uncover? Not that I've tried that hard, but still, I'm a cardinal and this is my life we're talking about. Yet, it's like the information is deliberately staying hidden!"

"Oyster Bay, Long Island," Al said. "Let's go there for a visit. See the place, get a feel for the situation, smell the water. Get to know the streets by the soles of our shoes. What do you say, Jason?"

"You're on," Frost replied, and after that, there was never any turning back.

Atlantic Ocean
June 1, 1946

The trip across the ocean was one of the worst experiences that Jason Frost ever had in his entire life. He was seasick from the beginning of the trip until shortly before they came into port. At that point, he made his exhausted way up to the deck, red eyed and haggard. The clothing that he wore hung on his skinny frame like a sack, and he had the appearance of someone who could use a lot of food and motherly love. Up until then, food had been scarce, since getting a portion was dependent on being strong and making sure that you were taken care of: two things at which Frost wasn't that good. The ship twisted and danced on the ocean waters. Frost lay on the top bunk and stared out the cabin porthole for hours on end, as the sun rose and set, turning the waters crimson and gold with the reflections of the fiery ball.

He stared out the window and dreamed of the new world: a place where he would become a new person, where he'd become someone important. He had a burning goal to succeed. In his heart he knew that he wanted to work in a position of authority, where people would come to him for advice and assistance. He would be able to help them out. He would be full of ideas, and he would be the type of person who would always know what to do in any given situation. He wanted people to feel that they could share their problems and life challenges with him.

Unfortunately, his mind was the only thing that had remained steady, since he couldn't keep any of his food down. Whatever little bit of food the other boys managed to bring him from the dining room would come up almost as soon as it went down. Eventually, he gave up even trying to eat since it just wasn't worth the effort. The trip was pure agony, and he tossed and turned night after night in an attempt to find a comfortable position. But try as he might, he could find no peace. It was only when he was so tired that he couldn't keep his eyes open for another second, that the young boy would fall asleep. But it was never for a long time, and it was never a restful sleep. He would awake sweating and in pain, and lean out the porthole heaving, as the ship pitched and plunged in the rough sea troughs.

And then, just as he was resigning himself to being eternally hungry and sick, the ship entered a stretch of calmer waters, and he found that he was able to stand up and walk without falling on the floor in agony. He made his way out of the cabin and up the stairs to the dining area where he was finally able to eat a light meal without feeling like he was going to explode.

Things were much better after that. From that moment on, he was able to go to every meal, and he began to get his appetite back. In fact, he began to find the constant roll of the waves soothing. Now that he was hungry again, he was determined to make up for the many days that he hadn't been able to eat at all, and he became a force to be reckoned with in the dining area. The sea air gave him an unceasing appetite, and he was the first to enter for breakfast and one of the last to leave.

Whereas he hadn't been able to leave his cabin until then, now he couldn't bring himself to go back there. Instead, he roamed the ship from port to stern and back again, exploring every nook and cranny, and exclaiming in boyish delight any time he found something that struck his fancy. He met the captain and the cook and charmed them both. The bosun took a liking to the impish boy, and asked him if he wanted to help around the ship, an offer he promptly accepted. He was very bright and good with his hands. The bosun trusted him because he had the kind of nature that inspired trust, and because he proved to be reliable and hard working. He had come aboard ship with a number of other orphans who were all headed to the same orphanage in the States. They were all sweet kids, but there was something special and original about the boy who answered to the name Jason Frost.

From the moment the seasickness left him, Jason Frost didn't sleep in his room again. Instead, he found a lifeboat in a little-frequented corner of the ship, and claimed it as his own. He'd lie in the tiny craft at night, covered by his thin blanket, but not feeling any cold at all, despite the stiff sea breeze. He stayed awake for hours staring at the cosmos, his alert eye discerning patterns in the stars above him.

When he would finally drift off to sleep, it was with a smile on his face, because he knew that he was leaving Europe. Even at his tender age, he knew that he never wanted to live there again. He was going to America, the land of the free, the country where people went to escape the tyrannies of history.

The night before the ship was scheduled to dock at Ellis Island, Jason was so excited that he barely slept at all. It was near the end of the night when he finally dozed off. It seemed as if it was just a few minutes later that he was awakened by the sounds of clapping and cheering as the sun rose over the ocean. The boatload from Europe got their first glance of the United States.

It was a pivotal moment for the young Jason Frost. As he peered over the side of his lifeboat, he received his first glimpse of New York Harbor. There, standing proudly and majestically, framed and wreathed in the golden morning sunlight, was Lady Liberty. Jason Leonard Frost knew that if he lived for 100 years, he would never see another sight like the one he had seen that morning, touching him more then anything else he could remember.

Slowly but surely, the ship edged into the harbor as the crowds of European refugees stood on the deck watching, shoulder to shoulder. Jason, too, emerged from his lifeboat. After much squeezing and maneuvering, he found himself at the railing where he could see the swirling brown waters of the harbor disappearing under the ship as it inched inside closer to the dock. It was a chilly morning, and the sea breeze was sharp and blew right through his thin shirt. But Jason wouldn't have dreamed of leaving that deck. This was a moment to remember, and he would be there to store it in his memory bank.

The sailors were working furiously, their muscles heaving and straining as they coiled the ropes and cursed roughly. Those on board broke into spontaneous applause as they bumped into the side of the pier. The sound of their clapping and whistling filled the deck and reverberated throughout the harbor. The ropes were fastened to the metal rings on the dock, and the sailors lowered the gangplank. There were the sounds of arguments as the people began rushing here and there, to put together their luggage and disembark as quickly as they possibly could. They had finally arrived in the United States and they were still standing on the ship! Everyone suddenly realized how much they wanted to be Americans already. What had been a unified crowd of crying refugees became an uncivilized group of desperate people, all intent on getting their families off the ship and onto Ellis Island where they could begin their processing.

Jason didn't have very much in the way of earthly possessions. In fact, aside from the clothing he wore, he owned a grand total of one travel bag filled with all his earthly possessions. But he couldn't disembark until the group he was traveling with was ready. So he waited, while the orphans' chaperons made sure that everyone had what they needed. He watched person after person leaving the ship with huge smiles on their faces as they stepped onto the ground of "the promised land." It seemed to take forever, but his group was ready at last, and it was their turn to disembark. Jason rushed forward with his bag slung over his shoulder and led the way, as the orphans filed off the boat and onto American soil.

He looked at the stern faces of the American immigration officials, and was happy that he was there legally and that all his papers were in order. He was happy that these mean-looking men wouldn't have any cause to get angry at him. The orphans realized that they had arrived at their destination, and that they would never have to relocate if they chose not to. They entered a cavernous building with a great hall where the group of refugees was cordoned off into sections by men in starched uniforms who never smiled, and who kept order in a rigid manner. This was a world as far from Europe as was humanly possible.

The refugees kept a wary eye on the men in uniforms, used as they were to the uniformed men of Europe who were always corrupt and out to demean whomever they could. The lines moved slowly as the refugees were processed and their papers examined closely. Many were taken off to the side to be questioned on the extent of their knowledge of the English language and their ability to earn a living in the States. The American government wanted to make very sure that these people wouldn't end up as a burden on the government.

This was all besides the point for young Jason Frost, who had all the papers he needed, and was able to speak enough English to charm anyone he met. He stood and watched the scene before him with wide-eyed wonder, enjoying the hustle and bustle of all the people coming and going. The huge room echoed a cacophony of noise and frenzy as the officers directed the crowd to line up single file, the sounds of their shouts echoing throughout the cavern. The orphans waited patiently for their turn, not saying much of anything — not even talking among themselves — content to wait until it was their turn to pass before the stern-faced immigration people, answer their questions and then walk as soon-to-be Americans into the streets of the greatest country in the world.

Eventually, they were escorted to a separate room where they were welcomed by a man in a neat suit and watch with a golden chain peeking out of his vest pocket. He addressed the crowd of orphans with sincere and sensitive tones.

"Children," he began, "this is a great day for America. Do you know why?"

They shook their heads and wondered why indeed this was a great day for America.

"Because," the man continued, "because," he said once more, "you children have crossed the ocean to come and live in this great country! America is a land that was built by millions of people from hundreds of lands. Every newcomer, whether young or old, male or female, has an integral and important role in the building of this great country. Every one of you sitting in front of me today can become a leader of industry, a lawyer, or a doctor, who will go on to discover the cure to an illness that has been plaguing the world for hundreds of years. It's up to you, children. You are the future of America! Welcome!"

And even though Jason Frost was young, he was still very touched by the idea that he could fulfill his dreams and go on to become a power in this great land. The children gave the man a rousing ovation, and then they filed from the room. They went through customs and were given their luggage. They were given immunizations by a doctor with a dour complexion who made no attempt to spare them pain. It didn't matter. They were in America, and whatever happened along the way to becoming an American was worthwhile and not something to complain about.

Finally they were finished doing everything that needed to be done, and they were able to leave the building, on the way to becoming brand-new American citizens. They were going to go forth and change the world. It was up to them. Their minds were full of the slogans they had just been fed by the official spokesman for the American government. For that first hour, they truly believed that they could cause positive change just by virtue of who they were.

Jason found the streets of New York more amazing then anything he had ever seen before. He had been in many more places than a kid his age had any need to have been. But this first glimpse of an American street was way more than he had ever expected. The sheer vitality of the people doing business, the conglomeration of dialects that assailed his ears from all sides came together in one earth-shattering revelation. This was the place to be. The new world rose up from the ashes of dusty old Europe, to take its place as the leader of civilization.

The children stood on the sidewalk and gawked in dumbfounded awe. Only Jason approached one of the chaperons and asked her when they were going to eat, because he was starving and they hadn't been given food for a long time. Inside he was amazed at the change that had come over him since he'd arrived in America. He had suddenly become brave and had the confidence to speak to those in authority. He followed the peddlers with their pushcarts in fascination, and breathed in the smell of the delicacies that rose from those corner stands. The peddlers' hoarse voices merged with the roar of the traffic. Jason saw the nuns/chaperons go over to one of the carts that sold hot dogs and place their orders.

Within minutes, the food was ready and they each received a hot dog in a bun. They were allowed to put on as much ketchup, mustard and sauerkraut as they wanted. They walked to a neighboring park where they sat underneath the leafy overhang of the solid oaks, and enjoyed their first meal on American soil. Jason would never forget the taste of that first American hot dog. He bit into it and the sizzling juice popped out and dribbled down his chin, and the ketchup oozed out of the bun. The soda was cold and fizzy enough that it tickled his nose. For the moment, he was blissfully happy with his life.

Many of the children fell asleep on the grass after they finished eating. The rest lay on their sides pulling the blades of grass from the moist earth until their fingers had turned a bright green and their clothing was stained. They were content for the first time in a long time. The nuns made sure that they were all cleaned up after their first experience with a New York hot dog. Then they boarded the buses that had arrived. They were taken to their new home in Long Island, where they would be picking up the pieces of their lives under the auspices of the Catholic Church of America, department of orphanages.

5
Moshe Amoni

Teveria, Israel
February 6, 2009

Moshe Amoni was a hardened man in his late 50's. He had spent the majority of his life fighting for a cause and a country in which he believed. He was deeply tanned from spending so much of his youth out of doors, and the muscles in his biceps were taut like oaken strands.

He had fought in the Six-Day and Yom Kippur Wars, and was an unleashed animal on the battlefield. He had commanded the squadron of tanks that had taken control of the Syrian officers' headquarters in the Golan. He was a chain-smoker and loved to sing old Israeli songs from his early pioneer days. He was father of five and grandfather of three, and was supremely proud of all of them.

He had done many things in his life, but wasn't happy about all of them. He had been a farmer, and had grown grapes for wine making and celery for export to Europe. He had killed in the service of his country and was still a colonel in the reserves. And now, after his colorful and interesting life, he had found peace of mind working for Mekorot, the national water company based in Teveria on the banks of Lake Kinneret.

It was actually where he was at the moment. He lifted a bronze-colored cup and carried a water sample to a machine for testing. He waited till the machine gave a final reading. Recently they had received reports about foreign substances in the water, and they were running all sorts of checks to ensure that it didn't occur again.

David, his co-worker and good friend, emerged from the office at the back of the building, and made a few jokes while he waited for Moshe to finish what he was doing.

"So the head of the U.N. and the head of Hamas get pushed off the roof of a building in Beirut. Who hits the ground first?"

"Who?" Moshe asked.

"Who cares?" David replied.

Moshe chuckled. "Very funny," he said.

David was on a roll. "How many *baalei teshuvah* does it take to change a lightbulb?" he asked Moshe.

"*Nu*?" Moshe asked.

"Are we allowed to?"

Moshe laughed at that. "Are you ready to leave yet?" David asked him.

"In a sec," he mumbled, poking his head into to the machine, peering at the graph on the side that indicated the level of purity in red letters. David left, took two bottles of beer from the fridge and went outside to warm up the car. Moshe finished what he was doing and looked at his watch. Leora was waiting at home to go out for their anniversary, and he was late. He waved goodbye to the few workers remaining in the lobby and rushed outside to the car, where David was impatiently leaning on the horn.

He nodded to his friend and got into the car. With a practiced motion, he flipped the cap of the beer bottle out the window and drank deeply from the icy bottle. It had been a long day, and it was time to go home. He relaxed in the air-conditioned car, massaging the kinks from his neck and upper back, as the cool gusts of air made the hairs on his arms stand up. They left Mekorot's grounds behind them in a cloud of exhaust and drove along the side road leading to the kibbutz where they had lived for the past 30 years. David concentrated on the road while Moshe rested, head nodding on his arms.

They pulled into the kibbutz, past the guard booth where Elisha sat listening to the radio, puffs of smoke drifting upward from his ever-present cigarette. Elisha knew full well that he was holding a death sentence in his own hands, but for all his toughness, smoking was an addiction that even the strongest of humans found hard to conquer. They drove down the winding paths, David admiring the massive amounts of flora that the kibbutz had planted so generously all over the streets. He took the road bumps slowly so as not to wake Moshe up with a sudden jolt, finally pulling up outside the Amoni's modest home. A hinged sign with the family name hung suspended from a eucalyptus tree, swinging in the slight evening breeze. Moshe's dog Nimrod ran out, barking in delight at the sight of his master. Moshe awoke with a grunt and stretched and yawned. Then thanking his friend for the ride, he got out of the car.

"See you tomorrow," he said waving goodbye.

David honked the horn in response and pulled away into the sunset of the golden evening. Moshe turned and entered the comfortable home that had seen a generation of kids grow up. He paused for a moment at the hallway mirror, running a sunburned hand through his patch of unruly hair, and flipped through the pile of mail resting there. Then he put down the satchel carrying his work files, and went to the fridge for a drink. From upstairs came the sounds of his wife preparing for their evening out. He shrugged his tired shoulders, and took a can of Coke out to the deck in the backyard. This was where he went when he wanted to think quietly, undisturbed.

It was a verdant paradise out there. There were palm trees, a pomegranate tree and an *aravos* bush. It was a heady mixture of all sorts of smells, and he loved the peacefulness. He popped the top of the can and took a drink, the bubbles making his nose twitch. From inside, he could hear the sound of Leora's heels, and knew that she'd be calling him any moment now. He finished the can and went inside. Five minutes later they were on their way to a restaurant that a friend of hers had recommended in Moshav Amirim. He drove, wearing sunglasses to shield his eyes from the final rays of the setting sun, and hummed tunelessly to himself.

Leora was full of good cheer as befitting their anniversary, and he slowly found himself succumbing to her charm and laughter. The car sped smoothly, as it ate up the miles. Twilight was turning into night, and the shadows alongside the road became deeper and more elongated until there was nothing left to see aside from the road in front of him.

They were smiling at each other as they pulled into Amirim. There were brightly colored lights suspended over the restaurant's garden, and they were greeted by the tinkling of wind chimes moving lightly in the breeze. There was a festive atmosphere, and the bottle of wine that came with the meal made it even better. The food was excellent, and they found themselves rehashing their many years of marriage.

"Remember the time that Nachi fell into the well?" Leora asked him, referring to the time their oldest child had climbed into an abandoned well at the edge of the kibbutz, on a dare from one of his friends, and had not been able to climb out.

"Do you remember when Ruti finished high school and entered the army?" Moshe asked her. "I couldn't sleep for months. I was so worried about her!"

The talk rambled on as the hour grew steadily later. They had black-forest cake with vanilla ice cream for dessert, and one more coffee each. Then it was time to go. The air was whistling mournfully as they left the restaurant. The ride was over before he knew it, and he was in bed and out like a light.

It felt like a few minutes, but must have been a good few hours later when the phone rang. For Moshe Amoni, super-patriot of Israel, things would never be the same. The voice on the other end was fairly young. It spoke carefully, deliberately. It had an accent that Moshe wasn't able to place. He was groggy; he wasn't his usual quick-witted self. It had been a deep sleep. The voice was smooth, conveying trust. It spoke softly, saying every word with direct emphasis.

"Mr. Amoni," the voice said.

"Yes," Moshe replied.

"From what I understand," said the strange voice, "there is a problem with one of your purifying machines." He paused for a moment. "You should check it out." There was a click as the other man hung up his phone.

It was the middle of the night, but Moshe stood up in a matter of seconds. His wife looked up at him and asked who called, and he mumbled something about a wrong number. Then he left the room.

He hurried downstairs, taking them two at a time. He stopped at the hall closet, reaching to the uppermost shelf where his wife never cleaned. He removed a canvas bag containing a change of clothing that he had left there just in case the phone rang in the middle of the night and he couldn't get dressed upstairs. He removed his pajamas and put on the shirt and pants that had sat inside this bag for over a year and a half — ever since he had taken his current job with Mekorot. Then he slipped on a jacket over that. The canvas bag contained some other things as well, besides the clothing. He slung the bag over his shoulder as he slid open the sliding doors leading to the patio at the back of the house.

He left his house with nary a backward glance. The engine started on the first try. He kept the lights off until he was a distance away from his house. Shifting from first to second, he drove down the deserted roads, slowing as he encountered the guard booth for the fourth time that day. Elisha stuck his head out of the booth at the sound of his engine, peering into the eerie night as was his job. When he realized that it was only Moshe, he went back to his magazine, pressing the button for the bar to rise.

Moshe drove out into the darkness of a night in the hills. There were no streetlamps to illuminate the roads, no headlights from approaching vehicles to surprise him. He was on his own. He drove with the window opened, the night-time air feeling like an electric shaver on his jaw. He wasn't thinking; he was reacting. He took side roads for as much of the way as he could, then hit the highway and felt vulnerable for a while. The wait by the traffic lights was immeasurably long. He was going out of his mind.

All too soon, there was a sign for Mekorot, and he swung left. It led down a straight road to the company, empty this time of night, save for a night watchman and the guard who sat in the entrance booth. He sped down the road, the wind whistling through the car like the crescendo of an opera, and stayed focused on what needed to be done. The guard booth was in front of him, and he slowed down and honked. The guard came out of the booth, not expecting anyone this time of night. Moshe waved at the older man and honked his horn another time for good measure. The guard studied him for quite some time almost as if he didn't recognize him. Then Moshe realized that he really didn't know him at all since he came on the night-time shift after Moshe had usually gone home. Maybe they had met once or twice.

Finally he bade Moshe to approach, and then he asked him what the matter was.

"Nothing is the matter," Moshe told him. "I couldn't sleep. I was involved earlier today with a project that I didn't have a chance to finish, so I figured that I would come on down and take care of it, while the place is nice and quiet."

The guard looked at him dubiously, but Moshe maintained his innocent look, until the man shrugged, walked over to the gate and swung it open for his car. Breathing a sigh of relief that he hadn't had to kill the man, Moshe continued driving through the complex, passing water tanks holding sufficient water for the entire north of Israel for a few weeks. Then, not wasting any time, he drove right, straight toward the factory that held the purifying tanks.

He parked his car in one of the reserved parking spots — not that this mattered at that time of night — and carrying a flashlight in his hand as well as the canvas bag, he made his way up to the double-glass doors that led into the building. There was a code pad at the side of the door, and he tapped in the private code that would allow him immediate access.

He moved down the long hallways quietly, making no unnecessary noise. Dim lightbulbs cast their weak glow on the hallway floor as he moved on to the purifying room. It was filled to capacity with large tanks and machinery; it was easily the largest room in the entire building, and the busiest one in the middle of the day. Now the silence was unnerving. He didn't hesitate; it was too late for that. Like a loyal soldier, he pressed on for his mission, not knowing why, but understanding that it must be so.

He reached the first tank, climbed the metal ladder beside it and opened the access window at the top. He unzipped the canvas bag and removed a medium-size bottle which he gingerly unscrewed. Using the flashlight, he measured a specific amount of liquid into a small cup. Taking no time to reflect on what he was doing, he poured the liquid into the tank. Then he climbed down the ladder and, treading softly so as not to be heard, he moved on to the next tank and the next one after that. By the time he had finished the contents of the bottle, the back of his shirt was sticking to him and he felt as if his head was on fire.

He backed down the steep ladder, taking the steps carefully and measuring his every movement. It wouldn't pay for him to fall and break his hip and have the night guard find him there, defenseless and in pain. So he took his time. When he reached the bottom, he moved quickly, with purpose and fluidity. His mind was clear despite the lateness of the hour. He knew that the morrow would bring forth only agony and an attempt at damage control. But that would arrive too little and too late.

He turned the final bend in the hallway, and saw a guard sitting at the front desk. The guard looked up with a squint, taking in the rushing figure approaching him, his hand in the depths of his jacket pocket. He didn't recognize the man coming at him, and there was no earthly reason for this man being here in the first place at this time of night. He was just picking up the phone to dial security, when Moshe made a graceful leap through the air, landing smack on the desk where he kicked the phone out of his hand with one well-placed heel.

The guard's hand went for his gun.

Moshe's hand exited his jacket pocket with a clean forward movement. There was a whirlwind of hand coordination, and Moshe brought a little mallet crashing down on the guard's head so quickly that the guard was still reaching for his gun. He slumped forward in his chair and ceased reaching for anything. Moshe pushed him off the chair and under the desk. He continued on his way without a backward glance as the echoes of the swivel chair turning slowly faded into the distance.

Outside the building, the air tasted frosty and fresh like mint, and the crickets kept up a steady stream of song. Moshe swiftly moved to his car, blending into the shadows with nonchalance and ease. He turned on the ignition and drove out of the gate, the guard giving him one sleepy look before raising the bar for him. He drove in the direction of Teveria and an old abandoned section of the Kinneret, where he had stored a small boat a long time before. He drove at a fast clip, right under the speed limit. Moshe was pulling into the small and narrow inlet before he had a chance to reconsider what he was doing.

Hiding the car under the low-hanging boughs of an old eucalyptus tree, he stepped out after opening the trunk from inside. It opened with a tiny clicking sound. A small light went on in the interior, and Moshe was able to find what he needed. Rapidly, he lifted out two oars. Then walking to the side of the abandoned beach, he reached a large pile of branches and brambles with which he struggled. Eventually he uncovered a boat which he dragged across the rocks to the shallow water. He tested the boat for holes and found it secure. Then without another wasted movement, Moshe Amoni, veteran war hero of Israel, maneuvered his craft completely into the water, and jumped in after it. He clicked the oars into place and shoved off from the beach. The little flashlight he had attached to the front of the boat provided sufficient light for night-time "fishing."

He set course for a harbor inlet, not too far away. It would take him only a little more than an hour to get there, but it was worlds away. His next stop was Jordan, and they would be waiting for him there; he was sure of it.

At 10 o'clock in the morning, the first of the cases arrived at the emergency room, to be followed by more and more people, all suffering terribly, all throwing up and experiencing the strangest sensations. The scandal of the poisoned water had begun. It didn't take the police long to arrive at the Amoni home where a reluctant Mrs. Amoni answered that Moshe had indeed received a phone call in the middle of the night. No, she didn't have the slightest clue who it could have been. And no, he had not given her the slightest clue of what he was about to do. Even worse, she had no idea where in the world he had disappeared to.

6 Kobi Shapiro

Buenos Aires, Argentina
May 2, 1960

How do I look?" Kobi Shapiro asked his silent, taciturn partner. Shalom took a look at him, nodded and grunted in his usual fashion before turning back to his papers. Kobi studied himself in the dirty, cracked mirror that was part of the furnishings in the low-budget motel room. He saw a medium-sized man with black hair, green eyes and an oil smudge along one cheek. He was wearing a pair of coveralls which stated the name of the company for which he worked, and a cap worn low obscuring his face. He had a studied, almost careless appearance as he whistled to himself, before nodding at his reflection in the mirror. When he finished his preparations, he looked at his watch. From the distance came the tinny sounds of a guitar playing the blues.

"It's almost time to go," he said, more to himself than to his partner. They locked the door and left a hair on the knob. There was a piece of tape on the inside as well. They would know if an intruder had broken in when they were away. They took the stairs to the lobby, making eye contact with no one. They were completely anonymous, unrecognizable wallflowers, people who blended into their surroundings. They were not memorable, and that was exactly what they wanted. The lobby was deserted, and they moved through on rubber-soled shoes alerting nobody to their presence. The bus stop was located about seven minutes from the hotel, and they blended in with the locals waiting for the bus to arrive.

A woman waited nearby, pushing a baby carriage holding twins. One of the babies was crying loudly, screaming at the top of his lungs, while the other slept soundly, used to the disturbance. The people looked hot, tired and sweaty. No one gave them a second glance. Five minutes later, the bus appeared at the corner, got caught at a red light, then pulled up to the stop and discharged 10 people, before allowing the newcomers on. They boarded separately. Kobi was the third person onto the bus, Shalom got on second to last. They sat apart and paid no attention to each other. The bus pulled away from the stop in a cloud of exhaust, belching smoke and heat at the passersby. It was summertime in Buenos Aires, and a cloud of smog hung over the city. The people endured the bumpy bus ride lethargic as ever. But Kobi waited tensely knowing that he had to be on the alert, that there was no place for error, not after so many years of hunting.

They left the downtown area. The bus made a sharp right turn, went under an overpass and down into a tunnel. Soon they were on the city's outskirts and the pace was much slower. Up at the front of the bus Shalom coughed once, then again and stood up to get off the bus. They were in a seedier neighborhood now with homes built closer together. The people walking the streets were dressed even more shabbily than at the motel. Shalom got off the front of the bus while Kobi used the back door. Still, without any recognition, they contrived to walk 10 feet apart from each other. Up ahead, Kobi could see a bar, and he knew that the moment he had anticipated had arrived. Would he be there, or not? Was this the man they were searching for so long?

Shalom entered first while Kobi took his time scanning the street for anything out of the ordinary. There was nothing even mildly suspicious. A mother yelled at her kids from the open window of a third-floor apartment, and the mail truck pulled up at the corner to collect the mail. Other than that, the street was quiet. Shrugging his shoulders, Kobi steeled himself and walked into the bar. It was cool inside the long wood-paneled room. A bartender stood at the polished bar taking orders. There was a jukebox playing what sounded like rock and roll, and a few older men sat on round bar stools at the counter looking morose and making little conversation. Shalom took a seat at the bar in front of the mirror that gave him a clear view of the entire room, while Kobi sat himself at the back of the room. It was almost time.

A waiter came by to take his order, and he ordered a tequila with extra lime and a bag of peanuts. On the opposite wall, a fan moved lazily, doing its best to circulate the pungent-smelling air. His drink arrived, and the waiter busied himself arranging things to his satisfaction. Kobi glanced surreptitiously at his watch, mentally willing the waiter to finish already and stop blocking his view of the front door.

The man finally moved out of his way, and when Kobi glanced up again after sticking his wallet back into his pocket, there was a shadow at the entrance and someone was walking into the establishment. He was an older man who appeared to be rather sickly. He was wearing nondescript loose-fitting clothing, a pair of thick-framed eyeglasses that magnified his eyes to many times their true size. His head, or what Kobi could see of it from under the cap he wore, was bald. He moved with a kind of furtiveness, and reminded Kobi of a ferret.

He settled into the second booth from the door, his eyes moving from his drink to the door and back again every few minutes. If you didn't know that he had good reason to watch the door, you wouldn't have guessed that he was doing so. He was not in any way obvious about what he was doing, but the fact that he was acting this way made Kobi even more certain that they were looking at the right man. His blood boiled, and with a casual glance from over his glass he eyed the man who was nursing a beer. Such a simple-looking man. Such a far cry from the prince that he'd been in a different life! Picking up some nuts with his left hand, Kobi slipped his right hand into his pocket. Removing his wallet, which he went through on the pretense of searching for more money, he compared the man near the door with a photo that had been given to them just a few days earlier by someone claiming to be his son. The picture matched the shabby man. They would still have to ascertain that that was the man they were looking for, but the chances were very good. *Strip them of their power and see the difference,* he said to himself, still not daring to believe that the end to his search might be in sight.

In his mind, he tried to superimpose the two men on top of each other. The shabby older man of the here and now over the picture of the dashing officer, the arrogant psychopath, the sadistic mastermind of the most satanic tortures ever devised by man. Could it be the same person?

His son claimed he was. In fact, the man in the picture did share some of the same features of the man they were searching for. For now that would have to be enough. They now had adequate information to risk bringing the main team down from Israel. They would shadow him, check his dental records and they would verify 100 percent that this was the right man. When that was done and he was brought to Israel, they would have laid a million people's nightmares to rest.

The rest of the agents arrived in Buenos Aires from several different directions and continents. They had done their job in many forsaken places around the world, where men of great evil had thought they were safe, but had learned with horror that they were far from safe. The team was well experienced with South America by now, since almost every man they had hunted down had gone there to live (no surprise when you took into consideration the fact that Argentina had no extradition treaty with either America or Israel). Kobi or Shalom picked them up at the airport and drove them into the derelict part of town they called home. The men looked around them with interest, and made sure that certain pieces of their luggage had arrived intact and were at hand, ready for action.

They were professionals and oozed supreme confidence. Each one possessed the special talent that gave him the ability to mask hard work with what appeared to be indifference. Kobi and Shalom briefed them. Slowly the men began setting a plan in place. There was absolutely no room for error. They did not want this one getting away. If they lost him, he would be gone forever, and they would never forgive themselves. One of them verbalized their thoughts while absentmindedly rubbing the number on his arm.

They prepared a plan, a back-up plan and a safe house for when the plan succeeded. They spent considerate time determining how to handle the man after they had him in their grasp, and how to control the more unrestrained of their team who would happily gut his entrails and hang him from the nearest lamppost. There was to be none of that. This man was to be an example of what they could do if they put their minds to it. The entire world would know about their exploit, and that there was nowhere safe for those who were enemies of the team. That was the goal. They went to sleep the night before with heartburn in the gut of more than one of them. This was scary. One misstep could prove fatal. It had in the past. They were weary, so they slept.

The morning of the operation, they needed every last bit of strength they could muster. One by one they left the safe house, and made their collective way to their respective posts. It was early in the morning, and the hazy smog of Buenos Aires had thus far not put in an appearance.

Buenos Aires, Argentina
May 11, 1960

The car was in place. The team in charge of that facet of the operation took up their spots in the live drama they were producing. The car was experiencing severe "stomach pains," and its hood was up in the air with two men huddled around examining its innards with rapt attention. Another man was riding the bus along with the man who called himself Ricardo Klement, just in case something went wrong and he didn't get off. Zero hour was fast approaching. The minutes ticked by on their synchronized watches, and they waited with tenseness and hope, tinged by the cynicism their job had taught them over the years. They had grown used to disappointment, so much so, that any success, however small, became the cause for great celebration. After a while, they stopped muttering among themselves. They couldn't talk. Their emotions were running much too high. The critical hour had arrived and nobody had anything more to say.

Would Ricardo Klement be on the next bus or the one after that, or would he perhaps not arrive at all? Had he been warned by the organization named Odessa, which specialized in smuggling people like Klement far away and out of the clutches of the Israelis? An oversized rusty bus began cresting the hill in their direction. But it was still early, and they weren't expecting him yet. First he would enjoy his daily pit stop at the friendly and quiet bar that Kobi and Shalom had staked out. Then when he was just a little soused, enough that his memories would only be good ones, Ricardo would leave the bar and board another bus in the direction of his simple home. It was odd that a man who had been so successful should have ended up here, in the run-down suburbs of this sprawling metropolis. But that was none of their concern.

The minutes passed with agonizing slowness, as if the hands on the clock had ceased moving. The men wiped the sweat from their brows and got under the car. They tinkered with the parts, cursing from frustration and impatience. It was almost time.

They could hear the ancient rumble from afar as the aging monolith began wheezing its way up the hill, groaning with the effort. Clouds of black oily smoke belched from its exhaust pipe as it strained against gravity. This was it; all these months of planning, coming to a culmination right then. The bus came to a creaking halt, shifting back and forth on its haunches as it opened its doors to allow the passengers to exit. Five people got off the bus: two elderly women, a young boy licking an ice-cream cone, a teenager wearing jeans, pausing from time to time to hoist his backpack farther up his back. And the man. The man who called himself Ricardo Klement, the man who worked as a foreman at the local Mercedes-Benz factory.

He was walking slowly, intently measuring one small footstep after another. It was the man from the bar, and he looked like a loser. The two men under the car were ready. Everyone was ready. The operation was a go. The elderly women had vanished from sight. The young boy was intent on his cone, and wouldn't have paid attention if an earthquake had come his way. The teenager turned into one of the nearby homes. Still, the man with the balding crown came closer, not knowing that the devil was waiting for him. When he was fairly close to the car, Zvi Aharoni stepped up to him and asked him for a cigarette. As he reached into his pocket, the men who had been tinkering under the car rolled out and attacked him, attempting to take him down. He fought back. Peter Malkin, a Polish Jew with a black belt in karate, knocked Klement unconscious with a chop to the back of his neck. They bundled the silent form into the car.

Kobi quickly closed the hood. The agent in the driver's seat turned on the ignition. They drove out of the suburbs, until the houses were few and far between, and their safe house was close by. They had arrived. Their quarry was still oblivious when they carried him out of the car and into the simply furnished house. He was put to bed in a room with no furniture other than a bed and chair. He was handcuffed to the bed, and the room was searched before they locked him in.

It was morning before they entered his room. Kobi and one of the other agents went into the room. The man was lying on the bed facing the wall. His cap was off and they could see little tufts of hair sticking up on all sides. He looked pathetic and miserable, and for a second Kobi thought that maybe they had made a mistake, that maybe this was the wrong man.

"Good morning," Kobi said in pleasant tones. "I trust you had a restful evening and are ready to answer a few simple questions." While he spoke, he unlatched windows, and released the handcuffs. The man trembled as he stood up. Kobi grasped his arm so he wouldn't fall over, even though touching the man filled his entire being with a tremendous loathing. They brought the man downstairs to the basement, and sat him down on a hard wooden chair. A harsh light was turned on, aimed directly at the man's face. The questioning began:

"What is your name?"

"Ricardo Klement," the man answered.

"What is your name?" the question was delivered again, with more bite in the tone.

The same response. The man's hands were trembling. He was shaking like a leaf. It was clear that he knew there could be only one winner in this game.

"WHAT IS YOUR NAME?" Kobi screamed at the man.

"Ricardo Kle ..." the man tried to say.

Kobi ripped the man's shirtsleeve and pulled it up his arm with extra force, enjoying the feeling of terror that he was inflicting on the man. He pulled the sleeve up to the man's shoulder, and forced off his shirt on one side of his body. When he was sufficiently exposed, Kobi lifted the skinny naked arm so the others could see underneath. There it was, the dreaded symbol of the SS, the tattoo that every officer had under his arm.

The man was now quivering in his seat. His eyes were rolling in his head. He was crying. Kobi looked into those dark eyes. Those twin pits of destruction. The eyes that had sent millions of Jews to their deaths without blinking, without thinking twice.

"Your name," Kobi went on remorselessly.

"Ricardo Klement," the man said again in a hoarse voice that was almost a cry. Kobi grabbed his mouth and forced it opened while other members of the team compared "Klement's" actual dental work to what their records said should be there. It was a 1,000 percent match. He had the dental work. He had the tattoo. His eyes were the right color, as was his hair — or what was left of it. There was no doubt in Kobi's mind that he was their man.

Kobi took out a gun from his pocket and approached the man slouching in the wooden chair. He pointed the gun at the man, and placed it against his skull. He spoke in a very soft voice, which somehow seemed a lot scarier than the screaming that had gone on previously.

"For the last time," he said as he pressed the snub-nosed revolver into the back of the man's head, "what is your name?"

The man sat still for what seemed like forever, but was more like two minutes. Then he spoke in German: "My name is Adolph Eichmann."

It was a miracle! They had apprehended the number-one man, the architect of the Wannsee Conference, the colonel who had masterminded the mass destruction of almost all the Jews of Hungary. He was in Israeli hands and he was as good as dead!

They flew him to Israel dressed in an EL AL uniform, supporting him between two stewards, as if he were inebriated to the point that he couldn't walk. He was drugged, and they weren't expecting any trouble. They knew their job and they would do it well. The monster would be coming back to Israel, where millions of people would face the demons of their pasts in what would become an intense courtroom drama never seen before in the Holy Land. They had identified him conclusively; there was no doubt that this was Adolph Eichmann. He was going to hang for his crimes.

The trial would be a chance for a festering wound to be opened, and for the pus to be let out. All the survivors who hadn't been able to discuss the Holocaust and what they had been through would finally be able to talk. Nobody had been interested in listening to them. People were actually embarrassed of them, calling them sheep, preferring to identify with the new breed of Sabras — the warriors — rather than with people who had gone to their deaths without putting up a fight. But this trial was going to change all of that.

By the time that the trial would be underway, the Israeli public was going to have acquired a much better insight into what had really occurred during the darkest period in European history. Names and faces from the past would come alive in that Jerusalem courtroom, as survivor after survivor stood up and testified against the archfiend. The world press was there en masse. Photographers, journalists, every major news' network in the world had arrived. Eichmann's face was plastered across the front cover of every publication around the globe. It would last for quite a while, and the entire nation would mourn collectively once again. Then would come a catharsis and they would be able to be healed. Closure, that was what they were all seeking. Closure.

They hanged him around midnight on May 31, 1962 at Ramle Prison. He was unrepentant and supremely evil until the end, saying that he felt no need to apologize for what he had done. They hanged him, and everyone breathed a sigh of relief, because the face of evil had been unmasked and destroyed. Now they could return to their everyday lives with a feeling that there was hope after all. But for Kobi and Shalom and the entire team, this was just the beginning. There was so much more work to be done.

After the amazing coup they had pulled off with the capture of Adolph Eichmann, and the subsequent hanging of one of the Jewish nation's archfiends, the group's appetite was whetted for more success. They had done it! Finally one of the modern-day Hamans had been unmasked and brought to Israel to stand trial for his crimes. There had been some accountability, and the people wanted more. In the op-ed pieces in the national papers, the editors wondered why such captures and trials weren't happening more frequently.

"Why is it," asked the editor of *Davar*, in rhetorical tones, "if the Mossad is capable of orchestrating such original, daring and successful operations, they are content to rest on their laurels? So many other ex-Nazis who have committed the most heinous atrocities against the Jewish nation sit unpunished and unrepentant in the Germany of today and all over South America. How is it possible for the government of the Jewish nation to sit passively and allow such a disturbing pattern to continue unchallenged? It is incumbent on the Mossad, who has shown what its capabilities are, to pursue this course until the people of Israel know that the murderers have finally been brought to justice!"

The Mossad had been, of course, unavailable for comment. That further fueled the paper's desire to write more, to see if they could get the Mossad to crack and make some sort of comment, but that did not happen. The Mossad was unassailable, granitelike and unimpressed by the writings of newspaper editors with papers to sell. They would carry out operations if and when they were deemed viable, for the security of the Jewish nation. Until that point, the Mossad would sit silently and ignore all the big mouths of the press.

But the reality was that there were many in the Mossad itself who agreed with the Israeli press on this topic. They knew firsthand how difficult it was to plan an operation of this magnitude. They also knew of all the failures, and that the chances of success on any one given operation were slim indeed. But they were still of the opinion that the State of Israel owed their people to at least attempt to carry out some reprisals against those who had done such harm. This movement within the agency grew on a daily basis. Finally the superiors in the organization came to the conclusion that it would be beneficial for company morale were they to take such a mission to a successful conclusion.

It was clear to one and all how difficult this was going to be. First, after the Eichmann operation, the remaining Nazis on the run had taken precautions so that they too didn't end up in the same Israeli noose that had put an end to Eichmann. The spider's web, known as the "Odessa network," was now working overtime to ensure that any Nazis who weren't sufficiently protected would receive whatever assistance they needed, whether financial, diplomatic or otherwise. Plastic surgery was used for the more familiar faces, and Odessa provided the necessary documents for anyone who wanted to leave Europe for friendlier shores.

Secondly, the biggest fish were already firmly entrenched in whatever location they had chosen for themselves. Either they were scientists, military or economic experts, who made themselves indispensable to their respective governments, thereby making their host countries unwilling to assist the Israelis. There was always some area of expertise that the former Nazis possessed. They had been trained so well and were so efficient, that they were held in high esteem in whichever country they had chosen. Even in the United States, stories had been told of Nazi scientists who had helped NASA in its ongoing cold war with Russian, helping America maintain its number-one status by being the first to put a man on the moon.

Yet, taking all that into consideration, the Mossad still felt that this was the right thing to do. It would be the perfect salve for a nation that was constantly on the receiving end from the Arabs around them. Furthermore, it would provide an extremely strong deterrent for Israel's enemies, by showing the world that Israel's intelligence agencies were able to carry out the type of missions that no other country could. So, after much consideration and thought had gone into the decision-making process — and everyone who needed to had given their consent — a team was put together for one express purpose: the capture of one man.

Tel Aviv, Israel
January 2, 1972

"Kobi," the man known as "S" said genially.

They were sitting in one of the Mossad offices for operation planning. Kobi had been called into the boss's office where he waited patiently to find out what the boss wanted from him. He was in no rush. If there was anything that Kobi had learned over the years, it was that the Mossad told you what you needed to know only on a need-to-know basis. Even then, they rarely apprised you of all the facts. So he sat in front of his boss's desk and reread the signs and studied the pictures hanging on the wall directly over the desk. He played a game with himself, studying each picture for 10 seconds, seeing how many details he could remember after glancing at it for a short amount of time.

Meanwhile "S" was on the phone talking to someone while smoking a cigar. Kobi wished that he would finish the cigar already because he was polluting the atmosphere in the office. Every so often, the boss would wave his cigar through the air, as though accentuating a point. The ash would fall onto the desk, the worn-out carpet, or on the papers on his desktop. Then there would be frantic scurrying to make sure that nothing caught fire. Kobi just watched with a bemused air. He was used to the boss's antics, and he had tremendous respect for the man and for everything he had done for the country.

"S" was a short man on the rotund side. He had thinning black hair and a hangdog look to him. The clothing that he wore looked like they had been purchased at a thrift shop. But take one good look at the man's eyes, and you realize why he stood at the helm of one of the most respected of all intelligence agencies in the world. There was a fire in those eyes. This man had brains. The operations he had planned and directed had been so incredibly daring, so full of originality and spirit, that he had been catapulted up the promotion ladder relatively quickly. Today he was the boss of all bosses. He had been the brains behind the Eichmann operation. Whereas Rafael Eitan had actually carried out the mission, this man had planned the operation from beginning to end.

The phone conversation came to end. Kobi watched as "S" replaced the receiver in its cradle, and took one last deep drag on his pungent-smelling cigar before grinding it out in the overflowing ashtray on his desk.

"Kobi, *motek*," the boss sighed, "I'm sorry for making you wait. Those shleppers in Algeria can't get anything done right. I even considered sending you down there to straighten them out. But at the last moment, I decided that you are too important to be wasted on some dead-end job in Algeria. No, I have something much more important for you to take care of, Kobileh."

The man paused. Kobi waited silently. He never interrupted. That was one of the things the big boys liked about him. Besides, you could learn so much from the body language of the man briefing you: if he was sitting straight or hunched over; if his fingers were steepled on the desk or clasped together. Kobi was usually able to tell if the mission stood a good chance of success from his briefing. Was the boss nervous or calm, and how much was he smoking while they talked? Was he giving his agent the whole picture or was he leaving out crucial information?

"Kobi," the boss said again, "this is going to be a very tough operation. I hesitate to send you out into the field, knowing that you have mostly been focusing on the planning side of things for the last few years. But Kobi, this is the kind of mission that an agent receives only once every few years; that's if he's lucky.

"You carried out your role in the Eichmann operation wonderfully. *Kol Hakavod*! But everyone has agreed that it's time for the next stage — to hook the next big fish — and you're the guy they want to reel him in. One more successful operation and you get moved upstairs with a promotion. You know how it goes."

"What's the objective?" Kobi asked.

"You tell me, *motek*," the boss replied. "Think about it for a moment. After Eichmann, who would we want the most? Whose capture would mean the most to the citizens of Israel?"

Kobi thought, and he felt that old familiar stirring of excitement that had once provided the adrenalin that he had needed to exist. For the first time in a long time, Kobi felt the old fire coming back. It was the way he had felt before the whole attack had happened, before his entire world had collapsed before his eyes. He recalled the anger and the fear, the immense pain that had invaded his being, that had removed his will to live. But now it flared up again — red hot and razor sharp — as if it had just occurred a few moments before. Suddenly he knew that it was up to him to even out the score, and to make it up to Shalom. That was what Shalom would have wanted him to do.

"S" was watching carefully as the emotions battled it out inside of him. The boss hid his own emotions, since Kobi was having enough trouble making the right choice without having to deal with the boss's pain and regret as well. Then, with tears glistening in his eyes, Kobi looked the boss straight in the eyes. He said that if they were going to go after the man he thought the boss was talking about, he didn't see that he had much choice but to agree to take on the mission, for his country.

"Who do you think it is?" asked the man in charge.

"Josef Mengele," answered Kobi, in as quiet a voice as he had ever spoken. The boss nodded in agreement, because that was the person of whom he was speaking.

"How did you know?" he asked Kobi.

Kobi gave a short little bark of laughter and replied that he didn't even have to answer that question. The one man more evil than Eichmann (if that were possible) was Mengele, and it would be a privilege and honor to bring the man to justice.

"But," said Kobi, "I have a question. How is it possible that nobody ever came close to capturing the man?"

"That's a good question," the boss said, "but unfortunately I don't have a very good answer. Somehow Dr. Mengele escaped after the war without a trace. No doubt he is a very smart man, and he uses every bit of brains that he was born with for devilish purposes. Nobody who has ever met the man could forget him, could possibly delete the impression that he made. Those gray eyes, like a reptile. No humanity within them, no warmth, no empathy or sadness. Nothing even close to emotion. The man was a psychopath — an emotionally sick and twisted man – who was possessed of an incurable desire to harm and hurt other people. In a different lifetime, the doctor might have been incarcerated in a mental institution. But this was World War II, and unbalanced dangerous people had become the rulers of society."

In such an unhinged world, Dr. Josef Mengele reigned supreme. This was where his unique talents were appreciated, and where he was promoted until he was given the right to decide who would live and who would die. Everything happened at his whim. He sent millions of innocent people to the death chambers: men, women and children, babies, the infirmed, the elderly, the mentally ill, the strong and the weak; it made no difference to the "doctor." The voices cried out from the ground, even after so many years. They cried out for the man to be found, for his face to be shown to the world.

Now, here was Kobi's chance to bring this man to justice in Jerusalem! So he turned a grave-looking countenance to the boss and nodded twice, in effect saying that he was accepting this mission for the good and for the bad, knowing the possible consequences, realizing the risks.

As he walked out of the office on the way back to his little cubicle, Kobi couldn't help but remember that it should have been both of them walking out of the office to plan the operation. If not for that one night, everything might have been so different. But that was all in the past, and there was no going back. Still, there were times when Shalom's face intruded on his thoughts, and this was one of those times.

Yes, Shalom, he whispered, *how excited you would have been to be assigned such a mission. You would have considered it such an honor. You would have danced down the stairs in your quiet way. But I knew, I always knew what was going through your head. I know that you would have been ecstatic to be granted such an opportunity. But that's life, Shalom.*

Kobi walked down the hallway to his office and, after closing the blinds, took a seat by his desk. He laid his head on his arms and remembered that night. The tears came once again, and he tried to wipe them away. He rubbed his fists into his eyes and whispered quietly to himself, *Stop being such a baby.* But that didn't help, of course, and before he knew what was happening, he was remembering every detail of the night he had tried so hard to forget. That was the night that Shalom was taken from him; the night when he had stopped living for a while. Time lost all meaning, and he would never know how long he sat at the desk and cried. But eventually he fell asleep on his arms, and the next thing he knew, he was reliving it all over again.

~

When they returned triumphantly from the Eichmann operation, there had been a celebration at Mossad headquarters for the team that had pulled off such an incredible coup. There had been a catered meal in the dining room, and all the agents had been there to celebrate along with them. This had been a triumph for all of them, and the drinks ran like water and the boys had gotten tipsy. Such a successful operation would be dissected and discussed by intelligence agencies around the world for years to come. The day after had come the debriefing, and they had gone over the entire operation from start to finish, looking for the holes in the strategy, searching for the mistakes that had been made. They were especially focused on the fact that one of the agents had tripped and almost made a botch of the entire operation due to his untied shoelaces.

Conclusions were drawn, promotions received and the proud team was given tickets so that they could watch the trial. They observed the trial in silence, reliving those final tense and agonizing moments when they weren't certain that it was Eichmann. They remembered the capture and the interrogation, and they heard the reams of testimony, until their blood boiled with hatred and disgust against this simple-looking man. They watched until he received the death sentence. Then they knew that it was time to go home. They had done all they could to bring the murderer to justice. They had succeeded, and now they could go home and take a well-deserved break. So they had gone back to their moshav, back to the oasis of peace that beckoned to them, calling out to them to return home. Home. How beautiful the word sounded!

Most of the team lived in a moshav in the north of the country that overlooked the Kinneret. It was a wonderful place to live. It was quiet and peaceful there. There were plenty of fruit and palm trees and you could see Mount Hermon from your window in the morning when the fog lifted. The moshav was inhabited almost entirely by Holocaust survivors and their families. A *simchah* in the moshav was something that was celebrated by every single family, because they could still remember a time when they never thought they would experience a *simchah* ever again. A birth, bar mitzvah, or wedding was a full-fledged celebration for every one of them. It was another victory over the Nazis. The members of Moshav Arazim belonged to families that had, for the most part, been decimated in Europe, and had arrived in Israel as refugees with nothing more than the shirts on their backs. They had rebuilt their lives with new families — new wives and children — new memories to replace the old ones.

This, then, was the home of the Nazi hunters. It was easy to become a Nazi hunter if you lived in this moshav. All you had to do was look around you, into the eyes of the survivors, and you could see firsthand what the Nazis had done to the Jewish nation. From there, to deciding on a career in the service was a short step away. Obviously, not everyone who wanted to join the Mossad was accepted, and not everyone who was accepted for the early tests made it through the entire training. You had to possess nerves of steel to survive the kind of training to which they subjected their agents. Most of the people who were recruited by the Mossad realized that they would have to find another way to serve their country, because it was almost impossible to complete the training with flying colors.

But every so often, there were one or two who made it through; who were emotionally healthy and physically strong enough to get through the training. Of those who made it to the end, a disproportionate number came from Moshav Arazim: home to the agents who were willing to do whatever it took to bring the killers to justice. That was why the moshav was so peaceful. No matter how violent and scary their personal lives could become, when they arrived back at the moshav, they shed that part of themselves and reverted to the seemingly carefree, playful people they had been before they were recruited. They relished the quiet of the tree-lined paths, the joy of a night, listening to music under the stars, or having a conversation in the playground. This was their real life, the rest was just their job. It was what they did, not who they were. The moshav was who they were. It meant the world to them. It was the place that had allowed them to rebuild their lives after the Holocaust, granting them the serenity they needed to come back to themselves.

They lived for their moshav, but if necessary, they would die for it as well.

Shali Loeberbaum

Caesarea, Israel
March 3, 2009

"How much does it cost for a plane ride over Israel for about an hour?" asked the sandy-haired girl to the young man standing at the counter.

"It's $300 for an hour's private flight," he answered. "We encourage our customers to book in advance because there are not always sufficient planes to satisfy the demand." He spoke in precise English. The sandy-haired girl thanked him and returned to the corner of the room where her friends were standing, studying the pictures on the walls. The pictures had been taken from the cockpit of a private plane belonging to the company.

"Should we do it?" the girl asked her friends.

"I think we should," said a petite girl with freckles. "This will be something to show everyone back home. Israel," she spread her arms wide, "the uncensored view." They all laughed.

"Okay," the girl with sandy hair told the guy at the desk. "We'll book a one-hour flight."

"Fine," he replied. "Just fill out this paperwork, and we can have you up in the air within 20 minutes."

"I can't believe I'm even thinking about doing this," said the petite girl again. "What's wrong with me? I didn't throw up enough times on the way to this country, I should make myself throw up on purpose?! What's wrong with me?" They laughed at her and told her she was crazy. They all agreed. Twenty minutes later, they were on the runway and ready to go.

They had a great time.

In fact everyone always had a great time at Shali's flying school. Whether they were the recipients of flying lessons, or just taking a brief pleasure flight up in the clouds over Israel, Shali's flying school provided the finest service for the best price. Shali himself had an impeccable record. He had flown recon for the Israeli Air Force, distinguishing himself with his military performance. For years he had been considered one of the greatest pilots in the IAF, and had been in line to be the top air force general, when he had been injured in a freak accident. But that didn't mean that Shali gave up flying. Not at all. He still flew many hours a week, by himself, with passengers and with his family. His firm had grown until they possessed 10 small aircraft. There were numerous clients who kept their planes at his airfield, just because they trusted Shali to do their maintenance the way it should be done.

Shali himself was a very friendly man in late middle age. He could make the most serious person laugh, and everyone enjoyed his company. There was a restaurant on the flight-school premises, and there were many nights when a crowd of older Israelis could be found in the restaurant, singing Israeli folk songs for hours, to the accompaniment of a bongo and a few guitars. The walls of the restaurant were plastered with pictures of Shali together with the air force greats: Ezer Weizman, Dan Chalutz, all there with their arms around everyone's favorite pilot. And if the air field was in close proximity to one of the army's most security-conscious bases, nobody thought much about it, because if anyone had the security clearance and was trusted to be near such an establishment, it was Shali Loeberbaum.

But the flight school never took their students over that army base. Even Shali Loeberbaum, the ace of the air force, did not have clearance to fly over such a sensitive area. Even if it were Shali himself, the situation could very well deteriorate, because flyovers were discouraged even by the toast of the air force. So the students and the tourists flew over other areas. Shali was an honest man, making an honest living, bringing happiness to the people around him. That was the way everyone would have described Shali; at least until the morning of the day that he went berserk.

It was 9:25 in the morning when the phone rang. The secretary, a woman who had served under Shali in the air force, answered the phone.

"Flight school," she said.

"Please ask the boss if the four Piper Cubs that were ordered for this afternoon have been serviced yet," the voice said.

Sarit had taken down stranger messages than this, and wrote it on the message board. It was at that moment that Shali entered the office in his flying gear and holding his helmet, about to depart on a two-hour flight with some tourists. Sarit passed on the message. She was never sure what exactly happened after that. Shali went from a joking mood to stone seriousness in two seconds.

"Tell me the message again," he said to her, and Sarit, never having seen him this way, nevertheless repeated the message. Shali placed his helmet on the desk and exited the club. He got into his jeep and rode out to the farthest hanger on the field where he had kept his private plane for years. It was in mint condition, and no wonder, since Shali spent every Sunday night making sure that the engine was in fine working order. Shali got out of the jeep, stood for a moment contemplating the business that he had put together over the past 10 years, turned and got into the plane.

That was the last time that anyone ever spoke to Shali Loeberbaum, flying legend of the Israeli Air Force.

He didn't bother waiting for clearance, violating every rule he had spent years drumming into his crew. He simply took off, heading straight for that top-secret army base that was a mere four minutes distance by plane. The alarms went off as soon as he entered the airspace of the base, and became loud enough to raise the dead when they realized that the plane didn't have any intention of stopping. Far down below, the sentries heard the alarm and raised their binoculars to scan the skies.

Boaz Shachar was the second line of defense. In a normal situation things would have never gotten this far, but the fact that the plane was recognized as coming from Shali's school complicated matters considerably. Nobody wanted to be the one to shoot down some kid learning to be a pilot in a moment of overzealousness. Besides, the school was so close to the base that the plane was almost overhead before they knew what was going on. Thus, the sentry in the first line of defense missed his opportunity to become a hero. Shachar was watching the little dot in the sky as it got closer and closer. He didn't like this one bit. Why wasn't anyone shooting this guy down? Even if it was one of the students from next door, that didn't change anything! *In fact,* thought Shachar to himself, *if they shot him down, he'd probably never do something so stupid again.* In fact, the chances of someone surviving a direct confrontation with the shoulder missile that Shachar was pointing at the little plane was not very promising at all.

Not that that made any difference at all. It didn't. Nobody should be flying over this army base. The material on this base was much too sensitive to be subjected to any scrutiny by outsiders. So when the small plane continued flying against all warnings of the Israeli army, Boaz Shachar simply raised the personal missile launcher on his shoulder until it was positioned just right. He waited the extra second until he was sure that he had the plane locked in his sights, and then he pressed down on the trigger. Two seconds later, the plane blew up in a cloud of smoke and exhaust. It was a strange thing, but instead of the plane just blowing up when the gas tank exploded, it was much more than that.

The plane exploded in a cloud of black smoke, then it did it again and again. Fireball after fireball rose, and the stench and decay of destruction was everywhere. It was almost as if that plane had been filled with napalm, and one match was sufficient to send off the continuing shock waves. The plane was charred beyond belief. There was almost nothing recognizable, certainly not the body inside the cockpit. There was nothing left to identify.

"Shachar!"

"Yes, sir!"

"Stand down, soldier. What the blazes happened out there?"

"Sir, I was at my lookout point when I noticed an approaching aircraft flying very quickly toward the base's most sensitive location. He was coming in so quickly that the lookout at the first location missed him. It was up to me to take him out with my missile launcher. So I put that big boy on my shoulder and let it rip, just the way that the manual says!"

"What if it was an accident, Shachar? Did you think about that?"

"Yes, sir, I did think about that, sir! But the alternative not to fire was far more detrimental. This is why they put me here, sir: to make sure that nobody gets through our airspace. Not the Iranians, the Pakistanis or some dumb kid from Shali's school."

"Okay, Shachar," the commander said. "I will forward your account of the event to the proper authorities. You did well, son, and I will be putting in a recommendation for a promotion for you. *Kol Hakavod*, soldier!"

"Thank you, sir."

~

Not too many people knew that the plane was headed for Section E of the air base, nor would they have comprehended what that meant, even if they would have known. But Commander Benny Alon knew that there would have been no other destination for a plane crammed with explosives other than E. Home to a host of experiments by the scientific department of the Israeli army, Section E was brimful of biological and nuclear components, as well as an entire array of the latest in a plethora of nerve diseases, which would have resulted in a breakdown in society if they would have been exposed to the light of day. But here was the big question. Why would anyone, least of all somebody with the record and history of Shali Loeberbaum, fly a plane full of explosives heading to blow up some of the most sensitive military material in the country? What on earth was going on here, and who exactly was Shali Loeberbaum?

~

Since this wasn't the first attack on a strategic Israeli location in the past few months, the Shin-Bet and other lesser-known intelligence agencies got right onto the situation. They met at Shin-Bet Headquarters. The giant conference room was occupied by as many as 40 agents, who were drinking coffee by the gallon and had sunglasses clipped to their shirt pockets. At the moment, they were mostly milling about, talking to one another. But that came to a halt when the agent in charge of the operation entered the room. Dror Lapid was a real tough boss, and no one wanted to get on his bad side. At least not this early into the investigation.

"What do we have so far?" he asked the assembled in rhetorical tones as he stood at the lectern and stared them down. When nobody answered his question, he said, "That's what I thought."

"O.K., first of all, there was that incident in Teveria with Moshe Amoni, a loyal patriot, if there ever was one. He fought in numerous wars, was a family man; couple of kids, loyal husband and father. Good man until he went nuts and broke into the Mekorot processing plant in the middle of the night, whacked some of the people and poisoned a whole slew of the water towers. No explanation comes to mind as to why such a stable good-hearted man would do such a crazy thing and then disappear." Those seated around the table looked at him with raised eyebrows.

"Amoni and his wife got home late after going out to celebrate their anniversary, went to sleep and sometime in the middle of the night a phone call came in. Amoni got up, left the house without telling his wife where he was going, drove his car to Mekorot and did what he did. He never came home. To be honest with you, I find it pretty hard to imagine that we'll be able to find the man, given the fact that he's been around the entire country, and knows it like the back of his hand. In fact, something tells me that Mr. Amoni isn't even in the country anymore." He paused for breath.

"The question here is: Why? Why would someone like Amoni do this? Which brings us to person number two, which is even stranger! I mean, Shali Loeberbaum was an honest-to-goodness hero! The man was one of the pilots whom the air force intended to send to bomb the nuclear reactor in Iraq. Shali was on so many missions and saw so much combat that he was nicknamed 'Jagged Ice' by the boys because they said that he never lost his cool, no matter what was going on around him. This man made the air force his career. This man almost died for his country 20 times. He always went back in when they asked him. They kept on asking him to go back in, until that terrible day when his plane went into a tail-spin, and they had to pull him out of the ocean. That was when he came to the realization that his air force days were over.

"And you know what?" Dror asked the crowd, as the agents wrote feverishly, trying to keep with his rapid speech. "Every kid who enters the air force wants to be a carbon copy of Shali. That's what they want. Ezer Weizman is cool; they're all cool. But Shali is the man they idolized. So what on earth happened here?!

"This is a tough situation. We don't want to risk antagonizing Shali's family by digging too obviously into his past. On the other hand, we can't afford not to dig into his past. So we are going to dig, and we won't be obvious about it, and everyone will be happy. Understood?"

"Understood," they all chorused. With a scowl, Lapid closed his notebook with one quick motion, and went to the corner of the room to speak with one of the agents. The rest of the group congregated by the coffeemaker to compare notes and discuss the case. This was going to be one tough case. They had to be very sensitive to the family on the one hand, while being even more sensitive to Israeli security on the other. But there was no choice. There was a force in motion to undermine the country, and they had to discover who it was. Five minutes later, the room was quiet once again, as the agents headed to their own offices and investigations, each hoping that he would be the one to make the crucial break.

8
Rafi Ganim

Rishon LeTzion, Israel
August 21, 1985

The morning radio show opened with a poignant violin piece. The music soared out of the speakers leaving its indelible impact on all who heard it. It was Verdi they were playing, but it made no difference at all. It was the kind of music they played whenever there was a crisis, whenever people had been hurt in an attack of some kind. Rafi Ganim adjusted the volume and waited tensely for the piece to end, for the talk-show host to begin his early-morning show. Four minutes later, he had heard the latest news. It was far from good. Two soldiers had been killed on the Lebanese border at 11 p.m. the previous evening. Hezbollah had taken responsibility at 6 o'clock in the morning, and the whole country was in mourning.

Once again there was sad music on the radio. Once again, the nation wore grief etched on their faces. It was the price they paid for living in Israel. The violin sang out its mournful tune, and Rafi found himself crying along with the music, picturing a house full of people waiting for their son/brother/husband/father to return, soon to discover that they would never see him again. He turned the volume up a little higher. He threw himself into the music. Rafi closed his eyes, letting the music wash over him, as if it were ocean waves. The piece came to an end. He shut the radio. It was time to face the day, and Rafi began to pull himself together. It was time to go to school. Without wasting any more time, he got dressed and went into the kitchen for breakfast. The tune he had heard reverberated through his mind, the mournful cry refusing to relinquish its tenuous hold on him.

~

"What instrument do you plan to study?" his mother asked him as they stood outside the music store. Rafi gazed through the window at the large assortment of beautiful instruments masterfully displayed to their best advantage. A drum set held center stage, five guitars next to that, and several of the newest keyboards. There was a piccolo and a French horn, and what looked like an entire brass section. He could feel his fingers tingling with the excitement of it all.

"I want a violin," he told his mother. He could visualize the radio in his room, and he heard the announcer speaking in somber tones about the murdered soldiers. He recalled the emotional turmoil of a country so inured to such acts as to have become callous and thick skinned in response.

~

Rafi had begun purchasing tapes while still a young teenager. He would listen to the concertos for hours at a time; the music, a soothing healing balm for a country so wounded. The more he listened, the more he knew that one day he would learn to play the violin, would master that most complex of instruments.

The money had been a gift from his grandparents, and that was how they found themselves browsing through the music store. His mother thought he was studying the violins before making his choice. He took one look and knew that he had found what he was looking for. There, resting on a music stand was the violin of his dreams: its wood glossy with a special finish, its strings taut in the stillness of the display. It was calling out to him, and instinctively he knew that this violin was going to become his.

"There it is, Ima," he told his mother while pointing at the violin. His mother looked from his face to the violin, saw the confidence and surety on him, and knew that he would be unyielding on the subject. They had inquired as to the price. The salesman took one look at them and decided that today was his day.

"You have to understand," he began, "that there are a wide range of violins in the world. To make what I'm going to tell you a little easier to comprehend, let me speak to you as if I was talking about cars. On the one hand, there are the Mercedes Benz and the BMW: top-valued cars for top price. On the other hand, there is the 15-year-old Subaru: flakes of rust falling off its body every time you slam the trunk closed. Then there are those in the middle, like the Toyota or Buick. Those are respectable vehicles, and they go for a price that most people consider fair. It's the same thing in violins," he said. "It just happens to be that the violin you've selected falls into the top category available. There are cheaper ones of course ..." Here he paused, knowing by the look in Rafi's eyes that they weren't an option.

Rafi had done his homework, however, and wasn't blown away by the little speech. "I have to beg your pardon," he told the salesman, "but the violin I have chosen is from the medium-price range." The salesman began to protest, and Rafi cut him off midsentence. "No, really," he told the dumbfounded man. "You know as well as I do that this isn't a top-of-the-line violin. But if you really want to make a fuss about it, we can always go to a different store where they won't try to pass off midlevel merchandise for what it's not." The salesman was beaten.

"Use it in good health," he wished them, as they exited the store. Rafi gave the salesman a brilliant smile and said that that was exactly what he intended to do. He knew that it would be part and parcel of his future.

~

The dream came again that night. It surfaced about once a month. Rafi was not surprised that it had come again. It wasn't a scary dream, it wasn't a sad dream. It was just a dream that appeared fairly often, and for which he had no explanation. In the dream, he would be visited by an old man. The man was extremely pious; that was obvious. He was also tormented. That was without question. There was such a look of pain in those wise and ancient eyes that Rafi would feel a pang of sorrow whenever he looked into them in the dream. He never wanted to gaze at those eyes, but somehow, he always gave in to his desire to look at the holy man. There was something pushing him, drawing him back when he pulled away. In the end, he would find himself at the mercy of those timeless eyes, of that gentle smile and the whitest of beards. When the rabbi had his attention (somehow Rafi knew the man was a rabbi), he would begin to speak to Rafi. It was always the same thing:

"Please find him," the rabbi would say. "Please bring him back to his home! I suffer so much from the knowledge that he is so far away. Please find him and bring him home! Please ... "

And then the rabbi would begin to sing in a faraway voice. He would hear the first snatches of the most incredible song. It would rise up at him like a phantom, like an angel singing. But then, just as the song reached the higher part and the sound became incredibly beautiful, just then the dream would end with the rabbi's face gradually become more and more misty and distant, until it blended into the walls of the room, and then Rafi was spinning through a void, spinning, spinning, spinning, down into the depths of his mind. When he finally surfaced, he found himself in his bedroom staring at the ceiling, trying for the hundredth time to understand why this was happening to him, who the old man was and what the dream meant.

Then he did what he always did when he awoke and the dream was still lingering in his mind: He got out of his warm comfortable bed and went across the room to where his violin rested on its stand: a prince of splendor on a throne of glory. He rubbed his hand lovingly on the shining wood. Rafi took the violin and placed it under his chin. Reverently, he lifted the bow and stood there for a moment framed in the earliest rays of morning, as the sun rose and the weak light filtered through the shades and highlighted the teenager standing motionless in the center of the room. Holding his violin as if it was a baby, he brought the bow up to the violin and ran it across the strings, drawing forth a series of velvety sounds from the instrument.

He would play his violin. He would play the exact song he always heard in his dream. He felt the need to play it now, because somehow, try as he might, the song would eventually slip away. But he savored the moment. His fingers ran up and down the strings, the bow moved with a life of its own, and the music that wafted upward sounded heavenly. Soon he found that his pulse began calming down, that he was feeling better. He would have liked to go back to bed for a few minutes, but he knew that morning had arrived. Walking to the window, he flung the curtains apart and let the sunlight stream into the room in waves. It was time to wake up and face the world.

June 2, 2004

Through the speaker on the console, the man behind the glass told the orchestra, "Let's take that from the top." The members of the orchestra gave the technician a nod, to show that they understood what he was saying.

"O.K.," the technician said, and the music began flowing through his earphones. Rafi Ganim was a member of the Israeli Philharmonic Orchestra, and the orchestra was currently working on a special project in tandem with one of most famous and sought-after conductors in the world of classical music. He was a German, but that didn't stop the Israelis from working with him. Every lift of his baton, every motion with his hands had meaning. Rafi was able to appreciate the difference between this man and almost anyone else with whom he had ever worked. This maestro was special. There was an innate chemistry between him and the members of his orchestra. When he gave the flutist a look, the man knew instinctively what needed to be done even if they hadn't already discussed it. Some had it and some didn't, and this conductor had it in abundance.

They were doing a complex concert by Chopin, and with anybody else, the orchestra would have given up, but this conductor inspired them to heights they would have never thought possible. There was a violin solo that each of the eight violinists were pining for. The conductor had auditioned each of them, and they all sounded incredible. But the solo was for one violin only, and there was but one solo. They had gone into the studio this evening to record the piece before the actual concert, since the show's producer planned to sell the recording at the actual show. Tonight was the night when they would find out who was going to get that solo.

The piece opened with soft piano music before being joined by an oboe. They harmonized briefly and then the string section kicked in: violins, violas and cellos all racing like the wind, all choreographed from beginning to end. The conductor waved his hands: bassoons, flutes and French horns, all swept in crisply, building the piece to a crescendo of vibrant music that flowed steadily higher and higher, as the conductor raised his baton. It was time for the violin solo, and as all eight violinists held their breath and hoped for the best, Daniel Dagenheim pointed at Rafi with his baton and motioned for him to take the solo.

Rafi lifted his violin to his chin and positioned the bow. His hands trembled for a moment as if they, too, realized the overwhelming responsibility they had just been given. If he received the solo on the album, then he would receive the solo in the concert hall as well, and when that occurred, Rafi would be catapulted to instant stardom. To have been chosen by the maestro himself, by the great Dagenheim, was just about the greatest compliment an aspiring violinist could hope for. He realized that his entire future hinged on this solo. He played it like it was the last piece he would ever play. It came alive. His violin cried, shimmered and hummed with every movement of the bow. This was music at its best and the members of the orchestra found themselves immersed in the sheer beauty and stopped breathing. The violin was a baby, helpless and alone. It was a lost child crying for its mother. It was music. The notes flowed like a dream, and Rafi found himself rising to the occasion. Then the grand moment passed, and the great Dagenheim himself gave him a rare half-smile. The entire orchestra threw themselves into the rest of the piece, committed to be worthy of their eminent conductor.

Rafi finished the piece in a daze. He couldn't believe what had just happened. He was the youngest of them all, the one with the least amount of experience. Yet, he had been given the coveted solo. He sat in his seat and accepted the accolades that were poured on him, and just enjoyed being alive. It had been a supreme moment for him, and he intended to savor it. All around him, the musicians were putting away their instruments, tidying up and discussing the upcoming concert. Rafi listened with half an ear, still thinking about that wonderful solo and the way he had played it. Dagenheim himself came over to tell him what an enchanting job he had done. Everyone knew that Rafi has just made musical history. He placed his violin lovingly in its leather case, and covered it with its velvet cloth just so. Then he joined the rest of the orchestra filing out of the studio.

"See you at the concert," said one of the other violinists to him, and he wished the man well. The man told him the he had never heard this particular piece played so beautifully in his entire life. Rafi was on cloud nine. He had made a superb impression on Dagenheim. He had been granted a solo worth killing for, and the concert was in just a few more days. Life was looking mighty fine right then.

That night he had the dream again.

It was the same old man: the same old man with the long white beard and the righteous-looking eyes that bespoke purity and oneness with G-d.

But the man was crying, and he looked so sad, as if he would never be happy again. He was sitting on a low three-legged stool, and he appeared to be in mourning. He crooned a soft tune to himself. But Rafi could hear the barest outline of the tune, a note here and there, and he recognized the music because he had heard it before. It was the song of his dream; the music of his heart.

It felt like forever. The old man, the *tzaddik*, was looking at him, beseeching him with those holy eyes that had never seen impurity. Begging him to find the man, rescue him, deliver him from the depths of evil. Please save his soul! Even though the man wasn't speaking at all, Rafi understood everything he was thinking, as if they shared some form of telepathy, and the old man was able to convey his thoughts to Rafi without even opening his mouth. But he didn't know whom he was supposed to save, or how to go about it. He wished that the old man would be more specific about his mission. Then the tune filled the dream and stirred a sense of passion within him. He was filled with a longing for something intangible that he knew that he wanted, but didn't know how to obtain.

The old man receded into the background, and soon only his outline was visible. Rafi felt himself being transported out of his dream and back to reality. He awoke gradually, the sounds of the song still fresh in his mind. He jumped out of bed, ran to his violin case and opened it with trembling fingers and shaking hands. He held the violin to his chin and lifted the bow, pausing for a moment allowing the music to wash over him. Then he began to play the song from his dream.

He finally understood that his soul had received something from this tune that accompanied him wherever he went, and took part in every note of music that he played. It had been with him during the violin solo earlier that day as well, and it would always be with him. He switched on the tape recorder to record it, and he played the piece over again, and he knew that he would never forget this evening. But still, he wished he knew what the old man wanted from him.

Mordy Kahane

Jerusalem, Israel
March 16, 2009

Several hours had passed by the time Mordy finished telling me the first part of his story. I sat on the wooden bench, my hands thrust deep into the pockets of my trench coat, and my hat resting low on my forehead. The afternoon had lost all semblance of warmth, and a stiff wind had picked up, racing in from across the valley and lashing at us.

"It was at this point that I experienced my first run in with anti-Semitism," Mordy said. "I was still Matt Kahane, but I had lost my naive and innocent outlook on life. It had been supplanted with a cynicism that most children will never know. I had been badly burned by the people I had trusted the most. The kids I had grown up with, with whom I had played ball for years, had all turned against me when the tide shifted. All it had taken was one loud kid with a big mouth, before everyone I had liked and felt comfortable with wouldn't look me in the eye."

I shook my head sympathetically.

"Yes, Reb Zack, I'm not exaggerating in the slightest. I wish I was. I wish that this whole crazy scenario had never taken place. But they turned into a pack of wild animals and I had barely escaped. Look, I was lucky that in the end it was only Brian who I'd had to fight against. I don't even want to think about what it would have been like if it had been all five of them at once. They would have killed me!" He paused for a minute, before continuing, "Maybe I look like a pretty confident guy, and maybe I am. But this is years later. The truth is I was kind of a sensitive kid. When I was popular, it didn't matter. But when this episode happened, it completely shattered my self-confidence. I had gone from being a popular, happy-go-lucky person to a kid who was scared of his own shadow. It would be years before I would climb out of this rut.

"My perceptions told me that the fact that such an incident could occur in my hometown, among the very people who had been my friends, meant that no one was safe. Let's face it. If the right leader should arise from among Middle America with the right rhetoric, it shouldn't be impossible to arouse the entire country to do the same things that my friends had done to me. It had happened in Germany not long before, and there was no reason that the same exact thing couldn't happen in America. That made me very scared. I had seen the video clips of Adolph Hitler at those massive Nazi rallies, and I knew that it had been a miracle that an uneducated housepainter had been able to accomplish what he did. He had pulled together an entire nation of 80 million people! Nearly every one of them had come to agree with him and to do his bidding.

"I shuddered at the thought that the same thing might happen in the United States. My childish imagination expanded the frightening fantasy in my mind. I could picture a blond-haired politician with a ready grin and family connections. He would be an incredible speaker, charismatic and interesting. In the beginning, he would present himself as a friend of everyone, as the future president of America. But the closer the country would get to the elections and with the more support that he garnered, the people would desire to know the real truth about this person in whom they believed. What were his policies and the ideals that he believed in? They would dig, and eventually the media would discover the truth, or the truth would be leaked.

And," Mordy went on, "my mind told me that when the American people heard what the man truly believed in, a large portion of them would find what he was saying to be really amazing. They would identify with such a person.

"Reb Zack," he said earnestly, "can you understand what I was feeling? I had been through such a terrible experience, and I could see it happening on a much greater scale all over the country. I became a person who was constantly afraid of the world. My parents looked on in dismay as their formerly confident son changed before their eyes. I refused to return to my old school. How could I return to the place where everyone hated me, where they had turned against me?

"This time, instead of forcing me to go back and saying that everything would be O.K., my parents agreed to send me to a private school in a different city. Nobody knew me or cared about the Ithacan baseball season." Here he stopped talking for a few minutes and we sat silently. There were still a few mothers in the park with their kids and the sounds of the children playing became peripheral noise, because we were completely engrossed in our own little world.

Mordy had opened up to me, and I could see the scared little boy running, running away from the pack of kids, all wanting to beat him up. It was really getting colder now, and Mordy was shivering in his white shirt. I was ready to find a warm place to listen to the rest of this.

"Are you hungry?" I asked him.

He nodded his head in the affirmative. He was hungry and so was I. It was time to go home for a good meal.

"Come home with me for supper," I told him and he agreed. I waited for him at the entrance of the building, and soon he came out the door wearing a sweatshirt. He reached my side and we walked through the streets together. I found myself intrigued by what I had heard so far. He was from Ithaca, of all places; a baseball star. But Hashem had had other plans for this guy, that was clear to me. I was really curious to hear what the rest of his story would be like. Somehow I had a feeling that it didn't get any less interesting. But now it was time to have something to eat.

Avigail was at a *shiur* in the neighborhood, and one of the neighbor's daughters was watching the kids. I thanked her, paid her and sent her home. I was going to babysit tonight. There were still some leftovers from Shabbos which I wasn't in the mood for, so I opened up the freezer and discovered an unopened package of steaks half-buried in the back under a bag of frozen broccoli and some green beans. Steak seemed like a good idea tonight. I slipped a few of them into the broiler and found half a potato kugel on the bottom shelf of the fridge that had been somehow overlooked. I toasted some pitas and brought out the hummus, pickles and the coleslaw, and we got down to some serious business.

Outside the weather was going from bad to worse, and it seemed like we were in for one stormy evening. But inside the house, it was warm and friendly, and the wonderful tantalizing aroma of broiling meat filled the kitchen. I heard one of the kids talking in his sleep. I went into the children's room and Yeshaya was having a bad dream, twisting and turning, whimpering and half-crying. His curly brown hair was messily arranged on the pillow, his chubby arm clutching his pet octopus very tightly. I said his name a few times, gently calling out to him, and calmed him. I rubbed his back until he began settling down and his breathing returned to normal. There was a half-smile on his face as I ran my hand through his hair. Then I returned to the kitchen.

Mordy had made a salad and soon the steaks were ready. Everything was really delicious. But I couldn't completely enjoy the meal because I was waiting for the next installment, wanting to know what happened next to little Matt Kahane, and how he had turned into such an enigmatic guy. We didn't talk much as we ate. When we finished and had *bentched,* we cleaned up the kitchen. Then I took Mordy into my office where we could talk privately.

My office is my domain, my space, a place where I can write my *chiddushim* on the computer, make any business-related phone calls, or just sit and read the newspaper. It was the perfect place to continue our earlier conversation. I flicked on the light, and Mordy followed me into the small room. My office doubles as a guest room, so we purchased a high-riser several years ago. That was where Mordy took a seat. I sank into my swivel chair and twirled around a few times.

"Good food?" I asked him.

"Good food," he confirmed with a smile. "You really are the all-around man, aren't you?" he said. "The *mashgiach*, the counselor and the cook all in one."

"Wait until you see me on the basketball court," I said. He smiled.

"So where were we?" I asked him.

"Well," he drawled, "after I got to my new school I realized that there were many things I had loved about my old school, but it was too late to go back there. Besides, the whole school hated me now for losing that game in the closing moments. Somehow they had forgotten all the times I had pulled in the victory for them, all the times I had led the team to glory. Now that was all history, and I was going to have to start all over again, which I did. I tried out for the teams, both baseball and basketball, and began making friends. This school was far enough away that nobody knew me. We hit it off pretty good, even though I was still depressed by what had happened.

"But over the next few months, my depression began to lift and I started getting into things again. I told no one that I was Jewish, but I think they figured it out anyway. I mean, 'Matt Kahane'? That's about as Jewish a name as a person can get! But the whole thing wasn't an issue. We did our work and had our fun, and that was not something that was spoken about at all. The year ended, and I decided to remain in the same town for high school. I liked the kids, the teachers were knowledgeable and fair, and it was a good place. Two years passed this way. In my third year of high school, I tried out for the high-school debating team and was accepted. We traveled around the state attending debating competitions, and it was there that I really began to develop a style of speaking.

"Now one of my best friends on the debating team was a guy named Josh Sebring. He played hockey as well, and we'd go to the ice-skating rinks for some really wild games. He was an awesome guy to hang with, and full of great ideas for a good time. Life was never boring when Josh was around. So we became good friends, and I even told him about what had happened at my old school. He took me to the 7-Eleven and bought me a giant Slurpy to make me feel better.

"The Sebring family owned a home near the ocean, and sometimes during vacation the entire family would go down there for two or three weeks. Since Josh and I were such good friends, they invited me to come along. It was a great house. And since Josh was such a great guy and I was no slouch myself, all the kids in the area used to come and hang out at the Sebring place."

I was watching Matt speak and he was animated, reliving the past, thrust into the character of the person he had been years before. He caught me studying him, and he smiled for a second and said, "You know, those were really super days! They had this boat and we would motor out onto the bay and run full throttle, taking the kind of stupid risks that kids love to take. We almost capsized a whole bunch of times. But Josh was really professional with the boat, and he knew how to bring it back under control.

"So that's the way it went that summer. It was almost time to leave and go back home when I experienced the day of the storm. I can still recall waking up the morning of the big day and getting ready to hike out to the beach house. The sand was still damp when we set out, and the smell of the ocean was very strong. I was wearing a windbreaker against the early morning chill, and I wrapped it tighter around me. The ancient beach house was about 10 miles away, perched on the end of a pier that jutted out into the bay. The pier was built on stilts and the wood had loads of rotting spots and holes. The house always looked as if it was going to topple over at any moment. The kids liked to say that sometimes when they looked at the beach house from their homes in the middle of the night, they could see what looked like candlelight coming from the old broken windows. You can imagine the rumors: Criminals, kidnappers, you name it; we thought it about the old beach house.

"We were going to cap our vacation with a night's stay in that run-down house. It took Josh a week to convince me, but by the time we were set to go, I was as pumped up about it as he was. We packed everything we were going to need for the night. Josh claimed that this was the perfect way to wrap up what had been the most amazing vacation either of us had ever had. I had fallen in love with nature by this point. We had been hiking some pretty tough trails over the past few weeks. We were going to face our fears and emerge braver men from the experience. Or at least that was what Josh said.

"We ate a hearty breakfast before we left, and as we hiked along the beach we could taste the salty air and we could feel the chill factor. But then the sun became stronger, and by the time we had stopped for lunch, it was a beautiful day. We passed the time on the hike singing old songs and telling jokes. It was getting dark by the time we had reached the dirt path that led to the old beach house. We could hear the roar of the ocean by now, and the sound of the water breaking on the rocks made the whole walk much more exciting.

"The path to the beach house was lined by tangled underbrush and bushes. In some parts of the path, the brush had become thick and overgrown, reaching above our heads, obscuring the moon and turning the trail very dark. It was a relief to reach the open expanse of beach that lay between us and the beach house. Our sneakers sank into the damp piles of sand, and we walked quickly toward the house, wanting to get inside so we could set down our gear, get out the food and find a spot to get a fire going. The beach house loomed up in front of us like an ancient boat that had been run aground. We felt small and vulnerable as we walked down the listing pier toward the house. We had to be very careful where we trod, because the holes in the pier were pretty big, and we could easily fall through them into the freezing water below. It was at that point that the night turned nasty. We had listened to the weather report for a few days prior to setting out, and no one had mentioned a storm. But here we were, on the rotting pier of the scariest house around, and a storm was heading in.

"First to arrive was a bright bolt of lightning followed by loud thunder. It sounded like the crack of a whip. It rolled across the bay like a drumroll, and we braced ourselves for the impact. When it came, it was kind of hard to stay steady on our feet." Mordy looked at me as he spoke and gave me a wry glance. "It was really scary," he finally said. "Really!" I simply nodded. I would definitely have been scared in such a situation. But then again, I would have never put myself into such a situation in the first place, so I didn't count.

"Then the wind began to whistle," Mordy went on. "Normally when you hear wind whistling, you hear it as it rushes between buildings and around trees and cars, and all those things that come between the power of the wind and you. But this location was completely open. So when it began to whistle, we began to run toward the shelter of the house, flimsy as that was. The pier was shaking back and forth in the fierce wind. We reached the house and pulled opened the doors in a frenzy. Down beneath us, the water was roiling, in a show of seemingly unprecedented strength. It looked like there was going to be another flood, and here we were in what was probably the flimsiest house on the bay, which just happened to be sitting on a broken pier, shaking dangerously in the wind!

"But there we were and we had to make the best of it. If the house had stood this long, it would hopefully continue to hold up, and we would have the most incredible story of our lives to tell. If we survived the experience, that is. We were absolutely frozen by now, and we needed to warm up. We ran through a hallway and entered what had obviously been a sitting room. But the whole place was constructed out of wood. So we went into the bathroom and made a small fire in the enamel bathtub. This was fast becoming the worst adventure of my life.

"We crouched near the edge of that bathtub and roasted hot dogs. We ate the slightly charred hot dogs with fresh rolls, ketchup and sauerkraut. For a moment there, it felt truly amazing. All the time, we kept an eye on the fire to make sure that it didn't become more than we could handle. That bathtub was a complete mess by the time we finished. We were well satiated and happy, and we were warm in the small room. But just then, there was a tremendous BOOM of thunder right outside the small bathroom window, and the entire house shook from top to bottom and the rain came down in torrents.

"It wouldn't have been so terrible if it had been raining in a normal way. Rain is fine. I have gotten wet before and I can handle it. This was something completely different. It didn't come down in drops, it came down in sheets! It was a torrential downpour. The rain didn't ping on the roof. It hit the roof hard without mercy, as if we were being struck with bowling balls! It felt as if the roof was going to cave in at any moment. We wanted to leave the beach house, we wanted to escape. But the pier was full of holes and shaking from the continuous onslaught. The wind was so strong that I was afraid that we would be blown off the pier if we tried to walk to dry land. Meanwhile, the weather was deteriorating.

"But the beach house hadn't stood for so long without being stronger than it looked. It had been built a long time ago, when workmanship meant something and quality had been highly valued. The roof held up and the bathroom remained dry. We finished our cookout and left the relative safety of the bathroom in search of a bedroom where we could spend the night.

"Every so often, when the thunder boomed particularly loudly and the lightning crackled with a sizzle, we could feel the entire house quivering on its foundation. But we found a room where we could roll out our sleeping bags. Josh had brought a small transistor radio in his pack. We lit candles, listened to the music and ate cookies, and felt very proud of ourselves. I mean, here we were sitting in the eye of the storm so to speak and actually enjoying ourselves. It was pretty amazing!

"It was still kind of early in the evening, too early to go to sleep, so we decided to explore the house. By now, we had become accustomed to the storm, and the thunder felt like a slap on the back from a good friend. The lightning was providing the most incredible views of the bay. I looked out the window. It was truly frightening what the ocean was capable of, when given the chance. I snapped a few pictures of the scene of crashing waves which I will never forget.

"It was a large house and it took us a while to explore, but we trooped from attic to basement and back again. You would think that being abandoned, the beach house would have been completely vandalized and destroyed, but that wasn't the case. Somehow, the teenagers who used the house from time to time treated it with a certain amount of respect. The house, although mostly emptied of furniture, aside from the living room, was in surprisingly good condition. Then we came to the most amazing room in the entire house. It was on the first floor and it was built in such a way that it was hanging over the edge of the pier and over the water. Standing there in that room, we could hear the water directly below us. I don't know if the architect of the beach house had left out the insulation in that one room, but it was as if we were actually standing on the edge of the pier, while the water pounded away at those rocks, trying to pulverize them.

"There was a picture window at the end of the room, and we looked through it and stared in awe at the frothing bay. Then, suddenly, the storm intensified, if that were possible. The wind went from its roar to a high-pitched whistle that was much more frightening than anything we had heard yet. The storm kind of ceased for a few moments, and the air seemed highly charged, and the night felt electric. I looked at Josh and he looked back at me, and there was fear in our eyes. We knew that very soon this storm was going to move up to the next level, and we really didn't want to be there when that happened.

"We stared at each other undecided," Mordy said. "Should we attempt to make a run for it? To get out while the calm in the middle of the storm lasted? But before we came to a decision, it was made for us. At that very second, it was like the end of the world had come! The waves were absolutely tremendous, slashing the pier and reaching almost as high as the window! It was a terrifying experience. I opened my mouth and screamed like a crazy man as the thunder repeatedly exploded all around us. The lightning crackled across the ocean, lighting up a sea gone insane.

"And then," Mordy took a long pause, "and then it happened. Suddenly we felt this huge shift, as if the house itself was moving — which it was — and the floor we were standing on began to shift. I know it seems far-fetched, but the entire front of the room we were standing in came apart from the house — window and wood — and fell into the ocean below. And up came this tremendous wave that threatened to engulf us in its grasp. As that giant wave came storming toward me, it was as if I could see G-d up above looking down at me, and He was saying, 'See Matt, this is all My creation. I'm the One in charge!'

"Then that wave entered the beach house, and we realized that the house was finally going down. The water tossed us back and forth. Even though we tried to grab onto things to hold out against its force, there was nothing we could do. We were swept out of the beach house and into the bay below, sucked into the undertow, swimming, trying to stay afloat. I was underwater for a while, and Josh was fighting it out somewhere else. I must have swallowed lots of water. I felt myself tiring, and I knew that I couldn't fight this much longer, but I still wanted to live. I didn't want to die just because Josh had talked me into spending the wrong night in the beach house! The water was playing with me like I was a ball, tossing me back and forth.

"By now the water had maneuvered us away from the beach house. We could still see it when the waves shifted. There was this creaking sound, and the next thing I knew, the pier cracked. The beach house was falling down, down, down, in slow motion. I opened my mouth to scream, and the water went inside and I lost whatever control I had had until then. The water swept me under and it was then that I knew."

"What did you know?" I asked him.

"I knew that there was no way I was going to survive this night if G-d didn't want that to happen. As I was tossed about on the waves like a piece of chalk, I realized that I believed in G-d and wanted to be saved. I knew that He could do it if He wanted to. I don't think that it was sheer luck that swirled me over to one of the few remaining pier supports and allowed me to find a little shelf where two boards were still attached to their stone supports. I sat on that tiny ledge for what seemed like an eternity. For the first time in my life, I actually prayed.

"That entire miserable and incredible night I had to remain awake," Mordy said, "because if I drifted off to sleep for even a minute, chances were that I would loosen my grip on the stone pilings and then the ocean would claim me. I worried about Josh and I cried a ton. My tears mixed with the salty water of the bay. I was freezing cold and utterly fatigued. But I had realized that there was a G-d up there, and He saw me. And for whatever reason, He desired that my life not be as simple as all the lives around me.

"Eventually, the night passed as all nights pass, and the storm calmed down as all storms do. Once it was over, I still clutched the pier support because I had no strength to drag myself to shore. I must have drifted off to sleep, my salt-encrusted head leaning against the stone. The next thing I knew, I was being shaken awake by some rescue worker in a rowboat who dragged me into his boat and was asking me all sorts of questions about other survivors. I was still shell shocked from my experience. I couldn't understand how much the world had changed from one day to the next. Beach house. Gone. Josh. Gone. Me. Almost gone, but not quite.

"In the end they told me that they had found Josh washed up on the beach about a mile away. They had worked on him until he began spitting up all the seawater that he had swallowed. He was in the hospital recuperating from his ordeal. They made me go to the hospital as well. I knew that somehow, somewhere, I had changed, become a different person. Maybe I was still searching because I didn't have a clue as to what my life was all about, but I had come this close to dying, and I was a different person than I had been the day before.

"But I still didn't know who I was."

We sat in silence for quite some time after Mordy finished the next part of his story. "So you and Josh were rescued and it was quite the narrow escape," I said.

"You could say that again," he said.

"Something tells me that this is not the end of the story," I said grinning.

He smiled back and said, "Nope, but we did get a good chunk done. Continue tomorrow then?"

I realized that now that he had finally begun opening up, he was probably finding it a catharsis. I was glad. It's always an amazing feeling when you know that you've connected with a *talmid*. Ask any educator, they will tell you the same thing.

"How about right after Shacharis?" I asked him. "You'll join me for breakfast and more Mordy history in my office. O.K.?"

"Wonderful," he replied, "I'm looking forward to getting through the whole story with someone. You know, I've been holding this history inside me for so many years now, the good parts and the not such good parts, and I don't know how healthy that was. I feel like this is such a relief for me. Thank you so much! For supper too!" He was such a good kid. So earnest. But I wasn't sure that I would be able to fall asleep now. I wanted to know the end of the book! Not such an easy thing when the book is alive.

We left my office and I walked him a little way down the street. It was drizzling again, so he pulled the hood of his sweatshirt over his head and ran. I went to the big neighborhood shul that had continual *minyanim* for Maariv. I had missed night *seder* listening to his story. But something told me that doing so had not been a mistake. Both his story by itself and the decisions that he was debating were extremely important. I knew that I should stand by his side and help him in any way that I could. There was a *minyan* beginning as I entered the shul, and I davened a long and inspired *Shemoneh Esrei*: long because I felt guilty for missing night *seder*, and inspired because Mordy did that to me. I wasn't sure why, but he did. I finished after everyone else, and I walked home through the quiet Yerushalayim streets, enjoying the solitude that allowed me free reign with my thoughts.

Jerusalem, Israel
March 17, 2009

"So where were we?" I asked Mordy as we sat companionably together the next morning over breakfast in the *mashgiach's* room. I was kidding around. There was no way I could have forgotten what he had told me the day before. On the way to yeshivah that morning, I had tried to imagine what he could possibly add to what he had told me up until then. I tried to envision the twists and turns of his life, but then I decided that I would just wait to hear it from the source. The cool part was that I was really hooked on his story! It had confirmed my suspicions that there was something really deep about Mordy Kahane, and as he revealed more of himself, I could see that my original impression had been on target. *Who are you, Mordy Kahane?* I thought for the umpteenth time.

I made him a cup of coffee, which he cradled in his palms, and then he shook his head as if to clear the cobwebs. He began talking almost as if he'd been in the middle of a thought and was turning on the sound.

"After that night," Mordy said, "Josh and I stopped being such good friends. I could understand it; I mean we had come mighty close to ending up on the ocean floor, and I guess it just kind of messed up the relationship. I was sad, of course. I mean, I had really liked Josh, and don't forget this had come after the whole debacle in my old school. So I was beginning to wonder if I was destined to go through life without friends.

I kept to myself for the next year and concentrated on my schoolwork, ignoring the whole party scene around me. I really didn't want to party. I guess when a person almost dies, he realizes that it's not all about the partying."

I looked at him in admiration, because I knew that there were plenty of people in this world who had come pretty close to dying but didn't let that change their lives in the slightest!

"Anyway," he went on, "I had concentrated so well on my SAT's, making up for not having a social life, I guess, that I was able to finish high school one year before everyone else in my class. At that point, I earned scholarships from some of the best universities in the country: Harvard, Yale, Stanford, Princeton. They all wanted me. In the end I chose the school I felt most suitable, packed my bags and off I went. By this point, not having friends didn't bother me as much as it used to, and I had developed other hobbies with which to fill my spare time. One of those was photography. I loved going out to the open spaces, finding something special on which to focus, then capturing that moment on film. I took pictures of birds, wildlife, sunsets and spectacular moons, and people, of course.

"I turned a closet in my dorm room into a darkroom and began developing my own pictures whenever I had a free moment. I discovered that I was really good at it. I had a knack for catching those special moments. Soon there was no room left on the bulletin board in my darkroom to display all my favorites, so out of necessity I began displaying them on the wall above my bed. More and more people saw my pictures and liked them. There was one amazing picture I had taken of an eagle: wings spread wide, cruising the skies, searching for something. That picture became famous at the school. So famous, in fact, that it led to everyone at school calling me 'Eagle.'

"At a major university, to have a well-known nickname at college is a major status symbol. But I was wary of this type of thing, knowing from past experience that just because people liked you one day didn't necessarily mean that they would continue to like you the next. I didn't pursue any friendships. It was fine that everyone was being nice to me, but that was as far as it went. I had been burned in elementary school, and my friendship with Josh Sebring hadn't survived the rigors of high school, so who could blame me for losing trust in society? But then I was offered the position of editor of photography for the university newspaper. After thinking it over, I decided to accept. I loved taking pictures and I enjoyed the world of journalism. Being able to spend time combining both of those activities seemed like a dream come true." He paused for a second, before saying dryly, "It's funny how often in life, people's favorite dreams become their worst nightmares.

"So I thought it over for a while and then I accepted. Listen, it was a prestigious position. Many of the people who had worked at this college newspaper had gone on to work for the big boys at The New York Times and The Wall Street Journal. I was proud that my work was highly regarded by people with discerning taste. Nobody even knew my real name anymore. Everybody called me 'Eagle.' 'Eagle, did you go over those pictures yet?' Eagle this, Eagle that. I almost forgot that my name was Matt Kahane. But in the end, I wasn't allowed to forget. Again I was tasting the sweet taste of camaraderie — of belonging. I enjoyed it so much that I allowed myself to forget how swiftly that drink can become bitter.

"We'd go out for meals and discuss our views on the world over beer and burgers. We had our favorite watering holes, and the whole campus knew that we were the journalists.

"Months passed this way. I made the dean's list. I was elected to the students' council. I had so much on my plate that sometimes I knew that I was overdoing it. Why was I piling so much work on myself? But I loved the frenzy of the newsroom. I loved the constant action, the deadlines, the black ink stains on my fingers. I loved seeing my pictures in the paper.

"Then it began to snow, and the world was simply beautiful in a stark, pristine sort of way. I loved standing on my balcony late at night as the wind blew those swirling snowflakes and they drifted down on me. There were days when there was enough snow to build forts and to have snowball fights. And if you think that college students are above this kind of thing, then you are greatly mistaken.

"Then one morning, a few days before winter vacation, I woke up in the morning to discover a giant swastika placed in the snow right across the front lawn of my dormitory. It was big and bent and black and cold. I looked at it, my blood ran cold and I thought, *It is also here? Will it never end*?! I grabbed my camera and I began snapping away. Take the pictures, show the world, put it on the front page of the college paper. Get some rage going among the Jews on campus! I wrote the editorial that day and it was a thing of raging beauty: the anger and hurt of the liberal Jew.

But nobody cared! I thought that the big papers would pick it up as they sometimes picked up news that was especially good, but they weren't interested. It was just another hate crime and nobody cared."

Mordy had tears in his eyes as he talked, and I could see how this whole thing had affected him.

"Two days later," he went on, "almost everyone left school for winter vacation. I chose to remain and work on some stuff that I'd been meaning to do for a while that I hadn't had the opportunity to take care of. It was also a good time to chill with my journalist pals on the paper. Almost all of them had elected to remain on campus as well. We had work to do. Our fraternity house had a working fireplace and we could sit and argue politics in front of the crackling logs for hours at a time without getting bored. There were plenty of soft drinks available, a kitchen loaded with food, my camera to take pictures of the snow, and people who I thought had the same goals as I had. We were all set to have a great time.

"I watched the cars exiting out of the parking lots. Students waving goodbye at one another. Locking up. Pulling out. Slowly but surely the campus was quieting down for vacation. I smiled as I looked at my car. It had been my parents' gift to me for finishing high school in three years. I kept that car in mint condition. I was very careful with it and didn't bang it around the way other students treated their vehicles. I went inside to make myself a sandwich. The fire was keeping the room deliciously warm. The atmosphere was terrific. Everyone was having a wonderful time; trading ideas for future issues of the paper, making jokes, roasting hot dogs on the fire.

"'Let's go out and have a snowball fight,' Elliot suggested, and everyone loved the idea. We divided up into two teams and built forts. We made piles of snowballs. We blasted music through the windows, and it was tons of fun. Then someone threw one snowball, and suddenly the air was filled with massive numbers of snowballs flying across the divide. In the end one of the teams won the fight, and the other team had to cook dinner. We walked back upstairs soaked and laughing, poking fun at the losing team. It was good-natured bantering, and everyone was having a terrific time. It was great to be alive! I changed into clean sweats and sneakers, and put my car keys in my pocket just in case I decided to go for a ride and get some more food.

It was a Kodak moment with the guys playing Risk on the floor in front of the fire. I came out of my room to join them, jangling the keys in my pocket, thinking that I wasn't sure that my car would be able to make it out of the snow, even if I decided to actually try. And then everything changed. In one second, everything shifted, like a castle made of sand."

"Why?" I asked him.

"Because right then there was a knock on the door. I wondered who could be knocking. Those of us on campus were indoors; it was snowing outside. I went to open the door and found myself staring into the face of Brian McHalten, my old enemy from elementary school! I could feel the blood rushing to my face at the very sight of him. He had grown into a real big guy, way broader in the shoulders than I was; probably a lot stronger too. He had this washed-out blond look. He wore his hair almost down to his shoulders. I tensed myself for the confrontation that was sure to come. Nothing happened. He smiled at me. I was floored! Brian McHalten smiling at me. That had never happened before!

"'Is Rocky in?' he asked in a pleasant voice, and I realized that he had come to visit one of the guys and hadn't recognized me.

"'In the main room on the floor playing Risk,' I told him. He stared at me for a second as if he were trying to place me, as if he recalled my voice from somewhere far away, but couldn't identify it for the life of him.

"'Have we met before?' he asked me. I could feel my heart start to beat furiously because I was afraid of this much bigger and probably armed Brian. I doubted that his hatred had lessened since we had last parted. If anything, he was probably an even bigger anti-Semite and racist than he had been when I had known him.

"'Nope,' I answered, fingering the car keys in my pocket, trying to decide whether I should leave the moment he turned his back or not.

"'O.K.,' he said at last, turned and went into the fraternity dorm. I couldn't follow him inside. I couldn't do anything! I was totally shaken by this encounter. I hated this person with all my heart! This kid had ruined my life! I retreated into the bathroom, looking for something that would calm me down. I tried opening the medicine cabinet, but my fingers were shaking so badly that I just gave up. I perched on the edge of the bathtub and tried to decide what to do next. Finally I came to the conclusion that I would just walk through the living room where everyone was playing, go to my room, pack some of my stuff and just go for a long drive.

"I began walking back toward the living room when I heard him speaking. I paused in my tracks right outside the room, wanting to hear what he was going to say.

"'I heard about that giant swastika they found in the snow here a few days ago,' he said with a laugh. 'I heard that there were a couple of those in a dozen colleges at least. Serves those Jews right! But it's good for the paper, gets people to read it. Otherwise nobody would look at the rag you guys put out. You know what? The newspaper crew probably built it themselves to have something to write about! Am I right?! C'mon, I'm right.'

"They were all laughing now, captivated by his personality. I mean, as evil as it was, he had something there, something that hooked people.

"'Rocky,' he said to his friend, the only guy on the paper whom I didn't like, 'who is that guy who opened the door for me?'

"'That's Eagle,' Rocky said.

"'Eagle,' Brian repeated. 'No, I mean what's his real name? Does anyone know his real name?' I stood there shaking in the hallway. Now what? Should I run? Nobody spoke for a while; I guess they were trying to recall my name. I had been Eagle for so long that it was hard to remember what it was before that.

"'I think his name is Matt or some ....' Brian didn't wait for the kid to finish his sentence.

"'Matt Kahane,' he exhaled, 'I knew our paths would cross again!'

"I heard him rise from the floor and run to the living-room door. I heard it, but I didn't see it. I was too busy running to the fire escape at the other end of the hallway. He would be searching for me near the entrance of the building. I could hear him screaming my name, how I should come out and fight him like a man. Like two men who had a debt to settle. Interestingly enough, not one of my friends on the paper staff thought of coming to my rescue. I climbed out onto the fire escape, clad in a trench coat, sweats and sneakers. It was freezing outside, and the fire escape was treacherously slippery with snow and ice. I hadn't thought to bring gloves, and I couldn't let my hands grab onto a railing for too long or they would stick to it! There was no time for niceties. I ran down the metal steps of the fire escape, slipping almost at the bottom and catching myself on the wall of the building. There were three flights of stairs to get down. I was descending the one closest to the ground when Brian appeared at the door of the fire escape three flights above.

"'Running away again,' he taunted me. 'The scared Jewboy, always running.' Then he began coming down after me.

"'What are you going to do when you get to the bottom?' he jeered at me.

"I didn't bother replying that I had my car keys in my pocket. I reached the bottom of the fire escape and stepped onto the ladder which slid down to the ground. I jumped off when it was close enough, and then I began running to my car. When he realized that I had an escape plan in mind, Brian became frantic, running down the last flight of the fire escape like a madman! He tripped and banged his head. I saw that he was bleeding. Served him right! It didn't stop him though. He kept on coming, and I fumbled with my car keys, desperate to get the door open on the first try.

"It actually took me two tries. I jumped into the car, stuck the key in the ignition and turned it on, praying that the engine would turn over, even though the hood was covered by snow. The engine caught on.

"Brian was approaching fast. He was a mess. He was bleeding and he had that mad look in his eye. He would smash the window if I gave him the chance. I tried to reverse out of his path. The car was stuck in the snow, and the wheels spun uselessly! I would have to go forward. I pressed down on the gas, motioning him to get out of the way. He wouldn't listen. He was going to smash the window if he could. He had a snow-covered rock in his hand. I turned the steering wheel, and the car cut across the snowy parking lot, while giving him a non-too-gentle shove as it passed him by, gathering speed and traction. He kept on running after me, and I was content to let him run now that I was in a moving car. Then he picked up the rock and let it fly, but I swerved at the last second and it flew harmlessly into the distance. I cut across the parking lot, skidding over speed bumps, snow, ice and sleet and shot through the gate, out of his life, hoping never to see him again.

"The last I saw, he was standing outside my dorm in a polo shirt and jeans, his face a bloodied mess, holding some sort of weapon in his hands. By then, I was too far away to see what it was. As I left the campus, I realized that I really didn't know where to go next. So I drove to a motel about an hour away, checked in and did whatever I could to calm myself down. And this thought kept going through my mind: *Is this how my life is going to be, always running away from something?*"

The coffee was long cold now. Mordy had been telling me the story with his eyes closed, and now he opened them up again and he said, "It really happened like this. I'm not making it up."

"I believe you, Mordy," I said. "I doubt that anyone has that much originality." He gave me a thin smile.

I knew that he was going to have to tell me the rest of the story right then and there, no more bits and pieces. Then, he'd tell me his dilemma, and then a decision. But first I wanted him to eat some breakfast. And I wasn't going to say no to a heaping bowl of cornflakes myself.

Jason Leonard Frost

Oyster Bay, Long Island
December 12, 2008

They decided to take Al's car for the drive down to Oyster Bay, Long Island, not because it was better than Frost's, but because Al was in charge of this mission. Since he was the boss, they would take his car. Privately, Frost ruminated that since the church seemed to know just about everything that was happening in his life, they would find out about this pretty quickly as well. So it was a good thing that Al was the leader in this escapade.

Al's car was in tip-top shape, and Frost, tired out from the last few weeks of introspection and worries, let himself drift off into a dreamworld as Al sang along with the radio. He dreamed of a time long ago when life was different, and there was something elusive that he couldn't place. That familiar tune swirled through his mind, still there after all this time, yet he still didn't know why. He began to think back on the memories of all those years, to recall …

Oyster Bay, Long Island
1946, 1947

The next few years passed in a flurry of growing up. For Jason Leonard Frost, they were years that he would look back on and remember with fond memories. The teachers at the orphanage were well-meaning nuns, and they did their best to develop the kids' minds. They dedicated considerable classroom time and developed many projects with the express goal of helping their students to excel. The church orphanage was located on a beautiful campus in an exclusive area deep in Long Island. For the most part, Frost was happy with his life and dedicated to his school.

He often wondered what it would be like to have parents to come home to after school. But he didn't let the fact that he was an orphan get him down. Simply put, Jason Frost loved life and lived it to the fullest. He was a great sportsman who gave his all to his team in every sport that he played: from wrestling to football to rowing. In many ways, he was the nearly quintessential student: polite to his teachers and popular with his peers. He was a leader who led by the magnetic force of his personality. He sparkled in a way that couldn't be ignored, and his teachers reached out to the precocious youth and focused a lot of attention on him.

There were two activities in the school that stood out for Frost in opposite ways. One he hated more then anything, the other he loved with the same intensity. A passionate person in general, his passion, both for the positive and the negative, could be overwhelming at times. The activity that he disliked most was anything to do with the religious programs of the school. From the moment that he entered the chapel, he had taken a quick, but extremely intense dislike to the service and everything else about the religion. It didn't take long for the instructors and the nuns to come to the realization that Master Jason Frost was not impressed.

The thundering sermons of Father Fitzgerald, which left every other student wide eyed and impressed, did absolutely nothing for Frost. He became disenchanted and bored, and before anyone knew what was happening, the boredom had spread to tricks of many types and styles. Frost never did the same type of trick twice. He began with the classic frogs-in-the-Father's-robes' kind of tricks, and then he quickly graduated to more complicated and original stunts that bore his trademark and style. There was one prank that was talked about long after Frost had left the school. It was his most daring and original stunt of all. Students would discuss his handiwork in reverent tones as they tried to come up with something that would best the great Frost.

It was the middle of the night when Frost got out of bed. The cold stone floor sent shivers up his spine, and he gave a mighty yawn as he quickly slipped the black sweatshirt over his head. Next came the sweatpants. There was a hood and that went over his head. Not that this would make any difference if he were caught. But he liked the drama of it. He stuck a tiny flashlight in his belt just in case he needed it. As popular as he was, Frost always operated alone. He left the dormitory without anybody having any idea that he was up to no good. He had discovered early on that the less people involved in any nefarious activity, the less chance there was that someone would crack and give up names of the people involved. He had no intention of becoming a martyr. He did this strictly for kicks and to show the school how he felt about the Friday-morning service and the abysmally long speech to which the student body was subjected.

In his hand he held a satchel. He moved through the quiet corridors with a kind of cagey grace. His feet led him toward the auditorium where the Friday-morning assembly took place at 9 o'clock sharp. Father Fitzgerald, or "Fitz" as Jason liked to call him, would be standing on the podium pontificating to the entire student body.

But they would be in for a surprise.

Frost entered the darkened room. The auditorium was completely dark except for two small lights that dimly illuminated the stage. He slipped down the aisle and ran up the stairs to the stage. He maneuvered a chair over to the podium and, without wasting any time, got straight to work. Balancing on the podium, he fiddled with the ceiling panel directly above the speaker's place, until he was standing with his head inside the ceiling, setting the stage for the following morning. He removed the contents of his bag, and finished putting the final touches on the morrow's entertainment.

Friday morning was cloudy as if in preparation for the storm that was about to hit the school. The students ate breakfast and were instructed to make their way directly to the auditorium for assembly. Frost was among the crowd of students jostling one another as they entered the wide-swinging auditorium doors. There was nothing on his face that indicated that he was up to no good. Frost had perfected the art of the innocent look. Every grade took their assigned seats, and the Friday-morning assembly got underway. All eyes were on "Fitz" as he made his way down the long carpeted aisle toward the stage. He walked with a pompous gait, deep pride in the arch of his neck. He was in fine form. He reached the stage and climbed the few stairs. He walked to the podium and opened the bible to the story of Joshua assuming the leadership of the Children of Israel. He was a master orator, and even now he waited that extra second to begin. There was complete silence in the room as the students waited to hear what old "Fitz" had to say. He began his speech in the ringing tones of a prophet of old, and the students were mesmerized.

Then, just as he was hitting his stride, there was a creaking sound. The ceiling panel above his head moved slightly aside, and the entire student body got a quick glimpse of a bucket shifting. A steady stream of white began pouring out of that bucket and directly onto the head of the astounded Father Fitzgerald. He was so surprised by the attack that he didn't get out of the way in time and was completely covered by an entire coat of white paint. The uproar that followed had never before been witnessed in the entire annals of the history of the school. "Fitz" would never forgive the student who carried out the surprise attack. But the culprit was never found. Nobody knew who did it. Everybody suspected one person, though credit was never taken for the escapade. As far as the student body was concerned, there was only one person capable of carrying out such a trick. Their esteem for that individual rose considerably that day.

~

There was also the matter of Jason's positive passion and the joy that it brought to his life. Jason had never even dreamed of the joy he would discover when he opened the lid of the piano in the auditorium. One moment, he was standing, fingers gently touching the keys, getting the feel of the black and white keys on his fingertips. The next second, a rich chord was echoing through the rows of seats and up onto the stage where Steve Max, the orphanage's musical director, was adjusting the sound system.

"Who made that sound?" Mr. Max demanded.

The students who had been clustering around the piano in good-natured nonchalance looked at one another in surprise. Frost spoke up, "It was me, sir."

There was a new look in Mr. Max's eyes as he stared back at Frost in surprise. "How is it that I never heard you play?" he asked the boy.

"Because I don't know how to play, sir," Frost answered flustered and a little taken aback by the way this conversation had suddenly become an interrogation.

"Nonsense, Jason," Steve Max replied. "Anyone who can play a chord like that, without even trying, has real talent. You have a gift, young man, and it's my job to make sure that gifts like those aren't wasted. I want you to meet me here after school hours, and we will see what you can do."

"But sir ..." Frost attempted to speak up.

"That will do for now, Jason," Mr. Max said firmly.

Frost knew that he would have to miss part of his after-school free time. But there was really nothing he could do, because at the Catholic orphanage, a teacher's command was law.

That evening after dinner, Frost returned to the auditorium for what he imagined would be a short talk with Mr. Max where he would politely explain that music didn't really interest him. Mr. Max would sigh and say that if he ever changed his mind, the door would always be open. In fact, that was not what happened.

From afar, he could hear the piano notes wafting out the auditorium door and down the hall, brushing his cheek warmly, beckoning to him with golden wings. He turned the corner and stood before the large doors, listening closely to the music Mr. Max was playing. Silently, he entered the large room and stood at the back watching and listening. He saw the older man sitting ramrod straight on the piano bench, hands upright as his fingers flew over the keys and the most heartfelt and beautiful music came pouring out of the baby grand. There was a spell in the room that had been created by the music's effect, and Jason didn't want to shatter it. Barely moving, he eased into one of the plush seats and simply watched as Mr. Max played. In his mind, Jason could almost envision the notes rising from the piano and heading upward. Jason hadn't even been aware that the song had finished, so absorbed had he been in the music of the moment.

"Frost," Mr. Max said, and Jason jumped in surprise.

"Yes, sir," he said.

"Frost, come up on the stage." Mr. Max said all this without even turning around, indicating that he had been aware that Jason had entered the room. It was as if he possessed a clairvoyance of some kind that provided him with the ability to see what others couldn't.

Jason moved onto the stage as if he were in a dream. His legs felt heavy and his fingers felt strange. Listening to that music had opened up possibilities that he hadn't even imagined. Unbidden, a tune began to echo in his head, begging to be played. Suddenly Jason knew that there was music in his soul waiting to come out. Hearing the music that Mr. Max had played stirred something within him. It had been the first time he had ever listened, really listened to music, and it was like a calling, like the walls of an enclosure had come down at last, and the way to the pot of gold lay open and ready for him.

The tune was now stronger in his mind, and although it came and went, he was seeing it through the mists of daybreak.

"Sit down, son," Mr. Max said. Jason obeyed him as if in a dream.

"Play," Mr. Max commanded. Jason, instead of protesting that he didn't know how, raised his fingers over the keys. As he looked at the gleaming baby grand, there was a small voice inside his head telling him that he could do this. His essence had music in it. He couldn't believe that he hadn't realized it until this moment.

He touched the keys of the piano reverently. The notes reverberated through the room, the acoustics magnifying the sounds, making them larger than life. He pressed both hands down on the keys, and somehow, he knew exactly what to do. He was playing the piano without even trying! He could feel the music running through his veins, coursing through his bloodstream and exiting through his fingers. He was playing — with both hands — chords, arpeggios. He was really playing, and he couldn't believe his own eyes. It felt so right.

First he played simple songs that he had grown up with: the nursery rhymes and children's tunes that everyone knew. "It's Raining, It's Pouring" took on rich tones as he played the simple notes. "London Bridge," "Happy Birthday" — every song was instinctive and natural. He played by ear, and the ease with which the music flowed made Steve Max look on with his mouth hanging open. He'd never, in all his years teaching at the orphanage, come across a student with such amazing talent and natural affinity for the piano. The songs just kept coming, one after the other. Mr. Max stood there silent, in shock, and Jason played as if his life depended on it, as if he couldn't understand how he had forgotten about music for all these years. Because that was exactly the way it seemed; that Frost had forgotten about his talent.

Then, that misty piece of music bubbled up from somewhere deep within him. He reached out and tried to play it. He began the first few chords to the tune that only he could hear, but this strange and unhappy feeling overcame him. He tried to vanquish it with the music, but he could only recall part of the song. The rest was floating away from him, even as he played. He tried to find the notes, to take the song to the second part, but the song had left him. He remained with his hands on the piano and a misty recollection of music that he could not recall. He had gone from the highest of highs to nothing in a matter of moments. Now the pleasure was all gone. He felt shattered. He placed a trembling hand on his forehead and felt clammy. He tried to understand why he felt this way, why playing the piano had made him feel as if he was suffering an anxiety attack.

Steve Max was looking at him closely when he came down to earth from wherever it was that the music had carried him.

"You O.K., Frost?" he asked Jason.

Jason, feeling less O.K. than he had ever felt in life, raised a shaky hand to his head and said, "Yes, of course I'm O.K. Why shouldn't I be O.K.? I was just playing the piano."

But they both knew that this had been an intense experience for Jason Frost. He slid off the small wooden bench and shook Mr. Max's hand and thanked him for allowing him to play. Even though it had been somehow traumatic and overwhelming in some way that he didn't understand, it also had been an experience that had shaken him in a tremendously positive way. It had opened up a new world for him. The world of music was a different reality, a different dimension than anything he had done before. It felt as if he was coming home, as if his soul was sending him a message of relief.

Suddenly, he was like a thirsty person, who couldn't curtail his need or desire for a drink. Now that he finally understood the connection he possessed to the world of music, he found that he couldn't stop thinking about it. It had been both a positive and negative experience. But the positive side of the experience far outweighed the negative side. From that day on, music became an integral component in the life of Jason Leonard Frost.

Oyster Bay, Long Island
December 12, 2008

Frost snapped out of his trance when they were almost there, and took a deep breath of ocean air. They stopped for gas, and Frost bought one of those high-energy drinks which really kicked him awake. Al concentrated on the directions, and soon they were taking the turnoff to Oyster Bay, Long Island, to the orphanage/monastery where Frost had spent his formative years. As they approached the ancient stone building that had been built long before Oyster Bay had become the upper-class residential area that it was today, memories of his time spent in the school filled his mind and he smiled. He had been a popular student, and it had been a fun-filled time for an orphan boy.

"Having fun, Jason?" Al asked him. Frost winked at him. The streets were lined with poplar and sycamore trees which shaded them from the strong overhead sun. They followed the town's main avenue until they reached the school, situated right on the town's border. It looked exactly the same as Frost remembered, down to the ivy climbing the walls and the geraniums and tulips in the flower baskets on the windowsills. They parked the car in the parking lot. Frost felt as if the years were slipping away from him and he was a mere boy once again, late for Brother Timothy's mathematics class. The students were everywhere, laughing, running, whooping it up with the high spirits of youth. Down on the lake they could hear the school's rowing team singing as they plowed forward.

It was cooler inside the stone edifice. They reached the offices and asked the nun where the archives were located.

"What's this for, Father?" she inquired, staring at Frost with unabashed curiosity.

"Confessional-related business," he replied, giving her the most self-righteous stare he could come up with.

"O.K., Father," she said, managing to sound both impressed and cynical at the same time. "Whatever you say. Just sign the book." Frost signed the book, and she checked the name and exclaimed, "Welcome back, Father. You haven't been around for quite some time!"

"I've missed the school every day that I've been away," Frost answered her in jocular tones, letting her know that the interrogation was over and that he was ready to begin doing whatever he had arrived to do.

"I'm sorry for keeping you from your task, Father," she said. "I'm going to let you go now. I just want you to know, on behalf of the entire student body and staff, how proud we all were about the fact that one of our alumni was a candidate for the papacy!"

"Thank you," he replied.

She asked one of the students to take them to the school's records department. They were issued passes for one day. They followed the student to the building housing the archives. Frost explained what he was seeking to the man sitting in the back room watching old reruns on his portable black-and-white television set. The man got wheezily to his feet and lumbered over to the farthest corner of the room, where they were surrounded by shelf upon shelf of files.

"Here you are," the man said brightly. "These are the years you requested. I'm sure you'll find him here."

They thanked him profusely and began their search. The files were in order of class and year, and were organized very specifically. Frost was impressed by the amount of work which had clearly gone into making the information readily accessible. But his happiness abated fairly quickly, when neither he nor Al was able to discover any file with a reference to a young boy named Jason Leonard Frost! Nothing! It was as if Frost had never been a student at the school, never graduated with honors in all the fields, never been sent to the principal's office. What on earth was going on here?

They returned to the man and interrupted his solitude once again. He rose, sighing, and asked them what the matter was. They explained to him, that try as they might, they were not finding the file that they needed. Frost asked the man if perhaps there were other files, and if it would be possible to see those. The man got a crafty look on his face. Frost realized that it was going to cost him, but money wasn't going to stop him from finding out what he wanted to know. So he reached into his pocket and, taking out his wallet, handed the man a $50 bill.

"There is another section," said the man. "It's a restricted section, which means that you can't make any copies of the information you find there."

They agreed to make no copies. The man led them out to the hall, up a flight of stairs and then down another hall. They entered another room that was full of shelves as well. This time, he didn't leave them, but took a seat watching them as they began their search. Sure enough, after looking for five minutes, they found a record of one Frost, Jason Leonard. But the file was empty, and the only information inside was a note that read: "This file has been moved to the main archives in Boston." They realized that for now, their search had come to end.

11 Kobi

Moshav Arazim, Israel
January 10, 1966

They entered Lod Airport like thousands of tourists from all over the world. They did not appear to be of any particular nationality; all had a vaguely Mediterranean look. They looked as innocent as any group of young men in their 20's. They arrived separately on various airlines. Some flew Olympic Airlines, others Sabena and one took Air France. The group had been well trained, and had practiced their operation for a very long time to be sure of success. Nobody was taking any chances. Two of them met at the luggage carousel. They exited the main terminal and were not stopped by the customs agents.

The remainder of the group went through passport control at different times without being stopped, and exited the airport to the balmy spring weather. They stuck to public transportation as opposed to taxis, whose drivers might conceivably remember them at a later date. They traveled lightly: a backpack or two and nothing more. Their clothing was specially chosen to blend into the general surroundings as much as possible. Their haircuts, body language and everything about them were nondescript. The rendezvous was at a house that had been rented for them five months earlier on Tel Aviv's Allenby Street in an old building that was shabby and unobtrusive. They rented two vehicles for the operation from two different car rentals, using documents that had been procured for them by the people bankrolling the operation. Another two cars had been rented for them as well, by other people they did not know, and would probably never meet. By Thursday night, they had all arrived and had recuperated from their traveling fatigue. The operation was slated for the following evening.

Although Moshav Arazim was not a religious moshav, it was not anti-religious either; consequently, the inhabitants would be celebrating the Sabbath — at least to some degree — and there would be a lowering of their guard. The British, when warring with the Jewish nation during the years proceeding 1948, had assimilated this fact as well, and had let down their own guard on the Sabbath, due to the Irgun's tendency to rest on the seventh day. That policy had led to several deadly Irgun attacks on British bases specifically on the Sabbath. There were devastating outcomes for the British due to that mistake. Now however, it was a peaceful year, and the moshav would be enjoying the weekend.

The leader of the operation was a man by the name of Rupert Henry. He was a charming individual when he needed to be, yet he could sweet-talk an alligator out of a goat carcass. They were all veterans of various terrorist organizations who lived for their cause. Their cause was money. They worked for whoever paid them the most. Since they were very good at what they did, they were constantly working. They did not know who was behind the intermediary who had hired them, nor did they care. Their one interest was in getting in, doing the job, getting out and receiving their money. They did not know what this particular moshav had done to warrant such incredibly harsh treatment and didn't much care.

Friday was a beautiful day. The sun rose in all its glory and shone on the Mediterranean beachfront city in a benevolent way. Rupert made his way from room to room waking up the guys. Ten minutes later they were all up, dressed and eating breakfast. Rupert instructed them to check their weapons and make sure they were in working order, and that they had sufficient ammunition for any unforeseen emergency. Rupert handed each of them a hefty wad of cash just in case the situation turned dangerous and it was every man for himself. They went over the plan one more time in detail before loading the cars. Every man knew his part. Every man knew what to do if one of them was shot and the rest had to compensate. It was a brilliant operation, and Rupert was justifiably proud of himself.

By 10 o'clock they had gone through the apartment one last time to make sure that they had left nothing behind that might incriminate them. It was spotless.

They got into their cars, three men to a vehicle. Rupert rode in the first car, a white Subaru. The second car was a Fiat. Both cars had souped-up engines that could outmaneuver any patrol car that might give chase. Rupert took the coastal highway, taking the exit toward Zichron Yaakov. The Fiat took the highway all the way through Haifa and on to Acco. They would rendezvous in Tiberias near Lake Kinneret at a restaurant called David's Harp. If all went according to schedule, they would all be there by 2 o'clock that afternoon.

They drove with the windows down, and scrupulously followed their maps. Nobody wanted to get lost and end up in Jordan. They reached David's Harp 45-minutes apart, and sat at different tables.

It was never a good idea to begin an operation on a full stomach, but they had many hours to go, and they would need a good meal to tide them over. Somehow, after the meal, the two groups merged together under the leafy trellises where they blew smoke rings out over the lake, and discussed the operation one last time. When they left the premises the shadows were lengthening on the lake all around them.

Rupert had rented a nondescript safe house, about eight minutes out of the city on a bluff overlooking the lake. They crowded together on the back porch, as the sun sank down and the evening became night. They were quieter now — more introspective — the way they became before the onset of an operation. Rupert told them to get some rest. They set their alarms for 10 o'clock that night. They slept.

The city down below grew quieter, as the night gradually took over, emptying out the streets and sending people home. It had been a long day. At 10 o'clock their alarms went off and they got out of bed, alert and ready for action. There was a professionalism about the way they put together their weapons that bespoke hours of practice. At 1 o'clock in the morning, they set out for the 10-minute drive to Moshav Arazim, home of the Nazi hunters of Israel. It was about to be attacked; for the hunters were about to become the hunted.

~

Yaakov Mishon had lived through some of the most hellish experiences the war had given anyone, and had emerged stronger because of it. A survivor of Treblinka and Bergen-Belsen, Mishon had arrived to what had been British-controlled Palestine, on an old and rickety boat belonging to the Hagganah. They had been spotted by a British navy patrol and had been forced to swim ashore in the dark of night. Mishon had been one of the few who succeeded in evading the search lights, and made it to shore. The rest of them had been sent to Cyprus. He, on the other hand, had reached Hertzalia at 3 o'clock in the morning and never looked back. He was a tall man with a confident manner, who loved children and was loved in return.

He was on guard duty that night at the entrance to Arazim. It was not like the early days of the State when one had to be constantly on guard against Arab marauders. But Mishon had learned to take nothing for granted. He liked listening to classical music as he peered out of the guardhouse window toward the lake. A few lit-up boats were on the water, and if he strained hard, he could still hear the sounds of singing emanating from the cafes on the shore. He loved his life and the country that he had helped build.

At 2:30 in the morning, as he was struggling to stay awake, he heard the sounds of an approaching motor. Wearily he got to his feet and watched as a white Subaru crested the road leading to the entrance of the moshav. The car had music playing, and he surmised that the people inside were youngsters either coming or going to Teveria who had had too much to drink, had gotten lost and were looking for directions. They did not appear to be suspicious in the slightest, and Mishon was totally unprepared for what was about to happen.

Carrying his rifle in his arms in a relaxed stance, he exited the guardhouse and walked across the paved expanse to the vehicle. The Subaru's engine was idling, and the driver slid his window down and waved at Mishon with an expression of embarrassment and apology for disturbing him in the middle of the night.

"Yo man, you speak English?" the long-haired guy said through the window of the car.

Mishon shook his head in the negative. "No so good," he replied as he approached the car, ready to help the kids find the place they were looking for. The moment he reached the window and bent down to see the man better, he found himself staring into the barrel of a silencer.

"Goodbye, sir," Rupert said. The silencer went off with a popping sound as Yaakov Mishon, veteran and survivor of five years in *Gehinnom,* slid to the ground with a very surprised look on his face. Rupert got out of the vehicle, went around to the trunk and removed something which he placed on the grass directly in front of the "Welcome to Arazim" sign that was situated there. It was big and white and made of wood that had been varnished with a flammable substance. He left it there and got back into his car.

Rupert spoke into the walkie-talkie he was carrying. "We're in. It's all systems go," he said. The Subaru pulled away from the spot with a roar of its souped-up motor and a squeal of tires. From down on the highway came the sound of another car as the Fiat raced to join the Subaru. The guardhouse looked eerily empty as they drove down the tar-paved road in the direction of the moshav proper.

When the early members of the moshav first planned Arazim, much thought was given to the matter of protection. Because they had suffered through the worst possible experiences a person could possibly endure, they were unwilling to take any chances. They came to the conclusion that it made sense to build the moshav on top of a hill, thereby giving them the edge in the advent of an attack.

The layout would be as follows: first guardhouse number one, then a long stretch of road, followed by another guardhouse, and then the moshav. The second guardhouse was usually manned by a pair of guards: — one who remained in the hut at all times, and the second, who patrolled the perimeter of the moshav throughout the night. These precautions had worked up until now. The Arabs who had attacked the moshav in the past had learned at their cost, that there were plenty of less adequately guarded moshavim in the area that were easier to attack.

The moshav hadn't bargained on Rupert and his men.

The two cars drove up the long road toward the moshav at normal speed, not wanting to attract any more attention than was needed. The Subaru was the first to reach guardhouse number two. It gave a little honk, and the man exited the hut and approached the gate. Rupert waved to him from the window of his car and the man glared at him suspiciously. Finally he spoke.

"*Ken*?" he asked.

"I don't know what that means, man," Rupert said back to him, pretending not to understand at all. Shrugging his shoulders, the man turned and went back into the hut, returning with his walkie-talkie, which he was using to talk to someone, probably his partner.

"Why Yaakov no call to say you come?" he finally asked at them.

Rupert shrugged his shoulders. As the guard tried to call Mishon on the radio, he was suddenly surrounded by three more men who had suddenly materialized from the shadows. The Fiat had parked a short distance back, and the men had continued on foot, scaled the fence and overpowered the guard with the minimum of fuss. With two guards completely out of commission, and the third unaware that he was perched on the cusp of disaster, the group broke into a run in the direction of the closest cluster of houses to the entrance.

They were in fine shape, having spent months working out, and they had fine-tuned the plan down to the last detail. Consequently, they worked in tandem like a well-oiled machine. They fanned out through the moshav, concentrating on the homes of those individuals who were the main Nazi hunters and recruiters. The other homes were ignored. They carried jerry cans of gasoline with them. Every one of the six men reached their assigned home and ran around the perimeter spraying gasoline. They did not miss a spot. They sprayed the walls and the ground in the immediate vicinity. Rupert was in contact with each of them on their walkie-talkies. When they had finished soaking the bases of the houses, Rupert told them to open the window nearest them and toss in the grenades.

This was a moshav, and no matter how security-conscious it is, the people usually don't lock their windows. This was why they had three patrolmen; so that they could sleep with the windows unlocked! The men slid the windows open quietly. In the case of one of them, they cut it open with a glass cutter. Then together, all working in tandem according to Rupert's instructions, each man removed two grenades from his bag. Wasting no time, the pins were pulled and the activated grenades tossed into the houses. They then threw a lit match to the line of gasoline and ran.

The gasoline caught fire instantaneously, flaring up in a tremendous arc of destruction, causing the homes to become death traps in a matter of seconds. The fire was still outside when the grenades detonated almost in unison. BOOM! BOOM! Twelve huge explosions, one following the next. From inside the homes came the sounds of screaming, as the inhabitants woke up from the scorching heat and the explosions. All around them, lights were being turned on, and people were running out of their homes clutching weapons in their hands, searching to punish those who had caused the latest tragedy to befall them. Some called the fire department;

others ran toward the burning homes, knowing inside their hearts that it was already too late to do anything. The probability of anyone surviving such an inferno was next to nil, but they all wanted to do something: to save someone, anyone.

They tried using their fire hoses, but the fire had spread to the upper stories. While some of the people inside the homes managed to jump, most of them were too disoriented from the smoke, the shouting and just waking up to be able to do anything to save themselves. The screaming was the worst part about the whole thing. These people had lived through the worst inferno the world had ever visited on humanity. It was such a tragedy that they were meeting their end in an inferno brought into their homes.

Rupert and company were far away from the horrible scene by the time the majority of the people had exited their homes. They were running through the forest in the direction of the guardhouse at the bottom of the hill, when the sounds of an undulating siren caused them to look at one another in dismay. They hadn't been counting on that. But it didn't really matter. They were almost at the bottom of the hill, near the first guardhouse, which they had left unattended behind them. They ran like crazed men toward the small break in the trees that opened up on the parking lot adjacent to the guardhouse.

They came out on the gravel lot beside the guardhouse. Lights were blazing from the doorway and windows as they ran past it. All six of them could hear the alarm from behind them rising in pitch. They were about to cross the road and head to where two new cars awaited them, when suddenly a man emerged from the forest holding a rifle in his arms which he used to begin spraying them with bullets.

Right away, he hit one of the terrorists in the stomach. He fell to the ground in a pool of blood. The man stood stoically and continued to shoot at them completely unmoved by the carnage. He stood there like a giant, and used that gun with the lightest touch. The moment the bullets were used up, he ejected the spent cartridge and inserted a fresh one in the rifle, as he carried on with his shooting. It was Kobi.

He had been the third man on duty that fateful night. He had been trying to call his fellow guards when he had heard the first of the explosions. His job was to circle the border of the moshav, and to drive past the farthest homes from time to time. Nobody had called his attention to anything wrong, but he had been in the Mossad long enough to have developed some sort of instinct for trouble. Now too, he had simply known that something was very wrong. He tried to raise Yaakov on the radio, but there had been no answer. He tried brushing that off, by telling himself that Yaakov was an older man; maybe he'd fallen asleep. But deep inside, he knew that wasn't what had happened, because Yaakov Mishon had been on guard duty many times before, and he had never fallen asleep on the job. Everyone in the moshav had to be able to rely on the guard at the gate. The guards knew this, and they never let their people down.

Next he tried calling the guard at the second guardhouse. Here, as well, there was no answer. That was when he had known with certainty that something terrible was happening. Kobi hadn't wasted too much time trying to figure out what was going on. His training kicked in, and he remembered the doctrine that had been drummed into his brain by a host of instructors.

"In the event of an attack," one instructor has stressed over and over, "make sure you cut them off. If you don't know where they are and have no chance of finding them without giving yourself away, then go directly to the spot where they have to pass you by. You'll be able to cut them off." It was too late by this point to get to them and prevent whatever it was that they had come to do. He heard the gunfire and the moshavniks' response. Someone in Arazim was fighting back. He could hear a gun battle now. Soon enough they would realize that they couldn't hold off an entire moshav. When they came running by to try and escape, he'd be waiting for them. He called the army on his radio and was relieved when a voice answered on the first try.

"We are under attack in Arazim," he bellowed into the radio. "Get here as soon as you can!"

"When did the attack begin?" the soldier wanted to know. But Kobi couldn't be bothered with talking any longer. He couldn't answer any questions now. He had to get to the entrance of Arazim and prevent them from getting away. They had to be professionals. Anyone who had gotten past the security at Moshav Arazim would have to be top in the field. But he was going to get them before they left the grounds. He was going to lie in wait at the entrance, and before they left, they would receive a surprise, just the same way that they had given one to everyone there.

He drove to the entrance using the jeep trails, which allowed him to circle the moshav, with no one seeing him as he approached. It would be a surprise ambush. He left the jeep in the underbrush and found the ideal spot to wait for them. With his rifle cocked and ready for action and a couple of extra magazines at hand, Kobi waited for them.

Now he was shooting at them nonstop, knowing that he couldn't lose the edge. But already, they were rolling on the ground into the underbrush and getting out their own weapons. He took a moment to steady his shaking hands and aimed at one of the prostrated forms on the ground. He let loose a barrage at the form, and was satisfied that he had hit it. He had killed two so far. The rest were already shooting at him. One shot as the rest ran forward in classic military style. He, too, had taken cover behind one of the bigger bushes, and kept on shooting from there, changing the magazine when it was finished. Eventually, he hit one more man. But then he felt a stinging sensation on his cheek, and the next thing he knew, he was down on the ground and couldn't move. Then his eyes closed and he saw nothing after that.

Rupert and the remaining two men paused for one more moment at the white form on the grass. He struck a match and the white thing burst into flame. It was an awful, yet mesmerizing sight: the white wood burning against a backdrop of emerald green grass. They turned and left, running across the street and down the highway where another two cars were waiting for them. They left, driving straight to the safe house they had rented, where they would wait until the hunt for them had petered out.

Kobi lay unconscious and helpless on the muddy ground as the army arrived and roared into the moshav and the ambulances and fire trucks came storming through the gates. The police would only discover him in the hours to come, when the detectives arrived on the scene and began examining the bodies lying on the ground. For the three killers, it was too late, but Kobi had received a grazing wound, which had knocked him out due to loss of blood. They loaded Kobi into an ambulance and drove out of the moshav toward the hospital, where he would recuperate from his physical wounds. But the emotional wounds that had opened up that night would take a much longer time to heal. It was on that night that his best friend and partner, Shalom, was killed. His house had been one of those that went up in smoke on that fateful evening. Kobi would never see the sweet face or hear the soft-spoken words ever again.

Nobody knew who was behind the attack on Moshav Arazim. There was no note explaining the motive, no shred of evidence on the bodies of the people who had been killed. There was just one thing that gave some clue to the identity of the men and the motive behind the bloodthirsty attack. That was the white wooden thing which kept on burning on the green grass. The white wooden swastika lay illuminated by the spotlights and by its own burning mass, until someone found the time to douse the flames. But the outline of the swastika had burned itself into the grass, and would remain there implanted forever, until the moshav finally had to rip it all up and replant the grass anew.

The funerals were shocking to the members of Arazim. They couldn't believe that after surviving the Holocaust they would be subjected to another attack by the Nazis, for that was clearly what this had been. Six houses had been burned down, and far too many people had been killed and maimed. The best of the hunters had been bested by the hunted, and some of them would never hunt again. And Shalom was gone as well. Kobi was in shock. He had always pictured Shalom as a cat with nine lives. They had been through many daring missions together and had always escaped unscathed. Kobi couldn't believe that he would never see his best friend again. He stood at the back of the crowd in the cemetery wearing sunglasses, so that nobody could witness his tears.

Each family that had been targeted in the attack had held their own private funeral service. At Shalom's service, Shalom's wife and young sons watched Kobi anxiously from the corner of their eyes, wondering what was going through his mind. Miraculously, they had been away the night of the attack, visiting relatives in Tel Aviv. Their house had been burnt to the ground, but they all escaped through the luck of circumstances. Kobi was not much of a speaker at the best of times, but since the attack, he had almost completely ceased communicating. His wife was very worried about him.

The crowd slowly began shuffling to the exit. Kobi motioned to his wife and sons to go on without him, saying that he wanted to remain behind for a little bit. As the cemetery emptied out, he approached the grave and stood at its foot, his sunglasses firmly in place. His mind took him back to the first time they had met years before. He pictured the younger Shalom, still laconic and silent, but with a half-hidden smile that lit up the world when it finally broke through. Shalom had been his best friend for so many years, the man with whom he had traveled the world, the man who had taught him how to accept whatever happened as the will of G-d. They had been so at ease with each other. They hadn't had to make conversation. They could sit for hours over a game of chess, barely exchanging two words. Their wives had seen the joy the friendship brought them, and became good friends as well.

They spent hundreds, if not thousands, of hours on missions together; sitting in wait for the men they were stalking to make a mistake, to let down their guard and become vulnerable. They had been partners for so long, how could he even think of working with anyone else? They were so accustomed to each other. He was going to have to work on his own from now on, heading a team of agents, if he could ever bring himself to go back to work. The way he was feeling right now, he wasn't too sure that he would ever return to the field.

When it had come to internal security, the Mossad had failed to detect a threat. The cars had been recovered free of prints. The burning swastika had been slathered in a flammable substance, and there had been no identifying clues. The investigation was still ongoing, but Kobi didn't think that anything was going to come from it. The three men who had been killed had been wearing clothing that had been purchased in Israel. They had been equipped with forged identities. As of now, the police weren't at all sure if they would be getting any help at all from the bodies. Meanwhile, many people had been killed and wounded, and the shock and the trauma that this attack had wrought on the moshav were incalculable.

Memories of *Kristalnacht*, of shattering glass and crying, bloodcurdling screams and burning shuls and houses had been visited on Moshav Arazim, home to the survivors, who suddenly needed to learn how to survive again. He crouched near the gravesite.

"So I guess this is it, buddy," he said at last. "Maybe one day we'll meet again when this is all over, and you'll tell me about the way it is up there. But until then, you should know that I will always miss you and the times we had." Placing his hand on his heart, he looked down and said, "I'll miss you, my friend." He studied the short epitaph that had been written on a card placed on the grave: *Devoted husband and father. Dedicated member of Israel's security forces. Survivor of the Holocaust. A man who died in the service of his country.* He had been 33 years old. A man in the prime of his life with so much more to give.

As he turned to leave the cemetery, he was struck by such a sense of finality that he couldn't control himself any longer. The tears began rolling down his cheeks behind the sunglasses. He walked hunched over like an old man to his jeep — the solitary vehicle remaining in the cemetery parking lot. Solitary. Just like he was now.

For years he hadn't been able to let go of what had happened. He had lost the edge that was needed to do the work that he did. They pitied him at headquarters. They felt bad for him, and he was given paperwork to do: work that took little effort on his part, yet which seemed to take him forever. It was as he were swimming underwater all the time, and could never seem to rise to the surface. But now he had been given an opportunity that had brought the excitement back to the surface once again. He could feel the juices flowing for the first time in years. Capturing this particular man would be a penance to all those people who hadn't survived, and especially to Shalom.

In his mind, he could see Shalom grinning from ear to ear on the night they had captured Eichmann. He could see him laughing as they drove to the airport in Argentina: Eichmann drugged, sitting between them, not knowing a blessed thing, just obeying orders, leaning on them as they boarded the EL AL flight.

By the time they arrived at the terminal, Eichmann was alert and somewhat resigned to his fate. But that didn't stop him from glaring at his captors with a hatred that was chilling. Throughout it all, Shalom couldn't stop smiling. Eichmann was theirs. Let him hate. Let him glower at them with those bottomless eyes. Let him do whatever he wanted, for he was going to hang, and Shalom couldn't be happier.

But now Shalom was gone, never to smile again. Yet suddenly, Kobi could feel his strength returning. He felt capable to go where he was sent and to find those monsters once again. Shalom's face would be with him wherever he went. And Kobi would be a force to be reckoned with.

Welcome back, he whispered to himself. The look on his face would have chilled the blood of anyone who sought to oppose him.

Jason Leonard Frost

Boston, Massachusetts
December 15, 2008

The home of the central archives in Boston was an edifice that stood out from the buildings around it. Part church and part library/archives, it was an old impressive-looking building that had been built over 100 years earlier. Frost and Al parked their car in the church's parking lot, and made their way to the entrance of the archives' part of the building. Frost pressed the buzzer. A security camera curved around and pointed down at them as a voice asked them to identify themselves.

"Cardinal Jason Frost and friend," Frost said into the intercom. That must have satisfied the cameraman, because there was a click and they pushed the door open. They sat for five minutes in the waiting room and then the inner door opened up and their guide emerged to escort them inside.

"Eminence," he said in a thick Irish brogue as he introduced himself. "Cunningham's the name. Heard about you and am mighty pleased to finally meet you in person!"

"Thank you," Frost said.

"Now then, how can I be of assistance?" Cunningham asked.

"Well," Frost said, "I'm actually here to see the files for children who were cared for at the Catholic orphanage in Oyster Bay, Long Island back in the late 40's, early 50's. Do you think I would be able to see those files?"

"Can I ask what this is about?" asked the man in a perfectly friendly tone.

"Certainly," Frost replied. "But the thing is, I'm bound by the confidentiality oath of the confessional in this particular case. Suffice it to say, my having access to these files will hopefully change a person's life for the better."

"Well I can't argue with that," the priest said. He led them down a long hallway to an elevator. "The archives are on the third floor. There are over 500,000 files in these archives," he announced proudly, "and we are extremely careful to keep them in mint condition."

Frost smiled and nodded. The man was a fool, but he was in charge and had to be humored. The elevator stopped on the third floor, and they emerged into a different world. Stacks of papers and leather-bound books rested neatly on shelves that stretched from one side of the room to the next.

"We're in the process of computerizing our files right now," the priest said somewhat apologetically, "so visitors will have to look information up in the actual files until the computer system is ready. I hope you don't mind."

"Mind?" said Frost. "I hate computers and love books: the feel of the old paper, the smell of the ink, the look of the faded letters on the ancient pages. I love everything about them. Computers on the other hand ...." he waved a depreciating hand at himself as he spoke. "The truth is," he went on, "that I can't even figure out the simplest things on the computer. I'm like a baby when it comes to penetrating the artificial brain."

While they walked, Cunningham's eyes were alertly searching the shelves for the files that he needed.

"Which names?" asked the priest.

"I need the files of all the boys in the classes of '49, '50 and '51 please," Frost said.

"No problem at all." He pulled over a ladder and removed a file from a high shelf. "Here it is," he crowed. "The Saint Helen Catholic School in Oyster Bay, Long Island. Here you go!" He climbed down the ladder and placed a carton of heavy files in Frost's hands, smiling at him, happy to have helped an actual cardinal of the Catholic Church of America. Then he climbed back up again and came down the ladder twice more for additional files. He handed them over with a smile each time. They placed the files on a table in the corner of the room and began searching through them for the picture of a young boy named Jason Frost. They turned to the section of names that began with "F" and turned the pages slowly, studying each picture carefully, before moving on to the next in line. It was painstaking work. They couldn't afford to skip a picture, thereby missing Frost.

There were quite a few "F's" that year, but not that many! There was no doubt about it; Frost's picture was definitely not among the "F" members of his class. But maybe he had been misplaced, and had been put somewhere else in the file by mistake. It was possible. So they searched and they searched. After an hour of going through all the files, they had to admit defeat. There was no indication of an orphan named Jason Frost.

"Look, Father," Frost said to the man who had accompanied them to the archives, "I'm looking for one specific child, and I'm not finding him. Are there any files that you're not showing me?"

The man lowered his voice and said, "Eminence, you of all people should know that sometimes the church chooses to keep certain information to itself. Maybe this is one of those times?"

"But I need to know," Frost persisted.

Cunningham sought to placate the distraught cardinal. "Look," he lectured, "I'm sure that you could make a big thing about this, and rake up all the dirt to get to the files you need. I'm sure you could. But, if you do that, you will irritate those in the upper echelons, and when you annoy people like that, it could be messy, if you know what I mean."

The priest looked Frost in the eyes.

"If the files are missing, then in my experience, it's usually for a good reason. And when people persist to look for information that they're not supposed to know, then nothing good can come from that. Listen to what I'm telling you, Eminence. I don't care how high up in the church you are. There are people a lot higher and more powerful than you. You should never forget that!" Suddenly, inexplicably, Frost found that he was afraid of the secret that he was slowly unraveling.

"I hear you," he said to a relieved-looking Father Cunningham. He called to Al who was still busy searching — had actually never ceased looking the entire time. Together they followed Cunningham from the archives room. Cunningham accompanied them to the parking lot saying how sorry he was that he hadn't been able to be of more assistance. Frost was gracious about the whole thing, merely stating that he had assisted him more then he had ever imagined. Al started the engine and they pulled out of the lot, Cunningham waving goodbye until they were out of sight.

"That was disappointing," Frost remarked to Al over the roar of the traffic and the drone of the radio.

"Maybe," Al replied cryptically.

Frost knew Al pretty well, and it was obvious to him that Al had discovered something in those archives, some bit of information that was making him smile broadly from side to side. "Out with it, Al," he said.

Al pulled a scrap of paper out of his shirt pocket, slowly, teasingly, and held it just out of Frost's reach. Frost grabbed the piece of paper and looked at it. For the most part, the paper was empty. But at the bottom, there was a little scrawl, as if someone had written the words in a hurry. He studied the words and found them hard to read.

"What does it say, Al?" he asked his friend.

"Notre Dame, Paris, 1948," Al replied.

"Where did you find this?" Frost doggedly persisted.

"Oh you know, while you and *Faaaather* Cuningham" — Al stretched out the word "father" contemptuously — "were hobnobbing with each other, I was still busy searching like the bloodhound that I am. I went back over the entire section beginning with the letter 'F,' and what do you know? I find that there's an empty page right between two names that probably surrounded yours on either side. Coincidence? I think not. My guess is that when they moved your file, they forgot two things: One, this little scrap of paper, since it was so small and was scrunched at the bottom of the plastic, and two, they forgot to move all the other files closer together. Anyway, their loss."

"Well, even if what you're saying is true and this scrap of paper is from my file, what does it mean?"

"You know," said Al, "for a cardinal you just ain't that bright. And I say this with the highest respect, Holy Eminence." He received an elbow in the ribs, and squealed in mock pain.

"It means," he went on, "that our trail is moving along nicely. In fact, we will soon be leaving for the city of Paris. I haven't been abroad for quite some time, and a little vacation will do me much good. I assume that you will be joining me in the ongoing quest into the background and makeup of Jason Leonard Frost. Correct?"

"Of course I'm joining you, Al," Frost said. "I just can't help but wonder what on earth is going on here, and where this whole thing is leading us. That's all."

"That's all, the man says," Al mumbled under his breath. They stopped at the nearest Dunkin' Donuts for coffee and a bag of doughnut holes. It was a long ride home, and they needed all their wits about them.

Cunningham walked back into the church and made his way to his office. He wasn't proud of the fact that he was a mole and had to report on people like Jason Frost whom he respected. But this was part of his job and the way he made the money that allowed him to live in the style he enjoyed.

He dialed the foreign area code and drummed his fingers on the table. The call finally went through and a voice with an accent picked up.

"Yes," it said.

"This is Cunningham in Boston. Frost was just here sniffing around with his friend. I thought that this is something you would like to know."

"Thank you for the information," the voice said. "I trust they didn't find anything."

"Nothing. I moved the file months ago," Cunningham said.

"Very good," said the voice, and the conversation came to an end.

13
Rafi Ganim

Tel Aviv, Israel
January 3, 2005

As the years passed, Rafi made a name for himself in the music world. His music had a freshness that made even the most cynical critic sit up and take notice. He was not the least bit religious, and the only time in life that he felt somewhat connected to G-d was when he was immersed in his musical passion. Though his family had been religious — even very religious — back in the old days, that had all ceased with his parents. He didn't even know his grandparents. His parents had made sure to keep him far away from anything that might possibly harm his chances of being the best in the music industry. Everyone knew that it was impossible to succeed in the world of musical entertainment if you kept Shabbos.

For Rafi, it wasn't even an issue to work on Shabbos. It never even occurred to him that there was another option. He enjoyed his music and that's what he wanted to do. He saw no reason not to pursue his dream. His family stood behind him 100 percent. They attended all his concerts, and made sure to join him in his dressing room after the show. Things were only getting better for the young man with the amazing future.

But the dreams still came once in a while. When they did, he fought back the urge to cry, because the old man still looked so sad, and he didn't have any way of knowing the reason. He had tried telling his parents about the dreams, but they laughed and said that dreams were just dreams, and didn't warrant any attention. Sometimes, he stopped for a moment and thought about real things, taking his mind off music for a second. That was when he was stumped. Why had he been born? Had he been put on this earth for the sole purpose of creating music and playing the works of other composers? What was the point of that? There had to be something more in life.

In the Israeli army, he had been given the option of joining the entertainment corps and had turned it down. He'd opted for a combat unit instead, and spent most of three years defending settlements in the West Bank. He was a model soldier, and the army had invited him to pursue the military as a career. But the army wasn't the life for him. He was going to be a musician; that was the only career that interested him. Three years after going in, it was time to be discharged. He was now going to devote his life to his musical career.

He rented his own place in Tel Aviv. It was a small apartment near the sea. He furnished it from secondhand shops and put together an eclectic look. Posters of old-time bands on the walls indicated that this was a musician's digs. He kept to himself for the most part, trying to discover who he was, what the point of it all was. It couldn't be that he had been created for the sole purpose of practicing the violin for 12 hours a day, so that he could get on a stage and entertain a few thousand people. Even if he achieved international renown, what then? It was still kind of pointless. There had to be something more.

The disquiet in his soul mushroomed to the point where he began finding it hard to play his violin for more than an hour at a time. Whereas in the past he had been able to sit and practice for four or five hours straight, now it was becoming an effort to even pick up his instrument. But if he couldn't play his violin, then what could he do? That was what he had always wanted to spend his time doing! If he didn't enjoy it, then what else could he do? So he forced himself to continue playing, and even enjoyed some measure of pleasure. But he knew that he had to find an answer soon.

He began taking long walks through the city. He found narrow alleyways that wound through neighborhoods with which none of his acquaintances were familiar. He strolled through the upscale part of the city, and explored the slums of Tel Aviv where the homeless begged on the streets. The people lived on welfare and many shadier sources of income. His mind broadened with its newfound education, and he began looking forward to his daily walks. His feet took him everywhere.

One Friday afternoon, he went out to buy a soda. Slipping into his T-shirt and cut-off jeans, he bought a Sprite from one of the seaside vendors. Somehow his feet took him in a different direction than any he'd taken up till then. Before he knew it, he was in unfamiliar territory, in a neighborhood that he had never been in before. This was still Tel Aviv, but a far cry from the bohemian city of night life. Although he didn't know it, this was the Tel Aviv of his grandfather's days. The apartment buildings were built close together in a haphazard collage that spoke of a time before building ordinances had been the law of the land. Buildings were constructed one on top of the other in this part of town. The atmosphere was more sedate and worn as well.

The neighborhood moved at a less frenzied pace. There was much less traffic, nowhere near as many cars as there were in other parts of town. And the people: he hadn't really met people like this close-up. But here they were in the flesh. He had seen people like this in Jerusalem, like those he sometimes encountered in Tel Aviv's central bus station on their way to Tzfas or Meron.

These were apple-cheeked kids with long side-curls and velvet caps. They laughed and shouted in a foreign tongue that reminded him of German, until he realized that it was Yiddish: the time-honored language of the Jewish people. From afar, he heard the wail of a siren. For a moment he thought that the Iraqis were attacking. But the families all around him weren't the least bit apprehensive, so he assumed that the siren was no cause for concern. Children began emerging from every doorway in every shape and size. There must have been thousands of them, and they were all cute and loud and intent on their games. Some of them played catch, and some sat on the sidewalks and played a game called five stones. The girls were jumping rope while their mothers sat and chatted on the benches off to the side. He stared at all of this in silent wonder, and was at a loss.

It was as different a scene as anything he had ever witnessed before. He had no idea how to relate to it at all. It could have been another planet for the amount of sense it was making. Some of the children noticed the stranger in their midst, and began nudging one another, pointing at him.

He realized that they were looking at the fact that he was oddly dressed, and for the first time in his life, he felt that the clothing he was wearing didn't adequately cover what was supposed to be covered. He tried to walk away from the accusing eyes, but felt rooted to the spot. He had feelings that he didn't recognize pounding inside him, pushing to come out. Still he couldn't linger all day. The people might suspect that he was a criminal and call the police on him! That was the last thing he wanted or needed!

He turned to go, and nearly collapsed with a tall bearded man wearing a fur-trimmed hat, and accompanied on both sides by two teenage boys wearing hats and long coats as well.

"I'm sorry," he stammered, as he apologized.

"Nothing to worry about," the man genially replied. "Nothing happened."

The man was friendly! He was speaking to him in Hebrew. He spoke his language!

"Are you here for Shabbat?" the man asked him.

"No," he replied, "I was at the beach, and I took a walk. Somehow, I'm not even sure how I ended up in this part of town. I've never been here before."

"Well, then," said the man, "if you're already here, you might as well stay for a while."

"Stay and do what?" he asked the man. The man sighed.

"What's your name?" he asked Rafi. Rafi told him his name.

"Listen, my friend," the man said. "Right now Shabbat is about to begin. Here's what I suggest. Since this is your first time in our part of town, why not join us for this Friday night and experience something different than anything you have every experienced before? What do you say? Are you up for trying something new? Do you want to see what we are all about? Come to the *beit knesset* with me and stay for the evening meal. You'll have a great time! I promise you!"

Rafi was about to politely refuse, but he suddenly remembered the lonely apartment that awaited him near the beach. So he decided that he wasn't going to miss this experience that life was throwing his way.

"O.K.," he finally agreed.

The man offered him his hand and introduced himself as Naftali Kenighofer. "Now let's hurry," he said, "davening is about to begin and we don't want to be late."

So they hastened down the street. It was a strange sight to say the least: three chassidic Jews, and one man in cut-off jeans and a T-shirt. Passersby stared in confusion, but they paid them no attention; there was a *minyan* to catch and it was late.

Kolodover Beis Midrash, Tel Aviv
January 30, 2005

The Kolodover shul was a beautiful edifice with tall white pillars supporting a facade carved out of stone. It was named after a rabbinic sect that Rafi had never heard of (not that he'd heard of too many!). As they neared the building, obviously religious Jews joined the stream entering the building. This was quite a popular place, and Rafi stood out like a lion at a bird sanctuary. His face was flushed due to his discomfort, and he thought about leaving, but Kenighofer placed a confident arm on his back and he thought better of it. They entered the building through the main doors and found themselves in a giant lobby filled with chassidim talking, gesturing and interacting with one another.

They walked through the swinging doors, and Rafi caught his breath. The *beit knesset* was absolutely magnificent, and he was enchanted. The ceiling soared and was painted a royal blue with golden stars like a sky studded with jewels. The floors were tiled in an expensive granite design with alternating colors. But his attention was drawn to the *aron kodesh* at the front of the huge room. It was taller than three men standing on top of one another, and was a blend of stone and wood. It commanded respect. In fact, the entire sanctuary did; the closest comparison Rafi could think of was a concert hall just before show time. There was a feeling of solemnity and anticipation in the air. For what could these people be waiting? What on earth was going to happen?

The rows surrounding them were almost completely filled by now, and yet more chassidim kept arriving. Somehow they all found a seat and joined the swaying mass of men dressed in black and white. Suddenly, a door at the front of the room opened, and everybody in the huge room stood up in unison. Rafi craned his neck to who commanded such awe. All he could make out was that the man was quite distinguished looking with a silvery beard and beautiful fur hat that was set off by the golden threads in the brocaded garment he wore. The moment the holy man took his seat beside the ark, another man clad in a white prayer shawl began leading the prayers. At this point, Rafi would have surely gotten lost. But Mr. Kenighofer made sure to keep him in the know, by repreatedly showing him the place in the siddur. He also indicated when to stand and when to sit, so that he wouldn't feel out of place.

But Rafi didn't feel out of place. The moment the prayers had begun, a wonderful soothing feeling had entered his heart, a feeling of peace, serenity and joy all at once. It was as if he had arrived home, to a place that had once been his. He was almost exultant, because there was something in this room, an elusive element that spoke to his soul. Maybe it was the musical connection, because the very air buzzed with a certain musical quality. The *chazzan* said the *kaddish*, and the entire congregation answered a thunderous *amen* in unison. It was a roar, a shout, an affirmation of spirit, and before Rafi could assimilate the feeling, they said it again. Then the entire shul erupted into *yehei shmei rabba*, and it was like a wave was hitting the shore, crashing against the rocks in a frenzied spray, rising in a crescendo of joyful sound that seemed as if it would never end. At the end of that *kaddish*, there was a sudden silence so intense that the seriousness struck him with an impact that was almost physical. The people he knew were never like this. They were always joking around, never just swaying and speaking to G-d! He had never seen anything like that before! They were actually speaking to G-d! Could one really speak to G-d? Was that possible?

He looked around the crowded room and realized that it was definitely possible, because that was exactly what they were doing. Speaking silently. Pouring out their hearts to the One Who possessed the ultimate connections and abilities, while there he stood saying nothing. What was wrong with him? This was an opportunity waiting to be grabbed, and he was just standing there like a mute. How often did he find himself in such a situation? He couldn't imagine a time that this would happen again. The fact that it had actually occurred in the first place was pretty close to miraculous. He had to take advantage of this chance to do something that he would probably never do again. But he couldn't pray from the book. No, those were prayers that other people had made up. If he was going to pray, then he would pray using his own words. He closed the siddur and looked around the huge hall. Nobody was paying any attention to him. Everyone was intent on his own prayer, and for all practical purposes he was truly alone.

G-d, he began, *help me find myself. Show me where to look. Show me my path. If it's music, that's all good and I will be a happy man. But G-d, I'm not at all sure that this is what You want me to be doing with my life. If this is my path, then I would feel so instinctively, and I would be content, because my heart would tell me that it's right for me. But I don't feel that way. Instead, I roam the boardwalk searching for inner satisfaction, and I come up empty handed. Maybe this is my chance to figure it all out. You guided my path into a situation that I would have never imagined. But here I am and it's pretty cool. So I'm not going to dismiss it right away. Maybe there's something here and this is my chance. In that case, I don't want to miss it, because it might be my one opportunity.*

Rafi was speaking to G-d! He had never done anything even remotely similar in his life. But with everyone around him doing more or less the same thing, it didn't feel strange. It rather felt as if he were having a conversation with a very longtime close friend. He was still having this strange conversation when the *chazzan* began his repetition of the *Shemoneh Esrei.* He sat down and listened to the crowd as they roared *amen* in unison, and he just took it all in. They finished Minchah and he said *Aleinu,* the concluding prayer. Then someone else approached the *amud* and began the next part of the prayers. He had a rich and magical voice that soared when he went for the high notes. Rafi felt that he could sit and listen to that voice forever.

They had reached a prayer called *Lechah Dodi.* The *chazzan* began a tune, and Rafi felt as if he was going to faint! Literally faint! It was a shock magnified many times over by the fact that it wasn't just one person singing the song, but hundreds of people harmonizing together. Rafi couldn't believe that he was finally hearing the song that had been a part of his life for so many years. He sang along full voice, and the people around him stared at him in wonder and shock. They couldn't comprehend how someone who looked like him was so familiar with their song. This song clearly belonged to this *chassidus*! He paid no heed to them, to their stares and looks. He lost himself, immersed himself, submerged himself in the music. He sang with his hands up in the air, with his eyes closed and his *neshamah* crying with happiness as it reconnected with its heritage.

So it wasn't just a dream. There was much more to this than met the eye. Whose song was this? Who had composed it? Where did it originate? He had to discover the history behind this piece that transcended all barriers for him and led him straight to the highest world of music.

Naftali Kenighofer was somewhat taken aback at the turnaround in his unexpected guest. But he shrugged it off to the fact that Rafi was seeing something so radically different from his own life for the first time, and was reacting accordingly.

And if his enthusiasm was a little bit over the top, well, who could blame him really? So the davening continued for a while. Even though the rest of it was nice and inspirational, it paled in comparison to the song they had sung in the middle. This had been an astouding experience. Rafi was kind of shell shocked from it all. After it was all over, the chassidim lined up to wish the holy rabbi who sat up front a *Gut Shabbos,* and be wished the same in return. Naftali led him to the end of the line. As they waited their turn, he began to explain the background of this particular sect and where they hailed from in Europe. Rafi listened with part of his mind while assimilating everything else around him with the other.

The warmth of the chassidim, the joy of the prayers, the welcoming in of the Shabbos — these were all feelings he wished were part of his life on an ongoing basis. These people seemed to have it all worked out. What did they have that he didn't? The line moved fairly quickly. Suddenly, they found themselves standing in front of the Rebbe. The Rebbe was in late middle age, yet radiated good health and a joyful demeanor. He sat in an elaborately carved wooden armchair and received everyone with a smile, a handshake and a brief blessing.

Rafi was nervous, and Naftali didn't understand what had overtaken the young man in the cut-off jeans. Was the sight of the Rebbe so powerful to someone who hadn't ever seen him before? There was no time to ask, however, because it was their turn to stand before the Rebbe and wish him a *Gut Shabbos.* They had been almost at the end of the line, so the Rebbe wasn't in as much a rush as he might have been. He looked at the disconcerted man standing before him in a T-shirt and cut-off jeans. He stuck out his hand and speaking in *Ivrit,* he inquired as to his name.

"My name is Rafi," he said.

"I see," the Rebbe said. He continued with a question, "Why do you look so perplexed?"

"Can I tell the rabbi something?" Rafi asked the man in front of him, the turmoil evident on his face.

"Anything you desire," answered the Rebbe with a warm smile.

"It might take some time," Rafi said. "In fact, I don't think that we will be able to discuss everything in 20 minutes. I think this is going to be a long conversation."

"You will go on home with Naftali," the Rebbe instructed him, "and after the *tish* tonight, we will have time to talk for as long as you need." The Rebbe saw his disappointed face and said, "Don't worry, we'll talk tonight. In the meanwhile, you will have the chance to spend some time with my Naftali. Believe me, that's a *z'chus* that not enough people have taken advantage of. This will be a night for you to remember."

Events were beyond his control, and Rafi submitted to the maneuvering of a higher power. Besides, it was Naftali the Rebbe was talking about. In the short time that they had been together, Rafi realized that there was much to be learned from the welcoming man with the auburn beard and the gold-flecked eyes. There was no reason to be nervous. The Rebbe would still be there when they returned that night, and they would talk. In the meanwhile, he would go home with Naftali and take things as they came; which, as it turned out, was not such a bad way to live.

Naftali lived in an old apartment building that was part of a row of 15 such buildings. They were shabby, and were badly in need of a fresh coat of paint, but no one seemed to notice. No bohemians lived around here; no people who thought they were the upcoming artists of the millennium. This was a neighborhood of quiet, unassuming people who were just simple, warm individuals. The front lobby was packed with more carriages than he had ever seen outside a carriage shop.

They could hear the sounds of the building's inhabitants singing *Shalom Aleichem.* The children's voices rose above the deeper voices of their fathers. It was a welcoming sound. They climbed several flights of stairs to the Kenighofer apartment and entered a brand-new world. A little girl about 5 years old opened the door in response to their knock, and ran to her father's side. There was a spectacular warmth in the house, and a delicious aroma wafted out of the kitchen. As Naftali entered the dining room, children rose from the couch while others entered the room from other parts of the house, all wishing their father *Gut Shabbos.* Everyone took their seats around the long table: white tablecloth, crystal bottle filled with ruby-red wine, golden-brown *challos* peeking from under a beautifully embroidered cloth. Rafi looked around the room and saw genuine happiness and contentment.

Naftali began to sing *Shalom Aleichem* in a tune that was half-song and half-chant. The older boys joined in, their voices still unchanged and undeveloped, yet that only made their inspiration more real. No one was trying to impress anyone at this table. Naftali poured the wine into his silver *becher* and recited the *kiddush* while focusing on the Shabbos candles. From time to time he closed his eyes in intense concentration and concentrated on the words. The entire family was quiet, even the little children. The *challah* was fresh and still warm from the oven. Rafi relished every bite. He knew that he would never forget this evening. Every aspect would be indelibly etched on his hard drive.

The father was singing with his children, the baritone merging with the sopranos and altos. When had his father ever sung with him? Never, not once could he remember such a thing happening! Yet here was a family, with many more children than his family and not only were they not stressed, the parents were spending quality time with their children as if that was their greatest joy in the world. Rafi knew they weren't putting on a show. The children helped their mother serve the food, and the meal moved by much too quickly for him. He didn't want it to end. He would have been happy to put off his meeting with the Rebbe. All he wanted was to sit and eat home-baked *challah* at a Shabbos table in a tiny apartment where the walls had childish scribbles on them, and the glow of the Shabbos candles shone with an otherworldly light.

But it had to come to an end, and eventually, they were eating dessert. There was one more song and then it was time to *bentch*. The meal was over, and Rafi felt an incredible sadness wash over him. He knew that they would invite him to return next week. He could tell that they liked him and wanted him to come again. But he didn't know if he would. Right now everything in his life was up in the air. He thanked the hostess for the wonderful meal and the chance to be surrounded by such charming and well-behaved children. Then Mr. Kenighofer and his sons donned their coats back for the walk back to the shul for the *tish*.

The streets were still now. All was quiet save the occasional whimper of a crying baby. As they walked, Naftali told his boys a story about one of the holy men of the previous generation. Their footsteps echoed in the stillness, and Naftali lowered his voice in deference to the special quality of the night. Then there was another chassid in *shtreimel* and *bekeshe*, and then another and another. Before they knew it, they were part of a crowd of *Yidden* all rushing back for their weekly dose of Shabbos inspiration.

Once again, for the second time that evening, Rafi was climbing the steps of a building he'd never imagined visiting. But this time, there was a hint of excitement and anticipation in the depths of his eyes.

Rafi, was shown to a spot in the bleachers diagonal to the Rebbe's chair. He watched as Naftali took his seat at the long wooden table alongside many other chassidim. Precisely to the minute printed on the Shabbos schedule, the door at the front of the *beis midrash* opened, and the Rebbe walked in closely followed by his *gabbai* and the *bachur* who lived in his house to attend to his needs. The entire assemblage stood up, and sat down only when the Rebbe himself was seated. The Rebbe was dressed in an exquisitely sewn caftan of the deepest purple, tinged with gold and silver. His silvery beard was in sharp contrast to the gold and purple. He lifted up his hand, and the chassidim began to sing a slow song filled with yearning.

Rafi caught on to the tune right away and created a complicated harmony on the spot. Several *bachurim* on the bleachers picked it up and joined in on the next round of the song, dispelling any traces of unease that he might have felt. The next few songs were unfamiliar pieces of music. But then one of the elderly chassidim was honored to begin the next song. He began singing in a quavering voice. It was his song again, straight from his dream. They were all singing it together, with harmony. He sang along full throated, and tried to understand how this was happening to him.

The next time passed in a blur of singing, and listening to words of Torah which he had no way of understanding. At intervals, he was passed some type of food: a sliver of fish, a sip of beer, some *arbes*. The sound of a room full of grown men singing unashamedly about Shabbos brought tears to his eyes, and he sang along with enthusiasm. Finally it was over. The chassidim wished the Rebbe *Gut Shabbos* as they filed out. When Rafi approached, the Rebbe bade him to wait at the side.

Naftali bade him farewell while inviting him back to their home whenever he chose. He told him that he should just drop in, and that he didn't even have to call first. Such wholehearted sweetness was so unusual that Rafi simply didn't know how to relate to it. He accepted the offer graciously and said that he hoped they would see each other again. Then the *gabbai* led him away from the crowds and into the Rebbe's private quarters, where he took a seat on the couch and waited for the Rebbe to finish giving *berachos* to all his chassidim. He wondered what the Rebbe was going to say when he told him about this particular *niggun* in his recurring dreams.

Then the door opened up and the Rebbe was coming through, walking slowly and leaning on his cane. When he caught site of Rafi, he broke into a beautifully genuine smile that made Rafi smile back at the holy face.

"What's on your mind, my young friend?" asked the Rebbe.

So Rafi told the Rebbe the entire story from beginning to end. He told about growing up in upper-class Rishon LeTzion, and how he wanted to learn the violin because of his love for music, and especially for one particular song that haunted him. There were times that the dreams ceased for a few months at a time, but never vanished totally. He related to the Rebbe how the music that was played after a terrorist attack inspired his love for music. How he was at the forefront of the industry today, and was a featured member of the most professional orchestra in the entire land. Yet, he couldn't figure out why his life was still so empty after all this time, even though he loved music and excelled at his chosen profession. He told how he walked the boardwalk and listened to the pounding of the waves when he wasn't practicing, and sometimes thought he was going crazy from the emptiness of the life that he led.

But the dreams had begun again with a vengeance. In the dream, the holy old Jew would cry and beg Rafi to save someone, but Rafi didn't know who. The hauntingly beautiful song would fill his dream, and he had never known from where this tune originated. But then he had gone out walking earlier this afternoon and had somehow ended up in this very neighborhood. He had been invited by Naftali to spend the evening. And then — and his face turned white as he relived the experience — when everyone began to sing the song from his dream, it was like a hidden world had opened up for him, and he didn't know what to do.

All this came pouring from the tormented young man in a torrent of painful gasps. Finally the Rebbe broke into the monologue.

"Wait a second," he commanded. "You recognized the song," he said, "but what about the face of the old man? Have you recognized that as well?"

Rafi was about to shake his head in the negative, but something caught his eye on the other side of the room. He looked over for a second, and suddenly he appeared to be on the verge of fainting. He tried to speak and a stutter emerged. He cleared his throat and tried again. All he could do was croak.

"Here, take a drink," the Rebbe advised. Rafi gratefully accepted the cold drink of water that had been waiting for the Rebbe on the edge of the desk.

"What did you see?" the Rebbe asked him in a fatherly voice that was filled with concern. Rafi pointed at the far wall across the room, where a portrait hung. It was the holy old man from the dream. His picture was on the wall in the Rebbe's chamber. How many surprises could one man absorb in the space of a couple of hours? This last one was just one too many. Rafi learned for the first time in his life how it felt to pass out.

~

When he came to, Rafi faced the Rebbe in shocked surprise.

"Who is that?" he managed to blurt out.

"That's my uncle, the previous Kolodover Rebbe from Europe," the Rebbe said in his soft-spoken voice.

"But he's the man from my dream," said Rafi.

"Are you sure?" the Rebbe asked him.

"How could I not be sure?" Rafi replied with growing excitement. "Since I was a little boy, I've been having these dreams. I've lived with them, knowing that regardless of how much time goes by without me having the dream, I know that eventually I will have it again.

"Look, my family is not religious in the slightest, but I know when someone is holy. You can see it in their eyes, and this man had the most compassionate eyes." The Rebbe was listening to Rafi with complete attention. He motioned him to carry on with his narrative.

"The thing is, he's crying, always crying. He wants me to do something, to save someone. He's always asking me to help him; begging me to save this man, this unidentified man! But as much as I want to help, I have no idea who he wants me to save or how I would go about saving him!" the Rebbe listened, his eyes piercing with the intensity of his gaze. "And another thing."

~

"What is it?" he asked.

"The song," Rafi said.

"What song?" asked the Rebbe.

"Every time I was visited by the dream, that song accompanied it, almost as if there was a soundtrack to the dream. It was the most incredible song, so musical and melodious, so touching, that it inspired me to great heights in my musical career. I was able to make my music so much better because of that inspiration. And yet, throughout the years, as much as I grew in my career and as famous as I became, there was still a part of me that couldn't understand who I was. I wanted to know what the point of it all was. Was it all about the music? But I wasn't playing the real music! I was playing the classical stuff. But the real music — the heart music — that was the stuff that I heard in my dream, and that wasn't where I had made my fame.

"And now, I ended up here tonight and I have no idea how that happened. As I stood in the shul tonight, I was struck by an overwhelming feeling of coming home, of a contentment just by virtue of being with these people. It didn't matter in the least that I had never met these people before. I was home. I was infused with excitement. But that was nothing compared to the feelings that coursed through me when they all began to sing."

"Why?" asked the Rebbe.

"Because," answered Rafi simply, "they were singing the song from my dream!"

The Rebbe's eyes were blazing now. "This is the song from your dream? That song was composed by the previous Rebbe, *zichrono l'v'rachah*, the man who you say appeared to you so many times. This is extremely puzzling! Why would the Rebbe appear to you, someone who never had any connection with him at all and request your assistance? It makes no sense. We must be missing something. Something important." They sat in silence for a while. The Rebbe stroked his beard thoughtfully, and Rafi watched him without making a sound. It was clear that the Rebbe was deep in thought. Finally he stopped stroking his beard and spoke to Rafi.

"Tell me a little bit about your family," he said.

Rafi was a bit puzzled by the request, but wasn't about to refuse this man anything.

"I grew up in Rishon LeTzion," he began. "My parents are well to do, and we lived in a comfortable home. I had pretty much anything I could ever want within reason. I have two sisters; the older one, Shira, is studying dentistry, and Tamar, the younger one, is a professional hypnotherapist," he said.

"For some reason, from the time I was very young, I felt extremely connected to the rest of the nation. I used to listen to the radio and cry whenever there was a terrorist attack. The music they played on the radio always touched me deeply. I think that was why I decided to become a musician: that and the fact that I was always having this dream, with this particular song constantly playing in my mind." Rafi paused for a moment and took a swallow of the drink on the desk in front of him.

"I'm not sure why," he continued, "but the instrument that I chose was the violin. Perhaps because it could be so sweet at times, while at other moments it could be demanding and strident. I felt that this was kind of like life itself."

The Rebbe was murmuring to himself, "Interesting, very interesting. You know, of course, that my uncle the *freerdige*, the previous Rebbe played the violin as well. But of course you don't know that!" he interrupted himself. "How could you? But that's a fact. My uncle played the violin magnificently. They said that one of the famous theater producers once heard him play the violin and made the Rebbe an offer on the spot to be first violinist in the Warsaw Symphony Orchestra. When he played, it was like the angels themselves were singing. But go on with your story."

"I purchased a violin," continued Rafi, "and took lessons. But the song that I most loved to play was the song from the prayers tonight, the song from my dream. I went to the army, serving with distinction in a combat unit, and I was invited by the army to take an officers' training course to make a career out of it. But I refused the offer and returned to the stage. And yet, even though my career has taken off to such a high degree, I never discovered the kind of satisfaction that I was looking for. So I wandered up and down the boardwalk late into the night searching for the meaning of life."

"Tell me," said the Rebbe, "your father, does he have anything to do with the Jewish religion, with his heritage?"

Rafi laughed. "My parents — actually, I should say my father has absolutely nothing to do with his heritage, whatsoever. In fact, when I was younger there were times that I asked him why he was so virulently against it. I mean, I learned about certain concepts and ideas in school, and they didn't seem so bad. He never answered me. He would get angry at me if I brought it up. So I learned to steer clear of the topic. But that's my family."

Again the Rebbe was quiet for a while. The silence seemed to stretch on and on, until Rafi began wondering if the Rebbe had fallen asleep.

Finally the Rebbe spoke, "Stay here for the rest of the Shabbos. There is something that I'd like to show you tomorrow night, O.K.? Will you remain here with us? We have plenty of room, and I am sure that the Rebbetzin won't mind."

Rafi looked at the Rebbe in shocked silence for a moment. "Of course I will stay," he said. "It would be the greatest pleasure for me to stay with you for Shabbos."

"Good, then that's settled," the Rebbe said. He glanced at the clock on the wall and said, "*Oy,* it's late. It will be hard for you to get up tomorrow."

"Just have someone knock on my door, and I will get up whenever it's time," Rafi said. They shook hands. It had been a powerfully charged night, and he still didn't know what the Rebbe wanted to show him. Whatever it was, it was going to have to wait until the following evening. The aged Rebbe led him out of his office and down a flight of stairs into his private apartment. He showed Rafi the empty room. The bed was made up and the kitchen was just down the hall if he was hungry or needed anything at all. He thanked the Rebbe as best as he could, and the Rebbe pinched his cheek, called him a *tiyera neshamaleh* (a precious soul), and wished him a heartfelt *Gut Shabbos.* He thought that it would take him a while to fall asleep. But he was out from the moment his head touched the pillow.

14

Kobi Shapiro

Herault, France
March 4, 1972

Kobi picked his team very carefully for the monumental undertaking of hunting down Mengele. As a Mossad agent, he had studied criminal psychology at length, and he knew the type of minds that usually chose the criminal world. The average criminal has a need to boast; a need for people to know what he has accomplished and of what he is capable. In other words, subconsciously, criminals weren't happy until they were caught. Because they had this subconscious need to be caught, they made mistakes that pointed those looking for them in the right direction. It all stemmed from that need to get caught. But some people were so sick, so emotionally scarred, such misfits, that they enjoyed being evil solely for the purpose of being evil. They didn't have the slightest interest in being caught. All they wanted was to inflict pain.

Josef Mengele was such a man. He wasn't looking to boast about his exploits in front of the cameras of the world. He couldn't care less about publicity. He had received enough publicity to last him the rest of his natural life. Millions of people knew his name and couldn't sleep at night because of his face. Now, he wanted to live out the remainder of his life in peace and quiet, deep in the jungles of South America, content to spend the majority of his time playing chess with his bodyguards. He was going to have to be smoked out of his hole, because he was so well hidden that it would be almost impossible to get to him otherwise.

There had been other teams, other agents, who had tried to get to the man, but they had failed. Some had even lost their lives in the attempt. Mengele was determined to live, and he didn't care if a few more Jews died because of him.

Kobi had pulled out all the stops for this investigation. For a few months, all he did was fly around the world searching for clues, sniffing out any lead. People, however, were afraid to talk. They were petrified of Odessa, the giant spider's web of intrigue and assistance to all the Nazis around the world. They knew that if they did give that bit of information and because of that Mengele was caught, then Odessa would hunt them down and murder them. It wouldn't be a bullet to the head, either. Traitors deserve slow torture. Consequently, nobody was talking.

There were also those people who wanted to talk. But they were even more frustrating than the first group of people, because you never knew when they were telling you the truth and when they were lying. There were moles and countermoles, and it was very difficult to know which direction to take and whom to trust. Kobi was beginning to fear that perhaps this was going to turn out to be a big waste of time. But then he met Leon, and that was when things began to get exciting.

Leon had been a French Nazi in the old days, and he professed to regret the things he had done under the French Vichy rule. He claimed that he didn't know what had come over him, and had tremendous angst for having sent so many people to their deaths. To make up for all the damage he had done, Leon decided to help those who sought revenge. He was an expensive informer, but there were those who felt that he deserved every penny that he asked for. The information that Leon provided was usually worth its weight in gold. Leon had heard that Kobi was looking everywhere for one man in particular. So they set up a meeting at a small cafe in a village called Herault in the south of France near the ancient family chalet that Leon called home. The cafe sat unobtrusively on the corner of an intersection, and that was where they were slated to meet.

Kobi was instructed to come to the meeting wearing a leather cap and holding a copy of that day's Le Figaro, with the picture of de Gaulle on the cover. Kobi purchased the newspaper and set off for the fateful meeting with the man who hopefully held the key to the missing Mengele. France was a beautiful country, and Kobi marveled at the scenery as he drove through the countryside from Orly Airport.

It took him quite a while to reach the village. He didn't want to fly because he enjoyed getting a feel for the land and its people. He was so proficient at reading maps that he never got lost. His French was passable enough to enable him to order food in a restaurant or speak to the natives in their own language. A Frenchman might know that he wasn't from France, but he wouldn't be able to figure out where he *was* from. He had studied languages at the academy for many years, and had a very good ear. Even now, it flowed naturally from his tongue. Languages were like driving; once you knew them, they were pretty much yours forever.

The meeting wasn't until 10 o'clock the following morning. He stopped for the night at a small hotel, and continued on his way the following morning, till he arrived in Herault. He was sitting and enjoying a buttered croissant and a cup of coffee while he waited for Leon to arrive. As he sat, he watched the village life go by. Two backup agents who had been staying in a different hotel kept watch from a distance, updating him any time someone new walked into the scene.

Ten o'clock came and went, and still there was no sign of the man. At 10:15, just as Kobi was about to give up and leave, he heard one of his agents warn him that a tall, heavyset man wearing sunglasses and a leather jacket was approaching. It sounded right. He remained seated and the man did in fact head his way, taking a seat across the table.

"Sorry that I'm late," he said in heavily accented English. "I just wanted to make sure that nobody was following me. They do that from time to time. Anyway, there was nobody there today. Let's go." Leon called for the bill, and throwing a 10 franc note on the table, he motioned to Kobi to follow him. His Land Rover was parked around the corner from the bistro in such a way that nobody was able to park next to him or box him in.

"Get in," he said. When Kobi didn't obey immediately, he barked at him, "Do you want to be spotted? Because if you do, then just stand there like an idiot-fool and look at the sky. That will give them plenty of opportunities to get a picture of your face! Let's go!"

Against his better judgment, Kobi got into the car wondering if he was making the mistake of a lifetime. Leon started the engine and the Land Rover purred into life. They pulled away from the curb, and Leon held the wheel lightly between two fingers and took the curves with ease. He was quiet most of the way, and Kobi was too busy holding on for dear life to want to talk. So the ride was spent in silence, until Leon slid a cassette of Pavarotti into the car's recorder, and the sounds of the operatic voice filled the confines of the car. They were driving in the hills now, and the view was magnificent. They passed people cantering on horses and others hard at work in their gardens.

Suddenly, they were turning off the main highway onto a small road that began to climb higher and higher until it was clinging onto the side of the hill. Leon was more relaxed now, and he began slowing down. He rolled down the window on the driver's side, lit up a cigarette and inhaled deeply.

"Ah, that feels good," he said, and coughed uncontrollably. "Picked up this rotten habit in the war," he said and coughed again. He offered one to Kobi, who accepted it just for the sake of companionship. They smoked for a while until they rounded one final curve, and Kobi stared in awe at the castle sitting in front of him. It was absolutely enchanting. It was more than a mansion. It was a castle, and it all belonged to Leon.

Leon parked the Land Rover carelessly in the circular driveway, and they got out of the car and entered the castle. Everything was grand; more than grand, grandiose. The carpets, the furniture, the artwork on the walls were antiques. It reeked of pretension, and Kobi was vaguely aware that he disliked his host on general principle.

"Follow me," Leon said, and they walked through the long, dimly lit hallways and huge rooms decorated with bear heads and deer antlers on the walls. Leon showed him into the modernized kitchen and told Kobi to make himself comfortable at an island surrounded by stools.

"Tea, coffee or juice?" he asked him.

"Juice," Kobi replied.

Leon placed two large glasses of orange juice on the island, and they sat sipping in silence. It was fresh-squeezed orange juice, and it reminded Kobi of the Israeli oranges he relished.

"O.K.," Leon finally said. "I was told whom you're looking for, and I hope you know that your chances of catching him are very slim. He is probably the most protected and vigilant man alive today. I don't say this lightly. Places and events that other less cautious men might attend wouldn't even be considered by this man. He remains at home in his fortress, and doesn't mind that the world is passing him by. He couldn't care less about socializing. The man is sick. He is a megalomaniac, and his bodyguards pay homage to him." Kobi was about to interrupt, but Leon held up his hand to cut him off before he even began.

"Look, friend," he said, "everyone in the world wants to get this guy. They want to hang him and chop him up into little pieces. They want to destroy him. You probably don't even know about all the attempts that have been made, all the bloody failures, all the people who perished in various attempts to capture him. Let me tell you about one of those attempts. This happened about 15 years ago. The Nazi hunters weren't as advanced back then as they are today, while Mengele was just as paranoid. The Mossad put together a team to capture the beast. They were good, very good. But Mengele was better. Scary, but true. The man has this innate understanding of the human mind. He has the best survival skills I've ever seen in a human. Sort of like a rat. Give him a challenge and he rises to it. After the war, he wasn't as well hidden as he is today. But all that changed the moment he realized they were coming after all of us."

Kobi gave him a strange look.

"Yes, me too," Leon said. "They were coming after me as well, until I got in touch with the right people over in Israel and convinced them that I sincerely regretted my actions during the war, and desired to make up for them by helping out the hunters in any way that I could. They flew me to Israel. I met some of your highest security people including Isser Harel. He had to decide if they were going to trust me when it came to these matters — matters of the highest national interest. In the end, after I was subjected to a battery of tests, they decided to accept me as an informer. I have helped out the Israelis so many times, I lost count.

"Anyway, back then Mengele was living in one of the smaller South American cities. A city is much easier to disappear in than a small village where every outsider stands out. The second he realized what was going on, he was gone. He picked up everything in the middle of the night and just left. For a while, nobody had any idea where he had gone. It was only a year or two later that we were given an inkling as to his whereabouts. One of his relatives pointed us in the right direction, and that was how we discovered that he was living in Paraguay. It was some little town at the edge of the world. It was the most forsaken place that you could imagine. He owned a ranch on the outskirts of this place, where anyone who entered the town without a legitimate reason stood out and was recognized in a microsecond. It was that kind of place.

"To get to the town, you needed to pass through rain forests. The ranch itself was built at the foot of this huge mountain range. Somehow, I was able to get this information to the interested parties."

"They were caught, weren't they?" Kobi said, looking at the informer with fire in his eyes.

"Yes, they were, " said the informer. "But before you get angry at me, you should just understand that the setup didn't originate with me. It came from somewhere in *your* organization."

"I don't know," Kobi said. "It just seems too convenient for you. Give the Mossad your information. The agents come and walk right into a trap. What does that say about you?"

"It says that I am human and I make mistakes, and that not every bit of information that comes my way is accurate, especially now that they suspect me! But if you think that you're in danger, you should just know that had I wanted you dead, you would have been dead before we left the village!"

"What do you mean?" Kobi asked him.

"I mean that there was a man with a high-powered rifle checking you out through a pair of field glasses pretty close to where you were sitting. If he had seen anything suspicious, and I mean anything at all, then he would have shot you, no questions asked. That would have been the end of you, buddy. That's what I mean! Get it? I'm not in the business of taking unnecessary risks, and neither are you. I assume you had your own precautions in place as well. I would be disappointed in you and the Mossad if you thought you could handle this all by yourself, because this is way bigger than all of us put together." Kobi was reeling from the sheer force of this man's personality.

"Here, come with me," Leon said. They went downstairs into a mini-theater. Leon switched on the screen with a flick of his finger, and slipped a video cassette into the slot.

"I took this footage after the fact, but it will give you a proper picture as to what you're dealing with." The screen was not very clear. Either the camera hadn't been of the highest quality, or the person shooting the video hadn't been the best in his field; maybe both. Either way the picture was grainy and of low quality. Kobi had to strain to discern a clear picture.

"O.K., if you look toward your left and up," Leon said narrating so Kobi would understand what he was seeing, "you'll see a big old house. That was where Josef Mengele used to live. Notice the bars on the windows, the way that it's built on top of the hill so they can see anyone who was approaching." The camera was obviously in a car, because it was moving closer and closer to the house.

"Look at the ground, and tell me what you see," Leon ordered him.

"There's a wire there," Kobi answered. "It gives off a signal to the house that someone had entered the grounds."

"That's right."

There were warnings for mines and barbed wire. The estate had some of the strongest security that Kobi had ever seen for a private individual.

"They wanted to come in by small craft through the lake," Leon told him in an ominous voice.

"What happened?" Kobi asked.

"What happened?" Leon repeated the question in an intense voice. "The underwater sensors picked up the movement and sent a message to the security forces that security had been breached. In the end, I'm told the agents were drowned in the lake. So there you have it, friend: the life of Dr. Mengele, the man who takes no chances. The man we have named 'Impossible to Kill.'"

"Wait a second," Kobi interjected. "I don't understand. If this is the situation, then why are we meeting? What possible outcome can come out of this meeting besides the deaths of more agents?"

Leon listened to his impassioned outburst with a little smile playing on the corners of his lips. "You're right," he said. "And if this was a week ago, then I would have never even agreed to meet with you. However, there have been developments."

He paused, then continued. "Here's the deal. There is going to be a meeting of a number of the highest-ranking Nazis in a few weeks' time in South America. It is going to take place at the home of a Nazi named Kurt Wolfgang Zeivald. He lives in a beautiful estate called The Palms, located on the border of Brazil and Paraguay. It's very hard to reach, and all the big boys are going to be there."

"Why?" asked Kobi. "What's the point?"

"The point?" parroted Leon. "The point is quite simply this: These people don't want to let the whole thing die. And I'll tell you something else. If you had any idea how much money they have, you would understand them. They stole the finances of Europe. They plundered the estates of millions of people. Money will never be a problem for any of them. So why not start the whole thing again? It's not just about starting again either. These people have plans, my friend, and I fear for anyone who gets in their way!"

"Yet, you're telling me their plans, basically handing me a blood-stained invitation. Why are you telling this to me, if you think I shouldn't go?!" Kobi exclaimed.

Leon started getting annoyed. "Listen, *mon ami,*" he said, "I don't know what you guys want. All I know is that I received a message that the Israelis are searching for information that will lead them to Mengele. I'm giving you what you want, and I'm also giving you my personal recommendation along with the information. I don't think you should go! That's what I feel. You do what you want."

"How will we know that Mengele is going to be there?"

"Nobody knows for sure, but ..." he held up his finger, "the word on the street is that the Doc will be addressing the gathering about our future goals. Nothing is definite. He might choose not to attend, and then Kurt Becher will speak in his place. But there is quite a good chance that he will be there."

"How will I get into town during this Nazi meeting?"

"That's up to you," Leon said. "The Mossad is quite professional. If there's a way to get in there, I'm sure that you'll find it. Anyway, this is what I have for you. A good chance at finding the man you're all looking for. Take the risks, don't take the risks, I don't care. I earned my money. Stay for dinner?"

Dinner was served in the grand dining room, even though it was just him and Leon. Leon sat in his carved armchair and looked like an emperor of old. Kobi sat on the hard wooden seat and felt very uncomfortable. Throughout the meal, he paid no attention to the splendid array of dishes that were served; the food just didn't interest him. There had to be a way. This would probably be their only chance for the next 10 years. If they missed this, that would be it. But how? The airport would be mobbed by Nazi security; the same for the ports. What was left? How could they nab this guy who lived out his days and laughed at his pursuers from the safety of his home?

He barely tasted the sorbet. Leon looked disappointed that Kobi was being such a poor guest, but his thoughts were all over the place. Get in, get out. Why were all those Nazis meeting? What could they be planning? They lost. The war was over. Move on.

Where could they take this thing from here, anyway? Someone was going to have to get in there and find out. Somebody would need to discover the secret and put a stop to them before they started again. The world had gone nuclear, and that boded no good for a country the size of Israel. What would happen if someone carrying even one tiny suitcase with a nuclear warhead managed to carry out a detonation right in the middle of Tel Aviv?! Then what!? He imagined Tel Aviv in flames, piles of dead and wounded, like Japan after the Americans bombed Nagasaki at the end of the war, and he shuddered. They would have to stop them sometime, otherwise when would all this end?

"Are you attending this meeting?" he asked his host.

"I haven't decided yet," Leon replied. "With all their suspicions of me, they might decide to kill me then and there as an example. That could be the only reason they even invited me. I don't know. Probably I'll stay home in the end, even at the risk of missing Mengele's speech. I'll live without it. I heard enough speeches during the war."

On the drive back to his hotel, Kobi thought about everything he had learned that day. In the end, it would be the decision of his superiors. But if they asked him to go, he would. Someone had to do the dirty work. It might as well be him. *Right, Shalom*? he asked his deceased partner.

15

Jason Leonard Frost

Oyster Bay, Long Island
Mid-1950's

School passed in a haze of fun and work for Frost. It was the best of times for someone who could not recall his early life. Try as he might, Frost had a very vague recollection of the way his life had been before he had reached America. His first solid memories began when he boarded the ship taking him and many other orphans to the United States. He was mischievous and full of fun, and he loved sports. He was very good at physical activities and he excelled in academics. He joined the orphanage's junior-high debating team, and was so good at it that he was elected captain. It was all about logic, and Frost excelled at that. In fact, part of him wanted to become a scientist because he didn't understand the religion with which they were constantly being indoctrinated.

The school was compassionate to the orphaned students. But when it came to religion they were inflexible. The rules could not be bent. Every student, with no exceptions whatsoever, was expected to be at mass on time. They had to remain for the sermon. If a student was late once, his infraction was overlooked. Twice, late meant a visit to the principal's office. Three times late meant some serious detention and the reduction of privileges and a paddling in the principal's office by the gym teacher, who had a very powerful arm.

Frost learned quickly. He didn't want to be beaten. After thinking it over, he came to the realization that since he was stuck at this school for the foreseeable future, he might as well come to terms with it and do what was expected of him and try to understand. So he tried; he really tried. For a while, he sat and listened carefully to every sermon that was delivered to the student body. He tried to follow the thread, but his keen mind kept on picking up contradictions from the many different religious texts. He ignored the doubts that assailed his mind, but they returned even stronger. He pushed them away and they returned again. In his senior year in high school Frost finally decided that the next time a priest came to speak to the students, he would make it his business to discuss his doubts with him. He was going to clear things up once and for all.

Three weeks after that resolution, Father Jeff McCormer, an alumni of the school who was well liked by one and all, arrived for an uscheduled visit. Frost felt that Father Jeff was the man he could trust to give him an honest answer to the questions that he had. So when the sermon was over and the students had all left the room for lunch, Frost approached Father Jeff and asked him if he could speak with him. Father Jeff was delighted to be of assistance in any way possible. They went for a walk near the soccer field after lunch.

Frost opened up under Father Jeff's silent encouragement, sharing his doubts and fears. The young priest tried his best to allay them all. His first answer went kind of flat, since Frost disproved his theory without trying too hard, by bringing a quote from the text he had learned. Jeff was stunned both by the depth of thought that Frost had shown and by the fact that the kid was actually right! Here Jeff had given him the standard answer provided by most of the theological experts that he knew, and the kid had demolished it with a wave of his hand. This kid was incredibly smart, and Jeff had been foolish for not noticing the contradiction the kid had picked up on.

"Listen," he told Frost, "you've asked a really good question!" Frost lifted his eyebrows dubiously.

"No, I'm serious," he said. "I don't know any other students your age who have as good a grasp on the material as you have. In fact, I cannot recall being asked a question as good as this one ever before. We're not going to give up. We're going to discover the answer together. Even if it means going to the biggest experts, we won't give up until we find the answer, O.K.?"

Frost was duly impressed by this declaration. He was accustomed to teachers telling him that they'd get back to him with an answer to his questions, when in the end they almost never did. For the most part, he'd let it go. He understood that he was very smart — almost abnormally so — and he didn't want to torment people with that. But this was different. This was religion, and if he couldn't count on that, what could he count on? It meant a lot to him that Father Jeff was taking this seriously. He was also impressed that the question bothered Jeff in the first place. That meant that Jeff was for real, and Frost liked and admired real people.

"So what's our first step?" he asked the dynamic priest in front of him.

"I think it's time to pay a visit to old Father Bargotti," Jeff replied. In response to the question in Frost's eyes, Jeff explained that Bargotti was one of the church's greatest experts on Christian writing. He would no doubt have a well-thought-out and conclusive answer for them. Frost was looking forward to the meeting. He imagined himself meeting an old and impressive priest: a man full of wisdom, an erudite crusader of truth. In fact, Bargotti was in some ways the exact opposite of what Frost had been expecting. Father Jeff had received special permission from the principal to take Frost out of school so he could meet the famous Father Bargotti. The principal respected Frost's intelligence, and didn't need much convincing.

The following morning found Frost in Father Jeff's old Chevy, making the drive to Long Beach where Bargotti lived. It was a pleasant day, and the car was saturated with the arome of pine needles and the stench of tobacco from the Lucky Strikes that Jeff smoked. Long Island was beautiful this time of year. As they drove, Jeff rolled down the windows, and breathed in so deeply he began to cough. He had to pull over to the side until the attack ceased.

"No more deep breathing for me," he said as he breathed in through his nose.

"Just stop smoking and you'll be fine!" Frost said to him. "I can't understand why any sane person does it. Really!"

"Well," said Jeff, "I got addicted like most people."

"So fight it," Frost responded. "You're a priest. You have to fight a lot of things. You're supposed to be on a higher level than most people, so just fight this thing and win!"

There was such conviction in his voice, that Jeff said, "You know something. One day you're going to be a real leader. I mean that! You have a sincerity that comes across in a real dynamic way."

Frost was going to remember those words: sincerity, dynamic. Important words for people who do important things, and he was going to be a person like that! Father Jeff believed in him! He felt like a million bucks. Father Jeff put on the radio, and they listened to a station that featured old-time band music for a while. Eventually Frost fell asleep, his head lying against the cushion, his brain enjoying the music even as he slept.

Jeff woke him when they arrived at Bargotti's street. It was a winding road surrounded on both sides by trees that had been planted over a hundred years earlier. Bargotti lived in a sprawling split-level ranch house, and he answered the door on the first knock. Frost was still slightly drowsy from the ride, but he woke up when he caught a glimpse of the man.

Father Bargotti was huge. He was over 6 feet tall with a large nearly bald head. When he smiled, his eyes crinkled up in the fleshy folds of his face, until they were almost lost from sight. His stomach rumbled when he laughed, which was often, and he shook with enjoyment and mirth. He did not look at all the way Frost had envisioned such a scholar, and Jason was pleasantly surprised.

"So you're the child genius," Bargotti said to him as they sat in his study.

"I don't know about that," Frost replied, "but I had this question, and Father Jeff tried to give me a couple of answers. There was something unconvincing about every one of them. I wasn't trying to find complications or contradictions, but they were just there, and I hate not knowing the answer!"

"I see," Bargotti said gravely, matching Frost's tone, treating him with the respect he deserved. "This question is quite a difficult one, and that's the truth. Many years ago, I stumbled on this question, and I tried to discover the answer. I went to speak to several of the men who were considered the experts back in those days, but nobody was able to give me a satisfactory response. I mean, they gave me answers but there was always something wrong with them: A contradiction from Mark, a question from Paul. I persevered and kept on searching for the answers. I said to myself, *This has to make sense*! A billion people live their lives according to this doctrine, and here I find a simple question and nobody that I speak to is able to give me an answer that satisfies me!"

"So what did you do?" Frost asked.

"What did I do?" asked Bargotti repeating the question. "I sent a letter to the pope." He leaned back in his chair with the air of someone who has vanquished all opposition.

"And," prompted Frost, "and then what?" In his impatience to hear the outcome of this exciting story, Frost accidentally tipped the Coke he'd been drinking. It spilled all over the couch. Father Jeff jumped to his feet and ran for a towel. Frost apologized over and over again as Bargotti laughed it off, his stomach shaking as he moved. When everything was back to normal, Frost took up where he had left off.

"So what did the pope write back to you?" he asked the priest.

"He wrote that there was a man who had devoted his entire life to this particular question and others like it, and had written down his conclusions in a book that was shown to people who had these same questions who weren't able to put them to rest. So of course I went to visit this man, this expert. I was so excited, because I just knew that I was going to discover a treasure trove of answers to my questions." Frost was sitting on the edge of his seat now.

"And," Frost breathed, "what did he say?"

"Well," Bargotti went on, "the man was a seedy-looking scholar in his 70's, with thick old-fashioned spectacles and a slow way of moving. But he had a razor-sharp mind. I told him all my problems and he went to get a copy of his book. But before he handed it to me, he prefaced it by telling me that I was headed for a disappointment, because the answers were by no means as complete as he would have liked them to be. I was sure that he was being modest, but it was true. He had presented all the questions in dry academic style leaving no room for error. Then he had attempted to answer them. But," said the older priest, "although he spent a lot of time on the calculations and really tried hard to make order, it was still not clear. I told him so. So he opened the back of the book and showed me what he had written there.

"He wrote that he knew that the questions remained, and that he hadn't given up. He invited everyone who read the book to attempt to figure things out on their own."

Frost had a very disappointed look on his face.

"So I took his advice," Bargotti said, "and I sat down and began doing my own research. After spending a long time traveling to the most obscure libraries, I discovered an ancient tome that addressed the issue. That led me to another ancient manuscript in Venice that was guarded under lock and key, and so on and so forth. I searched like a madman, and devoted nearly two years to this project. Eventually, I came to some conclusions that were entirely my own, and which I think answer this question satisfactorily."

"So tell me," urged Frost.

Bargotti raised his eyes heavenward as if asking for patience to deal with pushy teenagers and said, "Listen, this isn't a one-minute answer here. This is going to take a while."

"Fire away," Frost said.

Bargotti talked, and Frost listened. For the first time, Frost felt that maybe there was someone who had actually gotten to the bottom of things. Bargotti spoke with assurance and confidence; his words were precise, and historically and logistically correct. The case he was making was clearly original and was based on a daring premise. Frost listened closely, writing furiously as Bargotti spoke, interjecting questions, daring to challenge the huge man, to make him prove his theory. Bargotti fielded everything Frost threw at him with good humor, until the hour had grown very late.

Bargotti rose and began turning on the lights in the house. Frost realized that the hours had slipped by and it was time to leave. Jeff felt the same, and they were about to thank Bargotti for his time, when the priest asked them if they wanted to stay for supper. "It's the least I can do for an aspiring scholar so young," he said with a warm smile on his face. With so genuine an invitation, how could they say no?

Bargotti smiled. "I'm so pleased that you will join me. I have only simple fare to offer but you can have a choice. I have several frozen dinners that I can pop into the oven or we can make do with cheese and delicatessen sandwiches. Which do you prefer?"

Jason deferred to Father Jeff who opted for the sandwiches which were quickly assembled.

Jason sat at the table, and the three enjoyed their tasty repast. A bottle of hearty red wine accompanied the food and there was ice cream and cookies for dessert.

He looked around the small room and felt at peace in the company of these two men. Frost knew that when he got back to the school, he would be studying the sources and making sure that everything fit, until he was satisfied with all he had heard. Then he would write a counter-response and they would correspond with each other, because Father Bargotti was going to become his mentor. He was certainly smart enough. Instinctively, Frost felt that this was a man he could trust.

The drive home through the dark and calm Long Island roads was the perfect foil for the turmoil that had descended on Frost that evening. Until this point, he had been convinced that nobody had the answers and that there was no truth in the whole thing at all. Suddenly, he had met a person who definitely held the key to some of the answers, who had conviction and whom Frost could respect. It was a turnaround for the young boy. Father Jeff asked him his impression of Bargotti, and Frost deflected the conversation, because he wasn't interested in showing Jeff the depth of his feelings. He drifted off to sleep about halfway to the school and woke up as they were entering the school grounds. He thanked Jeff for the ride and told him that he would be very busy now, either proving or disproving Bargotti's theory. But either way, he appreciated being introduced to Bargotti more than Jeff would ever know.

When Jeff asked him why, he replied that finding a man who actually possessed a little bit of integrity was rare indeed. Then, leaving a puzzled Father Jeff in the parking lot, he turned and entered the school building instead of the dormitory and headed directly to the auditorium. It was late already, but there was only one thing that could calm him down right then. He needed to play some music. He opened the auditorium doors and stared in awe at the rows of plush red seats. He walked into the room and marched slowly down the endless aisle toward the stage. He reached the stage and walked up the steps quietly, and continued to the baby grand piano that was just waiting for him.

Reverently, he lifted the cover and pressed down softly on one of the shiny keys. The note chimed brightly in the gloom and silent darkness. He sat down on the piano bench, and then he played like he had never played before! It all came rushing out from his heart, all the uncertainties, anxieties and other feelings that he couldn't name. These were all overshadowed by happiness, because the key element in his fragile heart was a happiness so overwhelming as to be almost too much for him. He had found a mentor, and he hoped that the mentor understood that he had discovered a student tonight as well. The song that came out of those keys wafted through the still air of the majestic room, bringing a touch of freshness to the endless quiet. He didn't even realize that the song he'd been playing was the same one from long before, a song that emanated from his heart. It came from a place so distant that he couldn't recall where he had heard it first. Yet it brought a joy to his heart so strong that he wanted to cry.

So he did: the tears dripped on the black-and-white keys, until they were slippery from the wetness. The song in the great hall merged with the song in his heart. Then he closed the cover abruptly and left the auditorium. Somehow he found the dorm and his bedroom, and he went to bed, shaking from heat and cold, pulling the blanket up to his neck one moment and pushing it away the next. He tossed and turned for hours, mumbling in his sleep, until a roommate happened to wake up and saw the thrashing about and called the nurse from the infirmary. He was taken to the infirmary and given an injection, and finally he ceased moving so violently. A more gentle breathing took its place as a smile formed on his lips and his breathing evened out and he slept. But even then he knew that he was going to find the truth. Whatever it took, he was going to dig down and find it.

He remained in the infirmary for two days before convincing the nurse that he was back to himself. Father Jeff came to visit him, still unsure as to what had caused such a crazed reaction. Father Bargotti came as well, his giant presence a tangible comfort for the young man. If at first the nurse was displeased by the gentle giant's disturbance of her ward, she soon changed her mind when she realized how beneficial his being there was for her young charge. In fact, she soon came to encourage their conversations with each other, though they needed little encouragement. Without books at his disposal, Frost set his incredible mind to work attempting to disprove the older man's theory. He brought forth copious amounts of material by heart to back himself up.

Then Bargotti would have to rise from his chair once more, complaining and grumbling about his back and the strain that carrying all these books was taking on it. Then he would rush to the library and return with yet another pile of obscure reference tomes, and they would pour over the books together. The more they argued and investigated, the closer they became, even though the tide seemed to be turning in the direction of Frost. Frost was just too good, and his memory too strong to be stifled for long. All Bargotti had going for him was his greater experience, but that was not sufficient to stop the bloodhound in Frost. Their debates moved from the infirmary to his dorm room, where the piles of books on every available surface threatened to topple over. Finally, they came to the juncture where Frost had shown conclusively that Bargotti was wrong in almost every area. Bargotti stubbornly held onto those few points of merit, and they decided that they would send their questions to Rome for final arbitration, to settle the matter for good, one way or the other. And so, one cool spring day they sent the lengthy inquiry letter to Rome, and prepared to wait for a reply.

The Vatican, Italy
Mid-1950's

The man sat in the office deep in the Vatican, and went through the bundles of mail that arrived on a daily basis. Items of interest had been set aside to be dealt with by the proper parties involved. The name on the front of the envelope jumped out at him. He opened the letter and read the contents slowly and carefully. This was a matter for others to decide. Quickly he lifted the receiver and dialed the international number.

"*Ja*?" the voice replied.

"This is Carruso," he said, "and this is the situation."

"Thank you for bringing this to our attention," the voice said. "We will get back to you shortly with an answer." Carruso smiled and replaced the phone. Anything for the cause.

For months there was nothing. Even though Father Bargotti was a widely respected man of the cloth, and even though the questions were first rate, they had begun to give up on ever receiving a response. Finally the letter arrived at Bargotti's home. He called the orphanage, and Frost was pulled out of math class. He raced to the office and picked up the receiver breathlessly. "Jason Frost here," he said.

"Jason," Bargotti said, sounding positively delighted, "it came. I have it here waiting for you. I'm going to bring it to the school so we can open it together. Later then."

Jason couldn't concentrate for the remainder of the day. Math was a lost cause. Science couldn't hold a candle to the knowledge that Bargotti was coming to the school with a letter from the Vatican! Their question was good enough to be acknowledged! How could he even think about the mundane at a time like this! It was 7 o'clock when Bargotti arrived at the school. He parked his Buick in the lot and his big frame emerged. Then he strode toward the school, his massive stomach jouncing with every step. Jason was waiting at the door, and he ran over to the priest, much too excited to wait for him to cover the ground. They walked over to one of the picnic tables and sat down on the scratched wooden bench, the initials of countless students etched into the dirty wood.

Bargotti reached into his bag and pulled out the letter. It was a thick wine-colored envelope, and it was addressed to Father Bargotti and Jason Frost. His heart almost skipped a beat! That he, a poor, nobody orphan, had received a letter from the Vatican! Bargotti had brought a letter opener with him, and he slit the edge open carefully, making sure not to harm the letter that he was going to treasure for the remainder of his life. Inside the envelope was another smaller wine-colored envelope. He opened this one as well, and withdrew the heavy piece of stationery.

They read the letter together.

To Father Bargotti and novice Jason Leonard Frost,

We at the Vatican were extremely impressed by the depth of knowledge exhibited in your letter, showcasing an erudition not commonly found even among the priests, and certainly not among the youth. Therefore, we would like to extend an invitation to you, Father Bargotti, and to the young Jason Frost to visit us at the Vatican. We will set up a panel consisting of several of the church's greatest theological experts who will review the issues you have raised, until they have been aired and answered to your satisfaction. Please be in touch with us concerning the scheduling of timing, and the dates that you will be available to fly to Rome.

Sincerely yours,
Father Bartholomew Despondoseo

The contact information was located at the bottom of the letter along with the personal number of the Vatican's travel agent and the admonition to get this moving quickly. They looked at each other with joy in their eyes. What better way to get to the bottom of their quest than to meet with a team of the greatest experts that the Vatican had to offer, and set forth their issues before them? Of course they were going to go!

Father Bargotti would be taking complete responsibility for Frost on this trip. He had been recommended by Father Jeff, who was widely respected by the principal and the members of the school board, so that didn't pose any problem at all. Besides, what Catholic school would refuse a student the once-in-a-lifetime chance for a visit to the Vatican? In short order, the dates were agreed upon and their tickets were booked. Exactly one month later, Father Bargotti and Jason Leonard Frost were headed to the airport for their flight to Rome.

Rome, Italy, 1950's

Rome was a magical world for the two of them. Father Bargotti, although well read, had not traveled much. So to find himself in the city of his religion was the culmination of his life's dreams. Frost was so amazed by the sights, sounds and smells of the bustling city that he felt as if he never wanted to go to sleep again. The Alitalia plane landed at Ciampino Airport where they were met by a Vatican driver holding a sign with their names on it. The driver's name was Luigi, and he drove as if someone was pursuing him.

They passed through piazza after piazza, driving along streets crowded by the crush of the tourists following their guides, scattering them to the sides as they came rushing through the cobble-stoned squares with minimal warning. Luigi's hand was constantly on the horn and his foot on the pedal. They stopped for lunch at a quaint little restaurant. Luigi was welcomed to the eatery as if he were a long-lost brother. The owners kept on coming over and offering them advice about what special dishes to choose.

The waiter brought their covered dishes to the table, and when they lifted the tops, steam bellowed forth causing the other diners to look their way and smile at the ritual. It was the best linguine that Frost had ever eaten. From the moment that he lifted his fork and took that first wonderful bite, he barely paused for breath. They were served a light wine that tasted of raisins and cinnamon. He felt as if he could sit there forever.

Then they left the restaurant. The sun was shining brightly on the piazza. Luigi opened the door for them and Frost gratefully sank into the deep leather seats and was asleep before he knew what had come over him. It wasn't long before they arrived at the Vatican City walls, guarded by the famous Swiss Guards in their colorful uniforms, serious demeanors and full of pomp.

The next thing he knew, it was morning and he was waking up in a simple bed in a spartan room with a small window that let in the fresh morning air. He knew that soon they were going to learn the answers to all the theological questions that bothered them.

He got out of bed after a glance at the clock on the wall. Early morning had passed and it was time to get moving. They intended to go sightseeing this morning if they so desired. They were scheduled to meet with the panel that afternoon. The thought of meeting with such learned men was driving him mad with anticipation. He dressed, washed his hands and walked outside the room, finding himself on the third floor of a simple stone building. He went down to the courtyard where he found three priests sitting and talking under a plum tree. The priests were older men with brown skin, sunburned from years of sitting in the strong Italian sun. They greeted Frost with nods of their heads and wide smiles.

"*Buon giorno*," he said in response, and sat down on the edge of a little fountain outside the building, whose constant spray was sending forth cooling droplets on a day that was already extremely hot. Ten minutes later, Bargotti came downstairs, and he greeted Frost with a twinkle in his eye.

Vatican City was a big place. They didn't know their way around yet, so they waited until Luigi came to get them. They ate a simple breakfast; nothing as elaborate as the lunch of the day before. He drove them around to see a few of the places for which Rome was most famous. Frost decided that the Colosseum was just a bit overrated. Luigi glanced at his watch and said that it was time to return for their meeting with the panel.

Again, he drove like a madman. Not long afterward, they were pulling up at the building where their meeting was scheduled. They emerged from the car and entered the dimly lit building. A priest met them at the door with a somber gaze and a nod of his head.

"My name is Father Antonio Carruso," he said to them, "and you are to come with me." They had to follow him quickly as he strode on long legs down a seemingly endless hallway. Frost had to run to keep up with him. Bargotti was wheezing and coughing by the time they arrived at their destination. The priest knocked on the door with deference, and it was opened by another priest.

They were in a large chamber made of stone. There were windows set high up in the walls. The chamber had numerous bookcases crammed with thousands of books. At the far end of the room was a long table where five men were seated. Introductions were made. Two of them were cardinals, and the other three their assistants. The two remaining chairs were at the foot of the table, and it was to these that they were directed by Father Carruso. Having done his job, he turned and left, leaving them in the company of the five men who were all looking at them without speaking. Nothing was said until the priest had departed, at which point the older of the two men in the red robes began to speak.

"On behalf of my colleagues here at the Vatican we would like to welcome you to Rome. We were very impressed by your letter. In fact we came across the same questions in our years of research, and we felt obligated to try and answer you to the best of our collective abilities. Especially to you, our young friend," said the priest turning to Frost. "It is most uncommon to find such knowledge in one so young!

"And so," he said with an airy wave of his hand, "why don't we begin with you? Please tell us what's on your mind."

Frost began to speak of the questions that came to him on a frequent basis and how he had at first attempted to ignore them. But when he realized that that wasn't possible, he had begun to delve deeper into the historical sea of the past. He explained how he had come to meet Father Bargotti, an expert who shared his questions and had spent many years researching the very topics that bothered him. He told the priests how they had spent hours debating, until Bargotti had been forced to concur with Frost. That was when they decided to send their questions to the Vatican.

"I see," murmured the cardinal. "Father Sepium, this is your field." Attention turned to one of the younger priests with straight black hair and startling blue eyes, who looked at them and said, "Why don't you run your questions by me?"

And so they did. They took turns. Frost would ask a question and then Bargotti. They went on and on until the priest held up his hand and said, "That's enough to begin with."

From there, the conversation began moving very quickly. Books were pulled off the shelves at a rapid pace, and voices began rising higher and higher. Sepium had many original theories, but Frost was interested in facts, not theories. He was able to bring proof supporting himself by quoting extensively from the Old and New Testaments until he had shown that much of what Sepium was passing off as fact was actually wild conjecture. Frost had an almost photographic memory, and he could hold his own. It was unlikely for him to forget a source, and he used them now, quoting extensively from all over, showing how things just weren't making sense. He was, without a doubt, challenging the basic tenets of their faith.

Hours passed. Hours of debate in which Frost and Bargotti challenged a team of the finest scholars. When they finally broke for dinner, they were no closer to discovering a mutually satisfying answer than they had been when they had started many hours earlier.

Bargotti was enjoying himself, but Frost was getting the feeling that the longer they argued with these men the less patience they had for them. He began to get the feeling that their smiles belied sinister intentions. He felt that the atmosphere had gotten dangerous. There was nothing substantial on which he could base this feeling, but his stomach felt all knotted inside, and it was hard for him to swallow. There was something about these men that screamed: *We are not looking for the truth, and if you persist in your blasphemous talk, you will find yourselves in big trouble!* So he began to act as if he was being convinced by their arguments; not making a complete about-face or anything drastic like that, because they had fought for too long for that to have made sense. But slowly, imperceptibly, he began changing the rhythm of his arguments. They weren't going to agree with what he was saying, no matter how much truth there was. He should have understood that hours ago. Now it was simply a matter of getting out of this place unharmed. Somehow he comprehended that if they kept chipping away, they might not get out of this place alive.

Bargotti looked at him in a slightly puzzled way when he began to cave in, as if to say: *What, you're impressed by these arguments?! We thought of all this already*. But Frost didn't respond. Eventually Bargotti realized that there was something deeper happening here, and he too began acting as if they were convincing him as well. They finally wound up the "discussion" at about midnight, both sides agreeing to meet on the morrow once again. As they stepped outside the building and into a courtyard lit up by a glowing moon, Luigi emerged from the gloom to escort them back to their rooms. They were quiet on the drive back, not because they had nothing to say, but because they suddenly understood that they couldn't trust anyone around them. What they had thought was a wonderful offer from the Vatican for a joint quest for truth was something else entirely.

They didn't understand what was going on here, but they knew that they had stumbled into a dangerous situation. Maybe there was a secret group within the Vatican who kept track of people who were sufficiently intelligent to ask the kind of questions that plagued the minds of believers around the world, showing them that what they believed in was not necessarily the truth. When the Vatican heard of people like that, whether because they sent the Vatican a letter or because they were in the process of publishing a book, they invited them down to Rome so they could meet with them and convince them of the mistakes in their belief systems. *And maybe,* Frost's mind continued on relentlessly, *maybe when they weren't able to convince those people that they were incorrect, they resorted to harsher tactics. That was why you almost never heard of any opposition to the church. Anyone who tried to fight the general assumptions never made it all the way!*

The truth was, the way that he and Bargotti had been moving, they probably would have ended up writing a book. But now, here they were, and who knew how this was going to end? They went to their respective rooms, afraid that someone was watching them, and that it wouldn't be wise to talk together now. There was nothing concrete to put their fingers on. Nobody had been threatened in an overt manner, but there was something; Frost was sure of it! At this point, all he wanted to do was to agree with everything they said and then go home back to America. He just didn't feel safe here.

He tried to fall asleep on the hard mattress, but it was no use; his mind refused to shut off. It replayed the whole day for him, focusing on the looks the priests were giving one another whenever he was arguing passionately against what they were saying. Finally, he gave up and sat up in bed. There was a clamminess in the air, and he was sweating from the heat and from the helplessness that he felt right then. He swung his legs onto the floor and got dressed. He would go outside for a walk, explore a little bit. If he was in trouble then it wouldn't matter what he did or where he went.

He pulled the door to his room open and sniffed the air as if he were an animal sensing possible danger. The hallway was still and silent, the air stale and unmoving. There was a terrible stillness that filled him with foreboding. He stepped over the threshold and walked toward the staircase feeling as if he was drowning and dying for air. He held onto the banister like a blind man. He counted the steps as he descended and walked out of the building into the smoggy night. The moon was hiding behind a cloud, but from time to time the cloud thinned out and a shaft of light was visible, illuminating the marble fountain and three benches that surrounded it in the middle of the courtyard.

He took a seat on the fountain's edge and felt a little freshness from the water's spray. Without thinking, he rolled up his pants' legs and stepped into the fountain. The water was deliciously cold. He stooped down and threw handfuls of water over his head until he was wet all over. He bent down again for another handful of water, and as he was lifting his head back up, he saw them. Two men. They were here for him. He didn't know how he knew this fact, but he knew that it was true. They passed the fountain without taking the extra moment to check if someone was watching them, since there was no reason for them to imagine that he was going swimming in the fountain in the middle of the night! He watched as they entered the building. Then he stepped out of the fountain, silently rolled down his pants' legs and put his shoes back on.

He had to get away from here! Whatever it was that they wanted from him was something he could do without. But where would he go? His first time in Rome and he had to escape! How could this be? His mind raced as he ran to the entrance of the building's courtyard, slowly opened the heavy, sculpted steel doors and stepped out into the night. He was alone in a strange place and he didn't have a clue where to go. From behind him he could hear shouting and slamming doors. They must have realized that he had evaded them and were coming to look for him! He turned right and began to run. He had no idea where he was running. The main thing was to put distance between them and him. His chest was pounding and his mouth was dry. From behind him he could hear the two men running as well. His shoes made light, thumping sounds on the pavement, while their shoes were rubber and couldn't be heard at all. But he could hear their heavy breathing. He heard water. There was a bridge straight ahead and he ran for it, turning his head at the last second to get a glimpse of his attackers. They were not far behind and gaining on him. He ran onto the bridge and across two lanes of traffic; cars skidding to avoid him, angry honking as he almost caused a pileup. He was sorry. He was also scared to death!

The two men had split up.

One had crossed over to his side; the other was still on the other side just in case he changed his mind and crossed back. His heart was racing with adrenalin as he kept on running. He was almost at the end of the bridge. If he was going to escape, it would have to be now. There was no choice. He ran to the railing and scrambled up on the shallow wall that ran alongside the entire bridge. He stood there for a moment getting ready to dive. He looked down at the far-off water and he could not tell what was water and what was darkness. But he was an excellent swimmer and he was going to jump. He had no choice. His pursuers saw him balancing on the railing and sped up to stop him before he jumped. But he was quicker.

He jumped off the bridge before he could change his mind. Frost flew through the air ready for anything but what he landed on, because it certainly wasn't water. Instead of falling all the way down to the water, he had landed on the pedestrian walkway that was directly beneath the upper level. The lower level was wider than the upper level, and he had fallen onto the hard concrete without warning. The shock of the fall blinded him with the pain! He felt like he was broken. Swimming would have been fine. He could have gotten away. But this surprise fall was something else entirely. He tried to rise, to get up and run away again, but found that his strength vanished, and he couldn't get up.

Got to crawl … to get away from here before they come … can't move … in such pain … I can hear them coming! They're taking me away! Why? What do they want from me?? He couldn't resist them. He was powerless. They lifted him and carried him between them until they were off the bridge. Then they laid him down on the pavement while one of them went to get the car.

The other one made no attempt at conversation. Frost lay on the ground whimpering in agony, crying in pain as his body burned like fire. Minutes went by like this, and the pain was so intense that his mind left him for a while. From somewhere in the distance, he heard the car pull up and the door open. He was lifted and placed into the back seat. The seat was warm and soft, and the pain was throbbing less as he drifted off. The door closed and the car began to move. Someone adjusted him on the seat, covering him with a blanket. He passed out.

The next thing he knew, he was lying on a table under the glare of harsh lights. There was a doctor examining him carefully, probing him, pushing on the sore spots, ignoring his moans and cries. He tried to get up, but he was restrained by leather straps, which allowed the doctor to work undisturbed. There were no broken bones, but he was going to be sore for a long time. He was lucky that he was in such good physical condition, they told him, because his body was going to heal quickly and he'd be back to himself before he knew it. The question was: Why?! Why had they been chasing him? What did they want?

Eventually the doctor finished treating him, the pain had lessened, and he was allowed off the table and onto a couch in the next room. It was a pleasant room with a tall lamp that cast a warm glow on the carpet and a curved desk. There was a fish tank behind the desk, and he watched the tropical fish swimming back and forth, losing himself in the way that they moved, in the simplicity of their lives. Maybe it was better to be a fish? But even there in the beautiful world under the sea, there were plenty of predators to be faced. He took off his shoes, laid down full length on the couch and nodded off.

The man entered the room briskly and snapped his fingers until Frost woke up. He stared at the man trying to decide why he felt such a dislike toward him, although they had just met. The man had a flowing mane of white hair and bulging eyes. Frost thought that he looked like a frog.

"My name is Dr. Renaldo," he said, "and you are the troublesome Jason Frost; is that not so?"

Frost didn't answer. He had nothing to say to this man who seemed to know all about him. He didn't like him, and he wasn't going to talk to him.

"Come sit here at the table," instructed the doctor. Frost, knowing that he had no choice, took a seat on a hard-backed chair at a scratched oval table. He stared suspiciously at the doctor, wondering what the man was going to do next.

"As I told you," said the doctor, "my name is Dr. Renaldo, and together we are going to pay a visit to your past."

Frost didn't understand what the man was talking about, and his confusion showed in his eyes.

"You don't have to understand, Jason," the doctor said. "It's sufficient that I do. You are in good hands. Relax, young man, just relax."

As he spoke, he waved a handkerchief in front of Frost's face, and Jason felt his eyelids growing heavier and heavier. He was feeling very sleepy all of a sudden and he didn't know why. Dr. Renaldo proceeded to hypnotize Jason. He convinced him that though he is an intelligent person, not everything can be explained in a rational way. He was reverted to a previous uncomplicated existence.

When Jason would awake, he would find that the questions that bothered him in the past would cease to bother him. He was hypnotized to experience a simple devoted faith so he would not need to know why. He would enjoy life once again without worrying about irrelevant theological discussions. Dr. Renaldo told Jason that he would become great, and that they would see great things from him.

Dr. Renaldo also told him that his relationship with Father Bargotti was going to become a thing of the past. When they would arrive home, Jason would no longer feel the need to see him ever again. Finally, he told him that the reason he arrived in Rome was to experience a place where the greatest Christian members of history lived their memorable and holy lives. And he would return home with fond memories of his time spent in Rome.

It was an interesting fact, but from the moment Jason Frost and Father Bargotti returned to the United States, they were never seen in each other's company again. Some wondered why that was. Frost, however, wasn't one of them. The trip to Rome was forgotten as he moved forward in life, unburdened by complications in his belief system. And Bargotti? Those in the know said that after that trip, he was never the same again.

16 Dietrich Eberhart

Autobahn, Germany
May 17, 2009

Dietrich Eberhart accelerated the powerful vehicle with a slight touch to the gas pedal. The BMW responded with an internal purr as the needle of the speedometer flew considerably upward. Eberhart was going as fast as he wanted, since he was in the "no speed limit" lane on the Autobahn. He loved this highway, built just prior to Germany's emergence as a world power. Here, a man could drive a car as fast as he wanted and not have to worry about getting a ticket because he was five kilometers over the speed limit. He watched idly as the two specks in his rearview mirror gradually increased in size, until he was able to recognize them as the latest-model Porsche and Ferrari, respectively. In Dietrich's opinion, this road was probably the greatest road in the world. Where else could a person see a dozen of the most expensive and best-made cars in the universe in the space of one kilometer? This road tested the strength of a person's reflexes, his ability to maneuver and stay on top of any given situation. He drove this road by himself instead of using a chauffeur or taking the company helicopter, because it kept him sharp and in the game.

To his left, he watched as a Mercedes convertible attempted to pass him. He laughed and pressed the gas pedal, leaving the guy in the dust. His bodyguards Karl and Munich — nicknamed after the city of his birth — dozed in the backseat. They were accustomed to his driving and with the constant swerving and changing of lanes. The Autobahn was framed on both sides by rolling farmland and pastures, where cattle and sheep grazed contentedly on the lush green grass. Everything was neat and well tended; the German way. He stretched and yawned as he approached a highway sign indicating the exit for the suburban towns outside Hamburg.

Flipping the indicator to the right, he moved into the furthermost right-hand lane, passing a speeding Audi whose driver gesticulated furiously out the window at him. He laughed. He took the sharp curve at high speed, causing the BMW to nearly lose its grip on the road, and sending gravel flying in every direction. From here it was just another 40 kilometers till the Eberhart family estates. The actual mansion was set in solitary splendor in a forest that his grandfather had developed when he had increased his wealth years ago. The closest village was a good 10 kilometers from the estate, and he liked it just fine that way. Being solitary once in a while was desirable when you led a very busy social life the way he did. It was nice to come home and relax with nature. In the backseat, Karl stirred and cleared his throat.

"Are we there yet?" he asked, his voice thick with sleep.

"Are you 5 years old?" Eberhart asked him with a smile. "About 10 minutes," he said.

Karl leaned back into the upholstery and fell asleep again. Five minutes later, Dietrich turned left off the road and pressed down lightly on the gas pedal, taking the car to 130 kilometers per hour on the road he knew so well. The sun was beginning to set as he made the final turn onto the private road leading to the estate. The road was bordered by thick vegetation on either side, which was illuminated by tiny flickering lightbulbs.

As they approached the house, the bushes that grew over the road formed a welcoming canopy. He drove as canopy after canopy flashed overhead and disappeared into the darkness. The canopies gave way to a large open space, and the car roared forward like a giant panther. The mansion was shrouded in semidarkness. Dietrich drove around the house and pressed the button on the dashboard that opened the garage doors. The bodyguards got out of the car first, and he waited until they signaled him that everything was as it should be.

Munich entered the house first while Dietrich and Karl waited in the garage. Once Munich had deactivated the alarm and checked the premises, Dietrich entered the house and drew a deep breath. This was his house, the house he had grown up in, the place where he had been groomed for his future leadership role in the newly emerging Nazi Party.

"Dinner will be ready shortly," said Munich when he reappeared.

"Excellent," Dietrich said, "I'll be in my study. Call me when the table is set."

He headed down the hallway, perusing the artwork on the walls. These paintings had been hanging there since he was a child. Some of them were copies of *Der Fuhrer's* most famous paintings. *Such a brilliant man,* he mused to himself. *A master politician, an incredible tactician and an artist on top of everything else!* He passed through the giant living room, pausing to straighten a pillow, and continued on to his study at the farthermost corner of the house. He stepped into the room, slipping off his jacket as he walked. He placed it on a hanger behind the door, and went over to his desk. Sitting down, he reached into one of the drawers and removed several files, allowing himself access to a secret chamber that he had built into the desk.

He reached inside and removed a package. He placed it on the blotter and settled into the deep leather chair with a sigh of satisfaction. He was home, it was the end of the business week and everything was going quite well with the movement. Matters were moving according to the timetable he had set up for the major takeover. For a minute he debated with himself. Should he, shouldn't he? In the end he couldn't control himself and he opened the package. He took out a book and held it close to his heart. This book was the ultimate source of power. This book held the key to his country's reemergence as a world power like the United States or China. Until now, he had used the power sparingly, not wanting to give away too much at once. But the time was fast approaching where he would begin to use the power at closer intervals. As soon as that happened, the world would be plunged into confusion and chaos, as the people everyone had trusted would turn predatory and dangerous.

He licked his lips in anticipation of the feeling that using the book gave him: the feeling of playing master of the world, the awesome feeling of ultimate power and control over the lives of millions of people all around the world. They were all under his thumb, all under the Nazi Party! How proud *Der Fuhrer* would have been with the concept, by the amazing things he could accomplish from the safe confines of his study, without going to war and endangering troops, and without spending billions on military expenditures. The book took care of all of that. It was a brilliant concept. As he opened the book, his fingers tingled with excitement.

The first few times that he used the book, his hand had been shaking so hard he was barely able to dial the phone number. Now the feelings were less intense, but still very strong. He flipped through the pages debating whom to choose. Which country should he thrust into turmoil? Which city's infrastructure did he want to destroy? He studied the pages, his heart beating quickly, feeling like an emperor of old who was able to grant life or death with the flick of a finger. He was the emperor now, and it was his finger that decided who would live and who would die. And by extension, it was the power of the party.

Suddenly, growing impatient with his hesitancy to make a decision, he chose an entry and dialed the phone number that was neatly penciled in beside the name. He steadied his fingers and the call went through. He could hear the ringing on the other side. His heart felt like it was gong to explode through his chest and blow up the world. *Welcome back, power; welcome back, ultimate strength!* The phone rang twice more before someone picked up on the other side.

"Gunther Markson Military Base," said the precise voice at the end of the receiver.

"I would like to speak with General Dustin Mallory, extension 453, please."

"Yes, sir, one moment please," said the efficient voice.

The phone rang again. It was picked up on the third ring. The voice of another man, who was accustomed to commanding authority. Not a man to cross.

"Dustin Mallory," the man said. "How can I help you?"

Dietrich Eberhart spoke clearly and distinctly. "The new shipment of Tomahawk missiles should be arriving at any moment," he said. "Why don't you go outside and welcome them?"

That was it. That was all he had to say. And in an American army base halfway across the world, General Dustin Mallory got up from his desk, left his office and got into his jeep. Then, General Mallory, who had served with distinction throughout his entire military career, drove through the camp, only stopping when he reached a brick building in

Section Y. He parked the jeep and marched into the building. He passed the soldiers at the door who saluted him and he went down the stairs into the bowels of the earth. At Sub-Basement Number Two, he walked briskly down the long cement hallway, finally coming to a halt outside Room 30. He placed his thumb on the scanner outside the door. A green light flashed and the door opened up.

He entered the long white-washed room. He glared at the impressive array of the newest in missiles that the American army had to offer. And then, General Dustin Mallory proceeded to the closest missile, and began to fiddle with the wiring. As the commander of the base, he was an expert in the mechanics of the missiles. He knew precisely what to do to ensure that his rockets would cease being operational. Huge though they might be, and as powerful as they were, they were a delicate blend of technology. It was amazing what havoc a few well-chosen thrusts of the right tool could do to a missile. He worked slowly and methodically, making sure that he didn't make any mistakes. He had a mission to do and he was going to do it. Even though he was being careful, he was such an expert in the field of missile technology that he was able to move relatively quickly, destroying the wiring of missile after missile. He had taken out 20 of the newest American missiles at an estimated cost of $20 million per missile by the time the alarms began to ring.

Even then, he wasn't deterred. Nothing was going to stop him from doing his mission. As the sirens sounded and the alarms rang at full volume, Dustin Mallory continued working on those missiles, destroying them one by one. He wasn't disturbed by the noise; he had heard worse in the jungles of Vietnam and the deserts of Iraq. Even as they were breaking down the door, General Mallory was carrying out his vital work, completely ignoring the world around him. Nobody would ever speak of the firefight that broke out when they tried to apprehend him. Suffice it to say that General Mallory was an expert marksman, and the number of casualties was high. No papers reported these events. They were the internal affairs of the army, and not subject to the scrutiny of the press.

But Dietrich Eberhart knew from the general clampdown on all army bases later that day that his call had been successful. For a short time, there was a costly breach in the air defenses of the United States. And for the first time, the Pentagon had to agree that it seemed as if someone was declaring war on America. Why that would be and who that person was, nobody knew. But they understood that by the rate he was proceeding, they would begin to understand soon enough, and it terrified them.

~

Dietrich Eberhart enjoyed his filet mignon that evening.

The countdown was on.

He slept like a baby that night.

17
Jason Leonard Frost

Paris, France
February 28, 2009

Cardinal Jason Frost and his good friend Al boarded British Airways Flight 464 to Paris at 5 o'clock in the morning. Frost had wanted to pay for Al's ticket, but Al had adamantly refused. In the end, Frost had given in.

"Listen to me," Al said, "I made some money in my day. Now that I'm retired, I want to see the world. Is it O.K. with you if I take a trip over to Paris, without my good friend making me feel like a beggar by paying for my flight?"

Al was Al, and there was nothing to be done. Even though they were traveling to Paris to uncover his past, Frost felt that they might as well make the most of the visit. They were planning to rent a car and enjoy themselves. The flight was uneventful, and they arrived in Paris tired and disheveled after the trans-Atlantic journey. They collected their luggage, and made their way to the Hertz counter to rent a car.

Frost showed the woman his special clergy passport where he was officially identified as Cardinal Frost. Her entire demeanor changed to one of immense respect.

"You should have informed us of your estimated time of arrival, Your Eminence," she said. "We would have made sure to have a car befitting your stature waiting for you."

"I'm sorry for putting you on the spot," he replied. "It's just that I don't travel that often. When I do, it's usually to Rome, and then someone picks me up. It isn't very often that I have an opportunity to make all of my own travel arrangements."

She looked up from her computer screen and said, "Oh, you're in luck. Someone just returned the Jaguar. But don't worry," she said as she saw the look on his face, "Hertz wouldn't dream of charging you more than the basic rate. This is standard procedure for V.I.P.'s."

He protested that he was anything but a V.I.P., but she brushed his protests aside. Before they knew it, they found themselves sinking into incredibly comfortable leather car seats. He took this as an omen that their trip would be successful. Al was in a good mood. The smell of fresh croissants and coffee always put Al in a good mood, and there was no better place in the world for a croissant than Paris.

They drove out of the airport with Frost at the wheel and Al following the GPS. They found the roads clearly marked, and the GPS issued instructions in English. Before they knew it, they arrived at the hotel and were handing the car keys to a valet for parking.

Frost had never slept in a canopy bed before, and he awoke smiling and ready to face the new day. He took a long shower. He found Al at breakfast, working his steady way through a platter of croissants, various butters and jams, and a steaming pot of fresh-brewed coffee along with the International Herald Tribune. Frost helped himself to a croissant which he ate with marmalade. He was well rested and full, and it was time for them to continue their search.

Al set the GPS for Notre Dame and they were off. "I don't think that we need the actual church," he told Frost. "We'll probably find the orphanage in the area."

Frost was agreeable. Al was an ex-cop, and he had done more detective work in a month than Frost had done in his entire life. That was why they did whatever Al decided. They reached the vicinity of Notre Dame fairly quickly, and they asked a passerby for directions. Most of those they spoke to couldn't speak English. One who did respond directed them into a maze of neighborhood streets that must have been hundreds of years old. They bumped over stony roads, making cautious turns into narrow alleyways that barely gave them room to breathe, squeezing between buildings of yellow brick. Eventually, they emerged on a wider street, and Al suggested that they park the car and begin searching by foot. In a short while, Al pointed to a sign welded onto a corner of a nearby building.

"Notre Dame Orphanage," it read, and there was a curved arrow underneath pointing to a steep stairway. Narrow paths branched off the staircase on either side. One of them housed a thimble-sized cafe called "The Rainbow Parrot," where they paused for a break. The waiter brought menus, and they ordered soup and wine. When they finished, they left the cafe and continued to the bottom of the stairs.

They found themselves in a peaceful alleyway that turned and twisted. At some point there was another sign, and they knew that they were headed in the right direction. Then the road curved again. Just beyond the curve lay a green wooden door with a plaque affixed to the adjacent wall, upon which were embedded the words "Notre Dame Orphanage."

"This is it," said Al. Frost took a deep breath and pushed the door open.

They found themselves in an anteroom whose walls displayed pictures of the orphanage's history. Most of them were in black and white. They looked at the rows and rows of children all sitting and staring solemnly at the camera. Frost hoped they had arrived at the right place. There was a door across the room and they rang the bell. They were buzzed in, and they found themselves in a hallway with colorful murals on the walls depicting cartoon characters. Mickey Mouse danced with Donald Duck up and down, down and up, having fun and happy times. Nothing they had seen so far brought back any memories. There was an office off to the side, and they headed there first.

The man in the office wasn't old enough to know whether Frost had in fact lived at the orphanage, but after checking Frost's credentials, directed them to the small, windowless space in the basement, where metal filing cabinets nested one on top of the other, crammed with files, some dating back more than a century. They got down to business. It was tedious. This archive wasn't as organized as the others they had been to. It seemed like a lot of children had come and gone over the years.

"Well," said Al, "about what year do you think you would have been here, if you actually were here?"

Frost thought about it. "We docked at Ellis Island in 1946, which means that if I was here, it would probably have been before that."

"O.K.," said Al, "let's get cracking."

They began to plow through the files of those two years looking for Frost's name, his picture, or any relevant information. But there was no mention of a young boy named Jason Frost. None at all.

"I hate to say this, Jason," said Al, after a while, "but how do you even know that your name was Jason Frost while you were staying at this place, if in fact you ever actually stayed here?"

"Good point," said Frost. "But I seem to recall that that was my name upon arrival in America. I can't say this with any certainty, but that's the feeling that I have."

They resumed searching. Hours passed. They barely spoke. Lunch time came and went. They were jet lagged and hungry. The archive was so disorganized that even if his file was here, they probably wouldn't be able to find his picture. There were just so many kids who had been in the institution. It was 5 o'clock in the afternoon when they gave up and decided to call it a day. Frost felt as if he wanted to cry. They had come this far only to be met by an obstacle of disorganization. It would have been upsetting to find that his file had been removed, but at least it would have been another step in the ongoing saga. But somehow, knowing that his file could very well be in this room made things infinitely worse.

"We can come back tomorrow and the day after that if need be," Al said to him as they attempted to replace all the files they had looked at.

Frost thanked him and replied that maybe they would. But in his heart he knew that it was utterly hopeless. He sensed that even if they spent a month in this stuffy room, they wouldn't find anything, because someone (no clue who) didn't want him to know who he was! That filled him with anger! To think that some unknown stranger was removing the files of his life — blocking him from knowing who he was — made him feel such rage that he felt as if he was going to explode. This was his life they were stealing!

They gave the room one last wistful look before closing the door and making their way back upstairs. How was it possible that they had come this far only to be faced with failure? They were walking wearily through the brightly lit hallways when a bell suddenly clanged, and they watched as a swarm of children came running down the hallway on the way to the dining hall for dinner. They stood against the wall to avoid being trampled. When all the kids had passed, they continued walking toward the exit. But once they had found themselves in the room with all the pictures, Frost couldn't help himself, and he began examining them with a discerning eye.

"What are you doing, Jason?" Al asked him.

"What am I doing? I'll tell you what I'm doing," Frost said. "I'm refusing to give up! If I leave this place without discovering any clues, without finding any leads, then I will be beating myself up for the next 20 years! Are we crazy, Al? Did we come all the way to Paris to become discouraged just because some archive is too messy for us? What about all these pictures on the walls? Let's go through them right now!" Al realized that Frost had lost all rational thought.

"Fine," Al said. "Start on that side, and I'll start on the other side."

It was painstaking work. The walls were plastered with pictures over every available space. Many of them were quite old and badly faded. They were searching for someone whose name they didn't even know. But like Frost had said, they had come to Paris to find a little boy; they might as well do their utmost. For an hour, there was complete silence in the room. The only sounds were the ticking of their watches. Mainly, they looked at the pictures from the '40's. But there were many of them, and all the little kids looked the same. Al got excited at one point thinking that he'd found him, but Frost took one look at the child whom Al had pointed at and told him to keep on searching. Once again, it seemed like they had hit a dead end. But still, Frost refused to give up. He was famished, his head was spinning and he was dead tired. But something inside him — some stubborn streak — made him keep on going.

Eventually, Al decided to go back to the cafe where they had eaten earlier, and he said that he'd bring something back for Frost as well. Al left, and Frost remained behind, stubbornly searching. It was as he was reaching the end of one of the walls, and feeling dejected beyond words, that he heard someone clearing his throat behind him. Frost turned to see who it was. He saw an elderly man of about 90, who was dressed very formally. He was wearing a bow tie and tweed vest, and a gold chain that passed through a buttonhole in his vest and was attached to a gold watch. He was wearing thick spectacles that magnified his eyes, and he supported himself on a thick wooden cane.

"And who are you?" he asked Frost. He spoke in English with a heavy French accent. "They told me there were two of you here, but I guess your friend got tired, eh?"

He continued without giving Frost an opportunity to reply. "They told me that you came to see the archives. Big mess! I've been telling them for years that they need to reorganize the place, but there is so much to do ..." His voice trailed off as he studied Frost through those thick lenses. "So what is it?" he said again. "Who are you, and why have you returned?"

Frost was fascinated by the man. "My name is Jason Frost. How do you know that I've returned?" he asked.

"C'mon," the old man said impatiently. "You're studying the pictures on the walls as if you are hoping to find the pot of gold at the end of the rainbow. In my experience, nobody studies those pictures like that unless they spent some time in the orphanage. Those who stayed here will never forget what it means to be an orphan; to be completely alone in the universe. Those who grew up in traditional homes will never comprehend how lucky they were!"

"And you?" Frost asked him. "How long have you been around here?"

"I arrived as a child of 4," the man said, "and I've never left. I've been running the orphanage for over half a century. Before that, I worked in the office. Of course my memory isn't as good as it once was, but I can still recall how it was back in the old days. We had a grand time back then. After the war was over, the world was a different place, children constantly coming and going. We were a transit base for a while. But I'm getting ahead of myself. What did you say your name is, young man?" he smiled as he said it, because Frost was anything but a young man. At that moment Frost came to the realization that this old man was still sharp as a tack.

"You've been working hard for many hours," the man said. "Come to my office, take a break, and I'll make you a cup of coffee."

Taking Frost by the arm, he led him down a narrow passageway. The sounds of children yelling and laughing issued from behind closed doors. They reached the man's office. There was a little brass plaque beside the door engraved, Dr. Claude Sylvester, Dean. Dr. Sylvester waved Frost over to one of several comfortable armchairs. It wasn't an office in the conventional sense. There was no desk. There were couches, an exquisite Persian rug and an expresso machine. Sylvester proceeded to make them coffee which he would serve in tiny china cups. The machine hissed, sending a cloud of steam toward the ceiling every so often. Neither man spoke as they waited for the coffee to be ready.

Finally Sylvester took a seat across the rug from Frost. Perching the little china cup on his knee, he said, "So what year were you here, then?"

Frost found himself telling the old man the whole story: how he had arrived at Ellis Island after the war, and had been sent to an orphanage at Oyster Bay, Long Island. But his records had been missing when he had gone there to look for them. Their search had taken him to the main archive building in Boston, where once again, his file was not found. But they had discovered a tiny crumpled-up piece of paper that had evidently been left there by mistake. It contained a reference to the orphanage here at Notre Dame.

"But you don't remember being here?" Claude asked.

"Look, it was a very long time ago," Frost replied. "Everything is a blur. I moved around so often back then. Even if I was here, I feel as if I had been in other places as well ... Like this had been just one of the places on my journey! I mean, maybe I stayed here for a while, but it couldn't have been that long. I remember Oyster Bay clearly. Yet, everything before America is just one big blur."

"Allow me to sum up," Dr. Sylvester said. "You distinctly remember arriving in America. Everything prior to that time is unclear in your mind. For whatever reason, you have suddenly decided to track down your roots and have discovered that it's easier said than done. Files have disappeared and nobody is giving you straight answers. Probably this whole business began when they rejected you for the position of pope," he said triumphantly. "Am I right?"

Frost was speechless for a moment. "Look," said Sylvester, "I may be old and decrepit, but I'm not dead! I read the papers, I hear the news. I know that one Jason Frost was on the short list to become pope. And now, here you are in the flesh: Cardinal Jason Frost. You know what? I should be shocked that a cardinal doesn't have better connections than this?! But truthfully, I'm not that shocked, because you're not the first to come looking!" He delivered this line slowly, enunciating every word. He didn't wait for Frost to reply, but continued with his analysis, crossing one leg over the other while placing the empty coffee cup on a glass-and-chrome end table nearby.

"Your search brings you to the orphanage of Notre Dame," Claude said. "Here you are full of questions about the past. So I'm going to shock you a just a little bit and inform you that you are not the first person to find his way back to my orphanage. The men who come here are usually in your age bracket and are searching for their past, as well.

"I'll be honest with you and show you a class picture that I never wanted to hang up in the hallway. We will see if we can find one little boy who bears some resemblance to the Jason Frost that you recall."

He rose from his seat and shuffled over to a brown filing cabinet in the corner of the room. His hands fumbled with the key until Frost thought he was going to go out of his mind!

Frost watched as the old man reached into the cabinet and removed another framed picture from inside. "And here it is," he said with great fanfare. "Class of '46. Why don't you take a look and see if you recognize anyone?"

Frost needed no second invitation. He picked up the picture and studied it intently, staring at every one of the children in the picture. His eyes moved hungrily from one child to the next. Was he one of them? The children were all looking at the camera with serious eyes. Nobody smiled, as if taking a picture was an extremely important matter. Frost peered at the children, his eyes pleading with them to reveal themselves to him. A little boy with a cleft chin and straight dark hair held a sign in his hands that said "Class of '46" on it. Frost didn't know what to do. He sensed that this picture held the key to his search, but didn't know how to unlock the door keeping him out.

Sylvester, perhaps sensing his turmoil, suddenly turned the picture over. There on the cardboard back was a list of the initials of each child in the order they were sitting. He scanned the list quickly, until he stopped and pointed to the initials of the child in the center of the picture holding the sign. It clearly stated right there in black and white, JLF.

"But why?" Frost asked him when he had recovered from the dramatic moment. "Why don't you have the picture up in the hallway for everyone to see? What's going on here?"

Sylvester had a guilty look on his face now. "I couldn't keep this picture up on the wall along with all the others," he said, "because it's a constant reminder that we collaborated with some of the worst monsters in the world. Every time I look at this picture, I remember all the children who came, how young they were, how impressionable. Once again, I'm filled with anger at this orphanage that has done so much good, but failed those beautiful children, allowing those terrible men to use our facility as a holding stop. How could we have cooperated with people like that? But we did, and my actions sit on my conscience like a heavy stone."

"What are you talking about?" Frost asked the man.

"Sit back and I'll tell you all about it."

"I will never forget the day that he walked into this building," Claude said. "He was tall and muscular, he had a full head of hair, and his eyes shone with intelligence; a very fine-looking specimen of humanity. A man of the world. He was full of an obscene confidence, and he told the secretary that he needed to speak to the dean of the institution. I wasn't the dean back then. I was still just an assistant director, but I cared about the orphanage more than anything in the world. It was May 1945. The war in Europe had just been won, and the world was new and fresh.

"The dean wasn't in that day, and the secretary showed the man to my office. I invited him to take a seat. He shook my hand. I don't know why, but it felt like something had just crawled up my sleeve. He was smiling, but his eyes were like a block of ice. This was not a nice man.

"'I don't believe I caught your name, Herr ...?'

"'Von Clausen,' he supplied.

"'What can I do for you, Herr Von Clausen?' I asked him.

"Then he fed me this long story about a group of children from South America — war refugees — who needed a temporary place to stay in Paris just until their travel papers, visas and such, were sorted out for them.

"'We are a well-connected organization, and you do not have to be concerned that these children will remain in your hands for a long time. The plan, Mr. Sylvester, is for the children to move on to America and other places. We want them to leave Europe behind, giving them the chance to begin their lives in the new world; to take advantage of the opportunities they would never have access to in this part of the world.'

"'I don't understand,' I said. 'Why don't you keep them in South America until the travel documents come through? Why subject them to the whole ordeal of international travel, learning a new language, meeting new friends? Isn't it enough that they suffered so much as children? Why don't you make it easier for them?'

"He smiled. It wasn't pleasant to look at. 'Claude,' he said, 'you're an intelligent man. That seems pretty clear to me. We have a tremendous amount of money at our disposal. Allow me to make you an offer for your cooperation. You grant our children asylum in your facility for as long as we need it, and in return, we will show our appreciation in very generous monetary compensation. No more unnecessary questions. You assist us as best as you are able, and we will provide you with enough funding to turn this place into the best state-of-the-art orphanage in the city!'

"'But why don't you just open up your own facility?'

"'Look, I really hate having to spell things out,' he said to me. 'Suffice it to say that we need a legitimate orphanage as a springboard for our orphans' entry into countries like the United States and Canada.'

"He kept on talking while my mind tossed about his offer. *They were probably Nazi orphans,* I told myself. *But so what? Children are children. What would be so terrible if we provided a place for them to stay while they were in Paris, in return for which we received unlimited wealth? Was that so terrible?!* He was sitting there staring at me with those eyes like chips of jade. Inwardly, I shuddered.

"'Well, what's it going to be?' he pressured me. 'There are other orphanages, you know, who would be extremely pleased to be the beneficiaries of the amount of money that I am authorized to invest in your facility.'"

Dr. Sylvester stared at Frost.

"Cardinal Frost," he said, "I'm ashamed to tell you that I allowed my greed to win out over my morals. I agreed to grant asylum in my orphanage for whomever this mysterious organization wanted to send here, in return for which we were able to upgrade this institution tremendously."

"Wait a second," said Frost. "You don't mean to tell me that you feel so guilty just because you allowed some children to stay at your orphanage for a couple of months? No, that can't be it!" Suddenly Frost snapped his fingers in triumph. "I know," he said while Claude cringed. "You gave asylum to adults as well, didn't you? It wasn't just children who stayed here over the years, was it?" he asked in a soft voice. "That's why you feel so guilty, right? You gave criminals, terrible sick-minded people, a place to stay, and the ability to walk around as free men, while they waited for their arrangements to be made for them. And this transport of children was what started the whole thing off, wasn't it?" Dr. Sylvester nodded.

"Just tell me one thing," Frost said to the old man. "Who was the man in charge of this operation? Who was the mastermind, the man who wrote the checks? You must have found out who he was over the time the orphanage was involved with his organization. I have a right to know!"

There was silence in the room. Frost could see that the old man was still extremely paranoid about this shadowy organization from his past, that he was reluctant to give information that might come back to harm him.

"Listen," Frost told the man bluntly. "You are old, very old. You are going to die soon. Don't you think that I deserve to know who played around with my life and why? I'm not going to stop here. I'm going to take this and dig until I reach the bottom of everything. So why not just save me all that trouble and tell me the man's name!"

Dr. Sylvester sat silently for a few minutes rubbing his finger around and around his palm. Finally he nodded to himself as if he had arrived at a decision. "It was the Eberhart transport," he finally said, "under the auspices of Ludwig Eberhart — patriarch of the family and CEO of Eberhart Enterprises, Limited. And," he paused, "the transport arrived in Paris from Asuncion, the capital of Paraguay."

Frost left without shaking his hand.

~

Finally he had a name. Something to hold onto in the middle of the night. Ludwig Eberhart. This was something to celebrate! He couldn't believe that after all the travel, after all the searching, they had actually succeeded in uncovering a genuine kernel of information that might lead to even bigger fish. Who knew? Maybe he'd finally discover the truth?!

The song from long ago suddenly surfaced in his mind. No surprise there. It often did at stressful times. When he felt triumphant over something or unusually hopeful, the song would come to mind. When he was knocked down and in pain, the song would swim to the forefront of his brain to keep him company. And this was definitely something to celebrate.

He had heard of the Eberhart Empire. Who hadn't? World-famous leaders of industry and business. They were ruthless and cunning, and held the Midas touch. Whatever they turned their attention to escalated in value. Frost read an article recently describing the family's wealth and power in detail, giving a short rundown on their history, even touching on the fact that the family had been extremely influential on the Nazi scene during the war. It spoke of Heinrich, the grandfather, his son, Ludwig, and grandson, Dietrich who was a chip off the old block.

Now Frost knew that the history of the Eberhart family was somehow intertwined with his own. It was like a gigantic puzzle with pieces strewn around the world. It was his job to track them down and to put the puzzle together. He realized that somebody was guiding his search. Someone was giving him little hints, leaving tantalizing clues for him, just enough and no more. Sufficient information so that he would be able to move on, but never enough so that he would truly understand. But here it had been different. There was no way they (whoever "they" was) could have known that he and Sylvester would end up meeting, and that Claude would volunteer such sensitive information. Which meant, that for the first time, Al and he were on their own! It was a heady feeling!

The tiny alleyways of Notre Dame were deserted, and a stiff wind hit him with stunning force as he stumbled down the cobble-stoned road. He pulled the collar of his overcoat tighter around his neck and diverted his steps toward the bistro where Al was getting something to eat. As he walked, he wondered what was taking Al so long. It wasn't like him to spend so much time deliberating over his food. He reached the foot of the stone stairway, took a deep breath and began the climb. The bistro was located about halfway up the steep ascent. He was excitedly looking forward to sharing the news with Al. He gripped the banister tightly and climbed the stairs, envisioning the warmth of the bistro.

But halfway to the restaurant, he found his way blocked by an inanimate object lying sprawled across the steps. At first, he thought it was a drunk who had collapsed. Then he wasn't sure, because there was something familiar about the jacket the man was wearing. He was almost on top of the man, when he finally realized what he was looking at. That was when he screamed louder than he had ever screamed in his entire life. It was a scream of such bitterness, such despair, as to pierce the very heavens with its plaintive cry.

It was Al. His friend.

He was lying sideways, and there was a pool of blood under his body. Frost didn't have experience with this kind of thing, but it looked as if someone had stabbed Al with a knife and left him to bleed to death. It was as if Frost were looking down at the scene from high above, and someone was screaming. He didn't realize that that someone was him, but the screams grew louder and higher. Suddenly he looked up and saw that a crowd had gathered. He was hunched over on the stairway crying, racking sobs issuing from his chest.

Someone called an ambulance. When the paramedics finally arrived, they put Frost onto a stretcher and gave him a shot to calm him. He attempted to communicate to them that they should be focusing on Al, but the paramedic gave a rueful sigh and said, "I'm sorry, friend, but the gentleman has no need for ambulances. Right now, all he needs is the morgue."

After that, he had faded out only to wake up hours later in the white crispness of a hospital bed. He tried to open his eyes, tried to bring himself out of his drowsy state, but there was something out there — something so terrible that had happened, that every time he was about to awaken, his body thrust itself back into the black void.

He heard voices and felt something prick his arm. Then the cloud went away and he could discern a crowd of doctors around his bedside. One of them cleared his throat and said, "Oh, he's awake."

He glared at the man.

"How do you feel, Cardinal Frost?" the doctor asked him.

He sighed a giant sigh, and spoke in a thick voice, "Al?" he asked the group.

They looked away. He had his answer. Al had been murdered in Paris. He had gone abroad for the first time in his life and hadn't lived to talk about it! What made it all the worse for Frost was the certain knowledge that if he hadn't allowed Al to come along with him on his search for his identity, then Al would still be alive right this moment, probably setting up a game of chess in the park or reading a paperback. He would just be enjoying the simple things in a way that would never happen again. It was all his fault. He didn't want to think about the fact that he would never talk to Al again, never share a laugh or a drink. Al was lying in the cold morgue and his body would have to be shipped back to the States for burial.

"Cardinal Frost," the doctor said again, "how do you feel?"

Frost looked the doctor in the eye and said, "Unhook me, please."

"What?" said the doctor, startled.

"Remove these tubes," Frost said. "I will be leaving now."

The doctor's mouth dropped open.

"I am perfectly healthy and well," Frost went on. "There is no reason for me to remain here any longer. Consequently, I will be on my way." Resolutely, he swung his legs over the side of the bed, sending the nurses into a flurry of action. Within five minutes, he was up and dressed, and making his way down to the registration desk to inquire about payment.

"It was our privilege to host you, Cardinal Frost," said the woman at the desk.

"Be that as it may," he replied, holding out a copy of his travel insurance for her to take. He insisted on the right to pay for his treatment. She took it and began typing in the information.

It was only when he was safely back in his hotel room, sitting at the Chippendale desk, that he sought to place all the events in order. There could be only one conclusion. They had wanted to scare him off from searching further. They must have thought that with Al out of commission, he wouldn't know what to do to take the search to the next level. But they were wrong. They hadn't counted on Dr. Sylvester. They had thought themselves invincible, but had miscalculated badly. He had a clue, a very powerful clue, and he was going to use it. He was going to carry on, and he would make them pay for killing Al. Whereas before there had been a vague, unsatisfactory feeling inside him pushing him to discover who he really was, with the murder of Al, everything had changed. No more disquiet. There was an anger there now; a fierce, unyielding force of emotion that would push him to carry on until he would crack the code and find the answers.

From here on, he wasn't searching solely for himself. He was going to do this for Al.

Kobi Shapiro

The Palms, Brazil
January 5, 1973

It was called "Operation Jumping Jack," and it was planned down to the minutest detail. Obviously there would be many variables that could not be predicted. But whatever was in the Mossad's power to control was dissected and the plan was gone over with a fine-tooth comb. Their objective: the capture of Josef Mengele, although the Mossad would settle for documentation and photographs showing that he had been killed. The team members carried the requisite blue capsule with them as well, just in case they were captured. The agents on this operation knew too much to be taken alive; that went without saying, and was understood by all parties involved. It was a harsh fact, but part of the profession they had chosen.

There were four of them entering Kurt Wolfgang Zeivald's compound that evening. Each of the agents' dossiers had been examined with a fine tooth comb thoroughly by many high-ranking Mossad agents before they had been accepted for the mission. Kobi Shapiro was the agent in command. He had spent many hours with the other three men, briefing them on what to expect. All four spoke German fluently. They could hold a conversation in German, they could order a Bavarian bratwurst in German and they could sing 20 songs, recite 30 nursery rhymes and even discuss the latest in German entertainment should the need arise. In addition, they would be well armed and prepared to kill.

Kobi himself would be attending the party as General Konrad Ostermann, a notorious murderer who had recently been captured by the Mossad, in a little-publicized operation in the south of Germany. The Mossad knew that Ostermann had received an invitation to the gathering because they had intercepted his e-mail; they had taken the liberty of accepting in his name.

Kobi had spent many hours with Ostermann, getting to know the former general who had been commandant of a lesser-known concentration camp in Galicia. They were roughly the same build, which helped in preparing his disguise. He would have to cut his hair and to grow a mustache. There was a prominent scar on Ostermann's temple, but it was a simple feat for the makeup artists at Mossad headquarters to apply a latex prosthetic scar to Kobi's face. Learning to converse in the guttural tones of a general from Bavaria had been a much harder task. It wasn't just how the man spoke; it meant studying his mannerisms at length, how he ate, drank, how he held a cigarette. Did he blow smoke rings? Did he enjoy a good song or play an instrument? How did he laugh? Was he known for telling jokes? All the details had to be perfect before they could embark on this delicate operation.

Slowly but surely, Kobi learned all he needed to know about Herr Konrad Ostermann. Ostermann had been compelled to part with his prized possession: his SS dagger, inlaid with the twin lightning-bolt design in the handle and *Mein Ehre Heisst Treue* engraved on its blade. Kobi was to take that along with him, and thought it would be quite ironic if he ended up using an SS dagger to kill any of the neo-Nazis. *That would be a real twist*, he laughed inwardly.

The truth was, Ostermann had pretty much dropped out of the picture, with regard to getting together with his fellow Nazis. He had apparently been "rehabilitated" and had been employed as the CFO of a German import/export company when the Mossad had captured him. He had not been in touch with his fellow Nazi officers for quite some time. But meeting Josef Mengele provided a good reason to emerge from his self-imposed hibernation. This meeting was going to be impressive in the quality of its attendees. It seemed likely to be the most influential gathering of key Nazi players since Odessa had been organized back in '54.

The actual estate was located on the border separating Brazil and Argentina. The team would be leaving from the closest secure zone to the actual compound, directly across the border on the Brazilian side. They were going in via helicopter, and would land, commando-style, on the roof of the main house of the Zeivald estate. They wore formal suits under their flight gear and were equipped with the latest in night-vision.

They rested during the afternoon prior to the fateful evening. When they awoke they reviewed the plan again, checked to make sure that their ear pieces were completely operable and that their battery packs were fresh, and ate a light meal. Then they were driven to the helipad.

The helicopter was nothing like what they had been accustomed to. There were no military markings, and no stubby with twin guns mounted on then. It was strictly a utility vehicle. They loaded the rope ladder, 180 feet of sturdy nylon with loops for their feet knotted into it. The pilot took off as soon as it was dark enough. Within moments they had climbed a couple of hundred feet. Only the fact that they were strapped into their seats kept them from falling out of the flimsy flying machine.

This part of the world was sparsely inhabited, accounting for the fact that they could see very few lights on the ground below. The pilot had the exact location of the main house, and he would be circling above as they climbed down, one by one. As soon as all four agents were in place, he would land at a predetermined location, ready for their signal to return. All four were heavily armed, and would not hesitate to use their weapons. As they flew through the darkness, Kobi scanned the faces of his teammates. As the team leader, he had much invested emotionally and professionally in his men, and he prayed they would all return safely.

They appeared ready and confident. His gaze lingered on Roni. Kobi hadn't been sure about him. He was very young, and his enthusiasm sometimes got the better of him. But Roni reminded Kobi of himself in his early days so he had taken a chance, including him on this vital mission. Kobi hoped that he made the right decision, and yet, he couldn't help but be a little concerned. Were Roni to choose to act on his own initiative, ignoring the carefully planned agenda, things might get sticky. *Well, there was no point in worrying now,* Kobi thought, and tried to set to his doubts aside.

"We are approaching the house," the pilot said through his intercom. "I'm lowering the rope ladder. First agent, take your position."

Kobi approached the helicopter's open doorway, and grasped the frame, almost knocked off his feet by a gust of air that swirled through the aperture.

"Now!" the pilot commanded. Kobi grasped the first rung of the rope ladder and stepped off the helicopter. The wind whipped at his face as he quickly descended hand over hand, and the other agents followed close behind him, just seconds apart. From the corner of his eye, he noted the lights of the house. He had another few feet to go before he reached the roof. The celebrants would not be expecting visitors from the sky, and the Mossad agents thus had the element of surprise on their side.

As he neared the roof, he braced himself against the rope as it twisted in the wind. He landed lightly, and held the end of the ladder to stabilize it for the other three men. After they had all safely reached the roof, he rested for a moment against one of the chimneys of the house. They stripped off their flight gear, revealing a very handsome group of men clad in stylish formal attire. With weapons and ammunition ready for use, and ear pieces in transmitting order, they pried open the access door on the roof and walked softly down the interior stairs, one at a time, with Kobi taking the lead once again. When they reached a landing, Kobi cautiously turned the doorknob and peered into the hallway through the narrow opening as he held the door ajar. Seeing no one about, he motioned to the other agents to wait in the service passageway until he notified them to join him. He slipped through the door into a carpeted corridor and made his way to the stairwell.

~

Kobi/Ostermann walked down the carpeted staircase slowly, careful to stay in the shadows as long as possible. From below, he could hear the tinkle of tableware and glassware as the partygoers dined. He paused halfway down until he was sure that there was nobody in the hallway below waiting to intercept him. Then he moved. He spoke softly into his microphone, whispering instructions to the other agents to join him on the stairs. As soon as they appeared from the corridor, the team walked down from the bedroom wing, emerging onto a balcony of sorts that overlooked a grand ballroom. They took in the scene below for a few moments. Tables and couches had been provided for the guests to sit at and chat, and a well-stocked bar was already in full use. He checked his reflection in one of the mirrors that he passed, and was pleased. Ostermann was here, down to the frightening scar and the limp in his walk—a legacy of the war.

"Come on, men," he whispered. "Don't forget that I'm Ostermann now, and your 'fearless leader.'"

He patted the Luger in his shoulder holster and fingered the SS dagger in his belt. It was time to see if their plan to catch Mengele would succeed. He walked to the main staircase leading to the ballroom floor, feigning Ostermann's limp to maintain his disguise. Shoulders back, he walked out into the crowd, with an agent at either side and one at his back. They openly brandished their weapons, perfectly impersonating guards protecting a very important man. The surviving bigwigs of the wartime Nazi Party were all there. At a table off to the side, he could see Joseph Schwamberger sitting and laughing with a friend. Kurt Becher was holding court at the bar, a huge cigar clamped in his mouth, gesturing and laughing as he guzzled beer. The room was decorated in a Nazi motif. Huge blown-up photographs depicted Hitler in the Bavarian Alps, Himmler carrying out an inspection at Auschwitz, and Martin Bormann in conversation with Field Marshal Rommel. Then there were the bodyguards. For every ranking Nazi, there were at least two men, standing at attention and continuously scanning the room with cold eyes. His boys would fit right in.

Kurt Becher, CFO of the SS, was standing up now, motioning for quiet prior to making an announcement. He was the one who had been in charge of melting down the gold that was removed from the teeth of the millions who were murdered. He had given the orders to stuff German mattresses with the shorn tresses of the victims. He had directed that soap be manufactured from Jewish body fat. He had stolen hidden diamonds, commandeered jewelry that had been smuggled into the camps, confiscated priceless artwork. All of it had been under the control of Kurt Becher. He had wangled his freedom after the war and was now a top-level business man in modern Germany.

"My friends," he called out, "how about a song to celebrate this moment of togetherness?"

"*Jawohl*!" they shouted in unison.

"First, a toast, of course," he roared. "Fill your glasses, one and all!" Kobi reached for a flute of champagne, as well, taking it from the tray of a passing waiter.

"*Prosit*!" Becher screamed. "To all of you. To good health, to the imminent rise of the Fourth Reich, and most of all, to never being caught by the Israelis!"

"*Prosit*!!" They drank.

Becher gave the signal, and a group of musicians situated in a corner of the ballroom struck up the Horst Wessel song. Every man in the room stood at attention and sang along heartily. It was a powerful moment, and Kobi experienced a chill of horror as he realized viscerally something he had known intellectually for a long time: the Nazi Party was still alive and vibrant! These men missed the past, and longed for the days when the master race had been in control. He sang along on autopilot, trying to decide if he should forget about Mengele and just take out the entire room. He wished he had a few grenades as the song reverberated in his brain, and made the blood rush to his face. People would think that he had a little too much to drink. He could recall these same Nazis in the camps, drinking their beer, making sport of their prisoners and singing this hateful song. He wanted to vomit, he wanted, for once in his life, to act without weighing the consequences.

"Are you O.K., boss?" came the whisper in his ear.

He glanced to his left and saw Zev leaning toward him, concerned.

He nodded. He was more than O.K. He had it all under control. They had infiltrated the Nazi den. How much better could he get? The men were singing proudly, beads of sweat popping out on many a forehead. As the singers reached the last chorus, Kobi felt an arm hitting his shoulder.

"Well, well, if it isn't Konrad Ostermann," a voice said in a slightly inebriated tone.

Kobi turned around and found himself staring into the face of Kurt Wolfgang Zeivald. In his guise as a bodyguard, Zev stepped between the two men, and Kobi motioned him back.

"Zeivald," he rumbled back at his host, "how good to see you!"

"I received your e-mail saying you would come," said Zeivald, "but I had my doubts whether you would actually attend. It was really tricky to put this party together. Many people who'd been anxiously anticipating this gathering couldn't make it in the end. It's those infuriating Israelis. They have us hiding out like rats. It makes me sick!"

"I almost didn't come," said Kobi, "but then I remembered that I hadn't seen all my old friends for so long, and I was keen to hear the Herr Doktor speak, as well. I hope that worked out and he's managed to get here." He spoke in a querying tone, and was relieved when Zeivald replied.

"Oh, yes, Mengele's around here somewhere."

"Good."

A distinguished man suddenly approached Zeivald, and spoke to him earnestly for a few moments. Zeivald nodded his head and told the man to be careful, then gave him a friendly little shove and sent him on his way.

"Ludwig Eberhart," he said to Kobi/Ostermann. "A born leader and a true aristocrat."

"Heinrich's son," Kobi ventured a guess. "The industrialist and builder. Poor Eberhart. Such a shame. He was a good man, did so much for his country. He was a credit to Germany. I'm sure his son is the same way."

"Exactly," Zeivald said warmly. "I see your memory hasn't failed you. Still the same Ostermann, sharp as a dagger."

Kobi gave his host a penetrating look, trying to discern the intent behind his words. Zeivald had directed his gaze at the SS dagger prominently displayed at Kobi's waist.

"The Herr Doktor will be addressing the gathering shortly," Zeivald said. "I have to check that everything is under control. I'll see you later, Konrad."

Kobi nodded and the man hurried away. Kobi had to be honest with himself. It didn't look as if they would leave this place alive. Well, at least they could make sure that Dr. Mengele wouldn't either. Alcohol was flowing like water as toasts were proposed to the revival of the Nazi Party, to the health of Dr. Mengele and to the memory of Adolph. That was a good thing. After imbibing so much, the Nazis wouldn't be operating at full mental or physical capacity. On the other hand, the Nazi bodyguards weren't drinking. There were many fully armed men in total control of their senses.

The ushers were attempting to maneuver the unruly crowd into their seats, and bring some semblance of order to the ballroom before Mengele entered. This gathering had become something of a party! It made sense though, considering the fact that most of these men were constantly on the run, hiding from the Israelis; of course they would break loose when they had the opportunity!

Kobi spoke softly to the three agents flanking him. "As soon as Mengele enters the room, be on the highest alert! Everyone will be in the ballroom. Perfect opportunity. If we can get him out, we will! Otherwise, we shoot them all down. Now spread out so we can control more of the area. I'll take a seat near the stage."

His men stationed themselves as far apart as possible. They blended into their surroundings, as the real bodyguards also took positions against the wall, leaving their masters seated in front of the stage in the ballroom.

A massive flag displaying a huge swastika was suspended from the ceiling as a backdrop to the podium, which was illuminated by the footlights and the spotlights in the ceiling. Kobi was mesmerized by the flag: bloody red, ghastly white, stark black. A trumpet blast shook the room. Even the most rowdy guests finally took their seats, slightly sobered by the dramatic assault on their deadened senses.

Zeivald strode up the steps to the stage, chest puffed with pride because such a momentous occasion was taking place in his home! Bow tie slightly askew, hair disheveled and face flushed, he stepped up to the podium and tapped the microphone none too gently. A high-pitched squeal ripped through the room in response, and Zeivald apologized. He straightened his shoulders and commenced to utter his momentous announcement.

"It brings me tremendous pleasure to welcome to my home and to all of our hearts our illustrious colleague, Dr. Josef Mengele, the brilliant physician and research scientist."

Applause swept the ballroom. The men rose as one, clapping, stamping their feet, jostling one another to get closer to the double doors, to catch a glimpse of the man. The trumpets blared again, the doors were thrown open, and in walked the murderer himself. There were no bodyguards near him; there was no indication of fear. Mengele walked confidently to the podium, a wry smile on his face. He took his place after embracing Zeivald, and motioned his audience to resume their seats. An electric silence filled the room.

"My dear colleagues," he began, "your invitation brought me great pleasure, and I thank you for it ...."

But Kobi heard no more. He was too busy scanning the room, plotting the perfect course of action. From the corner of his eye, he could see Roni leaving the ballroom, and wondered where the agent was going. But there was nothing he could do about it now.

Roni knew that he had a few minutes before Kobi gave the order to attack. Until that happened, he considered this the perfect opportunity to check out Zeivald's office, to find out if there was anything there that the Mossad should know. Roni wanted to be a hero. He knew he had a problem following orders, but he had come to the conclusion long ago that it was acceptable to act independently, as long as you came up with the goods. He knew that Kobi was going to be displeased with him for leaving the ballroom for a few minutes. But this was just too good a chance to miss. Maybe he would uncover the source of Zeivald's power; would figure out why the Nazis had elected to hold this meeting in his home.

None of the guards were about. Every man in the house was in the ballroom listening open mouthed to the hypnotic words of their hero. He entered a narrow hallway, which he assumed led to Zeivald's office. A fine pair of antlers was mounted alongside the huge head of a black bear. Its glassy eyes seemed to follow him as he strode down the hallway. There were two doors at the end; only one had a lock. Zeivald obviously hadn't been concerned about infiltration, because the lock was a simple one, and Roni was inside the office in seconds.

Roni swept the room with eagle eyes. He missed nothing. He went through the desk drawers quickly. Nothing. The closet in the room contained only clothing. He snapped pictures with the miniature camera provided by the Mossad. There was a file cabinet adjacent to the desk. He picked the lock and slid it open, pulling out the bundles of files in one fluid motion. Most of the files were not important, seeming to hold information that was either business or personal. Here and there, he found papers that had to do with the cause. He snapped pictures of those documents. He had been in the room for nearly 10 minutes. Mengele wouldn't be speaking much longer. Roni had better get out now while the coast was still clear.

He was about to open the door when he heard footsteps approaching. There was no time to hide. Someone was coming toward the room. Who would be willing to miss Mengele's speech? He stood behind the door in utter silence. He turned off the light, plunging the room into complete darkness. The man outside inserted a key into the lock and opened the door. He stepped into the room and flicked on the light switch. As the light went on, Roni moved out from behind the door and hit the man in the throat, using a martial-arts technique he had learned during his training. The man fell forward onto the floor. Roni eased the door shut and turned the man over. He recognized his victim as a security guard, and, if he was supposed to check in with his superior, the agents were about to be discovered. Roni cursed himself for not having followed orders. Well, maybe the guard wouldn't be missed right away. Everyone was focusing on the speech, after all.

He turned to run back to the ballroom, but something caught his eye. A glass box on the other side of the room held a book. It was a small, simple notebook, and Roni assumed that it was being kept inside the glass for preservation. Well, if it was important enough for Zeivald to keep under glass, it was important enough for Roni to take. He smashed the glass, grabbed the book, and stuffed it into his pocket. An alarm began to ring. That did it. He had blown their cover! Kobi would have his head if the Nazis didn't get to him first!

Roni raced out of the room, down the hallway toward his position in the main ballroom. He got there just in time to hear Kobi calmly snapping out orders.

Kobi spoke into his microphone. "Yossi and Roni, commence firing on anyone armed. Zev, go commandere a vehicle."

"Copy, that."

The alarm was extremely loud, reverberating throughout the building. The room was a crazed war zone now. The older Nazis had imbibed too much alcohol that evening, and their reflexes were far from fast enough to keep up with the frenzied action. Kobi checked to make sure that his men were in position. Yossi and Roni had taken cover beside an upper exit on the balcony. They were peppering the crowd with a heavy volley of gunfire. Yossi concentrated on the sober armed guards, while Roni covered him by raking the entire gathering with a non stop barrage that kept everyone low.

Kobi spoke into his mike. "I think we missed Mengele," he said. "Shortly after the alarm went off, I shot at the stage, but he dropped to the floor as soon as he heard the alarm. I don't know if we got him. Keep shooting," Kobi said. "Hold them on the ground."

Here and there a bodyguard tried to get off a shot, but Yossi picked off anyone who lifted his head.

"We have about 30 seconds before reinforcements arrive and blow everything apart," Kobi said. "I'm going to try to find Mengele. Twenty seconds from now, I want each of you to blow this room apart with your grenades. Exit the building and meet me at the rendezvous point."

"Copy, that."

Roni kept up the constant gunfire, while Yossi picked off whomever he could. Kobi ran around the perimeter of the room toward the stage with his gun drawn, aware of the picture that he made. He hoped that the Nazis thought that General Konrad Ostermann was playing the hero he had always been. He ignored everyone and everything. There was unbelievable noise, the stench of gunpowder, the popping sound of bullets hitting the walls, gouging chips out of the plaster, the screams of agony from the wounded, the smell of the fear in the air. He ignored it all. He wanted to catch Mengele. Nothing else mattered to him.

Out of the corner of his eye, he saw Kurt Becher rise to his feet with a machine gun in his hand, only to be sent flying backward when a shot from Yossi hit him in the shoulder. Kobi raced around the smoke-filled room, taking the stairs to the stage two at a time. Mengele wasn't there. There was an exit door at the left of the stage. He ran through the door to find a metal staircase that led downward. He took the stairs quickly, his footsteps echoing as he ran. He reached the exit and stood to one side before throwing the door open.

The rear of the mansion was lit up. A helicopter on a helipad 300 feet away was about to lift off. The rotors were already turning, the engine was warm. A jeep was pulling up beside the helicopter. Someone emerged from the jeep. It was Mengele. He was climbing into the helicopter. He was getting away. This couldn't be! Kobi lifted his gun and took careful aim. The figure was stepping into the copter. He pressed down gently on the trigger. The bullet flew through the air as if on angel's wings. It hit the figure. He stumbled getting in. He'd been hit! There was a roar from the people around the helipad. They raised their weapons and began to fire randomly. Two more men jumped into the helicopter with the injured man, and the helicopter lifted off. From the mansion came the sounds of an explosion. His men had thrown the grenades. Time to get out.

Kobi was out of time. He hurried to the rendezvous point beside the garage. He heard gunfire before he actually rounded the corner, and saw them shooting. Yossi and Roni were covering Zev, who was smashing through the garage door in Zeivald's personal jeep, on loan to him from the Brazilian armed forces. Stealing the jeep was a brilliant twist on the plan. Kobi mentally gave Zev a pat on the back. They had planned to use one of the limousines that had brought the guests to the gathering, but the jeep was a safer vehicle. As an army issue, it was heavily armored and almost indestructible. But as they were piling inside, there was a moment when it seemed as if everyone in the world was shooting at them, and they thought that maybe it was too late. But Zev threw the door open and they jumped aboard.

Yossi climbed in first, and Roni was about to follow him, when Kobi heard him utter a strangled cry. He watched in horror as a bloodstain appeared on Roni's clothing. Kobi didn't waste a second. He raced forward, grabbed the young agent, heaved him over his shoulder, and found himself catching a book falling from the agent's pocket. Bullets were really flying and it was hailing death! He couldn't waste any more time. He threw both himself and Roni unceremoniously into the jeep, stuffing the bloodied book into his own suit pocket.

"Go!" he yelled at Zev. "Knock their fences down!

Zev floored it. They arrived at the gate to the estate, where a veritable army waited for them. But the jeep was bulletproof, and they plowed down anyone who dared to remain in its way. Then the fence came crashing down. They were out of the place, and Zev was pressing the gas pedal for all he was worth. All the while Roni was losing blood like a fountain, and Kobi's only hope was that they arrive at the helicopter in time to save his life. He tried to staunch the bleeding. He did whatever he could. But even as Zev pushed the speedometer to places it had never gone before, Roni's life was slipping away. Kobi ripped off a piece of his suit and pressed it tightly against the wound, but it was useless.

Kobi held the young man as his life oozed out of him. Kobi spoke soothingly as Roni rambled incoherently and feverishly. Zev was making the turn off the road toward their rendezvous where the Special Forces unit was waiting for them. If they had arrived even a few minutes earlier, Roni might have made it. But he was dead by the time they reached the helicopter, and they boarded with somber faces, thinking how different it could have been.

Many Nazis were dead and wounded. They had infiltrated a top-secret Nazi meeting. Kobi had a bloodstained notebook, which he would have to examine at a later date, when things had calmed down. But Mengele had succeeded in getting away. Yet they had dealt the Nazis a severe blow, hitting them right in the nerve center. Some of the worst enemies of the Jewish nation had been killed, proving to the remaining Nazis that the Israelis were going to track them all down. The evil monsters would be made to understand that they wouldn't be able to sleep at night. It could have been a huge success, if not for the foolish hero who lay dead in the back of the helicopter, who would never see the brilliant light of the Israeli day again. Why, oh, why, had he acted against orders?

Kobi flipped through the notebook, staring in surprise at the pages and pages of names written inside, wondering what it all meant. Kobi knew that he would always keep this book, stained with Roni's blood. And he would attempt to figure out its secret, a secret for which his young agent had given his life.

19
Jason Leonard Frost

Asunción, Paraguay
March 2, 2009

Frost landed at the Silvio Pettirossi International Airport at 7 o'clock Wednesday morning. He had been interested to read in the in-house flight magazine that the airport wasn't located in the city of Asunción itself, but rather some distance away in the city of Luque. The magazine assured its readers, however, that there was no cause for concern, since the transportation system was excellent. Getting to Asunción would be no problem whatsoever. The clerks at the information booth were extremely helpful and courteous, and they provided him with a comprehensive list of bus schedules to the city. As he exited the terminal, there was a bus to the capital idling by the stop, waiting for him to board.

The weather was on the clammy side, but the people were dressed much more formally than their European counterparts, despite the semi-tropical heat in the air. Asunción itself was situated on the left bank of the Paraguay River, and from there the city spread out, sprawling further and further in rectangular blocks.

Asunción's skyscrapers were all located in the newer, more modern, downtown part of the city. But it was clear to Frost, even in the short while that he had been in the country, that things moved at a slower pace in this part of the world. Pedestrians strolled down the broad leafy boulevards. Mothers pushed baby carriages and chatted with friends. The city had a unique flavor, a comforting pace, all its own. Nowhere was the hustle-bustle of a major metropolis.

Asunción was one of the oldest cities in South America, therefore it is known as the Mother of Cities. The bus drove through the city and let him off right in front of his hotel. His travel agent had researched the ideal hotel for him. It was quaint and charming, and Frost fell in love with it on sight.

A uniformed bellhop took his few pieces of luggage into the hotel for him. He looked around appreciatively at the beautifully furnished lobby. A short corridor led toward an inner courtyard with grapevines and well-tended flowerbeds. The guests relaxed over coffee and pipes, and a cloud of pungent smoke hung over the terrace. Frost followed the bellhop to the elevator. It was an old-fashioned brass elevator. It had an open-worked muted frame.

He had reserved a room with a view, and from his porch he could see the river in all its glory. It was a bustling scene, and as he watched, a truck pulled up and workers began unloading sacks of tobacco leaves. He unpacked, and went down to the terrace for an early lunch. He took another long look at the harbor before leaving his suite. All his life, he had read in the papers about South America and the bloody, violent overthrowing of governments that repeatedly occurred. But he was finding it positively idyllic. For a moment, he toyed with the idea of returning for good when this was all over.

He strolled through the hallway and out onto the terrace, hoping for an empty table.

"Can I help you, sir?" The question came from a man in formal attire, with a ready smile and a pleasant manner.

"I hope so," Frost replied. "Table for one, please."

"Right away, sir," the man said. He motioned to a waiter, who was hovering in the background.

"Carlos, show our guest to Table 14."

He followed the waiter to a wicker table at the edge of the terrace overlooking the pier, and accepted the leather-bound menu. After he ordered, the waiter uncorked the bottle at the table, and poured a small amount into a crystal glass for him to taste. He let a few drops of the

Merlot linger on his tongue and pronounced it perfect. He followed the waiter's recommendations, and was pleased with his dinner. When he was finished, he called for the check and left.

Frost headed back to the hotel where he approached the front desk and asked to see the manager.

"Cardinal Frost, I presume," the manager said. "It is a great honor to have you with us. In what way can I be of assistance to Your Eminence?"

"I'll tell you the truth," Frost said. "I need a list of the oldest shipping firms in the city; companies that have been operating for at least 60 years. Can you help me with that?"

"Of course, Cardinal Frost. I will be with you momentarily."

The man was true to his word. Within minutes, someone else was greeting new arrivals at the reception desk, and the manager was sitting with Frost at a coffee table at the rear of the lobby.

"Since the hotel is situated adjacent to the river's waterfront, this is the prime location for visiting as many shipping firms as you desire. Of course, not all of them meet the criteria that you set forth. But enough of them do to ensure that you will be very busy over the next few days."

Frost nodded.

The manager placed a Toshiba laptop on the table. He began typing very quickly, pausing from time to time to make sure that the information was accurate. When he finished, he pressed the print button. He left Frost and went over to the office to retrieve the printout. Then he gave Frost the list of addresses, and did his best to explain how to get around.

"Just remember," the manager finally said, "almost all the firms are located in this immediate vicinity. If you have any difficulty, just ask anyone you meet for directions. Everyone knows everything here in Paraguay. Have a successful afternoon. I hope to see you at our charcoal cookout this evening."

Frost thanked the man and went on his way.

There was a gentle breeze blowing in off the river, and he was grateful. He followed the directions, and was soon walking along a wide tree-lined avenue with many high-class boutiques from around the globe. They offered everything from Armani suits to Godiva chocolate. For a second, he thought that he was on Rodeo Drive. This was Asunción's shopping district, and he watched a steady stream of wealthy people flowing in and out of the various stores. He wasn't interested in that scene. Right now, he was interested in shipping firms only.

Eventually, the avenue branched off in two directions. He followed the split to the right, taking note as to how the neighborhood grew seedier with every step he took. This was old-time Asunción. Gone were the glittering showcases with their thousand-dollar handbags on display. This was a much tougher part of town.

Every other store was a bar, a used-clothing store, or a pawnshop. There were sailors everywhere, on shore leave with cash from their last paycheck, searching for action.

Frost checked the directions again, and found that he was nearing the street that was home to the headquarters of the majority of the Paraguayan shipping companies. Within five minutes, he spotted at least six different companies. The majority of the shipping firms had been around for quite some time. He headed for Pereira and Sons, Ltd. He entered the office.

The room had a musty smell to it, as if the occupants of this office hadn't moved for 20 years. The receptionist — a woman in her mid-60's — was on the phone as he walked in. She motioned for him to take a seat as she continued taking a message. Finally, she finished, thanked the caller and replaced the receiver in its cradle.

"How can I help you, senõr?" she asked him.

He replied that before he knew whether she could help him at all, he needed to know how long their firm had been in business.

"I will find out," she assured him, getting up and going into an office at the back of the room.

Frost glanced around the office. The pictures on the walls were of boats — modern-day yachts and ferries, interspersed with the more ancient sloops and cargo ships. An ancient fan circulated dank air. Frost picked up a newspaper from the chair next to him and fanned himself with it.

Finally the door of the office opened up and the woman returned.

"Senõr," she said, "the company was founded in the year 1956."

"Thank you very much," he replied and turned to leave.

"Wait one moment, please," he heard her say. She was clearly anxious to be of service. "If you tell me what you need, maybe I can be of assistance to you?"

"O.K.," Frost said, thinking that it was worth a shot. "I need to know which shipping firms have been around from the mid 40's, and are still open for business. If you could tell me which of those firms was the busiest and most influential firm back then, that would be an added bonus."

She sat down at her desk and said to him, "You know what? I'm going to call a friend. She had worked in this industry for years. She knows everything there is to know about the shipping business."

"I'll wait," he said.

She called her friend. There was much eye rolling and hand waving from her end. The rapid clip with which she spoke precluded him from understanding anything at all. As she talked, she wrote down the information. She thanked her friend and hung up the phone.

"These are your best bets," she said beaming at him. "They've been around for many years, and are highly successful. If anyone can help you, they can!"

She had been very kind, and he thanked her profusely for her time. Taking some money out of his pocket, he attempted to pay her for her help, but she adamantly refused. He left the establishment, gratefully took a deep breath, and headed for the first firm on his now considerably shorter list.

Another block, and he could see the sign for Carlos Shipping. It was a large sign with a golden lion cradling a ship in its paws. His intuition told him that this was not the place. Too ostentatious and flamboyant. He kept on walking. When he felt his shirt sticking to him, he realized that it was time for a drink. He went into a grocery store and bought himself a cold drink, sitting down on a bench to drink it. There were several old men playing chess at one of the nearby tables, and he thought of Al. He felt a sharp surge of anger course through him once again. It hurt so badly, he found that he couldn't even watch them play. He wondered if he would ever play chess again.

Dropping the empty bottle into a trash can, he continued down the block and around the corner, stopping in front of Ambrosia Shipping. The sign was a discreet and sober dark blue. There was a model sailing ship complete with rigging in the window. The words "Established in 1930" were written in diminutive letters on the corner of the sign. He had a good feeling about this place. Taking a deep breath, he pushed the door open and entered. It was a busy place. He could hear the buzz of telephones and fax machines, and the sounds of people chattering and laughing with one another. There was positive energy in this place. Maybe he'd be lucky.

A secretary sat at the front of the long rectangular room answering phone calls and typing on her computer. Frost hesitated to disturb her. Finally she had a free moment, and she called him over to her desk.

"Thank you for waiting," she said. "How can I help you?"

"Here's the thing," he said, "I have a question about events which might have to do with this firm; events that occurred a long time ago. Is there someone here at the office who would have this kind of knowledge?"

"You need Ramon," she told him with a smile. "Ramon is our resident expert on anything in the shipping business. He's been with the company for many years. In fact, he was actually hired by the original owner of the firm, Mr. Manoa, himself." She glanced at her watch. "Ramon usually comes in at about 11:30. He'll be here shortly. Why don't you take a seat in the conference room? I'll have him join you the moment he gets in."

He was touched by her friendliness. He had not informed them that he was a cardinal. They were just being nice because that was their nature. She showed him to a conference room with a buffet at the side, with freshly brewed coffee and delicious-looking pastries.

"Help yourself," she said, and departed.

He poured a cup of the strong brew, added sugar and milk, and walked to the window. There was a nice view of the water from the window, and he sipped his coffee. He thought how strange it was that he should find himself in the offices of a shipping firm in Asunción, of all places! The coffee was Colombian and very flavorful. He was pondering whether to make himself another cup, when the door opened and a man strode into the room. He knew instinctively that it was Ramon. He was old but vibrant, wrinkled yet vigorous, and he walked with a spring to his step. He was short, with a full head of curly black hair and the whitest teeth that sparkled when he smiled. He extended his hand to Frost.

"Ramon Garcia," he said. Frost liked him on the spot.

"Cardinal Jason Frost," he introduced himself, and Ramon was suitably impressed.

"I didn't know that I was in the presence of holiness," he said, and they laughed together.

"So how can I help you?" he asked a second later, suddenly all business. He had shifted into business mode. Frost was impressed with the ease with which he had done it.

They took seats across from each other at the conference table, and Ramon gave Frost his complete attention.

"I am in the midst of a life search," Frost began. "This quest has taken me from America, to Paris and finally to Paraguay. It goes back to May/June 1945."

Ramon whistled in amazement while running a dark hand through his hair. "That sure was a long time ago," he said. "What happened back then? What do you need to know?"

"A transport of children left Paraguay and headed for Paris in the spring of '45. I need to know if the people in charge of the transport used this firm."

"I see," said Ramon. "I will have to examine our records. One plus is the owner's reluctance to ever throw anything out. Every single shipping transaction run by Ambrosia was documented. The paperwork is still available, although much of it has been stored on microfilm to conserve space."

"Can you check your records, please?"

"C'mon," Ramon said. Frost followed him out of the conference room and down the hall to an elevator. They took the elevator down to the basement, and Frost followed Ramon into a large room filled with metal shelves stacked with files, computers and other electronic equipment for reading microfilm.

"O.K.," Ramon said, and he began bringing up the files on the computer screen. "All files prior to 1960 have been transferred to microfilm," he explained.

"1950 ... 1949 ... No, that's not early enough. 1947 ... O.K., 1946. Here we are. May, June, July, August. Let's see," Ramon said. "What was the name of the transport?"

"Well," Frost said, "the man in charge was a gentleman by the name of Eberhart. He ran the operation; probably funded it as well."

"I'm checking," Ramon said. He ran his fingers down the screen, shaking his head as he went from name to name. "No, no," he paused for a second and then said, "I'm sorry, Cardinal Frost. There doesn't seem to be any mention of an Eberhart in the files."

"What about any other German names?" Frost asked him grasping for straws.

"Well," Ramon drawled, "let's see. There was a transport of cotton for a Mr. Malloy. A transport of tobacco for the London Tobacco Company, coal and sugar headed for Brazil, and wait ... here's something," he said with rising excitement. "A transport headed to France on the 29th of May of '45. Doesn't say what was on the boat. It was ordered and paid for by a Senõr Kurt Shweber."

"Any address?" Frost asked him breathlessly.

"Yes," Ramon said. "The address is 116 Carlos Antonio Lopez Avenue, in the barrio of Sajonia, one of the upper-class neighborhoods in the city. I wouldn't get overly excited about this," he said over his shoulder to Frost. "I mean, this all happened a really long time ago. The chances of these people still being around and having any knowledge of what happened in '45 is almost nil!"

Frost stuck out his hand to the man. "Mr. Garcia," he said in his most formal voice, "I would like to thank you from the bottom of my heart for your help this morning. And if you are ever in the States and in need of anything at all, here is my card. I want you to contact me!"

Ramon clearly appreciated the gesture, and carefully stowed the business card in his wallet. They left the room, and Ramon accompanied Frost past all the cubicles to the street, where they shook hands one final time.

"O.K., Sajonia," Frost said as he hailed a taxi, "here I come."

The barrio of Sajonia was reminiscent of suburban America from 30 years earlier. Children played soccer, hooting and screaming in childish delight as the ball flew over the taxi. The houses sprawled over generous parcels of land. Tudor columns supported ornate porches overlooking green lawns, where dogs romped and flowers bloomed brightly. Many of the houses had patios where families gathered around picnic tables for the evening barbecue. They passed a Macy's style department store. Soon enough, the taxi turned onto Carlos Antonio Lopez Avenue. The driver cruised slowly past the buildings seeking the desired address. When they reached 110, Frost told the driver to stop. He paid him and tipped him generously. Then he exited the cab and began his approach.

He nonchalantly glanced around him, trying to give the impression that he was a regular in the neighborhood. It was interesting, but for the first time since he had arrived in Paraguay, he noticed that several signs were in German: a sign for a doctor's office, a grocery store, some of the advertisements on a nearby bulletin board — all in German. He wasn't surprised. Everyone knew that thousands of Germans had emigrated to South America. Many of them had found a comfortable haven in quiet, peaceful Paraguay. The inhabitants of this part of Sajonia had a decidedly European appearance, as well. Whereas the majority of the natives were swarthy and had black hair and eyes, there was a disproportionate amount of fair-haired people in this part of town.

Number. 116 was an unassuming ranch-style two-story building. The architect had created an illusion of space. There was no sign but Frost sensed that this was a club or restaurant; perhaps, a club for German expatriates.

There were a few young boys kicking a ball between them as they passed. With a quizzical look on his face, he hailed them and pantomimed that he was very thirsty and needed a drink. They pointed at the building, indicating to him that he could buy one there. He had guessed correctly. People here might know the answers to his questions. He figured that he'd go and do a little reconnaissance of the place, get a feel for the patrons, see if he could spot the people in charge. He was merely a thirsty tourist innocently stopping for a drink. There was no reason to be on guard.

There was a short flight of stairs leading to a ramp, which in turn led to a second short flight of stairs. He could either continue upward or enter the door nearby. He chose the door. Continuing upward would present him with a challenge if he had to explain why he, as an innocent tourist looking for a drink, hadn't gone into the first door. Taking a deep breath, he pushed it open and walked into another world.

The room was dimly lit, and there was a smoky haze in it. It took a minute for his eyes to adjust after the bright sun. The room was octagon shaped, the tables and chairs placed on the carpeted areas around the room's perimeter. A large section in the middle of the room was designated as a dance floor. But since it was midafternoon, the room was nearly empty. At the rear of the room was a mirrored bar where 10 older men sat and smoked cigars. Frost headed that way. The walls were covered with enlarged photographs, most in black and white. Although the majority of the photos were unfamiliar, he was able to recognize some of the more prominent subjects. The owners of the club, unlike Germany immediately after the war, were most definitely unashamed and unapologetic about their behavior during the war. In fact, this place was a shrine to the good-old days. There was a picture of Himmler at a ceremony of the Waffen SS, and there was a picture of Julius Streicher working at his desk at *Der Shturmer* — the official "news" organ of Nazi Germany.

Frost shivered as he suddenly came to the belated realization that perhaps, just maybe, he had bitten off more than he could chew. He had arrived with no clear plan and no backup. Al was dead, and he had stumbled all by himself into a den of people who considered the Nazi Party to be Germany's greatest accomplishment! The worst part was that he had been noticed and couldn't even leave.

A man detached himself from the group at the bar. He was in his 30's, very good looking in a tough-guy sort of way, blond and broad shouldered. He waved at Frost as he approached, and for a second, Frost thought he had been mistaken for someone else.

"Welcome to 'Club Salute.'" The man spoke with a German accent.

"Thank you," Frost replied. "It was very hot outside, so I asked some kids where I could find a drink. They kindly directed me here. I assume that you sell cold drinks as well as the hard stuff, right?"

"Of course," the man said. "Anything you want. Can I bring you a Coke?"

"Sounds good," Frost said.

"Take a seat over here," said the man pointing to an empty table not far from the bar, "and I'll be right with you. Oh by the way," he said, "my name is Jorge." He didn't bother waiting for Frost to reply — indicating that he knew *his* name, and didn't need Frost to tell him anything.

Frost sat at the table, trying to ignore the curious or hostile stares of the men at the bar. Jorge returned a minute later with an unopened bottle of Coke and a large glass filled with ice. He popped the cap of the bottle and filled the cup. "Take a drink," Jorge said, "and tell me what brings you here to Paraguay. Something important, I assume, for an obviously important man such as yourself from the States to come to South America! Come, drink up," he said, when he saw that Frost hadn't touched the Coke.

Frost took a sip. Despite himself, the Coke was frosty and good, and he felt refreshed.

"Look, Jorge," he finally said, "I came here because I've been searching for answers for a very long time. Somehow I think that the people here are in the position to provide them. So in response to your question, why am I here, the answer is: To discover who I am, as you obviously already know. Is that too much to ask? For a little information, to help me gain perspective on my life. Can you do that for me?"

Jorge's eyes were blank; there was no emotion in them at all.

"You ask very good questions," Jorge said. "But you know, I might have to kill you if I tell you the answers." Frost knew that old line, and he looked for the smile that usually went along with it. But Jorge was deadly serious.

"Come along with me, please," he said. It was an order. The men at the bar watched impassively as Jorge led him past the bar to a door at the rear.

"You are probably as curious as to what goes on upstairs, right?" he asked over his shoulder. "Well here's your chance to find out." They went up a staircase to the second floor, and Frost could feel his heart pounding. Jorge knocked at the door on the top of the landing, and it was opened by an imposing man who radiated both a sinister strength and the willingness to use it.

"Come in," the man said in German.

They had entered a conference room. There were six men seated around the table. They were all looking at Frost with an expectant stare.

"It's about time you arrived, Cardinal Frost," said the man at the head of the table. "It took you long enough to get here. I had given you more credit than you deserved. Welcome to the branch of my Club Salute in Paraguay. My name is Dietrich Eberhart. If you want to ask questions, this is probably the best place. I just have to warn you, cardinal, that I don't think you're going to be pleased with the answers."

Frost looked the man in the eye and said, "Why Al? What did he do to make him deserving of death?"

"He stuck his nose in where it didn't belong," Eberhart replied. "That's what he did. He was at the wrong place at the wrong time. That was Al."

"So you just murdered him?" asked Frost in disbelief.

"Yes," Eberhart said. "When someone oversteps the line he is eliminated."

The scene was reminiscent of something that had happened to him long, long before. Once again, just when he was on the cusp of discovering the truth, it had been swept out from under his feet. They were playing with his mind. Had his mind ever been his own? He had been so close to the source, and now he had nothing. He tasted the bitter taste of defeat. He could feel the tears of disappointment and despair about to emerge ... There was a man speaking to him with in a slow, calming voice, telling him to relax, to relax ... As if that was the only thing he needed to do right now. Relax, he was getting there ... Stop thinking so much, calm down ...

Why not? He might as well allow the soothing waves of the ocean wash over him and take him under ... He should listen to this man ...

"You are going under, Cardinal Frost ... You are under now ... You have a mission to fulfill and you are going to do it, come what may."

Jason Leonard Frost arrived back in the States uncertain as to what had exactly transpired over the last few weeks. One thing he did know, however. His life was rapidly swirling downward into a place where he was about to relinquish any remaining vestiges of control. The thing that scared him the most was that there was almost no one in the world whom he could trust. Almost no one at all.

Mordy Kahane

Jerusalem, Israel
March 17, 2009

I left Mordy in the office and went down to the dining room to get breakfast. Almost all the food was finished, and I didn't think Mordy was going to be interested in what remained. So I asked the cook, an old friend, if he could whip up a fresh batch of scrambled eggs for us, and he obligingly agreed. Ten minutes later, I was on my way back to "my" office with a tray of fresh steaming food. I have always found that people have a much easier time talking things out when there's food around.

"At your service, young man," I said, setting the tray down in front of him with a flourish.

As he ate, he asked questions: about my background, where I'd grown up and the yeshivos I had attended. I told him about the yeshivah in New Jersey, the place where I had spent my formative years where I had developed into a *ben Torah*. I told him how I hadn't wanted to leave yeshivah, how if it had been up to me, I would've remained there for a few more years. But the *Rosh Yeshivah* understood me better than I understood myself. He knew that I had gained tremendously from the yeshivah, but he also realized that it was time for me to move on. He pushed me higher, challenged me to grow in ways that I never even dreamed possible.

I explained to Mordy that I hadn't always been the kind of guy who people wanted to be friends with. I hadn't always been cool. But somehow, I had been able to change. It's amazing what the right rebbe can do for a person! The *Rosh Yeshivah* sent me to Eretz Yisrael, and I loved it at first sight.

"Mordy," I said, "I will never forget seeing Eretz Yisrael for the first time as we descended over the Mediterranean. We landed and disembarked. In those days the plane landed from the terminal. All the *bachurim* got down and kissed the ground. As I got back on my feet, I saw the palm trees swaying in the breeze. Something about them brought tears to my eyes. Then, I looked back at the people coming off that plane — young mothers strapping their babies into strollers, middle-aged businessmen, *yeshivah bachurim* and seminary girls, and the *bubbies* and *zeides* who were here to visit their *einiklach* in Yerushalayim. My heart sang because we were all one family. We didn't even know one another, but at that moment I felt a closeness unlike anything I had ever experienced before. I felt a longing and a warmth — a clarity and an unexpected surge of comprehension — and I knew I never wanted to leave my family again. I knew right then that I was going to make this place my home. My *Rosh Yeshivah* had known that I would react this way. He knew that I was well suited for life in Eretz Yisrael, and he sent me here because he understood me the way a rebbe should." Mordy was nodding as if he knew exactly what I was talking about.

I saw that he had finished eating and wanted to go on with his story. I understood what he was feeling. This was something that he had kept bottled up for so long. Finally, he was letting it all out and he couldn't stifle it. And I was astounded by his story! I mean, this kid had gone through a lot! People like Mordy whose life experience was unlike most of us, you just know that Hashem has something special in mind for them, a goal especially tailored for them. I nodded encouragingly, and he began to speak.

"After my university fiasco," Mordy went on, "I had the horrible feeling that my life would never be O.K.; that I would never fit in anywhere. I felt that it might work out for a few months — that my life would appear to be moving in a good direction — but I knew that such a thing would never last! I was destined to wander in the desert of loneliness. I would have a solitary existence. There was no reason to initiate a friendship because it wouldn't last.

"I returned to Ithaca, to my parents' home, back from the dorm, from my prestigious post as photo editor of the paper; back from school where everyone on campus had known and respected the boy called Eagle. They had revealed their true colors. Not one of them had stood up for me, tried to protect me or taken my side. They were nothing close to the way real friends should be. I was through with people like that. So I came home.

"But coming home was no longer comforting. Home had become a place to avoid. It had been quite a few years since that unforgettable baseball game. But the locals still remembered the story. They all knew me. I couldn't walk down the street without someone looking at me, scratching his head and saying to his friend in a voice that carried, 'Say Bob, isn't that Matt, the boy who lost us the championship?'

"They were stupid people who would never forgive me for not coming through for them. I couldn't walk into the drugstore without hearing some dumb comment. I couldn't go get my hair cut without having to listen to the barber explain how everything had gone haywire that day. My heart was filled with the betrayal and shame that I had encountered at the hands of this town."

Mordy paused for a second to take a drink. His voice was becoming hoarse from all the talking that he had been doing.

"I didn't have a clue how to get out of the rut into which I had fallen. I didn't even feel comfortable leaving my house anymore. I remained at home most of the day, venturing out when the sun was starting to set and people couldn't really see who I was. My life was really spiraling downward. And then, just as I began thinking that if this was the way my life was going to be like, that I wanted no part in it, just then, everything changed, from one moment to the next."

I could sense that we were approaching a turnaround in the story; a crucial, pivotal moment in the life of Matt Kahane.

"I awoke very early that morning," Mordy said. "I wasn't exactly sure what I was going to do, but the thoughts swirling through my mind were anything but healthy ones. I don't remember the exact details, but I was in a seriously bad place. I was walking down the street caught up in my own world, not looking around, when all of a sudden, a man who had been strolling along a few steps ahead of me just kind of keeled over clutching his arm! He was an older man, and I was suddenly propelled from my lethargy as if I'd been struck with a cattle prod! I realized that the man was experiencing a heart attack, and nobody was around. Nobody but me. I didn't want to get involved. It would mean having contact with the world again. I glanced around the empty streets hoping to see someone coming my way; someone responsible who could deal with the situation, leaving me free to slump off wallowing in my misery. But there was nobody. I would have to handle the situation and do my best to save the man.

"I began screaming, 'Help! Help! Someone's having a heart attack!'

"Then I ran to him. He was lying on the ground and his eyelids were fluttering. His face had an ashen color, and he looked absolutely terrible. He was obviously in excruciating pain. I got down on the ground and began CPR on him as best as I remembered from the First-Aid course I had taken years before. All the while I was screaming for an ambulance. Out of the corner of my eye I saw window shades being raised. It couldn't have been that long — although it felt like forever — before the ambulance arrived and the professionals took over. I guess I could have left after that. I mean, the EMT's knew what they were doing. There was no particular reason for me to remain. I could have headed into the distance. But I didn't leave. Something inside my heart was instructing me to remain by his side, to make sure that everything was okay before I left him and slipped back into my bleak existence.

"After they loaded the stretcher into the ambulance, I told the paramedics that he was my relative and that he had collapsed while we were walking together. I told them that I was accompanying them to the hospital. They agreed. I rode in the ambulance with him and I held his hand. For some inexplicable reason, I felt extremely close to this man. Maybe it was because I had saved his life. I didn't know for sure. But the fact was that I was suddenly filled with a feeling of contentment and happiness! I had saved someone's life. I had done something worthwhile once again! It had been so long since I had done anything that I was proud of. A few months had passed since my university debacle. No one had been able to get through to me, to penetrate the mask. But suddenly I felt free again. Free to spread my wings and fly, free to try again. The ride to the hospital was one of the best car rides of my life!

"I remained with him throughout the ordeal: through the bypass operation and for many hours afterward as he slept and his body healed. There was no next of kin. No family members came to visit him, but there were plenty of visitors from the church. Men in priests' garb came, and others who were clearly higher up in the ranking order of the church: bishops and cardinals. Apparently this older gentleman was a V.I.P. in the American church. The funny thing is, even after I discovered his line of work, I still felt the same way. Something about him connected with me on a very deep level, and I decided to remain with him until I got to know him.

"The older man awoke and was in full command of his faculties much quicker than any of the doctors anticipated. The nurses still thought that I was related to him, and when they saw how well we got along, nobody entertained any ideas of shooing me out of the recovery ward. He had fewer visitors now. When someone did come to see him, I would make myself scarce for the time that they were there. He had other friends who weren't connected to the church as well; men he played chess with or hung around with. Then too, I would make myself scarce. But after they left, I would return and then we would talk."

"But wasn't he surprised to see you when he gained consciousness?" I asked Mordy.

"Of course he was," Mordy replied. "But I explained who I was. I explained how I had been walking down the street behind him, just minding my own business, when he collapsed. I explained that I was the one who saved his life. Listen, Reb Zack, when you save someone's life, there's a bond, an unbreakable connection that's forged. That was exactly what happened with us. We just sat and spoke for hours, and never ran out of things to discuss. He is a fascinating man, a brilliant person and he is a fount of information. Obviously, he never married, he had no family, so he had filled his time amassing knowledge. And he has a memory like a steel trap. Just an incredible person all around.

"Slowly but surely, he drew me out of my shell, and I opened up and allowed him to get to know the real person within, the young boy who was still scared and vulnerable from the terrible events that had happened to him. He explained to me that everyone goes through their own personal set of harsh experiences in life. He explained that perhaps my lot was somewhat more difficult to deal with than most, but every person that I met had his share of hardships to overcome — his bag of challenges to face. I still hadn't shared with him the fact that I had saved his life while I was contemplating the direction mine would take.

"Then we began talking about him and the difficulties in his own life. He was an orphan and he couldn't even recall his parents. He told me about his youth, when he was shunted from one country to the next as if he was human luggage or something. He reminisced about the boat journey to America. It was obvious that even with all his friends and colleagues, this man was lonely. I could feel it in the way that he watched me, hungrily studying every detail of my face. I knew that he would cherish the time we spent together. The funny thing was, that I, who had never shown any interest in older people before, knew that the connection forged in that hospital ward would never be broken. It was an intuitive feeling, for we never spoke about what would be after he returned home. It was just an unspoken fact that I would stay with him until the doctors pronounced him fit to leave. And that's exactly what I did.

"My father came to the hospital with a change of clothing for me. He didn't have the slightest clue as to why I was devoting so much time to this old man. But then again, he had given up understanding me a long time before. I wouldn't have been able to explain it to him even if he would have asked, because I didn't really understand it myself. All I knew was that this was the right thing for me to be doing just then."

Mordy took a drink of coffee and grimaced slightly at the lukewarm yeshivah brew.

"For a man of his age," Mordy continued, "Cardinal Frost was in fairly good shape. He told me that he worked out on a regular basis and went jogging three times a week. He was a pretty active man. It wasn't long before he was almost completely back to himself and ready to leave. Both of us felt a certain sense of loss, because we both realized that once we left the hospital, our relationship wouldn't remain the same. But it was time for him to go. I helped him with his clothing that last morning, and then I hoisted a bag of his belongings onto my shoulder. We rode the elevator to the lobby together where he checked out. As we walked into the sunshine of a beautiful day, Cardinal Frost asked if I wanted to pick up a cup of coffee and go for a stroll in the park.

"Being as reluctant to leave this behind as he was, I immediately agreed to his suggestion. He told his driver to take us to the nearest Dunkin' Donuts, where he purchased two giant mugs of steaming vanilla coffee. He told me to choose the pastry that I desired. Then we left the store and headed to a nearby park. He nodded to many of the passersby; obviously, he was one of those people who was genuinely nice to everyone he met. There was something in his eyes that called out and said: *I like you. Let's be friends.* Children especially felt it, and whenever we passed a mother pushing a carriage, he would pause to play with the baby. He was like a kindly grandfather-type beloved by one and all.

"He took me to the chess enclosure, an area in the park where people, in his own words, 'old men like myself,' were playing chess. Everyone was happy to see him. They stopped their games and waved and made jokes and asked him who his babysitter (meaning me) was. He told them that I had saved his life and then remained with him in the hospital. They were all quiet for a minute until one of his friends asked how much I charged for my services. Then the jokes began again. He introduced me to his buddy, Al, a Jamaican native who smiled slowly and pretty seldom, but meant every one of them. Then we went for the walk.

"Sipping slowly on our no-longer steaming coffees, we meandered along the biking path. We barely spoke. I could tell that it was my turn to speak, to explain where I was coming from, what demons of the past I was attempting to run away from. But the words wouldn't come.

"'Hard to know where to begin sometimes, eh?' he said, and I nodded. 'It wasn't a coincidence that you just happened to be outside at 5:50 in the morning, right?' he went on. 'That's just not a usual time for most people to leave their homes. You must have been going somewhere, and fate put us together at the right moment for you to save my life.'

"'I left my house early since I was totally confused,' I told him.

"'Totally confused? You have your whole life ahead of you! You're talented and good looking and smart, even very smart! Your parents love you ... '

"He looked at me thoughtfully and said, 'Why don't you tell me the whole story. Don't worry; I'm a very good listener.'

"He was. We sat underneath one of those leafy trees for a few hours while I poured out my heart to this kind man. I described my early years in Ithaca and how happy I had been until Brian came along. I told him of my friends' subsequent betrayal, how quickly it had occurred, how rapidly they forgot about all the victories I had given them.

"I began to cry, and he handed me a handkerchief. I hadn't realized that there were still some people who used handkerchiefs anymore! Then I told him about Josh Sebring and our friendship, and how much it had meant to me after what had happened with Brian. I told him about the storm and how everything fell apart that night. He was properly sympathetic and fascinated at the same time.

"Through it all, Cardinal Frost sat and listened with everything he had. Complete attention focused on me.

"I told him how my life had been saved, but my friendship was over. Josh and I had barely ever spoken after that night. But on the other hand, I had prayed to G-d and He had answered me. I had discovered something incredible that night about belief; not only that, but I had come to comprehend that a Higher Being was running the world. But my friendship was gone, history. And I felt a great void.

"I told him about university and what had happened there: about my darkroom and the newspaper and all my friends on campus. And about meeting Brian again after all those years on a snowy day, when it was almost impossible to escape. I told him that the fact that I had gotten away was an open miracle. I felt the hatred again. I was feeling my Jewishness again, identifying with those people who had been killed in the Holocaust, because I knew what it was like to be singled out and persecuted regardless of the fact that I hadn't done anything wrong.

"That was when I returned home. The prodigal son coming back home to Ithaca, walking with my head down, facing the scorn of a town who still hadn't forgiven me for my crime of striking out. When I saw that I couldn't leave my house during daylight hours without encountering someone who had something negative to say, when I feared that I would spend the remainder of my life without any friends because that was the pattern that kept on happening, then I was at a loss. What was the point of living without friends?

"That was why I was wandering around in the early morning. Then, suddenly, I looked up and saw this man in front of me having a heart attack, and everything changed. A sense of purpose flowed through me. I was going to be a hero and save a life. It was a turning point for me.

"Now here we were sitting together, and I was filled with incredible feelings of gratitude for the desire to live again after all those months. I had a burning desire to make up for all the wasted time, for all those days filled with nothingness. I was ready to live again.

"The only question facing me now was: What should I be doing with my life? I had finished high school earlier than the rest of the kids that I knew, and I had messed up at university. Did I really want to start anew at a different college right now? Not particularly. What were my options? I told Cardinal Frost everything, all my dilemmas, how I didn't know where to go from here, what road to take. He listened to me, really listened, as if my conflicts were important to him. Then he said something that caught me completely by surprise.

"'Why don't you go to Israel?' he asked. I caught my breath for a second, because that was the last thing I was expecting.

"'Go to Israel,' he said again, 'and find yourself a place to study; a place where you can learn about your heritage.'

"'My heritage?' I said to him, not understanding what he was talking about. 'What heritage?'

"'The history of the Jewish nation,' he said, 'unless everyone has been mistaken and Matt Kahane isn't Jewish.' He delivered this line with a smile.

"I said, 'No, I'm Jewish.'

"'So go then, he said. 'Find a yeshivah for yourself and study about being a Jew.'

"'Find a what for myself?' I asked him, getting more and more confused as I watched this conversation spiraling totally out of control.

"'A yeshivah,' he said, 'is an institution of higher learning. It's a place where Jewish boys discover what it means to be Jewish.'

"I was shocked. 'Wait a minute,' I said to him. 'I don't understand. You're a cardinal of the Catholic Church. Why are you suggesting that I go further my Jewish education?'

"'Maybe because it's the right thing for you to do,' he answered me gently. 'Look, I have this feeling about you. I feel that everything that's repeatedly happening to you is because you are on the receiving end of a message from heaven. G-d wants you to think about your life and what has been happening. He wants you to ask: *Who am I? What am I doing here? Why was I created?* He wants you to search for answers. So what does He do? He turns your friends against you and makes them hate you. He puts you through that crazy storm where you almost die and lose your best friend again. The same thing happens in university. Obviously you are meant to ask yourself some serious questions, maybe change the direction of your life, because otherwise what would be the point of it all?'

"I thought about what he was saying and wanted to ask him, *Well, what about you? Why don't you ask some questions?* But I didn't ask. There are some things you can ask and some things that you can't. I guess this was one of those things that was out of bounds.

"'There's one big problem with what you're suggesting,' I said to him.

"'What's that?' he asked me.

"'The fact that my parents paid for university,' I said, 'and there is no way in the world that they will be willing to pay for me to go gallivanting off to Israel for a year to study ancient history, when it will cost them another whole clump of money.'

"That's when he shocked me in the hugest way. 'I'll pay for it,' he said. When he saw that I was about to protest and turn him down, he said, 'Look, it's the least I can do for you. Consider it my thanks to you for saving my life! I want you to go and I'm willing to fund it. You, my friend, are going to Israel, and that's final!'

"Reb Zack," said Mordy, "I didn't know if this was going to be the best thing for me. But it wasn't as if I had that many other options right then. So I went. And it *was* the best thing that could have ever happened to me."

"I arrived in Israel at the tail end of a heat wave," Mordy said. "The entire country was drenched in perspiration from head to toe. The heat hit me like a sledgehammer as I exited the terminal. The taxi drivers grumbled as they maneuvered the heavy suitcases into the cabs. I was fascinated by the Hebrew writing everywhere," Mordy said. "All my life, the sight of those squiggly letters had meant that we were at the synagogue for Yom Kippur. Suddenly the letters were everywhere — on the taxi stand, on the coke machines and even on the billboards — and I found this disconcerting to say the least!

"I had the address for the yeshivah that I was going to be attending in my pocket. I was looking forward to meeting all the new people. Cardinal Frost had done some research on the subject, and he had ultimately been the one who had picked the yeshivah! When I look back, I recall that something about that also struck me as funny — that my yeshivah had been selected for me by a priest!

"The name of the yeshivah was Moreh Derech, and it was located in a quiet out-of-the-way neighborhood of Yerushalayim. The streets were peaceful, the air was invigoring. We were close enough that you could see the Old City walls. I especially loved them at night when they were lit up. It was an oasis of serenity in the midst of the hustle and bustle of the city. I loved Yerushalayim on sight. I wasn't as sure about my feelings for the yeshivah. It wasn't something I could pinpoint. Everyone was nice enough. Most of the guys went out of their way to greet me when I arrived. The rooms were nice and airy, and the food in the dining room was plentiful and delicious. It had all been handpicked for me by a cardinal of the Catholic Church!

"For the first time in my life, I realized that there was something in those dusty scrolls that actually pertained to me. It came as a tremendous surprise. All my life, I had pictured myself following in my father's footsteps with regard to religion. I would donate generously to the UJA, I would be a solid supporter of Israel, I would attend synagogue on the major holidays. I would profess extreme pride in the fact that I was Jewish, regardless of the fact that I knew next to nothing about what being Jewish truly meant.

"On the first day in my new school, I was encouraged to attend a class on the subject of G-d and the creation of the world. For the first time in my life, I found myself thinking, really thinking. It was daunting. I had been challenged by what the rabbi was saying. I had never devoted any thought to the whole concept of Hashem. I mean, I knew that He existed, especially after that wild night when I rode the waves and survived. But now I returned to my dorm room, looked into the mirror and realized that if I didn't do anything to consolidate my newfound understanding, then I wouldn't be true to myself. I had never been a faker before. But if I accepted the premise that Hashem was the Ruler and Creator of the world, and if he had written a guidebook, then it was incumbent on me to follow the rules in the guidebook. Otherwise, I was not being true to myself.

"I began attending the beginners' classes on a daily basis, taking copious notes and going over everything I was learning, until I had gained a clarity in the assorted concepts and ideas. For the first time in my life, people were actually prepared to discuss difficult concepts. They wanted to clarify the most complex thought-processes. They thrived on debate. They weren't afraid of being bested and shown where they were wrong. My parents had excelled at the art of brushing off questions, while here they excelled at the art of anticipating them. They wanted me to ask and to ask again until all my questions had been satisfactorily answered, until my doubts were all gone and I was free to devote myself to moving on toward mastering the sea of Torah.

"It didn't take me long to get a handle on the beginners' level. I felt this burning desire to move more quickly than I was moving. I felt stymied and frustrated. I wanted to know everything all at once, but there was only a certain number of hours in every day, and that meant that things were going to take time. I compromised by going to the classes that the rabbis recommended, but I made sure to speak to each of the rabbis every moment I could. I was insatiable and couldn't get enough. I wanted to know everything all at once. All the Bible, all of *halachah*.

"In the end, the rabbis made me realize that I would have to take it one day at a time. I would have to leave the broader picture alone for a while and focus on the smaller pieces that made up my life. So that's what I did. I stayed in the *beis midrash* for many hours every day, pausing for meals and sleep. I was on a roll. I had found my rhythm and I reveled in it. Every day brought new exciting discoveries, new revelations. I was constantly finding myself amazed by the things I was learning. It wasn't long before I had conquered the basics. I will never forget the joy I had on the night when I read my first *pasuk* of *Chumash* in the holy language in which it was written. It was an incredible feeling. I wanted to celebrate. My rebbeim encouraged me to go out and treat myself to something special. I left the *beis midrash* a little bit early that night and found a coffee shop tucked away in an alleyway. I ordered an ice-cream sundae that tasted wonderfully sweet, just like my success.

"With every spoonful, I allowed myself to slip backward into the memories of the last few months: months of sweating until late at night, months of not giving up on my dreams, months full of moments when I thought that I'd never be successful, that I would never learn to read. Then all at once it had come, and now I could read the language with a degree of fluency. Now I would be able to move on to the next stage. I was going to start to really learn. I was going to become a *talmid chacham*.

"I know you probably think I'm being overly dramatic, Reb Zack," Mordy said. "You're probably thinking, *How is it possible that he had such an appreciation of Torah when he'd only been in yeshivah for a few months?* But that's the truth! I had gained such insight into the fascinating and illuminating world of Torah that I knew beyond a shadow of a doubt that this was the path for me.

"I returned to the dorm as the night grew steadily darker. I was proud and happy with what I had accomplished in such a short time. It was an uplifting moment for me. I felt ready to face the challenges of the future. I went to sleep that night in a very healthy state of mind, and it only got better.

"From learning the *aleph beis*, I moved on from the beginners' level. That was where I discovered something precious about myself."

I looked at him with curiosity. What had he found out?

"The moment I opened that Gemara the first time, I understood that the Gemara and myself were inexplicably connected. As the rebbe began to explain that first Mishnah, my mind opened up and I was able to see the entire picture in a way that I had never experienced previously. Not only was I *chapping* everything he was saying, my mind was developing its own line of thought. At first I tried ignoring what I was thinking. I couldn't imagine that my thoughts held any merit. I mean, I had just started learning Gemara! I was a complete novice. How was it possible that I had something to add? But my thoughts included questions and answers that were logical.

"I didn't interrupt the class. Instead I waited for it to be over and the other students — young *baalei teshuvah* like myself — had left the room. Then I turned to the rebbe, a sweet middle-aged man with a brown beard and big glasses, and I asked him if it was possible for me to share a few of my thoughts on the *sugya* with him.

"He smiled and probably thought to himself, *What could this kid have to say?* But of course he invited me to take a seat at the desk, and I launched into the thoughts that had come to mind during the *shiur*. I must have talked for quite some time. The more I talked, the more excited he became. He made me repeat my thoughts over and over, and he dissected them. I could see that he was taking them seriously. Then he walked to the bookcase. It was crammed with *sefarim*. He removed an aged *sefer* from one of the packed shelves which was a well-used *sefer*. The binding was cracked and the pages were yellowed and crumbling.

" 'This is the Ketzos,' he told me. 'A tremendous *talmid chacham* wrote this *sefer*.' I nodded, wondering what the Ketzos and I had in common.

" 'I'm almost positive,' he went on, 'that the very question you just asked is one that he discusses in depth.' As he spoke, he flipped through the pages until he had found what he was looking for. He held the *sefer* up triumphantly.

" 'Here it is,' he said exultantly.

"He proceeded to translate a few lines aloud, I realized that the Ketzos (whoever that was) was asking my question, only in a much clearer and more comprehensive way. But we were asking the same question. We had thought along the same lines! It was clear proof that my gut feelings had been correct. I was cut out for this way of life! The rabbi closed the *sefer* and looked at me and his eyes were shining as he said, 'I've been teaching at this yeshivah for almost 15 years, and never have I met a *bachur* like you: someone who has only just begun to learn Gemara and has enough of an understanding to ask the Ketzos's *kasha*. *Ashrei yoladitcha*! Praised be those who bore you!'

"Then he grabbed my hands and we began to dance together, overcome by what had just transpired between us. He twirled me around the room as if this was the happiest day of his life. He sang *Amar Rabbi Akiva, amar Rabbi Akiva, ashreichem Yisrael.* Again and again, he sang this song. The joy that filled my heart was so great that I thought it might burst from the sheer magnitude of *simchah* that we were both experiencing.

"When we finally slowed down, he said, 'O.K., Matt, you asked the Ketzos's *kasha*. What about an answer? Give me a *terutz*. I want an answer, Matt, right now!'

"So I thought for a minute, gave my head a chance to calm down from the spiritual dancing that had swept me away, and then I began to tell him my thoughts on the subject. They hadn't been as worked through as the question had been. It was only an inkling of an idea that hadn't even begun to germinate yet. But as I spoke, I suddenly started to understand the depth of the *sugya*. It was absolutely crazy! I didn't possess the *yeshivish* lingo at all, but the major components were there. I could feel the truth in what I was saying. My rebbe was looking at me with an almost apprehensive, albeit stunned, look because he knew it too.

"'Are you sure that you never learned in a yeshivah before?' he asked me.

"I had to laugh because not only had I never studied in a yeshivah before, I had barely known I was Jewish until I was sent to Israel by a Catholic priest! The rebbe found my answer in the Ritva. He told me right then and there that we were going to become *chavrusos* from that day onward. And that's exactly what happened.

"Now I'm not going to tell you that I became a *gaon olam* (a world-class scholar) in one day, because that's not even slightly true. In fact, the miracle that occurred that morning rarely happened again. But on the days that I was hot, I was really hot. When my brain opened up, I was on the mark. The questions I would ask were usually straight out of Reb Baruch Ber or the Kehillas Yaakov, and my answers were *mamash* good! And this was all without knowing how to read a Gemara.

"This development didn't make me feel conceited. I looked at it as if it were a gift, so to speak, from heaven. It was Hashem's way of showing me how rich my learning could be all the time if I really put in the effort."

"So what happened?" I asked him. "How did you get from Moreh

Derech to our yeshivah?" Implicit in the question was another, unspoken, query: Where were you for all those months after you left your first yeshivah and before you came to us?

"Reb Zack," Mordy said patiently, "people don't really understand *baalei teshuvah*. They cannot realize how difficult, how utterly challenging it is to leave your former life behind just because it's the right thing to do. Yes, I loved learning more than anything in the entire world. Yes, that was what I wanted to spend the remainder of my life doing. But that didn't stop me from experiencing a sense of loneliness and longing when I walked outside and saw a flock of birds overhead, when I caught a glimpse of a huge silvery orb hanging over my head at *kiddush levanah*, and all I wanted to do was drop everything, grab my camera and take picture after picture. But some of the guys at Moreh Derech would have never been able to appreciate such a concept. They would have scorned my behavior. They would have given me *mussar*. They would have said, 'How is it possible that such a future Torah scholar would waste so much time on something so banal as taking photos?'

"Now, I had seen them do this kind of thing to some of the other *bachurim* about the hobbies they enjoyed, and I didn't want to be next. I'm not saying that all *baalei teshuvah* are like this. But I was putting in 12-hour days, immersing myself in the Gemara. I was studying with my morning-*seder* rebbe, and I was learning with a bunch of other guys, constantly straining my brain to get to the root of the complexities. After a while, I had to unwind, and the only activity I really wanted to do was grab my camera and get out to the untamed wilderness to capture it on film.

"You know how it is, Reb Zack. A person can try to suppress his feelings, and maybe he'll be successful at first, like a person who is holding onto a rope that's keeping him from falling down a mountain. But eventually the rope is going to fray until it just rips apart. Then it takes everything he has just to hold onto a ledge until helps comes.

"I didn't want that to happen. I had been at the yeshivah for quite a while, probably close to a year. I decided that I needed a break. I convinced myself that it would be easy for me to be *frum* when I was out by myself in the middle of nowhere. The more I thought about this, the more convinced I became that this was something I had to do. When I finally worked up the courage to discuss my plan with my rebbe, he took one look at my face and realized that I had made up my mind and I just wanted him to rubber-stamp it for me. Well, he refused. He told me that when I was being successful and happy in my learning, I shouldn't leave for an extended period. He suggested that I take a week off instead, but I rejected that idea. I ended up walking out of his office and slamming the door on my way out."

"Where did you go?" I asked.

"I went to the wilderness," he replied, "trying to discover myself in the deserts of Israel. I volunteered for the society that guards Israel's natural sites and reserves. Sometimes I was posted at Nachal David, which is adjacent to Ein Gedi. Sometimes I was sent over to the Judean Desert. It was our job to make sure that people didn't litter or harm the environment. We drove around in jeeps and ensured that everybody left the hiking trails before it became too dark to see. We fed the wild goats and gave detailed reports to the government agency overseeing us. It was a completely different, yet strangely satisfying life out there under the open skies. The interesting thing was that I saw Hashem everywhere I turned. He was at the top of the mountains, in the glittering flowers that sprouted everywhere I turned and in the dark and dusty earth that produced so much with a little bit of work. Sometimes I even led groups, showing them sights off the beaten track. It was a good, busy life.

"But as much as I denied it to myself, I wasn't really happy. Yes, I had the opportunity to take as many photos as I wanted and they were wonderful. But the truth was, I simply missed learning. I missed straining my brain over a *svara,* missed dueling with my rebbe or study partner. I missed the intellectually stimulating and challenging yeshivah environment. On the other hand, I loved the freedom of being able to be whoever I wanted to be. Bottom line, I was filled with serious conflict. I felt differently about it every day. One day, I would decide to return to Jerusalem that evening, and then I'd photograph an amazing sunset and be filled with such awe that I'd change my mind again. It was tearing me apart inside! I just kept on pushing off my return."

"So what brought you back?" I asked him. "What was the turning point that made you realize that yeshivah was the life for you?"

"I'm getting there," he told me. "I'm getting there." He stopped talking for a second and lifted his coffee mug as if he was going to take another swallow. He glanced down into the mug and realized that it probably wasn't going to taste so good after all this time. He set it down on the desk and resumed talking.

"Remember those yeshivah guys who got lost in the mountains

a while back?" he asked me. I nodded my head as I remembered the *Tehillim* that was said in every yeshivah and seminary until the boys had been found.

"Well I was part of the team that found them."

"They were foolhardy kids in many ways, sure that they were invincible," Mordy said. "They figured that they knew everything about survival, so they evaded the patrols that check all the major hiking areas at the end of the day. But they flaunted the rules. They didn't realize that they were supposed to return at a certain hour. They didn't know that they had turned off the regular path. They thought they knew everything but knew nothing. They figured that they would climb up to the summit of the nearest mountain and spend the night there, make a barbecue, enjoy themselves, sleep out in the middle of nature. But when it got dark, it got really dark. Suddenly they weren't feeling so brave anymore. Most of the *bachurim* realized that they weren't that keen on spending the night among the mountain lions. Then one of them slipped while climbing and almost fell off a 50-foot drop to his death. That got them really scared. They were scared enough that they decided to face whatever punishment they would be given so that they could be rescued. But it wasn't that simple.

"You have to understand," Mordy said, "the cell phone companies don't usually put up antennas in the middle of the wilderness. Why should they? Almost nobody walks around there so why tangle with the environmentalists over an area where they won't make money anyway? This translates into a reality of no signal. You can't make or receive a call. It's as if you're cut off from the whole universe. That's what happened to those kids. When they got scared and tried to call, their phones didn't work. They couldn't get a signal, and that really freaked them out! They decided to continue to the summit, which they conservatively estimated to be not more than an hour away. But they were mistaken. It would have taken them more than three hours to get there, if everything would have gone right, which of course it didn't.

"One of them had a flashlight. They used it sparingly to conserve the batteries. But they were trekking through an undeveloped area with an extremely weak light. One of them tripped over a root and twisted his ankle. He tried to walk and collapsed in a heap. They were clueless when it came to first aid, but even they could tell this was serious. That's when they understood that they wouldn't be able to go any further. They would have to remain right where they were, on the side of the mountain, at least until morning arrived, and some of them could go for help. They were afraid of the wild animals, and hungry as well. So they decided to clear a large space, move away all the underbrush and rustle up a major bonfire. This way they would be able to cook their food and maybe someone would see the fire and realize that there were people lost out in the mountains. They ended up building a huge fire in the middle of a nature reserve. I will give them credit and say that they definitely attempted to keep the fire under control. But the winds were somewhat fierce that night, and somehow, some of the adjacent underbrush had caught fire before they even realized it. Within minutes, there was a blaze going!

"It did not take us long to realize that there was an emergency happening in real time right along the side of the mountain. The only way to get there in time to stop the fire from spreading was by helicopter. That meant that the army would be getting involved. But by this point, there was no choice. The army sent a helicopter that was specially designed for fighting fires.

"They got there in time to put out the fire, but there was no place for them to land. They had to fight the fire from the air. Eventually, they got it under control. But since there was no clearing where they could land, the kids would have to remain by themselves on the edge of the mountain in an area acrid with smoke and waterlogged ground. I could only imagine how distraught they must have been feeling. Two of us volunteered to hike over to them with some food, and to keep them company until the morning. I knew my way around the mountains since I had rescued people before.

"It took us a few hours to get to them. They were far off the beaten track and it was the middle of the night. After a while, we began to smell the smoke, and we knew that we were getting closer. You should have seen their faces when we stepped out from between the trees, faces plastered in sweat, arms and legs cut and bruised from our hike through the mountains. They surrounded us, overjoyed that someone had arrived. They were desperate to know what was going on. I informed them that a lot of people had been really worried about them for a while, especially while the fire was rapidly spreading. Some of their friends, who hadn't gone on the night hike, had alerted the yeshivos and parents as soon as they realized that their friends were out of signal range. Then, when they heard about the fire, everyone had gone crazy. Nobody knew what was going on. The police had no idea, and we hadn't known anything either, because the boys had purposely eluded us and hid until we were gone.

"I treated the boy with the sprained ankle. Then we handed out the food we had brought, and everyone finally began to relax after the traumatic night. But the young boy with the swollen ankle was in an extreme state of pain. It was a bad sprain, just short of a break actually. Whatever painkillers I gave him didn't do the trick. He was crying quietly, trying to be brave, and it broke my heart. But there was nothing I could do for him. And then the most extraordinary thing occurred. I saw a pocket-sized Gemara sticking out of his backpack. I asked him if it was his, trying to divert his mind from the pain. When he said that it was, I then asked him if he wanted to learn with me. The boy, whose name was Yaakov, was shocked that I was *frum* and capable of learning, but he immediately agreed. I would have done anything to help him. The fact that he wanted to learn was an added bonus. I hadn't learned for quite some time and I missed it keenly.

"He had a pocket-sized *Mesechta Horayos,* and we set a goal for ourselves to cover as much of the tractate as we could that night. He had studied it before, so we didn't have to spend a lot of time figuring out *p'shat.* Yaakov was a very serious *bachur* who had never done such an irresponsible thing before. He felt like a real fool, especially since he would be returning home in an injured state. But he definitely knew how to learn. This kid read the Gemara fluidly; he almost never had to pause. He really knew his stuff and was able to explain it. We stayed up and studied while everyone else went to sleep. As the night passed and the smoke dissipated, we climbed the internal mountain. I found myself extremely impressed with him. I could tell that he was fatigued beyond belief, both from his earlier climb and the fact that he was injured. Now he was throwing himself into the Gemara and he was happy and forgetting his pain. I enjoyed that learning, that sweet sweet learning, more than anything I had done since I had left yeshivah months before.

"We made a *siyum* on the *mesechta* as the sun started to rise over the desert mountains, illuminating the barren hills. That was when we began to talk and he asked me what I was doing volunteering in a rescue unit. I had nothing to say in my defense. All the arguments that had been so clear suddenly seemed like the biggest fluff in the dim morning light. I knew that if I tried any of them on him, he would just blow them out of the water. Suddenly I understood that I had made a big mistake. I motioned for his Gemara, and I held it up and kissed it. I knew that for the rest of my life and it wouldn't matter how long I lived, I would love that tractate with all my heart. For it was *Horayos* that saved my life, showed me the error of my ways.

"He looked into my eyes and he knew that I had seen the light, and he was happy. I knew that I was going to make *Horayos* into my *Olam Haba* tractate. I was going to study it again and again until I knew it backward and forward. I would bring it along with me to the World to Come. The whole night was one of those rare moments of true clarity. A few hours later the experience was over. A bunch of rescue personnel arrived and evacuated my friend. Eventually I arrived back at my room, took a shower and, since I had been up the entire night, tried to sleep. But sleep wouldn't come. Every time I closed my eyes, all I saw was Yaakov sitting with his Gemara, swaying as he chanted the words. I knew that I had to go back to the place where it all began. I couldn't go on this way anymore.

"But I didn't want to return to the same yeshivah. I wanted to go to a yeshivah where the guys had been learning for years, where they came from families and backgrounds where learning was familiar to them. It was now or never. I realized that I was going to have to make a major decision right then, before my life reverted back to its normal routine and my night-time experience just became a memory of the past. I sat down on my bed, closed my eyes and thought things through. I wanted to go back to learning, that much was clear to me. But the place should be more relaxed, the guys should want to have a good time after they finished *seder*. I wanted to enjoy the yeshivah experience and Moreh Derech had been much too intense. I was going to find myself another yeshivah. I was definitely good enough for almost anywhere I decided to go. Even after all the time I had spent trekking through the wilderness, I could still recall many of the *sugyos* I had studied in depth.

"That's when I remembered Kedushas Yisroel, your yeshivah. I recalled going there with a friend one Thursday evening. Even then I picked up on the relaxed atmosphere, how every guy was accepted for who he was. I thought about all the guys who had been learning seriously in the *beis midrash* while I was there. I also thought about some of the other guys who had been sitting in one of the *shiur* rooms hanging out for a while before going back inside to learn some more. And I knew that Kedushas Yisroel was the place for me. So I came.

"Right off the bat, I could sense that you and I would become close, Reb Zack. I just knew it. I could see it in the way you related to the guys and in how they related to you. I could see it in the bottle of Coke that you keep under your chair. How you cared for every guy. How the *bachurim* and the administration trusted you. You were clearly very special, and I was content to allow the relationship to develop over time. It probably would have taken us even longer to become so close, if not for that e-mail. You realized that I was troubled. You *chapped* right away, precisely because you are so attuned to the needs of the *bachurim* around you. I knew that here was a man to whom I could open up, who would give me good advice. It didn't even matter that we only know each other for such a short time, because after speaking to you in learning and spending that memorable Friday-night meal at your home, I knew that we would be talking to each other in the near future." He paused for breath, and I felt my cheeks burning from his complimentary words. Was I blushing?

"The e-mail was from my mentor Cardinal Jason Frost. He sends me e-mails from time to time and I write back. It's the least I can do for the man who sent me to study Torah, who changed my life with his persistence and dedication to my welfare. His e-mails are normally cheerful and fun, but suddenly everything has changed. I can sense it between the lines. Something is wrong in his life, and I know that he's trying to tell me that. But at the same time, he doesn't want to disturb my learning. I'm just not sure what to do. Maybe I should go home and visit him. I haven't been back for a while. Maybe this would be a good time to go. I mean, he's an old man. If it's a health issue, then I should be there for him. Even if it's something else, I should probably go. It's just that I was finally getting back into it ... I don't know what to do."

He stopped talking, having run out of steam, and sat there looking at me, earnestly waiting to hear the nonexistent words of wisdom that he was sure I would say.

"You are obviously very worried about your friend," I said to him. "I think that your concerns are justified. I just think you should call first, reply to his e-mail, maybe even ask him point-blank if there's something wrong. Then, based on his answer, you'll know if you have to go back to America or not." His eyes were on me searching, troubled, anxious.

"Don't worry, Mordy," I said, "I'm sure you'll figure this thing out over the next few days. Go out now and learn for a few hours. When it's afternoon in America, come back to this office and use this phone to call the cardinal. O.K.?" I knew that one way or another, we'd be getting to the bottom of this very soon.

~

I gave Mordy the key to the office and told him to make the call whenever it was convenient for him. It was a good day of learning. Afterward I made my way home.

Avigail was waiting for me outside the building. We were going out to a restaurant for dinner.

By the time we left the restaurant it was nearing 11 o'clock.

And then as we got into the taxi, I felt my phone vibrating. I looked at the screen and saw that Mordy had sent me a text message from his phone. I read it in shocked disbelief.

Frost in the middle of crisis. Needs me to be there for him as soon as possible. Am booking a ticket on the next flight home. Be in touch. Mordy.

Suddenly I was struck by a feeling that things were spiraling out of control. I don't know why, but I wondered what other bad news would be hitting us in the near future.

Dietrich Eberhart

Liverpool, England
June 14, 2009

The room was long and narrow, with a floor made of plywood with a cheap finish. The furniture was simple. A bare scratched table set squarely in the middle of the room surrounded by heavy chairs. The men around the table looked as if they had been in and out of jail, which was probably true. While they waited, they drank. The more they drank, the more the room smelled. It was not a pleasant aroma. This was the Neo-Nazi headquarters of the United Kingdom. They were a large group, but mostly unorganized. This meeting had been called because that needed to change.

There was no time for meaningless pleasures like beating up innocent old people on the trains any longer. There was no time for roaring down quiet suburban streets on motorcycles without mufflers. They needed to organize and begin carrying out specific goal-oriented tasks designed by the organization's leaders. The eight men sitting and drinking in the stifling room were the accepted heavyweights in this part of England. They needed to be told what to do because they weren't the brightest individuals. They were coarse, tough guys with tattooed torsos. Most of them were uneducated, but every one of them was street smart. They could follow instructions if given the proper incentive.

~

The BMW sped through the Liverpool streets toward the sprawling warehouse near the docks. The tires drove through puddles pooling at the corners near the drains, spraying water in every direction. Passersby looked curiously at the car. But the tinted windows precluded anything more than that. Dietrich Eberhart sat in the backseat with Karl beside him. Munich drove. He was in a hurry, and it was evident in the way he handled the car. Munich had programmed the GPS, and he followed the detailed instructions, taking turn after turn into a labyrinth of tiny streets sandwiched between huge factories.

The last street ended in a cul-de-sac, where a large factory held court. There was a chain spread across the entranceway, and Munich impatiently beeped his horn. Two figures emerged from the side of the yard: giant men in leather vests, short-cropped hair illuminated under the dull light of a solitary streetlight. Munich stuck his head out the window and told them to move the chain aside so he could drive in. The bigger man took one look into the car and told the second man to move the chain. The car moved forward, finally coming to a halt outside a loading dock at the rear of the yard.

Karl and Munich got out first and inspected the yard. As they turned back to the car, a light went on over the dock, and a small door to the side of the main entrance was opened. A man stepped out into the night, hands outstretched in greeting.

"Mr. Eberhart," he called out in delight, "good to see you again."

This was Ian Thonson, second in command to the leader of Liverpool's underworld. His organization ran most of the illegal operations in this part of the country. He directed the Neo-Nazis on a whim, consequently it didn't run as efficiently as the rest of his operations. Dietrich was here to change that. Thonson was about half a head taller than Munich, and he regarded the German through squinting eyes. Munich led the way with Dietrich and Karl following behind as Thonson directed them into the warehouse proper.

They walked through darkened rooms, ignoring the scurry of the rats in the shadows. Thonson led them to a door. Munich and Karl scanned the room from side to side as they accompanied Dietrich, who didn't seem the least bit nervous. Thonson pushed the door open and they entered the back office. The men seated around the table rose and welcomed them warmly. Dietrich was a king to them. They respected his ideals and they admired his business sense. They all knew of his empire and would have loved to work for him. He took the place at the head of the table that had been left vacant for him, and the men sat down, following his every move with eager eyes.

"We have spoken in the past," Dietrich said in crisp English, the merest hint of an accent accompanying the words. "Back then it still wasn't time to commence action. But now we are much closer to a time when everything will come out into the open. It's time to crank it up a notch." The men nodded, hungrily waiting for instructions. They knew that if Dietrich Eberhart said it was time, then it was time. Nobody second-guessed Dietrich Eberhart.

"It is time for the skinheads to be seen," Dietrich said decisively. "I want the people of England to know that something is going to happen. Everywhere around the world, the Neo-Nazi movement will be gathering steam. I want Britain to know that you are no longer afraid of getting caught by the police. You are acting from a position of power. Whatever they can do to you cannot be matched by what we can do to them!"

"What *can* we do to them?" asked a swarthy man known as Jack Sting.

"I can't reveal everything yet," Dietrich said. "But believe me that it's as simple as reading instructions out of a book." That was a cryptic line, and the men sitting around the table weren't convinced.

"Look, gentlemen," Dietrich said, "how many of you heard about the general in America who went crazy and disabled all of those missiles, leaving a large section of the United States unprotected? Who heard about that? Anyone?" One of the men raised his hand.

"I heard whispers," he said. "What about it?"

"I made it happen," Dietrich said quietly. Most men when making such a statement would have been laughed out of the room. But when Dietrich made such a claim, it was utterly believable.

"You wouldn't believe the power we have right at this very moment," he said, continuing to talk in that same serenely quiet, yet unmistakably powerful voice.

"I could turn the world upside down right this second. But that would be pointless and we would be wasting resources that should be saved for the proper time. Are you in? Decision time, gentlemen. What's it going to be? If you give me a yes, then I want to hear about the skinheads in the newspaper every single day. I want to hear about them smashing car windows. I want to hear about the people they beat up and the stores they break into, and the fact that the Jewish community is afraid to walk outside their homes. If you refuse, then you will never hear from me again. What's it going to be?"

The vote was unanimously in favor of Eberhart. The rise of Neo-Nazism in England and on the Continent was about to begin. This was just his first stop. He would be addressing the Americans in just a few short days, and he was confident of the outcome. They would come aboard just as the Europeans had fallen in line. It wouldn't be long before everyone would start to see things their way. The Fourth Reich was about to show itself.

22

Rafi Ganim

The Kolodover Rebbe's Home
January 31, 2005

That Shabbos was the most wonderful experience Rafi ever had in his entire life. Spending it at the Rebbe's home was an added bonus. He had fallen asleep under the warm European-style feather quilt in a matter of minutes, and he had never felt anything quite as comfortable. As he drifted off, his mind replayed the encounter with the Rebbe. He saw the Rebbe's warm eyes as they conversed together. He pictured the moment when he first realized he was looking at a portrait of the very man who had appeared to him in so many dreams. He recalled the song the chassidim had sung; a song that still coursed through him like a magical elixir. However he thought about it, he still couldn't believe that the previous evening had actually happened: From meeting Naftali Kenighofer and getting an invitation to his home and life, to ending up in a bed at the Kolodover Rebbe's home, it had been nothing other than miraculous.

Then he slept.

The next thing he knew, sunlight was streaming through the window waking him up gently. The lace curtains bobbed in the breeze entering from the street outside. Rafi looked at his watch, worried that he had overslept and that it was already noontime. He breathed a sigh of relief when he saw that it was only 7:30. He didn't want to miss any part of this special day. He stretched luxuriously under the silken sheets and sighed with pleasure. Then he forced himself out of the bed and into the white shirt and black pants the Rebbe had provided for him to wear. He was relieved that he wouldn't stand out in his cut-off jeans as he did the night before. He left the room and found the kitchen. There was cake on a platter, an urn with hot water and coffee off to the side. He made himself a cup of coffee, and took a thick slice of the yeast cake, wondering if anyone who saw him would be annoyed that he had made himself at home. He was just about finished when a young *bachur* walked into the kitchen and stopped short when he saw Rafi there. It was the Rebbe's grandson. He asked Rafi if he wanted to come to the *beis midrash* with him. Rafi realized that this Shabbos was going to be extremely spiritual. He followed the boy toward the Kolodover *beis midrash*. He could hear a low rumble coming from the building as they approached. He wondered what the sound was.

"The Rebbe asks the chassidim to recite *Tehillim* every Shabbos morning before davening. That's what that sound is," the boy said.

The boy showed him to a seat near the front of the giant room, not far from the Rebbe's leather chair, handed him a *Tehillim* and withdrew. He opened it and quietly began saying the words to himself. He said each word slowly, savoring the taste, as if it was a particularly enjoyable piece of candy. He could understand the literal meaning of the words, but knew he was missing the essence. He was so engrossed in what he was saying, that he didn't even realize that the majority of the chassidim had finished and were donning their *talleisim*. The man sitting next to him handed him a *siddur* opened to the right place. Rafi began to daven the Shabbos morning davening for the first time in his life.

The davening proceeded without any major surprises. But by *Keil Adon* when the *chazzan* tried singing one tune, the Rebbe motioned him over. The next thing Rafi knew, they were all singing his *niggun* once again. The *beis midrash* was filled with an uplifting exalted song, and his heart danced and his mouth sang with fervor. He wished that it would never end. The remainder of the davening was beautiful, as well. Then there was a *kiddush*, and the Rebbe wished each and every one of his chassidim a personal *Gut Shabbos*.

Rafi was invited to join the Rebbe and his family for the morning meal. He found the *chulent* to be other worldly. The Rebbe sang *zemiros* in a rasping voice that was full of yearning. By the time they *bentched,* it was the middle of the afternoon. The house became still as everyone took a short nap. A peaceful silence descended on a contented world. The same boy woke him up for Minchah, and he joined the chassidim for *Shalosh Seudos* afterward. The Rebbe spoke, as the day came to a close, and Rafi strained to hear what the holy man was saying, the hoarse voice sending shivers down his spine. After they sang one last song, they *bentched.* Just as they finished, the lights of the main *beis midrash* came on bright and strong. All at once, Shabbos was over. The Rebbe made *havdalah,* after which he motioned Rafi to follow him into his private study once again.

A wall fan oscillated with a soothing hum as the Rebbe finished a simple *melaveh malkah* of a piece of *challah,* a portion of fish and a cup of coffee. He had invited Rafi to join him; but now that the critical moment was at hand, Rafi discovered that he was much too overwrought to eat. The Rebbe spoke little as he ate, glancing into an old *sefer.* From time to time, he hummed a fragment of song to himself. When the meal was over, he washed his hands and *bentched.* Then he got up from his chair, went to the closet in the corner and asked Rafi to bring over a chair.

The Rebbe told him to climb on the chair and to reach up to the highest shelf and to bring him what he found there. Rafi did as he was told and strained himself, reaching further and further back until his fingers touched on something at the far corner of the shelf. He withdrew it from the closet and saw that it was a photo album: a large, old-fashioned photo album, discolored metal rings holding it together.

"Is this what you want?" he asked the Rebbe.

The Rebbe nodded.

"Come here," the Rebbe said. "Sit down beside me at the desk."

The Rebbe opened the album carefully, separating those pages that had fused together from years of disuse.

"You say that your family lives in Rishon LeTzion," the Rebbe said. "That's very interesting. Here, look at this." Triumphantly he moved the album toward Rafi, who peered inside expectantly. Whatever he had been expecting, this hadn't been it! Several teenaged boys stared back at them. One of them was clearly religious as evidenced by long *peyos* framing his face, and a straggly beard. He was smiling in a gentle way, one arm around the boy standing beside him. The other boy was *chassidish* as well, but you could tell that it wasn't going to last. His *peyos* were very short, almost imperceptible, and the beard was trimmed. There was a look of melancholy in this boy's eyes; it was clear that he was not a happy person. But his arm was around the other boy as well, and the bond between them was clearly very strong.

"That was me and David," the Rebbe said.

"David who?" Rafi asked as a sudden clarity hit him full force.

"David, my brother," the Rebbe replied.

There was something so familiar about the teenager, and for a long moment, Rafi couldn't figure out what it was. But suddenly, he pictured the boy in an army uniform and beret, and his breath caught and he felt faint.

"David, my brother," the Rebbe said again. "The man you probably call Abba. Welcome to the family!" He embraced Rafi, and he trembled as he did so. Rafi knew that the older man was crying.

"But if you are my uncle, how come we have never met until this Shabbos?" Rafi whispered. "How could it be that I missed out on such a wonderful life? Why did I grow up with no knowledge whatsoever of what Shabbos was? I should have been a part of all this. This should have been my life!! How could I not know anything about anything?!"

He was crying bitterly now, the tears rolling down his cheeks, weeping, his shoulders heaving with remorse for all the missing years. There were times when he had felt there was something missing, some emptiness, yet he did not have a clue where to start looking for the answer. All the time, it had been here, waiting for him. He had a family that knew the truth, that had the answers, that were truly happy. They didn't deny the fact that there was a G-d as his father did. How could such a thing have happened? How could a boy who had been raised in such a wonderful family have given it all up and thrown it all away like a bag of trash. How? And why had his family allowed him to disown them?

"How could you have let him go?" he asked the Rebbe reproachfully. "How come you didn't go after him, beg him to return, remind him who he was? How could something like this have happened?"

The Rebbe walked over to the closet and removed a leather case from a lower shelf. "Here," he said to Rafi, "this is my uncle's violin. I want you to play the *niggun* right now!"

Rafi opened the case and picked up the violin, placing it tenderly beneath his chin, holding it like a baby. He lifted the bow to the instrument and ran it lovingly over the violin, which emitted a sobbing sound. Then he played the *niggun*, and the sound soared through the room, like an angel singing, rich notes of music come to life. Both of them were crying together as if they would never stop.

The Rebbe said, "You think we didn't try to bring him back? You think I didn't go after him to his army base, to try to bring him home?! Of course I went. Of course I tried. But he was a lost cause. The war ruined so many, and those who were left were stolen by the kibbutzim. David, my beloved brother, was stolen from us. Yet, here you are.

"It's all come together like *Der Feter hut gezugt vet zein* (like the Uncle said it would). But who can really understand why people do what they do? Here, sit down at the desk. I'll ask your cousin to bring us some tea, and then we'll talk. I'll tell you everything I know, and then, you'll finally have some idea of our family's past. But even I don't know everything. Even I don't know why the *goyim* decided to become part of our lives." He sighed heavily. "Sit here beside me. You're part of my *mishpachah*. I feel almost as if my long-lost son just returned home from far away. Ah, *Baruch Hashem* for Naftali Kenighofer. What a *tzaddik*! Come sit down and I will tell you. But I must warn you, Rafi. The immediate history of our family is a sad story. There was happiness as well, but there is so much sadness, so much pain. You're listening? Good. Listen and learn from the deeds of the righteous what we should and shouldn't do. Because even the *tzaddikim* can make mistakes, and when that occurs, the ramifications can be catastrophic."

PART TWO

23
Heinrich Eberhart

Hamburg, Germany
April 12, 1935

"Come in, Dieter. Come in and have a seat."

"Thank you, Heinrich."

"What brings such a distinguished businessman to my office? Truly a great honor!"

"Please, Heinrich, the honor is all mine. I have been looking around for quite some time for the perfect partner for a new venture that I would like to launch in the immediate future. You have been recommended by many as an honest businessman with astute ingenuity. I'm impressed with what I have heard."

"Gerta," Heinrich called out. An older woman appeared in the doorway of the office. "Please bring Herr Sernteiner a tall tanker of beer and some pastry. Other than that, I do not wish to be disturbed. Thank you. Now, Dieter, why don't you tell me about this proposition of yours. I am all ears."

"Thank you, Herr Eberhart." Sernteiner said. He took a deep breath, cleared his throat and looked around the office briefly before continuing. "As you know," he said, "my construction company has been developing successfully over these last few years. In fact, the government has recently contacted me regarding an exciting new project, which I think could prove beneficial for both of us."

"And that is ..." prompted Eberhart.

"They have commissioned my firm to design the planned extension of the Autobahn, Germany's premier highway."

"Most impressive, Dieter," Eberhart said. "I have to congratulate you on procuring such an important contract. Obviously, it's a reflection of the prestige you and your firm have earned in the business community."

"Thank you, Heinrich," Dieter said, inclining his head graciously. "I must tell you, when I received the call from the government, I understood immediately what they intended. Quite a number of firms have tendered bids for the job, and I realized that my offer must have been the one accepted. I was thrilled, but I was also slightly apprehensive at the same time. On the one hand, a successful outcome would catapult my firm among the top construction firms in the country. You know as well as I do that with the ongoing recession, this is like manna from heaven. But on the other hand, I know what a tremendous task this is going to be. I know how many tractors, steamrollers and other types of equipment will be needed to facilitate an efficient operation. I could imagine the amount of money this is going to take. For a moment, I panicked, wondering if I would be able to make this happen.

"Then I decided to make you an offer." Dieter sat up a little straighter in the chair and looked Heinrich right in the eye.

"Heinrich Eberhart," he said, "your firm is nearly as large as mine. You have almost as much equipment as I do. You possess a well-deserved reputation as an honest man. I would like you to join with me on this project; to become my partner in the construction of this next phase of the Autobahn. Are you interested in my offer? Will you consider it?"

Eberhart wasn't caught unawares by the offer. It was true that they were bitter business rivals. But it was eminently clear to him that Dieter Sernteiner's firm couldn't pull this project off without him. He was surprised that it had taken Dieter this long to make him an offer.

"We will be fifty-fifty partners, Heinrich," Sernteiner said. Heinrich nodded, knowing he could probably squeeze the man sitting in front of him for a few more percentage points if he was so inclined. He didn't do that. He appreciated how difficult it had been for Sernteiner to swallow his pride and ask Eberhart for assistance. There was no point in rubbing it in. And besides, just because Sernteiner needed help today didn't mean that the same would be true in the future.

"On behalf of my firm, I thank you for your kind offer, and I will get back to you by this time tomorrow. I appreciate your coming to see me," Heinrich said graciously.

"It was my pleasure," Serteiner said. "And I hope to hear from you soon with good news."

Eberhart called him the following day with his acceptance. He had known all along that this would be an option, and had done significant research on the project just in case, thereby enabling his board to come to a surprisingly rapid decision. They approved and gave their wholehearted blessings. Eberhart Construction Company was going places. And who knew, with the way that the new winds were blowing in Germany, this could be the beginning of great things to come. He had very high hopes.

Autobahn, groundbreaking
April 27, 1935

The day of the groundbreaking ceremony was overcast and cloudy. The smell of rain was in the air as Eberhart and Sernteiner rode to the construction site. From afar they could see the gaily colored balloons and the freshly painted podium festooned with streamers and drapery.

"Take a look at the contract," Sernteiner said, as he handed Eberhart a thick sheave of papers. "There have been some minor revisions. Read it when you get a chance."

"I will. Don't worry about that."

The Mercedes came to a halt alongside a row of luxury cars and government vehicles, most sporting swastika flags. The two businessmen emerged from the car to the applause of the assembled, and made their way up to the dais where the officials were already seated.

"There's Goebbels!" Eberhart said, putting a hand to his mouth. "This is most impressive. How did you get him to attend the event?"

"Oh, I know Goebbels from way back," Sernteiner said nonchalantly. "He's helped me tremendously in the past. He is here as a representative of the government. This is a great day for Germany, and a realization of the Fuhrer's dreams for his nation: a car for every family, and money, jobs and prosperity, and of course a first-rate highway. He will be addressing the crowd later. Come with me and I'll introduce you to him."

They walked through the crowd greeting people they knew and

were greeted in return. It seemed like almost everyone to whom they had sent an invitation had opted to attend. The movers and shakers were there, the big businessmen and their assistants. Eberhart noticed several bankers rubbing shoulders with the architects and lawyers. It was gearing up perfectly. The sun was peeking out from behind the clouds as they approached Goebbels. He was conversing with another man, but he smiled at Sernteiner and motioned for him to wait until he finished. Two minutes later, he came over to them. Putting his arm around Sernteiner, he asked for an introduction.

"Ahhh ... Eberhart," he said. "Heinrich, am I right? I knew your cousin. We went to school together. Yes, those were good times, hanging out in the village pub with Ulrich Eberhart, whenever we had a free period. We used to go rowing together on the lake. Those were the days, all right. It's a pleasure to meet you. I've heard a lot about you from Dieter here, and I understand that your firm is moving along in the right direction. If this goes well, there will be no limit to the projects that could come your way." They conversed for a few more minutes, before Goebbels was pulled away by another government official.

"He was more pleasant than I thought," Eberhart said.

"When he wants to be charming, there's no one nicer. But when he's in a rotten mood, watch out. He turns into a holy terror," Sernteiner said with a grimace. "I wouldn't rely on Goebbels telling Hitler about us," he continued. "But Himmler's a different story. You never know, maybe we could end up working for the SS."

"No end to the amounts of money there," Eberhart said. "Anyway, one thing at a time."

They headed to the dais and were warmly welcomed by the assembled. The master of ceremonies introduced the mayor of the nearby town, who gave the opening address. Goebbels sat through the speeches, impassive and uninterested, his mind clearly elsewhere, as the leaders of industry and commerce praised the government and construction firms for taking the next step toward a more modern Germany. When Goebbels spoke, it was uninspiring and lasted for exactly five minutes. Nobody was overly impressed. Eberhart and Sernteiner cut the ribbon, and shoveled some earth. The assembled broke for lunch. All in all, the day was most definitely a feather in their caps.

1935 and 1936 were good years for the Eberhart firm. A small percentage of German Jews came to the realization that their future in the country appeared bleak, indeed. Most elected to remain in the homeland of their fathers, disregarding the risk. Some decided to sell their assets and leave while they still could. One wealthy businessman was Willie Meyeroff, partial owner of Hamburg shipping yards and Meyeroff construction. The banks appraised his assorted properties and real estate into categories, after which they were placed on the market to become the possession of the highest bidder. Eberhart's firm was the first company to make a respectable offer. Apparently, it was the best offer, as well, because it was accepted. Eberhart had jumped at the opportunity, using nearly his entire cash reserve in the process, and he became the proud owner of one of the oldest established construction firms in the country. With no spare money in case of emergencies, however, he had left himself vulnerable and open to takeover, if he wasn't careful.

Riding high on the crest of success, Eberhart wasn't particularly worried about the prospect of being put out of business. He continued investing whatever money his firm was making in a wide range of projects: from the purchase of a diamond mine to the development of a new weapon for the army that was lighter and easier to use than any other weapon of its day. It seemed as if he had the Midas touch, because every venture that he turned to became wildly successful almost overnight. The world was moving toward war, and if there's one thing that can put an end to a depression, it's a good, long war. War means production, and suddenly there were jobs galore and money began to be of value again.

These were good times for the Eberhart family. Heinrich would bring his son, Ludwig, to the actual construction sites so that Ludwig would learn about all aspects of the business. The firm was so successful that Heinrich was even invited to meet with Himmler regarding the construction of a future base for the Waffen SS in a secluded area in Bavaria near Hitler's headquarters. Heinrich traveled to Berlin for the meeting, inwardly unnerved by the idea that he was on his way to a meeting with the man who controlled Germany's secret police.

Berlin, Germany
February 18, 1936

Berlin was vibrantly alive again after suffering for so long during the post-World War I depression. Heinrich looked around him in amazement. All around, the city was undergoing change: monuments were being erected, buildings were being cleaned and renovated, their facades cleaned of 30 years of grime until they gleamed. The sidewalks were packed with crowds of Berliners going about their affairs. The restaurants and cafes were doing a brisk business and he stopped on the major thoroughfare for lunch. But the lighthearted lift in the air was offset by the omnipresent armed men in black uniforms everywhere one turned. Bands of Hitler Youth roamed the streets, as well, intent on finding someone to torment.

They took one look at Heinrich and knew that this was someone with whom they had better not start up. Although he was dressed in a suit, and his shoes were highly polished, he still had the appearance of a man who could snap a plank of wood with his bare hands. In the short time that he walked the boulevards of Berlin, he witnessed no less than 10 people stopped and asked to show their identification papers. Berlin had become an army camp, and the average citizen toed the line. He searched for the address of the Gestapo headquarters. As he approached the building, he realized that although this was one of the city's most beautiful and well-planned thoroughfares, there was almost no one walking there. It was almost as if the people of Berlin didn't want to tempt the devil. Consequently, they stayed away from his lair.

Heinrich, on the other hand, had an appointment with the devil.

He was challenged for the first time by a tough-looking soldier of the Waffen SS, and ordered to produce his papers and the letter confirming his meeting with Himmler. Upon seeing that the letter was genuine, the soldier's suspicion changed to admiration and respect at the fact that he had been invited to meet with the great Himmler himself, third most powerful man in the Nazi regime, after Martin Bormann and Hitler himself. He walked up the stairs with dignity, while inwardly his heart beat like a drumroll. How many people had entered this building and never left? That was a question better left unanswered. He had to show his papers to a series of guards, until he was finally shown to an anteroom and told to wait until the great man was available. He sat on a hard straight-backed chair and perused the latest copy of the SS in-house publication, while the sergeant on duty looked on with eagle eyes. When he was finally called, he lifted his attache case and made his way toward the office, calmer now that he was inside the devil's home.

Himmler was standing at the window. He turned and watched as Eberhart entered, and motioned for him to take a seat. Eberhart looked with interest at the man who held the country in the palm of his hand. He was short and unimpressive. His stomach bulged against the fabric of his uniform, and his features were not memorable. But when he stared Himmler in the eye, he saw a fire inside, a fanaticism that likely explained the source of the man's power and mystery.

"My people tell me you are a great builder," Himmler began. "They say you are an architect as well — an original thinker, a great mind. I have heard many nice compliments ... " His voice drifted off, as if he were allowing Eberhart to realize how privileged he was to be conversing with the great Himmler himself.

"I am honored that I have been the recipient of such warm words," Eberhart said, choosing each word that he uttered carefully.

"Yes," Himmler said, waving his hand again. It was almost as if he couldn't keep his hand still. *What could he expect from someone who had been a chicken farmer?* Eberhart thought to himself.

"I want to construct the greatest army base ever," Himmler was telling him. "I want this base to include training areas for all sorts of operations. This is to be an all-around, all-purpose base, where I will be able to send Waffen SS recruits, and turn them into the hardest of men, ready to serve the Fatherland with all their considerable might. You are an architect. Think now. Tell me this moment what comes to your mind. What is your gut reaction? Open your mind to me. Show me a vision."

Eberhart already had a pad of architectural sketching paper on the giant desk and was beginning to sketch. The more Himmler talked, the more Eberhart drew. The picture that was beginning to emerge was highly intriguing. When Himmler finished speaking, he glanced down at the paper lying on the desk in front of him and was astonished to see a full outline for a comprehensive army base.

"You could do all of that?" he asked.

Eberhart was amused. "I'm a professional. I could have this done in a matter of months, with the assistance of the army's corps of engineers and a little help when it comes to cutting through the normal red tape associated with a project of this magnitude. After that, it's purely a matter of manpower. The more men I put on the project, the faster it gets built."

Himmler nodded his head, listening and agreeing with every word Eberhart was saying.

"I see," he said. "Would you mind leaving the plans here with me so I could look them over when I have some free time?"

"It would be my pleasure," Eberhart said.

"You're partners with Sernteiner in building the Autobahn, correct?" Himmler asked him, evidence of the memory for which he was famous.

"That's correct," Eberhart said.

"Well then," Himmler said, "thank you for coming to Berlin. We will be in touch. Germany needs talented people like you to build the Fatherland. Heil Hitler!"

Heinrich Eberhart walked out of the dreaded building with a bounce to his step and joy in his heart. He had made it! To become Himmler's protégé was like reaching the absolute pinnacle of success in the Germany of the '30s. Eberhart was as good as there already!

Even as he built more and more, and overextended himself much more than was prudent for a company such as his, and certainly more than his father would have ever done, Heinrich Eberhart placated himself with the certainty that the orders were going to arrive from Berlin any day, informing him that he was in charge of a huge new project of maximum security. But those papers never arrived. Instead, others came, and those changed everything.

He had arrived at the office early that morning, energized and ready to face the world. He had been about to enjoy a cigar when his secretary brought in the mail. The majority of it was standard material, but there was one official-looking package, stamped with official-looking stamps. The envelope was made of expensive, embossed vellum. Eberhart felt a rush of excitement as he reached for it first. *It must be from Berlin informing me of a meeting to discuss the army base; it must be!* But instead, the letter contained news of the absolute worst kind. The letter was written on official Reich stationery by some functionary in the Ministry of Highways for the Third Reich. The detailed information it contained had to be a mistake.

He read the letter in disbelief. The cigar fell from his lips, cartwheeling down the front of his shirt and almost burning a hole in it. He read the words with an ashen face, his heart beating wildly, feeling as if he was going to keel over and die at any moment from the shock. And yet, he couldn't prevent himself from rereading the letter.

April 15, 1936

To Herr Heinrich Eberhart,
President of Eberhart Construction Company

The order to build the new phase of the highway has been superseded by a direct order from Reichsfuhrer Heinrich Himmler. As of this coming Monday, all work on the project will be diverted. The area slated for the development of the Autobahn has been deemed appropriate for a new army base. Consequently, the highway must make a major detour around said area.

Geological testing must be undertaken by your company to determine whether the land around the future base is suitable for construction. Since your company is in charge of this project, it is your responsibility to provide the funding for the continuation of the project. This decision is not open to negotiation and we expect your firm to carry out all directives posthaste.

Heil Hitler
Franz Dambach
Secretary to the Minister of Highways

Eberhart sat back against the seat dazed by what he had just read. He could barely believe that this was not some sort of cruel joke! How could this be?! Why would the government revise the planned site of the army base and insist that he bear the costs of the change in plans, notwithstanding that he was building something for them and the fact that he had already invested millions into the development of the highway? The future looked bleak! Just repositioning all the equipment presently located in the construction area would be absurdly expensive. He was looking at imminent bankruptcy!

Another thought occurred to him: He had met with Himmler regarding the construction of the ultimate army base. Himmler had never gotten back to him on that. Suddenly, an army base was going to be built on the exact location that he was being ordered to vacate, while receiving nothing in the way of compensation. What was going on here?!

Automatically, his fingers lifted the receiver to call his partner, but Dieter Sernteiner was conspicuously out of town and unreachable.

Suspicions raced through his mind as he tried working out what had happened here. Somehow he sensed that Sernteiner must have sold him out. Sernteiner had convinced Eberhart to invest heavily in the Autobahn project. Now when he, Eberhart, would be forced to declare bankruptcy, Sernteiner would be free to pick up the pieces of the business. Eberhart couldn't fool himself. He had miscalculated in a bad way. He had sunk much too much money into the Autobahn project. There was no way for him to pull out now, or even to move in another direction. Anything new would mean much more money, and that meant failure.

Sernteiner with his limitless cash flow would step right into Eberhart's place as the number-one man on the German construction scene. Eberhart sensed, as well, that they would be using *his* plans to build the army base; the outline that he had left in Himmler's office at his personal request. Sernteiner, being unencumbered, would be the one granted the monumental project of constructing Himmler's ultimate army base. Their contract had a contingency clause to sever the partnership of a bankruptcy, and that was exactly what this was. Sernteiner would be legally able to terminate their relationship, as if his actions had been aboveboard the entire time. But Eberhart realized that the plot was all sinister from the start.

He couldn't know these things for sure, but all the parts fit. He had been a fool to enter into such a close partnership with someone who had always been a rival. What had happened to the famed Eberhart business sense? He envisioned Sernteiner on the phone with Goebbels, requesting that he temporarily abort the highway project, repositioned in another direction, so that he, Sernteiner, could be awarded the army-base project. Sernteiner had probably called in all his cards on this one, and now Eberhart was left with a shattered vision and a company that was as good as gone! Sernteiner need not be concerned about the money that he had invested, because the army-base project was tremendous! It meant a long-term lucractive government contract, paying enormous dividends that would dwarf anything the Autobahn project would have brought in. It was more than worth it for Sernteiner to sink his teeth into this new project, leaving Eberhart floundering without a life jacket!

He had entered the office that morning in an exuberant mood as a man with a glowing future, and left it a broken man. As he entered his car, he looked around at all the machinery still breaking ground for the highway, and he began to weep. Then, without another word, he drove away from the site, trying to figure out what to do.

Autobahn, construction site
April 17, 1936

As he drove from the site, it began to rain. The ground around him turned quickly to mud. He heard the tires squelching through the muck as they splattered the windows with muddy water. The weather matched his mood 100 percent. He was finished. It was the end of the line. He didn't know where he was driving. He just drove without thought, trying to put as much space between his project and himself as possible. He imagined Sernteiner laughing to himself as he thought about how well his plan had worked. Just the idea of that scene made his blood boil, and he wanted to kill the man.

Maybe I'm just making this up, he told himself halfheartedly. But he knew that his gut feeling was right. There had been no plausible reason for Sernteiner to have come to him in the first place, and the fact that he had, should have made him leery. Perhaps Sernteiner hadn't known about the army-base proposal at the time, but had wanted Eberhart as close to him as possible, so that he could disable him when the right opportunity presented itself, like the Mafia credo, "Keep your friends close and your enemies closer." Eberhart had stepped right into the trap. What an idiot he had been. He bashed his fist on the dashboard and barely felt the throbbing.

What was he going to do? What could he do? He didn't want to kill himself, but there was no possible way that he was going to be able to pay off his creditors. In a few days, they would be banging down his door, wanting their money back. What would he say: that the blunder was all the government's fault? Nobody would care. He might as well drive the car off a bridge right this second. He drove for hours, not knowing where he was, not caring, crying the entire way, as the car slid effortlessly down the hilly country roads. The weather cleared and the sun emerged from behind a cloud. He felt the beginnings of hunger pains since he hadn't eaten breakfast that morning and now it was past lunchtime. There was no point in starving to death. If he was going to kill himself, he would do it in a much quicker fashion.

Off in the distance he could see a village situated among the rolling hills. The image before him brought the tears back to his eyes. Ah, his beloved Germany! What a beautiful country. How corrupt were her leaders! He could see the red-roofed houses nestled among the trees, and there was smoke coming from many chimneys. He imagined a welcoming scene of a *frau* baking bread, raising her eyes to greet her husband as he returned from the fields for lunch. He felt a wave of desperation sweep over him as he turned the car toward the village, wanting to be among people, to drown his sorrows in a tall jug of German ale.

He was driving down a long winding road. He could see children frolicking outside near the haystacks. For a moment, he recalled his childhood and the somewhat carefree time it had been. It hadn't been completely carefree; he had been an Eberhart after all. But even an Eberhart was occasionally permitted to play with the other children. They had romped in the woods and climbed the tallest trees they could find, and had gone swimming in the cold lake.

The houses gradually inched closer together until he was in the middle of the village. He turned onto the main street of the village and drove slowly until he found the local tavern. He hoped this one served a decent lunch, and in fact, it did. He settled himself into a nook in the corner of the room. He ordered a tankard of ale along with the meal and began drinking as soon as it arrived. For all his hunger pangs, he picked at his food. All he wanted to do was to drown his sorrows in mug after mug of the spicy ale, until things began taking on a different perspective, and he made his peace with the situation. The landlord refilled the pitcher when he asked him to, and the other patrons either ignored him or looked at him with sorrow in their eyes for his plight.

It was all good. He was going to make it. Rising unsteadily to his feet, he held onto the table for support and made his way to the counter, placing one foot in front of the other very carefully, so as not to fall. He handed the man a large bill and told him to keep the change, and brushed off the man's heartfelt thanks. He figured that his money would be gone soon anyway, so he might as well do some good deeds with it while he still had it. Then, wishing everyone in the pub a good day, he swung open the door and strolled out into the peaceful and pleasant spring-afternoon air. The sky was clear now and the sun was beginning its descent as Heinrich Eberhart slowly made his way across the village street, toward a park on the other side.

Even from afar, he could hear the sounds of a spirited soccer match going on. Despite himself, he could feel his spirits lift at the prospect of watching a soccer game in progress. It had been years since he'd had the time or the inclination to spend the afternoon just relaxing, and he figured that he would indulge himself. He made his way along a pebble-strewn path to the patch of grass where the game was played. Boys were scrambling in every direction chasing the ball, kicking it, butting it with their heads and tripping one another. The goalies were being kept exceptionally busy fending off the attackers who kept on returning to try again. Eventually one team scored, and the boys pranced about jumping up and down and teasing the opposing team. Eberhart found himself increasingly sober and wanting to play. Yes, he was much older than them, but he could still show these kids a thing or two about how to play a good game of soccer.

Shyly, he made his way over to the knot of boys and asked them if he could play. One of the boys wanted to leave the game due to a slight injury, so the captain — after looking him up and down — told Eberhart that he could join them on a trial basis. But he could only play if he knew what he was doing. Eberhart grinned at that remark and took his position. From the moment the ball went into play, he was a different man. He was back in his youth, hair flying in the breeze, jersey out, skimming the ground as he ran without a care in the world. His entire goal was to get that soccer ball into the net. He dribbled the ball between his legs like the most talented player, and he tripped one kid after another until they realized that he was very good. They all ganged up on him, and even then he was able to put up a good fight, until he was overpowered by sheer numbers. They were about to get the ball away from him when he passed it to a teammate. Then, the captain got hold of it and moved it forward. Heinrich ran over to the goal and got into position. The captain passed it to Heinrich and he faked the goalie and swish! The ball flew into the net with a satisfying thump. Heinrich was surrounded by ecstatic youngsters all jumping on him and begging him to do that again, because the other team always won and they wanted to win that day.

He wanted nothing more than to remain right where he was and play ball. He was a child living a dream. He was enjoying himself so much that he thought about running away, moving to the village and playing soccer all day. The boys asked him to give them some lessons, and he showed them how to maneuver around their opponents. But it was growing dark, and the children began drifting home. Eberhart stayed where he was, content for the first time in a long time, having finally discovered something that made him happy. He wasn't chasing the money dream; he was simply living life in a real way, and that made him smile. He lay back in the fragrant grass, closed his eyes and smiled. Slowly but surely, probably due to the sheer amount of ale in his system, he drifted off to sleep right there in the middle of the soccer patch.

It was a sleep such as he hadn't experienced in a very long time; the type of sleep that children have. It was a restful slumber after a day spent in physical exertion. He was emotionally exhausted as well, having spent many hours driving while crying. The result of the two, combined with the fact that he had drunk many cups of ale and played a rough game of soccer, put him into a deep slumber. Everything was peaceful and calm and sweet. But suddenly, his mind began to wander off into the dangerous waters of what had happened that day, and was held in the grip of a nightmare.

He was moaning and sweating, as he saw the letter in his dream. He was opening the letter, and it was covered in blood, his blood. He wanted to scream and run away, away forever, to never return. But something was forcing him to open it up, and now there was blood on his hand and he screamed with horrifying force as he saw the first words on the page. He tried to thrust the letter out of his hand, but it was stuck and wouldn't go away. He cried out in his sleep right there in the middle of the grassy patch, beside the town square. The passersby looked askance at the figure lying on the grass having a bad dream, begging for help, for someone to have mercy on him and put him out of his misery. But nobody stopped to help the suffering man. Nobody really cared. They thought he was drunk, and Germans are no strangers to drunken men.

Then he really began to cry and to yell. He was sliding down an endless tunnel, heading toward an abyss from which he would never be able to emerge. Someone was shaking him by the shoulder, and he was being pulled away from the edge of that gaping hole, just seconds before he would have continued falling forever. He could hear the man's voice calling out, "*Bitte, Mein Herr*, wake up, *bitte*, please, wake up."

Slowly, with tremendous effort, he sat up and looked around himself groggily, not even sure where he was for a second.

"You're in a little village called Bendheim," the man said. "You are lying beside the town square. You were playing soccer before. I saw you. You were good. But obviously there is something wrong. You were crying in your sleep. You were clearly suffering. It seemed like waking you up was the right thing to do. I hope that it was."

"Oh, it's ... fine ... " Eberhart said. "I didn't know that I was carrying on like that."

"Well, you were sleeping. You couldn't have known. Is there something I can do to help you? Please, why don't you come to my home for dinner and a good night's sleep? I don't think that you're in any position to drive right now. Judging from your attire, you are not from around here, am I right?"

"Yes." Eberhart said, "I'm from Hamburg."

"You are quite a distance from home," the stranger said. "Allow me to introduce myself. My name is Joshua Weinberger. My family has lived in the village of Bendheim for nearly 250 years. Why don't you come home with me and tell me about your *tzaros*."

"My what?" Eberhart said.

"*Tzaros*," Joshua replied. "Your problems. Whatever it is that's making you so upset."

"Who said that I'm upset?" Eberhart asked the man.

"I can tell. Your clothing indicates that you are a successful man. But I can tell that you have received some devastating news recently. I don't know why, but I feel this. Am I wrong?"

The question was delivered with such sincerity, the eyes were so honest and friendly, that Eberhart felt that he could bare his heart to this stranger whom he had never before met. What difference did it make? He could speak it out, spill all and nobody would ever know. He was going to leave the village soon, never see these people again. Why not take advantage of the kind offer and unburden his soul to the man? Besides, this was the first time he could remember receiving an offer from someone who didn't know that he was a big businessman and didn't have an ulterior motive, didn't want anything from him. On the contrary, the man was offering him shelter in his home, a warm meal, a comfortable bed and he expected nothing in return! Suddenly, Eberhart was struck with suspicion.

"Why are you doing this?" he asked the man. "This has never happened to me before. Nobody does this kind of thing. This is unheard of, to offer someone a meal for no reason, to bring them into your home when they're lying drunk on the ground! How do you know that I'm an honest man? How could you do this to your family?"

"I know that you're an honest man. I understand your puzzlement at my behavior. But rest assured, in the Jewish world, this is the normal way to behave. My religion says be kind to your fellow man, assist him when he's in a bad state. And you, my friend, are in a bad situation if I ever saw one! Don't worry, you can trust me."

It was the first time in his life that Heinrich had met a religious Jew, and he was unsure how to respond to the warmth. It was uncomplicated. He was just being nice. It was difficult for Heinrich to comprehend the concept, especially after what had just happened to him that morning. But the steam had gone out of him. Gone were the questions, the suspicions, the fear that this man wanted to take advantage of him. He suddenly felt ready to go home with the man and get some healthy home-cooked food into his system. There were no more questions. He was just going to go. So they went.

They walked through the village. Wherever they went, the people looked at Joshua, smiled and wished him well, even though it was 1936 in Germany, and the Nazi Party had made sure that the Jews felt themselves extremely unwelcome in the homeland of their fathers.

They were a few feet away from Joshua's home, when a band of Hitler Youth passed them in the road, clad in their well-pressed uniforms, shiny daggers at their sides. Eberhart stiffened at the prospect of what lay ahead, because he'd seen the Hitler Youth in action countless times before, and knew what they were like when they were out of control. But the boys simply smiled at Joshua and wished him a pleasant evening.

"How come they aren't attacking you?" he asked the man as soon as the boys had walked passed.

"Here in Bendheim," Joshua said, "everyone still gets along. I don't know how much longer this will last, but for now, we are still on good terms with our neighbors. We hope that things will remain this way."

"That's the first ridiculous statement you have made since I met you," Eberhart said. "Haven't you heard of the Gestapo and the SS? Don't you know what they are doing to the Jews all around the country?

"This is one town where the troubles have not had any impact," Joshua replied with pride. "It says something about us, doesn't it?"

"Leave, man," Eberhart told him. "Leave while you still can get out. There are still some countries giving visas to Jews who want to emigrate. Take advantage of it!"

Joshua stared at Eberhart for a second. "I appreciate your sentiment," he said gently, "but enough about me for now. Let's get you settled for the night. My wife will serve you dinner, and then when you feel back to yourself, maybe we'll continue the conversation."

He motioned for Eberhart to follow him through a whitewashed gate and into a well-tended garden. In front of them was a spacious home in solitary splendor under a canopy of trees that were clearly hundreds of years old. There was signs of tender loving care on this property, from the carved wooden knocker on the door to the birdhouse in the trees. This domicile was a home above all else. Joshua led him into the house, down a long, dimly lit hallway, past a drawing room and living/dining room and into a warm and old-fashioned kitchen painted a cheerful yellow and white.

"Make yourself comfortable," he instructed his guest. Heinrich did just that, despite the fact that he was in the home of a man who had been a complete stranger, and despite the fact that the man was a Jew, and therefore, at least according to the state, someone to be despised. Eberhart had never been a man to care about the whole racial issue one way or another. It hadn't really mattered to him, or made a difference to his life. His line of work hardly ever brought him in contact with Jews. So the Jewish problem — as the papers called it — barely crossed his mind. He supposed he could understand why the Nazis were so vehemently against the Jews. There hadn't been sufficient jobs for the German people for a very long time, and many Jews held lucrative positions. It was a matter of jealousy and racism. He, being rich, hadn't devoted much thought to where he stood on the whole issue. But this Jew was unlike anyone he had ever met before. Heinrich was astounded by the respect and caring the man was showing him. Joshua was so caring to a man who didn't share the same religion, and who was a member of the nation that was so tormenting the Jewish people!

For a moment, Heinrich Eberhart felt intense shame at what the German people were doing to people such as Joshua Weinberger.

"Eat," his host urged him. Suddenly Eberhart realized how hungry he was. His host served him a delicious meal. Everything was so tasty that he wanted the meal to go on forever. For desert, Joshua served him a big slice of apple kuchen. He found, to his dismay, he was too stuffed to finish it. When he couldn't eat another bite, Joshua led him away from the table and up a short flight of stairs to a bedroom with a large bed, sporting thick quilts and feather pillows. He was provided with a pair of pajamas, and wished a good night. The moment his head touched the pillow, he was asleep.

Bendheim, Germany
April 18, 1936

Sunlight streamed into the room through a pair of blue-and-white checkered curtains. Disoriented, Eberhart awoke and looked around the room, trying to recall where he was and how he had ended up there. Then it all came back to him: the long drive away from the construction site, the crying as he drove, the drinking in the tavern, the soccer game with the village kids and Joshua taking him home with him. Joshua, a Jew, took a total stranger into his home and lifted him up when he was in the worst place he had ever been. He tried moving his arms and legs, and realized that they ached. He had strained his muscles playing soccer.

He swung himself to the side of the bed his body protesting with every move he made. Slowly he rose from the bed like a very old man and proceeded to get dressed. When he finished, he went to the window and moving aside the curtains, he peered outside with interest. The village was spread out before him, and he saw children on their way to school, jauntily swinging their briefcases and chatting with their friends. He heard the birds twittering gently from branch to branch and the sounds of their chattering and beeping made him smile. He was in a good mood. He didn't know what he was going to do to save himself from utter devastation, but that didn't mean that the solution wasn't lying right there in front of him. Sometimes, a person was just looking for it in the wrong place.

He hummed a tune as he showered, washing away the tension of the previous day. Relaxed, he was ready to go down the stairs and he took them two at a time. He sat at the kitchen table, and Joshua's wife proceeded to cook breakfast. His host returned from prayers while he was eating. Joshua greeted Eberhart warmly, inquiring whether he'd had a comfortable night. They ate together, and Eberhart found himself unburdening his heart to the kindly Jewish man.

He, a person who had always been so closed, so cold, so distant, was discovering that he was very similar to the man sitting next to him. Everyone had problems, everyone had *tzaros*. The only difference was how one dealt with those problems. What did a person do when caught in a web?

Heinrich told him everything. Joshua Weinberger listened closely to everything he had to say. When he finished relating the entire sorry saga from beginning to end, his host sat up and snapped his fingers together with a click that made Eberhart jump. He said, "There is one thing you can do!"

"And that is ..." Eberhart prompted him.

"You can visit the miracle worker and ask him for a *berachah*."

"The who?" Eberhart asked confused. "Ask him for what?"

"The miracle worker," Joshua explained. "He is one of the greatest *Rabbiners* of the Jewish people. He is a man who has assisted countless individuals from around the world who arrive at his door looking for a blessing for every manner of complication in their lives. People have traveled for months to visit the *Rabbiner* and to receive his blessing. Childless couples come for a blessing for children. Sick people ask for a blessing for good health. Poor people ask him to pray for them to receive financial assistance from heaven. And people whose entire worlds have collapsed around their feet have traveled to him, poured out their hearts to him and asked him to pray for them: to pray and intercede on their behalf, to ask G-d to revert everything back to the good. Nothing is out of G-d's reach, you know," he said to the stunned Eberhart. "If He decided to cast you down from your lofty position, He can bring you right back up to the top, just as easily!"

"Where does this *Rabbiner* live," Eberhart asked, "if I were to decide to travel to ask him for his blessing?"

"He resides in Poland," Joshua replied.

"But why would the *Rabbiner* give me a blessing?" Eberhart wondered. "I'm not a Jew. Why should he do such a thing for me?"

"Look," said Joshua, "I cannot promise you that he'll give you a blessing. That's up to him. But the fact that you aren't Jewish will not make him treat you any differently. He might not give you the blessing that you desire. But if that's the case, then he will have reasons for his actions, and *that* was definitely the best thing for you. I, for one, feel that it's worth a try."

"What's the name of his village?" Eberhart asked, not understanding himself anymore; not comprehending the drastic changes that had occurred in the mindset of the pragmatic, hard-nosed businessman that he had been just one day earlier.

"He lives in a small village called Kolodov. Lodz is the closest large city. That is where you need to go. From Lodz, you will have to hire a horse and wagon, and drive to Kolodov. But make no mistake, my friend," Joshua said, "the *Rabbiner* who dwells in Kolodov has helped many people in all sorts of ways."

Heinrich Eberhart reflected on the fact that a religious Jew had just called him "friend." He was struck by how strange the world could be at times.

"Why are you being so nice?" he asked his host. "Why did you take me into your wonderful home and treat me like a king? You fed me and gave me a bed in which to sleep. You don't even know me. I am a German, a member of the so-called 'Master Race,' the very same people who are tormenting your brothers. Why would you be so kind?"

Joshua smiled back at him, and he held out his hand to Eberhart and said, "Our forefather, Abraham, taught us to be hospitable and warm to one and all. I am merely attempting to live up to his expectations. Come, allow me to escort you to your car."

And Joshua Weinberger accompanied him to the automobile that was still patiently awaiting its owner near the town square. They shook hands silently, neither of them knowing what to say. Before Eberhart drove off, he turned to Joshua and told him that no matter how long he lived, he would never forget the man who had helped him on the day he lost everything.

The Kolodover Rabbiner

Kolodov, Poland
April 9, 1936

The train ride took an eternity, and provided Heinrich Eberhart with more than enough time to berate himself for taking such an unlikely step. He had considered driving to Kolodov in his Mercedes but he had never driven in Poland before, and he feared that were he to get lost in the middle of nowhere, he'd end up losing his car to some Polish bandits. So instead, he elected to take a train. Before taking off on this wild-goose chase he had phoned his wife to tell her that he had some business to transact that would take him out of the country for a little more than a week.

The train traveled through Germany, and he was reinvigorated by the change in the air. The average man walked with purpose these days. Gone were the days when a man would have to fill a wheelbarrow with cash just to pay for a loaf of bread; for that's how little money had been worth back then. Now people were earning a living wage once again. There was a feeling in the air that spoke of industry, that promised renewal and prosperity for everyone. The further he went, the prouder he became. He had always been a wealthy man, had come from a family that had always been wealthy. But the feeling of despondency that had held Germany firmly in its grip had succeeded in making itself felt all the way to the highest echelon. The average man had been left with no ambition and with no reason to live. Hope was what Adolf Hitler had given the German nation. For that, Eberhart was grateful, even though he didn't think another great war was what Germany needed at the moment.

The train passed through border control, and there was an hour's wait while the border guards fanned out through the train, checking people's documentation. They barely gave him a glance. The wait on the Polish side of the border was a joke. The Polish border guards were clueless at their job, and they couldn't have cared less. It was clearly about bribery as far as they were concerned.

Then it entered another country. Primitive. That was the word that screamed out to him. Somewhere along the way, the passengers had switched trains. The new train didn't have sleeping compartments. He was placed in "First Class," but that didn't stop the "upper-class" peasants from falling asleep on his shoulder as they snored their way across the countryside. The atmosphere was one of drunkenness. Eberhart thought to himself that if Germany ever needed to attack Poland, the battle wouldn't last more than three days. The only reason it would take that long was just because Poland was so big. The aroma of vodka permeated the train. The majority of the travelers didn't have the funds or the inclination to spend their hard-earned cash on bought provisions, so they made due with home-made sausages, black bread and herring all washed down by deep swigs from the vodka jug. The train reeked from the sea of unwashed humanity combined with their preferences in eating habits. Suffice it to say, it did not make for a pleasant traveling experience.

Yet, he wasn't in Poland for pleasure. So he gritted his teeth and pretended that he wasn't utterly disgusted by the people around him. He treated them politely, and they smiled at him with their rotting gold-capped teeth, and took another swig. He turned away in disgust. The train repeatedly broke down, and they were forced to spend time in a number of prime Polish locations. Eberhardt saw the utter poverty and a social order that was light-years behind their fellow Europeans in almost every way, as he lay down to rest in yet another dingy Polish inn.

Then the train would be repaired, and the conductor would finally locate the engineer and try to rouse him after a night spent swimming in vodka. That meant another delay. Finally the train would be on its way again and something else would happen, and the train would be forced to stop again. Through it all, he gritted his teeth and thought about why he was doing this; why he was putting himself through this. Eventually he learned how to sleep through the noise. He became inured to the odor and it ceased bothering him so much. Finally, the train approached the outskirts of Lodz, and it was time to alight.

~

Lodz, Poland
April 23, 1936

Lodz was a major metropolis, and Eberhart was impressed by the sea of people that surrounded him when he left the station. However the sensible thing to do was to get to Kolodov, so he could request a blessing, either be given one or not, and then leave and never return. This was no place for a civilized person. There was no culture here; no understanding of the finer things in life. These people were boors, and he was going to take care of what he needed to do and hurry home. He had no problem communicating with the people around him due to a Polish maid who had once been employed at his ancestral home. She had spoken to him in her mother tongue, and he had picked it up and could converse fluently, although it had been some years since he had spoken it. He asked a passerby for directions to the nearest wagon driver's depot. It was another world for him. He searched for a wagon driver who looked sober enough to trust. It was a hard search.

On the other side of the depot there was an old-style marketplace with multiple stands displaying a modest assortment of produce. The owner of every stand was calling out to the passersby to come and make their purchases at his stand because the produce was fresher and of better quality than everywhere else. The stands were doing a brisk business, and Eberhart watched as the peasants haggled and struck bargains, and then went off to throw the money away on beer and vodka. He was hungry, but he wasn't hungry enough to buy anything that had been cooked. He found a stand selling apples, and he purchased two of them. There was a tree with low-hanging branches off to the side, and he settled down underneath its shade to eat his apples and to watch the scene with amazement.

He returned to the wagon depot and noticed a wagon that looked somewhat less seedy than its fellow wagons. It had been freshly painted black with gold trim. The driver had a serious look on his face, his beard was trimmed and the cigarette he was smoking smelled a little less foul than those of the other drivers. Eberhart decided that he was going to be the one to take him to Kolodov.

"Kolodov," he said to the driver, while attempting to lift himself up onto the high seat beside the man.

The man mumbled something which Eberhart presumed was a refusal, since he was shaking his head at the same time. Removing a thick wad of zlotys from his pocket, Eberhart showed the man the money and asked, "How much to Kolodov?"

The driver licked his lips, glanced at the sun and began muttering to himself as he contemplated the offer. Eberhart removed a few bills and placed them on the seat. The man still hesitated. Removing two more bills, Eberhart laid them alongside the rest of the money and made it clear that this was his final offer. The man finally gave in and motioned grudgingly for Eberhart to take his place on the high seat. Then with a flick of the reins, the wagon moved away from the depot, in the direction of the road exiting the city. The wagon driver drove impatiently, driving the horses through the crowded streets as if he would not hesitate to mow down anyone in his way. But the citizens of Lodz were apparently used to such antics, and no one seemed overly concerned by the driver's lack of road manners. The crowd seemed to part effortlessly as they came crashing by, only to merge once again as the wagon trundled past.

As soon as they were out of the city, the driver allowed the panting horses to slow their pace, almost as if he felt that there was no point in rushing now that there were no pedestrians to harass. They were leisurely traveling along unpaved roads. Eberhart was thankful for the pace. The driver picked his teeth with a wooden twig for a while, and then began singing an old folk song. His voice merged with the birds' calls as the trees on either side of the road gave way to golden fields of grain. Eberhart watched the endless road and rubbed his eyes to keep from giving in to sleep. But the reflection of the sun on the horizon was playing tricks on his eyes, and he closed them briefly.

He was awakened by the feeling of a sharp object sticking into his side. He opened his eyes in pain and indignation, ready to retaliate. But there was nobody there besides the driver, and it was he who was jabbing Eberhart with the edge of a very sharp-looking knife. The driver was demanding the remainder of Eberhart's cash. If the money wasn't forthcoming within seconds, the driver continued, the birds would be pecking on his flesh, and no one would ever be the wiser.

It was unfortunate for the driver that he had underestimated his passenger, Eberhart reflected to himself, in the brief moment between arriving at complete wakefulness and the time it had taken him to formulate a plan of action. Due to family connections, Heinrich Eberhart had served Germany during World War I as a commissioned officer. He had undergone sufficient training to know how to deal with a Polish peasant who was getting a little too big for his breeches. Sighing, as if reluctant to comply, but afraid not to do so, Eberhart made a motion as if to reach into his pocket to take out the cash. The driver leaned forward as well, the better to see the money that would soon be his. In that precious window of opportunity, Eberhart struck.

Grabbing the driver's knife hand with both of his, he gave a sharp twist — so sharp that he heard the crack of the bone, as the knife was released and fell out of the driver's hand and onto the wagon floor. The driver opened his mouth to scream and utter some choice words. Eberhart put his fist solidly inside it, knocking out half his teeth in the process. The driver was crying in pain now. Eberhart reached to the floor, picked up the knife and slipped it into his own pocket, in case he had to deal with a similar scenario at a later time. Then having established that they were both able to understand each other, Eberhart ordered the man to drive without any more funny business, or he would have to throw him off the wagon and maybe break a few of his bones on the way down. The driver protested that his hand was broken and he couldn't hold the reins. Eberhart told him that he'd better, because if there were any other issues, he would simply confiscate the wagon and drive to Kolodov himself, regardless of the fact that he didn't know the way.

Once they had come to a mutual understanding of who had the upper hand, things settled down. The driver drove the wagon grimacing and keeping the injured hand in his lap while gripping the reins with his other hand. Now it was Eberhart's chance to sing. He made sure to keep a close watch on the driver. It wasn't long before the driver sullenly announced that they were approaching Kolodov. Eberhart thanked him for being such a great driver, and remarked that it was a shame that he had stopped singing, since that had added so much to the general ambiance.

Indeed, a village was coming into sight, but this one was so ragged looking that Eberhart doubted he would be able to find anywhere comfortable enough in which to stay. It was not the kind of place that he would normally choose to visit. But then he reminded himself why he was here in the first place. So the subject of where he would be staying ceased to preoccupy his mind, and his thoughts turned instead to the question of whether the *Rabbiner* would see fit to give him a blessing.

Eberhart disembarked from the wagon. He held out his hand and the driver immediately understood what he wanted. So the driver reached into his own pocket and took out the money that Eberhart had given him earlier. Cursing under his breath, the driver placed the zlotys into Eberhart's outstretched palm. Then, he swung the wagon around and whipped the horses until they broke into a trot. Within minutes, horses and wagon were out of sight, and Heinrich Eberhart stood by himself in the center of the poorest town he had ever seen. He wondered what the townspeople would think when he told them that he needed directions to the home of the *Rabbiner*.

It was a Shabbos to remember forever. Even though it was so soon after Pesach, Kolodover chassidim had arrived in the village from all over Poland and the neighboring countries, for the fame of Rav David Zushe of Kolodov had spread far and wide. Some chassidim had even arrived from far-off Hungary and Czechoslovakia bearing bottles of the finest Hungarian wine for the Rebbe's *tish*. It was a special Shabbos in the Kolodover *chassidus*. A Shabbos spent in the company of the Rebbe and chassidim in commemoration of the *yahrzeit* of the Rebbe's illustrious grandfather, the founder of the dynasty. It was heartfelt moments like these that kept the average Kolodover chassid going and able to serve Hashem properly throughout the long, brutal Polish winters. A Shabbos at the home of the Rebbe was like a cup of steaming tea in the midst of a winter's day. The singing would resound long into the night at the Friday-night *tish*, and each davening would last for many hours. The meals would be replete with incredible *divrei Torah, chiddushim, gematriyos* and *vertlach* that would make the eyes of the chassidim open wide in wonder, as they listened spellbound to every word that emerged from the Rebbe's holy mouth.

The Kolodover *beis midrash* was packed beyond belief. It seemed that every spot in the vast hall had been staked out by a loyal chassid who guarded his *makom* (place) throughout Shabbos. The chassidim had begun to arrive Thursday morning and afternoon, with the majority entering the town late that night. The stragglers had arrived on Friday morning. By the time Friday afternoon had arrived, every chassid was resting up from the journey in anticipation of the holy and joyous day to come.

As the afternoon wore on, more and more of the chassidim began making their way to the *beis midrash*, some walking alone, the majority in groups. They were very excited. They talked animatedly exclaiming with interest over the newest *vort* that someone had said. In general they were full of merriment and *simchas hachaim*, joy of life. The huge *beis midrash* embraced them, and once again, the street was still, save for the occasional chassid who, upon waking up late from his nap, was running down the cobblestones, tripping over his shoelaces in his haste to get to the shul and see the Rebbe. It was such a *z'chus* to have a chance to see Rav David Zushe face to face and to unburden oneself, and to walk out of the inner chamber a new man, worries and cares diminished.

Not all the chassidim would be able to get a private audience with the Rebbe on Friday. Most would have to wait patiently until *Motzaei Shabbos*. Even then, some would remain behind on Sunday and even Monday, until everyone who had come to Kolodov had received his opportunity to meet the Rebbe. When they experienced a Shabbos at the Rebbe's house, the glow would last them through the months to come, until they came back once again for another injection of holiness.

When the hour grew late on Friday, the *gabbai* would come knocking on Rav David Zushe's door informing him that it was time for the davening to start. Every chassid would run to his place in the *beis midrash*. The Rebbe, who was clad in a lustrous golden satin *bekeshe*, walked into the room slowly and majestically, his long blond coiled *peyos* framing a face which glowed with *kedushah*. There would be a gasp of awe when he looked at them and they saw the holy eyes, which had seen nothing impure throughout their entire sojourn on this earth. The Rebbe would take his seat.

The Rebbe would motion to the *chazzan* to begin. Like the roar of the ocean, the room would be full of noise, as every chassid began to pray in full voice, until the davening erupted into one tremendous maelstrom of *kavannah*. There was an unbelievable feeling of *achdus*, of togetherness, in the electrically charged air.

Then came the *shtille Shemoneh Esrei*. There was a hum, as everyone kept their voices to a murmur. But here and there, someone inspired by his surroundings felt that his heart was breaking because he wasn't the kind of *Yid* that he should be. So he would start to cry to himself as he said the words slowly and with deep concentration.

Before they knew it, *Kabbalas Shabbos* began. When they arrived at *Lechah Dodi*, there was a hush as everyone waited for the *niggun* to start. This was one of the highlights of the entire Shabbos davening. The *niggun* was the centerpiece of the *Kabbalas Shabbos*. When the chassidim sang that song, their hearts would soar to the heavens. Rav David Zushe sat in his place and sang along with the *chazzan*, his hoarse voice filled with such emotion, such poignancy, that tears would begin to flow. Then Rav David Zushe moved his hand a little bit upward. The chassidim knew that he wanted them to sing louder, and they would respond immediately by lustily singing the song they loved so much. At every *tefillah*, by every *tish*, and while they were learning by themselves over the course of the Shabbos, the chassidim would sing this *niggun* over and over. It never became boring. It never lost its charm. It inspired them to reach upward to the highest places inside themselves, to believe that they could make a positive difference to the world, through the power of music and their devotion to their Rebbe.

When the davening came to an end and the final *amen* had quieted down, then the chassidim would file into the large hall that was used for gatherings such as this. They would wash their hands and eat some *challah*, a little fish, a small portion of soup, a tiny morsel of chicken. The shabbos meal was accompanied by *divrei Torah*. Nobody thought about what they were eating because they were so inspired by the davening and the company that they were above the unimportant things like food. They were flying now, and the Rebbe was the pilot of the plane. When they finished *bentching*, everyone ran back to the *beis midrash* for the *tish*.

Then all of a sudden, the glorious night had come to an end, and it was time to go to sleep so they could waken and begin the second part of the Shabbos of togetherness. Almost the entire day was spent either davening, learning, eating the Shabbos meals and singing the special *niggun*. Sometimes the chassidim couldn't comprehend how the roof wasn't flying off into the heavens from the power of the singing beneath it.

Then came the final *tish* of the day: the *tish* of the third meal, where the chassidim sat in utter stillness as the darkness took over the day and the candles had long since burned out. The Rebbe talked and tried to give them the tools to deal with *galus*, as they allowed the Torah that he said to penetrate into their beings. They soaked up every word as if it was the sweetest of wine. After all that, it was time to sing the *niggun* one more time. That was the absolute highest point of Shabbos. It was said that if a chassid was able to achieve the proper concentration during that final song, then it was guaranteed that he would become a truly holy Jew.

That was a Shabbos with the Rebbe of Kolodov, and that was when Heinrich Eberhart had chosen to come and receive an audience to meet Rav David Zushe, the Kolodover Rebbe, in all his heavenly glory.

⁂

It was late Saturday afternoon, and Eberhart stood in the village square. He looked around not knowing where to go. The roads were empty and there was nobody in sight. *Well,* he said to himself, *if all the Jews were tucked away in their corner, then it stood to reason that the peasants were probably tucked away in their little corner, as well.* He was pretty sure that he could figure out where that was. He decided to just follow his nose. It didn't take him long to discover the place where the fine Polish citizens of Kolodov went to unwind.

Situated in a small building with a simple thatched roof, the building stank even from afar of cheap wine and potato vodka: vital staples in the diet of the average Pole. Eberhart pushed the door open and walked confidently into the village tavern. Head held high, his steely gaze met the eye of every man in the dank, smelly, dimly lit room. Most of the individuals shrank away from his look, having suffered in the past from men with similar looks. Striding straight to the bar, he ordered a pitcher of beer. Then he sat down and began knocking back the beer.

The men at the bar were watching his every move, although they pretended to be absorbed in their own conversations. Eberhart knew that this was the kind of place where strangers often ended up in a brawl against uneven numbers. This time, however, they had met their match in him. An ex-officer in the German Army could take down any number of these boors, and he worked out his plan of action as he pretended to keep on drinking. It wouldn't hurt if they thought he was a little drunk and unsteady on his feet. It would give him an advantage which he intended to use. There was no rush. He had all the time in the world. He sat at the table in a relaxed pose, at ease, as if he had no clue that there were people sitting not 10 feet away who were planning on liberating him from his purse. He drank a small quantity of the beer and found that he wanted to throw up. It was ghastly stuff. The rest of it he either poured on the floor underneath his table or left in the pitcher. Then slowly, as if he were having trouble getting to his feet, giving the impression that the world was spinning around him, Heinrich Eberhart headed in the direction of the door and fresh air.

Out of the corner of his eye, he noticed that three of the men sitting at the bar had risen as well and were starting to walk toward the entrance. Quickly, he pushed opened the door and walked out into the twilight. The sun was close to disappearing for the night, and he moved quickly toward a tree with a thick trunk that afforded him a place to hide until he deemed it the right time to emerge. He was just in time. The three men emerged from the pub, blinking in the dim light, looking in every direction as if searching for something they had lost.

"Where'd he go?" one of them growled at their leader, a solid-looking Pole with a bushy mustache and small devious-looking eyes.

"He can't be far," he said in a rough voice that grated on Eberhart's nerves. They were walking in a tight little knot as they approached the tree. When he felt that the time was right, he reached into his pocket and felt the knife that he had confiscated from the hapless wagon driver. It seemed like a million years ago now. The men didn't know what hit them. They, unlike Eberhart, had been drinking, and their reflexes were much too slow for a fighter like himself.

He kicked the biggest one right under the kneecap, and followed that up with a solid punch straight to the jaw. The man hadn't even hit the ground when Eberhart had already started on his friend. He whirled around and smashed his elbow straight into the side of the man's head. It connected with a satisfying crunch. There was a gagging sound as the man hit the ground. The entire battle had taken place in the space of 10 seconds. The leader stood there dumbfounded, not understanding what had happened; not comprehending that his two friends had been knocked out by one man so quickly.

Next, Eberhart turned his attention to him. Pulling the wicked-looking knife out of his pocket, he placed it right under the man's throat, letting the point jab the skin, pressing softly and with a little more pressure, easing up and applying the point once again until the big man had a look of intense fear in his eyes.

"Is this how you treat every stranger that comes to your village?" Eberhart asked the man, knowing the answer, and also knowing what the man was going to say.

"We weren't going to do anything to you," the man replied indignantly.

"Do you think I'm stupid?" Eberhart asked him pressing the blade into the man's throat with a little more pressure.

"I'm sorry, I'm sorry," the man said. "I didn't realize that you work for the police department. I will never do something like this again. I swear! Please believe me! We thought you were a simple stranger." So they thought he was a policeman!

"What's your name?" Eberhart asked the man.

"Stephan," he replied.

"Listen, Stephan," he said. "You're right. I work for the police department, and we have received complaints from many people who have visited this village. I hope that what happened here today will teach you a lesson. But understand that if it doesn't, I will be back and I will gut you like a fish. Do you understand me?" Stephan was shaking uncontrollably and murmuring to himself as Eberhart released him. He watched as the big man sank slowly to the ground.

"I haven't seen any Jews around today," Eberhart remarked nonchalantly to the prostrate form in front of him. "Where are they all hiding? Last time I was here, this place was crawling with them?"

"They are all with the *Rabbiner* in the synagogue for the big gathering," Stephan managed to get out. "Some special Saturday, when Jews come from all over Poland to spend time with the *Rabbiner*."

"Thank you, Stephan," Eberhart replied, "and do not, under any circumstances, forget what I warned you!"

Then leaving all three of them lying on the ground, Heinrich Eberhart turned and walked away, down a muddy path toward the big building a few streets away, from which emanated a low hum of many voices merging together in one pleasant medley.

It was time for him to meet the *Rabbiner*. If it was a special Sabbath, he wouldn't be able to get in to actually meet with him, but he could sneak into the synagogue and see him, try to gauge the type of person he was. He still couldn't believe that such a pragmatic person as himself had elected to travel a great distance on the off-chance that a *Rabbiner* would give him a blessing! He had never believed in blessings from anyone. But maybe he had been wrong. Anyway he was here now, so hopefully he had been wrong.

His future hung in the balance. There was nothing else. If this didn't work out, he might as well not even bother going home. There was nothing waiting for him there, just colossal failure and a host of creditors waiting for their chance to grab a piece of Eberhart Construction Company.

It began to rain without warning. One moment it was a warm evening, and the next second, the rain began pelting downward. He ran the remaining block toward the *beis midrash,* the sounds of singing issuing warm and inviting from the darkened building. He paused for an extra moment on the doorstep, and then he pushed the doors open and stepped into another world.

He was in a large anteroom filled with benches piled with coats. Off to the side there was a kitchen where a number of men were setting food out on trays and whisking them off toward the main sanctuary where the *Rabbiner* was. There was an enormous vat of boiling hot water bubbling merrily away, and a number of metal cups strewn about. Eberhart ignored all this, finding himself drawn to the main room from where the noise was emanating. He stepped over the threshold of the large room, struck by the beauty and holiness that were so obviously there. But more than that, there was a spontaneity in the air. They weren't serving G-d with the rigidity that Eberhart normally associated with prayer. In his church back in Hamburg, people sat in their pews and were very serious about their prayer time. They were so serious, in fact, that it was a boring, uninspiring few hours — so unlike what he was seeing here.

He had entered the room in the middle of a song, and the sound that burst forth from the hundreds of lips was so fresh, so vital, so intensely connected, that Eberhart wanted to cry. He, the most rational of men! He couldn't see anything in front of him due to the density of the crowd. The hall was packed to capacity. He wanted to see the *Rabbiner*, but there were a series of bleachers running around the edge of the room, and every spot had been taken.

Then, he spotted a gap in the crowd and he pushed his way through. Nobody knew that he didn't belong because it was dark in the room. They didn't notice that a gentile had made his way inside. He was near the front of the room, and for the first time, there was a small opening by his side. He shouldered someone aside and felt an almost physical jolt when he caught sight of the *Rabbiner* sitting at the head of the table at the front of the room. There was no doubt who the *Rabbiner* was, no doubt at all. He was so obviously holy, such a radiance shone from his eyes, that Eberhart wanted to run away and hide. He was struck with a sudden fear, with a feeling that he had made a terrible mistake by coming here. He felt that he was in the presence of greatness and had no business being there. But it was too late, because the *Rabbiner* had turned his way and his eyes met Eberhart's with a piercing sizzle. Eberhart blanched silently, because the man's gaze had been so intense as to be almost palpable!

He couldn't understand what was going on here! The room was shrouded in darkness. It was almost impossible to recognize anyone sitting in the shadows. And yet, the *Rabbiner* had looked his way and seen him — recognized that he didn't belong there, that he wasn't a follower, and had given him a look telling him as much. Did the look mean that the *Rabbiner* wanted him to leave? Should he escape while he still had the opportunity, or was this all mere foolishness on his part, and he had imagined the whole thing? But no, he could still feel the burning sensation where their eyes had locked and he knew that the Rabbiner knew. But he had come for a blessing, because he had no other choice. There was no way he could return to Germany empty handed with things remaining the way they currently were. He would be an embarrassment to his illustrious ancestry.

The Eberhart family had always been rich; they had always been leaders of industry. For him to go back in defeat and disgrace meant being stripped of his riches, his savings and properties. Everything would be lost to him, Marianne would leave him and his son would be brokenhearted that he'd let him down. Did he have a choice? The only honorable choice he'd have left would be for him to take a pistol from the rack of antique pistols in his home in Hamburg and to blow his brains out. But Heinrich Eberhart still wanted to live. And Joshua Weinberger had all but promised him that a blessing from the *Rabbiner* would be more than enough to save him. So he trusted Joshua and knew instinctively that he had only his best interests in mind.

He was going to stay, he decided, and whatever was meant to be, would be. No point worrying about it any longer. Then he turned back to the festivities in front of him, and allowed himself to sink into the most uplifting, yet strangest religious experience that he had ever seen. It was a roomful of Jewish bearded men in fur hats and long black coats and Heinrich Eberhart, shaven face, no hat, no long coat and someone who belonged to the Protestant Church! Here they were together! But the singing was so soulful and melodic, so full of fluidity and love. It was so different from a service back home. He was conditioned to sit ramrod straight, pretending to be completely focused on the clergyman delivering the sermon. When this *Rabbiner* spoke, the people listened because they really wanted to hear what he had to say. They truly believed that they could grow into better people if they followed his advice and integrated his lessons into their hearts. It was all so different.

So Heinrich Eberhart, German construction mogul, stood alongside the Kolodover chassidim as the Rebbe spoke at the final meal of the day, listening in hushed silence along with everyone else. He stood there quietly through all the talking and the singing, and found himself a corner to sit in when everyone joined in one last spirited dance after Maariv. He watched the *havdalah* ceremony from his little corner, not knowing what to make of the candle and the pouch they were smelling, or why the *Rabbiner* was chanting something over a cup of wine. Only when the *shamash* began lighting the oil lamps in the main sanctuary did Eberhart slip out of the shul and return to the lonely road.

It was completely dark now outside the shul, and Eberhart felt very alone. A slight drizzle was coming down from a sky laden with dense, low-hanging clouds. He realized that he was going to have to find some sort of shelter for the night. For a second, he toyed with the idea of returning to the tavern he had entered earlier, but he knew that it wasn't a smart idea. There would be others there now, friends of the men he had beaten up earlier that evening. No, going back wasn't an option.

Instead, he walked down the endless, lonely roads, using the weak light of the moon to guide him in his search of shelter. Spotting a barn, he left the road and began to trek through the muddy field ahead of him, cursing under his breath as he walked, slipping and sliding on the muddy ground. Finally, he reached the incline leading to the barn, and he collapsed against the red wooden building, grateful for the shelter that was protecting him from the drizzle that had intensified as he walked. But now he was safe at last, even though he was famished.

With a sigh of relief, he pushed open the doors and stumbled inside the structure. It was warm in the barn and smelled of farm animals. Reassuring noises filled the room as the cows lolled and snorted, while the horses made whinnying sounds to themselves as they caught the scent of a stranger who had invaded their domain. Eberhart peeled off his sodden jacket and placed it on a pile of hay. Then he looked around for something with which to dry himself.

In a little alcove off to the side he discovered a veritable treasure trove of items that he was able to use. There were a number of towels, some dirty, the majority clean, a variety of knives and household tools and a three-legged stool which he decided to use for milking one of the cows. He was so hungry, he thought he might faint if he didn't get something into his system. He had never milked a cow before, but millions of people did it every day, and they weren't smarter than he was. If they could do it, then so could he. He was going to milk the cow. He wasn't sure where he was supposed to sit, and he didn't know how hard to squeeze. After repeatedly trying, he finally began to get the hang of it. When he had half a bucket of milk, the cow swung its tail with blistering aim and sent that bucket flying halfway across the barn in a shower of milk. It made such a ruckus that he thought it was a miracle that the farmer didn't come see what all the noise was about.

After that, he tried another cow. This one cooperated right away. Soon he had enough milk to drink. It was warm and frothy and delicious. He felt satiated and happy and full of ambitious plans. He decided that he would leave the barn at the crack of dawn and make his way back to the synagogue where he would hang around until most of the Jews had left the city. He would ask the man in charge for an audience with the *Rabbiner*. That was what he was going to do. Having a plan of action made him feel more secure. He climbed the rickety ladder leading to the loft, and made himself a bed from a pile of straw. He had cleaned up after himself as best as he was able. He felt reasonably sure that everything appeared to be the same as when he had walked into the barn not long before.

Then, he curled up in the pile of hay and before he knew it, he was drifting off to sleep. It felt so good, because he hadn't slept in days — not a real, genuine sleep — just some catnaps from time to time.

The next thing he knew, he was awake and a pale sun was shining listlessly through the small window in the roof of the barn. He knew that he had overslept, and now he would have to be more careful when he left the barn. He wasted no time. He ran down the ladder twice as fast as when he had gone up. He slipped on his jacket which was sufficiently dried, and then he made his unobtrusive way out of the barn and down the incline toward the road again. The farmer and his sons were busy out in the fields, and nobody paid him any heed. He realized that he had slept through the morning milking, and was extremely thankful that they hadn't put two and two together. An unfamiliar jacket lying around on top of one of the hay piles and a less-than-usual quantity of milk in two of their cows meant a possible intruder. Dumb Poles! Lucky for him!

He decided that he could return to the tavern for breakfast because the really tough guys would be sleeping it off, and the regular breakfast clientele were probably wimps. He was right. The moment he walked into the place, he was treated just like any other customer. He ordered a loaf of bread, kasha and eggs and washed it all down with plain water from the spring outside. Then satiated, he paid the man at the counter and headed toward the home of the Kolodover Rebbe. It was time to ask the *Rabbiner* for a blessing. That was why he had come, and besides, every day that passed meant more and more possible changes back home. He had to get back to Germany before irreversible damage took place.

Here and there, groups of Jews passed him, on the way to the main highway where he surmised they were hoping to hitch rides from people heading out of town. It appeared that most of the Jews had left the previous evening, and he was pleased. The less people he had to interact with, the better. He walked with confidence, and he met the eye of every Jew who passed, knowing that they were staring at him, wanting to know why he was coming their way, why he was entering the Jewish part of town. But no one challenged him. He paused at the entrance of the big prayer house where he had been so inspired the night before. Shrugging his shoulders, he pushed the doors open and entered the anteroom.

It was still in disarray, and he looked on in amazement, not believing the mess before his eyes. Here and there, a chassid or two were moving the benches to their proper places. He knew that he needed to speak to someone with some degree of authority. Stopping a young boy who was carrying a mop and a bucket full of sudsy water and heading toward a big stain on the floor, he asked in German who he should speak to so that he would be able to meet with the *Rabbiner*. The boy put down his stuff and motioned to Eberhart to follow him. They went past the double doors leading into the main sanctuary and down a long hallway, until they emerged into a small room off to the side with benches for people to sit on. He saw a burly man guarding the *Rabbiner's* inner sanctum. The boy spoke earnestly to the huge man, while the man looked back at Eberhart once or twice, apparently sizing him up as he listened to what the boy had to say. When the boy had finished speaking, the big man called Eberhart over with the crook of his finger.

"Why do you want to see the Rebbe?" he asked Eberhart in Yiddish.

Since Yiddish was similar to German, Eberhart was able to understand what the man was saying. He tried his best to explain that he was in urgent need of a blessing from the *Rabbiner*; that it was an emergency.

"Are you Jewish?" asked the man, twirling one of his sidelocks between his fingers as he looked Eberhart up and down.

"No," Eberhart answered. There was no point in lying to the man. Even if this man was fooled and thought that he was just some uneducated, irreligious Jew, the *Rabbiner* would most definitely not be fooled, so what would he have gained? No, honesty was the best approach in this particular situation. He was sure of that.

"Who told you to come here?" the burly man asked him next. Eberhart explained how he had met a German Jew by the name of Joshua Weinberger who had told him that the best thing he could do for himself was to travel to the *Rabbiner*.

"Where do you live?" the man asked Eberhart incredulously.

"Hamburg," he answered.

"This is very strange," the man said. "I don't think I can recall something even remotely similar in all my years serving as *gabbai* for the Rebbe. I will go into the Rebbe and ask him what he wants me to do with you."

Turning, the man knocked lightly on the Rebbe's door. Then pushing it open, he entered, shutting the door, leaving Eberhart wondering if, after everything he had gone through to make it to this point, he was going to merit a blessing or not. It was probably the longest five-minute wait of his entire life. Every eye in the room was upon him, some full of curiosity, some hostile, some just amused, while Heinrich just stood there and didn't know where to put himself. The door opened and the *gabbai* motioned for him to enter. Heaving a huge sigh of relief, he hastened to the *Rabbiner's* room.

The moment before he stepped over the threshold and into the *Rabbiner's* room, the *gabbai* stopped him by gently placing his tremendous paw in the center of his chest.

"Calm down," he said. "Walk in slowly, show respect. This is a great man, and you are very privileged to be meeting with him. You will tell your children about this one day." Then he let Eberhart pass him and go into the room, shutting the door quietly behind him.

The air in the room was redolent with the smell of a pipe that had since gone out, and was resting on an ashtray on the *Rabbiner's* desk. A cooling glass of tea sent up little wisps of smoke into the air. Two of the walls were covered with floor-to-ceiling bookcases. They were packed with books. Eberhart had never seen anything like it before. There were so many books that they were crammed into the shelves like sardines in a can. It was incredible. There had been a library in his home, but those books had been leather bound and color coded and mostly for show. These books on the other hand, were anything but that. They were there to be used. They were actually falling apart. The binding of every one of them was cracked and splitting. Several of them were in a pile on the *Rabbiner's* desk. Three were opened, and the *Rabbiner* appeared to be reading from one of them as he waited for Eberhart to get his bearings.

Heinrich Eberhart wanted to speak, but his heart was still beating strongly. He gave himself an extra moment to calm down before he even tried. At that moment, the *Rabbiner* looked up at him and smiled. Eberhart knew that he didn't have to be afraid; that this was a good man who helped people, and that if it were within his power, he would assist him, as well.

"What can I do for you, young man?" the *Rabbiner* asked him in a surprisingly upper-class German, while motioning to Eberhart to take a seat.

Heinrich Eberhart, who never permitted anyone to see him weep, broke down then and there in the study of the Kolodover Rabbiner. He didn't know why he broke down; maybe it was nerves. But he just couldn't control himself, and he began to cry, while the *Rabbiner* looked on and said not a word. He didn't try to tell him it would be all right, or to comfort him in any way. He just waited for the storm to subside. Eventually, Eberhart felt better, and he began relating his tale of woe to the *Rabbiner*.

He told him how he had foolishly entered into a partnership with his greatest business enemy, and how that man had very probably caused his business enterprise to collapse. That was going to occur as soon as his suppliers realized that he was in desperate straits and would no longer be able to pay his bills. This would probably mean that he would never again be awarded a government contract. He told the *Rabbiner* how he had run from the building site like a frightened mouse, exhibiting behavior so unlike his normal mode of being. He told of fleeing to the tiny village, meeting Joshua while he was drunk, being helped in a way that he had never experienced before, and how Joshua had instructed him to come to Poland to beg the *Rabbiner* for a blessing.

He told the *Rabbiner* about the moment he had walked into the tavern, how he understood that he was going to be robbed or maybe even killed.

"What did you do?" the *Rabbiner* asked him, a worried look marring the serenity of his features. Eberhart realized that by acting the way he had, he might have endangered the Jewish community of Kolodov. So he hastened to reassure the *Rabbiner* that the people he had beaten up thought he was a policeman, and wouldn't dare take revenge on the Jews because of him.

"You don't know them," the *Rabbiner* answered him. "But they are not your problem."

"*Rabbiner*," Eberhart said, "I can assure you that those men are so frightened of the police that they would never think that I had any connection to the Jews. "

The *Rabbiner* smiled.

"It was twilight when I arrived at the synagogue last night," Eberhart said and he proceeded to describe to the *Rabbiner* what he had felt as he had experienced the *tish*. He spoke of being inspired, of the glow that had emanated from each and every one of the chassidim there. He hadn't wanted to leave, but knew that he had to. So he came back in the morning to speak to the *Rabbiner* face to face, to beg him for his blessing.

It was quiet in the room after he finished his impassioned outburst, and Eberhart didn't know where to look. He was suddenly extremely uncomfortable with how he had spoken, with the way that he had bared his soul to this Jewish man. He didn't know what to do with himself. The *Rabbiner* sat quietly, humming a tune to himself, while glancing into one of the open books on his desk. Outside, it began to rain again, and Eberhart realized how much he loathed Poland! He thought how miserable it was in this dank and unfriendly land, and he waited for the *Rabbiner* to say something.

"Herr Eberhart," the Rabbiner finally said.

"Yes," he answered.

"I can't give you an answer this second. I suggest that you return here tomorrow morning at which time I will give you my answer."

"But why?" asked Eberhart, even as he knew that he couldn't demand an answer from the *Rabbiner*. But he was shocked all the same. He had expected either a yes or a no. Why did he have to come back? That meant remaining in this horrible village for the rest of the day and another night. He absolutely hated this place with a passion! He had dared to dream that the *Rabbiner* would grant him a blessing right away, and he would leave the house, walk to the highway and hire someone to drive him back to Lodz. But obviously that was not going to happen. He was going to have to wait. It was tough for him to have to hide his disappointment. But he thanked the *Rabbiner* for his time, turned and walked out of the *Rabbiner's* room into the waiting room which was still packed with waiting chassidim. All the newcomers blinked in amazement when they saw who had just walked out of the Rebbe's personal study. Every man in the room was wondering what business such a man had with the holy *tzaddik*, Rav David Zushe of Kolodov.

Eberhart left the grand edifice and headed out into the rain, not knowing what to expect, almost despairing of the blessing for which he had been waiting. He wasn't sure where he would stay until the morrow. But of one thing he was certain; he had gotten this far, he would remain and hear the *Rabbiner's* answer. There was no other way. Any other option led to an antique pistol and a bullet that would do the job almost too well.

The moment Herr Eberhart had exited his study, Rav David Zushe called for the *gabbai*.

"Hirsch Ber," he said.

"Yes, Rebbe," his devoted *gabbai* answered.

"Go to Reb Chaim Schoenblum's house where my brother Rav Anshel is staying, and kindly ask my brother to come here at once. There is something I need to discuss with him immediately!"

Hirsch Ber understood that this had something to do with the appearance of the gentile, but he tactfully refrained from asking any questions. It was not his job to question the Rebbe. His job was to obey, and that was exactly what he did. Rav Anshel was eating breakfast, the remains of a herring and some black bread sat in front of him, and he was drinking a glass of tea and perusing a *sefer* in between delicate sips, when Hirsh Ber arrived to summon him to his brother.

"The Rebbe would like Rav Anshel to come to his study as soon as he can," Hirsch Ber told Rav Anshel with deference. It was widely known that Rav Anshel was one of the *gedolim* of the generation. He was an exceedingly humble man, never foisting his opinion on anyone. He listened carefully when others spoke, treating them with the utmost respect. He shared many of his features with his brother Rav David Zushe, but Rav Anshel's eyes were a darker shade of brown, and his beard was more sparse and with fewer gray hairs. The brothers respected and loved each other deeply, and it was known throughout Europe that when one wanted to give an example of true love, one spoke of the relationship between Rav David Zushe and his brother Rav Anshel.

"Tell the Rebbe that I will be there as soon as I *bentch*," Rav Anshel told Hirsch Ber.

The *gabbai* turned and left the room, heading to the main *beis midrash* to relay the message. When Rav Anshel finished *bentching*, he rose from his seat and, wishing his host a wonderful day, left the house and walked with very quick steps to the Rebbe's study. As he walked, he reviewed *mishnayos* from memory, saying the words in a constant flow of Torah thought. Rav Anshel had a photographic memory, and he usually didn't have to read a *sefer* more than twice before it was indelibly printed in his mind. But that didn't satisfy him. He reviewed constantly, etching the words of the Torah onto his heart. He had married very young and had nine children by the time he was 32. But his admiration for his esteemed brother knew no bounds. He admired him and craved to reach his levels in fear of heaven.

Rav Anshel approached the *beis midrash* and walked inside, quickly moving through the building until he reached the waiting room which was still packed with chassidim awaiting an audience with his brother. The assembled stood up when Rav Anshel entered the room, but he barely noticed. It was typical of Rav Anshel to pay no attention to gestures of honor. They were repugnant to him, and he resolved to keep them far away from his mind. Hirsch Ber led him into the Rebbe's room, and he entered with head held low in appropriate deference for his brother.

Rav David Zushe greeted his brother warmly and asked him to sit down across from him.

"I had a visitor this morning," he began without preamble. "A gentile." Rav Anshel listened without commenting, the normal manner of someone who doesn't talk until he comprehends the entire situation from beginning to end.

"The gentile comes from Germany," Rav David Zushe continued. "He is going through a very difficult time in his life right now." When no response was forthcoming, the Rebbe launched into the sad story that Heinrich Eberhart had told him. "When he comprehended what was going on," the Rebbe continued, "he ran away from the building site and ended up in some small village at the edge of Germany, a place where he had no friends, no place to stay for the night. He was lying drunk in the middle of the town square when he was approached by a *Yid*, helped up and brought to his home. The *Yid* fed him and provided him with a warm comfortable bed for the night.

"Then," the Rebbe gave a significant pause, "right before he was going to leave the man's home, the *Yid* suggested to him that he travel to Poland, to the Kolodover Rebbe where he should ask for a *berachah* for himself. So he traveled to Poland to Lodz, almost getting robbed twice by the locals. He snuck into the *beis midrash* during the *tish* last night, an experience which he found extremely inspiring." Rav Anshel's eyebrows rose upon hearing the last revelation.

"Then this morning," Rav David Zushe went on, "Herr Eberhart approached Hirsch Ber and requested a private audience with me so he could ask for a *berachah*. We spoke for a while, Anshel, and he truly has *tzaros* right now. The fact that he is a descendent of one of Germany's most influential families makes it all the worse, because the embarrassment will be that much greater. After telling me the whole story, he asked me for a *berachah*. I told him to return tomorrow because I wasn't sure how to handle this situation."

The Rebbe paused for a long five seconds before continuing.

"You, Rav Anshel, my dear brother, know that when I accepted the mantle of spiritual leader of Kolodov, I was granted special abilities which accompany the role. You have seen, many times, the *siyata dishmaya* that has come my way, granting me the knowledge time and again, in almost every situation, showing me how to handle myself, granting me the *daas* to know what to do. But this time, I am at a loss how to respond."

Rav Anshel looked at his holy brother in wonder and said not a word.

"I am at a loss," continued the Kolodover Rebbe to his younger brother, "because of the advice that our *Zeide* gave to all his descendants; advice by which they lived. He said, '*Mein kinderlach*, my precious children, do not waste your *berachos* on the gentiles who come to ask for them. Save your blessings for the *Yidden* who come and need to be saved; for the *almanos* and *yisomim*.' And in fact, our father never gave a *berachah* to a gentile. In truth, neither did I. What the *Zeide* said was sufficient for me, until today."

Rav Anshel finally spoke up. *"Ich farshtei nisht,"* he said, "I don't understand. What is so special about this gentile than any other gentile? Why are you hesitating so much over this one man, when you never worried about this before? In the past, you never had any doubts, you knew what you had to do and that was that! Suddenly, you don't know what to do? What does this gentile have that none of the others had? You just sent the others away with kind words of reassurance, but never with a *berachah*. Why him?"

Rav David Zushe was quiet for a very long time. The silence resounded in the small chamber as the two brothers sat across from each other; one searching for the proper words to say, the other searching for the right way to accept whatever his older brother might do.

Suddenly, Rav David Zushe laid his head on the desk and wept. He was sobbing like a small child in need of reassurance. Rav Anshel looked at his holy brother and felt a tremendous fear begin to pervade his body. He didn't understand. What was going on? He had never seen his brother like this. He was usually so serene, so sure of his *derech hachaim*. Suddenly, his head was down and he was crying as if his very heart was breaking into a million pieces! Rav Anshel sat still while he waited for his brother to regain control over his emotions.

Eventually Rav David Zushe lifted his head off the table. Rav Anshel stared in awe at his tear-filled visage, not knowing how to react to the sight of his holy brother in such acute pain.

"Anshele," the Rebbe said, using the name he had used when they were children. "There is going to be a massacre."

He stated this in a flat voice — in a voice that was completely sure of what it was saying. A voice that held no doubt.

"What do you mean?" Rav Anshel asked him, the chill that had hit him earlier suddenly penetrating even deeper into his heart.

"I mean that the persecutions that we *Yidden* have been suffering over the last few thousand years are going to pale in comparison with the massacre that will be coming our way sooner than we know!" Rav David Zushe's voice trembled and his eyes suddenly became shiny as a bright light shone forth. Rav Anshel stared at his brother mesmerized, thinking that in his *tallis,* his brother appeared to be speaking like an angel of Hasem.

"What type of persecutions?" asked Rav Anshel, his voice quivering.

"Like the horrors of *tach v'tat*, when the Cossacks rose up like the sea and rode from community to community butchering the *Yidden* in every place. Rivers of Jewish blood streamed over the cobblestones of Europe at that time. That was *tach v'tat,* and that was nothing compared to what is on its way.

"It will be like the Inquisition and the Crusades, and like every terrible thing the gentiles did to us throughout the years here on this blood-drenched earth. But it will be worse, much worse. We can't even imagine how much worse it is going to get! And where will it come from?" the Rebbe asked.

He pointed out the window as he spoke in a ragged voice. "From Germany, the Gemara tells us. That's where the evil will come from. Are we blind? Do we not see it? Right now in Germany, a man, a reincarnation of *Amalek,* has arisen. His entire goal, the reason he lives, is to destroy the Jewish people. That is something that isn't possible. But he will try, and he will succeed in inflicting much damage. Right now, the Jewish population of Germany is in grave danger. They are sitting atop a keg of gunpowder, yet only individuals attempt to escape the evil. The majority will stay until the end, deluding themselves as Satan laughs. So now you know my difficulty.

"If I know that this great calamity is going to befall our people, is it not incumbent on me to assist this man, who has the ability to be very powerful in Germany? Should I not give him a blessing which will hopefully be effective? I can give him a blessing that I make dependent on the way that he treats the Jews who will work for him. He is desperate for help. He is crying for salvation. I can give him a *berachah,* but one that comes with a price tag. The price: the hiring of many Jewish workers, his protection of them and making sure that they come to no harm. That will be the price that he pays for the blessing that he receives. And yet, *Zeide* told us, 'No! Do not give them a blessing,' and that is the way it has always been. Am I to be the one to break the chain? Anshel, help me! Give me some advice! Tell me what to do!"

Anshel didn't know what to say. He was grateful that it was not his responsibility, that he didn't know the horrors that awaited the Jewish people. But Anshel knew one thing. One didn't second guess the *Zeide.* What the *Zeide* had said, then, applied just as much today. And here his brother, the holy Rav David Zushe, was going to disobey his advice with the loftiest of intentions. The very thought of such a thing was burning a hole in his chest.

"My dear brother," he finally said, "the *Zeide* said no. How can you even think that this is a good idea if the *Zeide* said no?"

"But how can I not do it, if this could be a help? It can be a salvation to many *Yidden*. This man will become great, I can sense it. I know that he is destined for great things. But he needs the *berachah* to receive them. Without that, he will not be able to do anything!"

"But the *Zeide* said no," screamed Rav Anshel at his older brother — at the *tzaddik* of Kolodov. "That means that giving a *berachah* to him will be a bad thing for us, a bad thing for the family, for the dynasty. Who knows? It could return and harm our children. Who knows what the *Zeide* knew when he gave the *eitzah*? How could you, Rav David Zushe, go against his wishes especially on his *yahrzeit*, and do precisely the one thing he said not to do?"

Rav David Zushe stood up behind the desk and his face burned with an internal flame.

"Rav Anshel," he said, his voice quiet, yet the conviction that rang forth was so genuine as to slice through the air and bury itself deep into his brother's heart.

"Rav Anshel," he said again, "I have a responsibility to my people. If my giving this man a *berachah* will save some of them, then that is what the *Zeide* would have wanted me to do. I must give the *berachah*!!"

"But what of our family? What if this causes them pain and suffering?" The words hung in the air, reverberating through the room like sharpened arrows.

"Then I will bear the consequences," said his brother, "for I am the Rebbe. The possible saving of my people comes before my personal needs. Because that is what a Rebbe does."

It was at that very moment that the lives of Rav David Zushe and his brother, Rav Anshel, split into two separate directions. Right then. This was only the beginning, but the seed took root at that very moment. For Rav Anshel suddenly knew with a complete understanding that his brother was right in his assessment of the horrors to come, just as much as he was wrong in disobeying the *Zeide's eitzah*.

That was when Rav Anshel decided to leave Poland and journey with his entire family to Eretz Yisrael, leaving the blood and tear soil of Europe far behind him forever.

Heinrich Eberhart

Kolodov, Poland
April 25, 1936

Heinrich Eberhart spent the day on the outskirts of the village, doing his best to stay out of the way. He didn't want the peasants to see him, because that could only lead to a negative outcome for all involved. Consequently, he found himself a quiet field at the edge of town. There were haystacks there and he sat at the foot of one of them and dreamed of a positive answer. The very fact that the *Rabbiner* hadn't given him a blessing on the spot made him feel as if the blessing was worth infinitely more than he had imagined when he had first arrived. The day passed in a haze of sunshine and drizzle. It was only in the late afternoon that he dared to venture into the town proper to find something to eat. He purchased food from a peddler woman, and then, he returned to the barn where he had stayed the previous night, checking his back frequently to make sure that no one was following him.

This was his last night in the barn, come what may. He looked around him, at the weather-beaten walls and the slumbering animals, and knew that as long as he lived, he would never forget this place. He drifted off to sleep in the early evening and arose with the first light of dawn, determined not to stick around any longer then absolutely necessary. He left the barn and strode off into the early-morning mist in the direction of the *Rabbiner*, who would hopefully grant him the blessing he so needed.

The *beis midrash* was busy even at so early an hour. He took a seat in the waiting room, determined to remain there until he was able to see the *Rabbiner*. He was able to hear the sounds of heartfelt prayer through the wall beside him, and he found himself wondering, once again, why the prayers that were being said here were so much more intense than anything he ever heard in his place of worship back home. Apparently, nearly all those who had come to the village for Shabbos had left, since there were fewer people about. Still, whoever was there made sure to stare at Eberhart with puzzlement. He longed to get what he came for and be gone and out of the proximity of those stares already!

It was an hour before Hirsch Ber told him that he could see the *Rabbiner*. He entered the room with hesitant steps. This was it, the moment of truth. The *Rabbiner* sat before his desk, immersed in one of his sacred books. A steaming cup of tea and a few pieces of bread sat beside him. Eberhart studied the *Rabbiner*. Just at that moment, the *Rabbiner* met his gaze for one moment, and he felt his blood chill before the stare of the holy man.

"Sit," the *Rabbiner* said, and Eberhart sat.

"You are a descendant of an aristocratic family?" the *Rabbiner* asked him in pleasant tones.

"That is true," he acknowledged.

"I am going to give you a blessing, Herr Eberhart," the *Rabbiner* continued, "and I expect you to follow my instructions to the letter, as well." The *Rabbiner* paused for a long moment before speaking again.

"You know better than I of the troubles taking place in Germany for my Jewish brothers. I know that you personally are not a hater of the Jews, or you wouldn't be here requesting a blessing from a *Rabbiner*. However, since I am going to provide you with a blessing, I expect you to promise me something in return."

Eberhart looked at the *Rabbiner* expectantly. *What could he ask of me?*

"I want you to promise me that you will employ as many Jews in your company as you possibly can."

Eberhart hurried to nod his head in agreement, but the *Rabbiner* held up his hand and kept on talking.

"Not only that," he said. "I want you to promise me that not only will you hire these Jewish people, who incidentally will be the best possible workers that you'll ever have, but you will watch over them, protect them and enable them to keep on working for you. In essence, you will protect as many of my brothers as you can and save them. This will be your guarantee that the blessing will be effective. Basically, your success will be contingent on the amount of assistance you provide to the people who need it most right now. Do you understand?"

Eberhart searched within himself and realized that he didn't hate the Jewish people. He knew that he could do what the *Rabbiner* was asking of him. He knew, as well, that nobody liked starting up with success. If the blessing brought him material success, then he would be sitting on top of the world, and then it would not be overly difficult to use many people as workers, to disguise them as gentiles, to shift them around the countryside from project to project. Everyone would want his money and his influence. Nobody would be concerned about the men who were working under him and who were the driving force behind his shining star.

So Herr Heinrich Eberhart turned to Rav David Zushe, and with bowed head and humble manner he promised him that he would employ, protect and watch over as many Jews as he was able to without putting himself in a life-threatening position.

And so the *Rabbiner* gave him a blessing in exchange for his promise. He gave the blessing even though the words felt extremely dry in his mouth and had to be practically forced out of him. But he was the Rebbe, and the Rebbe had to take care of his nation, regardless of the consequences. Eberhart left the room overjoyed, thanking the *Rabbiner* again and again. But Rav David Zushe sat in his place and felt as if his whole world was crashing down around him. In the dimmest recesses of his mind, there was a constant echo of the *Zeide's* voice saying, "Never give a *berachah* to a gentile. Never give a *berachah* to a gentile."

There was one thing Eberhart had to do before he could leave the village. Upon receiving the priceless blessing, he hurried to the road exiting the village and waited there for the first passing wagon. It was a farmer transporting a load of geese to market in Lodz. Eberhart showed him his wad of money, and told him to get moving. Then he left the town of Kolodov behind him forever.

Eberhart allowed the farmer one good look at his knife, wanting the man to know that there was no point in getting his hopes up. Then he drifted off to sleep, bone weary from his uncomfortable stay in Kolodov. It seemed as if it was only a few minutes before he found himself at the wagon depot in Lodz once again. From there to the train station was a five-minute walk. He booked himself a "First Class" ticket, and sat down to wait for the train. He boarded the train with all the other passengers, and when they began singing a while into the journey, Heinrich Eberhart raised his voice and joined in for a chorus or two.

Hamburg, Germany
April 17, 1936

The Mercedes bearing Heinrich Eberhart rolled smoothly along the country road in the direction of his ancestral home. He was back from Poland, and had never loved Germany more. The moment his train had crossed the border into the fatherland, he had felt as if a huge weight had been lifted from his shoulders. He told himself that he was never going back. What a backward country! What a bunch of thieves! How wonderful it was to return home. It was almost worth leaving just so he could experience the absolute joy of coming back! The telegram that he had sent had arrived in time, despite the fact that it had been sent from some bungling Polish post office. His aide and his freshly waxed Mercedes had been there to welcome him at the station.

Gunther rushed to take his suitcase from him and, after depositing it in the trunk, ran to open the door for him. Eberhart settled himself into the cracked-leather seat, and was about to light his cigarette when Gunther reached over and lit it for him. Then they drove out of the station and onto the roads leading to the estate. Eberhart waited somewhat tensely for Gunther to tell him the news from the time he had been away. Had anything untoward happened? Had they received any threatening letters in the mail? But then he remembered that he had left instructions not to open the mail. Marianne would have followed his orders. She had been well trained by her military father.

He leaned back into the seat with a sigh of relief, the nervous feelings still there. Yet it had only been a week and a half. That wasn't sufficient time for the vultures. It would take his rivals a little more time until they realized that he was ruined; or maybe not. Maybe the blessing had already begun its work! Maybe everything was going to work out somehow. He couldn't imagine how things would fall into place, but the *Rabbiner* had made him a promise and he trusted the holy man's word. There must be something to the blessing. *Well,* he told himself as he drifted off to sleep, *I'll find out soon enough. No point worrying about it now.*

The next thing he knew, Gunther was turning the car into the sweeping driveway that led up to the old manor house. Eberhart had spent the formative years of his life in this elegant house, and he recalled many of his childhood activities with a warm smile. Gunther drove rapidly, as if he, too, was happy to have Eberhart back, and wanted to get him home as quickly as possible. Within moments they drove around a bend in the hilly road, and the mansion appeared before their eyes.

It had been constructed in the 18th century by the second Eberhart, whose deeds had been recorded in history. Holy Roman Emperor Charles VI had granted him this property and mansion as a gift in recognition of their friendship, and the Eberhart family had lived there ever since.

Gunther drove the car up to the stately granite steps, and told Eberhart that he was going to park the car. Heinrich headed up the stairs, not knowing what to expect when he got inside. At the top he paused, unsure for a moment, anxiety filling his heart, not knowing what unexpected surprises would be there to greet him. Taking a deep breath, he steeled himself and was about to knock on the door when the wide double doors were thrown open. Marianne Eberhart stood there framed in the late evening light.

"Heinrich," she called out in delight, "we've been waiting for hours! What happened?" Marianne Eberhart was descended from a family just as prestigious as the Eberharts, and almost as wealthy. She was the daughter of the man who had been the commanding officer of Eberhart's legion in the German Army. They had met when the officer had invited him to a formal dinner in his home. The most terrifying day of his life had been the day he'd had to request permission from his future father-in-law to court his daughter. He still recalled that moment and felt the shivers go down his spine.

"A bit of a delay at the border," he said, gratified by the warm welcome.

"Well, you're home now," she said. "Come in, the cook has prepared a special dinner in honor of your return." Still no word of anything out of the ordinary. Everyone was obviously under the impression that he had traveled to Poland on a business trip. So far so good. He entered the grand entrance hall, taking a deep breath of the familiar scent of home. There was nothing like it.

Marianne walked by his side, thrilled to have him back, knowing nothing of the torment he had experienced over the past week. He had always kept her sheltered from the anxieties and challenges that he faced in the business arena. That had worked well for all concerned. He was the provider and she ran the home. He made his tired way up to the master bedroom on the third floor for a relaxing bath, his usual means of unwinding. This was when he returned home from business trips, successful or otherwise.

"We'll serve dinner as soon as you come down," she said, and he nodded. The smells that were wafting toward him from the kitchen gave promise of a delicious meal, made all the better due to the fact that he had barely eaten for the past week. He had lost quite a few kilos on this trip to Poland. As he undressed and chose a fluffy white towel and donned his robe, he was waiting for something to happen; for someone to come bursting into his room waving a letter from his bank saying that they were going to foreclose on his house. But nothing happened. Everything was silent, relaxing and wonderful. This was his home and life was the way he preferred it to be.

What about the Autobahn deal? a little voice inside his head whispered.

The Rabbiner gave me a blessing, he answered the little voice sharply, but it refused to back down.

So he gave you a blessing, so what! Are you so sure that it worked? Do you know for a fact that everything is fine? No! I've absolutely never seen you as worked up about anything as you have been over this!

He decided that there was no point in trying to relax. He wouldn't be able to enjoy the bath at this point anyway. He might as well shower, put on his smoking jacket and go down to his study to read the mail, assess the damage and find out if he was going to make it through this. He took a very quick shower. Then he strode briskly through the house and entered his office, pausing in the doorway like a condemned man on the way to the gallows. If any room in the house was his, this was it. Marianne had the run of the mansion and the estate when it came to decor, but Heinrich put his foot down when it came to his office.

This was his domain, an island of masculinity in a feminine world. A heavy wooden desk sat squarely in the middle of the room. There was a pile of mail in the center of the blotter left there by Gunther. He felt his heart rate begin to speed up. This was it. His creditors had caught on to his situation. They were demanding payment from the firm, money that he didn't have. This was the beginning of the end. What was he going to do?

Wait, he told himself, *you don't know that for sure. Go look at your mail."*

He sat in the black leather chair behind the desk, and reached with trembling hands for the mail. He lifted the pile. It was heavy, and for a moment he imagined that there was a bomb in one of the packages. He set the mail down on the desk and opened the envelopes one by one: An invitation to a dance being held at the Museum of Culture and Sport, a letter from Jorg Haider, an old army friend, two bills and a few miscellaneous items. There underneath it all lay a large envelope bearing the insignia of Reichsfuhrer Himmler's office.

He picked up the envelope and with a letter opener, he slit it open neatly. There was one piece of paper inside the envelope, and he laid it out neatly on his desk. He read in disbelief:

> *To Herr Heinrich Eberhart,*
>
> *You are summoned to meet with the Reichsfuhrer regarding the continuation of your earlier discussion. Bring any and all pertinent information that would be appropriate in the furthering of the discussion. The Reichsfuhrer wishes to facilitate construction of the ultimate army base, and requests your presence in his Berlin office on the sixth of May at noon. Please confirm that you will attend as soon as you receive this letter.*
>
> *Heil Hitler,*
> *Konrad Papenheim*
> *Office of the Reichsfuhrer*

Wordlessly, Eberhart reached for the phone, his heart singing with joy and a feeling of deliverance. Somehow, it was all working out. He was going to Berlin! He didn't understand, but he didn't need to. What was important was that everything had worked out. Himmler hadn't sold him out for Sernteiner. The Autobahn project was still on track, and with him in charge of the army-base project, there was no way that the government would be diverting the Autobahn from its planned route. No, they would build the army base without destroying anything along the way.

Maybe you imagined the whole thing, the little voice said sarcastically. *Some dumb clerk in the Ministry of Highways made a mistake and sent you that first letter, and you went crazy, all for nothing.*

But Eberhart knew that it wasn't true. There was no way the Ministry of Highways would have done something like that without being ordered to do so from high up. Very high up. Roadways such as the Autobahn didn't get shifted around on a whim, even to build an army base. There was too much work involved. There had been millions invested in the geological surveys that had been conducted. A team of the most-qualified engineers had met to decide on the exact place to place exposives to bore through mountains, where to level off valleys. No, the order to divert the road in place of the army base had definitely been a deliberate order from someone extremely high up in the Nazi Party. Somehow Himmler had been convinced as well. Sernteiner had to have been behind the whole thing. The proof of that was when Eberhart had tried to reach him, Sernteiner had been constantly unavailable. Now, Sernteiner was suffering the consequences.

He stood up from his desk in a daze. His future glowed brightly before his eyes. The Autobahn project was still on. His creditors would be waiting patiently for their money. The banks would not be pressing him or trying to foreclose. The army base was a project of his office. Himmler wanted to meet with him, not with Sernteiner. It was a miracle! As if in a dream he recalled the words of the *Rabbiner* who sat in a tiny village, yet who saw the entire picture. Once again, he pledged that he would fulfill his promise to the *Rabbiner* and he would hire many Jews as long as he was able to do so without endangering himself. He practically danced out of his office. Marianne stood outside the study door as he came into the hallway. She looked at him as if he was a complete stranger.

"Heinrich?" she asked him bewildered.

"Yes!" he replied.

"Are you O.K.? Is everything all right?" She had never seen him so happy, so utterly at peace with himself and the world around him.

"Yes, Marianne," he said, "everything is amazing, better than amazing! It's going to be a grand ride from here on!" And he danced to the dining room for dinner. Marianne was accustomed to dour Teutonic men. But what was wrong with being happy? Did it make her husband any less of a provider? On the contrary, it made life so much more enjoyable, didn't it? And so she joined her husband in the great dining hall for what was obviously a celebratory feast of some kind. It didn't really matter to her either way. She didn't involve herself in the business. It was better that way. She would continue running the household. If he wanted to share his good news with her, then he would. But oh, how nice it was to see him in such a good mood. He was always so serious, his thoughts focused on the firm. But now, just look at him! He was smiling from ear to ear; he even had a mischievous look on his face. She could not for the life of her recall when she had seen this youthful side of him last.

Over dinner, Eberhart presented his wife with a belated anniversary gift. The look on her face when she opened the velvet box was well worth the price of the present. He had purchased the expensive piece of jewelry shortly before his world had collapsed. At that time, he hesitated to give it to her, knowing that he might have to bring it back to the store if he wasn't the recipient of a miracle. But the miracle had arrived, and Marianne gazed down at the gold-and-emerald necklace with wonder on her face. Words failed her. Eberhart, normally a man who kept his emotions hidden away from his family behind a stone wall, looked at her and said, "May we brighten each other's worlds, just like they do. Happy anniversary."

He hadn't known how weighed down he had been feeling until the weights had been removed. He felt unshackled, unfettered, free! He could fly again. The world was his oyster. He could conquer everything. But he had a promise to keep and he couldn't forget that. He wouldn't allow himself to forget that. He would have Gunther look into the matter in his usual discreet way. With the latest series of harsh decrees, he was sure that many more Jews had lost their sources of livelihood. The government no longer permitted gentiles to employ Jews, which severely limited their ability to earn a living. Gunther would have to circumvent the new legislation but he was certain he would succeed. Things would be changing around here pretty soon. It was the least he could do for the *Rabbiner* — the man who had changed his life for the good.

Marianne gave the signal, and the servants began bringing in the courses, bountiful and so delicious that Heinrich wanted seconds. For the first time in years, he finished everything he was served and even asked for more. Marianne was speechless and couldn't understand what had happened to him.

The following morning found Eberhart sitting in his study catching up on the news that he'd missed during the time he had been away. It was while he was reading the four-day-old newspaper that he came across a very interesting tidbit in the national news section. The article read as follows:

Industrialist Arrested For Involvement In Communist Plot

Herr Dieter Sernteiner of Stuttgart was arraigned yesterday on a charge of involvement in a Communist overthrow of the government. Sernteiner did not resist arrest, but was quite vocal in his protestations of innocence. The 45-year-old industrialist has connections in high places, but they were loath to defend him, as the evidence against Sernteiner continually mounted.

"We are conducting a thorough investigation," said Stuttgart chief of police, Wolfgang Shterner, "and hope to go to trial shortly."

Meanwhile, the German Communist Party circulated a letter denying the allegations of a plot, and calling it a pack of lies. "Serteiner was never one of us," said Ludwig Schaefer, head of the German Communist Party, speaking from an unknown location.

Sernteiner remains in jail, and will be facing the prospect of a harsh jail sentence in the event of a conviction.

As he read the words, his eyes swam with tears of joy. Not because he thought that Sernteiner had been framed; on the contrary, the accusations were very possibly true. But because of the miracle that had happened to him and his family. He was a free man, he had great things to look forward to and he would be traveling to Berlin, the following week. Yes, he had a lot to be thankful for and he knew it. A certain *Rabbiner* in a little town in the Polish countryside knew it, too.

Berlin, Germany
May 3, 1936

Berlin was still the same. Even though the regime had taken control of all aspects of life, there were still some things that resisted change, and the atmosphere of Berlin was one of them. Eberhart, serious as he was, loved it. Ludwig was in school at Offenbach, one of Germany's finest institutions, and Heinrich decided to bring Marianne along for the trip. She was a homebody, and she spent half the trip staring out the window of the first-class coach with wide-eyed wonder, and the second half commenting excitedly to Heinrich about the sights she had seen.

Something in the middle-aged man had changed. He had always treated his wife with politeness, and provided wonderfully for her, but his heart hadn't been there. But inexplicably, Heinrich Eberhart had become a different person, and Marianne was the chief beneficiary of her husband's altered personality. They checked into The Majestic, one of Berlin's finer hotels. They spent several days wining and dining all over the town.

The morning of his second meeting with Himmler dawned cloudy with a solid drizzle that showed no signs of abating. Eberhart donned his finest suit for the occasion and wore a cashmere coat over it. He whistled as he brushed his thick brown hair and knotted his tie. Marianne told him that he looked very handsome. A taxi was waiting for him at the appointed hour, and he set off toward the Reichsfuhrer's office, stomach all a-flutter. The cab pulled up to the curb, and Eberhart jumped out, ready and eager for his meeting. He carried a folder under his arm bursting with several plans and ideas to show the Reichsfuhrer.

Once again, he was challenged by the sentries on duty. Once again, he was allowed inside after a brief interrogation. This place was obviously off limits to most civilians. In fact, Heinrich was one of the few men in the entire building who wasn't wearing a uniform. He didn't feel out of place, though. Twenty years earlier, he had gone to war for his country, and would do so again if that was what his country needed. He was not a coward. A steely-eyed soldier motioned for him to come along, and Heinrich obeyed without question.

He followed the man up a staircase. Neither man spoke. Although it was a massive building, and there were hundreds of people working there, Eberhart couldn't hear a sound. An overall sense of fear pervaded the atmosphere. From far away, he could hear what sounded like cries of pain. Animal like, they echoed through the hallways, the very sound raising goose bumps on his arms. He recalled hearing about the infamous basement at this address. On his previous visit, he had been too awestruck by his surroundings to recognize the screams for what they were. But now, they seemed to float up from the building's depths and resounded with a seamless cry.

The soldier didn't pay attention. He was probably hardened to them and didn't give them a second thought. But as they climbed higher and higher, Eberhart imagined that he could still hear them, and the sound was painful. Security had been extensively increased since his previous visit, and he wondered if an attempt on Himmler's life was the reason for the additional soldiers. His folders were searched thoroughly, but there was nothing there aside from his drafts. Eventually they were handed back to him and they were on their way. There was no waiting this time. The moment they arrived at Himmler's office, he was told to enter.

Himmler was sitting at his desk when Eberhart entered the room. He was perusing some papers with a thoughtful expression on his face. Eberhart wondered how many corpses were the stepping-stones for this man's bloody ascent to power. Himmler glanced at Eberhart and his eyes lit up with anticipation. Scrawling his signature on a few of the papers, he placed them into a drawer, effectively clearing his desk for the presentation to come.

"Good of you to come, Herr Eberhart," he said.

"It was my pleasure, Reichsfuhrer," he replied. Himmler nodded.

"O.K., let's see those plans," he said, rubbing his hands together.

Eberhart unrolled a sheaf of architectural designs on his desk, and began walking the man through them step-by-step. He explained the purpose of each section and the incredible amount of attention on the seemingly endless details that had been required. Himmler was clearly impressed and complimented him on the originality of the designs more than once. The meeting lasted for well over three hours, with Himmler delineating a number of additional sections that he wanted, while Eberhart took copious notes.

"Pity about Sernteiner being a Communist, eh?" Himmler commented to Eberhart. Eberhart smiled weakly in return. It seemed from the look of things that Himmler liked him, and that he hadn't liked Sernteiner enough, or maybe there had been a power play between him and Goebbels, and Goebbels had lost. Who knew the truth? Suddenly, he wasn't so sure how he felt about this business development, but there was nothing he could do. If the Third Reich desired him as their public servant, refusal just wasn't an option. If he had any questions about how they treated those who displeased them, all he had to do was think of Sernteiner.

Over the next few years, the influence of the Eberhart Construction Company became somewhat legendary in German government circles as a company that could be relied on to get the job done for the best price and on time. The Autobahn project had been completed, using two additional firms in place of Sernteiner. The contract had been as air tight as Eberhart's lawyers could make it. The other firms were just content to be part of such an auspicious deal, and accepted every clause on which he insisted. The Sernteiner debacle had taught him a huge lesson about business, and he never forgot it. Never trust anyone! That was his motto, and he found no reason to think differently. The ultimate army base was a bit trickier, especially due to the fact that Himmler kept on changing his mind as to what he wanted. But Eberhart kept his cool, flattered the stocky man and pulled off a brilliant job in the end.

The government had insisted on the job being done as fast as humanly possible, so they had put the army on it, with a stream of never-ending labor available at any hour of the day and night. He was able to build the base so that it met the highest, most-exacting criteria. Himmler was ecstatic, and the honor of the cutting of the ribbon at the opening was given to *Der Fuhrer* himself, who gave a rousing speech that was carried live over the airwaves. Eberhart was accorded a seat on the dais. He surprised his son, Ludwig, by driving down to Offenbach, picking him up and taking him to the ceremony. He watched with great amusement as Ludwig's mouth fell open and remained that way. The dais was a veritable sea of celebrities, ranging from Hitler and Himmler to other lesser-known party officials.

Ludwig, who was by now a strapping youth, made a wonderful impression on the bigwigs of the Nazi Party. Himmler himself gave him the once-over and pronounced him "a fine specimen of German manhood, perfect material for the Waffen SS." Ludwig saw the esteem and respect his father was given and was excited about that as well. Marianne was overwhelmed by how beautiful their lives had become. In her wildest dreams she had never imagined her husband as the darling of the Nazi Party.

They stopped off at a charming little place to eat on the way home, and Heinrich seized the opportunity to discuss Ludwig's future, now that they were all together.

"So I was thinking, Ludwig," he began, as the waiter served their appetizers and the meal got underway, "it's time to begin thinking about the next stage of your education. Your mother and I agree that the University of Vienna presents a very solid place for you to realize your dreams. It's also where I was educated. What do you think?"

Subconsciously Eberhart found himself leaning forward as he

spoke, trying to convince his son with the earnest style he used while talking business.

"Papa," Ludwig said, "I'm sorry, I don't think the University of Vienna is the right place for me right now." Eberhart was about to protest, but Ludwig wasn't finished yet.

"Not only that," he went on, "but I don't think that the climate of the Germany of today is suitable for attending university at all!" Ludwig was speaking passionately now. *"Der Fuhrer* has explained the political situation time and again, and I think it's very clear what I should be doing with the next few years of my life."

"And that is —" prompted his father.

"The army, the navy, or the air force; something to do with the military," Ludwig said. "With the situation as dangerous as it is, and the army being forced to go on high alert, it seems clear to me that I have no choice but to enlist. And," he paused, "having met the Reichsfuhrer today, it seems pretty obvious to me that a word from you, Father, in the right ears would open the doors to the Waffen SS. In my opinion, there is no better place to serve." He spoke with the conviction of youth. Heinrich was proud of him despite the disappointment that he felt.

"You're still below draft age," he said slowly, trying to find the words to keep his only, beloved son out of the military for at least a while longer.

"Papa," Ludwig said, "does it really matter? It's only a matter of time until I'm old enough. This way I get a head start. I could be an officer by the time we are at war." Eberhart knew that his son's heart was made up. His son was stubborn in that way. Once he had decided on something, it was like talking to a rock; a very handsome rock.

"Now that Austria has been annexed," Ludwig continued his political analysis, "it's only a matter of time before Czechoslovakia becomes part of Germany, finally returning what is ours."

Eberhart was astounded. Ludwig had always been apolitical in the past, showing virtually zero interest in current events. This was a first, and Heinrich was very surprised.

"Finally showing an interest in politics, eh?" he commented, but Ludwig spoke sharply.

"Don't make fun of me, Papa," he said. *"Der Fuhrer* is the greatest man to have risen in Germany since Martin Luther and Bismarck! When he speaks, the entire country listens. The man is a gift from above. For once everyone realizes it and maybe that's the greatest miracle of all!"

"But Ludwig," his father interjected, "you are young and you think war is a good thing. I'm a little older than you and I will never forget the time I spent serving at the front during the Great War. Those were the coldest months of my life! We lay in those trenches, surrounded by rats that bit us and infected us with life-threatening diseases. The cold seeped into our very marrow. We sang patriotic songs, but deep inside each and every one of us, there was one desire, just one. Do you know what that was? To see our dear country again, to return home alive and in one piece. So many of those boys didn't make it. Almost an entire generation of European youth lost their lives on the battlefields of Europe. I tasted the mustard gas, Ludwig! It was my eyes that burned and my tongue that felt like ash. I saw my best friends dying needlessly over a few inches of useless farmland. For what? For what purpose, Ludwig? Don't you understand, son, that war is a terrible, terrible thing, and the country is much better off without it!"

"*Der Fuhrer* says there's not going to be another war if our neighbors come to understand that we mean what we say and we will not back down anymore," Ludwig countered.

"But you said before that you could be an officer by the time there's another war! That means that you understand that it's not out of the realm of possibility. We are definitely moving in that direction, son, it's only a matter of time. But don't think that it's enjoyable or exciting. It's plain horrible, scary and dangerous. When you're lying face down in the mud, it's as unglamorous as any activity can be! So realize what you're getting yourself into!"

"I don't care, Papa," Ludwig said, raising his voice and bashing his fist down on the table in a vicious fury. "*Der Fuhrer* has lifted this country out of the hole into which it had sunk. He is a miracle man and he has rescued us. He deserves my support. He has it because I believe in him. Anyway, Papa, you are doing more work for the Reich than anyone else I know. If you don't think that the policy of the government is right for the country, then why do you support its efforts with your work?"

The other patrons in the restaurant were discreetly eavesdropping, wondering at the scene. Heinrich was suddenly afraid of the wrong people overhearing the conversation.

"You misunderstood me," he said to his son, laying a soothing hand on his arm. "Of course I think that *Der Fuhrer* is the best thing for this country. He is a great man and I will follow him in whichever direction he takes us." Ludwig was visibly calming down.

"However, I want you to use your mind as well, son, and think about the consequences of your actions. Being a soldier is not just about the glamour, that's all I'm saying. Having a war is a tough thing. Ask any veteran and they'll tell you the same. Even Hitler himself would tell you that. He suffered terribly during World War I! I want you to think about your decision a bit more before you rush off to the nearest recruitment office to sign up. If, after you have given the matter sufficient thought, you still decide that you want to join the Waffen SS or any other division, I will give you my blessing and put in a word with anyone that you want me to. How does that sound?"

Ludwig smiled at his father and began to cut his steak.

"Sounds great," he said. "I'll do some thinking. But you get ready to speak to the men in charge, because Ludwig Eberhart is coming to town."

June 8, 1938

It hadn't been easy, but he had kept his promise to the *Rabbiner*. While the situation for the Jews of Germany had gone from bad to worse, things were very different in the world of Heinrich Eberhart. In a way, he had benefited from the cruel edicts that were constantly being decreed against the Jews. Due to the numerous decrees, it was very hard for a Jew — even an educated Jew — to find a job. Gentiles weren't allowed to work for them, and hiring them was frowned upon. But using them as slave labor was something which the government approved of. So Heinrich reported that his employees were being paid next to nothing and that their services were vital for the projects he undertook for the fatherland.

Then one day he entered the dining hall during lunch hour, and heard the workers talking in agitated tones. They quieted down the moment he entered the room in a way that made him very curious. He waited half an hour, then called one of them into his office.

"Jacob," he said, "what's going on?"

"Herr Eberhart," answered the man, "didn't you hear what happened last night?"

"Obviously not," he replied.

"Quite a number of German Jews were woken up in the middle of the night and deported, taken away, just like that, in their pajamas. They were given time to pack a few essentials, and then they were taken away.

Some of them were taken to Dachau," he said in a sudden whisper, his voice trembling with fear.

Eberhart had heard about Dachau. It was an infamous camp where the government sent anyone who disagreed with their policies. Jews were sent there simply because they were Jews. Himmler had even wanted to commission him to build a concentration camp, but luckily for him, Himmler realized he had too much on his plate at the time to do a good job.

"I have to tell you something, Herr Eberhart," Jacob said to him.

"Yes, Jacob?"

"We're all extremely grateful for your protection here at the company. It's somewhat of a known fact that anyone who works for the Eberhart Company is untouchable. When we show our papers, the soldiers even treat us with respect. It's an amazing thing, and we owe you tremendous thanks."

"You just better pray that they continue giving me projects, so I need my team of qualified architects and bookkeepers, and everyone else who is involved. You're not just here because I took pity on you," Eberhart said, in an attempt to put the man at ease. "Each one of you is here because you're an expert in your field, and I need you to help make the work of Eberhart Construction the best in the market. It's not for nothing that we are still sitting on top, you know! A good company is only as good as its workers. I value every one of you. I want you to tell that to all my friends out there."

Jacob's eyes were moist as he looked at his boss with gratitude.

"It's good that there are some people like you left in Germany," he said, "otherwise, we would all give up right now!" Then he turned and left the office.

~

Months passed. Everything had changed. Ludwig had finished high school and had chosen to make a career out of the army. More than anything, he wanted to be part of the Waffen SS, so Heinrich had called in a few favors. It had not been necessary, however. The officers had been as impressed with him as he was with them. Ludwig was full of admiration for the men leading his brigade. Only the fittest were chosen. The weeding-out process was grueling! They had been made to swim laps. They swam and swam, until the majority had dropped out. Even after that, the officers made them swim some more. Only those who kept on going until they nearly drowned were chosen.

They piled sandbags on their legs and made them do push-ups until their bodies ached as they had never ached before! They ran obstacle courses and burrowed under barbed-wire fences, and survived without food for long periods of time. They ran in the heat and were deprived of sleep for hours at a time. Only the fittest were chosen, and Ludwig was one of those. They were the future of Germany, the cream of the crop. The young boy whom Himmler had said "was a perfect specimen of German manhood" had arrived. He was taught how to be a leader. It was a trait that was inborn in him, but it was cultivated and it flourished.

Heinrich and Marianne attended the graduation ceremony. Ludwig stood at 6-foot-3 inches, light-blond hair parted on the left, looking extremely grown up in his gray-green uniform with the silver buttons, and SS rune on the collar. Himmler himself attended the ceremony, and delivered a truly uninspiring speech. Eberhart hugged his son to his heart when he received the coveted dagger, and examined it with pride. He knew that his inner feelings were extremely ambivalent.

He had never been prouder of his son, his country or the German people, in his entire life. He had never been more fulfilled at work either. The company had become the dominating force on the scene. What they had accomplished was incredible. To think that Germany had gone from being an impoverished land under the heel of the depression to the industrial giant it was today was so amazing that there were no words. On the other hand, there were the atrocities, and Eberhart couldn't fool himself about that. They existed. He had heard about the camps and about many of the experiments that were being conducted on a certain segment of the population.

The fact that the Eberhart firm did so much business with the office of the Reichsfuhrer meant that he found himself in Berlin more and more frequently. It also meant that he was meeting new people on a constant basis. Some of those people enjoyed boasting of their devilish accomplishments. It was that simple. But it meant that Eberhart couldn't fall asleep. At least he was able to partially console himself with the knowledge that his firm was still managing to employ a significant number of Jews. In the end, they hadn't been able to remain in their homes. That had proven to be too problematic to swing. So Eberhart had cordoned off a portion of one of the company's properties and turned it into a place for his employees and their families to live. And so, while the Germans were beginning their systematic annihilation of European

Jewry, the Eberhart firm was doing its best to protect the Jews who were employed there.

And yet, how could he not help but be proud of the German soldiers?

They had taken Poland in a few days, just as he had foreseen three years earlier. The Poles had come out with their cavalry and horses, and had been blown to bits by the tanks and the troops on their motorcycles. The Polish troops turned tail and ran. They removed their uniforms and put on civilian clothing so they could deny that they had fought in the army. The German troops easily took control. But Hitler wasn't satisfied. He was going all the way. A part of Eberhart believed that he might succeed. Would the Thousand-Year Reich actually endure? They had been welcomed into Austria with showers of flowers, and were granted control of Czechoslovakia by the cowardly leaders of the West who were now learning, to their chagrin, that Adolf Hitler was not the paper tiger they had thought he was.

Ludwig was a captain by now, and had been awarded several prestigious medals for showing incredible bravery under fire. One of the generals on Himmler's staff had casually mentioned to Heinrich that Himmler himself had his eye on the young man. He just knew that there were great times ahead for his son. Such bravery and sound reasoning under fire did not go unnoticed for long. Marianne was proud of her son, yet frightened for him as well. Eberhart knew of the many nights she had lain awake, too enveloped in fear to sleep.

At least he was able to lose himself in his work. No matter how many projects the firm did, there was always something else to build, always another task to complete. There was always an air-force base to design and build, an underground bunker for *Der Fuhrer* and his staff to use in the event of an attack, resort villas for the top officials of the Nazi Party. There were more roads to build, especially in the occupied lands, and Eberhart found himself traveling extensively to oversee the construction of his numerous projects. Through it all, the money was pouring in. He was an honest man and never skimmed off the top.

But even without dishonesty, his bank account had grown and swelled to the point where he opened a new account at a bank in Zurich. He accomplished that the next time he had to travel to Switzerland on government business. Yes, life was good for the Eberhart family: richer than ever before, with a son more successful than they had ever dreamed of, and still keeping his word to the *Rabbiner*.

26
Ludwig Eberhart

Hamburg, Germany
September 2, 1944

There was something he hadn't done, though, and his conscience wouldn't leave him alone about it. He owed it all — every inch of his success — to a simple man, who had taken him into his home when he had been down, had fed him, had given him a bed and had pointed him in the right direction. Joshua Weinberger. Heinrich had never forgotten him despite all the time that had gone by. On the train returning back from Poland, he had told himself that as soon as he saw that the *Rabbiner's* blessing had come true, he was going to get into his car and go pay the man a visit. But he hadn't done it. He was beholden to someone, and he had never done a thing about it! What was wrong with him? Eberhart men were noted for their sense of indebtedness, and here he owed this man his life, and in his eyes the debt just kept piling up.

The years had gone by. He told himself a least once a day that he would find out how Joshua was — tomorrow. He was going to go visit him and repay the man for all the good he had done for the Eberhart family. But he hadn't gone. That had been back in the seminormal days when the Jews were still living in their homes. These days, the majority of German Jewry were no longer in Germany. Those who were still alive were in ghettos or concentration camps. They were in Auschwitz and Bergen-Belsen, in Dachau and Treblinka. They were shoveling coal in the Carpathian forests and laying railroad tracks in Yugoslavia.

Yet, Heinrich owed the man too much for him to just ignore. He tried to still his guilt-ridden soul by treating his workers even better than before. They appreciated it, but he didn't feel any better inside. Joshua Weinberger was the first thing he thought about when he awoke in the morning, and the last thing he thought about before he fell asleep at night. He dreamed about the man. Ultimately he decided to search for Joshua's whereabouts and think of a plan that would allow him to help the man. It wouldn't be easy, but this was something he felt he had to do. There was no pushing it off any longer. How would he feel if he finally got around to looking for his old friend and discovered that he'd been gassed to death a few days earlier?! He would never forgive himself if he found out that he could have saved him, if he had just cared a bit more!

He was going to find the man. Easier said than done. But he was Eberhart after all, and by this time, there were many government officials who owed him a slew of favors. He had been helpful over the years — always happy to assist in any way possible — and now everyone was anxious to repay him. It took him a while, but in the end he was able to discover which office kept track of the whereabouts of the European Jews. He had always known something like this existed; there was simply no way that an obsessive-compulsive people like the Germans would lose out on an opportunity to keep thousands of lists bearing millions of names. This was heaven to many Germans, and of course there was such a bureau. It was one of the more secretive offices, away from the public eye.

Government reasoning went as follows: The mass destruction and murder of the Jewish nation clearly did not disturb the majority of the German people. But it was easier for them to feel that way when the subject wasn't coming up to slap them in the face. Out of sight, out of mind, went the motto, and it made sense. But it existed, and that was enough for him.

He kept his cover story simple. He was searching for one of his employees who had been arrested and deported before he had a chance to intervene. This man was an expert in his field, and Eberhart needed him back. His absence was affecting the firm in a bad way. No one wished to stand in the way of such a giant. It was like starting up with Krupp. You had to be crazy to do something like that. He had always believed that the simple approach was the best way to go about doing anything. He just showed up at this particular office and gave them a job: Track down one Joshua Weinberger and do it fast!

The clerks were nothing if not efficient. They got onto it immediately, and within 12 hours they had discovered that while Joshua and his family had originally been sent to Dachau, they had been transferred over the years, first to Bergen-Belsen and then to Auschwitz, where he was engaged in hard labor while his wife worked at the munitions factory. Most of their children were no longer alive. It was time to pay the man back for saving his life, and Eberhart was in a position to do so. Being actively involved in projects across Europe meant that he could drive wherever he wanted without arousing suspicion. Jewish people along for the ride didn't signify anything wrong; they were merely his employees. So one morning Eberhart set off on a cross-country inspection trip. His itinerary stated exactly where he was to be found on any given day. It just happened to be that he would be visiting Auschwitz instead of a nearby construction site.

Nobody knew what he had planned. No cloud of suspicion hovered over him whatsoever. Everyone admired Eberhart. Himmler invited him to his office from time to time just to discuss world history and the German impact on it. Hermann Goering, chief of the Luftwaffe, was indebted to him for the many airfields his firm had built on demand, and the speed with which they had completed the job. He was everyone's favorite; consequently, no one challenged him. He carried papers of the highest order, and his security clearance was from the highest in the Reich due to the fact that his firm had constructed the majority of the most sensitive military projects throughout the war. And so, he drove without hindrance, crossing the Polish border with confident ease.

It was strange to be returning to Poland, a land he had sworn never to reenter. This time, there were no corrupt Polish border guards to riffle through his belongings and demand illegal bribery for the privilege of visiting the backward country. No, this time he drove straight up to the border in his Mercedes. He showed his ID to the soldiers, who smiled and offered him a drink. He handed out packages of cigarettes to all the soldiers, and stopped for a few minutes to shoot the breeze. A few of them had served with Ludwig, and they spoke of him in reverential tones. Eberhart hadn't known that his son was such a legend, but almost every one of them had a story to tell about Ludwig. When he drove away a few hours later, he was prouder of his son than he had ever been.

He drove through the countryside remembering the way it had been all those years before. The peacefulness was no more. The highways were crowded with military traffic whizzing by. Armored cars, soldiers on motorcycles, and the occasional tank all shared the roads with the few civilians who had the clearance and the means to fill up a tank of gas in those days of rationed gasoline. But Eberhart always got whatever he needed. "Gasoline? No problem. Take as much as you want. Oil for the engine? Please take as much as you need!"

He made good time, and stayed at Eberhart Construction sites along the way. He was given the royal treatment, and he caught a few blunders that he was able to correct.

He reached Auschwitz in the early evening. From afar he could see the watchtowers. The roads were clearly marked with big warning signs sporting red, block lettering telling passersby that they were approaching a restricted area. The security was high. The guards were regular SS, and he knew better than to mention his son to these men. The rivalry between the regular SS and the Waffen SS was as intense as it had ever been. The Waffen SS considered the regular SS parasites who spent their time away from the danger at the front lines, and they were extremely contemptuous of them. The regular SS called the Waffen SS a bunch of arrogant buffoons, and there was no love lost between the two.

As he approached the sprawling complex that was Auschwitz, Eberhart thought about the time he had met the commandant of Auschwitz, and what a deplorable impression he had made on him. Rudolf Hess was a psychopath in his opinion and as mentally deranged as they came. This man was responsible for a camp that killed thousands of human beings on a daily basis! How did the man sleep at night? What had this war done to the German people? What had that madman Hitler done to the collective conscience of the nation? A people that had loved children were shooting them in their heads. A nation that revered poetry was burning people and books as quickly as they could get their hands on them. What was the world coming to?

The road on which he was driving ran parallel to train tracks. A short distance away he could see a cattle train pulling into the camp. From between the barred openings he caught a glimpse of a little girl waving a red handkerchief at him. He felt a lump rising in his throat at the knowledge that she was going to be ashes in a matter of hours. He could hear the shouting of the guards as they directed the train into the camp, as he turned the car onto the separate road leading into the parking area. Here as well, he had to pass through a roadblock manned by tough-looking soldiers. But he showed them his identification, and they waved him through with the minimum of fuss.

This part of the camp was completely different from the other sections. Flowers bloomed in planters, and tall trees waved their branches in the breeze. The sky was turning red with the setting sun, and he thought how appropriate the color was for this part of the world; red, blood red. *Welcome to hell. I'm the angel of death, coming to show you around.* In a few minutes, he found himself at an administrative center clerked by civilians in civilian clothes. Eberhart was taken aback by how normal even the most horrific activities could be made to appear. It was all about the staging.

"*A gutten tag*," he said to the girl behind the desk. "I have an appointment to meet with Major Wilhelm Danknar at 6:30."

"Who should I say is here for him, sir?" she asked him.

"Heinrich Eberhart," he said. In a matter of minutes, the screen door of the administrative building burst open, and Major Danknar came running in.

"Herr Eberhart," he said, giving Heinrich a warm welcome. "What can I do for you?"

They had met when Willie had been attached to the security detail at the Reich Planning and Zoning Offices. Eberhart had always been pleasant to the young man, and he apparently remembered that.

"Good to see you, Willie," he told the man, who glowed with pride at the fact that a man as important as Eberhart was calling him by his first name. "I came down here for a specific reason."

"Anything," Willie said. "Whatever you need, just say the word and it's yours."

"O.K.," Eberhart removed a notebook from his pocket, and pretended to consult with it for a second before turning back to Danknar again.

"Here's the thing," he said. "I had this amazing worker — actually one of my foremen on numerous projects for the Reich; a man with incredible capabilities. He had the respect of the workers. You name it, this guy did it. He was the perfect worker. Anyway, what happens? One day, this guy is walking in the market and is stopped by a pair of military police. Now it happens to be," here he stopped for a second and gave an embarrassed laugh, "that I'm not the strictest of bosses. I have always felt that I get much more out of my workers with gentler treatment than the other kind, if you know what I mean."

Willie assured him that he did.

"That being the case, my workers feel safe to walk the streets around the places where they live, since they are known as my workers, and nobody starts up with them. But these policemen were new on the beat, and they didn't know the score. So when my foreman was found to have been walking around without his identification pass, they went crazy. Next thing I knew, he's being shipped off to Poland with his entire family, and I need him back. I've let this thing lag for a while, because I've just been so busy. But I was finally down in this part of the country, and I said to myself, 'Now you have an opportunity to get him back to his job.' So here I am.

"I'm in a huge rush, Willie, so the quicker you can get the paperwork taken care of, the better. And I won't forget it either! The names are Joshua and Miriam Weinberger."

Willie was already opening files and going through lists.

"Listen," he told Eberhart, "this is going to take a while. The camp is absolutely huge. I mean, there aren't only Jews in this place. There are Gypsies, Russians, Poles and others. You'll have to give me an hour or two. Go on over to the cafeteria in the meanwhile, get yourself some strudel and coffee. I think there's a musical troupe performing tonight for the boys. I'm sure you'll enjoy that, O.K.?"

Eberhart thanked him for the wonderful idea, and Willie explained how to get there. Then he left. The weather was balmy and warm, and he strolled down an attractive pathway in the direction of the cafeteria. It was easy to forget where you were in this part of the camp. But there was a smell here — a stench of death — a sickly sweet aroma of the chemicals used by the monsters who ran this institution. From somewhere not too far away, he heard the sounds of a loudspeaker blaring orders. On a sudden whim, he decided that instead of going to the cafeteria for something to eat, he might as well utilize this opportunity to take a good look at the actual camp, not just the part they showed tourists.

He had the requisite security pass; there was nothing impeding his movements. Without investing too much additional thought in the matter, he changed direction and began walking the other way toward the gate leading into the camp proper. He showed his ID to anyone who asked. Nobody was about to challenge a pass that had been issued straight out of Himmler's office, so he was able to walk freely with no concerns. The barracks on either sides of him were shrouded in semidarkness and were partially illuminated from the spotlights that were constantly rotating, sending bright shafts of light in every direction. The fences were plastered with notices that they were electrified. The warnings were written in several languages, and there was a picture of skull and crossbones along with the words in case someone didn't know how to read.

Every so often he passed pairs of officers on guard duty, accompanied by a ferocious German shepherd on a leash. The young men smiled at him and wished him a good evening. Try as he might, he couldn't fathom why these men believed the Jewish inmates deserved to be thrust like so many animals into a cage. Why? He longed to shout at their complacent faces: How are they different than you? But this was Auschwitz. You kept quiet and were happy that you were allowed to leave! From time to time he noticed shapes on the fences, and realized on closer inspection that they were bodies; the bodies of people who couldn't take it any longer and just wanted to get it over with. And he shuddered.

He reached the end of a section. It was much quieter here, much darker. The strobe of the inspection light didn't penetrate as strongly here. He was about to turn around when he noticed a figure detach himself from the shadow of the final barrack. The man was starting to run, and Eberhart sized up the situation in a microsecond. The man was going to run at the fence. He was going to kill himself! He watched in horror as the figure came closer, and then when the man was about 10 feet away, he caught a glimpse of his face and turned white with shock! It was Joshua Weinberger and he was charging at the fence with all his might, attempting to reach it before a soldier spotted him and shot him down.

Weinberger saw him too, and in that moment their eyes met. Eberhart saw that he recognized him as well. In that split second, they shared a look that transcended everything: the war, the barracks, the fact that Eberhart had surprised his friend just as he was trying to kill himself. He lifted his hand and whispered for him to stop. At the last moment before he would have hit the fence, Joshua threw himself down on the ground, and rolled away from the electrical currents, rolled away from the place where he had almost ended it all.

Eberhart had moved to the fence and wanted nothing more than to break through the fence and pick Joshua up off the floor. But there was nothing he could do at that second, besides for calling out to him softly. Suddenly, he noticed the shadows of the two guards returning. They were coming back the way they had come by earlier. Eberhart didn't know what would happen if they spotted him talking to a prisoner at the electric fence in the middle of Auschwitz. Whatever they would think wouldn't be good.

"Quick," he whispered sharply to Joshua, "run back to the shadows of your barrack now!"

"I don't care if they see me," Joshua said. "I want to die anyway! I can't live like this anymore!"

"Please," said Eberhart, "listen to me. Don't let them catch you now. Run away and come back when they're gone. I want to tell you something. Now go!!"

Joshua stood there for what seemed an eternity, and Eberhart was sure that it was too late. But finally, Joshua turned and ran like the wind, into the shadows of the barracks, just as the guards came into speaking distance from Eberhart.

Their dog began straining on his leash, and one of the guards looked at Eberhart strangely and asked, "Did you see anything out of the ordinary now? Anyone out where they weren't supposed to be?"

"Nope," he replied. "Sorry."

They watched him for a moment, clearly suspicious of this civilian who didn't have any legitimate reason for being where he was. Then they turned and went off in another direction. Eberhart waited until the sound of their footsteps had vanished in the distance, and then he whistled softly. Joshua came back to the fence. He was emaciated, as frail as a little child, and his beard was gone. In fact, Eberhart wasn't sure how he had recognized him at all. He looked so different! But it was definitely Joshua.

"Listen to me," he whispered to the shell of a man standing before him. "I came here to get you out of the camp tonight. So go back to your barracks and hold tight. Hopefully this will be your last few hours in this hellhole, O.K.?" He was rewarded with a tiny ghost of a smile. But Joshua shook his head for a second.

"What about my wife?" he asked Eberhart. "I can't leave without her!"

Eberhart wanted to say that he had just been about to kill himself without his wife, but he held his tongue, and said that it was being taken care of as they were speaking. Joshua turned without another word.

Eberhart retraced his steps in the direction of the cafeteria, seeking a hot, strong glass of coffee to calm his nerves. The cafeteria was mostly empty by the time he entered, and he could hear the music emanating from the auditorium next door. He walked into the auditorium for a minute and wanted to throw up.

Five soldiers were singing and dancing on the stage, while a four-piece band threatened to bring down the house. The audience was loving it, and suddenly, he couldn't hold it in any longer. Heinrich Eberhart ran out of the room and down the hall to the nearest bathroom where he proceeded to throw up everything in his system.

What was wrong with these people?! What kind of people were they? Killing others like it was no big deal, then eating dinner and seeing a show! Was there no justice in the world at all?!

He cleaned himself up as best he could, then left the bathroom and drank a cup of plain black coffee, which was pretty much the only thing he felt able to keep down. Sipping it slowly, he sat on the nearby couch and made a concerted effort to pull himself together. Then, not allowing himself to think, he left the cafeteria and returned to the administration offices where Willie was waiting triumphantly to greet him.

"I found the man," he told Eberhart cheerfully, "and I've just sent two soldiers to his barracks and another two to his wife's. They'll be here shortly. Did you have something to eat yet?"

"Plenty," Eberhart said dryly.

"Great," Willie answered. "The food is not bad in this place. I mean, you'd think, that it wouldn't be so good ..." his voice trailed off as he noticed the pale color on Eberhart's cheeks.

"Are you all right?" he asked anxiously.

"I'm fine," Eberhart said. "I'm just in a rush to get out of here. I've got several other sites to inspect, and then it's back to Germany for me, and a meeting with Martin Bormann. You get the picture."

There was a sudden noise, and then the outside door was pushed open. Joshua and his wife were escorted into the room. They were emaciated, skeletons in almost every way. He thought about mentioning the kids, but on second thought decided not to. He couldn't imagine that they had lasted this long in Auschwitz. He had to fill out quite a number of forms. Willie wasn't taking any chances even if it was Eberhart. But eventually he was finished. Willie handed them civilian clothing. When they were dressed and ready to go, he walked with them to the car.

"Well, good seeing you again, Herr Eberhart," he said as they shook hands. Eberhart waved as he drove out of Auschwitz proper, and turned left onto the road that would take them out of this hideous place. When he reached the highway, he pressed the gas pedal and floored it. He opened the window and let the wind blow his hair around and felt sicker then he had ever felt. He kept on driving until the feeling receded, as the Weinbergers fell asleep in the backseat of the car, and the slaughtering grounds of Poland disappeared behind them in a cloud of exhaust.

As he gazed at the huddled forms in the back of his car, he whispered to himself, *At least I did something good. At least I saved Joshua.*

Then, everything began falling apart. Who can pinpoint where the problems began? Many say that Hitler's decision to attack Russia was at the root of the German disaster, and their overwhelming defeat at Stalingrad was the final nail in their coffin. But regardless of the reasons, somehow, suddenly, the super Germany, the invincible Germany of the late 30's and early 40's was gone. And in its place a Germany that some of the older citizens recalled came to the forefront. It was the Germany of defeat. Once again, they were on the run. They were retreating, and it was only a matter of time before the Americans, the British and the Russians would come pounding over the channel, intent on battering Germany to smithereens.

Yet, while this was going on, the people surprisingly enough did not stand up and rebel. They kept on fighting for their leader, who by this time was absolutely certifiably crazy. The man belonged in a mental institution, and it came to the point where some people decided to take a stand. Thus began a spate of assassination attempts. But they didn't succeed, not one of them. There were those that nearly succeeded. But somehow Hitler was always one step ahead of them, and the plots failed one after the other. Those who planned them were put to death in the most horrible ways. Still, the nation of Germany fought on, in a struggle to the end. Yet all this was not the first priority for Eberhart, because Ludwig had returned home on furlough, and once again, they weren't seeing eye to eye.

Hamburg, Germany
February 4, 1945

He had known that Ludwig had been successful in the army, but he hadn't known how much of a success he actually was. The son who stepped over the threshold of the Eberhart mansion was a changed man from the youngster who had left home. Battle scarred and hard as a rock, Ludwig Eberhart was an officer's officer, and far more than that! He had been promoted to lieutenant colonel, and had rows of medals pinned across his chest in a way that spoke of courage and bravery in the face of overwhelming odds. Clearly, Ludwig Eberhart was a hero, and his country appreciated that. And yet, there was something in those eyes, something intangible and distant, that frightened Eberhart in a way that he couldn't identify. For he sensed that something inside his little boy had changed; that he was a different person with different values. He knew that they did not share the same worldview any longer.

The meal began as usual. The servants served them a duck appetizer in a plum sauce, and Ludwig complimented the cook over and over until she blushed. There was bountiful food, even though everything was rationed these days. In the Eberhart home, there was always enough. It was over the brandied mousse that the arguments began.

Ludwig spoke of missions he had undertaken for the Reichsfuhrer, and informed his parents that he had been chosen by Himmler to spearhead a select group of brilliant young officers — the stars of the next generation — in a number of major operations.

"To allow us to continue into the next century," is how Himmler put it, Ludwig said. His voice was icy calm, the voice of an officer in full control of his senses. Eberhart wasn't happy about the direction the conversation had taken.

"Ludwig," he said, "why don't we wind up over here and continue this conversation in my study?" They moved to the study. Marianne begged off, stating tiredness as an excuse. But the truth was, the looks in her husband's and son's eyes made her uneasy, and she wanted no part in the upcoming "discussion."

"I see that you have been awarded the Iron Cross — Germany's highest medal," Heinrich said proudly. "You must have done something significant to merit one of those! And when did you become so close to the Reichsfuhrer?"

"He has had his eye on me for a while," Ludwig replied. "When he decided I was ready for bigger things, he plucked me out of my platoon and attached me to his personal staff. I've been reporting solely to Himmler for some time already. The missions that I've carried out for him have made the battles I was in look like kid stuff."

Heinrich Eberhart searched for the childish boastfulness in the words, but there was none. His son was serious about what he was saying. There was the sound of pride in his voice: the sense of being chosen, of the fulfillment of destiny.

"You were involved with the Mussolini rescue?" he guessed suddenly, remembering a spectacular coup that had been pulled off for the Italian dictator. "That's probably what earned you the Iron Cross, am I right?"

"Well that played a little part in it," Ludwig said, taking a deep puff on his cigar. "But let me tell you about it at my own pace."

"You were saying that Himmler thinks we're going to lose the war," Heinrich reminded his son.

"You know what, Papa," his son said. "We could have won the war, easily. But *Der Fuhrer* is so intent on his mission against the Jews that the more mundane concerns like fighting the actual war become insignificant when compared to the greater goal of destroying the Jewish people. Bottom line, Hitler is not a military man. But he won't listen to reason. Any general who disagrees with his tactics, his military policy, or anything at all is shot or hanged and accused of being a traitor. Is there any wonder that nobody states their opinion anymore? Not that I disagree with him regarding the Jews. He is correct about that! But this is no way to fight a war! He should let the SS focus on the Jews, while he focuses on the war, and he should listen to the military men. But no, he insists on doing it his way and then we get incinerated at Stalingrad. Then he suspects Rommel of being a traitor, so he kills him as if he's a common criminal. After that, there's no way this country is going to win the war!"

"What about your missions out of the country?" Heinrich asked his son.

"A Band-Aid, nothing more than that. But it's a real shame. Because if we would have won this war, we could have carried on with our mission until we actually finished it!"

"What are you talking about?" Eberhart asked.

"I'm talking about the only thing Hitler really got right: the need to destroy the Jews. They are parasites, bloodsuckers. Didn't you read *Mein Kampf* where he blames all the world's ills on the Jews?" Ludwig asked his father.

"No," Eberhart replied shaking his head. "I never had the time."

"Only for the hundreds of other books in your library, right?" his son challenged him.

"I don't think the Jews are so terrible." he said, staring his son in the eyes. "Does that make me such a bad person?"

"Papa," Ludwig spoke, and every word was razor sharp. "You just don't get it! We had a historic opportunity here. The German nation has been trying to destroy the Jews for thousands of years already. Look at history. You're the history buff, aren't you? Germany threw out their Jews numerous times. We have always hated the Jews! In every war, it was the Jews who are killed. The Hapsburg Dynasty threw the Jews out of Vienna. Every province banished them. We kept them locked in ghettos; they had to wear clothing with special identifying marks. Then what happened to Germany?

"Modern days arrived, emancipation, equal opportunities for the Jewish citizens. What a load of hogwash! But the world was ready for change and the Jews were ready as well. They threw away their religion and simply exchanged their synagogues for temples complete with organs. They gave their children good German names. But what did they think? Did they think that the Germans would like them now? Once a Jew, always a Jew." Eberhart sat in shocked silence listening as his only son spewed forth such horrific hatred.

"Then *Der Fuhrer* came to power," Ludwig said. "It was a miracle that a painter from an Austrian homeless shelter could rise to such dizzying heights. But he did. How could they have taken him seriously? But they did; all of them. The aristocrats of Germany adored the man. Do you know why, Papa? Because he was voicing the feelings, the emotions of the entire German people. That's why they loved him so much. That's why they still love him, even while he leads them straight to the edge of the cliff. They don't care. As long as they are allowed to murder Jews on the way down, they are happy. The war has been secondary from the start. It's always been about the destruction of the Jews. Don't you see that, Papa? It's what the people want. The Reichsfuhrer sees the greater picture."

"What greater picture are you talking about?" Eberhart asked him curiously.

"I mean that I have been assigned by the Reichsfuhrer to a team that he created with a specific goal in mind."

"And that is —" prompted his father.

"Look, Papa," sighed Ludwig, "we thought for years that Hitler would be able to pull it off. We thought that Germany would finally be able to conquer the world, be the masters of our own destiny. But let's face it, that's not going to happen any time soon. We are going to lose the war. The war is too far gone for any kind of comeback. Even with Hitler out of the picture, the Allies are never going to forget. The English will never forgive us for what we did to London, and the Russians will definitely not forgive us for the devastation of their country.

"But the Reichsfuhrer is a man with a far-reaching vision," Ludwig continued, "and he knows that sometimes you have to plan far in advance. He understood what I was saying when I presented my plan to him. He not only listened to what I had to say, he decided to actually develop the plan, and put it into action. He threw the entire resources of the SS behind me, gave me the backing to go wherever I wanted and to requisition anything I needed to turn what had been a fanciful plan into a reality."

"And all this is against the Jews, Ludwig?" Eberhart asked.

"Well, technically, it's actually a plan to ensure that Germany will be able to assert itself in the future. We will have the ability to become a dominant power on the international scene at the time we deem to be right."

"And the Jews?" Eberhart asked.

"They have a place in my plan as well, "Ludwig said, "an important place actually. I mean without them I probably wouldn't be able to carry out this plan at all."

"How did you come up with this amazing plan?" Eberhart finally asked his son.

"It was when Himmler sent me to Japan," he answered. "It was then that I realized that the way we were looking at things wasn't necessarily the proper way to go about our goals. The Oriental race has an entirely different way of looking at things. It would be good for us to adopt some direction from them. It was then that I came up with my plan — the plan that Himmler calls 'Operation Eberhart.'

"I arrived in Japan as part of a team sent by the Reichsfuhrer to meet with our Japanese counterparts and to learn from them, and to discover a solution to the Jewish problem. You had no idea," Ludwig said to his father, "and I never wanted to tell you, being that I knew how much you liked the Jews. But I had been an active participant at the Wannsee Conference where the leaders of Germany convened to find a final solution to the menace facing us from the Jews."

"Come on, Ludwig," Eberhart interrupted his son. "You can't honestly believe that these ideas are right!"

"Whether I believe it or not makes no difference, practically speaking," Ludwig said. "Germany is my country and this is our life right now. I was a secretary at the conference, adding comments to the file. I never dreamed that he would pay attention to my comments. But believe it or not, two weeks after the conference, Himmler called me into his office for a meeting. He told me that he had enjoyed reading my remarks and felt that they had been both insightful and accurate.

"He told me that he admired my analytical and physical abilities, and that I was to receive a promotion. He told me that I would be joining a team that would be working to convert the theories of the Wannsee Conference into realistic goals and ideas that could actually be implemented. That, Papa, was how I began working for Heinrich Himmler. I was sent on many missions. I was selected to oversee extremely sensitive operations even though I was very young. I had become Himmler's golden boy. Then he decided to send me to Japan to meet with my counterpart."

"How did you get to Japan?" Eberhart asked him.

"That was the fascinating part," Ludwig told his father. "We traveled to Japan by submarine. None of the Navy men on board knew our mission. We were given the royal treatment and I personally found myself fascinated by the myriad workings of the submarine. I found myself overwhelmed by the way they were able to cram such a tremendous amount of machinery into such a small space. Papa, you have never seen such a thing in your life!

"While in Japan, I spent time with my Japanese diplomatic partner. He explained that one of the reasons the Japanese remained unimpressed with the Western countries, including Germany, was because of their seeming inability to have any sense of long-term vision. Miyake (that was his name) said with great sincerity that this was and probably would remain a deep-seated difference between our mind sets in the future. He also said that were we to come to the realization that it didn't always pay to rush into things, that sometimes it was better to plan for the long-time eventuality we would be able to accomplish much more on the world stage.

"'You must learn to think 50 years down the line,' he said to me. 'Of course you will not be able to predict even a fraction of the world events that will occur over the course of the next 50 years, but that doesn't really matter. If you have a vision and everything you do is directed to carrying out that vision, then you will update your goals and plans as you move with the times. Whenever you feel that you have become sufficiently powerful, you can make your move. When you strike after 50 years of preparation, it's a completely different situation.'

"Papa," Ludwig continued, "Miyake felt most strongly that if Germany would have waited another three years before attacking our enemies, we would have been undefeatable.

"Now all that is debatable. But the theory he put forth opened my mind in a big way. Suddenly, I was full of ideas. And not just ideas that were applicable right now. On the contrary. An idea was developing in my mind — a way to make a comeback.

"If we were going to lose, we would just have to prepare for the next conflict. And our preparation would have to be in such a way that when we finally got around to going to battle, there would be no way that we could lose. Because we would have taken our time, thought out and covered every eventuality, as we adapted our plan to the events of time and the politics of whichever time period we were operating in. All this came to me directly in the middle of his speech to me. He was speaking so passionately about this idea of his, and all the while, my mind was moving full speed ahead. I had just come up with the most incredible idea. It was a wonderful concept, breathtaking in its scope, and I was properly amazed at what I had come up with all by myself.

"For my plan to succeed," Ludwig went on, "I needed to touch base with a number of Germany's most eminent scientists. I explained the concept to these men and they were properly enthusiastic. These were men used to dealing with futuristic concepts. The imagination presented by men like Hitler and Himmler went unmatched by other world leaders, except maybe Churchill. They were constantly hatching new far-fetched plans, and asking the scientists if they were feasible. In short, they weren't fazed by the concept of failure. I presented my concept to them on a rainy afternoon in Dusseldorf, and they got back to me three weeks later with a comprehensive study. According to their analysis, it had an excellent chance of succeeding. But it would mean a longterm plan in the extreme. I didn't mind. The short term was unimportant. From then on, I would begin to think in terms of how my present actions were affecting the remainder of my life."

Eberhart watched his son as he talked. Despite himself, despite the feeling that he had failed, that he had raised a son who was missing the most basic of qualities, despite all that, he was proud of his son. Himmler respected him enough to take him so seriously. He watched as Ludwig strode from one end of his office to the other, reliving his conversation with the third most powerful man in the country.

"Gone were the days that I had to wait a long time to see the Reichsfuhrer," he said. "I merely told the officer on duty that he should schedule an hour for me for later that afternoon. There were no questions asked. They knew who I was, how high I stood in his favor and nobody wanted to cross me. I arrived well equipped for my upcoming meeting. I had the charts explaining my vision, and I was ready to face the cross-examination from the master himself.

"Himmler was in a rare good mood that day. He was chuckling to himself when I entered his office and his happiness only increased as our meeting went on.

"'Welcome, Ludwig,' he greeted me, and I saluted in return. 'So what's this incredible new idea that you had?' he asked me.

"I spread out my sheets on his desk, as if they were a business proposal he was scrutinizing. His brow was furrowed as he leaned over the sheets, studying them, with the utmost concentration.

"'Hmm, interesting,' he said to himself, 'very interesting. Yes, I see where you're going with this one ... aha ... ingenious, really.'

"He kept on making little comments to himself. I just sat there silently, allowing him to arrive at a judgment by himself. When he had finished reading the proposal for the fourth time, he said to me, 'O.K., now share your vision with me in your own words.'

"I was ready.

"'Reichsfuhrer,' I began, while standing at attention. 'You mentioned to me a number of times that in your opinion, the war is at an end, and that there is no way that we will win it.'

"He nodded sagely, managing to look very much like an owl.

"'That's correct,' he said. 'And I'm becoming surer of that every additional day.'

"'Well,' I went on, 'I have developed a plan that will allow Germany to make an eventual comeback. Even if we end up losing now, this plan will allow us to accept our defeat with the knowledge that we will reconquer in the future.'

"The Reichsfuhrer was listening intently to my every word. 'Go on,' he said.

"'I propose to set up a team which will commence an immediate investigation whose purpose will be to provide us with a comprehensive list of the 150 smartest Jewish families under our control. Upon the determination of said list, a special team, which I will lead, will forcibly abduct one child from each of those families, wherever they may be. These extremely intelligent children will be taken to a pre-arranged place where they will await transportation to a far-off country, where they will undergo intensive mind-altering treatment. They will undergo the most cutting-edge tactics science has developed as of yet. We will be focusing on manipulating them through extremely potent drugs, and a series of brainwashing and hypnosis sessions for each child, according to his needs and mind. By the time the child will emerge from our 'training program,' he will have completely forgotten his background, who he is, where he was born, who his parents were and almost anything else associated with his childhood up until that point. We will mold them, take them apart and put them back together in the mold of our choosing.'

"'And what will we have gained from this exercise?' Himmler asked me.

"'A tremendous amount,' I told him. 'Reichsfuhrer, picture this scene for a moment. After they have undergone intensive life-altering treatments as is needed, we take them out, reprogrammed and ready to be placed anywhere we want in the entire world. Like clay in our hands, we will have the ability to instill in these children the desire to be anything we want them to be. We can send them off to Palestine wanting nothing more than to become a minister in the government there. They will be sent to America where they will desire to join the United States Army and will rise in the ranks to become generals and admirals, because that is what we will put into their minds. They will have the ability to refuse to listen to what their own subconscious is telling them to do. We will send them to the church and they will rise in that organization. Who knows, maybe we'll decide to make one of them pope. We will then be able to manipulate the entire church through our people inside. We will have an entire ring of the smartest individuals, all compelled to carry out our will. None of them will be able to guess why on earth they want to do what they are doing. They will become a network: a worldwide network of agents all programmed to carry out our bidding, to accomplish our goals.'

"'But how will you be able to ensure that they carry out your precise wishes?' Himmler asked me.

"'I told him that it was simple. We keep the programming fairly straightforward. Each of them is given a basic goal to achieve without their knowledge, of course. They will be programmed, as well, with a need that will arise from time to time, say every 15 years or so, that will make them get in touch with some of our people, who will be keeping tabs on them throughout that time. We will never lose sight of these agents, because they will become our most valuable assets in the field.'" Ludwig paused for breath, and took the opportunity to look over at his father, trying to gauge his opinion of the plan. Heinrich Eberhart had a stony look on his face, his expression giving nothing away.

"'Anyway,' he went on, 'when they meet us after all those years, we will gauge the success of our hypnosis tactics, and renew and update whatever needs to be updated, to allow these brilliant people to become the kind of leaders that will eventually be placed in the proper places to do the maximum amount of damage for us when we deem it necessary. This might take many years, but time will be on our side. Just a little lesson I picked up in Japan.'

"'But how will we get these agents to act at the right time?' the Reichsfuhrer asked me.

"'Reichsfuhrer,' I said, 'that is the absolute brilliance of the plan. Picture the future for a moment. There are 150 brilliant agents scattered in the most sensitive, the most crucial spots in the intelligence world, placed at the jugular of as many nations as we can put them. They are all as motivated as humanly possible. The absolute beauty of the plan lies in the fact that none of them know that they are secret agents. They are so secret that they themselves don't even know who they are!'

"'And what *do* they know?' the Reichsfuhrer asked me.

"'They know that they have an inborn push steering them toward certain locations. They do not know why they feel the need to move to those places, or why they want to work in a particular line of work. They do many things without knowing why, without reasoning, just by instinct. And there they lie in wait, like the most dangerous of predators ready to spring.'

"'How do we set them off?' he asked me.

"'That,' I said, 'is the most breathtaking part of all. Because all it takes is a phone call!'

"'A phone call?' he asked in disbelief.

"'Exactly! One call. These children will be programmed with a mission. The mission will be updated as needed, throughout the years. As they grow older, as the situation changes around the world, we will need to bring them back to update them with their new missions, all programmed into their subconsciousness, ingrained on their minds with the most powerful and mind-altering hypnosis. When we are ready to use them, when we want to spring these agents on an unsuspecting world, then all we will need to do is to dial their phone number and say the code phrase that we programmed into their minds long before. That one line will send them on their way. Their programming will make them drop what they are doing the moment they receive this call. Wherever we have placed them, be it the most top-secret military installments, or ready to blow up a strategic dam, or in a position where they have the ability to poison the water supply of half a nation, they will go off and do their mission without thought or scruples for the people they are harming. You must admit,' I said, 'that if this works, it will be the most effective team of secret agents in the history of espionage.'

"And predictably enough, Himmler loved the idea.

"'What do you propose to call this operation?' Himmler asked me.

"'Operation Network, or just The Network,' I said.

"'Sounds good to me,' he said, 'but in my mind, I will always think of it as The Eberhart Plan.'

"And then, Papa," Luwig said, "the Reichsfuhrer looked me in the eye and said, 'You are a credit to your father, Heinrich. He will be very proud of you.'

"Then he walked over to his desk, opened one of the drawers and removed a wooden box. It was polished and fairly gleamed under the light. He flipped open the cover and my heart jumped inside my chest. There, sitting on a bed of velvet, lay an Iron Cross made of gold — Germany's highest military award. The Reichsfuhrer was giving it to me!!

"'Congratulations, General Ludwig Eberhart,' he said to me.

"I had just been promoted. It was a moment of supreme happiness. That, Papa, was when Himmler gave me the Iron Cross.

"'I know that you will make us proud,' Himmler said. 'You have my authorization to use my name for anything that you might need while carrying out your mission. I will put it in writing.'

"The next thing I knew, he had handed me a letter stating exactly that, with his personal stamp and signature. Such a letter was absolutely priceless, and it was mine. Then I finally understood how amazing my plan actually was. How 'The Network' was going to be the future savior of Germany and the forerunner of the Fourth Reich. Then, Papa, I walked out of his office and into my new mission.

"I put together a team of the best people in a number of fields. I needed researchers and investigators and then really tough soldiers who had seen it all and wouldn't turn sentimental on me in the crunch, because this was going to be a rough few weeks. The researchers had to determine who the smartest Jewish families were. The investigators had to sift through thousands, sometimes hundreds of thousands of records detailing where those families had been sent. It was a tremendous mess, truth be known. Yes, we are Germans and precise, and yes, there were records of everything. But don't forget, there is a war going on and those families are constantly being shifted from place to place: to ghettos, to concentration camps, to labor camps. It can be very hard to keep track of exactly where everyone is all the time. But when you have the ability to requisition anyone you want like I did, then that's just what you do. I got in touch with my contacts at the police department and in many government offices, and was able to put together a team of the best investigators almost immediately.

"But it was hard work. It meant interviewing the Jewish people under our control. Don't forget that they really didn't want to talk to us. So we had to force it out of them. Which was why I had recruited certain individuals that had served in the Waffen SS alongside me — men I knew who didn't cringe at the idea of using force to find out the information they needed. My men visited every ghetto, and found the people who were the weak links, and worked on them and cracked them open until they were spouting information like a faucet. Eventually, we began putting together our master list — our network — the names of all those who were now children, but who would grow up and when they did would serve as pawns for us in the ongoing battle.

"When the researchers would discover the right family and the investigators would trace their whereabouts, until they knew exactly where they were, it was my job to travel to wherever they were and make sure that the children were taken away — abducted from their parents, stolen for our cause."

"You were able to do such a thing? To pull a child away from his mother's arms?" Heinrich asked his son, his face white with silent rage.

"I was, Papa," his son answered. "This plan means a strong Germany in the future, and that's the most important thing! So yes, I was able to do it, and I sleep at nights. I don't have bad dreams even though I watched my soldiers pulling little children out of their mothers' arms. They are Jews after all is said and done, and who cares about the Jews anyway? They are here for us to use, so that is just what I did. I'm not apologizing for my actions. I feel no remorse, and I would do it another hundred times if that was what it took to make us win!"

Heinrich sat as still as a statue, silent as the grave, his glowering face the only sign that he was seething like a volcano inside. Ludwig continued to speak, not registering how much consternation his words were causing his father, not really caring either way.

"Over the next few months I was extremely busy carrying out my task. I could be in the Krakow ghetto one day and in the Warsaw ghetto the next. Sometimes our child had already been sent to Treblinka or Bergen-Belsen, and then we would have to beat the clock, because if they were sent to the camps, the chances of the children remaining alive by the time we arrived on the scene were far from good. The SS in the camps were extremely adept at sorting the chaff from the wheat at this point. Within hours of their arrival at almost any given camp, parents would be separated from children, healthy from sick, old from young. It was our job to find out where they had been sent and get there first, greet the train and pull the kids away from the SS before they could be sent to the gas chambers.

"There was one time we ended up chasing one family around for two weeks, since they had fallen off the radar and nobody knew where they were. We must have visited five concentration camps until we finally tracked them down. By that time, the kids had been sent off on some sort of children's transport. We finally found them in one of the divisions of Birkenau. But we found them. We almost always found them. Himmler was proud of the men involved in this mission. It made him look good in Hitler's eyes, and that in turn was a great thing for us. There were promotions for everyone involved, especially me and my deputy, a fine officer by the name of Kurt Wolfgang Zeivald."

"Ludwig," Heinrich said suddenly, the desperation evident in his voice. "There must have been some times where it was difficult for you to do this! You have a heart! You were born with a conscience! Tell me there was some element of hardship involved. Please!"

The dashing young officer stopped in his tracks, and his handsome features creased into a frown, as he tried to think of something that had been hard for him. Finally he remembered something.

"There was one episode that was eerie," he said. "I can't say that it was extremely difficult, but there were moments when I felt as if there was something really strange going on, as if I was only getting half the picture."

"Tell me about it," Heinrich urged his son.

"Well there was this one family that my team tracked down. Brilliant people. They were Hassidim from some village in the middle of rural Poland. Not a place that I would like to frequent if I didn't have to."

Suddenly Heinrich knew what place Ludwig was talking about, and his heart turned to stone.

"It was this tiny village named Kolodov in the Lodz region," Ludwig said.

"Kolodov!" Heinrich stammered. "That's where you went?!"

"Yes," Ludwig said. "There was a *Rabbiner* there that everyone knew of. He was supposed to be a really holy man; a *tzaddik* is what they called him. From what we were able to learn, this man had a son, a little boy, about 5 or 6, who was a real genius, a child prodigy. When we heard about this kid, we rushed down to the village through the swamps and the mud of glorious Poland, until we reached the place, and discovered to our dismay, that the Jews of Kolodov hadn't merited a ghetto of their own. They had been evacuated from their town and placed together with the Jews of all the surrounding towns into the giant ghetto of Lodz. Supposedly, this was where they were: the *Rabbiner*, his wife, their children and this wonder child, a little boy named Yaakov, the apple of the *Rabbiner's* eye.

"When we arrived at the ghetto, it was growing dark — the twilight zone of the day. The shadows did their best to swallow up the bodies of the emaciated children who were lying across the cobblestones, too weak to move out of the way. When they saw us, however, most of them managed. We had received the *Rabbiner's* address from one of our informers, who had revealed it for some extra food and hated himself for it, to the degree where he ended up refusing the food and cursed himself for having cooperated with us. But by then it was too late. We had the information that we needed. We approached the building silently, not wanting to stir up a hornet's nest, the way it sometimes happened. Because then the Jews would rush to their hiding places, and being the experts at survival that they were, their hiding places were rather inventive and ingenious and plenty hard to find. Needless to say, it was much easier to catch them unaware.

"As we were approaching the dingy building, we could hear the sounds of people who were living in close quarters making dinner, all at the same time: the smells of the food, the tinkle of the silverware. In a sense, it was very normal, but also surreal at the same time. We reached the building, and as if in a dream, I could hear this voice singing to himself. It was a voice that was filled with yearning and emotion, singing a song that was laden with poignancy. Suddenly I didn't want to interrupt these people and take their son away. I was filled with a sense of unease, that somehow what I was doing was wrong, that I would be punished for what I was about to do."

"Did the melody go something like this?" Heinrich asked his son, and without waiting for a reply, began to sing a tune in a quiet voice, almost to himself. Ludwig listened to the song his father was singing, and said in a surprised voice that it sounded very similar to what he had heard. He didn't notice that this bit of news made his father even paler than before.

"So I felt uneasy," Ludwig said. "It wasn't the first time in my life that I felt uneasy, and it wouldn't be the last. During the course of the war, I had been in numerous conflicts and I had never let my emotions get in the way.

"I motioned to my men to follow me into the stairwell of the decrepit building. It was so old and shabby, and it looked as if it was going to collapse any second. Some of the men were reluctant to put their feet on the stairs. Everything was going okay, but suddenly, this little kid on the fifth floor leaned over the railing and caught a glimpse of us climbing the stairs. Within moments, the peaceful building had become a scene of frantic bedlam, as Jews on every floor began ramming furniture against the doors in their apartments to delay the inevitable.

"We were used to this sort of thing, and weren't afraid. In a second, my men had taken charge of the building and were headed straight toward the *Rabbiner's* apartment, ignoring everyone else. They were able to bash the door down and rushed inside just as the *Rabbiner's* wife was handing their little son through the window to someone else across the alleyway in a different building. It wasn't going to help them. I was here for that kid — that brilliant child — and I was going to take him away come what may. While some of my men were sent over to the other building, I sat down with the *Rabbiner* and his wife and told them that by orders of the Reichsfuhrer, we would be taking their son, Yaakov, with us."

Heinrich Eberhart sat forward, his face white, and he wanted to throw up.

"The *Rabbiner's* wife began to cry, but the *Rabbiner* didn't say anything right away. All the time, he was looking at me, studying my features as if trying to make up his mind if he knows me from somewhere. Then just as Kurt Zeivald brought the struggling child back into the apartment, a glimmer of recognition crossed the *Rabbiner's* face. He looked me in the eye and said, 'You're Heinrich Eberhart's son, aren't you?'

"When I didn't answer right away, shocked as I was that he knew my identity, he raised his voice and he almost screamed, 'You are an Eberhart, are you not?'

"This time, I nodded my head, almost afraid of the consequences for me if I didn't acknowledge what he was saying. Because it was true, we look like each other, not an exact match, but close enough that someone would be able to see the resemblance. And you want to know something, Papa? He didn't look the least bit surprised when I walked through that door at the head of my men. It was more ... like a resigned look, almost as if he were expecting me. You know, it was all very strange.

"Zeivald held the kid in his hands, and he was struggling. Zeivald held him tighter. The *Rabbiner* looked at me and he motioned slightly with his head in my direction, telling me to have my soldier put the kid down. He knew he was going to have to give the kid up in the end, but until that happened, there was no reason for his son to be in the arms of a Nazi soldier. It didn't matter to me, so I gave Zeivald the order, and he put the kid down on the floor. He ran over to his father and buried his face in his father's lap. Even the most battle-toughened soldier among us felt something right then, as we stood there witnessing the love flowing between the two of them, unstoppable, just the love of a son to his father.

All the time, the *Rabbiner* was singing this song, this haunting melody, until one of my men pointed his gun at the *Rabbiner* prepared to shoot him. I motioned to him sharply to put his gun away. We didn't want to traumatize this kid more than he was already. So the man was singing! So what? We were going to allow him to finish his song, and then, we would take the kid and say goodbye.

"There was silence in the tiny apartment. The *Rabbiner's* wife and children gazed mournfully at their father not knowing what was going on, only that it wasn't good. Their lives were about to change again for the worse. There was no sound at all, just the plaintive cry of a holy man in pain. He finished his song. He looked at me. I felt as if his gaze was piercing my heart. It was almost as if he knew that he had done something wrong; that this was his punishment and he was willing to take it like a man.

"'We are taking your son,' I said to him. He nodded his head as if he knew that already. His wife opened her mouth to scream and fainted dead away in the arms of one of her children.

"'It's all my fault,' he said, so quietly that it was if he were talking to himself. 'It's all my fault. Anshel was right.'

"Very cryptic words. It sent shivers up and down my spine. Then the *Rabbiner* lifted his son onto his lap and held him close. He placed both his hands on the little boy's head and gave him a blessing, a farewell blessing. Then he looked at me, piercing me to the core with the full power of his gaze. Then he said, 'Maybe you have him, but it's not over yet. The world is a circle. What's up today is down tomorrow. It's not over yet.'

"Those were his exact words. And we took the child and left the apartment, left the ghetto, shaken as could be. And you know something?" Ludwig continued. "The *Rabbiner* and his family were shipped off to Auschwitz the next day. They're gone now."

Heinrich was shaking now. His face was completely pale, as if all the blood had drained from him. His hands were fluttering so badly that he couldn't hold them still, hard as he tried.

"But a Jew saved our family, Ludwig!!" Heinrich screamed. "You have no idea how bad it could have been! They were going to take everything away from us. I wanted to die. You would have grown up a pauper, the scum of the earth, if not for the advice of one Jew and the blessing of another! The blessing of the man whose son you took away!"

The room was silent as Ludwig assimilated that piece of news. He sat quietly thinking for a while. Finally he spoke.

"It doesn't matter to me, Papa. It doesn't change the way I think, the way I feel about life. I still hate them; I still want to destroy them. In fact, if a Jew really did save you and is the cause of all that's good in my life, then I only hate them more, because now I owe them something as well!"

Heinrich looked at his son through eyes that had never seen him before. This was not his son. A devil had invaded his body.

"Papa," his son said to him, "don't think that I don't know about all the Jews that work for us, how you treat them so nicely, so humanely. At least they do valuable work for us. I always thought it was a business decision. But now I understand the truth. You have been repaying the Jews all these years, haven't you?" He glared at his father with downright loathing, as if he couldn't believe that his father would have done such a terrible thing.

"Don't worry, Papa," he said to Heinrich, his voice dripping with disgust, "I won't rat on you. But you should just know that I'm going in as different a direction from you as a son can go!"

"Why?" Heinrich asked his son. "Why? What did the Jewish people ever do to you to deserve such animosity?"

"You are such a hypocrite," his son burst out. "For years you have been the main contractor for the German Army. You built army bases and navy bases all over Germany and in the occupied territories as well, never giving a thought to the fact that the destruction of the Jewish nation was able to be carried out due in great part to the infrastructure that your company provided! Now suddenly you're a bleeding heart! Who are you fooling, Papa! What do you care about the Jews, you big faker! If you cared about them, you would have made sure not to work so closely with the Reich. But you did work with the government. You worked with Himmler and Goering and Jodl and everyone who wanted to hire you and had the money to pay for your time. You assuaged your conscience by telling yourself that you weren't so bad, that you supported a whole bunch of Jews who would have been sent to their deaths if not for you. So do me a favor and give the whole sanctimonious act a break."

Heinrich was speechless with rage and humiliation as he listened to his son without comment, part of him furious at his son for speaking to him this way, but another part of him was even angrier at himself because he knew that there was a fair element of truth in the accusations Ludwig had made. He had known what the SS was doing to the Jews, and yet, he had built their army bases and developed their infrastructure, becoming richer and richer in the process, and ignoring the jabs coming at him from within, telling himself exactly what his son had accused him of.

"So what should I have done, Ludwig?" he asked his son in a quiet voice. "Would you rather that I would have been killed? Because Himmler would have sent me to Dachau if he sensed even a little bit of hesitance on my part. There is no mercy in the Reichsfuhrer's office. So they would have killed me. You would have grown up without a father. Is that what you would have preferred?"

They were both quiet for a minute.

"I have to go lie down," he told his son and stumbled out of the room toward his bedroom, his gait the walk of an old man, his posture slumped. He had raised a monster who had repaid kindness with outright cruelty. What choice remained, if any?

Very late that night, when everyone in the Eberhart palatial mansion was finally asleep, a lone light shone in the study of the master of the house. There was nothing else to do. He lifted the revolver to his head and didn't hesitate. His hand didn't waver. This was the way it had to be. There was no way he could ever hope to make amends now. Without allowing himself to think any more, Heinrich Eberhart pulled the trigger. The sound was swallowed up by the vastness of the gigantic mansion. Marianne discovered him in the morning. There was a note on the desk, which she read to herself.

Ludwig, You are going to suffer for what you did in Lodz. If not you, yourself, then your children, because nothing goes unpunished. Don't forget, it's not over yet.

I remain your heartbroken father,
Heinrich Eberhart

Marianne fell into a dead faint beside the body of her husband. They tried to revive her, but every time she was awakened, she would faint again. Apparently, the sight of him lying there like that had been too much for her sensitive soul. She never recovered. Heinrich Eberhart was buried in the Eberhart ancestral graveyard near the mansion he had loved so much. On his tombstone was inscribed:

Here lies a Compassionate Patriot

All this did nothing to stop their son. He had a mission to fulfill, and he was going to carry it out come what may. He was now the master of the mansion, the keeper of the wealth and he liked it just fine. But every once in a while, a little whisper of doubt crossed his mind, that maybe his father had been right, and in fact it really wasn't over yet. There was no way to know, however, so he was able to push those thoughts from his mind.

And the Network list lay hidden in his home, waiting for its time to come, as well.

PART THREE

27
Rafi Ganim

Tel Aviv, Israel
March 15, 2007

All it took was one night for things to change dramatically and forever. It was the evening of the greatest performance of Rafi's life; one for which he had practiced long and hard, and one in which he was featured as first violinist. He would be playing the solos that night. It was his night under the bright lights. Although the importance of his career was steadily diminishing in his eyes due to the influence of the Kolodover Rebbe and his chassidim, he was still a violinist and practiced accordingly. It was also the night that Kamal Gamal Mahmoud ibn Sardi, or Sardi as he was known to his friends, chose to carry out a terrorist attack. For reasons that would forever remain unknown, Sardi chose to attack a concert hall. And Heaven decreed that the paths of Rafi, the violinist, and Sardi, the terrorist, should converge.

The evening was devoted to the music of Strauss, and the revered conductor, Daniel Dagenheim, was presiding once again. Music lovers had gathered from around the country for this event.

Sardi chose this performance for the attack he had been planning for ages. He had done his reconnoitering by attending numerous concerts.

Hamas paid for his tickets. He had become a music lover in the process, but that didn't seem to be an issue. The attack would be music at its best in the most tragic of operas. He had learned to dress as a concert goer — wore dress pants and an open-necked shirt — and developed a little self-esteem in the process. He might eventually have changed his mind about killing himself, but that was never an option, not with Hamas calling the shots. While the various musicians performed night after night, Sardi glided along the corridors of the hall, planning the attack as best he could, gathering the information that would turn an evening of music and culture into a bloodbath instead.

It was also a concert that Kobi Shapiro, past Nazi hunter for the Mossad and one of the original team who had captured Eichmann, chose to attend. Kobi loved music. As he grew older he developed an appreciation for good concerts. It was great to get away from the condominium he called home on the Netanya beachfront, and spend an evening in the company of others who enjoyed music and the finer things in life. Never did he dream that he was subjecting himself to danger by attending a classical music concert. So he sat in his seat and read his program with interest, and waited with anticipation for the lights to dim and the curtain to rise.

Sardi gained entrance to the show that evening in disguise. ID clipped to the pocket of his uniform, he made his nondescript way through the vast auditorium complex, equipped with a flashlight and a sheaf of programs. He had been comprehensively tutored for his role by the owner of the ID, Yousaf, an Israeli-Arab from Ramle. Yousaf had outlined all the tasks that were expected of him and how to fulfill them perfectly. Sardi was a quick study and soaked it up like a sponge. The trick was getting his weapons into the auditorium without setting off a series of alarms on the way. But Sardi had a way of thinking out of the box that made him so invaluable.

He waited one block from the hall, a carton of Elite potato chips beside him on the ground. It was the type of carton that would momentarily be delivered to the hall for the big show. In fact, it wasn't long before an Elite truck turned the corner and parked. Without wasting a moment, Sardi hoisted the carton onto his shoulder, and walked quickly to the truck, emerged behind another worker who was likewise carrying a carton of Elite goodies into the hall, in anticipation of the evening's performance.

The doors were open, and the guards did not think it the least bit suspicious when he headed in the direction of the concession stands.

As soon as he was out of sight of the front entrance, he turned right down the long hallway leading toward the locker rooms, where the cleaning staff kept their supplies and personal belongings. Yousaf had supplied him with the key to his locker. *When will these Israelis learn not to employ Arabs?* he thought to himself. *Palestinians or Israelis, Arabs were Arabs. How is it that the Israelis haven't learned this yet?*

Down the hallway he went, showing no outward signs of anxiety whatsoever. *Breathe in, breathe out, show nothing. Do not be nervous. Walk with measured strides. Keep a smile near the surface. Just a man going about his work. Be cool, calm and collected. There is nothing to worry about.* Just before he reached the locker room, a middle-aged Arab stepped out.

"What are you doing here?" he asked Sardi in a slightly suspicious tone.

"Yousaf asked me to take over for him tonight," Sardi innocently explained.

"And the carton?" his interrogator mercilessly inquired. He could feel his heart beating, beads of sweat on his forehead.

"Nothing important," he replied. "Some of Yousaf's uniforms that he washed at home and asked me to bring back to his locker." There, that would explain why he had the key to Yousaf's locker.

"And who are you?" the man wanted to know. Clipped onto his jacket pocket was an ID card. Sardi realized that he was speaking with the head of the cleaning/usher detail himself.

"My name is Ahmed ibn Masua," he told the man. "Yousaf is a neighbor of mine in Ramle. He wasn't feeling well so he asked me to take over for him tonight. I hope that's O.K.." He spoke with feeling. The man believed him. His words were being accepted. People were so stupid. Boy, would this man kick himself later when he realized that he had had the terrorist in front of him and had allowed him to stow his weapons right under the noses of the Israelis. How ironic it all was! An Israeli-Arab, assisting the Israelis to keep the auditorium secure, questions a terrorist and fails miserably, taken in by his sincere and obsequious manner. He hoped that he would be alive to remember this on the morrow, but deep down he knew that the probabilities of his surviving were slim. It didn't concern him. He was ready to die for the cause. The head of the cleaning detail was busy and in a rush, and didn't have time to question Sardi further. He nodded his head and turned to leave.

"You can go on in," he told Sardi, "but tell Yousaf that I expect him to call me himself if he can't make it for whatever reason. Tell him, O.K.?"

"No problem," Sardi replied, thinking that the chances of Yousaf ever working in Tel Aviv after this evening were right up there with the Maccabi basketball team opening a stadium for their fans in the middle of Gaza city. Not happening.

He entered the empty locker room. Most of the staff hadn't arrived yet. He inserted the key into the locker. Then, latching the door to the room from the inside, he opened the carton and removed a vicious-looking submachine gun from underneath the pile of clothing that he had placed there as a precaution. Working speedily he placed the gun and the grenade on the floor of the lockers and covered them with the clothing. Then he shut the locker door and reopened the entrance to the locker room, just in time to admit several workers who were descending the stairs, intent on storing their belongings before heading toward their shifts. Carrying the empty carton, he smiled and went to buy a soft drink. Now that the immediate danger had passed, he found that he was parched.

Rafi was in the dressing room donning his tuxedo and bow tie. He studied his reflection in the mirror as he tied the knot, and redid it once or twice until he was satisfied. When he finished, he stood before the mirror cradling his precious instrument under his chin, in the stance he assumed when he performed. He saw a young man with jet-black hair and a ready smile. The corners of his mouth were upturned, evidence of an innate optimism. Since coming in contact with the Rebbe and his way of life, that part of his soul was slowly emerging. He was feeling more and more optimistic, feeling that things were changing for the good all around him. He felt as if he was standing on the threshold of life, about to discover his mission. He grinned and glanced at the tiny *kippah* in his hair. The musical director had done a double take when he caught a glimpse of that *kippah*, but other than a pair of pursed lips, had made no comment. He had no interest in disconcerting the star of the show with some banal comment.

Still smiling, he lifted the bow and drew it gently across the strings of his instrument, savoring the sound that emerged. Then he began skimming the strings, moving the bow, faster and faster, his fingers pressing here and there, playing the violin as if he were on stage that moment. He was the maestro dancing around the room as if in a trance, a tune emanating from the violin as if with a life of its own ... the tune from his dream, the most special of songs, the song of his soul. He had played this tune so often, and yet he never tired of it. It was a part of him. He looked at his watch. There was a half-hour until his performance. He wanted to eat something before taking his place on the stage. He felt his pulse race in anticipation and happiness. Then he glanced in the mirror once more, and decided to redo his bow tie one more time.

Tamar Ganim looked at her watch and realized that she had better hurry if she wanted to be on time for Rafi's concert. It wasn't every day that she went to one of his performances. When he asked her why she didn't attend more often, she explained that she was inundated with work and couldn't find the time.

"Everyone needs to relax, Tami," he had said. "Just tell me when it's convenient for you, and I'll send you as many tickets as you want."

The truth was that the reason she didn't attend his concerts was because she didn't enjoy listening to an orchestra playing that much. But the past week had been especially stressful, and she felt that an evening of classical music would help her relax and put the cares of work and everyday life behind her for a while. Besides, she was proud of her brother and loved watching him on stage. She loved seeing the focus in his eyes, the dexterity of his hands, the respect he was accorded by the rest of the orchestra and even the greatest conductors. He was something special, that was obvious. In the end, she hadn't take advantage of his offer for the free tickets, preferring to purchase a ticket and surprise him at his dressing-room door instead. Now it was time to leave.

Hastily, she put her notes in order and locked the office door behind her. Then she rushed out of the Tel Aviv building and hailed the first taxi in sight. It was a 10 minute drive to the hall. She spent the time unwinding in the air-conditioned vehicle. The taxi driver attempted to start a conversation, but she replied in monosyllables, and he gave up. They made good time. Before she knew it, they had pulled up at the concert hall. When she was in the vast auditorium, instead of taking her seat in the front section of the hall, she walked to the stage and climbed the small flight of stairs. She showed her ID to the guard and explained that she was Ganim's sister and wanted to surprise him. He stepped aside and she walked backstage into another world.

A world of coiled ropes were suspended from the ceiling and young men with long hair and black shirts called to one another as they confirmed that the intricate details were under control. She could hear the musicians tuning their instruments and the sound of soothing music playing over recessed speakers. Musicians carrying their instruments rushed by, too busy to pay attention to the woman who had no business being there. She walked confidently, until she reached the dressing rooms. At the end of the hall was one last door with two golden stars painted on it. She knocked. From inside, Tamar heard the sound of her brother playing his violin, music soaring, heartstrings being plucked. She knocked again, a little louder this time. She heard his footsteps approaching as he went to open the door.

"Tami!" he exclaimed in gratified surprise. "It's so great that you came!"

"Thank you," she said, touched that he was so pleased. "I know that you're busy now, so I figured I'd come by to say hello and then ... " her voice trailed off as she noticed something different about him.

"What?" he asked her. "Is everything O.K.?"

She didn't answer, just looked pointedly at the top of his head, where the *kippah* was all but hidden in the mountain of hair.

"Don't worry about that," he said to her. "We have so much to talk about. Why don't we get together after the show and have coffee, O.K.?"

"Sounds good," she said. "I guess then you'll tell me what this means, right?"

"You got it," he replied. There was a sudden beeping sound, and he said, "Oh, there's the warning bell. It's time for me to join the rest of the orchestra. We'll meet at the backstage entrance when the show is over. See you later."

Then with a wave of his hand he headed toward the stage. She watched him go, a brand-new confidence in his gait, a surety in the way that he carried himself that had never been there before. Suddenly she realized that if wearing this *kippah* was doing that for Rafi, then maybe it was a good thing. She rushed to take her seat. The lights were dimming as she sank into the plush cushion, and she studied the program intently, prouder of her brother then she had ever been before. He was going to shine tonight; she could feel it in the air.

~

Kobi was comfortable financially but far from wealthy. Consequently, he usually made do with the less-expensive seats in the balcony. It was not that he couldn't afford a better seat, but it didn't really matter to him. His eyesight was still perfect, and spending more money would have been a waste. He picked up a program and read about the esteemed Daniel Dagenheim and the members of the orchestra. The musician that interested him the most was Rafi Ganim. Kobi loved how he played that violin. He couldn't believe that anyone that young was able to play so professionally. Rafi Ganim was so sure of himself, so poised and dapper, sitting and playing ... no, playing wasn't the right word. He didn't play that instrument, he communicated with it until it responded in an almost humanlike way.

He nibbled on the corn chips he had purchased. On the surface, at least, he paid no attention to what was going on around him. In reality, despite the fact that he had aged considerably, Kobi Shapiro knew exactly what was going on around him. His peripheral vision was just as sharp as the rest of him, and the fact that he was seemingly engrossed in the program was not taking away from his perusal of the crowd from time to time. Having been in security his entire life meant that he took nothing for granted. Nothing. And that was why he could never truly relax. Now as well, his antenna was picking up the slightest vibes that there was something wrong. But not knowing why that should be so, he tried to shelf his feelings and read his program in peace. Eventually, the lights began to dim, and he leaned back in his seat, ready to enjoy the evening, completely alert and on guard at the same time. Just another day in the life of Kobi Shapiro, former-Mossad Nazi hunter.

Kamal Gamal Mahmoud ibn Sardi stood at one of the entrances, flashlight in hand, and led the latecomers to their seats. Dagenheim had already made his grand entrance, and the performance had begun. The exhilarating sounds of Strauss filled the huge hall with magical beauty. Sardi smiled at everyone who approached him and treated them politely; not overly polite, since that would have made him a touch too memorable. He had decided to attack after the first interval, when the audience would be mellow and relaxed. When everyone's guard would be down, he would leave his post, make his way to the locker room, bring the weapons to the auditorium and run between the stage and the front row, spraying the crowd with bullets.

Everyone in the hall would go berserk. There would be a frenzied exodus as the crowd would rush the doors, trampling one another in their hysteria. It would be a sight to remember. He licked his lips in anticipation. He was almost certainly going to die, but it would be worth it. What havoc he would inflict on his way out! All around him, the audience was becoming more and more relaxed. They were clearly enjoying the concert. The music was uplifting and the arrangements were brilliant. Sardi was sorry that Dagenheim had chosen this night of all nights to conduct, but that was his bad luck. He should never have agreed to lead an Israeli orchestra. Turncoat German!

He watched Dagenheim with admiration. What talent! How agile! How much energy he expended! He was completely immersed in the music, his mind focused entirely on the black notes on the lined sheets. The baton moved, the violins and cellos replied in chorus, their sweet voices answering him gently at times and then with passion. The French horns chimed in their approval, and the cadence of the big drums all merged together with a stunning sweetness. Then there was a sudden silence as the orchestra grew still, instruments in place poised to continue, temporarily at rest as the first violinist began his solo. The music rose and hung there suspended over the heads of the audience, as the solo crescendoed to its glorious conclusion. A thunderous storm of applause followed, though the piece was not yet over. When it died down, the orchestra continued playing the great works of Strauss as brought to life by Dagenheim.

The applause at the finale was prolonged, and held the ring of authenticity. The lights came on, and the crowd stood, many of them stretching. The majority headed to the concession stands and the gift shops, with more than a few people electing to remain in their seats during the intermission. Sardi nodded at everyone who went in and out, and answered questions with charm. Anyone studying those eyes, however, would have seen a look buried in the depths that spoke of an unbridgeable hatred. The trouble was, no one was looking.

Sardi thought of his parents, brothers and sisters all crammed into a tiny room in the slums of Gaza, with no money to buy food and no telephone, mattresses lining the floor from side to side. He knew that this was something that had to be done, because something so precious had been taken from his family. Sardi had been thoroughly indoctrinated. He believed that his family's awful lot was the fault of Israelis. He never understood that it was Hamas and his Arab brethren who had stolen any hope they had ever had for something better. With his confused values and fresh resolve, he waited for his moment, as the lights dimmed a few moments later and the people rushed to take their seats for the second half of the evening. Daniel Dagenheim raised his baton and the orchestra began as one. Exactly 10 minutes later, Sardi slipped out of the doors, and rapidly headed down the stairs toward the locker room and his instruments of death.

He was wild with excitement now. He was going to be a martyr, give it all up for the cause. He steadied himself on the wall, before continuing onward, building it up in his mind, seeing the fantasy of a brave warrior going on the attack. He reached the locker room and hurried inside, taking care not to slam the door. He rushed to the locker and stuck the key into the lock. His hands were shaking so much that it took him three tries to insert it. The door swung open, and there was his gun, his grenade. He slung the gun over his shoulder and released the safety mechanism. He placed the grenade in his belt where it was readily accessible.

Jihad, here I come, he thought. *Sweet paradise, your running waters are waiting for me!*

He left the room, walking as if in a dream, everything happening in slow motion. Each step felt like an eternity; every movement felt as if he was swimming. He brushed aside the weird sensations, and relentlessly continued on, no hesitating, no changing the course of destiny. And then, after months of careful planning, Sardi emerged from backstage, directly in front of the entrance through which he would launch his attack, changing the course of Israeli musical history forever.

He stood beside the doors and waited for a climactic moment. The orchestra was building up right then. He could see Dagenheim waving his baton like one possessed! There was a distant roll of drums, and the violas thundered in unison. Sardi could wait no longer. Moving his gun from side to side, he ran into the auditorium, a fearsome sight to behold. The submachine gun sweept the room from right to left. This was his show now! He stood right in front of the stage and let go with a barrage of bullets into the crowd. There was a moment of intense shock as the audience realized that they were under attack. Then the sounds of hysterical shouting began competing with the orchestra, some of whom were still playing. A lone bullet grazed Daniel Dagenheim's leg and he fell, still holding his baton, a look of excruciating pain on his face.

Sardi stood with his back to the stage, gun to the crowd and emptied his gun on the enemy: those he felt to be at fault for the ruined lives of his downtrodden people.

It took Rafi three seconds to realize what was happening. The moment that the man with the gun turned toward the crowd, Rafi ceased playing and dropped to the floor, taking refuge behind the conductor's platform. His years of army training had kicked in. He was a soldier once again, and he hit the floor, rolled and was behind the platform quicker than it takes to write about it. His violin was still clasped tightly in his hand. The terrorist was facing the audience, still shooting. While the majority of his shots were wildly off the mark, some of them were making contact. Rafi knew that he would have to stop the man right here, right now. The terrorist hadn't expected a threat from the direction of the stage. It was a serious miscalculation indeed.

Rafi wasted no more time. He was working on autopilot, no thinking, just fluid movement. Brandishing his violin high above his head, he ran toward the edge of the stage and took a flying leap straight at the terrorist. As he flew through the air, he brought his violin swinging downward, slicing the air like a sword, and shattered it as hard as he could directly on the man's skull! The gun clattered to the floor with a crash, as pieces of broken violin flew every which way. The terrorist slumped forward. But as he fell, Rafi saw him clutch the grenade in his hand and pull the pin. The terrorist's hand had come open, releasing the spherical object into the air, and it flew upward. Rafi knew that it was going to explode, and what the man hadn't been able to accomplish with his slipshod shooting, he would succeed in carrying out with the grenade.

Rafi was moving on pure adrenalin. There was no need for anyone to clarify matters, or to point out the options. He had never seen a clearer picture in his life. He saw his uncle's face for a second, and he was smiling at him. The tune that he loved so well was blasting through his head as if the speakers were on maximum. He leaped up using one of the seats to propel him into the air. He jumped as high as he could, and caught the grenade in midair and held it tightly in his fist as the sounds of utter hysteria increased by the second. He looked around, searching the ideal place to toss the grenade. Every exit was crammed with yelling, shoving, masses of hysterical humanity. There was no way he would be able to throw the grenade through one of those doorways. There were just too many people; he was bound to hit someone. He looked at the stage, past the panicking musicians lying face down on the floor to the deep space beyond where there was a storage room.

Without wasting any time, Rafi drew his hand back, held the live grenade in the center of his fist for a millisecond until he was sure of his aim, and let it fly like a missile, directly over the heads of the musicians, and into the deepest, darkest recesses of the side stage. There was a moment of silence, followed by a tremendous roar as the grenade exploded. Rafi knew that the pianos in the storage room were doomed. It didn't matter. What was a piano worth when it came to saving lives? Absolutely nothing. The terrorist was still lying on the floor moaning in pain. Rafi grabbed his arms and pulled them behind his back. Instinctively, he seized one of the cable lines that snaked around the floor of the stage. He tied the man's arms together as tightly as he was able. Then he threw him onto one of the seats and looked at the watch on his wrist that was shaking uncontrollably.

The entire ordeal had taken just minutes. From the distance came the wail of the ambulance sirens. The loudspeakers blasted as they ordered cars to let them pass. He wondered how Tami was doing as he made sure the terrorist didn't move. It was all just too much: the attack, the smashed violin still lying in fragments, the grenade, the close call. His heart was still racing wildly as the adrenalin continued surging unabated. Now though, the fear was subsiding. EMT's came rushing into the auditorium to evacuate the wounded. It was a miracle how few had been murdered by the terrorist. Most of the bullets had gone wild. Rafi knew that everything about those last four minutes was nothing less than miraculous. A continuous stream of security people was entering the room now, and they admired how he had taken charge of the situation.

"You're a hero," they praised.

There was a sudden ringing sound, and he turned to see from where it was coming. It dawned on him that it was coming from the terrorist's pocket. It was probably the terrorist's dispatcher calling to see if he had managed to escape. There was no point in answering the phone. Better to leave that to the security experts. Rafi handed the ringing phone over to one of the policemen and tried to rise to his feet. He couldn't walk. His legs wouldn't hold him. One of the paramedics noticed the pallor on his face, and rushed to him. They made him sit in one of the chairs and someone brought a cold Coke from the concession stand.

"Are you O.K.?" they wanted to know.

"I feel amazing," he said. "I feel great. This is the greatest day of my life! Do you have a phone I can use for a minute?"

"Sure," the medic said, "talk for as long as you want."

She answered on the second ring.

"Tami?" he asked questioningly. "Are you O.K.?"

"Rafi!" she replied. "Rafi!" There was admiration and respect in her voice. "I can't believe what you did in there! You were a hero. You were like *Shimshon HaGibor!* Smashing the violin down over his head! What an idea! How are you? Are you O.K.? Were you hurt at all?"

"I'm fine, *Baruch Hashem,*" he said. "I just wanted to make sure that you were safe. Let's meet tomorrow for dinner, O.K.?"

"Definitely," she said. "I'll call you tomorrow. And Rafi," she went on, "I am so relieved that you're O.K.. I love you so much, and I'm so proud of the way you reacted. I will never forget the sight of my brother flying off the stage holding that violin high in his hand and bringing it down on the terrorist's head. You are my hero! I will see you tomorrow. Goodbye."

He hung up with a bemused look on his face. Tami had never been so emotional before. Normally, it was all about science with her. She was a hypnotherapist, and her services were highly in demand. People came from all over the country to be treated by her, and her success rate was outstanding. He had been so worried that she would take one look at his *kippah* and choose to never speak with him again. Who could have ever guessed that a terrorist attack, of all things, would bring about a closeness between them? He was so exhausted and felt his eyes closing. He leaned back and sipped the Coke in contemplative silence.

The Coke was delicious, and he was grateful for the sugar — for the high it was giving him. He closed his eyes for a moment and lay with his head against the back of the chair. He had the eerie feeling that he was being watched. He opened his eyes and found himself looking up into the kind face of an older man who was studying him intently, as if he were trying to peer into the innermost workings of his soul.

"Hello," he greeted the man tiredly. "Can I help you?"

"We have to talk," answered the man in a terse tone of voice. "Not here and not now. Tomorrow morning, I want you to meet me om the boardwalk by to the Tel Aviv Marina. Can you make it there at 10 o'clock?"

Rafi was dumbfounded by the no-nonsense approach and strength of character that he saw in the man's wise eyes. He would have liked to answer no, that there was no earthly reason why he should agree to a meeting with him. But he didn't. Instead he looked the man in the eyes, and sitting up straight, he stuck out his hand to him.

"Rafi Ganim," he introduced himself.

"I know," the man replied impatiently. "You are very talented for one so young!"

He turned to leave, but Rafi called out, "What's your name?"

"Kobi," said the old man, and he was gone.

28
Rafi Ganim

Tel Aviv, Israel
March 15, 2007

Representatives of the radio and television media were waiting for him outside the hall. He wasn't in the mood to talk right then. He had a thumping headache, was lightheaded and famished, and felt weak and nauseous all at the same time. He wanted more than anything to get to his apartment, have a beer and go to bed. It wasn't meant to be.

"Mr. Ganim, it's Choni Roth from Channel Two!"

"Mr. Ganim, Dudu from *Kol Yisrael*."

"Rafi, Rafi, it's Guy from *Galei Tzahal*!"

And on and on. Realizing that he was going to have to say something or they would never let him go, he agreed to an impromptu news conference. He told them what had happened from his perspective, what he had seen, how he had reacted, etc. They were awestruck.

"You actually attacked the man with your prized violin?" asked the journalist from *Yediot Acharonot* in disbelief.

"Did I have a choice?" " he replied. "There wasn't anything else to use! But a violin is replaceable. I couldn't just stand by and do nothing as this terrorist tried to kill as many Jews as he could. Someone had to do something, yet nobody was doing anything. It was a miracle that so few people were hurt!"

"You could say that again," said Yaniv Ben Maimon, the top reporter for *Maariv*. "What a story! Someone even had the presence of mind to snap a picture of you flying off the stage like an angel of mercy, brandishing that violin in the air like a sword! Now that's a picture. That picture is going to win awards. *Kol Hakavod*!"

He answered several additional questions, and then bade them all a good night.

"Look out for the story tomorrow," they told him.

And he knew that he was going to be plastered on the front page of every news publication in the country over the next few days. He didn't care either way, but he understood that it was beneficial for the Israeli public to know that there were still those who were prepared to risk their lives for their friends and neighbors. A policeman drove him home, where his parents and relatives had left repeated messages on his answering machine. He called those that were most important; the others were just going to have to wait.

It was a strange night, full of extremely weird dreams. He was being chased down endless corridors, and then the tables turned and he was the aggressor chasing others down the same hallways. It was hard to know who was friend and who was foe. At 6 a.m. he gave up trying to sleep and got out of bed. He went to *Shacharis* at the Kolodover *beis midrash*, and to say good morning to his uncle and aunt, who no doubt had heard various twisted accounts as to what had exactly transpired at the concert. He would eat breakfast with them and use the opportunity for a quick talk with his uncle, and then head over to meet with the mysterious Kobi. He hadn't advanced to the point where he went to shul each morning yet, but if any one day merited a shul appearance, it was today.

Shacharis was davened with full of *kavannah* that morning. It was the type of prayer a person experiences after being granted a new lease on life. It was a glorious feeling. He tasted the words of the *tefillah*. Each and every word seemed to take on a deeper meaning than he had understood until then. How lucky he had been. It could have been so much worse. The terrorist could have kept his wits about him and harmed many more people. He could have thrown his grenade into the densely packed crowd. Rafi could have misjudged the distance between them and not hit him hard enough. He could have dropped the grenade. If his aim had been off, the grenade might have exploded in the crowd. So many details could have gone wrong with catastrophic results. Instead, Hashem had decided to grant nearly everyone in that hall another chance to live life the right way. And Rafi rejoiced, his heart sang. He wanted to dance, to cheer, to jump up and down and clap his hands and compose songs to Hashem and sing them and play them on his violin. Then he recalled that his violin had been smashed to smithereens. The memory made him laugh out loud, because he knew that if the same thing had happened to his violin for any other reason, he would have been heartbroken. But now he was ecstatic.

People were looking at him, wanting to hear the real story. True, these chassidim belonged to an insular community, but they weren't completely cut off from the news. The attack of the previous evening had been sufficient to shock the entire country out of its complacency! One of the men told him that after a harrowing experience such as this it would be appropriate for Rafi to *bentch gomel,* recite a blessing for surviving a life-threatening event. As he was winding the *tefillin* that Naftali Kenighofer had lent him, he was tapped on the shoulder by a *bachur* who informed him that the Rebbe wanted to see him in his residence following davening.

Rafi told his aunt the entire story from beginning to end at the breakfast table, and she cried and became emotional when she realized how close he had come to being murdered. She served him a substantial breakfast, and he ate until he was very full, perhaps feeling a subconscious desire to feel alive. Then he went in to see his uncle. The Rebbe was in his seat learning from an open Gemara. He broke into a joyous smile when Rafi entered the room.

"Rafi Ganim, *mein tei'-eire kind* (my beloved child). Come over here," his uncle said.

Rafi heard his uncle's voice and suddenly felt at ease. Here was someone who truly understood him; had understood him from the moment they had met, without Rafi even having to speak. His uncle, the Rebbe, had an intuitive comprehension of his feelings with no need for explanations. Just seeing him smile, just hearing his voice made Rafi smile and brought tears to his eyes at the same time. The previous night had been traumatic. The knowledge that the Rebbe was sitting beside him, comforting him, made him feel that everything would turn out all right in the end. He told the Rebbe everything: That Tami had been in the audience, and how worried he had been when he hadn't seen her immediately after the atack. He spared no details. He opened up about everything that happened. And his uncle listened patiently, with a silent understanding. When he finished describing the attack, he told his uncle of the stranger who had approached him and asked him to come to the boardwalk near the Tel Aviv Marina later that morning.

"Are you planning to go?" the Rebbe asked him.

"I think so," Rafi said. "The man came across as very astute, if somewhat eccentric. Somehow, I don't think a meeting with him will be a waste of time."

"Then you should go with *mazal*," his uncle said. "And tell your sister, Tami, that my wife and I want to meet her, as well."

Rafi agreed to relay the message, hoping that a connection with them would provide his sister with some of the same life-altering sustenance that he was receiving. But he had his doubts. Tami was a tough cookie who most resembled their father in many ways. He refused to give up, however. In this life, you just never knew.

Tel Aviv, Israel
March 16, 2007

Rafi was walking along the boardwalk toward the marina. There was a cool breeze from the Mediterranean, and he smelled the tang of the sea. He walked briskly in the fresh morning air, ignoring the joggers and the power walkers. Up ahead there was a restaurant crammed with people eating breakfast, and he could see the square-shaped Carlton Hotel perched on the edge of the shore. It was almost 10 o'clock, and as usual he was on time. He skirted the bar at the entrance to the marina, and walked across the wooden planking, passing a billiards hall and another seafood restaurant. As always, the sight of the boats bobbing in the water lifted his spirits. There was a party taking place on one of the bigger boats, and he could hear the sound of singing and laughter clear across to the other end.

There were a few benches scattered here and there, and he took a seat and waited. He could hardly recall what the elderly man had looked like, and didn't know where to wait. So he opted to take a seat and allow the man to come to him. His phone rang, and he reached down to answer it. He didn't recognize the number.

"Lesson number one," said the voice of the old man, "never sit in an exposed or vulnerable spot."

"What are you talking about?" Rafi asked the voice.

"Can you find me?" the voice continued, taunting him. Rafi looked around annoyed. He hadn't come here to play games.

"Look, mister," he said, "either tell me where you are or I'm going to leave! You hear me?"

"You're not going to leave," the voice said. "If you were going to leave, then you wouldn't have come in the first place. But here you are, which means that you are curious. And curious people never leave. Can you find me?"

Rafi looked around the crowded marina, at the people preparing to board, at the waiters and at the excited children, but mainly at the numerous boats docked alongside the pier. He shifted his eyes from boat to boat, taking them in one at a time, until he caught sight of someone sitting by himself on a boat that was docked behind a number of other boats, rendering him almost completely concealed. He was wearing dark glasses and a straw hat, and didn't look old or young or anything. He was just an anonymous person. But somehow Rafi knew that this was the old man he was supposed to meet. He didn't understand why they were playing this game, but it was clear that the old man was trying to tell him something; that he had an agenda.

Rafi decided to play along.

He waited until a party of four was passing in front of him on the way to their boat. When he was completely obscured by them, he jumped off the bench and kept abreast with the group, until he was standing behind another boat, and out of sight of the faceless stranger. Then he moved soundlessly from one boat to the next, until he was just one boat away from where the old man sat motionless, dark glasses in place, unmoving. Getting down on all fours, he crept out from behind the last boat, and crossed the distance separating him from his mark's craft. He waited for the perfect moment, and then he boarded.

"I hope you're satisfied," he said to the old man, who was still looking in the opposite direction. The man ignored him.

"Don't bother getting Eitan to talk," said the old man from a boat across the dock. "He hasn't spoken in a really long time, and besides," he said, walking over to the 'man' in the sunglasses, "it's not really an option for him in the first place." He proceeded to remove the sunglasses and the straw hat from the 'man.' Rafi realized that the 'man' he had been hiding from was actually an inflated doll!

"Kobi Shapiro," the old man introduced himself. He had the greenest eyes. "What you just saw was one of the oldest tricks in the book. But I can't blame you. You were never in the game before, and the way you stayed out of sight was almost first rate. I think we are going to get along just fine."

That was Rafi's real introduction to Kobi, ex-Mossad and mentor-to-be.

They sat on his boat and eyed each other.

"Let me tell you a little bit about myself," the old man said.

Those green eyes were really intense. Every time he looked at them, Rafi felt as if he was in Eilat, staring into the bottom of the sea.

"You have no idea what I want from you," Kobi said to the young man in front of him. "You live a nice normal life just like everyone else. The people you know are teachers, lawyers, *Bamba* distributors, and you are a fiddler. Just another guy on the stage of life. But if you take my offer, say goodbye to that. You will have to become a shadow." Rafi raised an eyebrow questioningly at that line.

"You are looking at a man who devoted his entire life — his entire existence in fact — to an ideal. I couldn't live with the fact that there were Nazis roaming the earth, prosperously going about their business, making money, traveling freely in their luxury cars, flying around the world in their private jets. How dare they live so peacefully with such enjoyment, when they had murdered so many innocent people without a second thought. It gave me no rest. I voiced my thoughts to people who presumably informed others about my hopes and aspirations, because eventually I was invited to a meeting at a run-down building on Karl Netter Street in Tel Aviv. The building was surrounded by dusty garbage bins, and it seemed as if all the cats of Tel Aviv were foraging there. I looked at the building and couldn't imagine who would be awaiting me inside. It was so utterly run down and forlorn; so unimpressive.

"I entered the building. There was a stench in that lobby that made me think of unlaundered clothing. There was a man loitering on the stairs, dressed casually. He was someone you would pass in the street and not notice at all, completely nondescript. He looked me over from head to toe and asked, 'Kobi Shapiro?'

"I answered in the affirmative.

"'Take the elevator,' he advised me. 'It's faster and it smells better.'

"I pressed the button, wondering at the fact that such a worn-out building had an elevator in the first place. It arrived almost immediately. It was obviously well maintained.

"'You want the fourth floor,' the man on the stairs said.

"'Thanks,' I said and stepped inside.

"I pressed the button for the fourth floor and the elevator rose swiftly. There was a pinging sound, and the door slid open to reveal a large carpeted space with couches and a magazine-covered coffee table. A desk faced the elevator. I told the receptionist I had a 2 o'clock appointment with a Mr. Mulam. She nodded and in a clipped voice told me to take a seat. Unbeknown to me, I had just entered Phase One of my induction to the Israeli Mossad, not knowing that the road ahead of me was going to be long and hard. I would find myself stymied at times, find myself wishing that I hadn't chosen to go down this path, tell myself that I would be quitting the agency the next day.

"The training was brutal. I will not try to whitewash the truth in any shape or form. I was young and brash and sure of myself, but they saw right through my confident facade. They tore me apart and rebuilt me into something formidable. In the end, I became one of the best agents the agency had. I was a Nazi-hunter supreme, and proud of what I did. I was part of the team that captured Eichmann in Argentina. That was a triumph for me, a high in my career. But there were lows as well.

"I don't know if you recall the attack on Moshav Arazim. It was hushed up, but maybe you heard something anyway?"

Rafi hadn't heard of it. This was a new world for him: the world of spies and espionage, the fastest cars and coolest gadgets. What did he know of this stuff? Kobi told him what had happened at Arazim and how it had transformed him from one of the most successful agents in the Mossad to someone who could only handle a desk job; and even that was a joke.

"Somehow I survived the massacre at Arazim. It wasn't easy. In the end, it was only the knowledge that my partner would have hated what I had become that pulled me back from the brink of abject despair. Part of what brought me back was the fact that the agency wanted to send me on the most daring mission I had ever heard of. We were planning to find Josef Mengele, and either bring him back to Israel with us or kill him if that wasn't possible."

"But Mengele was never caught or killed," Rafi interjected. "I'm pretty sure that he drowned or something."

"I know," Kobi said, giving Rafi a sharp look. "We didn't get him. We crashed a gathering of some of the biggest Nazi names, taking place at the home of a man named Zeivald. It was a brilliant operation, and yet we didn't gain our objective. I shot at Mengele, and I think he was injured. But he most definitely wasn't killed by an Israeli bullet. There *was* some sort of consolation that day, however."

"Why, what happened?" asked Rafi curiously.

"One of my agents, a young man by the name of Roni, found a book, a very interesting, yet cryptic book. It contained several lists, rows of names. When he opened the case it was in, an alarm went off! We barely escaped with our lives that night, and Roni died in my arms. But I took that book home with me. For years I have wondered what this book — that clearly contained extremely important and sensitive information — was doing at the home of someone of mediocre rank. Zeivald was a nobody!

"But that question paled alongside a much greater series of questions: What was the book of names? Whose names were they? What did it represent? There was almost nothing to go on; just page after page of clearly written names. It didn't say where the owners of those names lived or what they were up to. It didn't give any indication if these names were genuine names or code names. And so, for years I have wondered what this book means, what danger lies within it. This book, covered in the blood of my eternally young friend, spells danger to me. I don't know why, in what way, but I know that it's in there waiting.

"I wanted to put some agents onto the book, to see what they could come up with. But the agency didn't see it as I saw it. They sent the book to the Mossad code breakers, but nobody came up with anything. After that, the bosses at the agency didn't really see the urgency as I did. I think they felt that I was trying to make it up to Roni for letting him down. But it wasn't true. Deep down I felt that there was something there; something that needed investigating. But you can't fight City Hall.

"I didn't know what to do about the book. I tried to discover its meaning in every way that I knew how, but I constantly met with failure. Obviously, this was an extremely well-guarded secret to which only a few influential people were privy. But one of them was me. Those names meant something, I was sure of that. But the heads of the Mossad didn't share my sense of urgency.

"My career continued after that unfortunate escapade with other successes, other failures. While my mind and energy were focused on other ideas and projects, there was always a tiny niggling buzz at the back of my head reminding me that there was a crucial, mysterious book in my safe at Mossad Headquarters. I don't have to tell you," Kobi went on, "that my line of work entails an enormous amount of reading. There are always updates and new information. An agent has to remain on top of his game. That means processing a mind-boggling load of top-secret information on an ongoing basis."

"I'm sorry to interrupt you, Mr. Shapiro," Rafi said, "but I don't understand why you are telling me all this. I mean, it's fascinating and all, but isn't this classified? Won't you get in trouble if you speak of these things with people from outside the agency?"

The old man held up his hand and gave Rafi a placating smile. "Mr. Ganim," he said, "give me a few more minutes of your time, please, and you will understand everything."

"Where was I?" he asked.

"You have to read a lot of information in your line of work," Rafi reminded him.

"Right you are," the old man calling himself Kobi replied. But somehow Rafi knew that he hadn't forgotten anything at all. He was testing Rafi in some way.

"So one day I was studying a packet of updated information on several Nazis who could and would stand trial, if we caught them. What do I see? Someone had uncovered a veritable treasure trove of information on Herr Kurt Wolfgang Zeivald, the man I had always considered mediocre, a lackey, a nobody. It seems that Zeivald had been the deputy of a much-more influential man, one Ludwig Eberhart. That made me look at Zeivald in a completely different light. If Ludwig Eberhart had approved of Zeivald enough to have accepted him for a deputy, then Zeivald must have been pretty smart or resourceful, because Ludwig Eberhart was just about the best the Waffen SS had, and that's saying something."

Rafi was shocked to hear the name Eberhart. The Kolodover Rebbe of Tel Aviv had related to Rafi as many details of Heinrich Eberhart's visit to his uncle, the previous Rebbe, as he knew, in his attempt to show him why the Kolodover Rebbe and his brother had parted ways. This development inspired Reb Anshel to move to Eretz Yisrael, leaving Rav David Zushe to face the wrath of the Nazis by himself. It had been a man by the name of Heinrich Eberhart who had been the cause of that breakup. The two *tzaddikim* had disagreed as to whether to give him a blessing. In retrospect, it seemed that Rav David Zushe had been wrong; that giving Eberhart the blessing had backfired on him in a terrible way, resulting in a rift between the brothers, and to part in disagreement.

Kobi was still talking, and Rafi came back to the present and found himself listening with a sudden eagerness that had not been there before. Eberhart was involved! He was the cause of so much of his family's grief!

"It's a known fact that Ludwig Eberhart was Himmler's protégé," the old man was saying, "with Himmler sending him on the most sensitive missions on his behalf. And wherever Eberhart went," here he gave a little smile, "Zeivald wasn't far behind. This tidbit of information led me to a little assumption, but one which I feel is probably accurate."

The old man lowered his voice, and Rafi had to lean in much closer to hear what he was about to say. The wind was blowing, and the boat they were on was rocking back and forth in the water. Kobi wasn't paying any attention to the boat. He was focused solely on his tale.

"If Eberhart's deputy had a copy of this book," Kobi said, "then I can only assume that the actual book — the original document with the people's real names *and* their locations, the book that will allow us to understand who these people really are — is no doubt kept in a secure location by Eberhart himself." He smiled brightly, showing strong white teeth.

"This means what exactly?" asked Rafi.

"This means that while we still have no idea what the significance of this book is, at least we have a reasonable idea of where it can be found. Ludwig Eberhart's main sphere of influence with Himmler was near the war's end. But with the situation in Germany drastically deteriorating from week to week, and Eberhart out of the country much of that time, chances are that he was still running operations for the Reichsfuhrer when the Allies reached Berlin. Himmler probably left behind loads of unfinished business. It's highly probable that this book was one of them. Which brings us to another assumption, namely, that Eberhart might have been in the midst of an ongoing operation at war's end for Himmler, one which was supposed to continue after the war was over. As we all know, Himmler himself was afraid that Germany was not going to prevail against her enemies and win the war. This operation might have been the result of his fears."

"Assumptions, assumptions," Rafi said, caught up in the whole zany discussion despite himself.

"True!" said Kobi. "But if they were only assumptions," he went on, "then why would Zeivald keep a copy of the book, or the original, for all we know, under an alarm system?"

"Maybe because the book had sentimental value to him?" suggested Rafi. "Who knows? Who cares?"

"Possibly," the old man thundered, "it might be for sentimental reasons. But it's possible and I think even probable that the book has some sort of relevance even today. That's why Zeivald had it in his home under lock and key years after the war was over. That's why I am almost positive that Dietrich Eberhart is in possession of the book. Not Ludwig. He died of a heart attack five years ago. But I'm almost positive that his son, Dietrich, has the book — the complete book — and I'm sure that there is much to learn about this book. If we don't find out about it now when we have the chance, it might turn out to have been a big mistake!"

"Why?" Rafi asked heatedly. "So there's a book with some names. So what? What's the big deal? What could it be already?!"

The old man sat quietly. It was clear that his thoughts were in the past, remembering things, things from long ago, things he would much rather not have seen. When he spoke, there were tears in his eyes.

"Son," he said, "for a few months after we escaped with the book, our agents throughout Europe kept hearing rumors about the book. There was a lot of talk about it; low-key talk, like the Germans didn't want too much publicity. But the interest was there and the fear as well. They were afraid because the book was in our hands. Again, they kept the lid on it for the most part, but our experts picked up on it and sensed the urgency. That book is important!

"I'll tell you something else, son. You don't know the Germans like I know them. They say that they've changed. People think they've changed. They regret what they did. They feel sorry for their actions. So much guilt in Germany. Blah, blah, blah. It's bogus, son. They're good actors. They paid reparations to Israel. They bought themselves a clean conscience, but they didn't do that for themselves. They did it for the world. Personally, I don't think they even lost one night of sleep over what they did to the Jews. And I'll tell you something else, and you might laugh and you might think that I'm crazy. But I feel that they are only resting. Resting. When the right time comes, and they once again have the opportunity to hurt the Jews of the world, they will grab that opportunity with both hands and do what they can to destroy us, once and for all.

"You think I'm being melodramatic, don't you? I can see it in your eyes. Do you know how many of today's German youth identify with the neo-Nazis? It would shock you if I told you the numbers. The Nazi movement is growing by the day. Not just in Germany, either. They are on the rise again all over Europe. The reports are coming in all the time. We do our best to hush things up, to camouflage the truth. We don't want the Jews of the world walking around with the shadow of another Holocaust. But it's becoming harder and harder to keep things quiet. They are powerful, but divided in England, more powerful and less divided in France. Even Russia — who you would think would have cause to hate the concept of Nazism more than anyone after the millions of people they lost in the war — is swarming with youths who relate to the concept, and are obsessed with the clothing, the literature, the whole repugnant outlook.

"Do you want to know who stands at the head of this worldwide network of neo-Nazis, skinheads, etc.? Do you want to know?"

Slowly Rafi nodded his head.

"Herr Dietrich Eberhart," Kobi said, "Ludwig's son, the chairman of Eberhart Enterprises worldwide. He is the man who controls a large portion of the German ecnomy, despite the fact that he is young. He jets around the globe finalizing monumental business deals, and is respected by all. He is also the owner of Club Salute, an extremely popular Hamburg club that is always jammed, despite the fact that it's the most expensive club in the city. Club Salute is a front however," Kobi said. "The club fronts for something much bigger than people coming together to dance and have a good time. It's also a place where the supporters of the neo-Nazi renewal movement gather, all under Eberhart's auspices. His supporters might help fund the movement, but everything is overseen and all the major decisions are made by Dietrich himself. The movement is growing stronger by the day!"

He allowed the words to settle in, saying nothing for a minute or two. Not a word passed between them, the only sounds coming from the ocean waves that were splashing against the sides of the boat.

"O.K.," Rafi finally said, "say I agree that the theories that you put forth make sense at some level. Let's say there is a book. It's very probable that Dietrich Eberhart has it, and the book might contain dangerous information, and so on. What do you want from me? Why are you telling me this? I'm not an agent. Why are you singling me out like this? What do you want?"

"To put it bluntly," the old man said, "I want you!"

"What?!" Rafi sputtered.

"You heard me," Kobi said. "I have been waiting for years to find the perfect man, the perfect agent, to join me on this mission. I'm more or less retired now. I served my time, I put in much more than my time. But I never wanted to discuss the book as a mission with other agents. It had to be the perfect man for the job, someone who impressed me with his ability to think on his feet. When I saw you in action at the concert last night, I realized that you were the man for whom I was looking. What a brilliant idea to bash the guy over the head with your violin! That's called thinking out of the box, and you are the man I want to take on this mission."

"Wait a second," Rafi said. "I don't understand something. Why didn't you devote yourself to this mission all these years? You had this mysterious book in your safe at the office for so many years, and you never followed up on it. Why not? Why now?"

"That's a good question, and it deserves a proper answer," Kobi replied. "First of all, at the time that I discovered the book, the Nazis were beaten and in hiding, and I had many pressing operations on my desk. Many times over the years, I thought about getting my teeth into this matter. Every time I was about to sink my teeth into it, something else came up. When I would ask my boss, 'What about the book?' He'd say to me, 'The book, right. We really do need to get into that. But right now you need to track down Ulrich Krum, the commandant of Rakower.' And that's the way it went."

"So what changed?" Rafi asked.

"Everything changed," Kobi answered quietly. "The Nazi Party has risen once again. Out of the ashes, there had been a rebirth, a renewal. The neo-Nazis are here to stay. In the past, we were able to delude ourselves into thinking that it was one or two, or a thousand. Today we know that it's many thousands of people all over the world. They are constantly gathering strength. Their numbers are growing, their financial power is growing, and I don't doubt for a second that there are plans afoot for an emergence. From the way events are developing on the ground, I don't think that they are planning to wait that much longer. These people are ambitious; they are Germans, efficient and well thought out. That's why the time has arrived to finally get to the bottom of this. There is no more time to delay, to say that we'll deal with this tomorrow. That's why I'm meeting with you. I know that we have enough agents on board, and that

I don't have to recruit you. But I have a good feeling about this. I think you are the right man for the job, even if you don't have any experience in the world of espionage.

"You served in a top-notch unit while in the army, and you made your mark. You have a natural aptitude for this type of thing, and I have no doubt that if you decide to take this on, you will be extremely successful here as well."

"But I'm a violin player," Rafi protested, "not a spy or an agent!"

"And I wanted to be an actor," Kobi said, "but the situation didn't allow it, and I ended up moving in another direction.

"Look," he said, "think about it. If you decide that you want to join, I will send you for training immediately. You will become an agent, and I will stand by your side and mentor you myself until you're ready to go out in the field. Just remember, Dietrich Eberhart is not waiting for anyone. The man is extremely ambitious, charismatic and popular. He is taking the movement forward. For the first time in 60 years, the Nazis have a leader who may be able to pull it off. And if this book is a threat — and my gut is telling me that it is — then he is sure to have the original copy under lock and key.

"Look," Kobi finished off, "just think about it. What do you have to lose? You're young, not married, no major responsibilities. You can do this!"

"What I have to lose is my life but I'll think about it," Rafi said to the old man sitting in front of him. "If you believe in me, I'm going to consider this, talk to a few people who can advise me, give it some serious consideration."

"Just make sure that they're people you can trust. And remember, I'm expecting you to exercise clear judgment regarding the things that you share with them. This isn't a game, you know. Here is my phone number. I will answer it anytime you call. Please don't take too long."

With that Kobi Shapiro stood up. Refusing Rafi's attempt to help him off the boat, he moved onto the marina with surprisingly nimble feet. He didn't look back. Rafi followed the stooped shoulders and straw hat until he couldn't see them any longer. Then he arose as well and headed out of the marina and onto the busy Tel Aviv streets. A few more hours of sleep wouldn't hurt him right now.

Rafi had made up to meet her at a Chinese place a short distance from the Dan Panorama Hotel. It was a kosher restaurant, which was perfect for him, and classy enough that she wouldn't feel she was missing out by coming there. Tami was a professional, and used to the finer things in life. He didn't want her to think that just because he was becoming religious that he had to compromise on good food and service. He arrived early and found a bench overlooking the ocean, where he sat and waited for her. Five minutes later, a taxi pulled up alongside him, and Tami emerged, waving. She was holding about 10 newspapers and beaming like a lightbulb.

"Rafi," she called out, and he smiled at her. "I was planning to take the taxi straight to the restaurant, but then I saw you here and I figured, hey, we might as well begin right here. So here I am. And here you are!" She proceeded to hand him the newspapers, which were plastered with front-page photos of him in all sorts of poses. *Maariv* had him jumping off the stage, violin in the air. He looked positively dangerous.

"You remind me of Moshe Dayan," she said to him. "Mr. Brave, look at you, jumping through the air like a superhero. I'm telling you," she shuddered delicately, "I thought he was going to kill us all. But suddenly there you were flying to the rescue like an avenging angel. You have no idea how proud I was of you that second!"

"Even though I was wearing a *kippah*?" he ventured.

"Precisely because you were wearing a *kippah*," she assured him. "I suddenly understood that it has only made you better. I don't know. Something about you changed. You have this self-assurance that you never had before. I personally feel — and this is only my opinion – that I'm almost sure that the *kippah* has had a very positive impact on you."

"Thank you," he murmured, touched.

"You're welcome," she replied.

"Well, now that we're being so close and filled with brotherly love," Rafi said, "maybe you can give me your take on an offer that I just received this morning." He proceeded to tell her enough about his earlier meeting that she got the general idea. She was flabbergasted, as he had expected.

"But you don't have any training," she said to him at last.

"That's what I said as well," he replied. "But the old man said that he'd train me. It was obvious that he was in a league of his own, Tami. You should have seen him. He sat there ramrod straight, and his eyes were so sharp. They would have cut me if he would have let them. This guy was the real thing!"

"I don't know," she said. "It's so dangerous."

"As is the alternative," he said. "These people want to destroy us. If we do nothing about it, who knows what will happen. If G-d singled me out to save a concert hall of Jews, then He knew what He was doing. Because when I went on the attack against that terrorist, it felt right, like this was the right thing for me to be doing right then. You know what I mean?" She nodded.

"Well I'm kind of getting the same kind of feeling now. And I didn't even tell you about Eberhart, yet."

"Who is Eberhart?" she asked him. He smiled at her and began explaining all about the man in his recurrent dreams who kept telling him to help an unnamed person.

"The man from my dream turned out to be a relative of ours," he said to her. "I saw his portrait on the wall of the Kolodover Rebbe's study. And you want to know something else?" he went on not waiting for her reply. "He used to play the violin as well. And you want to know something even stranger?" Here he paused before going on. "Our father is the brother of the present-day Kolodover Rebbe!"

Her eyes widened in disbelief. "Get out!" she said.

"No, it's true. The Rebbe showed me pictures of them together when they were much younger. It was a very close family, but Abba went off the *derech* and chose his own way. It's very sad. The Rebbe told me some of our family history. It is very much intertwined with a German family called the Eberharts. Our great-uncle, the previous Kolodover Rebbe, gave Heinrich Eberhart a blessing for success after which he became wildly prosperous. But his son, Ludwig, was cut from a different cloth. At some point along the way, Heinrich died and Ludwig took over the family business. By all accounts, he was a fanatical Nazi, close to the ruling clique and a Himmler protégé. This blessing was the cause of our family's breakup. Our great-uncle and our grandfather disagreed over whether to give a *berachah* to a gentile. In the end, our great-uncle gave the blessing against our grandfather's wishes. Grandfather decided to leave the town of Kolodov and make *aliyah* to Eretz Yisrael, leaving his brother behind. I don't think the two brothers ever saw each other again, all because of a blessing."

"But it was a good thing," Tamar said, "because if our grandfather would not have emigrated, our entire family would have been murdered in the war. So in a sense, as much as the blessing was bad for one of them, it was a good thing for the other."

"But you can understand now, why when the man from the Mossad told me the entire history, and mentioned the Eberhart family, suddenly I couldn't help but feel that this was something I was meant to be doing! For years this old man has been coming to me in a dream, begging me to find this person. Suddenly I discover that he's related to me. There was this song that came along with the dream, sort of like the dream's music track. The first time I walked into the Kolodover *beis midrash* I heard the chassidim singing it. That's when I knew that there was an incredible amount that I didn't understand here. Now that I discover that Eberhart's involved, it's like a circle which has to be closed, and maybe I'm the one who is supposed to do the closing."

Tamar looked at him, and he could see a tear in her eye. "Listen," she said. "You know that I'm very good at what I do."

"I know," he said. "They say you're the best."

"It's true," she said. "False modesty aside, I am. But if this is a family thing, then I want to help out, as well. If at any point along the way, you feel that you need my help in any way whatsoever, then you must call me. Are we in agreement? I'm just as smart as you are, and I feel that my unique skills might end up being essential for your mission. If such a thing happens, and you do need me, then you call me, at any hour of the day or night, and I will get on the next plane to wherever you are, and I will help you rescue our family. I will close the circle along with you. You have no idea when you might need an expert hypnotherapist. Deal?" she asked.

Feeling closer to his sister than he had ever felt before, he stuck out his hand and they shook on it. He must have been crazy, but for some reason, he didn't feel as if he had a choice in the matter. He had never fathomed that a person's life could change so drastically from one hour to the next. But now he saw that it could very well do just that. Underneath it all, he knew that his uncle, the Rebbe, would agree with his decision, as well.

"Let's go eat," he said.

So they went to the restaurant and ordered half the menu. It might have been the final meal of the condemned, but it sure tasted good.

29

Rafi Ganim

Tel Aviv, Israel
Summer- Fall 2007

The moment Rafi Ganim gave Kobi Shapiro the go-ahead, it was as if he handed over control of his life. Kobi insisted that he leave his apartment near the waterfront and move into a flat belonging to the Mossad. Kobi was retired; he'd been very clear about that. But the man still carried the respect of the agency. Rafi learned very quickly that when Kobi wanted something to move, it moved. He had a power seldom seen. Here was an old man who had supposedly left the agency years ago, and unexpectedly he spots a young man whom he recruits for an operation that may, or may not, produce results. But nobody was challenging him at all. In fact, Kobi was provided with all the resources that he needed to train the violinist. Once again, it was time to pick a team, and Kobi had chosen well. These were the men who would be training Rafi, molding him, teaching him the tricks of the trade, and only the best would do.

Rafi had been taught the basics back in his army days, but his instructors now focused on the specifics in a way that he could never have picked up back then. They were experts in their craft and superb teachers. There was no mercy for him. He was expected to be tough, and he asked for nothing. They pounded away at him day after day. Slowly but surely there was a change. His fighting skills were honed, his technique developed, and within a few weeks he was a different man. Kobi had been correct as always. Rafi's reactive skills were far above the norm. He had the ability to assess a situation within moments, to make decisions on the spot, and charge forward with them. It was incredible to watch someone so young, maneuver so well.

His handlers took him to a main thoroughfare on a mission: to stroll down the street from one corner to the next, while counting the "enemy agents." He had to spot them in the windows of the three-story buildings, and he had to know if they were among the people waiting at the bus stops. In the end, he had identified all of them, except for one agent who had been walking a dog and had been the most natural seeming of them all. It may have been one mistake, but they pounded him for it. They wouldn't let him forget the fact that in the field, one mistake was sometimes all you got.

He learned to swim like a pro, underwater demolition, bomb assembly, survival courses and martial arts. They brushed up on his English, and grilled him on his German until it was coming out of his ears. It didn't have to be perfect. He was never going to present himself as a German national; that was out of the question. But he was going undercover as the descendant of a prominent German family, and it was essential that he have the ability to speak the rudiments of the language passably. Rafi was a man used to working hard. You didn't become the top violinist of any country without working. But he had never put in days like these! Eighteen-hour days was insane! Yet he persevered with no complaints. He took everything they threw at him like a man.

Four months later he began learning the history and culture of the Nazi Party. A wheezing professor from Hebrew University came every day for three hours. They carried on an interactive discussion, attempting to cover as much material as possible. There were music tapes to listen to and to learn — songs that no self-respecting Nazi family would have neglected to teach their children. Being as musical as he was, this posed no problem. He listened to the songs once, and was able to sing along with them, or accompany them on his violin; whatever the situation warranted. They taught him how to drink. He was clueless when it came to knocking back hard liquor. That was something he would need to learn in order to be a successful Nazi. The professor quizzed him on the important names like Himmler, Goebbels, Martin Bormann and Alfred Rosenberg.

He memorized their positions and knew exactly what happened to them after the war. They made him repeat the SS motto until it flowed off his tongue, even though he had clearly never served in the SS and clearly never would.

He was going to present himself as a fanatical, anti-Semitic neo-Nazi, and that meant that he would need to know an outlandish amount of Nazi trivia. The training took months and months, and he wasn't allowed to have outside contact during that time. He had told his parents what he was doing so they wouldn't be more worried than necessary, and the knowledge that Tamar was out there and proud of him helped, as well. He hadn't realized when she had made him promise to call her if he needed assistance, how much that gesture had meant to him. Every time he thought about it, he was suffused with a warm glow.

One night he and his handler drove to one of the upper-class neighborhoods in Caesarea. They stopped at a magnificent home. Before they got out of the car, his handler whispered to him, "Your name is Rolf Zimmer."

Rafi rolled it around his tongue: Rolf Zimmer. He tasted the words, trying them out again and again, familiarizing himself with them.

The door was opened by a patrician-looking gentleman, with a head of curly white hair and light blue eyes. He welcomed them into his home, and led the way past the kitchen and into a large living room. There was a baby grand on one side of the room, and a violin on a music stand beside it. This was clearly a music-loving family.

"*Sprechen sie Deutsche*?" the man asked Rafi.

Rafi answered "*Ja*."

The man immediately launched into a convoluted conversation, and Rafi had to work very hard to follow what the man was saying. Clearly he hadn't gotten far enough yet.

"What's your name?" the man asked him in German.

"Rolf Zimmer," he replied.

The man switched to English after that. "Your German isn't bad, but you're going to have to improve. This is no joke. The people you're going to be dealing with are not into playing around. One mistake — just one — and goodbye Rolf!

"Anyway," he paused for a moment, "allow me to introduce myself. My name is Helmut Zeigler. In my youth I served in the Waffen SS special troops where I distinguished myself with exemplary fighting skills. I was promoted a number of times due to my daring and bravery on the battlefield, and was a major by the war's end. Just to be very clear, I was never part of the SS that supervised the death camps. I was a soldier from day one, and I have nothing but contempt for the men who committed such outrageous atrocities, and then had the audacity to claim that they were only following orders. I felt guilt on behalf of my nation. I wanted to make amends, even though I didn't have anything to do with the Jews during the war. Just the fact that so many of my fellow Germans sold their souls with such glee was sufficient reason for me to want to embrace some form of repentance."

Zeigler walked over to a side bar. "Drink?" he asked Rafi, filling his own glass with a golden Scotch.

"No thanks," Rafi answered, reluctant to drink with a German — any German — no matter how repentant a man he was.

"Have a seat," the man said, motioning Rafi to a couch over on the other side of the room. Rafi sat. Zeigler seated himself on an antique armchair facing him. The agent who had brought him was flipping through some books in the library down the hall.

"You have to understand," Zeigler began, "that the average German soldier during World War II, could have knocked the stuffing out of five of his counterparts in any of the Allied armies. They were tough men, well trained and well armed. They were fighting because they believed in a cause. Whether the cause was right or wrong is debatable. But they believed. That gave them motivation and courage, and they were provided with skill and knowledge. The truth is, they could have won the war. If Himmler had been in charge instead of Hitler, the seat of world power today might have been in Berlin instead of Washington. But Hitler was a power maniac and insane when it came to the Jews, and he made terrible decisions regarding Russia. He never listened to his generals, and in the end, Germany paid the price. But the average man on the German street was more than equipped to win the war. They were in conquering mentality. This is typical of the Germans. They have an obsession about being on top, and they will do anything to make that happen.

"The scary thing about all this," Zeigler said, "is that millions of the German people yearn for their past days of glory. They would like nothing more than to resume their role of world aggressor. They bemoan that they were duped for the cameras of the world media, yet millions of their youth identify with the ideals and philosophy of Nazism. Hitler was the single largest catalyst of death in the history of Europe, yet scores of European teens revel and glorify themselves with Nazi paraphernalia!" He sighed.

"Go try and explain; there is no explanation. You have to assimilate the culture, the idea that the entire world was created to serve you; that you are a higher man with a better physique. If you don't cultivate the proper attitude, they will spot you a mile away. As of now, you haven't got it.

"Dietrich Eberhart is the biggest bigot of them all. The man firmly believes in Germany's right to world domination. And he has a plan. I still have friends in Germany. They are men who served with me back in my days in the Waffen SS, who are the leaders of German society today. They give me the scoop. Not only don't they feel bad for what they did, they would do it again if only they had a leader who could inspire and lead like old Adolph. The men I know are respected business leaders, industrialists, politicians, — Germans from across the spectrum. So many of them would welcome any opportunity to try again.

"Dietrich Eberhart is slowly but surely turning into that icon, that person to whom people listen. Many urge him to run for the Reichstag, but he remains so far uninterested. That, to me, signifies the fact that he possesses a plan of significance. He obviously feels he can gain control of the people without first acquiring a basis in the political arena. People are talking about this man. He comes from the right kind of family. Dietrich Eberhart is the only son of Ludwig and Trudy Eberhart. His grandfather, Heinrich, was a firm favorite of the party, and a contractor who built much of the infrastructure that allowed Germany to fight on other people's lands.

"Dietrich has more money then he will ever need, yet he continues to amass more and more, which he will no doubt use to firm up his popularity base. His nightclub, 'Club Salute,' is the most expensive club in Hamburg, yet remains the busiest at the same time. It's hard to explain, without taking a good hard look at Dietrich's magnetic personality. Unmarried so far, and Germany's most eligible bachelor, his handsome face beams from the glossy covers of Germany's news, fashion and culture magazines. His opinion is sought on every topic. People want to know his opinion on just about everything. Every theater company sends him complimentary tickets for their shows. He has a box at the opera, and Eberhart Enterprises owns its own jet. The man has everything a person could desire, and he makes no secret where his desires lie. Everyone knows that Ludwig Eberhart was a close confidant of Heinrich Himmler, and Dietrich makes no secret that his own ambitions are to emulate his old man. This is not some fringe group. He represents mainstream Germany! To sum it all up, friend, in order for you to break through, you're going to have to somehow endear yourself with Herr Eberhart. He is the key to the Germany of today. Do you understand what I am saying?"

Rafi nodded.

"Good. But you are not yet ready for this. I will speak with your handlers. They will increase your lessons and training. The language has to come more naturally, more fluently. Do you have some special talent, perhaps, that we can use as a tool?" He threw out this last thought casually.

"I play the violin," Rafi said.

"Do you play well?" the German demanded.

"Well enough that the great Dagenheim himself used me as a soloist in recordings and on the stage."

At the mention of Dagenheim, Zeigler's eyebrows arched upward in surprise. "You must be very good," he said, his tone a mixture of question and respect.

"Not bad, not bad," Rafi conceded.

"Show me," the German ordered him. "Go on, get over to that violin stand, pick it up and show me what you know how to do."

The handler, examining books over in the library, shook his head in amusement. This was sure getting interesting.

Rafi went to the violin stand and picked up the violin in his hands. It was a beautiful instrument, more than a 100 years old. He lifted the violin to his chin and ran a finger lovingly over the expensive wood, the carved surface, the painstaking attention to detail and the love that had gone into creating this one instrument. He raised the bow and began to play. The room became utterly still. The music soared upward to the lofty ceiling of the room and beyond. Rafi played as if his life depended on it. He hadn't thought about what he was going to play, and the music flowed out of him without a conscious decision on his part.

It was the song. The theme song of his life.

It was real music, and the German appreciated it. He threw back his head and closed his eyes, allowing the song to wash over him. Time seemed to hang suspended for a few minutes. Finally Rafi finished the song. Nobody moved. It was as if they were afraid to break the spell.

Zeigler was the first to talk.

"Amazing," Zeigler said. "Absolutely amazing. I haven't enjoyed a piece of music as much since ... I can't even remember when. Excellent, young man, excellent. Well, there's your answer."

"My answer?" Rafi was confused.

"Yes," the German said. "You were wondering how you can infiltrate the movement." The old man paused for a moment and coughed violently. "Well, here's a way in. Dietrich Eberhart loves music. In fact, one of the events that Club Salute is celebrated for is the fact that they host the greatest musicians from around the world. Can you play the Horst Wessel song?"

Rafi smiled.

"I take it that's a yes," the man said. "Let me hear it then."

Rafi played the hated song while Zeigler's eyes lit up at the military beat, and his foot tapped to the rhythm. He actually clapped at the end of the song.

"You are very good, young man," he said at the end. "Mark my words; you are going to be a huge hit at the club. This is your ticket. Use the music, use the songs. He will recognize you, though; he will have heard your name. Change your appearance; wear contact lenses that change the color of your eyes. It can be done. With music you will bridge the gap. Say that you're an American or Canadian with German heritage. Maybe you were studying at Juilliard when you heard the call. You're from a noble German family. Play your music, and you'll be in the door before you know it. That's the thing about great people like Dietrich Eberhart. They are so smart, it's hard for them to realize sometimes that there are other people who are just as smart as they are. I can see it now, your debut. You are going to knock them dead. I just wish I was there to witness it. But I'll be here in Caesarea rooting for you." The man picked up his glass of whiskey holding it up to the light. It sparkled under the faceted crystals of the chandelier. "A toast to your success," he said. "I wish you all the best. Just use the music and you'll be fine."

The handler materialized out of nowhere and it was time to go. They said goodbye, and Rafi realized that he was no longer nervous. He had been given a direction. In fact, this was really a good idea to play to his strengths. Why hadn't they realized it before? He sat in the backseat of the car on the way back to Tel Aviv and contemplated the developments of the past few months. He was amazed at the way everything had changed so quickly. Yet, he would still be a violinist, only playing on a different stage.

The agency hadn't allowed him to visit his uncle, the Rebbe, but they had brought the Rebbe to Rafi, and he understood what was happening. The circle was coming to a close after all this time, and it was only natural that it was a member of their family that did the closing. When Rafi thought about it sometimes after a long day in the gym, or working on his German, or engaged in espionage exercises, it seemed pretty ironic.

Two weeks later, Kobi came to Nordau Street to check on him. He watched as Rafi sparred with an instructor. Rafi held his own in the ring. Kobi looked on impassively as Rafi did 60 push-ups in rapid succession. He listened with silent interest as Rafi carried on an entire conversation in German. He had been pushed to the limit, and emerged victorious. The skills he had received in the army had been honed and sharpened. He had become a warrior. Once again, Kobi had followed his instincts and had been justified. Sometimes, he felt as if there was a sixth sense guiding his moves. The book was in existence, he had no doubt. Now it would be up to Rafi to find it. And once that happened and they uncovered the mystery, they would have to put a stop to their nefarious plan. Dietrich Eberhart played to win, and in the deepest recesses of his heart, Kobi was more than a little afraid for his young friend. But his heart told him, as well, that there was no choice.

After Rafi had finished demonstrating his proficiency in a plethora of essential skills, Kobi pulled him to the side.

"Very impressive," he said. "Come with me."

They walked down the hallway side by side, taking the elevator to the basement of the agency building. There was a 30-ish man with an attitude guarding the door.

"Kobi Shapiro," Kobi snapped at him, flipping an ID card at the guy for about a second.

"Take it easy," the man said. "Who's the kid?"

"He's with me," Kobi said, "and that's all you have to know. Now let us in."

The man looked as if he wanted to argue, but taking in the feistiness of the diminutive man standing in front of him, he relented and allowed them entry.

The room was long and narrow, replete with the most wonderfully ingenious assortment of weapons Rafi had ever imagined, and many that he had not had occasion to think about at all. Apparently, the agency took precautions that its people were protected.

Kobi gave Rafi a private tour, explaining the function of the majority of the weapons. There were some, however, that were new enough that he, himself, didn't know how they worked. That was when they needed to call the guy at the front for assistance. Rafi felt as if he had stumbled into the middle of a science-fiction film. The technology was incredible! Tough guy, once properly humbled, gave them the guided tour, explaining as he went along.

"What's that?" Kobi barked at the man, pointing at a long narrow object that was shaped like a pen.

"That is one of the agency's most up-to-date weapons." He picked it up tenderly. You could tell that he was sincerely proud of his job. "The agent keeps it in his pocket, just as if it was a pen of some sort. It really does write, just in case someone takes a more-than-casual interest in it. However, if the agent finds himself in trouble, if he is still in possession of the pen at that time, all he has to do is point it at his target and press this button," and he showed them a tiny button that was built into the base of the pen, "and then, boom! There's an explosion loud enough and sufficiently powerful to ensure that the agent will have sufficient time to either escape or reverse the situation to his advantage. Along with the explosion comes an incredibly bright light that will temporarily blind anyone that it's pointed at. The agent is ready and closes his eyes, but the enemy won't be ready and will be blinded, disoriented and harmed in the attack."

"What's this weapon called?" Rafi asked the man.

"It's called a Triple Blaster, because it can be used three times before it has to be recharged. But it's a guaranteed winner. We've had agents in sticky situations, where all their weapons had been taken away from them. The Blaster was all they had to rely on. Believe me, it was more than enough! How are your shooting skills?"

"He's spent enough time on the range," Kobi grunted. "Give him something light that won't slow him down. He probably won't even have the opportunity to use a gun most of the time. Anyway, the Triple Blaster packs a tremendous kick, and has the advantage of surprise."

They continued walking down the aisles of the warehouse-type room. It was like a candy store for an undercover agent. Rafi, who despite his training with guns had never really taken to them, did take slight comfort in the fact that he would be going in armed with something somewhat easier to use.

"Wait a second," tough guy suddenly said. "What kind of operation is he going on?"

Kobi gave him the watered-down version.

"I have just the thing for him," tough guy said confidently. He reached up to an uppermost shelf and took down a box of sunglasses.

"This," tough guy said, as he picked up one pair, "appears to be just your run-of-the-mill pair of Gucci sunglasses, and it is. However," he lifted up a finger, "it is also equipped with a function that is anything but normal. Take a good look at this edge." He was pointing to the tip of the glasses: to the part that curled over the ear, holding the glasses in place. "This," he said, "is the best spy weapon we've ever come up with. The end is very sharp, much sharper than it appears to be. When pressed against paper, any other material or flesh, it will slice through it with ease. Positioned beneath the sharpened tip is a cache of potent poison that will inflict the onset of death on the enemy within a five-second time span. All the agent has to do is to simply press the point of the sunglasses into the upper thigh of his opponent and withdraw. The enemy won't know what hit him, and won't have time to react. This is the ultimate killing weapon."

Rafi held the sunglasses in his hands and studied them intently. It was difficult to comprehend that death lay in this simple pair of glasses.

Kobi was enthusiastic regarding Israel's technological prowess, but Rafi felt strange as he held the murder weapon. He had never even given serious thought to the possibility that he might have to kill someone, and it made him uncomfortable. It wasn't that he had an ideological issue with doing so for the security of his nation, but still, the mission had suddenly become much more serious in his mind. He was going into this well-armed: a Triple Blaster, which he fully intended to keep with him at all times, and this pair of sunglasses that would come in handy in a pinch. Tough guy was explaining to Kobi how to unscrew the earpiece and refill the poison if need be. He paid serious attention. After all, boy scouts were always prepared.

30

Rafi Ganim

Ayalon Highway, Israel
January 17, 2008

Tamar Ganim steered her late-model Subaru to the right, taking the turnoff for Haifa. She had made good time for most of the drive, only catching the tail end of the traffic jam on the Ayalon Highway. After that, it had been smooth sailing for the remainder of the trip, and it wasn't long before she was pulling into the parking lot at Haifa University. She parked the car, turned off the engine and made her way to the university's main entrance, where she was greeted by a student representative of the university's Psychology Department.

"Dr. Ganim," the woman said, "Welcome. There is still time before your lecture. Can I take you to the cafeteria for a cup of coffee?"

"I could definitely use a cup of coffee," Tamar said. "It will revitalize me after that long drive." She followed the woman down the flight of stairs to the cafeteria, and accepted the steaming cup of coffee.

"It's such an honor that you agreed to lecture here at the university," the student representative said to her.

"On the contrary, Liron," Tamar said. "It's a great honor for me that the school even asked."

"How can you say that?" the student protested. "Your new book on hypnotherapy is an international best-seller. You're the hottest news in psychology departments around the globe. C'mon, I'm sure you get invitations to lecture all the time!"

"It's my pleasure," Tamar told her sincerely. "Really it is. There is nothing that would make me happier than if my lecture influences other young students to make more breakthroughs in the field. Hypnotherapy is a science which is yet still untapped to a large degree. There is so much going on under the surface that would change our life assumptions, if we only knew where to look for it. My goal is for hypnotherapy to be accepted by licensed medical practitioners as a tool to be used on a more widespread basis. Have you read the book?" she asked the girl.

"Three times," she replied. "The case studies are particularly fascinating. You were able to get inside the subjects' minds to such a degree! How did you convince them to allow you to use them as case studies?"

"Well," Tamar said, "most came to me first requesting my assistance in curing them of a host of assorted ailments. I asked those clients with whom I was particularly successful, if they would allow me to present their case studies in the book. Nearly all of them agreed. The complexities that we discovered along the way made for a more compelling manuscript at the end of the day."

"You stated in the fourth chapter that you found yourself drawn to the part of the brain that makes people take certain actions because other people want them to do those very things. You wrote that you were fascinated by the fact that so many otherwise intelligent people allow others to manipulate them into doing things that they really don't want to do. In several studies you focused on precisely that point. Do you feel that you were successful?"

"I definitely learned a lot," Tamar answered. "In a number of cases, I successfully relieved the need to please other people, and watched as my clients were actually able to get on with their lives without experiencing what had been a compulsion up until then. It alleviated an incredible number of guilt-related activities. The most complex science doesn't measure up to the level of activity that constantly goes on in the brain of every person!"

Liron glanced at her watch. "It's almost time," she said. "I'll take you to the auditorium. You're speaking in our largest lecture hall because so many have been waiting for this lecture with anticipation."

They entered a large auditorium packed with students who applauded as she entered. Every eye was on her as she adjusted the microphone and began her speech.

"On April 19, 1963," she began, "a young doctor of the mind discovered a secret that would form the cornerstone for the way medicine looked at hypnosis for the coming century."

The students leaned forward expectantly, waiting for the mind-blowing lecture that was soon to come. Tamar smiled as she spoke, because after practicing hypnotherapy, talking about practicing hypnotherapy was what she liked doing best of all.

February 2, 2008
Kennedy Airport

Rafi preferred not to fly a German airline, because he had always thought of them as "Nazi airlines." And yet, for the first time in his life, he was flying Lufthansa voluntarily. In his travel bag was a kit with his personal documents, including passport, driver's license, social insurance number and birth certificate, all made out to Ralph Zimmer. He was a Canadian citizen, all his papers were in order and he had never spent a day in Israel in his life. Although he had been named "Ralph" by German parents who were doing their best to help their children blend into the Canadian way of life, he called himself "Rolf," and told everyone he met to call him that as well. He had sent his Triple Blaster through the X-ray machine at Kennedy Airport without triggering any alarms.

It had begun, quite suddenly. After being nervous for months, he found that the nervous feeling was gone. It was akin to finally standing on stage after months of rehearsals. He was able to talk and joke with his seatmate, and after knocking down two of the complimentary drinks in First Class, he was positively jovial. He had spoken to the Kolodover Rebbe at length about his obligations with regard to kosher food, and the Rebbe advised that he should pass himself off as a vegetarian.

His hair and eyebrows had been dyed a dark blond, and his contact lenses had changed the warm brown color of his eyes to a stormy grey. All in all, he bore scant resemblance to the violinist who had been the toast of the Israeli classical music scene. He was now Rolf Zimmer, and he behaved exactly the way Rolf would behave. He stored his violin in the compartment above his head, and proceeded to enjoy the free alcohol. Kobi had explained that the average German really enjoyed his drinks, and that he would have to acclimate himself to their society if he wanted to fit in.

"The social life in that beastly country — as in all of Europe for that matter — revolves around drinking," Kobi had said.

So they taught him how to drink. It hadn't been easy. He detested mostly everything about alcohol: the smell, the taste and, most of all, the way people changed after they'd had one too many. But it was vital for his cover, so he forced himself to acquire the taste. Now he was able to knock back the booze without losing his cool.

"What language would you prefer in your headset, sir?" asked the steward.

"German, please," he replied in perfect German. The man was pleased, and adjusted the controls.

Rafi leaned back in the comfortable leather seat and reviewed his cover story. He was the descendant of an aristocratic Nazi family that had fled the country in the chaotic aftermath of the war, ably assisted by Odessa, the German network that had come into being expressly for that purpose. The family had reestablished themselves originally in South America, eventually moving to Ontario, Canada, away from the glut of German expatriates on the South American landscape. He had heard stories of his grandfather's exploits in the SS, and had been a closet member of a Canadian neo-Nazi group.

That was the way it had been until he had come to Germany five years earlier for a visit to get a feeling for his heritage. While there, he had developed friendships with people who had taken the opportunity to introduce him to a radical side he hadn't known existed. Although he returned to Canada to pursue a career in music, and although his teachers had all predicted great things for him if he opted for a concert career, he discovered that his heart wasn't in it. He loved music, but it would always take a backseat to the fiery discipline and rhetoric of the pre-war Nazi Party. In the end, he found that he could no longer continue living a lie. He wouldn't play the music of Bach and Mozart by day and attend Nazi rallies by night. Halfway measures were for other people, not for him. So, he relinquished his place in the prestigious music academy he had been attending, sold most of his possessions, said his goodbyes and boarded the next Lufthansa flight to Germany, intent on devoting the best years of his life to music, as well, but mainly to the cause which he felt most passionate about.

He was going to become a leader of the revival of Naziism. He had the leadership skills, the charisma and the ability to inspire a crowd. But his greatest asset was the fact that he truly believed in the cause. He had heard of Dietrich Eberhart. Who hadn't? He knew all the right names. His "family" still lived in Canada. There was no reason to question his background: Odessa network, South America, related to the Zimmer family in Bavaria. They didn't know that their cousin was on the way to meet them. There was no reason for them to doubt his sincerity. The Canadian Nazi movement, although small, was quite vocal and respected, but it wasn't enough. He didn't want to be a big fish in a little sea. He wanted the Atlantic.

A few "friends" were already in Germany and they would be more than happy to show him around. Most of them were assigned to the anti-terrorism desk of the Israeli Embassy. But even so, they all had connections that they would set in motion for his benefit.

Somehow, he would manage to meet Herr Eberhart.

The Kolodover Rebbe had given him a *berachah*, and that gave him a greater sense of security than all the vague promises that Kobi had made about backup and people watching out for him. He was on his own and as long as the One Above was watching out for him, everything would be O.K.

His eyes grew weary despite his churning thoughts. Eventually he drifted off, sprawled on the leather seat. The liquor put him into a deep sleep, and he slept for nearly four hours. They were over the ocean when he began to dream the same recurring dream. The previous Kolodover Rebbe was crying out to him with heartrending sobs, beseeching him for help ... to bring "him" back ... The tears were rolling down his cheeks and into his beard. Then *the song* began playing in stereo, and the sound of the violins overwhelmed the other instruments. In his dream, he was playing his violin along with the music. There were people singing, and he found himself in the Kolodover *beis midrash* in Tel Aviv. The entire congregation, a few hundred strong, was singing so movingly and they were all weeping. Naftali Kenighofer admonished him to stay strong. Suddenly the plane began bouncing and jolting from side to side, and the voice of the captain could be heard over the sound system requesting that everyone to take their seats due to turbulence. He awoke, moved his backrest into an upright position, and fastened his seat belt. A few hours later, the sun broke through the clouds, and he caught his first glimpse of Germany. The prodigal son had come home.

~

Hamburg, Germany
February 3, 2008

With his Canadian passport he encountered no trouble. Canada, it seemed, was on everybody's good list. If the Germans only knew how much he loathed their harsh accents, they would have ousted him on the spot. But he spoke to them in German, and smiled as he was processed. He headed to the conveyor belt to pick up his luggage. His violin case was strapped to his back and he took care not to jostle it. He wore a baseball cap that had Hyundai Getz, car of the future, scrawled across it. He didn't look Jewish at all. If you had to venture a guess as to his nationality, you would probably say French or Scandinavian. He went through customs and was not stopped, not for the pen in his pocket, which he removed before going through the electronic scanner, nor the pair of sunglasses that were clipped onto his shirt pocket. In the end he had chosen not to bring the gun.

He collected his luggage and wheeled it out of the terminal to a nearby Avis counter, where he rented a Volkswagen. A modest car, intended to blend in with all the others. He loaded his gear into the car and drove toward the apartment that had been rented for him. He programmed the GPS with the apartment's address, and followed the directions of the clipped Germanic voice. He left the Hamburg airport and confidently drove toward the center of the city.

He found his lodgings without difficulty. They were located in a spacious building that had been constructed in the early 1900's. There was an old-world charm that he delighted in. At least the agency didn't pinch pennies. He pictured Kobi yelling at some clerk who was trying to cut corners, and he smiled. There was no elevator, and he had to drag the suitcases up the sweeping flights of stairs to the apartment on the third floor. He was panting by the time everything was inside the door. He surveyed his new home. The rooms were large and well proportioned, but the furnishings were sparse. Everything was clean and ready to use.

There was hot water, and he took a long relaxing shower, allowing his weariness to wash down the drain along with the soapy water. He found himself singing his tune. The steamy room filled with the sound of his voice which competed with the rushing water. It was still hard for him to comprehend that he was finally there. After all this time, he had reached the place where it had all began. It was all coming around full circle: Eberhart on one side, the Rebbe of Kolodov on the other. Kobi had no idea that his family had a connection to the Eberharts from way back. He probably thought that he had delivered such an amazing pitch that Rafi had been blown away. The speech had been good, the theory made sense, all true. But the clincher was the fact that it was Eberhart who was involved. He was the man behind the family's split. Because of Eberhart, his father had gone off the *derech* of Torah. Because of Eberhart, he hadn't even known his own family. And that was why he felt compelled to get to the bottom of the whole story, and to find that book. The circle would be complete. *Let's finish what was begun so long ago.*

He prepared himself for sleep and said *Shema* with concentration. Then he turned off the lights, locked the door and burrowed under the delightfully cozy quilt. He was out like a light.

For the next few days, Rafi and the city of Hamburg became well acquainted. He mastered the transportation system with ease, and was pleasantly surprised by how efficient everything was. He drew no unnecessary attention from passersby and tried to soak in the culture — the pervading mind-set of society. Everyone was extremely polite, and he wanted to slap them. He drove around the city and even rented a boat to get to know the waterways, and he waited to be summoned. The signal came three days later. That afternoon, the phone rang twice. The caller hung up. Then the phone rang another two times. Rafi checked his mailbox late that night, and found the manila envelope inside.

He carried it up the broad staircase and opened it at the kitchen table. Holding it upside down, he watched as a bunch of glossy photos slid from the envelope. They were pictures of a building dominated by a Jewish star on the roof. The accompanying paper stated that the building was quite close by. He studied the photos and took note of the wanton desecration. Graffiti had been scrawled across the building's outer wall. Hate messages were painted on the surrounding wall and on the building itself. The team had done a thorough job. It looked genuine enough. His stomach turned when he realized that his team was responsible for the desecration this time. He was very uncomfortable with this part of the job, but he had been in on the planning stages and realized that there was no other way to infiltrate Eberhart's inner circle. He understood it was all part of the bigger picture. It had to be done.

He turned on the radio and waited for the news. The broadcaster gave the political news first, followed by the international business-related news. Then his voice became properly somber as he mentioned what appeared to be a neo-Nazi attack on one of the oldest remaining Jewish institutions in Germany. Windows had been broken, the building had been vandalized and swastikas had been spray-painted everywhere. The desecration was formidable, and the police had already begun their investigation.

The government had dispatched a team of workers to repair the building and the Jewish community was told to remain on high alert. He closed the radio, put on a windbreaker and left the house. The drive to the site didn't take more than half an hour. The wind was whistling mournfully through the trees as he stepped out of the car and walked up to the gate. He could see a crew of workers busily removing the graffiti and repairing the windows. His heart cried at the desecration. He stood there for a while longer tormented by his part in the destruction, and then as the wind picked up, he headed back to the warmth of his car.

From the distance, a man with a powerful Nikon snapped 10 photos of the man in the windbreaker. In the final frame, Rafi's face was clearly visible as he got back into his car. The man shrugged and sent the pictures off to be developed.

Over the following half a year, there was an outbreak of shocking attacks on the institutions of Jewish Europe. The Jewish Day School in Cologne was defaced, the Jewish Old Age Home of Antwerp was broken into and there were attacks on the Jewish Community Center in Paris and in Vienna. Here and there, a pedestrian was targeted, as well. No life-threatening injuries resulted, but several men were roughed up and mugged. The infamous Nazi swastika was prominently visible at the site of each and every one of the incidents. The police took the spate of racial attacks very seriously and investigated thoroughly including calling in markers and favors from the underground community throughout Europe. But nobody had seen anything or was able to help in any way.

Dietrich Eberhart was called to the police station for questioning, due to his neo-Nazi affiliation. But he convinced the police that he was just as much in the dark as they were — not that he didn't admire the people who had taken care of the arrangements. He didn't the share the fact that he possessed a picture of a certain stranger with the police; first, because he never shared anything with the police and second, because he had no idea if that picture was relevant to the case. The man might have been a complete stranger who just happened to drive by after he had heard the news and decided to look around. It was definitely possible. On the other hand, in Dietrich's experience, if a man happened to stop by a scene right after an attack had been carried out, then that person often had a link to the scene.

And yet, he hadn't been spotted at any of the other attacks, which meant that either he had gotten better at doing surveillance without being noticed, or that actually he had been there by coincidence. Regardless, it wasn't necessary to tell the police anything. So Dietrich only smiled frostily at them and repeated that he knew nothing. Seeing that this was just a waste of time, the interrogating officer told him he was free to go. Dietrich sarcastically promised to call them if anything relevant came up.

In the end, no one was convicted for the series of anti-Semitic attacks that raged across the capitals of Europe. No one was convicted, because nobody was caught, and no one was caught because there were no clues. It was as if everything was being done by an invisible man. It had taken a while, but the groundwork had been laid. It was now time for Stage Two to commence.

September 12, 2008
Hamburg, Germany

The night was cloaked by a dark and unfriendly fog that had swept in off the docks, and had lingered. Rafi was dressed warmly in brown corduroy pants, turtleneck sweater and boots. He wore a leather trench coat that nearly swept the floor. His hand was over the violin case as he drove toward the club. The weather was sufficiently evil that he wouldn't have been surprised if the club was only half full that night. He didn't need a huge crowd to make his point. All he wanted was to attract the attention of one particular person. He had put in quite a practice session that afternoon. He was a little rusty and wanted to be completely confident that evening. The agency claimed that Dietrich Eberhart was at home that evening. Well, this would be a test of their efficiency.

He had visited Club Salute a number of times over the past few months, wanting the doorman to get used to seeing his face. The entertainment that was regularly featured at the club really was top of the line; well worth the top dollar the club was charging. Tonight was "Open Mike" night, however, and the club was in for a surprise. Club Salute had an open stage night every once in a while. When they did, it was almost impossible to get a spot since every amateur band wanted a turn on their prestigious stage. But Rafi had made a point of befriending the bartender, whose job it was to pick the contestants. He had been one of the lucky ones. Once he got up there, he would blow them all away. A winner would be chosen from the group of performers. Dietrich Eberhart was usually on hand to present the check and trophy that the club gave the winner.

He found a parking lot a short walk from the club, and left his Volkswagen there. He then walked off into the fog, swinging his violin case in a manner that left no doubt as to who was going to take home the trophy that night. He cut through the parking lot and then took a shortcut through a local park, emerging across the avenue from the club's lit-up facade. Cars were constantly coming and going, and the crowd was waiting to get inside even now. Rafi was recognized, and the bouncer let him pass. Once inside, he took in the festive scene with wonder.

The club had been decorated with the rustic, rural look of a Bavarian pub. There was a huge sign hanging from the rafters welcoming one and all to the Club Salute Semi-annual "Open Mike" night. What made the evening's competition even more challenging was that the club never revealed the style of music to be performed until the very night of the competition. Rafi hadn't been concerned. He could handle a broad spectrum of musical styles. It was to be an evening dedicated to traditional German music. Rafi had just the piece for the man he was trying to impress. He said hello to his friend, the bartender, and took a seat on the side to await his turn. The musicians sat apart from the crowd, and he fingered his bow lightly, gearing up for the performance.

From his seat, he could see the legendary window that overlooked the dance floor. It was known as Eberhart's perch. From time to time, the patrons were able to catch a glimpse of the great man himself when he parted the curtains to survey his empire below. Now the curtains were closed, and Rafi imagined Eberhart eating dinner in the privacy of his office, surrounded by a bodyguard or two. Rafi was counting on Eberhart's security force to be as good as they were known to be.

The musicians around him were drinking beer, calming nerves and tuning instruments to pass the time and stay calm. Here and there a tussle broke out. But for the most part everyone was on their best behavior. It was a known rule that the winner of amateur night usually went on to become a household name throughout Germany. The event was not covered by any of the networks, due to Eberhart's strict insistence on barring them from his club. But that didn't make a difference. There were plenty of representatives from numerous recording companies waiting to see who would emerge the winner tonight.

Rafi was about to place his violin gently back in its case, when he caught a sudden movement out of the corner of his eye. Turning quickly, he looked up and saw Dietrich Eberhart surveying the packed house below. The man was dressed in the traditional Bavarian hunting costume. A smile hovered on his lips. Rafi studied the man. He was a classic Alpha Male, leader of the pack. But Rafi knew that he was more than capable of giving this man a run for his money. They would know tonight.

There was the sound of clapping as a portly man dressed as a Bavarian innkeeper climbed the steps to the stage. He had the round stomach of the jolly tavern keeper of yore, and the crowd greeted him with shouts and laughter.

"Ladies and gentlemen," he began, "welcome to the Bavarian village tavern. You have arrived just in time for the Semi-annual Music Festival. We have a great lineup planned for this evening, including a surprise appearance by one of Germany's up-and-coming hard rock groups, and we hope that you will enjoy yourselves in a big way. And now," he paused as a drumroll began to reverberate throughout the room, "please put your hands together and welcome 'Fishsticks,' one of the hottest bands on the German music scene today!"

The crowd erupted in a cacophony of applause. Whistles and wild clapping filled the room as the band took their places on the stage, dressed all in black. The leader of the band gave a signal, and the percussionist began smashing his drumstick on the cymbals, while the drummer started a heavy beat, and the guitarist joined in. Some of the crowd recognized the song. It was one of "Fishstick's" hits — a song called "Fresh Bread." As the singer took off, the entire crowd clapped along with him. The atmosphere was electric.

"Fresh bread!" the singer roared.

"Gotta get some fresh bread!" the crowd responded lustily.

They were rocking! It was an audience-participation show and everyone was into it. When the amateur talents had their turn it would be difficult to choose a winner, but Rafi wasn't worried. His act was so different from everyone else's that he was definitely going to stand out. Besides, he didn't need to win the contest tonight; he just needed to be recognized. If he won, that was an additional bonus, but it wasn't necessary. He watched as "Fishsticks" finished their song, received a rousing round of applause and left the stage satisfied with their performance and the crowd's response. He watched as the next three groups took their places on the stage and went all out for the audience. The drinks were flowing like water, but Rafi touched nothing. He needed to be completely in control tonight. When the sixth performer finished, the Bavarian tavern keeper announced a 15-minute intermission.

Rafi glanced upward during the show, and was rewarded by a glimpse of Eberhart from time to time. The man obviously took his music seriously, and Rafi understood. Music was an extremely powerful tool whether used in the right or wrong way. Certain songs have the absolute power to unite an entire people. That was one of many elements that gave the Third Reich such potency. He mused that Eberhart was probably searching for the perfect sound for his regime. It wasn't going to be easy developing the perfect combination of nationalistic and military sound. Fifteen minutes later, the master of ceremonies was back.

"And now," he said as he raised his arms in the air, "it gives me great pleasure to present a different kind of performance, one that has never graced our stage before. Here is something new. Ladies and gentlemen, please put your hands together and welcome violinist extraordinaire, Rolf Zimmer!"

There was an outburst of applause. Rafi walked onto the stage. He moved onto the stage directly under the warm glow of the spotlight. A high-backed stool had been placed there for him. Slowly, drawing everyone after him, he sat down. Reverently he studied the violin as if he had never seen it before. The crowd was watching him with bated breath, being drawn into the depth of his performance: the drama, the obvious emotion. Rafi lifted the microphone from the stand and spoke into it in a subdued voice. The crowd was completely hushed, waiting to hear what he was going to say.

"Some music is loud," he began, "other music is soft. But there is something called heart music: music that emanates from of the heart of one person and enters the heart of someone else. That's the music that I play." The crowd was mesmerized. "You all know this song," he said. "Get ready to rock with the song that won the hearts of your grandparents."

He rose from the stool. The light shone down on him, bathing him in a halo of gold. He lifted the violin to his chin, raised the bow and began to play. The sound was soft at first; tracing the air, as if requesting permission to hang around. The music grew steadily stronger and more demanding, strident, arrogant, besotted with itself, a hint of grandeur, a residue of longing for the past. There was a stir throughout the audience as the majority recognized the song. It was the Horst Wessel song. The people in the club had grown up with knowledge of that song, because that was the song more than any other that represented the power that had once belonged to the ancestors of the people sitting in this room. Although there was but one voice of music, there began a tapping across the floorboards as the audience joined in, keeping time with their feet. Their grandfathers had sung this very song as they marched off to war. The crowd felt the majesty of the music seeping into their bones, giving them a purpose, a goal, to make sure that the power never dies.

Rafi played that violin like a maestro. The bow flew over the strings; the music grew in mastery, maturity and emotion. The people couldn't remain in their seats. This was their song he was playing! How could they sit? He picked up the tempo playing it more rapidly, with more strength, more decisiveness, moving about the stage as if so immersed in the music that he didn't even know what he himself was doing! He danced about, bow vibrating up and down those strings, doing complicated harmonies that he was composing on the spot.

The crowd was roaring now. Suddenly he could see that the window near the ceiling was open wide, and Dietrich Eberhart was standing there, fully visible, singing along with the music. The crowd screamed the words, as well. For a moment, all he heard was the roar of wild voices shouting. But gradually, order swept the room, and once again, the plaintive cry of the violin was heard above the cries and adulation.

He laughed and brought the song to the highest note with everyone singing along. The audience erupted into a torrential burst of applause for his performance. The spotlight left the man standing on the stage, and moved higher and higher, finally coming to rest on Eberhart himself smiling deeply at the window. The light rested on his face, and he laughed and stuck both thumbs up out the window, as if he were congratulating Rafi right that moment. It was an exhilarating moment at Club Salute.

He had played the Horst Wessel song on his violin, and he felt sick to his stomach. He walked off the stage and swayed so that he had to catch hold of the railing to keep himself from falling on his face. The music had gone to his head. He was almost drunk with feeling. He sat down on the first unoccupied seat and couldn't move. His shirt was drenched with sweat. His face felt flushed and shiny from being under the lights. He felt weak and jittery and strong and powerful all at the same time. He had done it. The club was his. Dimly, as if from far away, he could hear the master of ceremonies introducing the next act and the music starting up. But he wasn't paying attention because he had done all that he could, and now he had to see if something would result from it.

Finally the last band of the evening played their final note, and the audience dutifully clapped for them. But their heart wasn't in it anymore. Everyone was waiting for the winner.

Suddenly there he was, the man himself! He entered the room from back stage, hair cut short, military style, shirt crisp. He held an envelope and the first-prize award in his hand. Dietrich Eberhart approached the microphone and coughed once. The room became instantly quiet. Anticipation filled the hall. Who would be the winner? There had been so many amazing bands tonight, so much quality music. But only one man had played by himself, and only one man had played the violin, and only one man had played the song of their fathers. Deep inside, they all knew who the winner was.

As Dietrich Eberhart began his winner's introduction, the crowd began tapping their feet on the floor, the way they had tapped as they accompanied Rafi in his rendition. Eberhart lifted the check up in his hands and said, "I see that I don't even have to announce the winner. You've all beaten me to it. Come on up to the stage, Rolf Zimmer!"

The crowd went berserk! As he handed Rafi the envelope and the award, he whispered in his ear, "Come up to my office when this is over. I want to have a little talk with you." Rafi knew that he was in.

The club had emptied. The people were gone, the sober supporting the drunk. So many of the patrons had come over to speak to him, to tell him how much his music had meant to them. They asked him why they had never heard of him before. He thanked them sincerely, explaining that he wasn't actually from Germany, but rather Canada, and that he hoped that they would be hearing a lot more from him in the upcoming months. He was their star. If he had possessed any doubts at all about the way these people thought, their reactions to the music silenced them forever. This was the land of the Nazis all over again. What did they think? That they would be allowed to try the same experiment again? That the world would allow them to begin training the same kind of army they had put together back in the 1930's, There was no way!

The room was almost empty. He sat in his seat and waited. He knew that someone would be coming for him. He was right. The man appeared suddenly: very muscular, closely shaved face, with a tiny scar directly above his right eyebrow. He motioned Rafi to follow him. They walked through an unobstrusive door at the side of the room, and left the Bavarian scene far behind. The atmosphere behind the wall was businesslike. There were a number of offices off to the side, lights off, screen savers on. On one of the screens a swastika floated endlessly. The hallway was unfurnished and plain. A metal staircase led upward, past another hallway that branched toward the left, eventually arriving at a heavy steel door. The man patted him down before reaching up to knock. Two knocks, and the door was opened for them. Rafi found himself in Eberhart's office: the man who held the future of Germany in his hand, the man some called a modern-day Bismarck.

He glanced around the office with interest: two suede couches in a corner, a coffee table strewn with magazines. He could see Eberhart's window directly across from where he stood. There was a sleek black desk positioned in the center of the room. Eberhart was seated behind it, studying him without making a motion, the way a snake might look at his prey before going on the attack. The bodyguard bade him to sit. He told himself to look Eberhart in the eye and tried to hold on, but in the end he couldn't. The man's stare was just too disconcerting for him to compete with. His eyes were a bright green, very intense. He radiated control.

"Rolf Zimmer," he said to Rafi, "so nice to meet you."

"Herr Eberhart," Rafi managed.

"Call me Dietrich," Eberhart said. "All my friends do."

"Thank you for the honor," Rafi said mechanically, going through the motions while trying to figure out his next move.

"You were incredible," Eberhart said to him. "Really amazing. I've seen talent before. They've all played on my stage. But your rendition of the Horst Wessel song had me going in a way that almost brought me to tears. You have a talent far beyond the norm. And I'll tell you something else," he went on, "there is no way that a man can play a song like that with the kind of emotion that you put on, without really meaning it. Have you ever played professionally?"

The question was fair, but Rafi wondered if Eberhart had ever heard a CD of one of his concerts and recognized his style of music.

"The truth is," he replied, "that I have been studying the violin for many years, and have just recently decided to begin performing on stage. I'm from Canada, but I've wanted to come live in Germany for quite some time now."

"Why is that?" Eberhart asked him.

"I visited the country about five years ago," Rafi said, "and ever since then, I've wanted to return and get in touch with my roots in a way that I was never able to in Canada."

"And what roots are those?" Eberhart inquired.

Rafi looked him squarely in the eye. "My German roots," he said. The words hung in the air.

"What do you mean?" Eberhart asked him.

"The Zimmer family," Rafi said, "my relatives. My grandfather, General Alois Zimmer."

"Alois Zimmer was your grandfather?" Eberhart asked surprised.

"Yes," he answered simply. "I never knew anything about Germany's glory growing up. My parents always told us we were Canadians. Yes, we were originally from Germany, but we lived in Ontario and were proud members of Canada. I played ice hockey, sang 'Oh Canada' and dreamed of joining the Royal Canadian Mounties after graduating college. I wanted to live in Quebec, play my violin for town holidays and teach my children to be patriotic. I loved Canada and never imagined wanting something different for myself."

"What happened to change all of that?" Eberhart inquired.

"I was cleaning out the attic one rainy afternoon when I came across a box that had been stuffed into the furthest corner. Overcome by curiosity, I cut the cord that bound it and pulled opened the flaps. I was utterly overcome by the treasure trove I discovered inside."

Despite himself, Eberhart was intrigued. "What did you find?" he asked.

Rafi lowered his voice a couple of notches, forcing his host to lean forward to hear better. "I found a box full of history right in front of my face. And I had never even known!"

"What do you mean?" Eberhart demanded.

"I mean," said Rafi, "things like this."

From his sock, he pulled out an old dagger — an SS dagger to be precise. "It was my grandfather's," he said, and tossed it on the desk for Eberhart to examine. Eberhart jumped slightly as the dagger landed on his desk. He turned murderous eyes on his bodyguard, and spoke in a quiet voice that made Rafi's blood chill.

"Didn't you frisk this man before allowing him into my office?"

"I swear I did, sir," the man said. It was clear that he was more frightened than he had ever been in his entire life.

"I will speak to you later," Eberhart told the man. "Now go!" The man left the room like a wounded puppy.

Eberhart turned his attention to the dagger. "General Zimmer's dagger, you say? Maybe so, maybe not.

"Munich," he snapped, "bring me the list of officers and their serial numbers."

The bodyguard named Munich jumped to attention, and went over to one of the many file cabinets lining the wall. There were numerous files on the shelves, and he lifted a thick one off the shelf, and laid it down carefully on Eberhart's desk. Eberhart flipped through the pages gently. From what Rafi could tell, it was a file with the names and serial numbers of the upper-ranking officers in the SS. Eberhart studied the dagger for a moment and wrote down the number that was inscribed on its side. Then he continued flipping through the pages until he found the names that began with the letter Z. Rafi kept still the entire time, inwardly praying that the boys over at the agency had done their job well and gotten the number right.

"Here we are," Eberhart said. "Zimmer, General Alois Zimmer. Serial number 35787." He looked at the number he had written and compared the two. "Intriguing," he said. "It's a match. This dagger really did belong to old Zimmer. My father told me about him. A tough warhorse, he was. He fought together with my father in Crete and Finland, among other places. They saved each other's lives a few times."

"I had no idea," Rafi said.

"And your parents never shared their heritage with you? They kept you in the dark?"

"It was safer that way, I guess," Rafi said. "But I have a feeling that my father wanted me to know about the past. That's why he sent me up to the attic to sort through those boxes. I think he felt that it was time for me to discover where my loyalties really belonged. It was a funny thing. Here he was, the son of one of the most respected officers ever to have fought in the SS, and he spends his life coaching Canadian high-school hockey games. Imagine how he felt? He probably walked around feeling guilty for rejecting his heritage. The general was long gone. He died while the family was still in South America, and never went to Canada with the rest of his family. Then his only son disregards almost everything he saw in his father's home. He didn't say a word to me about what my grandfather did during the war years, nothing. He was a secretive man.

"But then all of a sudden, here was this dagger with German words inscribed along the edge. There was a whole slew of medals and other bits of memorabilia. It was like walking into a World War II museum. It just blew me away. And the pictures were incredible! There was my grandfather with Jodl and Rommel, and there he was in *Der Shturmer's* office with Julius Streicher. He was a friend of Goebbels and Goring, a confidant of Himmler, an iron man who everyone respected."

"Do you have any of those pictures here with you?" Eberhart asked.

"Actually, there is one photograph that I carry around in my wallet," Rafi replied. He opened his wallet and removed a frayed photo from among a group of pictures. "Here, take a look."

There were several officers sitting around a table in a bar, celebrating something, maybe a victory, maybe something else. General Zimmer was sitting in the center holding a cigar in his hand and laughing at something that someone had said. Around him were arrayed the best and most brilliant crop of younger officers that Eberhart had ever seen in a photo together. He took a sharp look and then another. There in the back was a familiar face.

"That's my father," he shouted out. And it was. Ludwig Eberhart was looking at them from the corner of the photo, gelled hair slicked back, handsome and arrogant, the quintessential German soldier. There were tears in Eberhart's eyes. He studied the photo closely. "You resemble your grandfather," Eberhart said after a while.

"I know," Rafi answered. "That's what my father always said. He just didn't realize that I resembled him in my passion for the cause as well."

Eberhart was granite once again, and Rafi was impressed by his self-control. There was a mocking lilt to his voice as he looked Rafi straight in the eyes and said, "You mean to tell me that just because you found some old medals and other junk from 50 years ago, you decided to change your entire way of life?"

"Not that quickly, no." Rafi said. "But I did begin my quest right then. I wanted to know who my grandfather was. He looked like the closest thing to a hero that I would ever know. I wanted to meet the people that knew him, that loved him. That was when I decided to take a trip to Germany and meet the few men still living who had served under his command during the war. And I met them. They talked to me about the way it was, the magic of those times. I realized during that visit, as I traveled the country and saw the land of my fathers, that this was where I wanted to be, not back in Canada living a boring life. No! I wanted to return here and devote my life to the cause."

"You've been doing just that, haven't you?" Eberhart said, sliding a glossy picture across the surface of desk toward Rafi. "That's you, isn't it?"

Rafi took a good look at himself — at the young man standing outside the gates of the desecrated building — the wind whipping his hair up and around. There was a pensive look on his face as he surveyed the violation he had wrought.

"You were behind this, weren't you?" Danger in the quiet speech.

"Yes, I was, actually. So what?" A contemptuous sneer appeared on Rafi's face. "It's not as if you were doing anything! All your talk about the renewal and the rebirth and the power, blah, blah, blah. All it is, is just that. Talk. You haven't done a single thing for the cause in years! Tell me I'm wrong! Tell me! You saw the damage I inflicted on the Jews of Europe over the last half a year. You know the fear that pervades the Jewish communities since I've let my beasts out of their cages. Look at what I've managed to do without the police finding me, without anyone discovering who the ringleader is. Look at what you, the great Dietrich Eberhart, were able to do. All you were able to do was to find out who was behind it all!" He paused, then spoke softly. "But you didn't do anything yourself." There was anger in his voice and youthful passion.

"I'm glad that you are so smart," Eberhart said sarcastically, "but I have to tell you, I would have expected a lot more from the grandson of a man such as Alois Zimmer. The surest way to lose a battle is to rush headlong into it without making sure that you have a retreat or a backup plan. Losing battles was never something that my father or Alois Zimmer did. They planned, examined all the possibilities and, most importantly, didn't act rashly, because rashness leads to mistakes." Eberhart spoke slowly, patiently, as if lecturing a child. "Before you jump to conclusions and think that I'm a coward and keeping a low profile because I'm afraid to actually do something, I have to tell you that that is just not the case."

Rafi waited patiently.

"You know how the politicians always say that they know something that the average man on the street doesn't know? That the picture from where they are standing is radically different from the picture that the average person sees? Well that's the case with me. There's an element that you don't know, that changes the entire picture and makes it prudent for us to wait just a little bit longer before we take the gloves off and really shake the world."

"That's all great and everything, Dietrich," Rafi said. "But now I'm worried that you're just a regular politician. You have access to all the information that I, as a normal guy, don't have. You have access to all the facts. You have it all figured out. You're being prudent. It's all great. But I'm disappointed. Somehow I have this feeling that it's never going to be the right time; that the time for attack will never arrive, because there will always be another element that the little guy doesn't see that changes the picture and makes waiting the right course to take. But *I* have something to tell *you*.

"Hitler did not wait for the right time. Himmler didn't wait for the right time. Rosenberg, Bormann and von Rundstedt didn't wait. They took action and changed the world. If you wait for the right time, the results will be that you will accomplish nothing at all, while the perfect time passes you by. You will end up in the pages of obscurity, barely remembered as the man who could have been a threat, who would have made it happen if he had the guts to actually jump into the unknown." Rafi was speaking passionately, trying to get into the man's mind.

His plan had succeeded beyond his wildest dreams. Eberhart actually believed that he was the grandson of his father Ludwig's commanding officer. The picture with Alois Zimmer surrounded by all the boys had been the perfect touch. *Thank you, Kobi.* The photo that he had enabled Dietrich's men to take of him at the vandalized building had been another sweet touch. Manipulate the other side. Make them think that they're ahead of you. They always think that they're smarter than you. It's hard for them to remember that sometimes there are other people who are just as smart. And now Eberhart felt guilty. He felt as if he needed to explain to this younger man why he wasn't pulling out all the stops.

Rafi knew that there was a plan. It was obvious that Dietrich Eberhart was not a coward, that he was waiting for something specific to happen. But by pushing him, Rafi hoped to learn what that plan was, to see if it had something to do with the book that Kobi was talking about. Right now, there was nothing left to say. He had said it all. He had shown that he was an activist by carrying out operations over the past half-year. He could be trusted. He didn't brag. Nobody had known it was him, and they still had nothing on him aside from one picture. Even that only served to prove that he had an interest in vandalized Jewish institutions. He came from the right background. If they attempted to check out his "parents," they would find an older couple living quietly in Ontario, pursuing the Canadian dream. Yes, they were the children of General Zimmer; yes, they had a son who had gone completely off his rocker and wanted to return Germany to the way it had been before. No one would ever guess that this couple was working for the Mossad just as he was.

Eberhart was sitting with his head in his hands. He looked totally exhausted. There was silence in the room. The bodyguard looked apprehensively at his boss, and Rafi studied the floor. Finally Eberhart raised his head and looked across the desk at the brash violin player who had invaded his life. He seemed to be weighing something.

"I like you," he said to Rafi. "You remind me of the way I was a few years ago before I assumed the mantle of leadership. Then I thought that the main thing was to do the job, action, action, all the time. Just like you. But the truth is," and here he gave Rafi a hard look, "that all the action doesn't really accomplish everything meaningful in the long term. Sure you'll scare the Jews, and that's terrific. But if your goal is to create something concrete with your actions, then what have you accomplished? So I learned to change my mind-set, and so will you.

"The thing is, I understand you; I hear where you're coming from, and I empathize with your frustration. You want to see the end already. While I can't in good conscience give you too much information, I can give you more than you have. I can show you that there's a future. Come, let's get out of here. I'll take you to my house and show you around. If I'm not mistaken, Alois Zimmer attended quite a few dinner parties in my father's day. It will be like closing a circle.

"Karl, Munich, let's get moving!"

Already the bodyguards were up and gathering anything they needed before leaving. Munich went downstairs to bring the car around, and Karl brought Eberhart his coat. Rafi felt like a kid who was caught with his hand in the cookie jar. He could smell the cookies, he could see the cookies and he could almost taste them. He just wondered if all these cookies were a dangerous figment of his imagination. Quietly, he followed the men out of the office and into the elevator.

"I hope you don't mind that I won't be giving you back your knife while we're together," Eberhart said calmly. "I'm sorry, but it's against my better judgment to allow people around me to carry weapons. Call me paranoid, but there it is. Do you have a problem with that?"

Rafi, mentally fingering the Triple Blaster in his shirt pocket, said, "No, not at all. It's a sensible precaution."

"Dare I ask, are you carrying any other weapons on you now?" Eberhart questioned.

Rafi couldn't hesitate in the slightest, because any hesitation would have given him away. So he answered no, easily and with confidence.

"Good to have you aboard, then," Eberhart said. "Get inside." Indeed a BMW had appeared almost magically before them. As they seated themselves in the vehicle, Munich touched the gas pedal and the car shot forward.

"Drink?" Karl asked him. The next thing he knew, a shelf had opened in front of him, displaying an elaborate array of the finest whiskeys and soft drinks. He took a bottle of ginger ale and some ice, and found that he was having a hard time swallowing. All the time he had spent preparing for this moment seemed like an illusion, felt as if he was being thrown into the deep end of a swimming pool without knowing how to swim.

"Step on it, Munich," Dietrich Eberhart said.

The BMW surged forth onto the Autobahn, where the speedometer hit 140 km in three seconds. Rafi decided not to look out the window anymore. What for? If he had wanted to fly in a rocket, he would have joined NASA.

31

Rafi Ganim

Eberhart mansion
September 12, 2008

There was a traffic snarl half an hour into the journey due to a massive pileup, but they made good time once they had passed that point. Rafi dozed off in the comfortable seat. When he awoke, they had turned off the main highway and were traveling on a wooded country road. He felt the "pen" in his pocket, and was reassured by its solid presence. He regretted that he wasn't carrying the sunglasses, but it would have seemed odd for one to be carrying shades after nightfall.

Still, it would have been nice to know that he had another weapon in his arsenal. But he really hadn't thought that the meeting would go as well as it had. Who would have imagined that Dietrich Eberhart was going to invite him to his mansion? Yet here he was, going into the lion's den, so to speak, equipped with only a pen! He didn't even know if the thing worked! He trusted the agency, but it was all well and good when you were sitting in a nice warm office back home, and the techie nerd handed you this thing that looked and felt like a pen and said, "Here, buddy, this pen is the nuclear missile of the future!" But now that he might very well have to use it, it seemed more like an elaborate joke than anything else. The fact was he was scared. He had been in tough situations in his army days, but at least then there had been other soldiers with him. There was safety in numbers. But now he was just one man alone, equipped with — a pen, O.K., the most amazing pen ever to be invented. Somehow, it just didn't feel as if it was enough! But it was too late for regrets. They had arrived.

He watched in silent dread as the car left the country road and headed under a canopy of overhanging oak trees that shielded the road from the glow of the moon and stars. Eberhart's face was shadowy in the dim light of the car's interior. For a second, Rafi thought very seriously about throwing open the car door and making a run for it. But only for a second. They had a car and would hunt him down. They had guns and he possessed nothing but a Triple Blaster. Suddenly the car emerged from the leafy tunnel, and they were rushing across a paved area toward a large fountain that sat in solitary splendor in front of the Eberhart mansion. Home sweet home.

Karl got out first and opened the door for his master, while Rafi opened the door for himself. Munich drove off as soon as they were all out. The front door stood open in welcome. An older woman was standing just inside the door, face creased in a smile.

"Dietrich," she exclaimed joyfully as they entered the hall.

"Inge," he responded warmly, "how have you been?" He turned to Rafi and said, "Inge is the closest thing to a parent that I have." The woman beamed. "She was with my parents, and I hope that she will remain with me forever."

"But of course I will," she blushed.

"She is my housekeeper, my cook and my confidante," he went on, "and I have known her since I was a boy."

"I prepared something light for you and your guest," she said.

"Speaking for myself," he said, "I'm not hungry. But perhaps my guest would care to have a bite."

"No, thank you," said Rafi. "I'm still full from the last meal I ate. Besides, I try not to eat after 10 o'clock at night."

"I'm going to smoke a pipe," Eberhart said to Rafi. "If you're not too weary, then perhaps you'd care to join me?"

"I wouldn't say no to a nice sweet-smelling pipe right now," Rafi said.

He followed his host down a long wood-paneled hallway redolent with the aroma of brandy and furniture polish. They turned a corner, walked past a few closed doors and entered Eberhart's study. It was a pleasant masculine room. There were a number of pictures on the walls: Most featured leading Nazis of a bygone era. Several photographs appeared to have been taken in some sort of underground bunker. One photo didn't appear to fit in at all. It was a picture of a parking lot. Eberhart noticed him studying the photos.

"That's a place that speaks to me," he said simply. "Whenever I visit those few rooms, I can hear the voices of the past speaking to me, encouraging me. It's almost like a shrine. And when the right time comes, I will fight the next war from the most fitting place I can think of: a place with overwhelming historical significance for the German people, where our greatest leaders did their utmost for the cause. I'm a big believer in tradition, in knowing where you come from and acting accordingly."

"That's exactly the way I feel," Rafi said with sincerity. "A person without roots is like a ship lost at sea. He has no direction, no stability, no understanding of what is expected of him."

Eberhart was nodding his head as he prepared two pipes. When he finished tapping down the tobacco, he handed one of them to Rafi with a polite nod.

"Enjoy," he said "I use only the finest. This is a mixture of vanilla and cherry tobacco imported from Cuba." Rafi nodded, and Eberhart reached over to light it for him. A fragrance filled the room as the smoke began drifting upward. They sat in companionable silence for a few minutes, smoking and meditating, until Eberhart finally broke the solitude.

"O.K.," he said. "We're at the homestead. You had time to think on the way here, and I did as well. I'll be honest with you. I'm still not at all sure that you are who you say you are, but we'll let that be for the moment. I think it might be a good idea for you to remain with me for a while, and see what it actually is that I do. You have courage — that I know. You're a smart man; I can see it in your eyes. Honest — I'm not as sure about that yet. I need more time with you to make a complete assessment of your character.

"Now to get back to what we were talking about before, I would just like to say a few things. The world today has done a complete turnaround from when my father and your grandfather were running the show. The type of weapons, the amount of computer involvement in the wars of today and the shifts in the world economy are all supremely different than the way it was back then. Now follow my train of thought here for a second.

"The German nation is not ready for another war, especially anything along the lines of the two world wars. Sixty years might have passed since then, but the nation's soul has still not recovered completely. In fact," he said as he took a deep puff on his pipe, "the German people are afraid to move, to do the wrong thing. They are anxious to stay out of the limelight, not because they feel bad for what happened, because they don't feel bad. No. The reason they are keeping a low profile is because they know that just as they have not forgotten what transpired in this part of the world, the world still remembers as well. Russia remembers, because it was their manpower that won the war, and America definitely remembers, because they were the ones who footed the bill. And if there's one thing to be said about the people of America, it's that they are darn good businessmen — maybe not as good as the Japanese, but good enough.

"Are you still with me?" he asked. Rafi nodded.

"That being the case," he went on, "the next war will have to be something infinitely different. It will have to be something that will not require such a heavy commitment on the part of the nation; something that will allow us to return to power without spreading ourselves thin over the battlefields of Europe. It was my father who came up with the concept, and it was Himmler who approved it. Both the research that went into the plan and the amount of actual planning were enormous, but well worth it. Are you beginning to catch my drift yet?"

"Do you mean that you will be able to return to power with just a few men?" Rafi asked him carefully.

"In a manner of speaking, yes," Eberhart said. "Just a few men, but the right ones this time. A key brain in the right place is worth more than a thousand men on the battlefield. Why waste resources?"

"You have men who can do this?" Rafi asked in rising excitement, ever mindful of the role he was playing.

"Let's just say that with a few words, I could completely alter the world as we know it," Eberhart said. "Now you know why we are waiting. I am still setting the stage. But as soon as it's set, we will be in business and you will be a part of it.

"But enough of this for one night. I must tell you that I am honored to be sitting and discussing such a vital topic with the grandson of Alois

Zimmer. Your grandfather would have been proud." The pipes had gone cold. They placed them in a crystal dish on the desk.

"Well, time to turn in, I guess," Eberhart said as he closed the door to the study. "Let me show you to your room."

The room turned out to be a suite, furnished like a hunting lodge with elk antlers and a boar head on the walls. Rafi found a pair of pajamas on the pillow, and a plush and obviously expensive bathrobe hanging in the bathroom. He glanced at his watch. It was 3 o'clock in the morning and he was wide awake. He waited for close to an hour to give everyone a chance to fall asleep. Then he reached into the pocket in his trousers and pulled on a material tab. A hidden pocket that was sewn into the inner lining opened, and he took out a small plastic tube. He examined it carefully. It seemed to be in operable condition. Holding it aloft, he turned the knob of his room, and stepped into the hallway. His shoes made no noise at all. The house was utterly still. He presumed that there were no video cameras following his every move, but just in case, he gave a good look around him. Nothing.

He was reasonably certain that he was the sole occupant on his particular floor, since most of it was open floor space. This part of the house had obviously been designed with the guests' comfort in mind. There was one other room with a closed door. Easing open the door, he saw that it was a laundry room. He closed the door behind him. Stepping lightly, he walked quietly up the stairs to the next level. There were quite a few rooms on this floor, and he assumed many of them were bedrooms. He wasted no time, because there was no time to waste. He walked from door to door. Putting the tube to the spot where the door almost met the carpet, he gave a little squirt of liquid cloud into the room. He did this to every room on the floor. Then he walked down the two flights of stairs to the ground floor, and did the same thing to every room there. He looked at his watch. Ten minutes had passed from the time he had left his room. He could hear noise coming from a little room near the front of the house. He figured this was the guardpost where either Karl or Munich was taking a shift. He paused by the door, and gave a quick spray inside, then he moved on.

Two minutes later, he cautiously opened the door with a dampened towel over his mouth and nose, and found the muscular Karl slumped on the floor in front of the television set. He left it on. The house was now his to work in. Making no attempt to keep quiet, he retraced his steps to Dietrich Eberhart's office. He paused outside the door, petrified for a second, imagining silent alarms emitting their signal the moment he crossed the threshold. He turned the handle and was inside Dietrich Eberhart's office. He drew a deep breath in relief. How had he gotten this far? He knew one thing. There was no way that Eberhart was going to leave his copy of the book in plain view. And now that he had heard Eberhart's plan, it was more than likely that he had the original in his possession.

The question was: Where would he have put it? The thought crossed his mind that maybe Eberhart had it stored in a bank vault or another safe place, in which case the entire operation from start to finish was a waste of time. But he fervently hoped that this was not the case. He began searching the room. He looked behind pictures on the wall, he pulled up the carpet from the floor, he opened the closets and riffled through the shelves. He saw many interesting things, but no book, no notebook, no diary. Nothing appeared to be in any way connected to the object of his search. Maybe it wasn't in Eberhart's study. Maybe it was in his bedroom, along with his clothing and personal belongings. But if it that were so, it might be anywhere in the house, and this was a very large house. That would mean that he would have to continue his search the next day. Everyone in the house was bound to be suspicious when they didn't awaken at their usual hour.

No, he couldn't push it off. He racked his brain trying to remember what the instructors at the agency had taught him to do in these situations.

"Sometimes the walls are hollow." He repeated those words quite a number of times. "Sometimes the walls are hollow especially in older homes."

It was worth checking out. He walked around the room knocking on each of the walls in turn. One by one, they sounded solid. It was a centuries-old house. There were no hollow walls in this mansion. He had been searching for nearly an hour. He didn't have that much longer. If he didn't find the book soon, he was going to give up for the night and try again a different time. He looked around the room, studying it, trying to read it from a different perspective, from a different angle. His gut told him that if the book was in the house, it was in this room. His gaze fell on the desk situated inconspicuously near the wall. It was a handsome desk, perhaps the desk that Ludwig Eberhart had used as well. A fountain pen rested on the glass desktop. There was a pile of envelopes bearing the Eberhart family crest.

He opened the desk's center drawer. Nothing important was inside.

He tried the first drawer on the side. There were several contracts lying stacked with precision. He knew instinctively that this was just business and nothing more. There were checkbooks in the drawer underneath, and additional financial information, much like desk drawers all over the world. The same went for the remainder of the drawers as well. It was all very innocuous, nothing out of the ordinary, boring. But the desk appeared much deeper than the drawers he had looked into. He got down on his hands and knees and crouched into the crawl space underneath the desk. He ran his fingers all over the inside of the space searching for something out of the ordinary. Maybe there was a catch, a hidden lever, something to grab onto. There was nothing there; it was completely smooth. He crawled out and sank down into the executive chair, swiveling around, trying to organize his thoughts.

He glanced down at the desk again and pulled open the bottom drawer. It slid out smoothly, coming to a stop with a slight hiss. He measured the drawer with his hands. There was no question about it, the drawer was definitely not filling up the entire space. With rising excitement, he began emptying out the drawer, carefully. He had to make sure that Eberhart didn't know that he had been in this drawer. He piled everything on the desk exactly the way it had been stored inside the drawer: box of Havana cigars, box of Mont Blanc pens, a small pouch made of cracked leather. He flipped opened the lid and gasped. Inside was a most exquisite Iron Cross made out of pure gold! Underneath that, there was a row of medals from World War II.

When the drawer was empty, he reached in and used his fingertips to tap on the wood. At the top of the drawer, there were a series of ridges and bumps. He pressed them and tried to turn them. He did everything he could think of to make them open, but nothing did the trick. He kept on searching and discovered identical ridges on the other side of the drawer. With a silent prayer, he pressed the fingers of both hands on the two sets of bumps at the same time. He pressed down and twisted the bumps, there was an imperceptible click, and the back of the drawer came off without any warning. The drawer came shooting out of the desk, almost doubly as large as it had seemed originally. There was a medium-sized carton in the drawer that looked as if it had not been moved in ages. With trepidation, he lifted it and ran his hands around the edges, searching for the clasp.

There was a set of combination numbers built into the case. He realized that here was another setback that was going to take up at the barest minimum another half an hour to resolve. He was playing it mighty close. He had a special key with him that was able to open up any kind of lock. But that was no use with a combination lock. For a moment, he toyed very seriously about giving up and returning to his bedroom. But his innate stubbornness reasserted itself with a vengeance. Beside the row of numbers, there was a button that would open the case if it wasn't locked. He figured, why not? Might as well try. He pressed the button, expecting nothing. Instead, there was an unexpected easing of pressure, and the top of the case flew open. Eberhart had apparently not felt the need to lock the case, probably never imagining in his worst nightmares that the hiding place would be found. And there, inside the case, on a bed of red velvet, lay a book, one notebook. It was not a large book, either. The book was bound in black leather with gold lettering on the top.

He stared at the words. They were written in a fancy script. He wasn't totally fluent in reading German, and he mouthed the words slowly to himself.

"The Network," he read. This was it. He had found it. This was the book that held the future power of the party. He wasn't at all sure what "The Network" was capable of, but if one believed Eberhart — and he tended to do so — then the book that he was holding represented real danger. With trembling fingers, he opened the cover and looked at the first page. It was a list of names. The information on every name took up about 10 lines. There was what seemed to the person's original name, another name listed underneath the first (obviously the name by which he was presently known), the person's address and phone number, and another series of words about which he was clueless. He assumed those lines were some form of code. He had to take pictures of this. But before he did that, he would snap a few photos of the office since one never knew what was important and what wasn't.

He removed his watch from his wrist and positioned it so that the watch face was focused. Then he began to snap photos of the room: the paintings on the walls, and basically everything that Dietrich had on display. It didn't matter that it was taking time. It was vital that the agency got a handle on the neo-Nazi leader. He took pictures of the entire office from every angle.

He checked the pictures. Everything was clear. The camera was working. Morning was almost here. He began to move even more quickly, making sure to keep the work professional. He shot page after page of names. From time to time, he found a name that he recognized, someone famous, someone infamous. Some of the names were people in positions of tremendous power, military power, financial power, political power. He snapped away. Every name had a page to itself. There were 150 pages. By the time he had filmed 100 of those pages, he began to get a bad feeling in his gut, almost as if a sixth sense was warning him that it was taking him too long!

He went to the office door and cautiously eased it open. He left it slightly ajar, allowing him to hear if anyone approached. Then he resumed his picture taking. Beads of sweat were dripping down his forehead now. He could feel his shirt clinging to the small of his back. He wiped his brow with the back of his arm, and his shirtsleeve felt soggy and wet. He was almost finished. There were two more pages to go. Just two more and he had them all. But wait! What was that sound?! He strained for a moment, and then he knew that he hadn't imagined anything. There was definitely someone either entering or about to enter the house. The sounds were coming from the front door! Even though the office was down the hallway and around the bend from the front door, every sound was more than magnified in the middle of the night. He could hear someone mumbling to himself. In fact, it sounded like Dietrich and he sounded angry!

He didn't have time to photograph the final two pages. Not with Dietrich coming into the house and about to discover him in his office! He flipped the book closed and slipped it back in the velvet-lined case. He set the case back into its hidden drawer and clicked the panel back into place. It closed with a satisfying click. His nimble fingers were moving very quickly now. They were practically flying. He maneuvered Dietrich's personal belongings back into the drawer as quickly as he could, hoping that he had replaced them in the exact order they had been in before he removed them. There was no time to do any more than that. He could hear Dietrich entering the house! Thank heavens Dietrich's office was around a bend in the hallway and couldn't be seen from the front door!

He pushed the drawer shut with a gentle shove. It moved easily and smoothly right back into its place with finality. The room looked undisturbed. Nobody would ever know that he had been riffling through the closets and drawers, under the carpets and behind the paintings on the walls. His watch was back on his wrist, and he slid out the door. It was still dark outside, but Rafi could tell that dawn would soon be breaking. He had been up all night. His head pounded and he felt nauseous. He gently shut the heavy door behind him. His feet sank into the thick pile carpeting. He moved silently through the first floor of the house until he reached the kitchen. From behind him, he could hear Dietrich lumbering through the house, and he knew that the next few minutes would be crucial — especially considering that the bodyguards were unconscious!

Have to act natural! Like you were thirsty and needed a drink. Keep it simple! You know nothing!

He took a glass from the cabinet, and opening the fridge, removed a carton of orange juice. He poured a glassful, made a *berachah* and took a sip. The juice flowed down his throat like the sweetest nectar in the universe. The footsteps were getting closer now. And then, there he was. Dietrich Eberhart himself, standing at the kitchen door, glaring at him with murderous hatred in his eyes.

"Stay right where you are!" he ordered Rafi. "Don't move! I don't want to have to use this yet!" Rafi could see that he was brandishing a pistol, and that his hand wasn't wavering in the slightest.

"Karl," he called out. There was no response.

"Munich," he tried. Again nothing. The house was silent, resting, peaceful.

"What have you done to my men?!" he roared at Rafi. "What's going on here? Come with me!"

Rafi still hadn't said a word. There was nothing to say. Obviously, Eberhart suspected him. The main thing was that he was prepared to kill Rafi right now! Dietrich manhandled him down the corridor toward his office and continued on until they came to a halt outside the little room from where the sounds of the television still emanated. There was laughter, music. Dietrich pulled open the door and stared in horror at his bodyguard, who was slumped on the floor, out cold. But his hand never wavered on the gun. He was still as steady as ever.

He turned away from the door and ordered Rafi to walk ahead of him to his office. Rafi led the way, thinking the whole time how to turn the tables on this situation. After all, the sole weapon he possessed was the pen, and there was one very irate German man in extremely fit condition, who was pointing a gun directly at him, and who wanted nothing more than to tear him limb by limb. And Rafi? Rafi was equipped with a pen! But that was the reality of the situation. At least the pen was still in his pocket.

They entered the office. The room looked untouched. Rafi could discern no sign of anything out of its place, or any reason why Eberhart should be so upset. Eberhart sat down in his leather chair and pointing his gun at Rafi, ordered him down onto a hard seat facing the desk. There was very little chance to do anything, not with a gun pointed straight at him!

"Anyway, there I was," Eberhart began speaking, almost as if he was in the middle of a conversation and had just remembered to turn up the sound, "asleep in the guest house. Yes," he said, correctly interpreting the confused look on Rafi's face, "I often prefer to sleep there. Last night, I decided to crash in my bedroom there. So I was lying in bed, tossing and turning, trying to find a good position. But I couldn't seem to settle down. Then out of the blue, this thought popped into my mind.

"'Wait a second,' it says to me, 'You've seen this man before! You know you have.'

"I was racking my brain trying to recall where I had seen you before, when all of a sudden I remembered. It was a really amazing picture of you. It was somewhere in Israel, you were standing on a stage, not even standing on the stage, but actually jumping off the stage right onto this terrorist who had his back to you. Your violin was lifted in the air, and you were smashing it on the man's head. That was how you became a hero. You saved the day. It was you, wasn't it?!"

"Nope," said Rafi calmly. "I recall that story," he said to the German, "and I'm flattered that you think me capable of such quick and decisive action. But the truth is," a pause, "I have never been in Israel in my entire life! Unfortunately, you have confused me with someone else."

His hand was beside his pocket now, and he began motioning with his left hand as he spoke, to draw attention away from his right hand which was removing the pen from his pocket.

Eberhart laughed. "Do you think I'm stupid?" he asked Rafi. "Dumb question," he said a moment later. "Obviously you do. But here's a little newsflash. I'm not. Not in the least. So here's what I did, knowing that you were going to deny my accusations. I printed out the picture of you leaping from the stage with that violin in your hand, and put it through one of my computer programs that has the capability to compare facial structure and profiles. And what do you know, my computer concluded it's a complete, 100-percent match! Shocker, huh?! So I figured no point in rushing this thing. I'll give my security men a chance to catch a little rest from their exertions the night before. But when I finally came into the house to call them, I find you in the kitchen taking a drink, which means that you've been sneaking around my home. That's never a good sign in a guest. Not only that, but somehow Karl has fallen asleep on the floor of the office, and Munich is sleeping so deeply that he didn't even hear me call his name. That's something that has never, ever happened before!

"So what's the deal, Rolf, or should I just say Rafi Ganim?" He rose from his seat and walked around the desk toward Rafi. "Get those hands up in the air!"

Rafi wasn't sure what Eberhart was going to do next, but he didn't think that he was going to murder him right in the office. He tried to anticipate his next move. Eberhart would probably order him out of the house, and then they would go outside, to some barn or something, and then he would shove him against a bale of hay to muffle the sound. His mind had gotten carried away for a second. Now Eberhart was saying something, probably telling him to get up. But Rafi was already standing up — a move the other had not anticipated. As Eberhart lifted the pistol with intention to bring it down on Rafi's head, Rafi pulled his "pen" out of his pocket and pointed it in Eberhart's direction. His fingers found the little button on the bottom of the pen. Even as the gun was beginning its downward descent, Rafi covered his eyes with one hand and pressed the button with the other hand.

There was a tremendous explosion, magnified multiple times by the fact that it was happening in a contained space. An incredibly bright light shot out of the Triple Blaster in the direction of Dietrich Eberhart. The distance was so short and the blast so powerful that Eberhart collapsed on the floor of the office completely blinded, and began stumbling around the room on all fours, howling from the pain of the blast. But he was recovering quickly, and Rafi didn't intend to take any chance, so he aimed the Triple Blaster toward the blond man again and depressed the button a second time. The sound and light show happened all over again, except that this time, there was a crumbling sound and a shower of plaster came crashing down from the ceiling amid a fountain of paint flakes and dusty whiteness. Rafi turned around and ran for his life!

He couldn't even comprehend that he was no longer being held at gunpoint. But he knew that his freedom could easily be the most short-lived escape in history unless he managed to flee the Eberhart estate.

He had no gun. He regretted that he hadn't taken the extra second to relieve the bodyguards of one of their weapons. But he was already at the front door of the house. He threw open the hallway closet and found a warm jacket. He turned the handle of the door, while slipping on the jacket at the same time, and was confronted by a frigid blast of icy air. And then he ran.

It was very early morning now and he was running for his life! He didn't know to where he was running, and he didn't know what he was going to do when he arrived there. He ran around the corner of the mansion, and saw salvation staring him in the face. There was a man there, and that man was leading a horse by its reins. The horse was saddled and ready for an early-morning ride. There was no time for an explanation, and Rafi did something which he didn't want to do, something he had never wanted to have to do. He put both his hands together in a huge fist and brought it crashing down on the man's head. Then he grabbed the reins in one hand, stuck his foot into the metal stirrup and threw his leg over the horse's back. The horse, instinctively understanding that the man on its back was an expert horseman, responded to his every command as though they had been a riding team for years. He pressed his legs into the sides of the horse, it picked up speed, switching instantly from a trot into a gallop.

The ground became a blur as they merged into one. Up ahead, Rafi could see a bluish-whitish line, and he realized that he was looking at a wide stream that was partially frozen over. It would not be able to support their combined weight. They thundered toward the stream. There was no bridge in sight. Already the Eberhart estate was a speck on the horizon. Hooves flailing on the frozen ground, the horse approached the stream and began gearing up for the jump. He pressed his entire body flat down on the horse, breathing when the horse breathed, keeping a firm hold on the horse's neck.

They were almost upon the stream. He could see the water moving underneath the surface, through the cracks in the ice. The horse bounded forward. Almost flying now, it heaved its body into the air and sailed over the stream, where it landed on the shore, took an extra second to catch its balance and then, once again it was off and running.

Rafi was frozen, and every second that passed he seemed to become colder. But he kept going because he knew that Eberhart would be close behind. In the distance, he caught sight of a road, just a smidgen of black asphalt and yellow lines. They surged forth, the horse reading him, seeming to sense where he was headed.

They sped down the rolling hills, skimming the surface of the land, the horse finding its footing at the last second, time and again, almost losing its balance, almost causing them to plummet to their deaths. At last, they were on the top of a hill, looking down at the highway below them. Every jolt was fire and agony for Rafi now. The horse was tiring and inclined to lose its balance.

Now they were plodding down the mountainside in the direction of a rest stop. He had to urge the horse onward, making clicking sounds with his mouth, prodding the horse with his legs. The horse responded tiredly, doing what was necessary despite the chill and his fatigue. They picked up their speed. Finally the crest of the road came into view. There was a whizzing sound as car after car sped past them. Now that they were on a flat surface, the horse found it easier to run. Once again, he picked up speed and raced down the road.

Eventually, they entered the rest stop and came to a full stop outside the convenience store. There was a big jolly man clad in a spotless apron standing behind the counter. He bellowed good-naturedly at Rafi, "Good morning, young man. What do you need? A nice hot cup of coffee? A doughnut? What can I get for you?

"What kind of cookies would a horse enjoy most?" Rafi asked him. The man emerged from behind the counter, and selected a big box of cookies.

Rafi thanked him and the man scratched his head and said, "None of my business now, but why would you be needing cookies for a horse?"

"Actually," Rafi said, "my horse is tethered to a fence outside. He put in a good run this morning and I felt that he deserved a reward."

"Can I take a look at your horse?" the man asked all businesslike.

"Certainly," Rafi replied. So they walked outside into the biting air, and the horse was still there neighing and miserable. Rafi fed him the cookies and he quieted down.

The big man patted the horse's nose absentmindedly and said, "Listen, friend, this fellow needs to get into a warm stable as soon as possible."

"I know," Rafi said. "Would you like to buy this horse from me now? I'll give you a really good price."

"In a rush now, aren't you?" the big man replied, studying Rafi shrewdly from beneath hooded eyelids.

"Actually, I am in a big rush," Rafi said. "And I'm prepared to sell you this horse in return for a car ride to the nearest city." The man pondered the offer for a while.

"Someone is after you," he remarked flatly.

Rafi nodded his head and said nothing.

"O.K., I'll take you to the nearest city," the man finally said.

Rafi gave the horse the remainder of the cookies and patted his nose and face and whispered words of praise into his ear. Then the big man shouted to one of his workers, who led the horse away. Rafi climbed into the cab of the man's truck. It was an old Renault, and it took a while for it to crank into action. But once it rumbled to life it moved off down the highway at high speed. Twenty minutes later Rafi found himself in the city of Clausen, standing at the entrance to the Metro station where he purchased a train ticket to Berlin, leaving him with little cash in his wallet.

During most of his train trip to Berlin, Rafi hid in the restroom, emeging from time to time to buy something to eat and for a breath of fresh air. Hours later, the train pulled into the main terminal in Berlin. Rafi waited until all the passengers had exited the train before he too walked out through the doors and onto the bustling platform, blending anonymously into the crowd. He was another face in a busy world, and that suited him just fine. There was a line of taxis waiting outside the terminal. Rafi chose the nearest one in the line.

"Where to?" asked the cab driver.

"Just drive," Rafi answered tersely. For some reason the driver found this amusing but he did as he was told.

They drove for five blocks. Then Rafi directed him to go around a traffic circle and double back, and then he told him to do it again, making certain that the driver just caught the light at the corner. Finally when he was reasonably sure that no one was following him, he gave the driver directions to the Israeli Embassy. The driver drove up as close to the tall wrought-iron gates as he was allowed, and then Rafi emerged and ran for the entrance. It was only when he was finally standing on Israeli soil that he breathed a deep sigh of relief.

The guards listened to his story and led him through the hallways until he reached a door with the words Military Attaché on it. There he knocked and walked into the room. The secretary waved and smiled at him, but he barely noticed.

"Get me a secure line to Tel Aviv," he said to her, "and a quiet spot in a room that has been swept for all electronic eavesdropping devices. After I finish speaking on the phone, I need a bedroom with a comfortable bed and a decent kosher meal. I haven't eaten normally in quite some time."

"Go right in there to make your call," she said, directed him to an empty office, "and by the time you have finished speaking to Israel, everything else will be ready for you as well."

The phone rang twice. He heard the familiar voice speaking to him, a voice he thought he would never hear again.

"Rafi, is that you?" the voice asked incredulously.

"Of course it's me," he answered impatiently. "I have the book." There was a silence on the other end of the line.

"You have *the* book?" the voice said. "You have the book I have been searching for all these years?"

"Right inside my watch, Kobi," he said. "It's a long story, and I almost didn't make it out alive. But you can tell those boys down at the agency or wherever they come up with these brilliant ideas, that those Triple Blasters work really well! I'm going to take the next flight back to Israel, and then I'll tell you everything. There is so much great information, it's going to blow your mind! I just wanted to let you know what's been going on. I'll be in touch as soon as I land."

"Thank heaven," Kobi said simply. "I'll come pick you up at the airport. Just get me the flight numbers."

"The secretary will take care of it," Rafi promised, and they hung up.

Five hours later, Rafi Ganim was driven out of the Israeli Embassy in a BMW with dark tinted windows. Security personal escorted him to the airport, through passport control and into the executive lounge. Forty minutes later he was the first to board the plane. The entire First Class section had been reserved for him, and was closed off throughout the flight. It was only when the plane actually took off that Rafi was finally able to relax. He had been in accursed Germany for long enough; it was time to get back home — to his Rebbe, his violin and to Kobi Shapiro — but not necessarily in that order.

PART FOUR

Mordy, Cardinal Jason Frost, Rafi and Kobi

Ben-Gurion Airport, Israel
March 18, 2009

Mordy Kahane boarded British Airways Flight 343 at 5 o'clock in the morning. From the moment he had received the e-mail, he changed. He had no clue as to the nature of the emergency, but it didn't matter to him. Frost would never have asked him to come back from Israel without there being an excellent reason. As the taxi pulled up outside Ben-Gurion Airport, he felt a tremendous sadness overwhelm him. He was leaving Eretz Yisrael, the country that he had come to love. He had finally begun to feel at peace once again. He didn't want to go back to America, to Ithaca. He had such bad memories of the place! But he would do anything for Frost. He checked in, and reserved both a *mehadrin* kosher meal as well as an aisle seat.

What could have happened? he wondered again for the thousandth time. Frost was so level headed and controlled. He never allowed anything to upset him. Was he sick again? Was that why he wanted Mordy to come home, because his days were numbered? The questions raced through his mind like tiny granules of sand sifting between two fingers. He settled into his seat and tried listening to music. He was dreading the next 11 hours. He disliked flying intensely, but he had to get home. He decided to learn until he became too tired. By the time he closed the Gemara two hours later, he had managed to review several *blatt*. Then he leaned back in his seat, slipped on the earphones and he drifted off to sleep as the sounds of a smooth saxophone filled his ears.

New York was the same as always. Mordy followed the directions of a loud-voiced woman who told him and countless others to "Go to the left line, to the left line!" He passed through passport control rapidly. He walked out of the terminal at Kennedy and waited for his father to pick him up. A sleek SUV with tinted windows pulled up at the side of the curb. The window slid down, and Stan Kahane motioned him into the car.

Mordy piled his luggage into the back of the vehicle. He jumped into the front seat beside his Dad and they exchanged hellos. There was an awkward silence for a few minutes as they both were at a loss for what to say. He was thinking, *C'mon, Dad, you could ask how yeshivah is going!*

His father was thinking, *C'mon, son, you could at least pretend to be happy to be home. Just a little bit!*

There was a stiffness between them, and it was a relief for both of them when several hours later the signs for Ithaca appeared on the side of the highway. His father took the exit lane, and 10 minutes later, he parked in front of his house, which Mordy noticed had been remodeled. His father helped him with his luggage, and the car was emptied quickly.

The tension in the air was so thick one could slice it with a knife. Mordy could sense that his parents had still not made their peace with his decision to be *frum* and devote himself to learning in yeshivah.

"Mom's in the backyard," his father said. "We're going to have a barbecue to celebrate your homecoming later. In the meanwhile why don't you go say hello to your mother?"

It wasn't a request, it was an order. He grudgingly made his way to the back of the house where the grass had been freshly mowed, and there were 20 different species of flowers growing. His mother was sitting peacefully on a swing under the shade of a giant tree that had been begging for a tree house forever.

"Matt!" his mother called out happily when she caught sight of him. She made him sit down and tell her all about life in Jerusalem, and was fascinated by everything he had to say. She told him that she was very happy that he finally found himself; that she had known it was going to happen one of these years. She said that they would have to come and tour the country along with him when he returned.

He nodded, glad that she was being so positive, and told her that he had to go and visit the cardinal before dinner. His parents knew about the cardinal. They knew the cardinal had covered the expenses for his stay in Israel. They knew that they certainly weren't paying for him to study ancient studies at some fanatical academy. They weren't thrilled that their son was so close to a cardinal of the Catholic Church, but there had been odder friendships in the world. At least he had emerged from his shell after meeting the man.

He promised his mother that he would return a while later. As he walked through the house on his way to the street, he noted that his parents had compensated for his absence with a host of material objects until there was almost no room to maneuver. He shrugged. Whatever made them happy. His father had given him a key, so he locked the door and headed in the direction of the cardinal's home. The sun was out and the birds were chirping. He was feeling kind of cheerful, but full of anxiety as well.

What did the man want? What could it be? When he reached Frost's house, he stood on the pavement outside for a while, just looking at this home whose sole occupant had provided him with a desire to pick up the pieces and live. Then he walked onto the porch and rang the bell. He could hear the sound of the bell reverberating through the house. He waited but nobody answered. He stepped off the porch and walked to the back of the house, where he turned the knob of the back door and let himself in. From what he knew of the cardinal, he was probably in his study reading, oblivious to the world and to doorbells. He went through the kitchen, dining room and the living room, and approached the study. This was the cardinal's retreat from the world, a place where he could read the classics, write his speeches, answer his mail and do the thousand and one things that comprised his job.

Mordy knocked on the door. When there was no response, he turned the knob and entered the room. The cardinal was seated at his desk, his thoughts immersed in some ancient tome, brow furrowed and shoulders hunched. He was wearing earphones, and was listening to a symphony. Mordy gave a sigh of relief. Frost was fine. He was just concentrating so deeply that he hadn't heard the bell. He didn't want to frighten the man by interrupting him, so he took a seat and waited for the cardinal to catch sight of him. Five minutes later, the cardinal glanced up. When he noticed his guest, his face creased into a huge smile.

"Matt," he said excitedly, "or should I call you Mordy now?"

"Whatever works better for you, cardinal," Mordy replied.

"Am I glad to see you," Frost said. "You have no idea!"

"I really don't," Mordy said. "Talk to me. Tell me what's been going on since I've been away."

"I don't even know where to begin," Frost said. "I remember parts of what happened, but there are pieces that I can't recall for the life of me. It's all very confusing. Some times I remember more than other times. But there are days when everything seems to slip away, and then I'm hopelessly confused."

"How are you feeling now?" Mordy asked the older man.

"Today is actually a better day for me. I seem to be doing a little bit better in the remembering department than usual."

"That's great then," Mordy said, "because I'm here now, and I want to hear what's been going on since I left. Tell me everything that you remember."

"I'll try," the cardinal said, "but there's something wrong; something holding me back. You might be thinking that it's Alzheimer's or something similar, but it's not. It's almost as if my mind was invaded by someone whom I can't recall, who put some parts of my mind under lock and key, and I can't seem to get to them."

"So tell me about the parts that you do remember," Mordy said.

Cardinal Jason Frost leaned back in his chair and began talking, really talking, to the first person who genuinely cared since Al had been killed. Once he began, he found that he couldn't stop. But the more he spoke, the more questions Mordy had. As many times as Mordy asked, Frost could only shrug his shoulders in frustration and say that his mind was a blank.

Yes, he had decided to travel with Al. No, he couldn't remember why. Yes, they had gone to Paris. No, he couldn't remember why. Al had gotten killed. Why? He didn't know.

He'd been in some other countries as well, but couldn't recall for what reason. It was terribly confusing and disconcerting, and he was drowning in an extraordinary sadness that engulfed him for hours at a time. He knew that he had been on the verge of discovering something important about his life. But he was totally bewildered as to what that something was. Deep down, he could sense a warning signal telling him that catastrophic events were about to happen; that he was standing on the edge of a volcano that was going to erupt momentarily. He didn't know when and he didn't know why, and he no longer knew whom to trust. But there was one person that he knew he could trust, and that was why he had asked Mordy to return home. Because maybe together, they could solve this thing and help him figure out what on earth was happening in his life.

Mordy heard it all and was clueless as to how to proceed. The symptoms Frost was describing were pretty similar to any number of illnesses that affect the minds of millions of elderly people. Who was to say that the same thing was not happening in the mind of Cardinal Frost as well? Yes, he was a very intelligent man. But so many others were intelligent as well. Mordy had no training in the field of psychology, and if there was one person that would be able to help this man, it was someone who could actually get past the barriers that the conscious mind put up to protect a person, and focus on what was really going on in his subconscious mind; to discover the secrets that were haunting him for so many years, and to find out why he had gone to Paris and elsewhere. Someone needed to find out what had transpired in this man's life, to cause him to be so happy, learned and charismatic in some ways, and so miserable, and full of fear and anxiety in other ways. But Mordy couldn't be the one to do this. He could stand by the cardinal's side and hold his hand, but that was the extent of it. He only wished that there was more that he could do.

Tel Aviv, Israel
September 14, 2008

Kobi had aged considerably over the past few years. Whether due to the fact that he had just grown old, or due to the agency's failure to recognize his warnings as the truth, the aging process had definitely gained momentum. Rafi had seen it happening, and he bore a tremendous amount of anger to the people at the top who had seen fit to phase the old man out of any part of all current and ongoing operations. It all started when he returned from Europe with the information burning a hole through his watch. Kobi had stood over the technician as he worked, making sure that no extra copies were made of anything. Then together, they had closeted themselves in Kobi's office and reviewed the pages of names until they had memorized each and every one of them. Rafi apologized again and again for the fact that he hadn't managed to photograph the final two pages in the book, but Kobi quieted his apologies.

"We wouldn't have any names if it weren't for you and the amazing feat, that you did, so stop beating yourself up, and start feeling proud of yourself for carrying out the most incredible operation I've seen in years!"

"But we don't know who the last two people are," Rafi said. "I should have looked at the pages! Even if I didn't have time to photograph them, I could have looked at them and tried to memorize them. What was I thinking?"

"You weren't thinking," Kobi said. "You were terrified that Eberhart was going to catch you in the act of messing with his most prized possession, and then you wouldn't have gotten anything out of the whole mission. I'm glad that you didn't look and that you got out of there while you were able to. And don't forget, without you, we wouldn't know about any of them," Kobi finished. "You've done so well. It's just a shame that the entire country can't be told about your accomplishments!" And Rafi had blushed.

There were some very influential names on those pages; people who held some extremely sensitive positions in military forces around the world, men who wielded tremendous political power, who could influence Capitol Hill if they so desired. Quite a few of those were from Israel. One had been an ace in the air force, highly respected and motivated. He was a man whom many held up as a role model. There had been many others all across America, the guardians of security. They were all there along with their phone numbers and some sort of code written alongside their names. That part of the puzzle remained unexplained. But that didn't stop Kobi from marching into the chief of the Mossad with Rafi in tow, and showing him the book.

The chief was skeptical and equivocal. He congratulated Rafi on a job well done, but didn't understand what Kobi wanted him to do with this information.

"So there's a list of names. So what?" he'd screamed at Kobi. "What does that prove? Maybe this Eberhart wants to recruit these people to his cause. Who knows? But one thing I'm sure of is that a man like Shali

Loeberbaum, a genuine honest-to-goodness hero of the Israeli nation, is not in any way involved in anything to do with a man like Eberhart!"

"So why not call him down here or go talk to him and ask him why he thinks that his name is in Eberhart's book?" Kobi asked reasonably.

"No can do, friend," the chief said. "This man will not be happy if I decide to interrogate him for no good reason."

"But there is a good reason," Kobi yelled at the chief, finally losing his patience. "Look at the names on the list: Loeberbaum, a man who runs a flight school that happens to be adjacent to one of the most sensitive military bases in the country. How's that for a coincidence? Moshe Amoni, another army hero who works for Mekorot, another sensitive position."

"What could Amoni possibly do to harm the country?"

"I don't know," answered Kobi. "Maybe poison the water tanks or poison the Kinneret. There are countless possibilities and that's the point. We don't know what these people are up to. We know nothing. All we know is that Jason Leonard Frost, a man in line to become pope, has his name on the list as well. Maybe we should inform the Americans? Maybe they are entitled to know about this. And what about this man?" He pointed at the name of a man who was very high up in the German government. "Here's a man whom we all know and love. He's always been a sympathetic friend of Israel. But he's on the list. Doesn't that deserve some investigating?"

"No," the chief said, "it doesn't. You want to know why? Because absolutely nothing has happened, and there is no proof that anything will happen either."

"Try to use your brains," Kobi screamed at his boss, who was busy lighting a cigarette. "Think out of the box for a second. All these people on the list have either Jewish or Israeli names."

"So?" asked the chief with growing annoyance.

"So, here's a theory," said Kobi getting out of his chair and beginning to pace around the cramped office. "All these men and women are pretty much in the same range, right? The chief nodded. "Now imagine for a second that the Nazis kidnapped all of these people when they were kids, and placed them throughout the world with access to money and power and ..."

"Wait a second," interrupted the chief, "even if I accept your crazy theory that the Germans kidnapped all these Jewish kids, what would they gain from it? How could they be sure that the children would grow up and do exactly what they wanted them to do?"

"Good question," Kobi snapped. "I'm thrilled that you're finally beginning to ask intelligent questions. I don't know the answer to everything either. But there's enough here to convince you to question Shali Loeberbaum at least and take a good look at his past. See where he comes from, where he was brought up. Did he ever leave the country? How many times? That type of thing. And then we'll begin to get a handle on this thing. Because my gut is telling me that this is the source of Eberhart's future power."

"Eberhart is a little nothing," the chief said. "I mean he's a successful businessman and everything, but his neo-Nazi resurgence stuff is a joke!"

"He may be nothing," Kobi replied, "but he's a serious individual, and he's talking in such a way that he seems to be extremely confident that he'll be able to pull off everything he wants to pull off."

"And," Rafi interjected, "he told me himself that his plans will bring about a monumental victory for Germany without having to fight all over the battlefields of Europe. They will win a war without having to involve the lives of millions of men. It will be a smart war fought by a few. He has a plan!"

"One second," the chief interrupted. "Does Eberhart even know that you have the list?"

"To the best of my knowledge, no," Rafi answered.

"There's your answer," said the chief. "We wait until he does something. When one of these people on the list actually goes nuts and does something that could benefit a man like Eberhart, then we swing into action."

"A preemptive strike is one thousand times more effective than a defensive strike," Kobi snapped at the man. "You know that! Why are you talking this way? Get the agents out there and find out some background information. We did the hard part. All you have to do is some investigative work. Why is that such a big deal?!"

"Kobi, you know as well as I do that I don't have that kind of manpower. My agents are engaged in operations all around the globe. I just can't spare the manpower for such an operation."

"Fine," Kobi said, "so investigate *one* of these people. Start with one."

"I'm sorry, Kobi," the chief said. "No can do."

"Choni Dagan," Kobi said to the balding man across the desk, "have I ever steered you wrong before? Why all this opposition?"

"Because it's a waste of time, that's why," he replied, "and because everyone on that list would raise a major ruckus if I called them in for questioning, that's why. And because you're off the case, that's why!"

"I'm off the case?" Kobi yelled at the chief. "I *am* the case! I have pursued this case for years, and I'm telling you that there's something here."

"Listen," the chief said in a suddenly soft voice, "it's time to retire. Take it easy now. See the grandchildren for a while. You've served your country for long enough."

It was at that point that Kobi motioned for Rafi to follow him out of the office, and it was at that point that Kobi's fragile heart had been broken once again. He all but retired from the agency, and broke off all contact with everyone but Rafi. For a while Rafi had watched the old warrior driving himself to the grave. A man who had been the fieriest, feistiest firebrand had become a depressed old man, who was dying a little bit more every day. It had been especially difficult for Kobi to bear the humiliation, because the chief had appeared to have made the right call. There hadn't been any attacks connected with any of the names on the list. Eberhart himself had lowered his profile in a significant way, perhaps in response to the fact that he had been targeted, and had come to understand that he should close his mouth until he was ready to act.

Eberhart had bided his time. He waited for the perfect moment to trigger the first person listed in the book. It had to be in celebration of a special event. He wasn't committing himself to do that every time, since once he started, the pressure would be on and he would be forced to carry them out at a rapid pace. But at least the first child of the Network should be triggered on an auspicious date. It hadn't been easy for him to make a decision. There were so many important dates in the history of the party, after all. There was the conquering of Paris; the day that Poland fell; the moment the leaders of England and France had decided to grant the Germans Czechoslovakia, hoping that this would keep Hitler satisfied; the annexation of Austria. There were so many dates, so many memories.

In the end, he decided on the date of Hitler's first attempted coup in Munich so many years earlier. It was that failed coup that had sent *Der Fuhrer* to prison, and it was in prison that he had written his monumental work, *Mein Kampf*, My Struggle. In the end, a prison sentence had been extremely valuable for Hitler. But that was Hitler — Eberhart ruminated — always turning every situation to his advantage. They sent him to prison and he wrote a book to change the world's perceptions.

And so, Eberhart triggered the first of the names on that date from his office. The feeling of power that he experienced when he picked up the telephone was immense. He had the sensation of playing master of the world, choosing who lived and who died. To think that he held the future of the universe in his hands, that all he needed to alter the face of the earth was a phone, was mind boggling. Once again, he thought about his father, the genius who had thought up the concept in the first place.

He would never forget that first call. He chose a low-key target for his first attempt. The man that he called had gone immediately and destroyed the main grid that provided electricity and phone services to a major stretch of land, which included an important army base in the United States. It had left a large portion of the States undefended, until the army had been able to repair the damage. No one suspected foul play. No one even knew who had demolished the grid, since the video footage that would have provided that proof had been blown up in the attack as well. The experts had reasoned that there had been some sort of freak accident. But Eberhart knew what happened, and that was enough, because now he knew, beyond a shadow of a doubt, that all the money they had invested over the years was going to justify itself in a big way. The experiment worked! One phone call was all it took, one line of code to the right person's ear and the results were catastrophic. He had thrown a party that night.

The best part about the whole thing was that even if an agent was captured, it wouldn't make any difference at all, because none of them had any clue that he was a ticking time bomb. None of them knew anything at all. Even after one had carried out his attack, he would still be clueless as to why he had done such a thing. He wouldn't be able to defend himself or provide any satisfactory explanation. He would be incarcerated in a prison or an asylum for life. And he, Eberhart, would be free to continue triggering one of them wherever he lived, without any risk to him or his country.

After he had triggered the first one, he found it painfully difficult not to call a second one straight away. The urge to call and send someone out on a wave of destruction was overwhelmingly powerful. But the brilliant businessman from Hamburg controlled himself for a while. He didn't want the United States to know that they were being targeted just yet. There was no rush; time was on his side. The truth of the matter was that America wasn't his main objective in any case. He had other fish to fry. But by involving the States in this operation, he would be warning them through every additional phone call that they would do well to not become involved. The message was that they should not try and stop him, because the weapons at his disposal were too dangerous to mess with.

He had waited a week before triggering the next one. This time it had been a man in Denver, Colorado whose destructive action had caused a blackout to a tremendous area around the Rockies. Inside his heart, he wondered at his reasons for choosing two people from America instead of someone from Israel. He knew deep inside that he was simply afraid to do so. After that run-in with the Israeli agent, he pulled back for quite some time. He came to the realization that he acted foolishly by publicizing his goals so early in the campaign. So he toned down the rhetoric. *Yet even after that,* he wondered, if the violinist had found the Network? After the agent's daring escape on horseback, no less, something at which he never ceased marveling, he had checked the drawer and found everything inside it untouched, exactly the way he had left it. But the man had been so good, so professional. It was highly possible, even probable, that he had discovered the hidden drawer, found the case which hadn't even been locked, and taken pictures of the document inside.

Yes, he was leery of hitting Israel. But it had to be done. So after two attacks on American targets, he had chosen an Israeli and called him in the middle of the night. That had succeeded as well. Now Eberhart knew that time was of the essence, because the Israelis would put the pieces together quicker than the Americans. If there were any clues to be found, they would find them, and then they were going to come after him, and do their best to put an end to his power. That meant that he was going to have to start moving quicker, and that's exactly what he did: a target in England, a target in Belgium, another target in America. He spread it out, sowed the fear and reaped the benefits. He made it very clear that a new player with a lot of talent had come to town.

Tel Aviv, Israel
June 16, 2009

The atmosphere at the meeting was caustic; there was no other way to describe the tenseness or the bitter feelings that Kobi and the head of the Mossad felt for each other. Where once they had been close friends, the belittling tone with which the chief had spoken to Kobi Shapiro, going so far as to almost order him to retire, still rankled among the rank and file in the agency. Kobi Shapiro had accomplished so much for the Mossad in so many ways that it was almost unthinkable that such a thing could have happened. But there had been words, and they still festered. Kobi hadn't been at headquarters since that fateful day, and he was stooped and bent over now. But the fire in his eyes had not been extinguished.

He entered Mossad Headquarters like a returning king, nodding this way and that way. The agents surrounded him and smiled at him. He grunted at them and yelled at them in his gruff, good-natured way. He hadn't changed a bit, and if he had been asked downtown, it meant that his theory had been on target and finally been proven right. It didn't surprise them at all. He was almost always right. They were enjoying the pleasure of watching the chief eat his words. Rafi met Kobi at the entrance of the building, and they embraced with great emotion. Although there had been no rift between them — no argument or disagreement — Rafi was still an agent of the Mossad, and that meant that he had little to no time for socializing. He barely had an opportunity to see his uncle, the Kolodover Rebbe, and whatever free time he had left, he utilized for learning with Naftali Kenighofer. The man's talent was to learning what Rafi's talent was to the violin, and Rafi loved studying with him. They were well matched intellectually, and whenever they got together, their voices escalated, fingers pointed at each other, and the pleasure was clearly obvious on both faces. But the bottom line had been that he hadn't been in touch with Kobi for a while.

Kobi understood, however. He knew the schedule an agent of his rank kept, and he didn't hold it against him. Now he hugged him with real warmth, and then arm in arm they headed upstairs to the top floor, returning to the office of the man who had thrown Kobi out and now needed him back. There were a number of high-ranking officers in the room when they entered. The Mossad knew what kind of a nightmare they had on their hands. Thus far, none of the other security agencies knew anything, and they weren't sure when they were going to let them in on it. In Israel it often seems like everyone had a favorite nephew who's a journalist, and it's not uncommon for secrets of the highest national priority to end up as grist for the journalistic mill. That was not going to happen here. This secret was going to remain a secret for as long as they could keep it that way.

The chief was smoking. He shoved a pack toward Kobi when they entered the room.

"No thanks, Choni," Kobi said. "I don't smoke anymore."

There was a shocked silence in the room as the assembled digested *that* bit of news. Kobi Shapiro had been a chain-smoker for years. Could a leopard change his spots?

"Just kidding," he said and laughed. The others laughed as well. Kobi had always been famous for his practical jokes and sharp wit. He hadn't changed. Good. He was still as sharp as ever. Good. They needed every razor-edged brain they could get. The chief began first.

"I apologize for the way I treated you, Kobi," he began. This was another first. Nobody on Choni's staff could ever recall him apologizing to anyone. It was simply not done. And here he was sincerely asking Kobi for forgiveness. Obviously the situation was critical, and this was his way of letting Kobi know this. Just as obviously, Kobi knew it already. He wouldn't hold sharp words against the chief. Kobi knew that everyone made mistakes from time to time, but this one was a huge mistake. It was time for damage control.

"O.K., here's the situation," the chief began his briefing. "There have been a number of attacks over the last few months around the globe. None of my counterparts in Paris, London or New York have any clue to who is behind them. The only ones who have any idea at this point in time is us. We know. Now," said the chief holding his cigarette between his fingers and eyeballing every person sitting in the room, "I have to warn you, gentlemen. What we are about to discuss in this room is so sensitive that if any of it leaks to the wrong people, I will personally track down the man who let the cat out of the bag and make sure that he suffers long and horribly." There was no smile on the chief's face. "We cannot afford any slips to the media in this case! I hope that I have made myself perfectly clear here!" All heads nodded in acknowledgment of the chief's severe warning.

"O.K., now that that matter is settled, a little background about the case." He took a deep puff on his smoke, coughed harshly from deep in his lungs and took a drink of water from a glass on the table.

"About three years ago, Kobi Shapiro chose an agent to carry out a mission that had been troubling him for decades. I was a young agent when Kobi carried out a daring raid on a top-secret gathering of the most influential Nazis in South America. I was not one of the agents chosen to go along." Kobi favored the chief with a look of intense scrutiny. Maybe that was the reason Choni had been acting so bull headed? He had felt slighted; felt as if he'd missed his chance. How idiotic!

"The raid was successful and unsuccessful at the same time," Choni continued. "The goal of the operation had been to capture Josef Mengele. In this, they were unsuccessful. However, Kobi Shapiro managed to gain possession of a book that had been under alarm in Wolfgang Zeivald's office. The agents managed to escape with the book, although one of them was killed during the escape. When they arrived back in Israel, the higher-ups examined the book and determined there was too little information. They weren't familiar with any of the names in the book. It was written in code and there were no clues. It was simply a book of names. The mission to uncover the secret of the book was put on hold, as other more nationally high-priority operations came along. But Kobi held on to the book as the years and decades passed by. He knew that this book was important. There was a feeling deep inside his heart telling him that he must never forget the importance of the book. And he didn't.

"A few years ago, Kobi Shapiro recruited Rafi Ganim, world-famous violinist, as an agent to the Mossad, with the intention that he use his ingenuity and skills to uncover the secret of the book. Against his will, Rafi Ganim traveled to Germany and gained a reputation as the head of a splinter group of neo-Nazis, men who were not interested in waiting for Dietrich Eberhart to actually fulfill his many promises of action. In reality, the men under the command of Rafi Ganim were our agents. They carried out numerous attacks on Jewish institutions throughout Europe, taking every precaution to ensure that there was no loss of life while managing to make it appear as if the neo-Nazis were about to reemerge with great power. In the end, Eberhart and Rafi Ganim met at Eberhart's Club Salute.

"Eberhart was taken with Rafi, but Rafi challenged him to live up to his rhetoric. Eberhart invited Rafi to his estate and they had a conversation where Eberhart hinted at some future events. He boasted without revealing facts of his ability to fight a war on a tremendous scale without using a lot of men. They retired for the night. Rafi used a spray to put everyone in the house into a deep sleep, then broke into Eberhart's office and discovered the second copy of the book. This copy proved to be a fount of information. The title of the book was 'The Network.' There were names in the book, names of people located all over the world. Every country that fancies itself a world player had at least a few names.

"It was a network of agents. Every one of them was working in a position of power. Every one of them had the ability to commit significant acts of sabotage. We can only assume that Eberhart has begun with acts that cause less mayhem, and is moving steadily higher in his attempt at blackmailing the world, in his quest for the renewal of the Nazi dream. Interestingly enough, the agents listed in the book — and there are 150 of them — every one of them has a Jewish name! They were all Jewish, kidnapped by the Nazis as children and sent away from European shores to be raised as gentiles, and educated to fill any position the Nazis felt would prove to be most valuable. This is The Network, Eberhart's plan for world domination."

The chief paused for a few seconds. He was obviously very uncomfortable with what he had to say next.

"Kobi and Rafi Ganim brought me the information and the book on the Network, and I'm ashamed to say that I didn't take it seriously. I have always considered Eberhart to be slightly insane, and a man more concerned with his image than anything else. But I was wrong and Kobi was right. He said that we should send out agents to every name on the list, track them down — those whose names we recognize and those whom we don't — and put a stop to them before they put a stop to us. I objected on the grounds of manpower logistics, and because I didn't really believe that anything was going to happen. Not only that, but I forced Kobi into taking early retirement. I forced a legend, a miracle man, to leave a job that he loved and in which he was extremely valuable to us, because he made me uncomfortable. Ultimately, it was he who was proven right and not me.

"Thank G-d, it is still early in the game. Eberhart doesn't know whether we have the book or not. We can preempt him. I will be sending out over a hundred teams of agents around the world. Every team will have at least one or two top-notch agents, and one extremely qualified psychology professional. If the professional has studied hypnotherapy, all the better. We have to reach as many of the Network agents as we can before Eberhart calls and triggers them. We have ascertained that a phone call is the trigger but we could not break the code regarding the words used. We need to understand where they are coming from, get into their minds and penetrate their defenses. We must find out who they really are, and break through the barriers. We have to turn them around and make them see who the real enemy is, so that they disobey his command when he calls them up. That is the plan.

"Our agents will be briefed this evening. The Mossad has a list of the top-ranking, most successful psychiatrists in the country, and you will be getting in touch with the ones we need to work with, today. Within two days, the majority of the teams should be making their way to the homes of the remaining sleeper agents around the globe. It will be a difficult mission for everyone involved: for the agents and doctors because they are going to have to change a person's entire mind-set regarding who he or she is, and much more difficult for the actual people themselves, because it is they who are going to discover that they have been living a lie. They'll discover that they are extremely potent and dangerous weapons, and nothing like the people they thought they were.

"If G-d forbid, we are unable to actualize a change in their minds, then unfortunately the chance for them to continue to survive in their current state is not going to happen. In short, we are considering them extreme risks, and they will be taken away for medical examination. It goes without saying that if any of them are triggered during actual meetings with our agents, our men have permission to neutralize the threat in any way they see fit."

The chief gulped and swallowed before continuing. "Kobi Shapiro had been brought up to date on all phases of the operation and will be in charge from now on. You will all report to him. That's it for now. I want to hear good news soon!"

The chief stood and left the room while Kobi took over the briefing, assigning agents to different handlers, clarifying details and taking command, exactly the way it had always been. There was a calmness in the room, despite the feeling of danger in the air, because Kobi was back and in control. The men trusted him implicitly to take care of them in the best way that he knew how.

"When you leave this room," Kobi said, "you will brief the men under your command, again stressing complete and total secrecy. Breaches will not be tolerated in the slightest. When you finish, every team will drive to the office of the psychiatrist assigned to them and inform them they have been chosen to accompany the team. You can expect threats, displeasure and noncompliance on the part of the doctors, but you are authorized to use any means at your disposal to ensure that they acquiesce. Ultimately, they have no choice but to agree to accompany your men. They will, of course, be compensated for their time. We may be kidnapping them, but we will not be stealing from them. That's it. Every agent has received a list of instructions with the location and all known information on his principal. I expect to be updated every five hours. My phone will always be on, and you can reach me at any hour of the day or night. Thank you and get a move on."

There was a scrambling of chairs as the assembled rose and made a beeline for their offices. Mossad agents around the country were alerted to make their way to headquarters as soon as possible. This was a Red Alert situation, and that meant: Disregard all traffic laws and do whatever it took for you to get to the office as quickly as you could.

They came equipped with suitcases packed for a trip. They would receive a significant amount of cash, along with a credit card that could be used in time of emergency. When the light flashed Red Alert, you dropped everything and ran. And that's precisely what over 100 agents did.

Every cloud has a silver lining, and for Rafi the silver lining was pretty obvious. It even had a name. It was called Tamar or Tami. This was his opportunity to work with his sister: a sister whom he never thought would see the redeeming factors in the Jewish way of life, yet who had surprised him in her acceptance of whom he had become. She had come to feel pride in her "spiritual" brother.

Tamar was an expert hypnotherapist, one of a handful in the country who had earned international recognition. Rafi had read her books, and found that he couldn't put them down. Aside from her presentation of brand-new theories, her case files were fascinating. Tamar had an original style of writing, which caught her readers and pulled them into her books, turning dry factual material into a textbook that the average layman actually wanted to read.

So Rafi was going to make Tami a part of his team, and together they would be traveling in the weeks to come. It wasn't as if she had a choice. If it wasn't him, it would be someone else, that much was clear. This was a national emergency; there was no question of her refusal. Besides, she had on her own volition offered her assistance to him in the past. Now was the time to take her up on her offer.

He left the Mossad building and got into his car. Unmarried, he had saved his salary and purchased a better car than the agency provided. Consequently, he drove the latest model Jeep and loved it. He enjoyed sitting high up in traffic and felt that it was worth every dollar he had spent. He became trapped in traffic near her office for 20 minutes, but he called ahead and knew that she would be waiting for him whatever time he arrived. He parked in the office building's underground parking lot, and took the elevator up to the 23rd floor.

The secretary buzzed him in and he passed through a long corridor with doors leading to a number of other doctors' offices. Tami had the corner office with an amazing view of the sea. If this was his office, he wouldn't be able to get any work done at all. He'd be standing at the window, gazing at the sea for hours at a time. Tami sat with her back to the view. He admired her work ethic, and didn't try to persuade her otherwise. He was proud of her. It was amazing what she had accomplished in such a short time. To be internationally known at such a young age was an impressive accomplishment.

Tami was sitting at her desk and working on the computer when he entered her office. She indicated that he should take a seat, and he sank into one of the ultracomfortable chairs. The office had been designed with the patient's comfort and well-being in mind; it reflected the tremendous amount of thought that had been expended on it. She mouthed that she was just going to be a minute, and sure enough, within seconds she was shutting down the computer. Then she joined him on the couch.

"What's the big emergency?" she asked him, a jocular smile on her face. Ten minutes later, the smile was gone and was replaced with a look of intense concentration and worry.

"So you want me to cancel all my clients for the next few weeks, just like that, and waltz off with you to the States?" she asked him.

"Something like that," he said. "It's not just you, of course. Almost every big name in your field is being conscripted into the Mossad for this operation. They will all be compensated based on their usual fees. Obviously I wanted you since you're the best."

"Naturally," she replied, bobbing her head in mock acceptance of his compliment. "So now what?" she asked.

"Now we drive to your house, you pack your stuff — your professional gear, the amount of clothing you need for a week and a half — and then you take your well-worn passport and we hit the airport for the next available flight, which," he consulted his watch, "is leaving in exactly three hours. So we'd better hurry."

She walked to her desk. "Nava," she said to her secretary over the intercom, "please cancel all my clients for the next week and a half." She listened to the surprised voice on the other end.

"Tell them whatever you want," she said. "Tell them it's a family emergency; tell them I'm off on a secret mission. Make up something, be creative. You're the best!" She turned off the intercom.

"O.K.," she said. "I need my laptop, some of my books ... " She walked around the room mumbling to herself. Seven minutes later, she was ready to leave and they took the elevator to the parking lot. There they split up. Rafi drove his Jeep, and Tami her car, and they met at her home, where she packed and had something to eat, all in record time. Tami was a world traveler. She knew how to move when necessary. Neither wanted to leave a car in the airport's long-term parking lot, so they ordered a taxi. They didn't talk much on the way to the airport. Rafi was silent, because he knew that his sister had just experienced a rather startling afternoon, and needed time to digest the fact that she on her way to America for a completely unexpected trip.

They arrived at the airport, and Rafi made his confident way to an unobtrusive door at the back of Terminal A. He knocked, and they were ushered into a section of the airport that Tami had not known existed. Their passports were hurriedly scrutinized, and then they were taken to a special lounge adjacent to the departure gate, where they waited for the final call for their flight. When the lounge had emptied, they were ushered onto the plane and into the First Class section. It was unoccupied except for two businessmen who were busy on their laptops. Ten minutes later, the plane was already on the runway, engines rumbling in preparation for takeoff. Rafi was explaining the background to the entire situation.

"You might think that the origin of this trip can be traced to my courageous act of attacking the terrorist with my violin on the night of the show," he said to her. "But the truth is, the saga began a long, long time ago. The old man who recruited me had been waiting for many years to meet someone whom he felt was the right person to send to Eberhart. For some odd reason, which I still don't fully understand, he decided that I was the man for the job."

"And he just happened to be right," Tamar interjected.

"I'm sure that there are plenty of agents who could have done just as good a job as I did," Rafi said.

"Maybe, maybe not. Bottom line, you were the one who came home with the goods."

The conversation between them flowed for hours. Tamar took the opportunity to ask his opinion on some of the questions that had always plagued her about the religious lifestyle, and Rafi answered her as best as he could.

"Keep in mind that I'm just a beginner myself," he said more than once.

"It's O.K., for a beginner you know an incredible amount," she replied.

They were halfway through the flight before they decided to call it a night.

The next thing they knew, the pilot was instructing them to buckle their seat belts for the approaching landing at Kennedy Airport.

33

Rafi Ganim

Ithaca, New York
May 3, 2009

Mordy was spending an increasing amount of time at the home of Cardinal Frost. There was a good reason for this: Simply speaking, he was afraid that his friend would become so depressed that he would seek to end it all. He recounted his trip to Europe to Mordy, or at least whatever he could recall of his trip, and the whole thing seemed bizarre. Why didn't Frost remember everything? His mind was as clear as that of a 30-year old, and his memory was like a steel trap. There was no easy way to account for the fact that a man in such good health shouldn't be able to remember a simple thing such as his itinerary! Frost knew that traumatic events had occurred in the course of his travels, but he couldn't remember what they were. All he knew was that his life had changed considerably over the course of the trip. and things would never be the same.

Even if Frost had never been truly happy with his life of solitude as a priest, at least he had been able to console himself with his sharp brain. But since this was no longer the case, it was hard for him to see the point of living.

There was one consolation for the old man: Mordy and his refreshing outlook. Frost soaked up the stories that Mordy told him about Israel and yeshivah life in Jerusalem. He was fascinated by the whole learning approach, and he thought that Reb Zack was an amazing person. Mordy told Frost about his hiatus, when he left the yeshivah world to find himself, and how he had done just that on a mountaintop in the middle of the night, as he sat and studied Gemara alongside a wounded boy. Frost lapped it all up. It was clear that he was living vicariously through Mordy, now that he considered his own life to have come to an end, and that he didn't care what happened any longer.

"Too many disappointments," was how he put it to Mordy. But Mordy was no stranger to disappointments, and he knew how debilitating they could be for a person's mental and even physical health. So he did his best to keep the cardinal strong, and shared with him as many anecdotes as he could remember from yeshivah life. He talked and talked, trying to infuse as much joy into the cardinal's existence because he realized that Frost was toying with the idea of permanent retirement from life. He knew that the effective way to make someone happy was to share your happiness with them, and there were no moments in Mordy's life when he was happier than when he was learning Torah. So that's what he began talking about: How amazing and inspirational it was, and how much he had grown as a person since he began to learn.

It shouldn't have come as a surprise to him, but eventually Frost asked him if they could study Torah together. Mordy didn't know what to do. Frost wasn't Jewish and the *halachah* was quite clear that a Jew is not allowed to teach a gentile words of Torah. He also thought it was strange that a gentile — particularly a gentile who had spent all his adult years in the service of the church — would possess this desire to study Torah. He was a cardinal of the church!

So he called up Reb Zack and asked him to clarify the matter for him. Reb Zack called him back two days later with the *psak*. The *issur* of teaching Torah to a gentile was only an issue when it came to Torah that didn't pertain to the gentile. However, any portion of Torah that dealt with the seven commandments that a gentile is obligated to fulfill could be studied by a gentile, even in depth, which meant that Mordy was able to introduce Cardinal Jason Leonard Frost to the wonders of Gemara.

They focused on the *sugyas* that had to do with *avodah zarah* and the like: activities forbidden to Jew and gentile alike. Cardinal Frost took to Gemara like a fish to water. They would begin from the original Bible text and trace the steps until the actual Gemara, because Frost really wanted to understand how the rabbis had come to their rulings. He was enthralled! Mordy was reminded of a newly minted *baal teshuvah* discovering the treasure that awaits him for the first time. He hesitantly explained to Frost what his limitations were, worried that this might put a damper on his enthusiasm. But instead, the fact that there were boundaries and strict guidelines only made him more excited and enthusiastic about his newfound favorite activity. He had stopped studying Christian theology years before, having found that it did nothing for him. But this was like a newfound passion!

After studying together for over a week, Frost informed Mordy emphatically that there was no way he was going to go on studying from English translations. Instead, he had decided to teach himself to read and write Hebrew. The fact that he was an older man didn't scare him. Mordy looked on in amazement, because the Frost who was seated before him was a completely different person from the depressed Frost he had encountered on his return from Israel. There was an inner peace radiating from the man, a glow of contentment and satisfaction that Mordy knew could only be attributed to Torah learning. Seeing how much inner peace the cardinal was gaining by the day gave Mordy a feeling that soon he would be able to return to Israel and his own learning as well.

England
June 17, 2009

It took the neo-Nazis of England about one day to show everyone that they had become a force with whom to be reckoned. In Gateshead alone, the damage they inflicted on the Jewish community ran into the hundreds of thousands of pounds. It took the police a long time to respond, and by the time they arrived, the damage had been done. The majority of the storefronts in the Jewish neighborhoods had been shattered and utterly destroyed in a way that was reminiscent of *Kristallnacht*. A tremendous amount of looting had been done by the neo-Nazis, with the locals joining in with fervor. The Jews of the town had barricaded themselves into their homes, and were busy calling everyone from the prime minister on down. By the time the police put in a real appearance, the ring leaders were long gone, pockets bulging with money and goods. Spray-painted across every storefront was the slogan: *This is only the beginning. We'll be back, and that's a fact.*

The future of the Jews in England suddenly seemed grave indeed.

~

All over Europe, the Nazi party had erupted after decades of silence. They roamed the streets in packs, like rabid dogs, biting anyone they chose to bite, attacking anyone who looked at them the wrong way. The gentile populace was afraid to antagonize them, especially after the leading newspaper in Paris wrote an editorial condemning the Nazi renewal movement in the strongest terms, and the paper's offices were firebombed later that night in retaliation. The Jews of France were terrified to leave their homes. Many got into their cars, drove to the airport and boarded the first available flight for Israel. Others left the cities in droves, heading for the countryside and the relative peace that could be found there.

The private security firms had never had a better few weeks of business since their inception. They had been hired by every Jewish-owned business to guard their enterprises. But that turned out to be a bad move, since it proved conclusively which businesses were clearly Jewish, turning those stores into targets. The president of France called a press conference, where he declared a state of emergency and stated unequivocally that he was calling in the armed forces to restore peace to the streets of the nation.

The morning after the army pulled into Paris, the boulevards were full of armed soldiers patrolling. But there was no longer anything to do. All the rabble-rousers had disappeared, leaving behind slogans which had been neatly painted across the major streets in the Jewish neighborhoods: *Juden, we will be back, we promise. Move to Israel now!*

Many of the French Jews heeded their advice. There was no future for Jews in France anymore. The trouble was there were few places to go. The Jews of England were living in terrible fear of their neighbors, destroying any ideas of emigrating there, and the rest of the European continent was faring no better. Israel, as everyone knew, was in the midst of a daily missile war, and even the United States, which had once been the stronghold of a safe haven for people everywhere, had changed dramatically after its own incidents of anti-Semitism.

To make matters worse, no one was standing up to take responsibility for the vandalism and terrorism that was taking place. Everything needs a face, and the fact that there was no public face to the menace made things infinitely more terrifying! The name Dietrich Eberhart was on the lips of people everywhere, but he had not yet claimed responsibility for what was happening. There was no one to point to, no doorstep for the police to visit. The units of neo-Nazis were mobile, and as soon as they inflicted their damage on any one place, they got right back onto their motorcycles and moved on, always one step ahead of the police.

Through it all, every few days, the world was struck by another insane attack, initiated by someone who had been the pillar of his respective society. Men who held the most prominent positions were destroying themselves, as they committed acts of sabotage and mayhem that appeared to be completely disconnected from one another. But by now, too many of these attacks had occurred to be considered random happenings. And the name Eberhart was being whispered on more and more lips, but with a growing dread, because it seemed as if the man was capable of doing anything he set his mind to, with devastating results.

Members of the Nazi gangs were arrested. But the police were soon afraid to arrest more of them, when one of the prisons in Stuttgart was attacked by a large force of Nazis, the prison guards were overpowered and their prisoners released. Europe had become a playground for the mentally insane, and the longer things continued, the more incidents were attributed to Dietrich Eberhart and the powerful underground army that he controlled. The scariest detail of all was the fact that Eberhart was no longer visible. He had gone underground and was conducting his personal war from a safe house. No one other than the three people closest to him knew where he was, which might have helped if they hadn't disappeared as well.

Kennedy Airport, N.Y.
June 18, 2009

There was a car waiting for them when they arrived. They checked at the Hertz counter and it had been reserved for them. This operation was costing the Mossad a small fortune, but obviously there was no choice. Rafi decided that they needed a couple of hours to rest before heading out to Long Island and the home of the man the agency had assigned to them. Rafi booked two suites at the Airport Ramada, and insisted that they catch at least three hours of sleep. They were jet lagged right now, and danger or no danger, there was no point in driving to Long Island if they wouldn't be of any use once they reached their destination. Tamar told him that she was much too keyed up to sleep, but he gently insisted that she at least try. In the end, both of them yielded to exhaustion for a few hours. It helped. After showers, some food and strong coffee, they were in business and ready to drive out to Long Island and meet sleeper agent Kevin Barns.

Barns was one of a handful of men who was trusted with full access to a vast amount of extremely sensitive material. Serving as he did in the capacity of adviser to the chairman of the Federal Reserve, he was in the unique position of one who knew more about the finances of the United States than almost anyone else in the world. He also knew which buttons to press in order to scramble many of the complicated computer programs that were constantly working overtime as the Federal Reserve adjusted and readjusted the interest rates and monitored the dollar in relation to a host of foreign currencies all around the world. In short, Kevin Barns was in a position to cause infinite harm to American finances if he so desired.

At the moment, he was just fine. But that was subject to change.

~

The rental car drove smoothly. Rafi took the Southern State Parkway toward Long Island. The car was outfitted with a GPS system, and Rafi marveled at the world of today. No more getting lost and having to stop at a gas station to ask for directions; none of that. In his opinion, GPS was for cars what spell check was to computers. They made good time with little conversation along the way, and a stop for some junk food and energy drinks. As they approached the town of Great Neck, they planned their strategy. Basically, they were going to surprise this guy with the shock of a lifetime. Here he was a high-end executive with a major job in the financial sector, probably looking forward to his retirement, enjoying the occasional game of basketball with his kids. They were going to come waltzing in, just like that and inform him that he was not who he thought he was. Not at all.

He imagined himself to be Mr. Kevin Barns, but in reality, his name was Pinchus Kirschenbaum. He wouldn't remember that of course, but that's where Tamar entered into the picture. She would do her best to help him recall any fragments of the past that were still in his memory box. Then they would deprogram him, take him elsewhere, away from his phone and e-mail.

They had spoken to the witnesses of the first few attacks and they all said the same thing. A phone call had been the catalyst. The phone rang and the target answered. The target usually listened for a few seconds and then took off to carry out whatever it was that he had been programmed to do. So they had to get this guy away from a phone, put him somewhere he couldn't be reached. But he would have to believe them first. That would take time. They would have to be convincing and believable. Hopefully, he would agree to cooperate with them. The GPS indicated to turn left and another left, and they found themselves on a long, well-tended block, with houses that were close in size to mansions with expensive, foreign cars lining the driveways.

They pulled up to the curb and parked. The street was completely silent. Every lawn was covered with a blanket of lush green grass. It was still early enough in the day that Barns would be home. He usually went into the office late and remained until late at night. He was a workaholic, and he provided very nicely for his family. They headed up the pebbled walkway to the front door. From the side of the house came the thumping sound of a basketball hitting the pavement. There was a grunt and a heave. Whoever was playing shot the ball. There was the sound of the ball hitting the backboard and the shout of triumph. Rafi hoped that whoever was out there playing ball would be able to continue their idyllic lifestyle for a long time to come.

They reached the front door and Tamar rang the bell. They rang again, and the door was opened by a woman in an apron who introduced herself as Angela, the Barns' maid.

"Is Mr. Barns in?" Rafi asked.

"Yes, he is," she replied. "Who should I say wants to see him?"

"Tell him Dr. Tamar and Rafi Ganim are here to see him."

"Is he expecting you?"

"No, I'm afraid not, but it's extremely important that we see him right now!" Something in their demeanor must have been convincing, because she held the door open and said, "Please come in."

She led them into the house, past a living room with a long white couch and a baby grand piano at the end of the room. There were a number of family portraits displayed on its sparkling surface. They passed a dining room with a polished banquet-sized table. Rafi was not an art expert, but the pictures clearly were all originals. Overall, they were in a home that was well cared for and loved, and Rafi hesitated at being the one to destroy the preconceived notions of an educated family man such as Kevin Barns.

Angela led them through the house into Barns' office, an understated room filled with expensive electronic equipment. A Toshiba desktop held court in the center of the desk, as swirling pictures of the universe flew by on the screensaver. This man obviously knew his place in the overall scheme of things. He was a mover and a shaker; a man who got things done. How was he going to take the news that his entire life had been a lie, a sham, a mockery? How would he react to the news that he had not been born in Englewood, New Jersey, but rather Krakow, Poland; that his name was not really Kevin Barns, but rather Pinchus Kirschenbaum? They could hear footsteps approaching and a man's voice asking, "What are their names again?"

"Dr. Tamar and Rafi Ganim," the maid replied.

"Thank you, Angela," he said, his voice growing in volume as he approached the room. He entered the room with assurance. This was a man with presence. He was in the process of putting the finishing touches on his tie. His shirt was a light blue and crisply starched. His initials were embroidered on the cuffs. His hair was wavy, and a little bit longer than was stylish. The corners of his mouth were permanently turned up, suggesting a smile. His eyes were the color of topaz. He came across extremely affable, but he was clearly in a rush.

"Good morning," he said as he headed over to his desk.

"Good morning," they replied.

"To what do I owe the honor of your visit?" he asked them. "Have we perhaps met before?"

"I'm afraid not, Mr. Barns," Rafi said. "But nevertheless, believe me that what we have to tell you is probably the most important piece of news you have heard in 20 years."

"I'm all ears," Barns said.

"It would help if you would stop fiddling around," Tamar said to him sharply. "My name is Dr. Tamar Ganim, doctor of psychology and hypnotherapy in Tel Aviv. This is my brother, Rafi Ganim, who works in the field of Israeli intelligence. We are serious people and we appreciate how busy you are as well. You can rest assured that we wouldn't be here at all, if it wasn't absolutely necessary!"

Perhaps her tone of voice got through to him, for he gave them a good look for the first time and pulled out the leather chair that was behind the desk.

"O.K., what's going on?" he asked them in a mock defeated tone of voice.

"Mr. Barns," Rafi interjected, "what I'm about to tell you is going to shock you and make you angry and confused. You are not going to know how to deal with the news, but I assure you, that every word that I'm going to say is completely true."

Barns' eyes narrowed with suspicion. "What are you talking about?" he demanded. "You're being very dramatic. Just come to the point, because I have to get to the office!"

"Pinchus Kirschenbaum," Rafi yelled out suddenly. "Little Pinchus from Krakow. How did you become Kevin Barns?" The face of the man in front of them had become white.

"Whhaaatt ... " he stammered. "What are you talking about?"

Tamar took over. "There was once a little boy who lived in Krakow, Poland," she began. "He was a smart little boy and he was part of a loving family. But soon, events began happening all around him and he couldn't understand what was going on! He was so little that his parents weren't able to explain that their entire world was falling apart. All he knew was that their street had become a scary place, full of the heavy tread of soldiers in long coats with guns in their hands and menace on their faces ... "

She spoke in a monotone, keeping her voice perfectly even. He was shaking his head as the tears started coming to his eyes.

"Yes," he whispered. "Pinchus."

"You were taken away," she continued, "sent off to a faraway place, to be raised by strangers — strangers with blond hair and smiles — who told you all sorts of stories, yet nothing of the truth. You are Pinchus Kirschenbaum from Krakow, Poland. But you were raised by strangers who told you that your name was Kevin Barns. And they controlled your brain and made you study, and sent you off to learn all about numbers and how they apply to an economy. But deep inside your mind, you can still recall the way it really was back in the home of your youth ... "

She let her voice trail off, allowing his mind to go back in time, to find itself.

Rafi marveled at her power. She had been able to get past his defenses in a very short time. Now he was white faced, quiet, and remembering, and for the first time since they had set out on this mission, Rafi felt that maybe they had a chance to stop this thing. Barns' eyes were full of tears. The tears were poised on the brink, not falling. Rafi realized that he looked just like a little boy who wanted to cry, but was trying to hold himself back. Tamar had succeeded in regressing the man in front of her, pulling him back to his early years. She was amazing. They were going to get through to this guy. They were going to explain to him that his whole life had been one big manipulation, that he was a pawn in the hands of a shadowy group of people who had shaped his personality and put him right where they needed him most. They had so much to say and so much to explain. But they were getting through to him. It was incredible!

It was such an eerie moment: The two of them sitting there with Barns frozen across from them like a statue. They were on the verge of a breakthrough. It was at that exact moment that the worst possible thing happened.

The phone rang.

It wasn't the phone that sat on the desk in front of Barns. Rafi knew that if it had been that phone, Barns would have let the answering machine pick up. It was a red phone on a shelf behind his desk. Instinctively, Rafi knew that this was a terrible thing, and it was happening right before their very eyes. They watched as the terrified lost-child look left his eyes, replaced with a cold determination and a cunning intelligence. They had been dismissed without a second thought. The moment that phone rang, Barns had straightened his shoulders and was ready to leave on his mission, like a soldier reporting for war.

He jumped from his chair and answered the phone. He listened quietly. He replaced the phone in its cradle and turned to leave the room.

"Don't go," Rafi said to him.

"Don't go," Tamar warned him. "You're making a mistake!"

Rafi approached him, a friendly expression on his face, his body in a nonthreatening posture. He was about to hit the man with a body slam, but Barns saw it coming. Before Rafi had a chance to do anything, Barns punched him in the face and followed that up with a right hook to the stomach and kicked his feet out from underneath him! The man was in late middle age, but was fighting like a 20 year-old! Rafi fell to the floor. Barns stepped over him lightly and ran for the door. Tamar began to rise, but Barns didn't even bother looking at her. While Rafi struggled painfully to his feet, they could hear the sounds of their host running down the hallway toward the front door. Tamar helped Rafi into a chair, and then she ran outside in time to see Kevin Barns speeding out of the driveway in a Porsche Carrera. They would never be able to catch up to someone driving a car like that. The Carrera had enough horsepower to outrun almost anything, and Rafi was in no condition to drive at that point anyway.

Instead, Rafi picked up the phone in the study and placed a call to the Mossad switchboard emergency number that was being manned 24-hours a day.

"Yes," said the clipped voice on the other end.

"This is Rafi and Tamar Ganim," he said.

"Go on," said the voice.

"We were just with Kevin Barns, assistant to the chairman of the Federal Reserve. In the middle of our conversation with him, a phone rang, a separate line. He answered, listened for a few seconds and instantly changed his persona. When I tried to prevent him from leaving the house he attacked me and proved to be quite the fighter. He left me on the floor of his office, ran out of the house, got into his Porsche and was last seen headed to what I can only assume is his office and the bank of computers that he controls. This can only mean that he received his orders to throw at least part of the financial world into chaos."

"Go after him," said the unidentified voice.

"There is no way that we'll be able to catch this guy," Rafi said, getting more and more agitated at the turn the conversation was taking. "He was driving a Porsche and I have a rental car. He'll be out of sight by the time I hit the highway. It's pointless."

"I have no free agents in the vicinity," said the voice. "You're going to have to go after him yourselves."

"Where's Kobi Shapiro?" Rafi asked furiously. "Where's the agent in charge?"

"Agent Shapiro suffered a ministroke last night and has been hospitalized. He is unable to take any calls. Now stop wasting time and go after Barns!"

Rafi was so angry he threw the phone across the room, only realizing the moment after he threw it that he was going to need it again. Tamar was looking at him with a mixture of curiosity and fear on her face; fear at their situation, and curiosity, because she could see that he had some sort of plan up his sleeve and wanted to know what it was. He removed a tiny notebook from his jacket pocket and flipped through the pages, searching for a particular number. He moved his fingers down the lines of the page until he found the one he was looking for and then he dialed the number.

Tamar watched her brother in fascination, not recognizing him for a moment.

"Hello," Rafi said, "is this Nick Harrow, head of Homeland Security for the State of New York?" He listened carefully for a moment.

"Yes," Rafi said, "I know this is an unlisted number, and that should tell you something about the person who's calling you! It doesn't matter how I obtained this number, but believe me, what I'm about to tell you is crucial for the security of the City of New York and for the entire country as well. And no, I am not being dramatic or overstating anything!

"I am at the home of a suspect right now. The suspect has escaped and is heading toward the city in a silver Porsche Carrera as we speak. I do not know if he is armed, but would have to assume so. He is highly dangerous and mentally unstable. He is heading to his office right now. This is the address." He repeated the address twice. "I repeat: This is not a joke. This is the real thing. Suspect capable of anything! He might even have a bomb with him! The N.Y.P.D. must intercept the man before he does anything that cannot be rectified. His name is Barns, Kevin Barns, and he is employed by the Federal Reserve."

"And you are, sir?" asked a confused Nick Harrow.

"It doesn't matter. I cannot identify myself without compromising my cover. But this could have worldwide ramifications! Trust your gut on this one, sir. I'm sure there were times when you had to do that in the past. Listen to your heart and you'll know that I'm telling you the truth!" There was a moment of silence, of indecision. Finally the man spoke.

"O.K., sir, I will have them intercept him when he comes into the city. Any idea which direction he's coming from?"

"Stop asking questions," Rafi almost screamed. "Just get some cops over to the tunnel and the bridges and have some others waiting for him at his office just in case he manages to elude all of them and actually reaches his place of work. Do you hear me? This is Red Alert priority!"

Rafi hung up the phone. "Let's go," he said to Tamar, "right now! We certainly overstayed our welcome in this house."

They left the Barns' home, not sure where to go next. The fact that Kobi was in the hospital put a huge damper on the whole operation. Now there was some peon manning the phone, who was completely clueless.

"Listen," Tamar said to him, "we were originally supposed to go to the next person on our list if we weren't able to meet with Barns. Well, Barns is out of the picture now, so I say we move on to the next man on our list and get over there as soon as we can. Sounds good?"

"I don't really see that we have much of a choice, do we?" he said. "I just hope they manage to stop Barns in time, because he can really cause great havoc if he isn't caught. Who's the next name on our list?"

"That would be Father Jason Leonard Frost, cardinal of the State of New York."

"They like playing hardball, don't they?" he said. "Well then, let's play."

~

Undisclosed location in Berlin
June 18, 2009

The command center was located in a sprawling underground bunker that had been refurbished over the past two years. The bunker had been in existence for many, many years, resulting in cracks developing in the foundations of the buildings nearby. The Berlin Construction Company was called in to repair the area. If one delved into the ownership of the Berlin Consturction Company, by sifting through an intricate maze it was possible, but highly impossible to uncover that the parent company was Eberhart Construction. Consequently, they were able to go into the bunker and develop it further without anyone paying attention. There was so much mess around — so many boards and piles of bricks and cranes and all sorts of machinery — that nobody would have had any clue as to what was going on even if they had been on the lookout for something suspicious, which they hadn't. As much as Eberhart himself was under scrutiny by the security forces of West Germany for his obvious and open leanings to the far right, his company was still the most respected construction company in Germany. It had a reputation for excellence, and the police did not dream that he was mixing business activities with private action. That meant that Eberhart was safely ensconced under the ground in a place that had been made operable long before, and which he had renovated under the very noses of the West German police force.

If it hadn't been this place, it would have been somewhere else. The Eberhart company files contained thousands of building sites in the country, among them several bunkers they had built for the German high command in caves and underground caverns surrounding Berlin, in the Bavarian Alps and in many other locations. Eberhart had chosen the one location that spoke to his heart more than any other. It was a place rich with the whispers of history; a place where he could sit and contemplate the Germany that would soon be under his control. The entire area above ground was undergoing construction at the moment, and nobody even thought to enter a place lined with fences plastered with signs that read: *Danger! Construction Site!*

The inside of the bunker had been gutted and rebuilt from the floor up. It was a wonderful example of modern-day structural design. Any architecture magazine would have been more than thrilled to do a five-page spread on the place. There were bedrooms and a living room/dining room and a billiards room and a kitchen outfitted with everything necessary for a few months' long stay. Then there was the octagon-shaped command center.

The octagon-shaped command center was linked to the world in the most modern way. This was a room with access to every media network in existence, so that Eberhart knew what was going on at every minute of the day or night, in every part of the world that he was interested in. There was a picture of Adolph and Himmler on the wall, but the biggest portrait of all was one of Ludwig Eberhart, his father, and the man who had inspired him all his life. It was at this desk that Eberhart made his calls, one after another.

Knowing that with every touch of a button, with every phrase uttered, he was destroying the lives of people all over the world gave him the ultimate thrill of power. It didn't trouble him to destroy lives. A few lives for the many, that had always been his motto. Besides, most of the lives that were being ruined were those of Jews, and who cared about that.

So he sat at his desk and dialed the numbers. The phone signals were sent through scrambler after scrambler, until not even the top National Security Agency would have been able to decode the signals to discover from where they were issuing. He had just gotten off the phone with Kevin Barns, adviser to the chairman of the Federal Reserve, and he had spoken the few words that triggered his rush directly to his office and the computers that controlled much of the world's economy. Within a significantly short time, there would be serious trouble in the market as the Fed's main network computers began sending forth all manner of misinformation into the system. The moment that happened, chaos would erupt in the financial markets, and even greater chaos in the hallowed offices of law-enforcement agencies everywhere.

In the meanwhile, he had a few of the cable stations set to the lower Manhattan frequencies, ready to pick up anything out of the ordinary. So far, the plan had been working amazingly well with very few glitches. It was standing up under pressure, and Eberhart was proud of the way he had followed through with all the members of the Network over the years, taking over when his father passed away, ensuring that the road to greatness still lay open to them. At this precise moment, policemen all across the United States, Europe and Israel were waiting for the next disruption that was sure to come. He knew that his was the number-one name on everyone's lips, but then again, nobody was absolutely certain. And so, while the police were searching for him at his home, they weren't tearing apart the country to find him, because a person was innocent until proven guilty, wasn't he? And maybe, deep inside their hearts, the police wanted him to succeed.

So, while the neo-Nazis were running rampart throughout Europe completely out of control for the first time since the war, the Jews of America stayed locked up in their million-dollar homes, afraid of what lay in store for them in a land that had suddenly become hostile. And while Israel didn't know when or from where the next shot was coming, Eberhart sat at his desk and picked up the phone to call the next entry in the book. But before he had pressed the third button, something on one of the TV screens caught his eye. The police were covering the exit from all bridges into New York City, and the media cameras were already there. Somehow they had found out about the emergency. Ordinarily, he would have called the press vultures, but right now he was more than happy that they were there to cover the event. The phone dropped from his hand as he contemplated the screen before him with bated breath.

New York City
June 18, 2009

The police and National Guard had blocked off the exits from every bridge and tunnel leading into the city, and the exit from the tunnels was cordoned off as well. Eberhart watched and waited along with thousands of other people as the traffic began to slow and build up. The police were taking their time, checking every car that looked even remotely similar to Kevin Barns' silver Porsche Carrera.

Nobody wanted to be the one who allowed the suspect into the city. Every car that exited the bridge was given the once over by a vigilant group of eagle-eyed cops, and only then permitted to merge with outgoing traffic. The streets of New York City, which are never quiet, were becoming more and more congested. Suddenly, Eberhart caught sight of a silver Porsche Carrera exiting the bridge and inching toward the cops. There was no way that the car was going to be able to escape. There were too many cops and not enough room. Even if Kevin managed to evade the cops for a few blocks, he would be caught in traffic in the end. It would not be good for the Network if Kevin Barns was caught, not at all.

Kevin Barns drove off the bridge and into Manhattan. He had noticed that traffic had been slow for some time already, and was pretty sure that he knew the reason why. He was no longer thinking rationally. Ever since he had gotten that phone call, he shifted into autopilot, his subconscious mind making decisions for him. A gap opened in the traffic and he drove the Porsche right through it. Up ahead, he could see a group of police officers moving from car to car, looking inside and studying the drivers. He knew they were looking for him. It was sheer mayhem. All around him, drivers were beeping on their horns and pedestrians were studying the scene with interest. It was insane. He had to get out of the gridlock! Very slowly, he inched his way out of the mass of cars and positioned himself on the outside of the crush.

The policemen saw him idling there. The silver Porsche Carrera just sat there on the side of the mass of cars, daring them to do something about it. Here was the target.

They converged on the sleek little car, like bees at a pollen festival. About six cops made their calculated way to his car. He was in their grasp. They were about 10 feet away from him when everything changed. Kevin pressed down on the gas, taking the turbo-charged engine from zero to 70 miles an hour in less than five seconds. The cops scattered like feathers in the wind and ran for cover. The Porsche shot forward toward the police barrier. Instead of stopping, it drove right underneath the wooden pole. The Porsche was low enough to do that without even scratching the roof of the car. He was suddenly free of the traffic and he pressed on the gas, taking the car up to 90. He had never driven like this before, but a little voice told him this was something he had to do. Behind him, police were racing to their cars, jumping inside and gunning their engines, while journalists and photographers were running along the city streets hoping that he would be trapped and they'd get the shot of the century.

The Porsche didn't stop. Kevin was a maniac. He drove on sidewalks, around cars, the wrong way down one-way streets and didn't stop at traffic lights. He drove like a madman. From all over the city, police converged on the section of town where the action was, ready for anything. Soon he was nearing the downtown section where his office was located. He figured that he would ditch the Porsche since it was such a focus of attention. He drove down into one of the anonymous underground parking garages in the city. And then, Kevin Barns, executive assistant to the chairman of the Fed, walked down the street toward his office building, just like any other businessman in the city.

He approached the 73-story building with complete confidence. He doubted that they knew what he looked like yet, but just in case, he purchased an "I Love NY" cap from a street vendor, and shoved it down low on his head, obscuring his face. Next he entered a sporting goods store where he purchased a Yankees' jacket. Placing his suit jacket in the bag provided by the store, he walked right up to his office building and attempted to enter.

Officer Mario Perroni was scrutinizing every passerby, and the guy wearing the "I Love NY" hat and Yankees' jacket struck him as odd. Something was wrong. His shoes were at odds with the rest of his outfit. Perroni pulled him over to the side and asked the man for identification. The next thing Perroni knew, the man had shoved him to the ground and dashed through the door in the direction of the elevator bank. Five policemen took up the chase, cornering the man near the elevators, but at the last moment, he took the staircase leading to the upper floors and began racing upward. The policemen couldn't keep up with him, so they took the elevator up to the 10th floor and began running down in the stairwell hoping to meet up with the guy as he ascended. Policemen closed off all the exits to the building just in case he took the elevator back down to the street. Kevin surprised them by taking the elevator upward to his office instead. The two officers who were waiting outside his office on the 65th floor were not strong enough to overpower the crazed man, but they kept him from his computer, until other forces arrived on the scene. When Kevin Barns came to the realization that he wouldn't be able to carry out his mission due to the seven policemen it had taken to subdue him, he quieted down, thereby lulling the cops into thinking he was over the worst. They allowed him to sit to the side, while they decided what to do next. They hadn't counted on Barns.

At his first opportunity, Kevin Barns went running headlong through the nearest window, thus ending what had become a day that Manhattan would never forget.

Berlin, Germany
June 18, 2009

Eberhart hadn't been able to tear himself away from watching the news the entire time the chase had been in progress. From time to time, he received an update, and his heart was beating wildly as he waited to hear if his man would be caught or not. It would not be a good thing for Kevin to be caught. The Americans would put him through a psychological circus of doctors and hypnotherapists and who knew what else. By the time they finished with him, they would have a much better idea of what was going on than they had up until now.

Eberhart turned up the volume as the news flashed on the screen. The camera cut to a man with windblown hair standing in front of Barns' office building. He was given a signal to start, and he nodded at the camera and began to talk.

"Good afternoon from New York City. Willi Baylor with the latest. In an unprecedented chase through the streets of the city today, Kevin Barns, adviser to the chairman of the Fed, led a large posse of New York's finest on a chase. Nobody knows what put Barns in such a state, but the fact remains that he was trying to get to his office quickly and was prepared to lay his life on the line to realize his goal. Once there however, he was stopped a number of times, but managed to evade the police by every turn. The showdown came at his office where it took seven officers to hold him down. When they thought he had come to his senses and would sit still for a few moments while they decided what to do with him, he hurled himself through the window, leaving a room full of perplexed officers behind him."

The scene shifted from the reporter to the office with the camera focusing on the shattered panes in the large plate-glass window.

"Mrs. Barns," continued the reporter, "has not the faintest clue what has come over her normally mild-mannered husband. In their more than 20 years of marriage, he has never behaved this way before. She had seen him tearing out of the driveway in his Porsche. He drove like a maniac and she didn't know what to make of it. As of now, the police are trying to put the pieces together, but are having little luck. This is Willi Baylor with the latest from New York City."

Eberhart muted the screen and leaned back in his seat. So that was that. Barns had gone to his death with all his secrets intact. But things could change drastically within moments, as he saw today. It was time to push the timetable up a little bit. He reached for the phone once again and dialed the number from memory.

"Hello," the voice on the other end was rich and mellow, the voice of a man who enjoyed a good drink and was not afraid to admit it.

"Monsignor, it is I," Eberhart said.

"What can I do for you, my friend?" the man asked.

"Not only for me, but for my father whom you loved so much," Eberhart replied.

"Yes, yes, true, true, that I did. There was no one like Ludwig, that's for sure. What's on your mind, son?"

"It's time for the next step. I want you to finalize things with the Israelis and the pontiff. The groundwork has already been set in place. All the pieces of the puzzle are fitting together. All we really need is to make the announcement."

"Yes, you are correct," the priest said. "Now would be a perfect time for the conference."

"So we are in agreement?" Eberhart asked.

"One hundred percent," said the voice from Rome.

"Thank you, Father," Eberhart said. "You know how much I have valued your advice through the years, and the care and concern you have shown to my family. If there is anything I can do for you, anything at all, please don't hesitate to let me know."

"I'll keep that in mind," the voice said.

They hung up with best wishes on both sides.

The future had finally arrived. All the years of waiting for the plan had arrived. It was time to go for the finish line, and Eberhart was glad. No more worrying about whether it was actually going to work out. They would finally know.

In Vatican City, a certain priest with a rich and mellow voice made a few phone calls and prepared the text for the news conference. The Israelis weren't happy about the abruptness of the meeting, and had protested that there wasn't sufficient time to prepare. The police had said the same thing. It made no difference to him what anyone said. He loved Eberhart like a son and would do anything for him, as he had done for his father. He would always be their friend and a friend of the Network.

And as far as Father Antonio Carruso was concerned, any friend of his was a friend for life.

Rafi, Tamar, Mordy and Cardinal Jason Frost

New York
June 19, 2009

The world media was in a dither. It was a major breakthrough however one looked at it. The pope and the prime minister of Israel were heading for New York City for a historic meeting at the Waldorf-Astoria that would span the past, the present and the future. The world leaders will discuss the obligations shared by the two sovereign states from a moral, economic and historic point of view. The meeting will be conducted in an atmosphere of friendship, civility and understanding.

Time magazine called the meeting "a focal point for our civilization for many years to come." Newsweek called it, "meeting of the year." There was extensive coverage in The New York Times, The Washington Post and The Wall Street Journal. Much speculation was expended regarding precisely what the pope wanted to discuss, what concessions he was prepared to give and what he would request in return for being so magnanimous. The Jerusalem Post reported that the feeling on the Israeli street was that this meeting was not going to herald good tidings for Israel, and that the majority of the people fully expected the pope to pressure the prime minister into relinquishing a major piece of Jerusalem real estate in appreciation for the pope being so conciliatory. "There is no grassroots support for the meeting," continued the Post, "and the people are either apathetic or adamantly against the meeting, citing many examples of other 'historic meetings' and their outcomes."

However, all was light and smiles as Prime Minister Doron Chizkiyahu and his wife were being interviewed by journalists from every newspaper in the land. Maariv and Yediot Acharonot both ran three-page spreads in their weekend editions. All major channels of Israeli television as well as the Galei Tzahal and Kol Yisrael radio stations featured the story.

The meeting had been on the back burner for some time now, and the Vatican and the prime minister's office had finally reached agreement on a date that was convenient for both parties. The leaders would be staying at the Waldorf-Astoria Hotel, and the security arrangements on the part of the New York City Police Department were bound to be of the highest level. The N.Y.P.D. was well aware that both the pope and prime minister would have their own armed security personnel with them. Under the guide of staff members with the highest clearance these men would be accompanying their leaders. All in all, it promised to be a memorable event for all concerned. There was to be a parade up Fifth Avenue in honor of the pontiff's arrival, and both the mayor and governor of New York were slated to put in an appearance.

The Jews of America were not sure how to react to the meeting. One thing was definite; the upcoming meeting was the hottest topic of conversation at the moment, and was going to remain that way until it was over.

The fact that the meeting was scheduled right in the eye of a security storm was not making the security personnel any happier. They made no secret of their disapproval. In fact, the chief of the N.Y.P.D. stated in very disgruntled tones in an open interview with The New York Times that the last thing the city needed right now, coming on the heels of so many unexplained attacks, was such a high-profile meeting.

"What makes this meeting especially difficult for everyone," he explained, "is that we were given such short notice. It is of little interest to the police department that Vatican City had been discussing this meeting for years! We only learned about it a few days ago, and there is just not sufficient time for us to prepare the groundwork! The people from the Vatican told us that the reason we were only informed about the meeting two days in advance was for security reasons, but that is indefensible! You want security? You give the police enough time to get the job done! But," he finished, "the police will do their job, and ensure the safety of all concerned."

And so, New York City went into high-preparation mode, with everyone hoping that there would be no unpleasant surprises waiting for them on the big day.

New York
June 19, 2009

Rafi drove while Tamar fiddled with the radio, trying to find some program that interested her.

"O.K." he said, when it had become abundantly clear that she had tried every existing station. "Enough with the radio already! How are we handling this cardinal?"

"We aren't going to break down the door and come rushing in with guns blazing?" she asked.

"Very funny," he said, "Seriously, what's the plan?"

"Well," she drawled, thinking out loud, "first, you have to be on your guard against any phone calls coming in. You have to be prepared to take him down. We don't even know his mission. It's not like we can go to his objective and secure it. The most we can do is make sure that he doesn't leave his house to accomplish whatever terrible thing he's programmed to do."

"The best thing," Rafi said, "would be if the agency would allow us to give our list to the F.B.I. They would take them into custody and that would be the end of Eberhart's operation!"

"The more people knew how much information we have," she said, "the more likely it is that Eberhart will trigger all of them."

"So instead we show up at locations around with the world, with a few agents per location and hope for the best?!" he asked rhetorically.

"Exactly," she said. "Hopefully, I'll have enough time to make some inroads before the phone call. If the call does come at a crucial moment, you must be prepared to take him down!"

"I'll be ready, don't worry." Rafi reassured her.

Once again Rafi was relying on the GPS to find his way to Ithaca. The scenery was so incredibly beautiful that he wanted to lift his voice and sing. So he did just that. He taught Tami *the tune.* He sang it over and over, never tiring of the heartbreaking tune, until his voice began to get hoarse.

The GPS directed them off the highway, onto a scenic rural road, with pasture and hilly wooded areas on both sides of them. Here and there they passed "Deer Crossing," or "Sharp Curve" signs. Rafi kept both hands on the wheel and both eyes on the road. Tamar had drifted off to sleep a while back, and Rafi stopped at a gas station, where he filled up, and purchased soft drinks and chips. They had been driving a few hours and he was feeling more than ready for a break.

According to his map they were almost there, and indeed, a few minutes later they made a right off the road because they were approaching the town of Ithaca. Before he knew it, he was rolling onto the main street, past several small businesses and larger emporiums. He drove past a number of parks, and took note of all the people involved in sports activities. The tennis courts were full, and there were joggers and people biking. Soon enough they were turning onto a shady block where the houses were spread far apart. Most driveways had a basketball hoop attached to the side of the garage. There were kids outside playing ball. Rafi reflected that he wouldn't have minded being raised in such a place. There was a parking spot at the curb in front of the house, and Rafi took this as a good omen. They emerged from the car and walked toward a wooden porch with a swing and chimes that tinkled sweetly in the wind.

"Well, this is it," he said. Reaching down, he pressed the doorbell with assurance. The sound tolled deep within the house. Rafi was about to press it again, when he heard footsteps hurrying toward the door. The door swung open to reveal a young man in his early to mid 20's with a black *kippah* on his head and a ready smile on his face. The Ganim siblings were taken aback and obvioulsy flustered by this turn of events. This was the home of a cardinal of the church, wasn't it? Yet, the man who answered the door looked like a rabbi-in-training! What was going on?

"Hello," the young man greeted them with a smile.

"Hello," Rafi answered back automatically. "Is this the home of Cardinal Jason Frost?"

"Yes," the man answered. "Would you like to see the cardinal?" When they nodded, he said, "I'll just go check and see if he's available now."

He left them standing in the entrance way and returned within minutes.

"The cardinal can see you now," he said.

They followed him through rambling rooms filled with artwork, much of it Judaica, and books piled on every surface. Some were open and lying face down on the table as if the cardinal had been in the middle of reading them and been pulled away into something more fascinating, but would return momentarily. There were many pictures on the walls of the cardinal in his younger years attending assorted religious ceremonies, presiding over others, dressed in his robes and looking dignified. He certainly had the stature for the job. Yet here he was with a Jewish boy wearing a *kippah* on his head. How could this be?! Could he have become drawn to his roots without even knowing what they were?

The curtains were drawn on most of the windows, lending a perpetual state of shadow to the homey rooms. They stood in the doorway to the study and peered into the room at the broad figure sitting and studying at the desk. The cardinal's brow was creased as he concentrated intently on the book before him, eyes squinting under the lamp's bright light. Rafi's mouth dropped open when he realized that the cardinal was learning Talmud. This was quite an interesting situation! Here was a man of the Church, a man who had been in line to become pope, studying Gemara!

The young man, who introduced himself as Mordy, spoke softly to the cardinal, informing him that his visitors were waiting. The cardinal looked up. His eyes were bright and clear and filled with warmth. He had the most charming smile.

"Yes," he said. "What can I do for you?"

"I think the question is more like what can we can do for you, Cardinal," Rafi replied.

"Allow me to introduce myself. My name is Rafi Ganim, and I work for the Mossad. This is a member of my team, Dr. Tamar Ganim, my sister, and a noted hypnotherapist. It is our job to clarify certain things before your life swings completely out of control. Has anything strange in your life occurred that you haven't been able to explain? Do you have the feeling that you are not in control, that there are other forces manipulating you in all sorts of directions, anything like that?"

"Yes," mused the cardinal quietly. "Many things like that. You are from the Mossad? How interesting. It's finally coming full circle, isn't it?"

"Yes it is, cardinal," Rafi said, "and we're going to need your permission to get to the bottom of this."

"I'm willing to assist you in any way I can," he said.

"I'm happy to hear that," Rafi said. "Why don't we move to the living room where we can be a little more comfortable?"

"Can I see some identification, first?" the older man asked.

"Certainly," Rafi said. He pulled out his passport and showed it to the man. Tamar did the same. "You can call Israel if you'd like and confirm that we are who we say we are."

"That won't be necessary," the cardinal said, with a curt wave of his hand. "Come with me."

They followed him into the living room where Tamar asked the cardinal to take a seat in one of the soft-cushioned armchairs. She pulled up a hard-backed chair which she placed not far away. Mordy was hovering in the doorway of the room, taking in the events with a perplexed expression on his face.

"I'm going to have to ask you to leave," Rafi told him.

"No," the cardinal said. "He stays right here. If he has to leave then we don't do this."

"O.K.," Rafi said, "I didn't realize he was so close to you."

"I trust this boy with my life," the Cardinal said, "and I need him here with me, especially if I'm to undergo some sort of psychological analysis. Before we start, I'm going to need a little background, please. What made you pick me? How did you even know about me? Talk to me. Tell me what's going on!"

Rafi began, "It all began with a book," he said, "a book that was found and that would puzzle several people for years … "

Vatican City, Italy
June 19, 2009

The black stretch limousine pulled up alongside the entrance to the pope's private quarters. The driver stepped out of the car to stretch his legs while he waited for the pope to emerge. Sergio Velosi had been the driver for the previous pope, as well. He found Fernandez Mendoza to be a strong confident person with a healthy outlook on religion. He was a peaceful sort of man, who wasn't overly arrogant. Velosi adjusted the papal flag flying from the hood, and absentmindedly polished a smudge on one of the windows. He would not be accompanying the pontiff to the United States, and for that he was grateful. He had no desire to deal with the craziness that confronted the pope wherever he went. The crowds alone were enough to drive a person berserk.

No, he would drive the pope to the Vatican heliport and pick him up when he returned home. The papal helicopter would transport the pope to the airport where he would board the Vatican jet for his flight to the States. The door opened and the pontiff emerged from the building, accompanied by two cardinals and a bishop. The pope was resplendent in a white robe embroidered with gold thread, and he walked with the aid of a cane. A large white silk skullcap covered his head, and he walked majestically toward the car. Sergio opened the door, and the bishop assisted the pope into the vehicle. The cardinals entered from the other side. They were stern-looking men with stiff faces and forbidding looks. There was no merry twinkle in the eyes of these men. They were pure business.

As soon as everyone was seated, Sergio pressed lightly on the gas and drove the car through the Vatican City compound toward the helipad. The papal helicopter was already waiting on the pad, engines warming, propellers beginning to spin. A movable staircase led to the door of the helicopter. The bishop helped the pope up the stairs and into the helicopter. Sergio watched as the propellers began spinning even faster and the sleek helicopter began first to hover and then lifted off. When it was just a speck on the horizon, he turned and went back to his beloved car. He hoped all went well in America, because he, for one, just didn't feel that this trip was right.

Berlin, Germany
June 19, 2009

Dietrich Eberhart watched as the reporters jostled one another in their haste to get closer to the pope's helicopter. The television cameras were all focused on the papal aircraft as it came to a final stop on the ground and the door opened. The reporters who possessed the special permits needed in order to be permitted on the tarmac stood at rigid attention as the pope appeared at the door of the helicopter, looking happy but fatigued.

He watched as the pontiff walked carefully down the short flight of stairs and waved to the reporters. The media liked this pope. He treated them gently and they responded in turn. This pope was treated with kindness and caring. The helicopter had landed a short distance from the airplane, and the pope turned and waved one more time before climbing the longer flight of stairs to the plane. Then he disappeared into the rounded doorway, and the media party was over. An airport employee pushed the staircase away, the door was shut tightly and the plane began coasting along slowly in the direction of the international flights' runways.

Eberhart gave a sigh of pleasure at the way everything was moving along, and turned his attention to another screen, where a reporter in Moscow was speaking earnestly into the camera about the latest neo-Nazi attack in the capital. Snow was falling lightly behind him as he stood in front of the Moscow Jewish Center, and pointed to the swastikas that had been spray-painted all over the walls. The police, he said, were mounting an investigation and were hoping for results very soon.

"Good luck," said Eberhart, and flicked that screen closed as well. They were on a roll now, and stopping them wasn't an option any longer. It just wasn't. The equivalent would have been trying to stop Hitler after he overran Poland. It was just not happening. He reached for his book of names, and tried to decide whom to call while the pope was making his way over the Atlantic. It was a difficult decision.

Ithaca, New York
June 19, 2009

"And that's why the Mossad has sent out agents all around the world," Rafi told the cardinal, "to the homes of every one of the people whose names are in the book, to every member of the Network, hoping to stop them before they receive the phone call that will trigger their subconscious, turning them into human death machines. We recently paid a visit to the home of a man named Kevin Barns. You might have heard of him. The gentleman was the assistant to the chairman of the Federal Reserve. He was in line to become the chairman of the Fed when the present chairman retired. Shortly after we arrived at his home, the phone rang. He answered, listened for a few seconds, hung up, knocked me down before I could stop him from leaving and drove off toward the city in a terrible hurry.

"I don't know what his mission was, but since I do know what he did for a living, I can only surmise that it had something to do with harming Wall Street and the world economy from a place that would really hurt. Eberhart is pulling out all the stops now. He wants to show the world that he possesses the power to destroy them all if they don't give him what he wants."

"What does he want?" Frost wanted to know.

"We don't know yet," Rafi said. "Right now, he's just establishing a new worldwide reality. The police weren't even able to stop Barns and get him into custody, because he threw himself through the plate-glass window of his office and plummeted to his death! That indicates that every one of the people in the book has been subjected to the same kind of mind games that Barns was. That is why we have come to meet with you and help you resist this maniac. Dr. Ganim," he said, pointing to his sister, "is a world-known hypnotherapist who can deprogram you from everything you have undergone throughout the years."

"How do you know they met with me throughout the years?" asked Frost in a surprised voice.

"It's an obvious assessment," Rafi replied. "I mean, think about it: All the people in the book were kidnapped when they were young children. They were probably transported out of Europe." Frost nodded; this made sense to him. "They were subjected to months of in-depth hypnosis and mind-altering drugs. When the doctors overseeing the project deemed them ready, they were sent overseas and placed in whichever society the Nazis felt most suitable for the child's personality and for the Nazis' future needs. For example, the psychologists who tested Barns came to the correct conclusion that he would be most fulfilled working with numbers as an analyst. So they tampered with his mind and instilled within him the desire to become exactly that. Then they sat back and manipulated events to ensure that their man became an analyst in precisely the right environment."

"How?" asked Frost.

"By meeting with their subjects from time to time and reprogramming them once again, to reinforce their desire to become what the Nazis wanted them to become. Tell me something," Rafi said looking Frost straight in the eyes. "Aren't there any stretches of time where you can't recall exactly what you were doing? Was there a month here and there, a few weeks where things were blurry and you couldn't remember what was happening in your life right then? Does such a phenomenon ring a bell?"

Frost sat quietly, thinking deeply into what Rafi had just said. Finally he spoke.

"Yes," he said. "You are right. There are periods of time in my life that my memory isn't clear; times where a sort of fog has descended over my brain, closing off my memory."

"Like your last trip," the young man named Mordy interrupted. "I asked you all about the trip you took a short while ago, and you couldn't even tell me about it. You claimed that you didn't remember the details. At the time I attributed it to old age, but the truth is that your memory is just fine. Since I've returned from Israel we've spoken and studied for hours together, and you have related countless bits of information and many stories from your life and personal history. Nowhere did you exhibit even the slightest bit of hesitation except for those few times. Then you're a complete blank!"

"Somehow," Rafi went on, "they were able to get you to a place where they could ensure that your internal programming was untouched; that essentially you were still the agent they had built."

"And that would explain why I didn't become pope," Frost said in a tremulous voice. "They built me up, sending me higher and higher in the hierarchy of the church, plucking me out of my obscurity and elevating me to the most important of positions. But when they decided that they didn't want me to become pope, well then, I didn't become pope." There was an intense bitterness in his voice.

"This, Cardinal, is exactly what we need to determine," Rafi said. "That's why Dr. Ganim is here, to get to the root of the matter. Would you consider allowing her to put you under a hypnotic state so we can get to the bottom of this, so we can find out who you really are?"

"I need some time alone first," Frost said. And with that, he rose and walked slowly but steadily from the room.

They looked at each other in consternation. Mordy began apologizing for the cardinal, but Tamar waved him off.

"It makes complete sense that he feels this way," she said, "I would be surprised if he didn't want to be alone. The humiliation, the raw feeling of vulnerability. The knowledge that his entire life hangs on a phone call that could arrive at any moment. It's a terrible shock for the man. Give him some time, he'll come around. In the meanwhile, I want you to tell me everything you remember about the last trip the cardinal took to Europe, and whatever he told you about it, every last detail, the smallest piece of information, as trivial as it may seem. I need some ideas to use as a spark when he is ready for me to access his mind."

They sat in the living room and Mordy began to talk, while Tamar took notes. He went through everything he knew about the cardinal's trip: his reasons for going, his excitement, the fact that Al had gone along and been subsequently murdered — a fact that Frost himself seemed to have forgotten. Mordy spoke about every place on the cardinal's itinerary about which he had been told. Tamar wanted to know everything. Mordy told her all he had learned until he had talked himself out and there was nothing else.

In the meanwhile, Rafi was prowling around downstairs.

"How many phones does the cardinal have in the house?" he asked Mordy.

"Just one," Mordy replied.

"Good," Rafi said, "I'm going to put this phone out of commission for a while, until we determine the risks to the cardinal." He proceeded to do just that. He removed the phone cord from the wall.

"O.K., he's not in any immediate danger now, so he can take all the alone time that he needs. Now what?" They were all keyed up. Rafi began walking aimlessly through the house, searching for inspiration, while Mordy took a seat on the couch, where he sat opening and closing a book, trying to read but finding that he couldn't concentrate. Only Tamar seemed perfectly at ease. Rafi looked around the living room for something to do. The cardinal had an extensive library of interesting books on every subject under the sun, but Rafi couldn't get himself to sit down and read. There was a high table in the corner of the room that was covered with a blanket on which books were piled. Something about the shape of the table caught Rafi's eye, and he went closer to get a better look. He lifted a corner of the blanket and realized that it was in fact not a table. It was a piano. Music! That was something to do! A bridge, a way to get past the awkwardness.

"Mordy," he called out, the apathy gone in a wave of excitement. "Help me move these books."

Rafi began handing the piles of books to Mordy, and Mordy

transferred them to the floor. When all the books had been removed, Rafi removed the blanket and revealed a beautiful piano. The white keys gleamed in the room's dim lighting. There was no piano bench, so Rafi pulled over a chair. Somehow he sensed that music was the key here.

But what song should he play? He thought and thought, trying to decide what piece of music to play. He had studied piano over the years, and while he wasn't nearly as good at it as he was at the violin, he sometimes thought that maybe he had picked the wrong instrument. Not because violin was wrong for him, but because piano was also so right. He lifted his wrists above the keys and pressed down. The chord reverberated through the house, its richness dispelling the gloom. He pressed another chord and the music danced like golden sunlight through a prism. And then he knew what to play. It was so obvious!

And he began. It was the tune, the melody from his dream and from his uncle's shul in Tel Aviv. The song wafted joyously through the house, filling every corner and every heart with simple joy and hope for the future.

He hadn't played piano for such a long time. He was rusty. Yet, the sounds that he was managing to coax out of a piano that hadn't been tuned in years were just heavenly! He played the song from his dream in many versions and styles. He played it like it was a piece of classical music, Baroque, Modern and Jazz. The piano quivered with the effort and vibrated with the power, the force of his music. All of them, and especially Mordy, were deeply immersed in the music, in the feelings that were being invoked. But suddenly something made Rafi look toward the doorway, and there the cardinal stood, the same and yet a different man.

Everything stopped for a moment in time. The sounds echoed and reechoed, and when it was finally still, Frost spoke.

"That was my song," he said. "I know that tune. Here, listen," he said as if wanting to prove that he wasn't making it up, that he really did know the song. He began to sing. At first his voice was weak from lack of use. But by the time he had sung the song three times, his vocal chords had revived, and he was singing with power, with passion, in a surprisingly strong and rich voice. Rafi found himself singing along with the cardinal. After they had sung the song 10 times, Mordy knew it as well and was singing as if his life depended on it. Then Rafi was on his feet, and he grabbed the cardinal's hands and they began to dance around and around in a frenzy of musical emotion. Frost was crying mightily, not knowing why, not understanding what was happening to him, just giving himself up to the power of the moment. Mordy joined them as well, and they twirled around the room singing and singing, begging Hashem for help, for an answer. Tamar watched them with tears in her eyes, because this scene was one of the most incredible dramas she had ever witnessed.

Finally, when they were all spent, they sat down on the couch, and Frost looked at them and then at Mordy and he said, "No more alone time. Let's do this. I'm ready to uncover the truth and discover who I am."

There was nothing more to say. He was ready. Tamar took a deep breath and told him to make himself comfortable on the couch. She pulled up a chair and took a seat diagonally across from him.

"O.K.," she said. "Cardinal Frost, I'm going to put you under a hypnotic state. We are going to get to the bottom of this. We are going to find out who you really are." As she spoke in her soothing voice, they could see the cardinal beginning to slip away. His face was relaxing, going slack, and his eyes were unfocused. He was slipping under and his mind was open. It was time to begin.

"Welcome to the past," Tamar said. "You are a little boy living in Europe. Why don't you tell us your name, please?"

When he spoke, it was with the voice of a little boy. "I am Yaakov," he said in a childish tone. They were in. He was responding.

"Why don't you tell me a little bit about yourself?" she said. His features turned introspective. He was thinking about himself. When he finally began to unburden himself, the story was so sad that they couldn't keep from crying. He spoke of a wonderfully warm family, of a devoted mother and a distinguished father, of brothers and sisters, of a big beautiful edifice where his father was the *Rav*. He spoke of Shabbos and Yom Tov and the davening and the singing. Without any warning, he opened his mouth and began to sing the tune that Rafi had been playing on the piano. Again and again he sang the song, but he sang it in the voice of a child. It was most disconcerting, watching the older man singing a song with the voice of a child. "Tatty was a Rebbe," he kept on saying. "The Kolodover Rebbe. I'm his chassid. I sing his songs."

Rafi jumped when he heard that. He wanted to interrupt, to embrace the man — the cardinal — who was his cousin, the cardinal who was really Jewish, who could sing songs from the *tish* with the best of them.

Tamar held up her hand, motioning him to stay put. He couldn't believe his eyes. This was the son of his great-uncle. This was what the Nazis had done to him. They had taken a precious Jewish boy and made him spend his life in the service of the Catholic Church! This was how the Eberhart family had repaid the Rebbe for his blessing to them, by stealing their child prodigy and sending him to live as a gentile! It made his blood boil.

Tamar led Frost through his childhood. All at once things became terribly sad. He was sad now. The corners of his lips were turned downward because he was sad, because the men were bad men in black uniforms. They were frightening men who yelled a lot. The children were no longer permitted to play outdoors. The bad men were everywhere. There were hiding places prepared especially for kids like him. But the bad men came for him, just for him. They came for him because they had learned that he was smart. He overheard them speaking. His father had no choice. His mother cried and kissed him goodbye. His father gave him a *berachah* and a hug. The bad men carried him away, forever. Tears were pouring from his eyes.

He was placed with many other children, all very smart, all Jewish. They were on an estate near the water. At least they were never hungry now. There was always plenty of food for everyone. The children loved watching the water. There were waves, gigantic waves, always splashing the rocks. One child fell and almost drowned in the water, before the bad men in the black uniforms jumped in and saved him. It was cold near the water. They wore heavy clothing all the time. In the house it was warm, and the children were taught to speak a different language. They lived on the estate for what felt like a long time. Then the big black boat arrived to take them away.

It arose out of the water like a whale. The men were excited, yelling, yelling, all around. The kids were leaving. Everyone bundled up in their winter clothes. They were getting on the long boat that looked so scary because it was black just like the bad men. It emerged from the water like a monster. They walked onto the boat on a shaky bridge that swayed in the wind. Frost's face became frightened as he relived the memories of his earliest years. And then the boat ("It must have been a submarine," Tamar whispered to them) went down under the water and they cried and cried because they didn't know what was going to happen to them.

He continued in this vein while Tamar drew him out expertly. He said that they were transferred to a big boat, but still kept below deck and he told of their arrival in South America. He spoke of the treatments to which they were subjected. He spoke of the hypnosis. He was like a fountain that could not be stilled. He had so much to say. How it felt to be brought up by Nazis, by the same people who had killed his parents. Then they took them back to Europe to an orphanage in Paris, and then to America. Then he spoke about how it was growing up in Oyster Bay, Long Island. The session lasted for hours; the little boy could not be stopped.

Finally Tamar brought him around to his mission. Here he clammed up. Obviously, he had been programmed against just such an intrusion. But Tamar was an expert. She was able to recognize the barriers and get past them. But she hadn't counted on Frost. He refused to cooperate with her. He was loyal to those who had gotten there first. In the end, she decided that the session had carried on for long enough and she brought him out of it.

Mordy went out shopping and returned with bread, canned tuna, fresh vegetables along with juice and soda. Enough food to make a kosher meal for all of them. Tamar had wanted to protest that it didn't really matter to her, but then she looked around at the people around her and realized that maybe it did, just a bit. She looked at her brother who had given up a career as the darling of the classical music world so that he could help his nation find peace. She looked at Mordy, and was amazed by the devotion and respect he was showing an older man who was not even his relative. She understood that the behavior they were exhibiting stemmed from the fact that they cared about what they ate, and where they ate it.

She allowed Frost to rest for a couple of hours, and then they began again, when his mind was still sleepy and his guard was down. This time she began with his unexplained absences. She dug into his trips to Europe, searching for the thread, the elusive link that would open him up, allow him to share what had taken place on those past trips. She got into South America and there she struck gold, because it was all tangled up in his mind. His experiences in South America when he was young had merged with his experiences in South America of more recently. She had gotten inside his mind. He told her about his search to uncover the truth about why he had been bypassed for pope. They backtracked to Paris, and the discoveries that had led him toward the other side of the world. He had returned to Paraguay and described how he had entered the club and found all the men, saw the pictures on the walls and was taken upstairs where it all began again.

"What began again?" she asked him.

He wouldn't say. He couldn't say. The programming was too strong. She looked around the room for inspiration. Off in a corner of the room she could see a painting on the wall of a mother lighting two candles. There was nothing overtly religious about the painting, and yet she instinctively knew why he had purchased it. She knew that he recognized his mother in that picture, that it represented a yearning for days long gone, days of Shabbos candles and a mother who sang to him while he nestled in the safety and comfort of her lap.

She had an idea.

She didn't have to search very far for a pair of candlesticks. There were actually a number of sets to choose from. She took one particular set, an intricately designed set of brass candlesticks and found two candles in a kitchen cabinet. She placed them on the table before him. Then, for the first time in her life, Tamar Ganim lit Shabbos candles, despite the fact that it wasn't erev Shabbos and she had never imagined herself doing something like this at all.

She stood there in silence for a moment as the flame caught on the wick, and a tiny little fire began dancing on the first one and then the second candle. A serenity enveloped her soul. *It's just a candle,* she tried to tell herself. But a voice from the back of her mind whispered back that it wasn't just a candle. *You have just taken your place as a link in the chain of history,* the voice continued. *How proud your grandparents would have been!* She couldn't tear her eyes away from the candles. The flames signified who she really was, what was really important in her life, how she had finally discovered her role as a Jewish woman.

Frost sat at the table staring into the flames, seeing things that she had never seen. Then he looked at her and he said, "Mommy lighting candles for Shabbos," in that same childish voice. Rafi began to sing their song again, the song of the Rebbe of Kolodov, the song of the cousins, their family's song, the tune of their ancestors. They were locked in a circle comprised of two siblings from Eretz Yisrael and their cousin, a man who had spent his entire life in the service of the church, yet whose soul still cried out for the song of his youth.

Tamar began again. This time, he told her everything, almost as if his mind finally understood where his true loyalties belonged. Now she was able to get through his mind, to bypass the traps they had set up all those years ago, to uncover his part in the giant tapestry that was the Nazi plan to regain power and finish everything they had begun so long before. It was all coming together. They were still missing some of the pieces, but the more she dug, the more she uncovered. Maybe now they would be able to begin turning the tables around. Maybe he could repay the Eberhart family for the tortures they had put him through all these long and bitter years. As she worked, Frost's mission became clear to her, and she couldn't believe the absolute gall behind this mission. They were using people all over the world for their own purposes. How incredibly vile it all was.

Now that he was finally open to working with her, Tamar dug deeper and deeper into his subconscious. It was more like the inner workings of a very complicated computer than anything else. Just as a computer expert will eventually locate the source of a virus, delete it and then place protection in its place, that was exactly what Tamar proceeded to do. When the phone call would come — and it was definitely going to come, of that she had no doubts — Frost would be ready. He was more than ready. They had worked it all out. He was filled with such a tremendous desire to destroy them that he would have been willing to do almost anything as long as it hurt the creators of the Network.

"You can reconnect the phone now," she said to Rafi.

If Eberhart wanted to play ball, well then, batter up.

Tel Aviv, Israel
June 20, 2009

It was 1 o'clock in the morning when Kobi Shapiro got out of his hospital bed, put on his clothing and made sure that he had all his belongings. He had been in the hospital long enough, and it was time to leave. In fact, he couldn't remain any longer, not even another hour. He had to get out of this place. *You feel all better,* he told his reflection in the bathroom mirror, *all set to go into the race, right?!*

Right, his reflection answered back enthusiastically. Boy, was he looking old. He looked around the spartan room one last time. Everything was in his overnight bag that was slung over his shoulder. Moving quietly, he opened the door and stepped outside into the dimly lit corridor. The hospital was very quiet at this time of night. As he passed the nurses' station, he glanced automatically down the short hallway that lay beyond it. There was a bench at the end of the hallway, and a man was sleeping on that bench. It was hard work staying up all night with a family member or friend. Kobi knew all about it. He had done it himself more times than he could remember. He waited for a second to make sure that the man was truly asleep. When he stirred, snorted and turned over, searching for a more comfortable position on the hard bench, Kobi headed toward the elevators and freedom. He'd get his secretary to process his release from the hospital tomorrow. In the meanwhile, he'd better leave while he still could.

The air was brisk and cool as he exited the giant building and headed toward the main boulevard to hail a taxi. A bracing wind was blowing in from the Mediterranean, and he pulled his jacket around his frail body. There was a bus shelter at the corner. He stood in its embrace gazing at the walls, as if he was studying the multitude of posters that were plastered one on top of the other. Two minutes later there was a beeping sound, as a car came careening around the nearby corner, coming to a stop right alongside the stop.

"Taxi," said the young man driving the car, "hop aboard."

Kobi pulled the door open and jumped into the car.

"Where to?" asked the driver. Kobi gave an address in Yaffo, and the car pulled away from the curb in a gray cloud of exhaust. When they were a comfortable distance away from the hospital, Kobi pulled his cell phone from his pocket and dialed a long-distance number. The phone rang once, twice, three times. He was about to hang up when a voice answered.

"Rafi?" he asked.

"Kobi, is that you? They told me you were in the hospital."

"I was. I checked myself out. Tell me everything that's been happening. Don't leave out a detail. Talk to me now!"

Obviously Kobi hadn't changed in the least. The car drove through the deserted streets, as Rafi filled his mentor in on all the news that had happened since they had last spoken.

"Keep up the good work," Kobi finally said. "I will be in touch. From now on, if you have something to say, call this number and this number only. Got it?"

"Got it," Rafi said. But Kobi had already hung up the phone.

Prime Minister Chizkiyahu and the Pope

New York City
June 20, 2009

A teaming mass of humanity had gathered along Fifth Avenue to await the moment when the pope would pass by waving from his car. A contingent of policemen on horseback would be riding behind the motorcade. The media was of course covering the entire event from start to finish, and even the weather was cooperating wonderfully. Up above, network helicopters hovered, reporting live on the event.

All the hoopla and festivities on Fifth Avenue were in marked contrast to the welcome given the Israeli prime minister. Prime Minister Doron and Mrs. Chizkiyahu landed at Kennedy Airport, where the ambassador was waiting to greet them. The prime minister and his wife waited for their Secret Service people to be cleared through, as well, and were then bundled into the ambassador's waiting limousine.

The demonstrators who had gathered at the hotel entrance were very vocal. None had any illusions about the upcoming meeting. The crowd booing the entourage was decidedly critical. This meeting was considered by one and all to be a foolish decision. Nothing positive would be gained by meeting the pope. It was a lose-lose proposition anyway you looked at it. The Vatican treating the Israelis with respect meant that they would probably feel they could justifiably request a huge chunk of the Old City as compensation.

Stay away from the meeting!!! read one sign, held by a protester. *Jerusalem is not for sale*, read another one. *Say No to Pope*, read a third sign.

They booed Prime Minister Chizkiyahu as he emerged from the limousine. The prime minister reflected to himself that the last thing he really wanted to do was to meet with this pope, but the Vatican had insisted and really put on the pressure for reasons that only they knew, and in the end he had been compelled to agree. He was not happy about it, and all the smiles and nods were a front he was putting on. In reality, he was just as apprehensive as all the demonstrators. He hoped that he would be able to withstand the pressure, and return to Israel without having done any lasting harm.

Why did you want this job so badly anyway? he asked himself glumly, and waved at a protester holding a sign that said, *Go back to where you came from and stay there!!!*

Tel Aviv, Israel
June 20, 2009

There were two of them keeping watch on the building. One was dressed in shorts, T-shirt and sneakers, while the other one wore a suit, carried an expensive briefcase and spoke on the latest model cell phone. He was clearly a businessman. T-shirt sat in a falafel shop across the street from the building, eating slowly and wishing that it was a steak house instead. There was a clear plastic earpiece practically unnoticeable, emerging from his ear and trailing down into his shirt. His body language didn't encourage the kind of closeness that would have allowed anyone to get close enough to see it.

Briefcase wasn't eating. He was chewing gum and talking on the phone. Whoever he was speaking to was clearly fascinating, because the conversation was animated and he was laughing a lot. The two of them were a team, and occasionally they switched roles with each other. Briefcase looked at his watch and then glanced down the street toward the store where T-shirt was still toying with his food. He held up his palm. That meant that the man they had been waiting for would be emerging shortly, and they should be ready to move.

Five minutes later, the man exited the building, attaché case in hand. The agents were already in place: Briefcase at the wheel of a classy brand-new Mazda 6, and T-shirt on a motorcycle down the road. When the man pulled his late-model green Volvo into the street, the Mazda allowed four cars to go by before easing out into traffic. There was no chance of losing the man. They had placed a tracking device on his vehicle. They weren't taking any risks. The man to whom they reported expected perfection, and they knew better than to let him down.

Berlin, Germany
June 20, 2009

Eberhart sat in his chair and peered at the motorcades as they passed by on two different screens. The pope had aged since he had seen him last, which came as no surprise. Eberhart had seen it happen time and again. The moment a man assumed responsibility for a major concern about a business or a country, the obligations began weighing him down much quicker than he could have ever imagined. The elderly visibly aged, while the young put on weight and developed stress lines they never had previously.

The Catholic community was welcoming the pope with cheers and smiles, while the Jews were welcoming their leader with complaints and disapproval. *No surprises there,* he thought to himself, *it has been that way from the time of Moses.*

The pope had arrived at the Waldorf-Astoria first, and was helped from the car and into the hotel by the manager and the staff, who lined the stairs, bowing and curtsying the entire time. The pope was moving slowly, and his face was deeply creased, yet he smiled at everyone and shook their hands and blessed any baby that was handed to him. His security men surrounded him and looked menacingly in the direction of anything that moved.

Fifteen minutes after the pope was safely ensconced in the hotel, the Israeli leader's motorcade pulled up at the entrance, and the process repeated itself. Prime Minister Doron Chizkiyahu appeared trim and fit, while his wife accepted a bouquet of red roses from a delegation of the leading Zionist organization with a smile and a wave for the cameras. The

Israelis entered the five-star hotel, security forces surrounding the prime minister and his wife in a protective phalanx, eyes shielded by darkened sunglasses , faces devoid of expression.

Eberhart thought it a shame that Barns hadn't succeeded in carrying out his mission. What an unbelievable confusion that would have caused: the financial losses, the international panic. But somehow, it hadn't worked, and Eberhart didn't know why. He supposed Barns might have been spotted speeding by the traffic police. But that didn't account for the welcome that had been waiting for him when he got off the bridge. Someone had known he was coming. Someone knew about the Network. Once again he kicked himself mentally for allowing that Jew to get away from him. He should have killed him when he had the opportunity, with no questions, no interrogations, just death. The moment he had begun to suspect him should have been his last moment. Instead he had allowed himself to be taken in, hoodwinked by pictures and clever talk, and now he was paying the price.

He consoled himself, however, with the fact they weren't doing that great a job of tracking down the Network, because many of them had gotten through. He had sown fear around the world with the attacks, and when the right moment arrived, he would give his historic speech, and nothing would ever be the same again. It was the way of the world. They were on the rise now. The stage was set. The players were in place. He wouldn't permit himself to worry about unknowns at this point. He had to move forward and strive for the best, knowing that his cause was true. It would be all right. It had to be. Too much had been invested for it to be anything less than all right.

Opening the book, he placed it on the desk in front of him and lifted the receiver. Glancing across the room, he saw that the police chief of New York was being interviewed on CBS news, while another screen showed a recent anti-Semitic attack on a cemetery in Holland. The FOX news commentator showed pictures of the attack and said that Dietrich Eberhart was rumored to be behind the recent spate of attacks. Nobody knew where he was hiding, the reporter continued, and all attempts at tracking him down had so far failed.

Eberhart dialed the number for the house in Ithaca, New York, home to Cardinal Jason Leonard Frost. It was time for the cardinal to pay them back for all they had invested in him.

The phone rang once, twice, five times. Maybe the man wasn't home.

He was a cardinal, surely he was a busy man. He would have to try a little later. Still, he let the phone ring a few more times. It was picked up on the tenth ring.

"Hello." It was an elderly voice. Eberhart recognized it and his heart filled with elation. This was it.

"There are two people waiting for your services in the confessional booth at the Waldorf-Astoria Hotel," he said, enunciating each and every word.

"I'm on my way," the cardinal said.

Eberhart knew that the light was about to dawn.

Tel Aviv, Israel
June 20, 2009

Briefcase drove the Mazda the way he did everything else, with a devil-may-care attitude: two fingers on the steering wheel, talking on his cell and smoking all at the same time. Obviously nobody had informed him that smoking had ceased to be fashionable. T-shirt was holding his own on the motorcycle. They knew their mark; the man was good and there was no point in taking chances. One slip and he would recognize them. T-shirt allowed several cars to overtake him. The tracking device kept him in the game, allowing him to know exactly where the man was headed at all times. The Volvo left the city streets and got on the Ayalon Highway heading south. T-shirt caught up with him and with a sudden burst of power overtook him on the gas tanks. The man was talking on his car phone as T-shirt passed the vehicle, and he took the next exit and waited on the side of the road, giving the Volvo time to catch up. They would pick him up again pretty soon.

Briefcase kept the Volvo in his sights. He didn't like relying exclusively on technology. It was one thing to allow technology to assist you, but at the same time that he was manipulating the man, the man could be doing the same to him. These things worked both ways. He always tried to keep the suspect in his sights. The Volvo had a distinctive color, and he was able to keep an eye on it, while keeping the other eye on his mirrors, both rear view and sides. It was very possible that just as they were following the man, someone was following them. The suspect was devious and suspicious of everyone and everything. It was highly probable that he had agents watching his back, as well. He switched lanes a couple of times, dropped back and pulled forward, using every trick he knew to spot a possible tail.

There was nothing, or at least nothing that he could locate. It was possible that they were so good that he wasn't picking them up, but it certainly wasn't probable. Briefcase was one of the best in the field; that was why he had been chosen for this mission. Shrugging his shoulders, he pressed down on the gas pedal, and the Mazda ate up the road. Up ahead he could see the sunlight reflecting off the Volvo's roof. The Volvo's indicator showed that he was moving off the highway in the direction of Highway 6. From behind him he heard a sudden roar and looked out his window just in time to see the motorcycle pass him by. The T-shirt was nowhere in sight, having been replaced by a button-down shirt and leather jacket. The Volvo was clearly heading south, and the agent wondered if his boss's suspicions were on the mark.

Waldorf-Astoria Hotel, New York City
June 20, 2009

The taxi let Cardinal Frost out in front of the hotel. The street was cordoned off by police barriers, and it was impossible to get into the hotel without being subjected to a barrage of questions and security checks. Even then, most people were told that the hotel was off limits to anyone not registered there, or not directly connected with the parties staying there. Many potential patrons of the hotel's renowned restaurants, upon seeing the type of security in force, came to the obvious conclusion that they were going to move on and go elsewhere for a dinner instead. Cardinal Frost was not one to be turned away. On the contrary, he was welcomed with open arms. The manager came out to greet him with a big smile and handshake.

"Eminence," he said, "welcome to the Waldorf. Your visit brings us great pleasure. Is the pope expecting you?"

"Of course," Frost replied with warm affability.

"I will let the pope know that you are waiting, Eminence," the manager said. "Please allow me to seat you in the lounge. I'll have one of the waiters bring coffee while you wait."

"Thank you," Frost smiled at the man.

He took a seat in the nearby lounge while the manager scurried away to place a call to the penthouse suite informing the pope's men that Cardinal Jason Leonard Frost had arrived for a meeting with the pontiff. The phone was answered by one of the cardinals with the icy eyes. He thanked the manager for the message, and asked the man to inform Cardinal Frost that the pope was in the middle of a meeting, and would the cardinal mind waiting for another 10 minutes.

"Not a problem," answered Frost with a smile.

The manager smiled at Frost. He couldn't help it. He liked the man. Everyone did.

~

Rafi approached the hotel, showed the policeman on duty the American passport that had been supplied for him by the Mossad and explained that he was an assistant to Cardinal Frost, who had arrived at the hotel a short while earlier for a meeting with the pope. The policeman scrutinized his passport, and let him pass. He entered the building and looked around until he saw the cardinal sipping a cup of coffee in the lounge. Casually he sauntered toward his table and took a seat at the adjacent table. There was no communication between them, none at all. A waiter approached and inquired, "Would you like a drink?" Rafi ordered a diet Coke with a twist.

"Very well, sir," the waiter said.

He returned minutes later with the drink. Cardinal Frost was enjoying his coffee. The manager drew near to apprise the cardinal that the pope was ready to see him. He rose, made his way to the elevators and pressed the button for the top floor. A minute later Rafi rose as well, left some money on the table and took the elevator to the second-highest floor – a different floor than the one where the prime minister and his wife were staying. The elevator arrived in record time, he got inside, the doors closed and he felt himself being borne speedily upward.

~

The elevator opened up at the penthouse suite. Frost exited the elevator and found himself in a small anteroom between the two penthouse suites on the highest floor of the hotel. There was a desk directly opposite the elevator where a bishop was seated. A security guard stood beside him.

"Hello, Julio," Frost greeted the man.

"Jason," the man replied, "it's been too long, my friend. We really must get together more often."

"The pope?" inquired Frost with a raised eyebrow.

"Ready and waiting for you," answered the bishop.

"Thank you," Frost said. Without another word he walked to the door and knocked three times. The door was opened by one of the cardinals.

"Jason," the man said, "you've arrived! The holy father will be so pleased to see you. Why don't you go into the living room?"

"Thank you, Father Carruso," Frost replied. The man nodded, his icy eyes not missing a nuance. Frost walked on through the carpeted vestibule, past a bedroom with a closed door and into the living room. It was a large room with the most exquisite view of the city and the river. Two couches faced each other, and at a desk in the corner of the room, sat the pontiff, reading with the aid of a lamp. He turned at the sound of footsteps. He rose with difficulty, Frost hurrying to his side to assist him. The pope held out his hand, and Frost kissed the hand of the man he felt to be far less suited to be pope than himself.

"Why don't we sit down?" the pontiff asked in Italian, a language they both spoke.

Frost allowed himself to be led to one of the beige couches. They sat across from each other.

"So how have you been, my friend?" asked the pope.

"Fernandez," Frost said, "I want you to get the Israeli prime minister up here right now! It's a matter of crucial urgency! I mean it!" He lowered his voice and said, "Fernandez, instruct Julio to ask the prime minister to come upstairs right now!" The pope stared at him in surprise, suspicion obvious on his features.

"Our meeting isn't until tonight," he said.

"You're going to have to trust me on this one, old friend," Frost said. "Please do as I tell you. I promise you that I'm not leading you wrong. We know each other for what, 30 years, 35 years? Trust me, please, Fernandez. Make the call!"

The pope studied Frost for a minute without saying a word. Something about the urgency in his friend's voice must have convinced him, because he reached for the phone on the end table and dialed the number for the hall. He spoke a few terse words into the receiver.

"O.K.," he said, "It's done. Now what?"

"I'll tell you when he gets here," Frost said. "Until then, how has the papacy been treating you?"

⁂

The elevator came to a stop at the floor beneath the prime minister's suite, and wouldn't rise any further. There was no way for Rafi to get to the next floor without a special key. The doors slid open, and he exited into the corridor. Two members of the Israeli Secret Service stood on either side of the elevator. They had him moved to a corner of the hall before he had a chance to blink.

"Who are you?" the bigger of the two asked him.

"Stick your hand into my right pocket and take out my wallet, please," he said to the man. "In the inside pocket under the American driving license is my Mossad identification card."

The second guard followed his instructions and removed the wallet from his pocket. Within seconds they were examining his Mossad ID.

"Rafi Ganim," the bigger one read. "O.K., maybe you're in the Mossad. But we have a prime minister to protect. What's going on?"

"Sit down and I'll tell you exactly what's going on," Rafi said. "After I tell you everything that you need to know, you guys go down the hall and take as many weapons as you think you might need to control a possible situation."

"Talk to us," the man said, "and then we'll see about the guns."

"O.K., listen," Rafi said, "because we don't have a lot of time."

"What do you mean?" one of them asked. Rafi was about to answer, but just then the phone rang and one of the men rushed to answer it.

"That was the pope's aide on the line," he said as he replaced the receiver in its cradle. "The pontiff would like to hold the meeting right now."

"This is all extremely irregular," said one of the security men. "In fact, I have never heard of anything like this in my entire career with the prime minister's office!"

"Well, then sit down and I'll explain everything to you," Rafi said. "In fact, you need to understand exactly what's going on. Have a seat, because this is going to take a good few minutes to explain."

⁂

Israeli Prime Minister Doron Chizkiyahu walked toward the elevator surrounded by four of his Secret Service personnel. Rafi Ganim followed unobtrusively behind the party, staying out of the limelight as much as possible. In the end, they had brought Rafi to meet with Chizkiyahu himself, and the prime minister had grilled him over and over. The story was so fascinating and outlandish, so far fetched, that the prime minister had been hard pressed to believe it, and hadn't accepted his version until Rafi had called Kobi Shapiro at his personal number and Kobi had confirmed the truth of the situation. After another round of explanations, the prime minister had agreed to play his part, knowing as he did that there really wasn't much of a choice.

The Israelis were outfitted with sufficient weaponry to withstand a full-pronged attack. But Rafi explained that nothing close to that would be needed. The prime minister's entourage stepped into the elevator pressing the button for the penthouse suite on the uppermost floor. It was time to meet the pope.

The elevator doors slid open. Two of the prime minister's security team were the first to emerge. They checked the area to make sure there was nothing that posed a threat to the life of the Israeli leader. Only then did they allow him to enter the suite. The Israeli party was welcomed effusively by Bishop Julio D'Liviosi, personal secretary to the pope, and ushered into the suite. D'Liviosi led the way toward the living room, where the pope was still meeting with his friend, Cardinal Jason Frost of New York, who would be present for the upcoming meeting, according to the pope's express desire and request. As the party made their way through the opulent suite, three of the Mossad agents detached themselves from the rest of the group, and began fanning out through the rest of the rooms.

The doors leading to the living room were closed. Bishop Julio respectfully knocked on the door and waited for it to be opened. The man who answered the door was a familiar face to the incoming party.

"Cardinal Frost," the prime minister said. "What a pleasure!"

"The pleasure is all mine."

"Please come into the suite," Frost said to the dapper man. "The pope is ready for the meeting. Before we begin, I would just like to preface it with the fact that he had absolutely no idea about all the events here. He has a sincere desire to bridge the gap, and while your co-religionists may be unhappy about that, he had no interest at all in causing you harm in any way. He is as much a tool in this game as the rest of us."

The prime minister made his way into the living room where the pope was seated on the couch, an uneasy frown on his normally placid countenance.

"Welcome, friend," he said simply. The prime minister nodded in acknowledgment.

Outside in the hallway, Rafi turned to the fourth security man and said, "Secure the suite. Nobody goes in or out! The prime minister will be remaining with His Eminence for the immediate future. Make sure that none of the pope's men are anywhere near a telephone. As of now, both the prime minister and the pope are out of touch with the world, unreachable. Any telephone calls with be handled by myself, and myself alone. Is that clear?"

"Yes," answered the man, "we are temporarily unreachable."

From the direction of the bedrooms came the sounds of muffled shouts of outrage.

"Yes," the man repeated the words, "unreachable. That's us."

Berlin, Germany
June 20, 2009

Once again, Eberhart's hand reached for the phone. It was time to send a message that would never be forgotten. It was a message of such sheer strength that it would neither be ignored nor overlooked. It was a message that would change the world as mankind knew it; an act that would have never been condoned up until that day. But the actions that had taken place in a certain hotel room over the last few hours had made it all possible.

His fingers traced the buttons and pressed down lightly.

Far away, the phone rang with a buzzing sound.

"Hello," the man said.

"Let the fireworks begin," Eberhart said.

The words hung in the air like a weight that would come crashing down, shattering the unsuspecting earth forever.

The Media
June 20, 2009

The whispers began seemingly without cause. Nobody knew what was really going on. The news spread like wildfire, like a really hot flame in a field of the driest wheat. CNN picked it up first. ABC, NBC and Fox were hot on their heels, and then the rest of the networks took up the story. They all made sure to use a disclaimer, to report that the source could be unreliable, but that this was the story they had received. The rumors spread faster than a tsunami rolling in from the ocean. By midafternoon, the Internet was buzzing with information, theories and inaccuracies about the incident.

There had been an attack in the course of the historic meeting between the pope and the Israeli prime minister. It wasn't exactly clear what had transpired during the meeting, and the pope's suite was temporarily off limits to the press. But there seemed to be a general consensus that the Israeli prime minister had attacked the pope with malicious intent to do serious harm. Both leaders were in serious danger right now, and the situation was worsening by the hour. But again, the networks stressed, this was still conjecture, not fact. The analysts sat and pondered what this shocking development meant for Judeo-Christian relations. Even if there hadn't been an attack at all, even if it was just talk, what would this mean for future relations between the world's two oldest faiths?

Whether the prime minister had attacked the pope or it had happened the other way around didn't really make that much of a difference, being that both leaders had been critically wounded during the exchange of lethal blows. The source of the rumors was unclear, only saying that the pope had requested that all security forces leave the room while they spoke, due to the sensitive nature of the matters on the table. It was a request which the prime minister honored grudgingly, but which turned out to be possibly fatal. The pope had then locked the door of the suite and had begun bludgeoning Chizkiyahu with whatever items he could get his hands on. Another source said that sending the security men out of the room had likely been Chizkiyahu's idea, and that the pope had acquiesced unhappily. Chizkiyahu had then gone crazy, completely out of control, and using the skills he had acquired as a paratrooper in one of the elite army brigades 30 years before, he had beaten the pope senseless.

All agreed that nobody knew what was going on in real time, but that whatever it was that had transpired would serve as a setback for Israel's relationship with the Catholic world, perhaps forever. If it was true that an Israeli leader had attacked the head of the Catholic Church in as brutal a fashion as they were making it out to be, then the entire Western world would be forced to rethink their relationship with the homeland of the Jews. Maybe Israel didn't have a moral right to exist? On the other hand, it might have been the pope who had lost it and attacked the other first, in which case Israel would have to weigh the consequences of breaking off all diplomatic ties with the Vatican.

Every half an hour or so, the papers and networks would be given another update on the situation from the same mysterious source, who claimed to have a contact inside at the scene. The talk-show hosts wasted no time in bringing in the experts who all rushed to share their opinions with the millions of viewers.

"Things will never be the same between the Jews and the Catholics after this," said Father John Rosten, esteemed rector of the major theological seminary on the eastern seaboard. "The repercussions are going to be enormous. Nobody, and I mean nobody, could have ever foreseen anything even remotely close to something like this happening. It is insane that the pope should be attacked by another world leader. How could something like this have happened in today's world? Haven't we learned anything about how to solve our differences yet?" He went on and on in the same vein.

CNN had the top American theologians on the air, and questioned them about the attack. The trouble was that they didn't really know more than anyone else did. All they could say was that if the reports were really true, then this was something for which no Catholic would ever be able to forgive Israel. There was no justification for something like this, ever, period.

When the host reminded them that it was possible that the pope had been the instigator of the whole thing, they flatly refused to consider that as a possibility, reminding the talk-show host that the pope had always been a man of peace and a lover of mankind, and that there was absolutely no way on earth that he would have done something of this nature! There was nothing to discuss. It was impossible. It had to have happened the other way around, and they would never forgive this. The funeral, were the pope to die, would be the biggest event the world had ever seen. A new martyr had been found. And the Jews would be made to suffer for the error of their ways. The church had taken a soft line with the Jewish nation over the past 50 years. Obviously, that had been the wrong way to treat them, and their original method had been correct. It was time to revert to how it had been for thousands of years. Yes, they had apologized to the Jews. Well, they had been wrong for doing so.

The Vatican had no comment to make. The Israeli government likewise had no comment. Their spokesman merely said that the country of Israel reserved the right to withhold comment until the air had cleared and they really knew what had transpired.

A brigade of concerned Christians decided that it was incumbent upon themselves to take matters into their own hands, and discover what was really going on with the pontiff. They formed a brigade on the avenue outside the hotel in response to a chain letter that was going around the Internet urging all true Christians to gather and fight the 21st-century crusade. Equipped with weapons of all sorts, they formed a mob, and were about to storm the front of the hotel, when they were stopped by a unit of N.Y.P.D.'s antiterrorist squad. The police beat the mob back and sent more than a few of them to the hospital. This inflamed the populace of New York, which began gathering outside the hotel in greater and greater numbers. The Israeli Embassy and Consulate had both gone into full lock-down mode, with the gates locked tightly shut, cement roadblocks in place and everyone on the highest alert since 9/11.

A new rumor began circulating. There was no way for a Delta Force team to force its way to the suite, because the entire floor had been booby-trapped by the Israelis. Anyone who so much as attempted to enter the penthouse suite would be sending themselves off with a one-way ticket to the next world. And the truth was, the Israelis really had put in a call to the American authorities warning them to keep anything resembling a Delta Force team out of the hotel. They hadn't gone so far as to mention the words booby trap directly, but they hadn't needed to; the Americans were smart enough to figure that out by themselves.

Right now, the world needed to be kept in the dark.The Mossad couldn't afford any leaks at the moment. If a warning like this was what it would take to keep their floor nice and quiet, then so be it.

The entire boulevard in front of the Waldorf was packed with angry Catholics protesting the injustice of it all. It was a tinderbox set to go off. The Jews of New York barricaded themselves in their homes and stayed there. They didn't really believe that Prime Minister Chizkiyahu had done anything even remotely close to what was being said. But the fact that there was no way to discover what was going on inside the suite, combined with the ominous silence emerging from within, made their hearts tremble at the expected outcome.

For if Chizkiyahu had really been the one to attack the pope, life would become bitter for the Jewish people for a long time to come. It wouldn't matter why Chizkiyahu had done it. It wouldn't even make a difference if the pope had held a gun to his head. All that would matter was that a Jewish man, an Israeli, had dared harm the highest leader of the Catholic world, leader of a billion faithful worldwide. They would never be forgiven.

The media was outdoing itself. Ratings were what mattered. The president had already issue a call for the people to return to their homes until the matter was cleared up, but the people weren't listening. The people wanted to know how such a tragedy, such an outrage could have taken place in the midst of the city of New York. The president threatened to call out the National Guard, but even that threat wasn't sufficient to convince the mob to return home. Millions of Americans wanted to know why the army wasn't doing anything to get into that suite and rescue the pope from the man who had arrived from Israel. Even liberals were speaking of the death penalty, forgetting that it had been the Vatican that initiated the meeting.

In the meantime, as army helicopters flew overhead attempting to get a good look into the penthouse suite, the suite's curtains remained tightly shut. Security personnel were clueless and would remain that way for as long as whoever was in charge in the suite elected to keep them in the dark. That meant that the networks were still basing their coverage exclusively on the source supposedly from within the pope's suite; a fact that some journalists were beginning to find very troublesome. What if they had all been deceived? What if the whole incident had been a setup from the beginning?

But at the moment, there was no other information to go on, so they went with their only source and prayed that it was right: that the pope had indeed been the one who had been attacked, and that the Israeli was the aggressor, and the pope was the poor, innocent victim. Because if it was the other way around, who knew what the backlash would be?

There was just one source emanating from inside the Waldorf, and that was the one they were listening to. The story was just too good to be ignored. And the crowds continued to grow.

Berlin, Germany
June 21, 2009

The world's inhabitants were losing their minds, and it was entirely due to him! He couldn't help but admire the genius of the great men who had planned the entire operation: his father, who had conceived the concept in the first place, and all the others along the way who had aided and abetted the plan and the Network, with no thought to their safety or comfort, intent only on recreating German might as it had once been. By the time he carried out the plan, the entire world would know that the mighty power of World War II Germany had returned with a vengeance. It was all controlled and led by him, Dietrich Eberhart. Gone were the leaders sans backbone. That was a thing of the past. He would emerge as the leader of the Germany of today, strong, confident and victorious; unhesitating in its ability or willingness to take any action that would ensure its present or future dominance.

He was the source. He was the one feeding the media the information. He himself had called the cardinal. He had said the code words that would trigger him. His man had seen the cardinal entering the Waldorf, ostensibly on his way to carry out an attack on the pope and the prime minister. That was what he had been programmed to do. The cardinal wouldn't be capable of undoing his programming, of resisting in any way. He was hypnotized to fulfill a mission. He had no choice to act in any other way. He would carry out his mission like all those before him had done, and he would do a perfect job.

He had no doubts that the cardinal had done exactly as ordered. He had killed both the Israeli prime minister and the pope, or wounded them severely, thereby setting the Israelis off against the Catholic world, and the entire Catholic world against the Israelis and the rest of the Jews by extension. That was why he had spread the word. He knew that it must have happened that way, thereby setting the stage for what was to come. That was why the media was in a frenzy, because he had set the stage for the next phase of the war. It was all coming together even better than he could have ever hoped.

36

Cardinal Jason Frost

Over the Atlantic
June 21, 2009

Cardinal Jason Leonard Frost leaned back in the comfortable leather seat as the jetliner flew off into the purple evening sky. Frost thought over the events of the last 10 hours. They merged with one another in an endless sequence of sights and sounds. He smiled to himself as he pressed the button that would move the seat back to its maximum reclining position.

"A glass of wine, sir?" asked a passing stewardess.

"No, thank you," he replied. He wasn't in the mood for wine right now. He still couldn't get over the fact that he had managed to escape the Waldorf without anyone noticing. It had helped that he had departed before the majority of the crowd had begun gathering. They had known that Eberhart would begin publicizing the clash between the pope and the prime minister as soon as he believed it had occurred. With that in mind, Rafi had remained behind, in complete control of the papal suite, and Frost had exited the building before the news had leaked that something terribly wrong was happening. Fully equipped with another set of identity papers by the Mossad's documents department, Frost was traveling under the name of Henry Morgen. Right now, the N.Y.P.D. were under the assumption that Cardinal Frost was in the suite along with the pope and the prime minister. The moment they found out that he was not there, every policeman in the civilized world would be on the lookout for him.

The question facing the Mossad had been very simple. Where was Eberhart hiding? The Germans were denying any knowledge of his whereabouts, even going so far as to claim that he might not even be in the country at all. Interpol had not seen hide nor hair of him. The UK security had no idea where he might have gone. Records showed that he had been in England a few months before, but had not returned since. Eberhart had to be stopped, and Frost knew that he was the man for the job. He was one of the only people that Eberhart knew was on his side, because he had programmed him to be. If Frost were to suddenly appear at the Germans' hideaway, they were reasonably sure that Eberhart would be willing to see him, knowing as he did that Frost must have something very important to tell him. The only question was: Where was he hiding?

The fact was Eberhart could be anywhere at all. The Eberhart Construction Company had building sites all over Europe. Eberhart could be at any one of those. But that didn't make sense to any of them, especially Rafi. This was something that they had discussed for hours before they left for the Waldorf. Rafi had sat with Eberhart. He had heard him speak of a sense of destiny, a sense of importance, and he knew that there was no way that a man with such a sense of history as Eberhart had, would sit in some decrepit hole to carry out his mission. There was no way. But where was he? Rafi recalled every word of their discussion together.

"It's a place that speaks to me," Eberhart had said simply about the pictures on the wall. "Whenever I visit those few rooms, I can hear the voices of the past speaking to me, instructing me. It's almost like a shrine. When the right time comes, I will fight the next war from the most fitting place I can think of. It will be a place with tremendous historical importance for the German people; a place where other greater leaders than I sat and did their best for the cause."

Rafi had taken a series of photographs of the bunker from all the angles exhibited on the wall. Included in the photos of the bunker was one that held no seeming relevance, a photo of a nearby parking lot. He had all of this in his camera. He had shown them to Kobi, both of them pouring over the photographs for hours. This then was the place that Eberhart had chosen to finish the game. But where was it? Kobi had had the photo developed and enlarged. He had provided copies of the picture to some of the Mossad analysts without telling them why he needed to know.

"Just tell me where this is," Rafi instructed them.

They had gone to work. Kobi figured that it had to have something to do with Hitler or Himmler, and knowing of the Eberhart family's fixation with Himmler, it was probably the latter. The analysts had pulled up the files from the agency's basement. They found hundreds of pictures of old underground bunkers, pictures that had been taken after the war by the allied soldiers. There were bunkers that had been constructed throughout Germany, mostly by the Eberhart Construction Company. It would not be a difficult thing for Eberhart to rebuild one of them and have it refurbished just the way it had been before the end of the war to use as a command center. The analysts had come through for them, up to a point. They had narrowed it down to one of three possibilities. One of them was Himmler's secret bunker in the Bavarian forests. But it was difficult to reach, with few paved roads. It was hard to imagine that this was the place Eberhart had chosen for his "final solution."

The second choice was another bunker that had been built by the Eberhart firm for Himmler as well. Constructed under his headquarters, it spread out under the Berlin streets in a number of directions, providing a shelter for those Nazi bigwigs who had not chosen to spend the final days of the war together with Hitler and Eva Braun. The problem with that was that the bunker had collapsed at the war's end in a heap of rubble due to the Russian bombing, and had never been restored. It meant that although the pictures matched to some degree, the idea was highly improbable.

Then there was the *Fuhrerbunker*, Hitler's bunker and the place where he ostensibly committed suicide along with his wife, as the Russian Army bombed their way through the war-torn streets of Berlin. The rooms were more or less a match, and it made sense that Eberhart would want to taste victory — correct the injustice — right at the spot where the master of Germany had gone the way of all tyrants. But there was one problem: The site of the bunker in the garden of what had been the Third Reich Chancellery was under construction by the German government. They had received complaints that the way the bunker had been built was undermining the structure of many of the buildings above it. Engineers had concurred with the complaints. Some serious structural damage had occurred to the underground supports, and it had been under repair for the past two years. With all the comings and goings involved with the renovations, it was hard to imagine that Eberhart had chosen that bunker for his command center.

Nevertheless, Rafi instinctively felt that it was this third option. The pictures were the closest match, it was still operable and it was easy to access. Best of all, after some digging on the part of Mossad operatives in Berlin, they were able to discover that although the firm carrying out the construction was the Berlin Construction Company, there was a parent company and another company above that, leading to a tangled web that never seemed to end. Rafi was pretty sure that if one looked far enough, the Eberhart Construction Company would surface at the end of the chase. Most importantly, Kobi agreed with him. Not only that, but the *Fuhrerbunker* was covered over by a parking lot that looked mighty familiar. It had to be the one!

That was why Frost was on his way to Berlin; because it was going to boil down to Eberhart and himself. That was where Eberhart was, in the *Fuhrerbunker*, trying to turn the tide of history. It was up to Frost to make sure that that didn't occur. Frost was doing it for himself, a man whose entire life had been a lie, for his father, the Rabbi from Kolodov, whose child had been taken away, and for the song that had accompanied them both throughout their lives and was reverberating even now through his head as the plane winged its way through a darkness that never seemed to end.

Highway 6, Israel
June 21, 2009
Afternoon

Briefcase allowed the Volvo to surge far ahead of him. They had been following the man for quite some time now, and Briefcase was beginning to have grave doubts that anything was going to happen. Even the best in the business made mistakes sometimes. Still, despite the fact that he wasn't expecting any action in the near future, he still took every precaution to remain out of sight. T-shirt, who was now Leather jacket, was keeping far ahead of the Volvo, and would pull over to the side of the highway at some point with "engine trouble," giving the Volvo the opportunity to take the lead again. They were heading due south, to the part of the country that had never been fully developed: the Negev, Beersheva, Sdei Boker. Down south, there were empty tracks of land that

Israel had desired to develop for many years, but had never managed to do so. A minister had even been appointed to form the Negev Committee, specifically established to deal with the issue and create a solution to the situation.

As of yet, the problem had not been dealt with. Drugs filtered through porous holes in the border from the direction of the Sinai Desert, and the Bedouins were the real masters of the land despite the numerous communities that had been built by settlers who had devoted their lives to cultivating the arid land. Now the man was heading toward that part of the country. Once they exited the highway, they wouldn't be able to remain with the same vehicles. The highways down south were much smaller, less developed and without sufficient vehicular traffic to provide sufficient cover. A switch was the only option. Briefcase got on the phone and dialed the number from memory. The phone rang a few times before it was answered.

"Yes?" the boss asked, "what is it?

Briefcase outlined the situation to him and explained that they were going to need a change of vehicles.

"They will be waiting for you at the main Beersheva junction," the man said. "I will call you back with the pertinent information."

Two minutes later the phone rang. "A 2005 Subaru will be waiting for you at the junction and a 2000 Nissan van will be waiting for your motorcycle partner."

He hung up.

They continued driving. The Volvo was making good time on the potholed road. The motorcycle was suddenly struck by the unexpected casualty of an overheated engine. The driver pulled to the side and took out the bottle he kept for emergencies. Keeping a constant lookout on the road, he began pouring in a steady stream of cooling agent. As he stood alongside his motorcycle, with his eye on the side mirror, he could see the Volvo approaching fast, the grille in the front of the car glinting as it reflected the sunlight. His face was turned to the side, but his peripheral vision saw that the driver had noticed him. He knew that he had lost the edge of surprise. He couldn't continue here. He'd been burned.

He stood at the side of the road and used his phone to call the agent in charge.

"It's time to activate the next set of agents," he said.

"Activated," the man grunted. Leather jacket hung up the phone and closed the bottle of cooling fluid. He was done for today, as was his friend in the Mazda. There was no taking any chances with this one. Two other agents would pick him up when he hit the Beersheva region. And indeed, two agents were waiting to take over at the junction at precisely the time when the Volvo was expected to arrive. But no Volvo showed up.

The two new agents were dressed like students. One was driving a Hyundai Getz, the other a Suzuki. The Getz, a small car with an engine that wouldn't quit, was idling on the side of the highway ready to hit the asphalt as soon as he caught sight of either the Volvo or a driver that bore a resemblance to the man. Instead of a Volvo however, he caught sight of what appeared to be the subject in the driver's seat of a Ford Explorer. He waited a while and then burned rubber for several miles until the Explorer came into sight. Then he dropped back, allowing about six cars to remain between them. The Suzuki took an alternate route, and joined up with them as they were hitting the Netivot Road. He entered the two-lane highway ahead of the Explorer and waited for instructions from the Getz.

Because the Suzuki was ahead of the Explorer he had no idea that his target had turned off the road. He continued driving keeping well within the speed limit and eventually his partner in the Getz buzzed him to say that the Explorer had taken a sharp right off the highway at some point. There were only a few possibilities where the target could have turned off, and he was going to take the one he thought the most likely. There were no road signs, he said, and there was only a bumpy dirt road, but the GPS in his car informed him that they were in the vicinity of the Bedouin village of Hibbaya. He instructed the Suzuki to make a U-turn and park around the bend from the almost hidden road that he had taken. It was late afternoon, and wouldn't be long before twilight began settling in.

The driver of the Getz, disregarding the feelings of dread that were telling him to stay away from this abandoned road, pressed down hard on the gas. The Getz shot up the little hillock and crested the bend. He turned on his brights and drove after the Explorer toward the village, hoping that he wasn't too late. There were no streetlights on this road, and giant potholes made the Getz toss and twist as he fought to keep control of the wheel and move forward at the same time. The side of the road was littered with the frames of stripped vehicles, a clear sign that he was approaching a Bedouin encampment. The empty shells exuded a feeling of impending danger, and he could feel his heart beginning to beat faster. Up ahead, he caught sight of something lying across the road. It could be a rope, could be a chain. But he had a feeling that he knew what it was. He'd seen them often enough in his stint in the army. It was metal teeth. Place them across a road and any car that drove over them would find that all the air was knocked out of their tires, just like that.

That was when he knew that he had made a terrible mistake. He hesitated in indecision and was about to make a U-turn and get out of there, but then he glanced in his rearview mirror and saw the giant truck coming toward him, blocking the road. There was no point in turning around. He stepped on the gas like a maniac, hurtling the car forward, his teeth shattering from the bone-jarring shocks as they drove over the rock-strewn surface. He was approaching the row of metal teeth. They covered the roadway nearly from side to side, but there was a little gap. It was there that he directed the tiny car at top speed. He shot through the gap and over the top of a hill, and found himself gazing at the valley beneath him.

A village lay before him: a maze of huts with tin roofs and thatched huts and tents of all kinds. Here was Hibbaya in all its threadbare glory, and there was nowhere for him to go because the roads were narrow intended for donkeys and not for vehicles. He had no idea which way to head, and he would only get stuck in some dead end and be forced to turn around while hordes of unkempt and unruly children laughed and pointed.

"Send backup," he whispered into his phone.

He saw them coming toward the car, a whole bunch of them, and he knew that it would take a miracle for him to get out of this place alive.

Negev Highway, Israel
June 21, 2009
Early Evening

The Suzuki waited for his partner to come out of the road or for something to happen, when he heard the faint sounds coming from the phone, "Send backup." He wasted no time. He contacted the agent in charge and told him in terse language exactly what he knew. The agent promised to send reinforcements. Meanwhile, he should remain where he was.

He sat in the car and waited tensely for something, anything, to happen. Time was passing as slowly as it had ever passed for the young agent. He was in mental agony as he imagined the worst. He wondered if his colleague would escape or if he was holed up somewhere in the Bedouin encampment. He squinted out the window, trying to discern any signs of life. It was then that he saw the cloud of dust rising from behind the bend in the road; the sign of a vehicle moving in a hurry. The dust probably meant that there was another road out of the Bedouin village whereby cars could leave. He put the car into gear, clicked his lights off, and began driving toward the low-hanging cloud of dust, trying to bridge the gap before he even realized that he was in business again.

New York City
June 21, 2009

The crowds just kept on increasing in size as the hours dragged by. The police presence kept growing as well, as the mayor of New York sent more and more police to the Waldorf. At some point, the mayor realized that this was not going to work. The crowd was getting ready to storm the hotel and take out the Israelis who were holding the pope and his men hostage. The hostage situation had been in progress for hours already. Nobody knew anything. The supposed hostage division of the police department had tried contacting the papal suite numerous times to negotiate, but either the phone had been pulled out of the wall, or nobody was being allowed to answer, because they hadn't been able to get through.

The police chief and his staff didn't believe that the pope had been killed or even harmed by the Israelis, but they were heavily outnumbered by 100,000 Catholics in the street below. It was when he saw the crowd escalate into a mob that the mayor put in a call to the governor to send in the National Guard.

"With tanks?" asked the governor.

"Not a bad idea," the mayor replied. "We need to disperse this crowd without anybody getting hurt. If the army doesn't arrive soon, someone *is* going to get hurt, and it just might be the N.Y.P.D. "

"I will have a unit of the National Guard in the streets of New York within two hours," the governor promised.

From that moment on, the networks began warning the citizens of New York to disband, since the army was on its way to handle the situation. Just the idea that the army was heading their way was enough to convince a sizable portion of the mob to go home. But there were others who were made of tougher material, who weren't about to abandon their leader. Those people stood their ground and prepared to charge the Waldorf before the army arrived. A man by the name of Ethan McElroy stood up on a platform and, using a set of lungs that could have competed with the best sound system, began directing the mob to begin charging the police barriers at the front of the hotel. The policemen of New York are not known for their patience at the best of times, and this was most definitely not the best of times.

They took one look at the charging crowd, raised their tear-gas canisters and began spraying indiscriminately at the mob. The mob reacted with a roar of pain and rage, and ran in several directions trying to escape the clouds of gas that were coming at them in an unceasing surge of stinging air. The mob began to retreat, and many of them were leaving when a call from McElroy ordering them to remember why they were there made them turn around and begin charging the hotel again. This time the city police who were on horseback rushed into the melee delivering smacks with their billy clubs right and left, until the mob was forced to fall back again, hurt and bleeding. But both sides knew that if the army didn't arrive soon, the mob would eventually succeed in overpowering the police and gaining the advantage.

In the Waldorf penthouse suite, Prime Minister Doron Chizkiyahu was watching on television the utter bedlam taking place in the street below.

"How much longer?" he asked the Mossad agent who had all but taken him hostage.

"As long as it takes," Rafi replied.

"But look at that scene," the prime minister persisted. "There must be 100,000 people charging the hotel! Maybe it's time to go public now?"

"With all due respect, sir," Rafi said, "we are dealing with an extremely resourceful and dangerous enemy. He is watching his television set just as you are. He knows what is going on here just as we do. In fact, sir, he is the one who manipulated you into getting on a plane and agreeing to meet with the pope in the first place, against the wishes of many of your advisers who warned you to stay away from this meeting. He has men high up in the Vatican, some of whom may well be right here in this suite. If we make the situation clear at this point, he may very well trigger the rest of those names. And yes, although we do have people at every location who will probably make sure that nothing too destructive happens, there is every possibility that they will not be totally successful. Right now, Eberhart is in Germany, still imagining that he has some level of control over the situation. The moment you and the pope show yourselves, the element of surprise is lost, and then goodbye to any semblance of peace. Do we understand each other, prime minister? I know that it's your natural instinct to want to fix the situation, but sometimes it's not as simple as it seems. So sit down on the couch, close your eyes and try to go to sleep, and pray that when you wake up, this whole nightmare will be over.

"Don't worry," Rafi ended. "We'll know when it's the right time. Besides, Frost is almost there. So just hold on."

"Oh wow," said the prime minister, "an elderly cardinal is on his way to confront this mightiest of enemies, and that's supposed to make me feel better about the whole situation?!"

"I think he'll have a couple of friends along with him as well," Rafi replied.

Negev Highway, Israel
Early Evening
June 21, 2009

The agent in the Suzuki took off after the cloud of dust, and then squealed to a stop as he considered his next move. *Take your time*, an inner voice warned him, and he slowed to a stop on the shoulder of the road, because something was telling him to wait. He shouldn't chase after the vehicle that had emerged from what had been a hidden road. He shouldn't reveal himself, or be too hasty. Two minutes later, there was another cloud of dust. From his present position, he could see the Explorer and another car crossing a hill on the side of the road, about to coast back onto the highway. They were emerging from the unidentified road. He had been right to wait. He had been right in not following that first cloud of dust.

But now, he had a tough call to make. Should he follow the Explorer, or take on the second car, an old, run-down Subaru? This was a call for the agent in charge.

"So what should I do?" he asked breathlessly into the phone. "Should I stick with the Explorer or stay on the Subaru?"

"Stay on the Subaru," Kobi said. "I'll have someone pick up the Explorer along the way."

"Got ya," he replied, and the chase was on.

As he drove off into the warm and dusty night, he could see army cars with sirens blaring, heading toward him from the opposite direction. He knew that they were going to Hibbaya and the agent in the Getz. He just hoped they weren't too late. Little shards of glass sparkled in the middle of the road from an accident that had happened earlier that night. The Suzuki swerved to avoid them, and saw the Subaru up ahead, waiting for a traffic light to turn green. He remained about five cars behind, and hoped that the Subaru wouldn't place him. From where he was in the line of cars, the man in the Subaru's driver's seat appeared to be the man they had been chasing all that night, but he couldn't be sure.

The Subaru kept to the speed limit, and did nothing out of the ordinary. They had been driving for several hours, and were approaching Tel Aviv. The Suzuki began to fear that Kobi had made the wrong call, that maybe the Explorer was the right car, and he was following a decoy. But no, as soon as they had gotten onto the Tel Aviv Highway, the driver began putting on the speed and shifting from lane to lane. He did his best to keep up with him without putting his life in danger. Up ahead, he could see Tel Aviv proper, and he was ready when the Subaru took an exit without warning, cutting across three lanes of traffic and almost causing two accidents. He followed the car off the highway, and realized that he knew where the man was headed. Standing before him were the two tallest skyscrapers in the country: the two towers of Tel Aviv, one square, the other round, known as the Azrieli Center. Somehow he knew, he was sure that the madman was heading right there, with whatever "bundle of joy" he was carrying in the car along with him.

He watched the driver take the corners at top speed, and he stayed right behind him. The time for secrecy had passed. All he needed to do was to get to the Subaru in time to get the driver in cuffs, open up his trunk and see if he had the package that Kobi was worried about inside the car. If the trunk was empty, no problem. The man would be free to go. But if there was a package in the trunk, then the action would begin.

Promotions, fun and games ahead for everyone involved in this case. Up ahead of him, the Subaru across the road and headed toward the entrance to the Azrieli Center's underground parking lot. A guard made as if to stop him, but raised the bar at the last moment. The Subaru obviously had a pass for the basement parking lot plus some sort of official sticker that exempted the vehicle from inspection.

The bar came down after the Subaru, and now the Suzuki was waiting impatiently for the guard to get himself over to his window. Nothing happened. The man was taking his time.

He jumped out of the car and yelled at the guard while showing his identification card at the same time. The guard ran to press the button. The bar rose in the air and he shot down the ramp into the parking lot, down the steep ramp that coiled snakelike round and round, past the numerous cars parked one after another, each one so like the next. Where would the man have gone? He would need an elevator. Where was the elevator? He drove with one foot shifting from gas to break and back to gas, trying to see through the rows of cars, trying to use that special sense that top agents possessed. Down below, he could see a car that looked like the Subaru come to a stop. The driver jumped out and headed toward the elevator, with a black package under his arm!

This was it. The hour had come. Just as Kobi had predicted.

He could see the man waiting by the elevator door, and he jumped out of the car and ran down the ramp toward the man who was two levels below. He could see him reaching for the door. He wanted to jump down and tackle him, but it would have been suicide. He was frustrated, especially as he watched the man stroll into the elevator and the doors close. He raced up to the elevator and in mute horror he watched it moving upward. It was going from floor to floor, not stopping. He watched with his heart in his throat, knowing that it would come to a stop on the highest floor. That was exactly what happened.

The man had exited on the highest floor of the Azrieli Center carrying murderous baggage, and he was stuck in the parking lot! He kicked himself mentally; how hadn't he realized that this would be the target! Of course this was the target! The highest building in the country, the fallout would be tremendous from this spot. They should have known.

The elevator doors opened with a ping and he entered, pressing the button for the highest floor and praying desperately. For the most part, his prayers were answered. Except for one floor, where the elevator opened up and he had to shoo the people away with his official ID, it went directly to the top floor. He raced from the elevator, accosting people in the hallway, asking them, yelling at them, screaming at them to remember if they had seen an older man carrying a black package passing through the halls just minutes earlier.

When nobody remembered anything, he became frantic and he began ordering everyone to clear the floor because someone was in the building with a dangerous package. The people heard and became frightened and the news spread like wildfire. Sure enough, they started cramming themselves down the staircase and into the elevators. He began running the other way, into offices and conference rooms and anywhere else he could think of that a man might want to hide a nuclear device the size of a knapsack. But there were so many places and not enough time.

Down the hall, near the last bank of elevators, a distinguished-looking man in his late 50's, removed a batch of papers from a black knapsack and turned it inside out. Now it was red.

The man joined the rest of the unruly crowd rushing down the stairs. It was like the Twin Towers all over again, someone said, and everyone agreed.

The agent from the Suzuki came running down the hallway now in the opposite direction, and skidded to a sudden stop. There was the man from the Subaru. The knapsack he was holding had miraculously turned red. But other than that, he was the same. So the agent took hold of his arm and told him to come along with him. They went into one of the empty conference rooms, where the agent from the Suzuki learned to his great dismay that he had been following the wrong car. The Subaru had been the decoy, and the Explorer had been the real McCoy.

We lost, the agent thought to himself as he put a call through to Kobi. *We could have won, but we lost. At the last second, the man slipped through our fingers. How could something like this have happened?*

But Kobi Shapiro amazingly enough didn't seem at all discouraged by the fact that the man had slipped through their fingers. In fact, if he hadn't known better, the agent from the Suzuki would have thought that Kobi wasn't worried at all. As he escorted the cuffed gray-haired man with the red knapsack into custody, the agent didn't quite know what to think anymore.

~

The Waldorf-Astoria Hotel, New York
June 21, 2009

The mob watched stony faced as the police lined up in front of the hotel in full riot gear. Ambulances pulled up and the wounded were carried aboard moaning and crying from the tear gas in their eyes, and from ribs that had been smashed by police clubs. The chief of police got on the phone to the governor and warned him in a voice that sounded as harsh as a razor that if the National Guard wasn't at the Waldorf within 10 minutes, he would personally make sure that the governor wouldn't last out the week in office. The startled politician promised to do all he could, reassuring the chief of police that the army was on its way, and that he would be hearing the heavy tread of the tanks momentarily.

But just then, someone from the back of the mob threw a firebomb at the cordon of police lining the stairs. It hit the ground directly in front of them, bursting into flames. The police were startled and reacted badly. This time, there was a flood of tear gas directed toward the crowd, who backed off choking and crying from the gas. The flames were spreading out of control, and the fire department couldn't get through to put it out. The developments on the ground were deteriorating, and the chief of police ordered 10 of his men to fire their weapons into the air in one unified shot.

As the waiters and bellhops of the Waldorf Hotel began pouring buckets of water onto the flames, 10 officers of the N.Y.P.D. lifted their guns and, aiming at the sky, unleashed a barrage of gunfire at the moon. There was a sudden stillness, and the mob came to the realization that the police had begun firing their weapons. Not knowing that it had not been aimed at them, they rushed the stairs, fire and all, intent on making the police department pay for their mistake.

But before they got too far, the ground began to shake, as the first of a long line of tanks began rumbling into sight, accompanied by army jeeps. The tanks ground to a halt not far from the entrance to the hotel scattering the mob, who retreated in confusion at the sight of the army.

Cardinal Jason Frost, Dietrich Eberhart and Kobi

Berlin, Germany
Late Evening
June 21, 2009

Cardinal Jason Leonard Frost stepped off the plane and into the carpeted tunnel leading toward the arrivals gate. He moved with agility for his advanced years, and was passed rapidly through passport control and the customs line. It would have been quicker had he been able to use his diplomatic passport, but that would have prevented him from carrying out his mission. Two men met him at the sliding-glass doors. They ushered him into a modest Audi. The car sped from the airport and merged with traffic. The agents' faces were stonelike in the darkened interior.

"We'll be stationed at your back," the agent in charge said. "But unfortunately, only you will be able to enter the bunker. The moment the Germans see that someone else is accompanying you, everything will be lost. You are going to have to get inside on your own. Only then, when their attention is focused on you, will we be able to enter undetected. There are 10 agents here tonight — more than enough to handle whatever security they have inside the bunker. We're still not even sure that Eberhart is in the bunker. We hope he is. With G-d's help, you'll be able to get in, and hopefully everything will go smoothly once you're inside. This is a tough operation, and we commend you for your bravery and courage."

The car drove through the streets of Berlin. It was quiet outside. For the most part, the city slumbered.

"As soon as you judge that you have gotten far enough inside the bunker," said the agent, "press this button, and we will be right behind you." He handed Frost what appeared to be a coin of some kind. Frost stowed it in his pocket. The car drove past what had up until the late 80's been Checkpoint Charlie — the most famous crossing point in the Berlin Wall — the concrete divider built by the Russians to separate East and West Berlin. Adjacent to the wall were the remains of the Chancellery and the nearby garden, beneath which lay the remains of the *Fuhrerbunker*, or Hitler's bunker. That was the underground retreat where the mad dictator had spent his final days on earth.

As they approached the site, they could see it was obstructed by a hastily erected fence, with a sign that warned passersby in four languages that it was a construction site and off limits. But the gate was partially opened, and there was no one present to prevent them from entering. They separated at the gate, and Frost looked back at the men for one final glance. He then plunged into the twists, turns and the maze of concrete and bricks that littered the site. He slipped through the debris, eventually emerging at a closed-off entrance that was padlocked, and which appeared to have been left completely undisturbed. For a moment he was concerned that he was at the wrong place. Maybe they had just made the mistake of a lifetime. But that thought was shaken out of his mind when he felt a pair of arms grab him from behind and a hoarse voice whispered, "Name and password, now!"

This was it. He was going in.

"Cardinal Jason Leonard Frost with an urgent message for Herr Eberhart," he said. "And I don't know the password."

"Identification," the gruff voice demanded. Frost removed his wallet and showed him his American driver's license.

The man spoke softly into a radio that he held, the harsh guttural sounds of his voice barely heard. He waited for a response and then nodded satisfied.

"O.K.," he finally said, "come with me."

Pulling a key from his pocket, he inserted it into the lock and turned. The lock opened smoothly, as if it had just been oiled. Together they stepped into the *Fuhrerbunker*, the underground rooms where Adolph Hitler had spent his final days on earth.

They walked into a well-ventilated hallway, which came to an end at a staircase that appeared to descend into the very bowels of the earth. The guard held onto Frost and made sure that he didn't trip as they took the stairs one at a time. From the looks of it, not much construction was taking place in the bunker, notwithstanding the tremendous amount of machinery outside. They reached the first level beneath the surface, and Frost could see a corridor with numerous rooms branching off it to the sides. He recalled reading somewhere that Joseph and Magda Goebbels and their six children had lived here in the closing days of the war. There had been many others residing there as well: Hitler's secretaries, his Alsatian dog, Blondi, guards galore and a host of others coming and going at all times. Arthur Axmann, leader of the Hitler Youth, had been a guest as well, and Martin Bormann, Hitler's private secretary, had remained near his master until the bitter end.

As they walked through the low-ceilinged corridor, Frost imagined he could hear the ghosts of the past calling out to him and one another. He pictured the scene at the end of the war: soldiers rushing about, orders being issued in a continuous stream for the defense of Berlin, Hitler's final meal with his secretaries, the dramatic moment when Hitler discovered that Himmler had sold him out by attempting to sue for peace with the Allies. This was the place where it had all come to an end: Hitler's Thousand-Year Reich, coming to an unceremonious finish after little more than a decade. Frost could hear the air-conditioner unit working, straining to provide fresh air for the bunker.

They walked through the corridor, reaching a spiral staircase at the end. The guard gave him a gentle shove forward, and they began to descend another 20 feet into the ground, to the newer section that Hitler had ordered them build, even deeper than the first section, insulated from the bombing of Berlin. The humming of machinery grew louder and louder the lower they went. They were in the second set of rooms. There were 20 rooms in all, branching off from the main hallway. This was the hole where Hitler had spent his final days.

Then they reached the end of the hallway, and there was nowhere left to go. The guard opened a closet door, and they found themselves in what appeared to be a walk-in closet, large enough to have been a linen closet or food pantry in days gone by. There was a poster on the wall. The guard moved it aside revealing a hidden panel with buttons. Frost realized that they were in an elevator. They began descending, the elevator creaking and groaning as the ropes held strong. For the first time, he understood that someone had built an even lower level that nobody had known about.

The Eberhart family would have known about this additional floor, either because they had been the ones who owned the construction company who had developed it, or because Eberhart himself had had this level built years after the war, for this very moment. He reached into his pocket and pressed the coin, signaling them to come in now, because they were taking him somewhere they had no knowledge of and he wanted them to know that things were not under control.

The elevator went from ponderous movement to a suddenly rapid descent. Frost didn't realize they had stopped until he felt his stomach catch up with him. The door slid open, and again they were in yet another hallway, this one wood paneled and carpeted. There were several photographs of Hitler on display. Again, there were many doors and corridors branching off the main hallway in all directions. At the end of the hallway was a door with the words "Command Center" stenciled in black. This was the place where it would all come to an end, one way or another. He could hear other men talking from behind closed doors. There was a very tough-looking man standing near the door.

"Here he is, Karl," the guard said to the man, who nodded with distinct military directness.

"Did you see Munich on your way down here?" he asked the guard.

"Yes, sir," the guard replied. "He's patrolling the upper level."

Karl nodded, effectively dismissing the guard. Picking up his radio, he spoke a few words into the mouthpiece.

"Send him in," came the response from inside the room.

Karl frisked him, pausing for a moment when he discovered a pair of sunglasses in Frost's pants pocket.

"They're for my cornea," Frost explained. "Recently I've had some trouble with my eyes."

Karl examined them for a moment before handing them back and propelling him toward the door.

"You're on," he said. And Frost knew that this was it.

High above the underground bunker on the Berlin street across from the construction site, the 10 Mossad agents swung into action. Clad entirely in black, with infrared night goggles over their eyes, they secured the site's perimeter. It was almost impossible to pick them up on camera due to their speed and dark outfits, which blended in with the blackness of the evening. Five of them combed the construction site for any additional guards. The area appeared to be deserted. They gave the other agents the signal. It was time to go in. As they stood clustered around the entrance to the bunker, there was a sudden whistling sound and the ping of a bullet hitting the door above their heads. Immediately, they spread out. Five hit the ground and began to return fire with their silenced weapons, covering the agent who was working the lock. One agent remained outside, keeping up a steady stream of fire, while the rest of the agents entered the bunker, closing and locking the door behind them from the inside.

They were standing at one end of a 9-foot-wide corridor. On either side was room after room, one after another with their doors closed. They did not know what danger was lurking within, and were taking no chances. The agents spread out, each of them taking a room. The leader gave the signal and there was a sudden crash as they smashed in eight doors at exactly the same moment. Within seconds they were in the rooms, guns swinging from side to side, covering all directions, eyes probing for anything moving. The majority of the rooms were empty. Two of them had guards asleep in their beds. They left them sleeping forever.

They moved forward to the end of the corridor, finding themselves at the top of a staircase. Cautiously, they began their descent, moving forward on the balls of their feet, making no noise, guns outstretched in their hands, goggles off their faces, which had been daubed with camouflage paint. They looked fearsome, like angels of death on the move. They reached the foot of the staircase, and began streaming forward along the sides of the corridor, hugging the walls, ready for anything.

There was an open door at the end of the corridor, and they could hear people talking. They slid along, approaching the source of the noise. From the end of the hall came a whistling noise. The team dropped to the floor, but one of them had been hit in his vest-protected chest. The impact of the bullet knocked the breath out of him. He lay on the floor gagging and retching. Leaving one man to attend to him, they returned immediately to fighting mode, weapons drawn, spraying the hallway with bullets. The guards heard the commotion from inside the room and rushed out to see what was going on. The first guard was sent flying off his feet and was neutralized, never knowing what happened to him. The second guard immediately barricaded himself in his room and began shooting at the agents through the door.

Again the team split up. The majority of the agents moved on in the direction of the shots, searching for the pocket of resistence. Relentlessly, the agents advanced, compelled to finish what they had begun, returning fire, progressing slowly, having to retreat, some covering the others. They cornered the shooters, threw a minigrenade into the room, and doubled back. The sound of a miniexplosion filled the hall, as well as the screams of the wounded. The agents moved on, getting closer and closer to the end of the hallway. It didn't take them too long to discover the elevator, the last remaining obstacle to the rescue of Frost and the removal of Eberhart.

The leader gave the signal, and two of the agents entered the small elevator along with him.

"We'll send it back up for you," he said, and they nodded.

Without another word, the agent pushed the button for the lowest level, no expression on his face as the doors closed silently, and the elevator started to move on ropes of coiled steel.

Ben-Gurion Airport, Israel
Late Evening
June 21, 2009

Kobi entered the terminal at Ben-Gurion through the entrance used by the security force. He walked quickly for a man of his years, an extremely serious look taking the place of his generally relaxed demeanor. He strode through the hallways, past the offices of the security force's senior staff and into the large room that served as the computer center for visual security. The room was manned by a number of staff at all hours of the day and night, ensuring that any suspicious individual who passed the threshold of the airport was immediately pulled to the side for questioning. The guard at the door nodded at Kobi with a smile, and didn't bother asking for identification, because Kobi was a regular in the room, having been a Mossad liaison with airport security. It was Kobi who had assisted the staff at Ben-Gurion in creating a security system that was the envy of every country.

Kobi headed straight for the rear of the room, to the office of the man in charge. Bentzion Nachliel and Kobi Shapiro went back decades together, and he wouldn't question a request that Kobi made, no matter how strange it sounded.

"I need a bank of computers set up for me, so that I can see every entrance into the terminal building. I want to know the name and I want to see the face of every person who enters the terminal or heads out to the tarmac. It's a matter of national security!"

"Are we looking for anyone in particular?" Bentzion asked him.

"Yes," answered Kobi, "but I can't tell you who until he's actually here, because if I'm wrong, then it would have been a horrible thing to accuse him. But I don't think I'm wrong."

While they spoke, a technician had begun setting up the computers for him. He took a seat at the console, moving the mouse from screen to screen, turning them all on, keeping his sharp gaze focused on every screen at once. If he missed something, he pressed rewind and made sure to see who or what it had been.

"According to my calculations," Kobi said to Bentzion, "he should be here in the next few minutes. Take a moment to check the flight schedules. Is the next Lufthansa flight to Berlin departing on schedule?"

"One hour from now," Bentzion said. "It's right on time. That's Ben-Gurion Airport, never late." They shared a laugh.

"Well then," Kobi said, "keep your eyes peeled for a familiar face, someone you know quite well; someone you would have never guessed would be involved in a situation that would pose a danger for the country."

They sat quietly for a few minutes watching the pedestrian traffic flowing in and out of the terminal. Suddenly Bentzion stiffened and grabbed Kobi's arm.

"Look over there," he said in a whisper, pointing at one of the security entrances that only those with the highest security clearance were able to use by accessing a special code. Kobi turned and nodded his head.

"That's our man," he said. "I want you to get four security men down there now. Have him escorted to your office immediately. They should pay no attention whatsoever to anything he says, not threats, not bribery. Nothing!"

Bentzion issued the order on his radio. They tuned into a video camera that covered the ground-level hallway that had just been penetrated. Within 20 seconds, there were four agents dressed in airport security making their way down the hallway toward the suspect who was walking normally, displaying no sign of any uneasy behavior.

"Are you sure this is your man?" Bentzion asked his friend, "Because if you're wrong ... " his voice trailed off.

"I'm not wrong," Kobi answered tersely.

They watched as the security agents reached the man and surrounded him without a word. They saw the man begin talking to them. They saw him become angry and begin to yell. But the agents ignored him completely. They just maneuvered him in the direction of the elevator leading to the security offices. They could hear him even before the elevator door opened. He was screaming his head off.

"How would you boys like to go to prison for 10 years?" he was saying. "It will make quite a change from your cushy jobs at airport security, won't it?!" His voice was icy.

They moved him forward into the security zone. People watched the venerated man blustering, agents bent their heads toward the desk, not knowing what was going on, but wanting to spare the man any additional embarrassment. The agents didn't say a word. They allowed him to yell and threaten to his heart's content. Eventually they reached the office at the rear of the room. One of them pushed open the door, shoving him into the office as he did so.

The man looked around him, trying to determine who the source of this outrage was. He looked first at Bentzion, who shrugged and turned away. Then he saw Kobi and his face grew scarlet and white all at the same time.

"Choni Dagan," Kobi said, "I was wondering how long it would be before you showed up. You were accurate almost to the minute. But then your flight to Germany leaves within the hour, doesn't it? You were always a stickler for details. What's the matter, Choni?" Kobi said looking the chief of the Mossad in the eye. "Cat got your tongue?"

"You'll never be able to prove anything!" Dagan said to Kobi. "So don't even bother wasting your time. Just let me go like a nice old man, and everything will be fine."

Kobi's face had turned into something that was terrible to look at, and Bentzion flinched when he saw it.

"Is that so?" Kobi whispered to his erstwhile friend. "Is that so? I should just let you go so you can board a flight to Germany leaving a certain Ford Explorer behind in the airport's parking lot?! I don't think so!"

He turned and spoke sharply to two agents who were waiting for instructions. "Take an airport car and drive to the main parking lot right now. Take a bomb-defusing squad along with you, the full deal, all the equipment. I imagine we're talking nuclear! Go now!"

Dagan's face had gotten whiter and whiter as Kobi rapped out his instructions. He seemed to shrink in stature, as his posture crumbled in defeat. There was complete silence in the office. The only sound to be heard was the ticking of the wall clock. Kobi glared at the man he had worked with for the majority of his life, and wondered how it had come to this. Ten minutes later, one of the agents came racing into the room white faced and panting.

"Sir," he said, directing his gaze at Kobi, ignoring Dagan completely, "we found the Explorer in the parking lot just like you said. We broke the window and found a black box in the rear of the vehicle. The bomb squad is defusing it right now. They said it was a miracle that we discovered the bomb when we did, because it was set for three hours from now and —" here his voice trailed off and he couldn't continue for a minute or two until he got himself together. "They said," he tried again, "they said that there was enough bomb in that little box to have demolished the entire city of Tel Aviv and destroyed the country of Israel for the foreseeable future. Sir, it's a miracle! Thank G-d!"

Everyone in the room was hugging one another and crying as the reality sunk in. If it had been a few hours later, they would have all been dead! It had been that close.

But Dagan had gone utterly berserk. "The bomb, the bomb, the bomb," he kept on repeating, "the bomb must go off! I have failed. It has to work. They sent me to set it off. How could I have failed? The bomb, the bomb. What will be?!" He was wringing his hands in agony. Kobi watched Choni Dagan's smooth facade, the facade of a normal man, begin to disintegrate right before his eyes. Dagan was crying and cursing, and trying to get away from his captors. He began kicking and punching them, and his spittle flew as he yelled at the people around him, "Don't you see, it has to happen! I have a mission! The bomb must go off! I have failed, failed! What will they say?!"

Someone called out, "He's gone insane! He's talking as if he's been hypnotized!" Suddenly a light went on in Kobi's eyes, and he knew, he just knew that here was one of the missing pages standing in front of his eyes. Dagan was insane, out of his mind, because he had been triggered and yet hadn't been able to carry out his mission.

"Take him to the best private mental hospital in the country," he instructed a group of airport security in quiet tones.

They snapped the cuffs on Dagan and pulled him from the room, screaming and yelling, mouth frothing, eyes flashing, looking like a deranged madman, when all of a sudden, everything changed. Choni straightened up and reverted to his previous self for a minute, as if the last vestiges of his sanity were warring with the dark forces that had taken control of his mind. He stared at Kobi, a question dancing on the tip of his tongue, sanity and craziness fighting each other within that brilliant mind.

"How did you know?" he asked Kobi.

Kobi chose his words carefully. "Choni," he began, "remember how Rafi and I came to you with the list of names? I showed you everything, all the people on the list, all the members of the Network. I pointed out to you how dangerous they all were if they weren't taken into custody and neutralized immediately. You objected. You disagreed with my reasoning and refused to take control of the situation until it was too late. That was my first clue that something was wrong. I thought then that you had just made the wrong decision, nothing treasonous yet, but it was enough to put me on my guard, to decide to trail you and see what you were up to.

"I began to look into who you were, and discovered that there had been many questions regarding your conduct during your tenure as Mossad head in Berlin. There were whispers about some sort of liaison with the Eberhart family. You had claimed at the time that you were infiltrating their inner sanctum. But you know, Choni, sometimes the infiltrator can become the infiltrated.

"But," I said to myself, "you weren't on the list, were you? You weren't one of those people who had been brainwashed and hypnotized, right? There was nothing written about any Choni Dagan on that list, was there? But then I realized that just as the people on the list had had the right motivation to carry out the attacks, it was very possible that you had had the right motivation as well. But for you, I thought, the motivation had probably been for money instead. This was my assumption, and while incorrect, it brought me to the right place in the end, because from that point onward, the rest was easy.

"I entered the hospital, so you would think I was out of the way. I remained there for sufficient time so your suspicious mind would move on to other more important things. Then I checked myself out in the middle of the night, while the agent you had sent to keep an eye on me fell asleep on a bench. I continued tracking you. I learned a lot about you and the people that you were meeting with. I began to put things together. It wasn't that difficult. After all, I had been suspicious of you for quite some time. I had followed you many times before. I had taken numerous pictures of you at scores of meetings with a vast assortment of people over the years. Most of those people had been innocent of any wrongdoing. But there were those that weren't as innocent. An agent develops a sixth sense eventually. In this case, my alarms were shrieking!

"Now, after all this time, I finally understand the truth. Now I know what was going on. You, Choni, were one of the last two pages in the book of the Network; one of those two little kids whom we missed.

"You didn't help us because you had been hypnotized long ago by the Germans. You were a cog in their future destruction of Israel. That's why you instinctively sabotaged anything that went against their goals. It was your subconscious doing the dirty work. You didn't even know why you were so against tracking down all the kids. But how could you have tracked them down, when you yourself were one of those kids, even if we didn't know that yet! Thank G-d the Germans never met with you after we found the book, because you would have given them all the information without even meaning to. But nobody met you and nobody asked. Thank G-d!

"But then they triggered you, and that's when it all came together. My men, who were constantly watching you, followed you around the country. Do you understand, Choni, it wasn't your fault at all. You were programmed to do this. You were one of them, one of the Network. You were a missing page!"

Kobi was about to speak again, when Choni lost control and began straining and pushing the agents. Kobi understood that the madness had won out for the time being once again. He watched red eyed as they pulled Choni Dagan away.

Then turning to Bentzion he said, "I need you to organize a press conference right now. Every major journalist should be on hand. The finale will probably begin very soon. It's almost over now."

The Fuhrerbunker, Berlin
Late Evening
June 21, 2009

The Command Center had been set up for the press conference that Eberhart intended to give. Every major network would interrupt whatever it was they were in the middle of, when the message came through that the man behind the attacks was going to speak, to finally explain what he wanted. Off in a side room, the engineers sat and watched Eberhart through double-thick glass, awaiting his signal to begin transmitting. He had made his point very well. The entire world would know his name and the magnitude of his power. He had timed his speech to coincide with the groundbreaking news from Israel: a mega-attack, a nuclear attack! It would be the first one since the Americans bombed Hiroshima and Nagasaki in Japan in 1945. That bombing had finally put an end to World War II. This one would deter every nation from going to war against him.

Now they would finally understand who he was.

He was the new leader of Germany; a leader who didn't hesitate to use tremendous force if that was what was necessary. He thought of the reparations, all that money that had gone to Israel. What a waste.

He would explain to the world how he had decided to destroy the country of Israel in retaliation for what the Jews had done to the pope. It was an act of vengeance for the entire Christian world, notwithstanding the fact that it was he, not the Jews, who had been behind the attack. He expected America to deal with their Jews once and for all, no more games. And if they wouldn't cooperate, there would be war. They had to understand that he held the cards, and that the names in his book, the people of the Network, were so well placed that he had the power to destroy any country with a phone call. He spoke on an intercom to the technicians who were sitting in the outside room, separated from him by a thick glass wall.

"Peter," he said to the man who directed his private television studio.

"Yes, sir," the man replied, almost saluting.

"Get CNN on the line," Eberhart said. "Give them our frequencies, and tell them that we will begin broadcasting in 10 minutes. They will want to pick this up."

"What if they aren't interested?" asked the technician.

"They'll be interested," Eberhart said. "I promise you. They know who I am. They know what's going on. They know that this is the scoop of the century. Trust me; they're going to run with this."

He glanced at his watch and smiled. It was almost time to begin.

The Waldorf-Astoria Hotel, New York
June 21, 2009

Rafi had just gotten off the phone with Kobi Shapiro from Israel. There was an air of great happiness, of amazement on his face, as he turned to look at the two of them sitting side by side: The prime minister of Israel and the pope — two men who had endured so much together during the last 17 hours. Enough that they would never forget the time spent in each other's presence for the rest of their lives.

"That was my boss from Israel!" he said to them. "He has just prevented a nuclear attack on Ben-Gurion Airport!"

The impact of the words hit everyone in the room like a ton of bricks. "It's time for us to go outside and show ourselves to the world right now, to let everyone know who was behind the 'attack' on the pope. It is the same person who was using this 'attack' as an excuse to destroy the entire country of Israel. We played his bluff and he lost. There's no reason for him to trigger more of his secret agents now. It would be pointless. It's time to show ourselves. Let's go."

Arm in arm the prime minister and the pope exited the papal suite together to the incredulous stares of an army of armed men who stared in wide-eyed wonder.

"Should we take the elevator?" wondered the prime minister aloud.

"I think we should use the stairs," rejoined the pope. "All that sitting down, you know."

The Fuhrerbunker, Berlin
Late Evening
June 21, 2009

Frost stood outside the door to the Command Center, and steadied himself as he gathered his courage to go inside.

"Go on," Karl said to him, "he's expecting you."

Frost turned the handle, and pulled the door open. He walked into the room and locked the door behind him with an almost imperceptible click. He looked around in wonder. It was a broadcasting studio, and he seemed to be interrupting a live broadcast. The walls of the studio were plastered with a giant mural of a black swastika on a red-and-white background. Eberhart was seated at a desk and talking into a microphone. All the television screens were showing his face. Every network was playing Eberhart and his plans for the future of the world.

"And so," Eberhart was saying, "my father came to the conclusion that we needed a plan that would ensure the survival of the dream. Not just the survival," he paused as if searching for the right words, "but the celebration of our dream. This, my friends, is it! Just a phone call away."

Reaching down, he lifted the book of names in his hands as if daring the world to react. "So much power concentrated in the hands of a few," he said. "And I am a man who won't hesitate to use it. I have used this ultimate power today on Israel, which according to my calculations has another five minutes to exist in the way that we know it. I gave the order, and in a matter of minutes, it will be destroyed, just like that. I will not hesitate to do the same to any individual or nation who opposes us and our ideals. All it takes is a phone call and it is done. Remember that.

"I destroyed Israel because of what the prime minister of Israel did to the pope. I did it because I wanted to finish off more than half of the Jewish population still living today in one fell swoop. And I did it, because I want you all to understand that it could be you. I'm looking for cooperation, and this is an incentive if I ever saw one."

Eberhart turned and looked at Frost, then back at the camera. He motioned for the camera to focus on Frost for a moment, and then back to himself.

"This man," he said, "is one of the names in my book. His name is Cardinal Jason Leonard Frost, and he was with the pope when the prime minister of Israel went on the attack. He comes to me with a very important message."

"How did you know where to find me?" he asked Frost from behind his hand, moving closer to the man, the better to hear what he had to say.

"Regards from Rolf Zimmer," Frost said out loud, and smiled when he saw the understanding beginning to dawn in Eberhart's eyes.

A murderous rage had spread over the German's face. He wanted to jump up, to tear Frost limb from limb. But just then his broadcast was interrupted by a smooth media voice.

"We are sorry to interrupt this broadcast," the voice from CNN said, "but we bring you groundbreaking news from Israel and from New York, live!"

The picture of Eberhart and Frost was relegated to the bottom third of the screen, while the majority of the screen was split between two scenes: Kobi Shapiro standing at a lectern at the entrance to Ben-Gurion Airport, and a triumphant Israeli prime minister with the pope.

The Waldorf-Astoria Hotel, New York
June 21, 2009

A jubilant scene from New York filled one side of the screen. It was an unforgettable moment as Prime Minister Doron Chizkiyahu and Pope Fernandez Mendoza exited the front entrance of the Waldorf, arm in arm, smiling and laughing, obviously the greatest of friends. The mob, which had been ready to storm the hotel only moments before, went wild with shouts of joy, as cries of happiness filled the air and hats were tossed aloft.

Ben-Gurion Airport
Late Evening
June 21, 2009

Kobi Shapiro stood at the lectern, as journalists gathered around him watching with rapt silence as he gestured with his hands, speaking with assurance, laughing and making jokes, and pointing at a black knapsack that rested on a table in front of him.

"It was close, gentlemen," he said, "really close. But once again, G-d was on our side."

"Who was the inside man on the job?" asked the journalist from Reuters.

"That is a matter of state security, I'm afraid," Kobi said. "You will have to forgive me if I don't elaborate on that subject."

"How did the Mossad allow your prime minister to get into such a situation?" asked another reporter.

"The Mossad didn't know the facts until the prime minister was already on his way," Kobi replied. "At that point, all we could do was send our best agents and hope that it all worked out for the best. The fact is, Prime Minister Chizkiyahu was never in danger at any point, due to the outstanding performance of one particular agent who shall remain unnamed."

"But by calling Eberhart's bluff," interrupted another journalist, "you put the entire country in supreme danger! If that bomb would have exploded, it would've been the end of Israel!!"

"Well then, aren't you glad we found it," was Kobi's quick reply.

"Thank you, gentlemen, for joining me here this evening," he finished up. "The news lounge in the airport is open. Get in there and make your reports. Go on, don't waste time now."

The picture from Ben-Gurion faded away, to be replaced by the Command Center once again.

"Apparently there has been some sort of hitch in Herr Eberhart's plans for the world," said the smooth, polite media voice from the CNN studio, as the attention of the world reverted back to the Command Center for a moment, only to find that nothing was the same anymore.

The Command Center, Berlin
Late Evening
June 21, 2009

Cardinal Jason Frost and Herr Dietrich Eberhart were rolling around the Command Center floor fighting each other. Once again, the Nazi shrine filled the full screen as the cameras focused on the two men fighting for their lives before a background dominated by a huge swastika.

Eberhart was younger and in much better physical shape. But Frost had a fury that drove him just as strongly. People around the world gasped as they watched in wonder as the old man who had almost become pope pummeled the man who had ruined his life. Eberhart fought back, no holds barred. He kicked Frost in the head, and Frost took it and went flying to the floor. But Frost got unsteadily to his feet and jumped at the younger man and punched him in the face and picked up a chair and threw it at him. Eberhart laughed and caught the chair in one hand and threw it right back at the cardinal. It hit him hard. It was a heavy metal chair, and Frost staggered and almost fell. But as he slipped, he picked up the microphone from its stand and swinging it by its cord like a lasso, flinging the expensive recording microphone through the air, connecting with Eberhart's head in a solid shot that was heard all over the world.

Eberhart was hurt. Frost waited for a moment on the other side of the room, breathing heavily and in obvious pain. Then Eberhart raced at the old man once again. The second before he propelled himself at the cardinal, Frost bent over. Eberhart passed right over the spot where he had been standing, and Frost straightened up at the exact moment, and centered his elbow directly into Eberhart's ribs with a solid cracking sound. And still they fought on.

The next few minutes passed in a blur of action of men fighting for their lives, and of people who had gone crazy. From outside the studio came the sounds of Eberhart's bodyguards screaming in pain, of muffled shouting and gunshots. But inside the Command Center, nobody was paying any attention to anything besides their own survival.

When the dust cleared, Cardinal Jason Leonard Frost was lying in a heap on the floor of the room, while Dietrich Eberhart, his face bleeding and his suit ripped, stood at the desk, and spoke into the microphone which he was holding in his hand.

"It looks like it's over," he said in desperation. "There's no reason not to send the rest of the Network operatives off on their missions. There's nothing to save them for anymore."

He reached for the list of names, and lifted the phone receiver, ready to dial, his eyes on the numbers on the paper before him.

He began to dial slowly, deliberately, teasing all those people out there who knew what he was about to do, but had no way of stopping him.

The figure on the floor — the broken figure of Cardinal Frost — began crawling across the floor toward the man on the phone — the man who was paying him no attention. In his hand was a pair of sunglasses, just an average-looking pair of sunglasses, like those designed by Gucci or

Armani. The figure on the floor sidled closer to the man who was dialing the number, waiting to trigger an agent on a mission of destruction for the sheer wickedness of it. Eberhart glanced at Frost for a second, and a contemptuous smile lit his face as he laughed at the pathetic creature on the floor. He turned back to the phone. Frost lifted the end of the sunglasses as high as he could, and pointed the sharp end — that Rafi had shown him was filled with a lethal poison — at Eberhardt. Then he pressed it as deeply as his strength allowed into the leg of the murderer before him.

Eberhart looked down at him with curiosity as the phone rang on the other end and someone said, "Hello?" He wanted to speak, to say those words that would send the man to become the next victim of his madness. But the words died on his lips, as his face contorted into a mask of pain and acute agony. He slipped silently to the floor holding his leg, coming to rest not far away from the man whose life he had stolen so many years ago.

Then there was a tremendous crash as the door to the studio was blown open, and a team of Mossad agents came rushing in with raised guns. The lights were extinguished, and everyone knew that it was over; that the madness and danger had been averted, at least for now. And the world breathed a sigh of relief.

Epilogue

Mordy, Jason Frost and Rafi

A Few Days Later …

Mordy met Frost at Ben-Gurion Airport. It was an emotional meeting, to say the least, for all concerned. Mordy had flown in on the first available flight. Frost had spent some time recuperating in the Israeli Embassy in Berlin, where his wounds had been attended to by a team of the finest medical staff. He then took an El Al flight to Israel. Their embrace at the arrivals lounge was recorded for posterity, and would never be forgotten by anyone who had the good fortune to witness it.

There was so much they wanted to do together. First, Jason Frost wanted to see Jerusalem, from a Jewish perspective this time. They stayed at the King David Hotel, courtesy of the Israeli government. Frost had an incredible view of the Old City walls from the window of his room. They sat on the balcony watching the fiery sunset, breathing in the sights and sounds of the holy city. When they finally arrived at the *Kosel*, Mordy watched as Frost approached the ancient wall and was pulled into its embrace like a long-lost son returning home. His arms went to the wall, as if he was hugging the creviced stones to his heart. Tears streamed down his cheeks as he thanked Hashem for allowing him to reach this point in time.

They traveled to Tel Aviv, meeting Rafi at the home of his uncle, the Kolodover Rebbe and Frost's first cousin. It was an incredible moment in the life of a man who had lived the majority of his existence without the knowledge that he possessed the most wonderful family in the world. They sat inside the Rebbe's study discussing the miracles that had taken place for all of them. It was during this part of the conversation that Frost had looked up at the wall and spotted the picture of the previous Kolodover Rebbe, Rav David Zushe, and the words he was saying just stuck in his throat.

"*Tatte,*" he whispered, rising from his chair and walking over to the wall on trembling legs, his entire body shaking with emotion. "*Tatte,*" he said again, the word emanating from his mouth with raw feeling, like a man floating in a dream.

"How I loved you, *Tatte,*" he said. "How I missed you all these years. I would have been a good son. I would have brought you joy. It's not my fault! It's not my fault! I would have been a good son!"

Rafi's uncle, the Kolodover Rebbe, went to the closet, removed the violin, which had belonged to Rav David Zushe, and began to play. The music rose in the room like the purest of sound. They sang, all of them: Frost sang to his father, the Rebbe. Rafi sang to the old man who would never visit his dreams again, because Rafi had done what he'd been asking for. And if he did come, then he would be smiling because it was all good now. Mordy sang as well, because his dearest friend, the cardinal, was safe and sound and really, truly, happy for the first time since he had been kidnapped so long before.

There they sat singing the special tune from the halls of Kolodov with an indestructible bond. As for Kobi Shapiro, as he sat there in the study, he felt a genuine peace, for the first time since Shalom had been taken away.

See, Shalom, he whispered to his friend, *I got it right in the end. Thank you for helping me from Heaven.*

It was a singing so joyful and unique that it would never be forgotten.

Jerusalem
Six months later

"There are times in my life that I look back on with nostalgia and true emotion. And I knew that this wedding was one of those times. I would never forget this night for as long as I lived. I sat at the *chasan's tish* and watched all the people coming and going: the boys from the yeshivah — Mordy's friends — and all the relatives and chassidim from the courtyard of the Kolodover Rebbe. The Rebbe was going to be the *mesader kiddushin*. It was a perfect choice considering that it was his niece who was the *kallah*. Yes, Tamar and Mordy were *chasan* and *kallah*, soon to build a wonderful new home in *Klal Yisrael*.

"I had met them all over the last half a year: the elusive and reticent Kobi; Frost, a man so effusive and overflowing with love for the life he had missed all this time; and Rafi, bravery personified and a *baal teshuvah,* a returnee to Judaism, just as Mordy was, and who had become close with Mordy. Rafi had come to us for Shabbos, bringing his sister Tamar along. Avigail had hit it off with her right away, and Tamar had returned a few times. She was growing, and we were so impressed by the determination and truthfulness that looked us in the face.

"Then one day I brought it up to Mordy as we were sitting in the back of the *beis midrash* by my table, sharing a cup of Coke.

"'Mordy,' I said, 'how would you like me to set it up?'

"'What?' he asked.

"'A *shidduch* between you and Tamar.'

"'Reb Zack," he said, "how did you know?"

"I didn't know how I knew, but I had known from the first moment I had met her, and had hoped that it would come to fruition. I didn't even have to work that hard at convincing anyone. They were both convinced. It was a marriage made in heaven. We waited a few more months, but it was inevitable. They were going to get engaged. I was Mordy's *chasan* teacher and Avigail taught Tamar. The night we celebrated their *vort* was a night of such incredible happiness, it felt as if the sky was going to open up and shower us with stars.

"Mr. Ganim – Rafi's father — came as well. The Kolodover Rebbe's estranged brother came from Rechovot to join the *simchah*. It was hard for him, but there is a time for everything, and maybe it was finally time for the circle to come to a genuine close.

"From the distance I could hear the sounds of a violin playing a tune. It was accompanying the *chasan* to the *chupah*. I saw Mordy's parents walking him down the aisle, and I could see the history on their faces, and I understood what this meant for them; how they had never dreamed that this day would actually arrive. I held my son Yeshaya's hand and gave it a squeeze as the violin played their song, soaring toward the heavens. The *kallah* began her stately walk to join Mordy at the *chupah*. It was that tune they were playing, the connecting bridge that had brought us all together. I looked down at Yeshaya and he looked up at me, and he said in his little-boy voice, 'Tatty, why are you crying?'

"I smiled and said, 'Because sometimes, that's the only thing you can do when you are overwhelmed with joy.' "

About The Author

Rabbi Nachman Seltzer is the author of novels: *The Edge* and *The Link*. These were followed by: *In The Blink Of An Eye* and *Stories With A Twist,* books filled with wonderful and fascinating short stories. He has co-authored with Dr. Moshe Katz the biography, *Nine Out Of Ten*.

The Network is his third novel.

Rabbi Seltzer runs the Shira Chadasha Boys' Choir, which is based in Jerusalem, and has produced a number of recordings with his group. He spends his mornings learning at the Yeshivas Mir in Yerushalayim and teaches American boys in the afternoons.

He lives with his wonderful wife and kinderlach in Ramat Beit Shemesh.

He can be contacted at nachmans@netvision.net.il

GW01605937

by

Nik Pringle and Jim Treversh

This book is dedicated to the
"Victim Support Scheme"

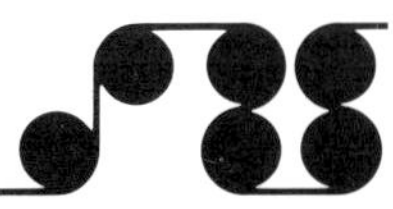

RADLEY-SHAW

ISBN 0 9517477 0 3

B.H. Skitt — Chief Constable, Hertfordshire Constabulary

M.G. Howley — Chief Superintendent, 'C' Division

1991

Foreword

It gives me the greatest pleasure to be asked to write the foreword for this commemorative book of the 150th Anniversary of the force.

I hope everyone reading it will share my enjoyment at the history of Hertfordshire policing revealed in its pages and equally congratulate the authors for their marvellous effort in producing such a useful account of the past and present.

As we move forward into the next century, I am sure our successors will read this book with equal interest. Congratulations to everyone concerned in its production.

B.H. Skitt
Chief Constable
Hertfordshire Constabulary

Contents

Our thanks to:

Book of Watford 1951,
Book of Watford By J.B. Nunn,
Constable Bill Wells
David Spain
Hertfordshire Constabulary
Archieves,
Photographic Department,
Inspector Barry Welch
Mrs A. Bishop,
Mr Ollie Philips, Watford Observer
Mr Rowe,
Rickmansworth Museum
Sergeant Mick Bonsor
Special Commandant Mould,
Story of Hertfordshire Police By Neil Osborn
Watford Library,
Watford Museum
Watford Observer,
Woman Constable Ann Evans

And all the people that have assisted in the production of this book.

The Constabulary must bear in mind that a heavy calendar, or numerous arrests, by no means proves the presence of a vigilant Police; the absence of the cause of arrests, commitals, and trials, best shows the well working of the Force; and where the evil-doer, from the dread of certain detection, abandons his malpractises and turns his hand to honest labour, or is driven from the County - there the influence of a good and efficient Police is most apparent.

A. Robertson. Chief Constable, Hertford County Constabulary, 1872.

Abbreviationss

A.C.C.	Assistant Chief Constable
C.C.	Chief Constable
C/INSP	Chief Inspector
C/SUPT	Chief Superintendent
D.C.C.	Deputy Chief Constable
G.O.	General Orders, Hertfordshire Constabulary.
INSP	Inspector
P.C.	Police Constable
S.O.	Standing Orders, Hertfordshire Constabulary.
SGT	Sergeant
SUPT.	Superintendent
W.O.	Watford Observer newspaper.
W.P.C.	Woman Police Constable

The Origins of Police

Saxon Times

In Saxon times, every freeman was bound by oath to "assist in preserving peace and order and repressing crime." This oath is still accepted in principle as part of the modern oath of allegiance taken by all constables on attestation of their post as Constable.

When the Saxons first settled in England, they introduced their own tribal system of policing by which the headman and the members of each settlement were answerable for each other's conduct and for the internal peace of their locality. Later on, as the country became more united under one king, who, in return for the allegiance and mutual good conduct of his subjects, guaranteed them a state of peace and security, which was known as the "King's Peace."

The Hundred

During the reign of Alfred the Great (870-901), an effective and new system was introduced. The King's Peace was made the responsibility of the Earls of the Provinces, who had their areas divided into Counties or Shires. Each Shire, had a Sheriff, who was responsible to his Earl. Obviously, it was impossible for the sheriff to maintain effective personal supervision of so large an area himself and so the Shires were further divided into "Hundreds", and further again into "Tithings". Each Tithing was made up of 10 families, and 10 Tithings made a Hundred. To ensure that the system was fully effective, every freeman over the age of 12 years was required to enrol his tithing and to give his pledge of surety, for the good behaviour of the other members of the tithing to which he belonged.

Tithingman

Each tithing had a "Tithingman" or "Headborough" in charge, who was responsible to the Sheriff for the peace and order of his tithing. Every freeman was therefore a policeman and bound by oath to assist in the preservation of the peace. The Tithingman in charge of his group had the responsibility of raising the "Hue and Cry" to collect his neighbours and pursue any criminal who had fled from the district. To ensure due vigilance was exercised in the pursuit of offenders it was decreed that if a tithing did not catch its criminals and so clear itself, all pledged members should be liable to a fine.

The Sheriff

The introduction of the feudal system following the Norman Conquest of 1066 eroded into this system of policing. William the Conqueror increased the powers of the Sheriff, but his main duty became the procuring of money for the King by the extraction of heavy fines. In addition to the Sheriff the feudal baron in his castle ruled absolutely over his retainers and serfs, with the result that law and order usually depended on the power and will of the local lord. The Lords also procured the King's consent to run local courts known as Court Leets.

Judges and Justices

In the reign of Henry the First (1100-1135), the old Saxon system was re-introduced and itinerant Justices or Judges appointed to decide cases in the Counties. During his reign, the King's Peace was maintained with such success the King was known as the "Lion of Justice", but it was followed by the reign of Stephen(1135-1154) which was characterised by anarchy and bloodshed. Henry II (1154-1189) had the support of the nation in the restoration of law and order and in his fight to end the feudal independence of the local Lords. His Assize of Clarendon in 1166 restored the system of pledges and the responsibility of seeing it was maintained was again placed on the Sheriffs. The "Hue and Cry" method of pursuing criminals was again adopted. The tithingman had by now become known as the "Headborough" and it was his responsibility to raise the "Hue and Cry". If a culprit passed from one district to another, the hue and cry was passed on until the culprit was brought to justice.

Watchmen

England then passed through another period of unsettlement, brought about by the absence of Richard I (Coeur de Lion), the misdeeds of King John and the weak rule of Henry III, covering the years 1189-1272, but the state of confusion was soon remedied by the rule of Edward the First. In 1285 his Statute of Westminster provided a definitive system for keeping the peace of the country. Firstly, the Hundred was made answerable for all offences committed in it. Every man between the ages of 15 and 60 had arms in his house, ready for use in keeping the peace. Secondly, the hue and cry was

A Watchman on his rounds

revived again. Sheriffs received instructions that law breakers were to be pursued relentlessly until they were caught, and if the hue and cry was not levied at once, the residents would be fined. Thirdly, watch and ward was to be kept in towns, it being directed that the gates of walled towns were to be shut between sunset and daybreak, with a watch of 6 men on guard at each gate. Every Borough was required to have a watch of 12 persons and smaller towns to have watchmen according to the population.

Wardens of the Peace

In 1195, Richard I had appointed knights whose duty it was to see that all males over 15 years took an oath to keep the peace. In 1360, Edward III took great interest in these knights or Wardens of the Peace as they had become known, taking care only to appoint good and loyal men and further authorised them to hear and determine all manners of crime. They became known as Justices of the Peace. The Tithingman became known as a Constable and it was he who supervised the watchmen, inquired into offences, served summonses, executed warrants, organised the hue and cry, took charge of prisoners, prosecuted them and generally obeyed the orders of the justices.

Every citizens duty

(Even today under Common Law, any person who is present when a felony or crime is committed is bound to arrest the offender. Further, every citizen is bound to assist a constable who demands his aid in the lawful taking of a criminal or in the suppression of an affray and any person who refuses without good excuse is liable to punishment.)

From this period, the duty of those who were bound by law to act as constables became eroded as they often appointed deputies to act for them on payment. These early paid officers did not generally rate very high in public esteem, as they were generally very poorly paid, often ignorant and sometimes too old to carry out their duties properly.

Then, came the Civil War, which left the country once again in a state of lawlessness. Cromwell, could not depend on the Justices who were chiefly country gentlemen and above all Loyalists so he had to rely on Military Rule. This he did through 12 Major-Generals who acted as the Police and Justices, utilising their force of over 6,000 soldiers each to act on their behalf. This lasted for a period of 2 years until the Restoration of 1660.

The Headborough

In 1673, Charles II empowered the justices to appoint constables every year. The Court Leets continued to function particularly in the smaller towns and appointed constables and a supervisor, the Headborough. These persons were usually men of standing in the district and who employed watchmen and thief takers to carry out their duties for them. Large towns began to appoint constables paid for out of town funds.

Strangers

During the reign of Queen Elizabeth I, St. Albans employed constables, one their tasks was performed monthly, when they had to search the town for strangers. Any stranger coming into the town had to bring with them a letter, written by a trustworthy person, saying that they were honest and reliable. The stranger also had to find someone in the town that would be responsible for their behaviour.

Strangers coming to St. Albans had to have a letter of introduction

The Highwaymen

Highwaymen, were the scourge of travellers in the eighteenth and early nineteenth centuries, holding up coaches often at gunpoint and robbing the occupiers of their treasured and valuable possessions. Hertfordshire, saw many of these highwaymen due to its proximity to London and the fact that it lay on the routes to the North.

The most famous highwayman of all of course was Dick Turpin. Turpin's wrong-doings started with his stealing of neighbours cattle after his apprenticeship as a butcher. Turpin was discovered as the thief, and fled later joining with a group of thieves and taking up robbery. The group, planned to go to houses they presumed contained valuable property, and whilst one would knock at the door, the others would wait in ambush for the door to be opened and then rush in to the house. The first offence of this nature, occurred in Watford, at the home of Mr Strype, an old man who kept a Chandler's shop in the town, whom they robbed of all his money, but were not violent in doing so. Later, the gang were to become more and more violent culminating in setting an old lady on fire when she refused to tell them where her money was hidden.

Highwaymen rob the mail

The last highwayman to be hung for his crimes, was Robert Snooks, who on Thursday 11th March 1802 was publicly executed at Boxmoor, Hemel Hempstead. Snooks, like Turpin before him had committed offences in Watford. The crime for which he was convicted, occurred when John Stevens, a postboy was carrying mail from Tring and Berkhamsted to Watford, as he approached the now Railway Bridge at Boxmoor near the Grand Union Canal, he claimed he was robbed and six leather mailbags were stolen from him, by a masked and heavily cloaked man with a pistol. The empty mailbags were found two days later near Chesham after the Hue and Cry had been raised. A reward of £300 was offered after it was discovered that the post contained a large number of valuables, one of the bags alone containing over £500. Another of the bags, contained large denomination notes issued by the Bank of Aylesbury. Snooks, took lodgings in Southwark and on leaving, gave a girl working in the kitchen at the hostelry a large denomination bank note. This raised suspicions, and was traced back to being one of the notes from the robbery. Some months later, Snooks turned up at Watford, where he witnessed an old woman being turned out of a cottage by its heartless owner, whilst another man burned her few possessions in front of her. Snooks reacted to this by threatening to shoot one and severely beating the other. He then gave the old woman money, before riding off. The incident was reported, and the description of Snooks was given by the two men. Further enquiries revealed that the money Snooks had given the old woman came from the Boxmoor robbery. He returned to his home town of Hungerford, where he was recognised and arrested. At Hertford, he was found guilty of highway robbery and the judge informed the High Constable John Page "to execute the prisoner at the scene of the crime and to hang his body in chains to rot at the roadside."

The people of Hemel Hempstead, complained at the sentence, for Snooks was a popular man and the authorities relented and gave permission for his corpse to be buried at the place of execution. It is said that Snooks met his death bravely, and his body was buried at the spot where he was hung. A few days later, some of his many friends exhumed his body to place it in a coffin before re-interring it in the same grave, which they marked with two gravestones. The stones, were later renewed, where they remain to this day in a field between

Boxmoor and Berkhamsted, under trees near the Railway Bridge at Boxmoor, Hemel Hempstead

Bow Street Runners

London, had its parish night watchmen and constables and also the Bow Street Foot and Horse Patrol, a force of paid men originated by Henry Fielding the novelist who was also a Magistrate from 1748-1754, who policed the streets and Highways leading out of London. Attached to the Bow Street Magistrates Court, were a dozen "Bow Street Runners", paid men attached to the Chief Magistrate who were engaged for the "Detection of crime".

A Bow Street Runner

The First Police Force

In 1792, the Middlesex Justices Act established seven new police offices, each of whom had three paid magistrates with six paid constables under their orders. This in effect, was the first officially recognised paid English Police Force. The word Police comes from the Greek "Polis" a city and the Latin "Politia" the condition of a state or government.

At the beginning of the 19th century there were therefore, many different kinds of Police Officers, controlled by many different and unconnected authorities. There was the parish constable, the deputy or petty constable who was paid by the constable to do his work for him, the constable and headborough appointed annually by the Leet Court, the constable appointed by the justices, the special constable who could be sworn in during an emergency, the paid watchmen, the Bow Street patrols and runners, the constables attached to the police offices and finally the water police. In spite of all this, crime and public disorder were prevalent and the law generally powerless. Even the severe penal laws of the time did not deter criminals.

Peelers

The necessity for an adequate and properly organised Police Service was recognised and following several commissions on the policing of London, Sir Robert Peel the then Home Secretary, was able, in 1829 to establish the Metropolitan Police Force by Act of Parliament. Sir Robert may therefore be regarded as the founder of the modern day Police Force, and the name "peeler" or "bobby" by which sometimes members of the force are known remain as memorials of his work. The Metropolitan Police was the first to be provided with a definite uniform, consisting of a blue swallow tailed coat with blue trousers strapped over boots, a leather top hat and a leather stock. White duck trousers were worn in summer. The helmet and tunic did not come into use until 1863.

Watford's First Constables

In 1829, Watford consisted of one main street, which ran from a toll gate at its Southern end near to where Bushey Arches now stand, along its present day route to terminate at what we now know as the Town Hall Roundabout.

Old Toll Gate, Bushey Arches. Photograph from Festival Book of Watford 1951

A number of alleyways and yards ran left and right from the High Street into which were crammed the dwellings of the indigenous population to what is now Beechen Grove on the one side and Exchange Rd on the other. Thereafter the landscape was dominated by farmland. The majority of the population of 2500 inhabited this small area in houses, lofts and cellars with no running water and no sanitation, except, if they were lucky a cess pit.

By and large those in employment worked on farms surrounding the town, although others found employment in the Breweries, Silk spinning and candle-making industries that had established themselves in the area.

Watford was a market town having been granted a charter to hold a weekly market by Henry I. Local farmers would drive their cattle, sheep and pigs along the High Street to the market place which was situated in the area between what is now Marks and Spencers and Boots the Chemist.

The Market place was dominated by the market house, built on stout wooden pillars with a large loft above, in which farmers stored unsold sacks of corn until the next market day. Adjacent to it were the stocks and old whipping post, together with the town water pump. Unfortunately the market house was destroyed by fire in 1853 despite valiant attempts to save it.

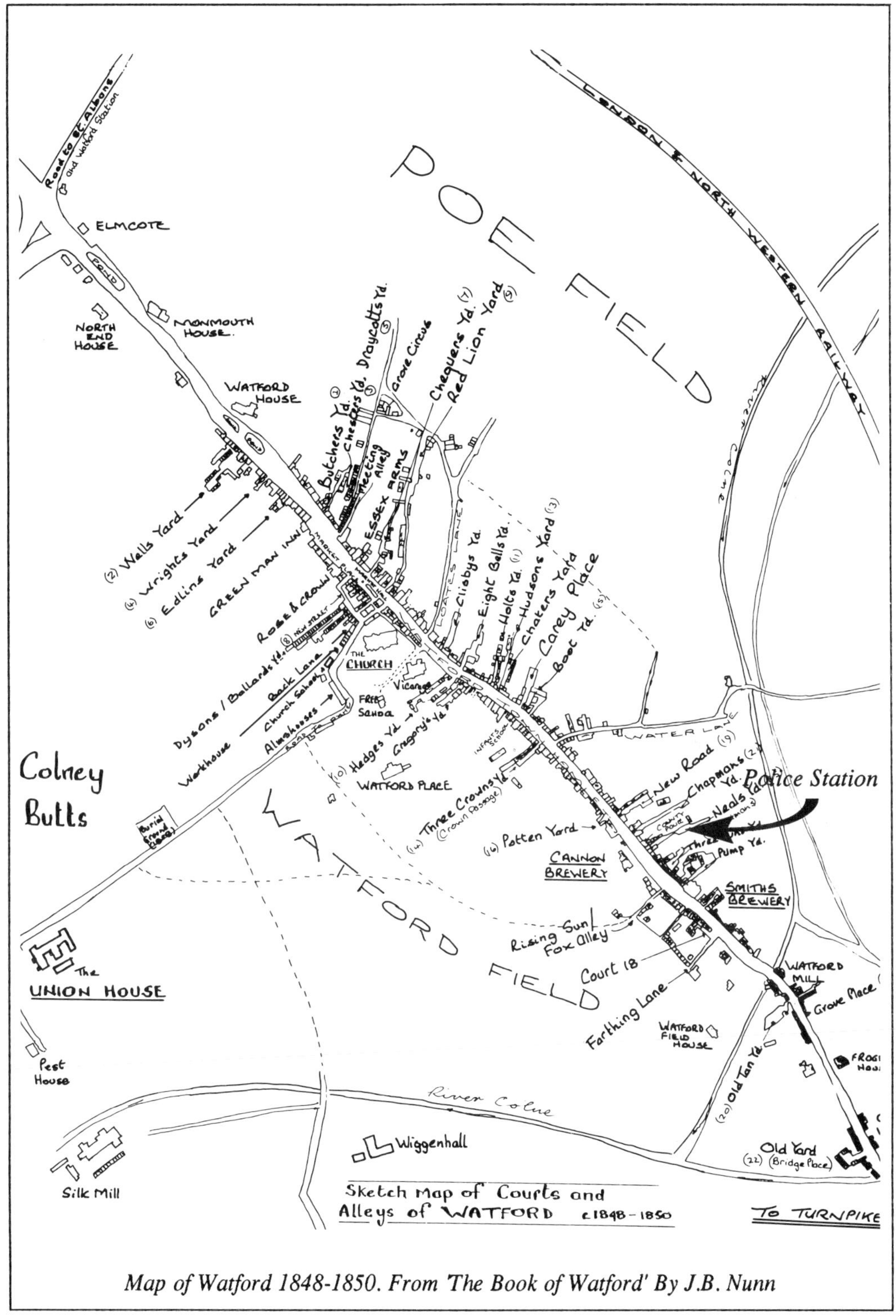

Map of Watford 1848-1850. From 'The Book of Watford' By J.B. Nunn

Drunkeness

Public houses were to be found in abundance. Certainly there were far too many to name here, but included the Eight Bells, The Fighting Cocks and the Leathersellers Arms. Additionally there were hotels and Inns catering for the coaching trade passing through the town. With no licensing trade to restrict opening hours and with drink being relatively cheap, droves of men and women flocked into these establishments day in day out, to seek some solace from their pitiful surroundings. Poverty, Vagrancy and Drunkenness were all much in evidence in 1829.

It was against this background that on Monday 19th January 1829, twenty local dignitaries including the Earl of Clarendon met in the Committee room of the Watford Poor House. The purpose of the meeting was to form a "Watch Committee" and to request the Magistrates to sanction and appoint two constables for the Town. One was to patrol during the day and the other at night to prevent as much as possible any act of Robbery or Vagrancy.

The Committee was formed under the chairmanship of the Vicar of the Parish Church of St. Marys, The Honourable and Reverend William Capel. Other meetings were convened during the next ten days at which two constables were subsequently appointed and details appertaining to their duties finalised. The Constables were to work under the direction of and were answerable to the "Watch Committee".

In order to finance the venture, the committee collected a subscription from local inhabitants which raised the sum of £245. The donations varied in amount from 10/- (50p) to £5.

The night patrol constable's tour of duty was to have been from 10pm to 4 am the following morning seven days a week for which he received 16/- a week (80p). It was decided that he would be accompanied each night by one of the subscribers who was to be known as the "Inspector". The day constable was furnished with an alphabetical list of all the subscribers and one of his duties was to inform each one as to the date they were to act as the Inspector.

Each constable was provided with a greatcoat and a wooden rattle. In addition the night constable was supplied with a lamp and "Oil supplied at the expense of the fund". He was also given a notebook in which to record incidents that occurred during the night.

In view of the fact that neither of the appointed constables Richard French or John Birch had any experience of such duties, an approach was made to Mr.Stafford the Chief Clerk of the Bow Street Police Office, London, for a Bow Street Runner to be seconded to Watford. The request was granted and in February, Mr Francis Fagan arrived to spend one week accompanying both constables about the town. It must have been a particularly quiet time, for his report to the Watch Committee on the 9th February merely stated that "Nothing particularly had occurred". The Reverend Capel thanked him for his conduct and sent a favourable report to the Bow Street Office.

Early days in Watford

During the days of the Watch Committee, the two constables patrolled the High Street on foot, calling out the hours of the night. During this time, it was said that a cannon-ball fired down the High Street after dark would hit no one, all honest folk would be indoors with their houses firmly shuttered. The Constables duties included the rounding up of all stray livestock and placing them in the Pound in St. Albans Rd. A common form of punishment during the time, was the clapping of wrong-doers into the stocks. The last recorded sufferer of this punishment was a drunken water cress seller known as 'Snoozer', who spent two hours in the stocks. The watchmen, also doubled as the Town's Criers. Following the burning down of the old Market House in 1853, a new Criers Bell was cast from the old Market Place Bell, although by this time the post of Town Crier had passed into history.

Rewards

In order to encourage the constables to go about their duties in an industrious manner, the Watch Committee of that time decided to reward them for acts carried out during their patrols as the merits of the case deserved. On one occasion a constable received a bounty of 5/- (25p) for apprehending two wood stealers and another received 3/9d (19p) for apprehending a man found on enclosed premises. As a means to involve the community in the venture, the committee printed and circulated a letter amongst the townsfolk which "recommended the inhabitants not to encourage vagrancy by giving alms to beggars, and with the object of assisting the measures of the association formed for suppressing burglary and other crimes in Watford and its neighbourhood, they will take the trouble of giving information to the constables whenever an act of vagrancy comes under their observation."

It is not surprising to discover that the constables of 1829 were frequently involved in matters relating to Public Houses as their early weekly reports to the committee show:-

16th February 1829

The constables reported that on the night of the 14th, drunken and riotous persons had come out of the George Hotel and that one of those persons had been warned by the magistrates and that the Landlord had been admonished.

2nd March 1829

The constables reported that on Sunday night they had apprehended Annie Stone and Maria Bell in Mr.Brittons Cottage in Red Lion Yard. Both females appeared before Magistrates on this day and were committed to St.Albans Gaol for one month, for being found in an unoccupied house.

16th March 1829

The constables reported that on Saturday night they had quelled a violent domestic disturbance at the Fighting Cocks.

As a result of this incident, both constables were issued with handcuffs.

1st June 1829

The constables reported that on Sunday night John Neville had been apprehended in a resident's back yard and committed to St.Albans Gaol for two months.

Vagrants also came in for attention from the patrols:-

16th March 1829

The constables reported that on Wednesday last, William Cole was apprehended for begging and committed to St.Albans Gaol for one month.

30th March 1829

That John Williams had been apprehended in

The Abbot's Langley and King's Langley

ASSOCIATION,

For the Preservation of the Peace, and Protection of the Persons and Property of the Subscribers.

In order to detect and bring to legal Punishment all Persons who may be guilty of the undermentioned Offences against the Persons and Property of the Subscribers, within the Parishes of Abbot's Langley, King's Langley, and its immediate Vicinity, the Association engages to give the following REWARDS, to be paid to the Person or Persons whose Information shall lead to the Apprehension and Conviction of any Person or Persons so offending, over and above any other Reward offered by Individuals or by Government:

For any High-way Robbery, Burglary, Setting Fire to any Dwelling House, or any other Building, or to any Stack of Corn or Hay,

TEN SOVEREIGNS;

For Stealing or Maiming any Horse, Cow or Sheep,

FIVE SOVEREIGNS;

For Stealing Corn, Hay, Coal, Shop Goods, or other Goods of Merchandize; or for wantonly Cutting down, Barking, or damaging Trees in any Garden or Plantation,

TWO SOVEREIGNS;

For Robbing any Orchard, or Garden; or Stealing or wantonly Damaging Underwood, or any Waggon, Cart, Plough, or other Implement of Husbandry, Gates, Fences, or any Iron-work belonging to such like Articles; or any Articles or Materials used in any Manufactory; for Cutting the Manes and Tails of Horses; or for Stealing or Maliciously Killing Pigs or Poultry,

ONE SOVEREIGN;

For Stealing Turnips or Turnip Tops, for Stealing or Breaking Hedges or Hurdles, or for wantonly throwing Gates off their Hinges,

HALF A SOVEREIGN;

And upon Conviction of Receivers of Stolen Goods, the Property of a Subscriber,

FIVE SOVEREIGNS:

And for any other Offence, not before specified, such Reward as the Committee shall think proper.

N. B. No expences except those on Summary Convictions, will be allowed by the Society, unless previous application be made to the Treasurer.

NAMES AND RESIDENCE OF THE MEMBERS.

THE RIGHT HONORABLE THE EARL OF CLARENDON, President.

Atkinson, R. H. Esq...... Troley House
Bailey, George............ Chipperfield
Bailey, John............... Bedmont
Bailey, Ezekiel............ Bedmont
Betts, John................ Balls Pond
Butt, The Rev. J. W...... King's Langley
Barnett, E. Nich. R....... Sarratt
Carpenter, John.......... Hunton Bridge
Cooper, Mrs............. Langley Hill
Carvell, Thomas.......... King's Langley
Currie, James Esq......... Hill Side
Dickinson, John Esq...... Abbot's Hill
Downer, William.......... Leavesden
Ebbern, Thomas.......... Lady Capel's Wharf
Edmonds, William........ Hyde Lane
Foskett, Captain.......... Rose Hill
Green, James.............. Waterdell
Grover, Matthew.......... Abbot's Langley
Groome, John Andrew.... King's Langley
Gulston, John.............. Hart Hall
Honour, John............. Chipperfield
Hatley, Newman.......... Langley Lodge
Hatley, George........... The Hyde
Hill, Joseph............... King's Langley
Hill, Daniel................ Micklefield
Janes, George............ Hunton Bridge
Kemp, John............... Chipperfield
Leach, James............ Grove Mill
Leach, George............ High Street Farm
Leach, Mrs................ King's Langley
Lewis, The Rev. William... Abbot's Langley
Longman, Charles Esq.... Nash Mills
Moate, Septimus......... West Wood
Maas, Jacob............. Chipperfield
Parsley, John Esq........ Chipperfield
Pocock, Samuel.......... Barns Farm
Reeve, Thomas........... Hunton Bridge
Slack, John............... Manor House
Sherwood, Mrs............ The Hill Farm
Squire, Miss.............. King's Langley
Solly, Samuel Reynolds Esq. Serge Hill
Saunders, John.......... Highwood Hill
Toovey, Thomas.......... King's Langley
Toovey, Benjamin........ Abbot's Langley
Tyers, William............ King's Langley
Vine, John................ Leavesden
Wotton, Richard.......... King's Langley
Winkfield, Joseph........ Longcroft
Yearby, Thomas.......... King's Langley

Rewards Poster Approximately 1830's (Courtesy David Spain)

an open field and had been committed to gaol for one month.

Despite their efforts the Watch Committee were not over impressed with the constables performance. On 15th June 1829 they were sent for and informed that complaints had been made of beggars laying about the town as much as ever and that disorderly women were about, leaving houses at improper times at night. The constables were ordered to pay more attention to stop this nuisance or other persons would be appointed in their place.

Corruption was soon to rear its ugly head. On August 31st of that year, Constable Birch was dismissed having admitted taking a bribe from a local pawnbroker for withol-ding information about him from the Watch Committee. A replacement was appointed the same day.

Rickmansworth's First Constables

In 23rd September 1818, the inhabitants of the District of Rickmansworth decided to form an Association for the protection of their property and the prosecution of felons and other offenders. A Fund was set up for the payment of rewards to any person giving information leading to the successful prose-cution of persons for arson, burglary and wanton damage etc. To this end, notices giving details of the Association and particu-lars of the rewards offered were exhibited in the High Street, Rickmansworth.A few years later two paid officers were employed to maintain law and order.

The Provincial Police Forces, came into being after the passing of the Rural Police Acts 1839/1840. Previous to this date, the 'policing' of a parish was in the hands of the parish constable nominated either by the vestry or the Court Leet. There is no reference in the Parish records of Rickmans-worth to the appointment of anyone to this office earlier than 1846. Before this date, the only records that survive are to be found in the records of the Court Leet of the Manor of Rickmansworth, and there it is noted that fourteen parish constables were appointed. The minutes for the 14th April 1841 show that there were three for the town, the same number for West Hyde, and two each for Mill End, Chorleywood, Croxley and Batch-worth. Their uniforms, consisted solely of a cloth top hat.

There is no local record that gives the date when the first uniformed policeman was appointed in Rickmansworth, but it is known that in 1846, the Chief Constable of the Hertfordshire Constabulary and his Inspector a Mr.Evans, visited the Town to confer with the vestry about renting the cage for the holding of offenders apprehended by his two men. The officers were granted the use of the cage at a peppercorn rent.

The cage had been built in 1757, and stored at the rear of the site of the old Beresford Almshouses and the old Fire Station, and it remained in use until 1864.

Special Constables

In 1831 The Special Constables Act was passed allowing for the nomination and appointment in times of emergency. It provides that when the oath is made by any credible witness before any two or more magistrates that an assault, riot or a felony has taken place, or may be reasonably apprehended in any place, within the divi-sion for which those justices act, and that the justices are satisfied that the strength of the regular police is insufficient to meet the needs for the protection of the inhabitants and the security of property, then they shall nominate and appoint so many as they shall think fit to act as special constables for such time and in such manner as they consider fit and proper.

William Graves

William Graves, was born in Norwich circa 1811. He moved to Watford, where he appears in the Watford Census Records living with his in-laws in the house of John Edlin. The Watford Observer of Saturday 6th December 1902, carries his obituary.

Death of Mr. William Graves - We regret to record the death of Mr. William Graves, who passed away on Monday at the age of 92 years at the George Hotel, the residence of his daughter Mrs. Noble. Up to two or three weeks ago Mr. Graves could be seen about the town. Coming to Watford as a young man, Mr Graves in his lifetime held several public appointments. He was, with the late Mr. James West, one of the old parish constables, these two being the sole custodians of the peace of the town in those days. Many amusing anecdotes could Mr. Graves tell of his experiences in this office. He afterwards assisted the late Mr. John Edlin in his duties as Assistant Overseer and collector of poor rates, and succeeded to that post in 1858. His general courtesy will be long remembered. In 1874, he was appointed registrar of births and deaths in succession to the late Mr. G. Poulton, and he continued in the office until some few years ago. Mr. Graves was an accomplished violinist and played almost to the last. His band was once in great request at parties round the town. Two of his sons, who predeceased him, were also well known as musicians, Mr. William T Graves as cornet player and Mr. John Graves as a harp player. The old gentleman was one of the oldest members of the local Oddfellows. His good eyesight remained until the last; he never wore glasses. The funeral took place on Friday.

James West

One of Watford's early Parish Constables (from 1832 until the coming of the County Police in 1841) was James West. He was also the Town Crier and Organ Blower at the Parish Church.

James West (1807 - 1893)
Photgraph from The Book of Watford 1951

The Constabulary is born

Desire to have a Police Force

The raising of the Provincial police forces appears to have been due to a request submitted to the Home Secretary by the magistrates of Shropshire, which stated that they were of the opinion that a body of constables appointed by the magistrates, paid out of county rates, and disposable at any part of the Shire where their services might be required would be highly desirable as providing in the most efficient manner for the prevention, as well as the detection of offences, for the security of property and persons, and for the constant preservation of public peace. A copy of this resolution was received by the Liberty Magistrates in February 1839, for their consideration. They were in favour of such a measure and wrote to the Home Secretary accordingly, but it transpired in subsequent correspondence with this Minister, that the Liberty of St.Alban was not included within the provisions of the proposed new Act.

On the 14th October 1839, a Committee was appointed at the General Quarter Sessions at Hertford to enquire into the expediency of adopting the provisions of the new Act, either partially or generally. A questionnaire was sent out to all Magistrates regarding the efficiency of the Policing in operation in their districts. The answers revealed some interesting facts, as well as showing a general dissatisfaction of the privately paid forces. It appeared that on average constables were paid one pound a week. The justices at Watford, go on record as having replied "We have the usual old women called Constables".

Discussion then took place with the Chairman of the County Sessions of Hertfordshire in order that the Liberty might be placed in a situation to adopt the Act. The outcome of these discussions was satisfactory, and steps were taken to establish a Constabulary Force for those parts of Hertfordshire and of the Liberty of St.Alban which were not included in the District of the Metropolitan Police. The parishes were then informed of this decision. It is interesting to note that a petition was submitted from Rickmansworth in February 1841, approving the adoption of the Rural Police Acts 2/3 Vict. and 3/4 Vict. 1839/1840.

First County Police

Soon after the passing of the Act, The Justices in Essex, formed the Essex County Police and shortly afterwards were followed by Suffolk and then Hertfordshire, who can therefore lay claim to be **the third oldest County Force in England.**

Liberty of St. Albans

A word or two about the Liberty of St. Alban, would not be out of place, and might explain why it was left out of the Act. The area administered by the Liberty Magistrates comprised all that part of Hertfordshire owned by the Abbot of St.Alban over which he had very full jurisdiction by virtue of many Royal Charters. Early Saxon and Norman Kings had granted full liberties and jurisdiction over the Abbot's territories to the exclusion of the Sheriff and King's Officer. In the reign of Edward IV, power was given to the Abbot to "do, execute and exercise all and singular those things which to the delivery of the prison of our said gaol pertain." This grant was confirmed by Henry VII, who also gave power to the Abbott to appoint his own justices, but these vast and dangerous powers were abolished by Henry VIII prior to the Dissolution of the Monasteries Act by Parliament which cancelled all Civil jurisdiction granted by the King's predecessors. One of the exceptions mentioned in this Act was the Borough of St.Alban. From the reign of Henry VIII onwards, therefore, the Liberty remained on the same standing as the County; the Liberty area could be roughly defined as the south-westerly part of the County. In 1874, the two jurisdictions were merged.

The County Police Force was to consist of a Chief Constable, with a salary of £300 a year with an allowance of £100 for keeping two horses and a gig, four Superintendents with a salary of £85 a year plus clothing and an additional £30 a year for a horse, 6 Inspectors, 30 Constables at 21/- per week and another 30 at 19/- a week, both these classes also recieved clothing. The cost of the force would be met by the levying of 3d in the £1 on the full value of the rateable property of the County and Liberty (Exclusive of those parishes within the Metropolitan Police Area and the Boroughs of Hertford and St.Alban), which amounted to £482,513; this would produce £6,030, the estimated cost for the first year. The rateable value of Rickmansworth at this time 1841, being £16,236.

Plans went forward - the Committee appointed by the Justices reported favourably, and in 1840 an advertisement appeared in the County Press for a Chief Constable. The following year, on 12th April 1841, Colonel A.Robertson was appointed to that position from a total of 24 candidates. The first Constable, Robert Dunn however was not appointed until 6th May 1841.

It will be noted that there were no sergeants in the newly created organisation. The men were stationed throughout the County in Towns and villages, and it is interesting to see that the establishment at that time shows what was considered to be the busiest parts of the County.

BERKHAMSTED	1 Superintendent	1 Constable
BISHOPS STORTFORD	1 Superintendent	2 Constables
HATFIELD	1 Superintendent	2 Constables
HITCHIN	1 Superintendent	2 Constables
WATFORD	1 Inspector	2 Constables
HEMEL HEMPSTEAD	1 Inspector	1 Constable
HERTFORD		1 Constable
ST.ALBANS		1 Constable

The total cost for the newly formed Hertford County Constabulary in it's first year of operation came to £5,851. During that first year, a total of 1642 arrests were made, which resulted in 1180 Convictions.

Not very much is known of the Hertfordshire Constabulary in its infancy, but apparently it did perform its duties well. Very few records of this period remain, as in 1900 the then Chief Constable ordered the destruction of all records prior to 1891.

Below are some of the stories and events that help to make up the interesting history of policing 'C' Division the Hertfordshire Constabulary.

First Constabulary Constables at Rickmansworth

In 1846, the first recorded Constable was stationed at Rickmansworth. His uniform consisted solely of a cloth top hat.

The census returns for 1851, show that there were two constables in the town, James Veitch, who lived in Mill End, and Elisha Tomlin at Batchworth.

Watford - 1851

By 1851, Watford had a total population of 3,826 people and was policed from a Police Station in the High Street under Superintendent George Cocksedge.

Watford Police 1863 - Photograph taken in Mr Downer's Loates Lane outdoor studio.

Prizefighting

On 23rd October 1863, the following article appeared in the Watford Observer.

"On Wednesday last the peace of the neighbourhood was broken by a band of ruffians from London who came to participate in and witness a prize fight. We repeat -a prize fight- and a most disgusting sight it must have been if all is true we hear, not fit for publication. It appears the fight commenced at Tring and after the men had fought for an hour the police put a stop to it. They then took a train for Watford and on arriving they sprang from the carriages without showing their tickets and ran across the fields to Loates Lane, where in a meadow adjoining the lane a ring was formed and the fight renewed. The police made their appearance and did their best to stop the fight, but there being only two of them it was of no avail. Unfortunately our Superintendent was out of town."

On October 31st 1863 the Watford Observer continued the story.

"We are sorry to find that our Police have got into trouble with regard to the prize fight that took place on Wednesday week. In consequence of representations made to the Chief Constable, Captain Robertson, our Superintendent, Mr. Hilsden, has been reduced to the rank of Inspector with a consequent loss in salary amounting to £20 per year; Constable Coulter was ordered to be dismissed from the force and the wages of Constable Farr have been reduced to 4 shillings per week.

Now we thinh it would be admitted that nothing but a gross dereliction of duty would warrant such a punishment as this. That such disgusting and brutalizing scenes as took place at Watford on Wednesday week should be put down by the arm of the law we must heartily affirm, and if the police have been guilty of negligence and cowardice it is right that such misconduct should not be passed over without reproof and punishment. Let us look, however at the facts and see whether they deserve such severe measures being adopted towards one of the most efficient Superintendents that we have ever had and towards two constables who have hitherto borne an excellent character in the police force..... The two policemen Coulter and Farr, who were the only two members of the force available, endeavoured to stop the fight. The ruffians, using the most horrible oaths and imprecations, threatened their lives if they dared to interfere, and the policemen seeing how great were the odds against them, gave up the attempt as hopeless. We cannot blame them for doing so; policemen are not expected to show superhuman courage in the discharge of their duties."

On April 14th 1863, the Watford Observer had carried a report about the conduct of Superintendent Hilsden. "After the swearing in of the parish Constables there was no criminal business or any other matter to occupy their worships' attention and there is very little doubt that the absence of crime and the present tranquility of the Watford District is in great measure attributable to the introduction here of Superintendent Hilsden from the Hertfordshire Constabulary. Through his vigilance and ability Watford has been thinned of its bad characters; he is well acquainted with his duties and they are ever fearlessly and faithfully fulfilled; his subordinates obey and respect him; they appear to serve with pleasure under his authority. Those who have watched him most admire him most. Nothing malignant could ever be traced in his character."

Robertson, relented finally in November, following a letter written to him by the Earl of Essex on behalf of the Watford Magistrates. He finally reinstated the officers to their original positions. However, the Watford Observer comments.

"We understand also that the Chief Constable has not offered to refund the loss incurred by the temporary reduction in salary of the Superintendent and Constable Farr and the dismissal of Constable Coulter, who we are informed has now been banished to a place called Wigginton-the Siberia of unfortunate policemen."

Talbot Road Police Station

Talbot Road Police Station 1864 - Drawing from the Rickmansworth Historian

In 1864 Hertford County Police purchase a house in Talbot Rd, Rickmansworth to use as a Police Station, onto which was built a cell, complete with a very small window with iron bars. This Police Station was in use until 1897, when a Police Station was built in the High Street, adjoining the Fire Station. The cell attached to the Talbot Rd House, was demolished in the early 1960's, but it's position on the building along with the Police Station sign can still be clearly seen today.

Framed Orders

In 1872 the Chief Constable issued his first orders and instructions to his constables. Some of which are quite harsh and reflect on the sort of life the constable had to endure at that time.

ORDERS AND INSTRUCTIONS FRAMED AND ISSUED FOR THE CONSTABLES OF THE HERTFORDSHIRE CONSTABULARY by A. ROBERTSON,

Captain H.-P. Unattached.
Chief Constable of Hertfordshire. 1872

Article 1

The Conditions upon which each person is to be admitted into the Hertfordshire Constabulary Force are stated here, that no complaint may be made hereafter upon their being enforced.

1. Each man shall devote his whole time to the service of the Hertfordshire Constabulary Force.

2. He shall serve and reside wherever he is directed.

3. He shall promptly obey all lawful orders, which he may receive from the persons placed in authority over him.

4. He shall conform himself to all the regulations which may be made from time to time concerning the service.

5. He shall not on any occasion, or under any pretence whatsoever, take money from any person without the express permission of the Chief Constable in writing.

6. He shall receive his pay on such days as shall be appointed.

7. He shall allow a deduction to be made from his pay when lodgings are found for him.

8. He shall not quit the Constabulary Force without giving one calendar month's notice in writing; in case he quit without such notice, all pay then due shall be forfeited. If he be dismissed the Hertfordshire Constabulary Force, the whole of his pay then due or unpaid is forfeited.

N.B.- By Act of Parliament, a Constable is further liable to one month's imprisonment for quitting the Force without giving one month's notice.

9. If any member of the Constabulary Force shall be absent from duty in consequence of ill health, the Chief Constable shall exercise his pleasure as to stopping any portion of his pay during such sickness.

10. Such debts owing by any of the Constabulary as the Chief Constable shall direct to be paid, shall be paid by them forthwith.

11. Each person in the force is liable to immediate dismissal for unfitness, negligence, or misconduct, or the Chief Constable may punish him, by suspension or fine.

12. Every member of the Constabulary Force will be prohibited from interfering directly or indirectly in any election for Members of Parliament.

13. All persons are to consider themselves for the first 56 days after entering the Hertfordshire Constabulary Force on probation and consequently will not be clothed earlier than the Chief Constable may deem desirable.

14. No member of the force shall keep a dog, pig, fowls, or any description of stock.

15. All clothing, appointments, or stores,

upon which may be lost, damaged, or spoilt, while in the possession of the person to whom they were issued, shall be made good by him out of his pay.

16.Everyman dismissed from the Hertfordshire Constabulary Force, or who shall resign his situation, shall, before he quits the service, take and deliver up every article of dress and all appointments which have been supplied to him, into the hands of the Superintendent or Inspector of his own division at the residence of such superior officer.

Pay and Clothing

1. Pay will be issued to the Constabulary once each fortnight, when all debts due by them must be discharged.

2. Any constable who shall not have received the exact amount for which he has signed the paysheet, three days after it is due, must report the same by letter direct to the Chief Constable, or he will be dismissed. The officers of every rank are forbidden, on pain of dismissal, to borrow, or to lend money one to the other.

3. Any member of the force who is reported as habitually in debt shall be dismissed.

4. A deduction of fourpence a week is made from the pay of each Constable, according to Act of Parliament, towards a superannuation fund.

5. The usual clothing will be issued to the Constabulary once in every year; it is to be understood that no part thereof will at any time become the property of the Constable, but all must be delivered over by him should he leave the force, or otherwise disposed of as directed.

6. Eighteenpence a month per man will be allowed in lieu of boots, and each constable must at all times be provided with two serviceable pairs.

7. All Police Officers attending Assizes or Quarter Sessions in any capacity, must appear in full uniform and without great coats; they must be clean and neat and well shaved, they must stand upright in the witness box with their hands down, and never lean or loll against the sides; they will give ready and distinct answers to the counsel on both sides; any laughter or impertinent conduct will on no account be allowed. Constables before being called to give evidence in court should refresh their memory from notes of the circumstances taken by them at the time of the examination before the magistrates, but such notes are never to be produced in court unless called for.

8. Constables are at all times to be dressed in their uniform, unless directed otherwise by a superior officer.

9. Each constable will be required to provide himself with a decent suit of plain clothes to be worn when so ordered.

10. No alteration whatsoever is to be made in the uniform issued to the constabulary.

11. THe great coat is never to be worn on patrol over the best body coat, and the cape is invariably to be carried by the constable when there is any appearance of wet, or when he has to proceed further than his own beat during the winter months.

12. Each constable will, on the first day of meeting in every month, bring with him to the station, for inspection, his staff, lantern, handcuffs, rattle, and instruction book. He will, at the same time, wear his great coat, old body coat, and old trowsers. On the

second day of meeting in the month, he will come in his new coat, best trowsers, cape, and belt (Without other appointments). The Superintendent or Inspector will minutely examine every article, and report any deficiency, or want of repair.

13. During the night patrol the old clothing and hats are to be worn, and also by day in wet weather.

14.No constable shall use, or allow to be used, the button marked "Herts Constabulary," except on the uniform coat of the force.

15. All members of the Constabulary will have their hair cut, at least once every month, nothing having a more slovenly appearance than wearing long hair with any sort of uniform.

16.The embroidery on the collar of the coat and great coat must be kept perfectly clean and white, which can easily be done by using a small soft brush with soap and warm water.

17. No constable will be retained in the force whose appearance and clothing are not neat and clean, and superiority in this respect will give a claim to first class pay,- without it no constable can ever hope for promotion.

Article II

The Instructions in article 2 are summarised.

Officers and Constables should endeavour to distinguish themselves by such vigilance and activity as may render it extremely difficult for any one to commit a crime within that proportion of the district under their charge.

When in any Division offences are frequently committed, there must be reason to suspect that the Constabulary is not in that Division properly conducted. The absence of crime will be considered the best proof of the complete efficiency of the Constabulary.

Every constable may hope to rise by activity, intelligence, and good conduct to the superior stations. He must make it his study to recommend himself to notice by a diligent discharge of his duties, and strict obedience to the commands of his superiors, recollecting that he who has been accustomed to submit to discipline will be considered best qualified to command.

It is indispensably necessary that he should make himself perfectly acquainted with all the parts of his beat. He will be expected to possess such a knowledge of the inhabitants of each house, as will enable him to recognise their persons.

If during his tour of duty he observes in the streets or roads anything likely to produce danger or public inconvenience, he must report it to his superior.

He will be civil and attentive to all persons of every rank and class.

While on duty he must not enter into conversation with any one, except on matters solely relating to his duty.

Any constable reported for endeavouring to conceal his number, or refusing to shew or tell it when asked, will be dismissed, as such concealment or refusal can only be caused by having done something that he is ashamed of.

Constables are not permitted to carry sticks or umbrellas.

Constables are always to take the outward side of the footpath, and it is particularly desired that constables when walking along the streets should not shoulder past respectable people, but give way in an a mild manner.

Any constable intermarrying with the family of a reputed bad character, or lodging in his house, or contracting an improper intimacy with him, will be dismissed the service.

Prisoners in custody are to be treated with kindness and lenity. They are to be permitted to purchase what refreshment (except spirituous or fermented liquors) they may choose; and when without money, are never to have less than two pounds of good bread for the day in which they are in confinement.

When toll shall be demanded of any member of the Constabulary Force who is on Police Duty, after having informed the gate keeper in general terms of the duty in which he is engaged, the toll shall be paid under protest, and the circumstances immediately reported to the Chief Constable.

Every constable, when his usual hours of patrol are over, will return to his own house or lodging, and remain therein, taking necessary rest; and unless called out to perform some service (the nature of which must be reported by him), it is expected that he shall be found at home until the hour for his again going on patrol arrives.

Each constable will take charge of and treat kindly all straying children, - take them to the nearest station, and make inquiry to whom they belong, and restore them, if possible, to their parents or friends.

They will give notice to all gipsies, trampers, beggars, and unlicensed hawkers to quit the County, noting their persons and appearance; and should any of those persons be met with a second time, they will arrest them, and take them before a magistrate. They will impound the horses, donkeys or mules of the aforesaid persons which they may find feeding by the roadsides, in lanes, or in fields, where they have no authority to be.

LASTLY. The Constabulary must bear in mind that a heavy calendar, or numerous arrests, by no means proves the presence of a vigilant Police; the absence of the cause of arrests, commitals, and trials, best shows the well working of the Force; and where the evil-doer, from the dread of certain detection, abandons his malpractises and turns his hand to honest labour, or is driven from the County - there the influence of a good and efficient Police is most apparent.

Crimes

In 1873 a total of 124 Crimes were reported throughout the County of which 72 were detected.

Force Strength - 1873

The strength of the Force stood at 117 Officers. There were 1,364 people per officer, and each officer was responsible for 3,152 Acres of the County.

Pitch and Toss (W.O. 18.3.1879)

At Watford Magistrates Court, George Bullen and George Spurr were charged with playing pitch and toss in a public path at Watford. Pc Mills, stated that on Sunday 9th March 1879, "at 5 o'clock in the afternoon I saw the defendants playing pitch and toss with a halfpence on a public footway in Cassiobury Park. I spoke to them and told them they should be ashamed of themselves for playing there on a Sunday. Their language was disgraceful. Complaints were made to me by several ladies who said they could not walk by without being insulted. The defendants told me that they hoped that I would forgive them."

The court heard that Bullen had a previous conviction for stealing a duck. The Court fined them 10/- each with 10/3d costs or in default of payment to 14 days imprisonment.

1st Divisions

On the first February 1881, the Force was reorganised into 5 Divisions and the duties of the Officers were laid down. For example, Sergeants will attend one or other of the Conference Points in his section every night and will be constantly on patrol looking after the working of the men on his section. He will attend the scene of every offence committed within his Section.

The New Divisions are:-

"A" or Ware Division.

"B" or Bishops Stortford Division.

"C" or St. Albans Division.

"D" or Hemel Hempstead Division.

"E" or Hitchin Division.

"R" or Reserve Division.

Groomboys

In 1881, the groomboys employed at the Police Stations were discharged and a Constable was detailed to look after the County Divisional Horse and Cart. The Constable appointed to these duties was also responsible for the Divisional lock-ups.

On 9th May 1881, the Secretary of State rearranged the strength and pay of the Hertford County Constabulary.

1 Chief Constable.

5 Superintendents at £120.

5 Inspectors at £95.

1 Inspector and Chief Clerk at £95.

15 Sergeants at 28/- per week.

112 Constables at 21/7d rising to 27/5d per week after 8 years service. Superannuation was taken back at Two and a half percent of pay. Married Constables were stopped 2/- a week if living in County owned Houses. One day a quarter was allowed as a rest day.

Promotion - 1882

The Chief Constable was promoted to Lieutenant Colonel.

Recruiting - 1882

Recruiting forms for the Force contained the question "Can the applicant read and write." Recruits were mainly drawn from Farm Labourers, Grooms, Gardeners and Wheelwrights. Very few Clerks applied to serve.

County Headquarters

Constabulary Headquarters moved from Hertford to Hatfield on 18th July 1883.

Fowl Stealing

On 10th September 1883, Pc 59 Hill having distinguished himself by his energy and ability in detecting offenders and procuring convictions in several cases of fowl stealing is permitted to receive a reward of £1 offered to him by the Steward to His Grace the Duke of Wellington.

Salvation Army

In 1883 the Chief Constable Issued the following Order:-

In the event of the body known as the Salvation Army holding meetings at any place or places in the County, it is the duty of the police to afford them proper protection and to prevent any disturbance being caused by opponents of that body. Any sign of exhibition of personal feeling or opinion on the matter of the Salvation Army on the part of any member of the Constabulary will be dealt with severely by the Chief Constable and as long as members of the Salvation Army confine themselves to their legal rights as citizens they are to receive that protection from Police to which the public is entitled.

Constable Weeden, Kings Langley constable circa 1883 - Photograph courtesey David Spain

Salvation Army II

William King, a builder and member of the Beechen Grove Baptist Church in Watford, decided that in 1883 that the down and out people of Watford needed Salvation. On Easter Sunday the "Salvation Army" entered Watford. A meeting was organised by King in a coffee tavern to dicuss the possibility of establishing a Salvation Army centre in the town. King enlisted the help of his brother Thomas and as result of their persuasion, the group sent a request to General William Booth, the General responded by sending Captain William Foster to the town. The Captain quickly assumed the nickname "Praying Billie" as he commenced his work.

The Captain was successful in converting many people to the Army, but not without meeting opposition from others including the Police. Such was the opposition, Henry Daniell was forced to issue an order reminding officers that however strongly they felt as individuals, that they must not show it to the public. The main opposition to the Salvation Army came from local publicans who soon commanded there own group of men who disrupted the Salvationists public meeting, by turning out lights at crowded meetings and they even resorted to releasing rats in the halls. The group finally turned to violence and several members of the new movement were injured. The Police reluctantly attended the next few meetings to protect the worshippers. After several more disruptions, a summons was issued against Captain Foster for "Breach of the Peace", and the Captain was sentenced to 14 days imprisonment, which he served at St.Albans Gaol. On his release, the Captain continued his work and eventually succeeded in converting his main protagonist a Mr. Stratford. With his main opposition now a convert, the opposition groups broke up.

Opposition by the Police however took longer to fade, in the 1890's, a constable who introduced a Salvationist to Captain Wymer the Superintendent at Watford as "Captain", was later summonsed to the Superintendent's Office. Captain Wymer is reputed to have said "Militia officers are bad, volunteer officers are a damn sight worse, but don't you ever show a Salvation Army officer in to me again."

Superintendent at St. Albans

In 1884, the Superintendent of Police for "C" Division, Captain H. Durrell was based at St. Albans. Inspector M.W. Hummerstone was in charge of the Estcourt Road Police Station. The Constabulary Sergeant at Watford was C. Purkis.

Free Beer

"The Chief Constable has information which leads him to believe that many of the Breweries in the County are practically open houses to the Police and at those breweries, members of the Force can obtain refreshment such as beer or stout free of charge. The Chief Constable desires it to be distinctly understood that this custom must cease at once.......the fact of accepting liquor without payment from a brewery tends to place the members of the Constabulary in the power of the breweries, gives the Police a deservedly bad name and most materially injures the efficiency of the Force." (12.11.1884)

Free Outing

13th July 1886. All members of the Force granted a free trip to the Colonial and Indian Exhibition at London, paid for by Magistrates and well-wishers.

Bedding

5th November 1886. Straw palliases supplied for the cells.

A.W.O.L.

Pc 14 Dunn "C" Division, absent without leave for 6 days, was sentenced to 3 months imprisonment at Hertford, for being found drunk and disorderly and for assaulting Police. (1886)

Inspection

The "C" and "D" Divisions of the Hertfordshire Constabulary were Inspected by Colonel Cobb at St. Albans on Saturday last. Lieutenant Colonel Daniell the Chief Constable was present. The men were complimented on their smartness. On examining the books of "C" Division, Colonel Cobb gave Superintendent Hummerstone great praise for the way in which they were kept. He was also pleased to notice a great decrease in cases of drunkenness, but was sorry to see an increase in cases of vagrancy. (W.O. 26.5.1888)

Ripper (No just Drunk)

There was intense excitement in Rickmansworth on Monday night, on it's becoming known that Sergeant Summerling and Constable Steers had arrested a man in Maple Cross who answered to the description of Jack the Ripper, and who had behaved in a most excited manner.

(The individual concerned appeared before the Magistrates the following day on a charge of being DRUNK.) (W.O. 1.12.1888)

New Police Station in Kings Street

Accommodation is very comprehensive, the ground floor comprises of a guard room forming the public entrance, the Superintendent's office to be used also as an occasional court, a small retiring room for Magistrates use, and a weights and measures room for testing and adjustment purposes. There are also 8 prisoners cells and a yard for their exercise. The stables embrace two stalls and a loose box, attached to which is a coach house, forage house and harness room.

Commencing with the guard room, it has two entrances, one from King Street having a lobby fitted with a seat, and one from the stable yard. The cells are approached from the guard room by a corridor running the entire length of the cells, the walls of which, like those of the cells are of massive construction with ceiling formed of brick arches filled with concrete. There are three open iron grates hung in the corridor which can be locked across it when required. This enables either 1, 3, or 5 cells to be shut off for females. The cells are each fitted with a wooden bench which forms a seat by day and bed by night. The heat of the cells can be regulated by the prisoners by opening or closing a grating. Each cell is fitted with an electric bell to communicate with the guard room. Cells are illuminated by night with gas lamps set into the wall. There are two W.C.'s, one at each end of the corridor. The exercise yard is paved with concrete and is 40 feet long enclosed with high brick walls. The Magistrates Retiring room is separated from from the Superintendent's office by a lobby having an entrance in Kings Street.

The first and second floors comprise of several residences viz Superintendents quarters comprising of two sitting rooms, kitchen, scullery, larder etc reached by a stone staircase from the stable yard and from the downstairs lobby. There are four bedrooms and a bathroom above. The Superintendent also has a separate yard with a concrete floor formed over the prisoners cells. Adjoining the Superintendent's quarters on the 1st and 2nd floors, are married Sergeant's quarters comprising a kitchen, scullery and three bedrooms. Next to those are married Constable's quarters containing the same accommodation. There are also rooms for single Constables adjoining the Sergeant's quarters.

King Street Police Station, 1889, wood cutting from Watford Observer

In addition, there is a wash house for general use and a large space over the cells and stables for use as a drying yard. Below the guard and harness rooms is a furnace room and two large cellars for coal and coke reached by a stone staircase from the stable yard.

The building is lit by gas throughout. Speaking tubes are provided for communication between the Superintendent's office and the guard room and from the guard room to the Superintendent's sitting room and bedroom, Sergeant's kitchen and bedroom and the Constable's kitchen and bedroom.

The building contract cost a total of £5,185.

On 29th January 1889, the Police Station was authorised for use as the occasional court house. (W.O. 12.1.1889)

Weights and Measures

Police were responsible for weights and measures, food and drugs and petroleum and explosives. Eight Officers were also appointed Assistant Relieving Officers for Tramps. (1889)

Unfit for Humans

Bishop Stortford Police Station was Closed as being unfit for human habitation. (1889)

Births

On 31st July 1889 at the Police Station Cottage, Talbot Road, Rickmansworth, to the wife of Police Constable James Bates a daughter.

Burglaries

On August 24th 1889, Daniel Hostler broke into the house of a Charles Harris at Watford, and stole a pair of boots and a tablecloth. He also broke into the house of a Mr. Austin a week later and stole a watch. His third housebreaking though proved his undoing as he broke into the home just as its Constable resident was returning home from duty. Hostler was subsequently sentenced to 5 years imprisonment. (W.O. 31.7.1889)

Testimonial - Supt. Hummerstone

On Wednesday evening a dinner was held at the Corn Exchange, Watford, the occasion being the presentation of a testimonial to Superintendent Hummerstone of "C" Division. Other members of "C" Division received recognition for their services in the past. The Superintendent's testimonial was in the form of a marble clock with chimes. This was the result of a general appreciation of the ability, hard work and tact of the officer. Donations were made by all classes in the neighbourhood and the amount subscribed not only permitted the purchase of the clock, but the gift of a purse of money between £40 and £50. In addition, a half sovereign in new coin was given to each man in the Division.

The Chief Constable Henry Daniell and Superintendent Pearson the Deputy Chief Constable were present together with various Sergeants, Inspectors and 25 Constables. A large number of local dignitaries completed the guest list.

Superintendent Hummerstone has served "C" Division for 8 years, previously he was stationed at Royston. (W.O. 30.11.1889)

Flogged

Chairman of the bench at Watford Petty Sessions, Mr. W. Woolrych sentenced 12 year old Herbert Hamill to be flogged with six strokes of a birch rod in the presence of the Inspector of Police for stealing milk from a Bushey Farmer. A Police Constable saw Hamill milking a cow into his hat while other boys stood around and watched. (W.O. 26.7.1890)

100 Years of C Division - Watford

The county of Hertfordshire was continuing to grow especially in the Watford area, and by 1891 it was necessary for the Chief Constable to review his manpower and the deployment of his constables. Below is an extract from the report that was produced:

Special Report to the Standing Joint Committee - 5th June 1891

In consequence of the urgent demands made upon me for a greater amount of Police protection in all parts of the County, it becomes necessary for me to submit to the Standing Joint Committee a comprehensive statement of the increase recommended by me to be made to the strength of the County Constabulary.

In most cases the increase is clearly demanded by a considerable augmentation of the population during the last 10 years.

In dealing with this subject I have also to suggest an alteration in the working of the 'C' or St. Albans Division, which will be found below in my report on the requirements of that Division.

'C' or St. Albans Division

(1) This division is decidedly in an unsatisfactory condition as regards the strength of the Force, in relation to the population and the value of the property under the care and protection of the Police.

(2) The population of Watford has increased in the last decade from 15,506 in 2,555 houses in 1881, to 21,000 inhabitants in 3,500 houses in 1891. At least 100 additional houses are at this moment in the course of construction, and there is no doubt that the population of the Watford Urban Sanitary District will continue to rise rapidly.

(3) During the past ten years the local Police Force has been from time to time augmented, and now consists of 1 Superintendent, 1 Inspector, 2 Sergeants, and 12 Constables. Of this force 1 Sergeant is stationed at Garston, 1 Constable is stationed at Hunton Bridge and 1 Constable is stationed at Bricket; leaving 1 Superintendent, 1 Inspector, 1 Sergeant and 9 Constables for duty at Watford. From these again must be deducted 1 Superintendent (who has the whole of a large division in his charge), 1 Clerk and Station Officer, 1 Constable Groom (in attendance on the Superintendent) and 1 Mounted Patrol; leaving for duty within the Watford Urban Sanitary District 1 Inspector, 1 Sergeant and 6 Constables. This number is manifestly and clearly insufficient for the population and area of the District, and an addition is required of 2 Sergeants and 4 Constables.

(4) The duty strength of the Force within the Urban Sanitary District will then be 1 Superintendent, 1 Inspector, 4 Sergeants and 14 Constables; 20 Total for the population of 21,000.

(5) RICKMANSWORTH.- The population of this Parish has increased from 5472 in 1881 to 6968 in 1891. The strength and distribution of the Force within the Parish is as follows:-Rickmansworth, 1 Sergeant and 1 Constable; Croxley Green, 1 Constable; Chorleywood, 1 Constable; and Mill End, 1 Constable. Total 1 Sergeant and 4 Constables; an addition of two constables is urgently needed.

(6) HARPENDEN:- The population of this parish has increased by nearly 1000 within the last decade, and now stands at 4000, while a considerable number of new houses are in course of erection and as yet unoccupied. The local Force consists of 1 Sergeant and one Constable. An additional Constable is required.

I have now to point out to the Committee the inconvenience and difficulty experienced in carrying on the duties of the Police, by the St. Albans Petty Sessional Division forming part of the Watford Division.

The Superintendent resides at Watford and cannot personally supervise with any degree of efficiency the Police of the St.Albans sub-division.

I recommend that the "C" or St.Albans Division should in future be called the "C" or Watford Division, and that the St.Albans Petty Sessional Division should be constituted a separate Sub-Division, with a 1st Class Inspector in charge, and that all the books, Returns and Reports, connected with the St.Albans Petty Sessional Division should be kept by the Inspector at St.Albans.

The Petty Sessional Division at St.Albans comprises part of St.Michael's, part of St.Stephen's, and part of St.Peter's, parishes of St.Albans, and parishes of Harpenden, Wheathampstead, Redbourn and Sandridge, all of them places of importance from a Police point of view, and rendered more difficult to work owing to the City of St.Albans having a separate Police Force, and therefore being unconcerned in the constant depradations of the bad characters of St.Albans, beyond the limits of their jurisdiction. If an office for the Inspector could be found in the Town Hall, it would be all that would be requisite.

Recommended Increase

The total increase to the Force recommended by me on the urgent application of Magistrates, County Councillors, Resident Gentry, Farmers, and my responsible Officers, is 1 Inspector, 3 Sergeants, 20 Constables.

First C.I.D. - 1892

1 year after the review, the first plain clothes officer was appointed to Watford, he was to be the first detective in the county. Watford at that time was considered to be the chief trouble spot in the county, and was also recognised as the busiest division. A 2nd detective was appointed in 1894.

Senior Division
Watford was also considered to be the senior division, and the Superintendent at Watford was recognised as the senior Divisional Commander and given the job of Deputy Chief Constable.

Typewriter - 1892

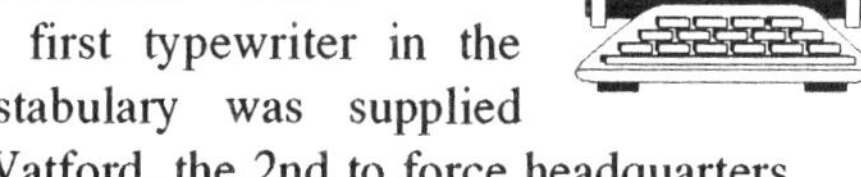

The first typewriter in the constabulary was supplied to Watford, the 2nd to force headquarters

Smallpox - 1893
In consequence of the danger to which Police Officers are subject by contact with vagrants or other persons infected with smallpox, all Officers are to be vaccinated. Wives and Children of all Officers residing in a Police Station or in a house rented or owned by the County are also to be vaccinated if required to do so by the Staff Surgeon. Officers whose wives refuse, are to vacate such House.

Telephones - 1893
Telephonic communication established between Watford and Bushey, Watford and Rickmansworth, Watford and St. Albans.

Coal Strike, Derbyshire - 1893
10th September 1893, Saw the first use of mutual co-operation between police forces, and the Hertfordshire Constabulary, when 30 picked Hertfordshire officers under the command of Superintendent John Reynolds, were sent to Derbyshire to help suppress riots there. The constables were armed with cutlasses.

Telephones - 1895
On 28th June 1895, telephonic communication established between Watford and the Telephone Exchange at Watford.

Street Gambling & Betting - 1895
At County Police Headquarters Archives, a folder of correspondence still exists, dealing with the problems of Street Gambling and Betting. The various letters are reproduced here.

On 26th September 1895, Lieutenant Colonel Henry Daniell the Chief Constable, sent a Memorandum to all his Superintendents.

Report at once if you have knowledge or suspicion of casual or habitual betting on races, occurring in the streets, or other highways or other public places in your Division.

All the Divisions except "C" replied they had no such knowledge of any betting taking place on the streets of their Divisions.

Captain Wymer the Deputy Chief Constable and Superintendent at "C" Division stationed at Watford replied on 1.10.1895.

Street betting and also betting on licensed premises has been systematically carried on in Watford for a period antecedent to my coming here and still continues, and I am Informed is also carried on at Rickmansworth by Bookmakers. I have not pursued any inquiries as to Rickmansworth for fear of hampering the prosecution which has been under notice with regard to the practices here.

I have the honour to be Sir,
Your obedient Servant
R.Wymer Capt.
DCC Herts

Captain Wymer sent a supplementary report on 5.10.1895.

At the "Railway Inn" Redbourn and in the village of Harpenden generally, betting on

licensed premises is believed to take place.

On the 16th May 1902 Superintendent W. Wood sent the Chief Constable a report.

Sir,
I beg to report that I am frequently receiving complaints of persons betting in the streets of Watford.

The bookmakers are well known to the Police, but so far as I can ascertain we have no power to take action in the matter.

In my opinion Bye Laws dealing with street betting would be very desirable.

I have the honour to be Sir,
Your obedient servant
W.Wood
Superintendent.

On 22nd May 1902, the following letter was received from the Clerk of the Peace Office, Hertford.

Dear Sir,

Street Betting
I am in receipt of your letter of the 17th Inst: enclosing letter from Superintendent Wood as to Street Betting.

If you are prepared to report to the Finance Committee that street betting exists to a considerable extent in the County I think they might perhaps be disposed to make a bye law dealing with the subject.

Up to the present they have not appeared so disposed to do this.

Please let me know whether you desire to press this forward.

From Superintendent Wood to the Chief Constable on 25.5.1902.

In reply to yours of 23rd May 1902 I beg to report that I have had a number of complaints with regard to street betting but have not kept notes of the dates. The last complaint was on 7th May 1902 from Mr. H.Williman of 37, Vicarage Rd, Watford, Missionary, who saw betting in a public urinal.

The Constables of Watford have often seen betting being carried on in the streets, and it is probably within your recollections that men have been sent here specially to detect betting in Public Houses.

I know of no other town in Hertfordshire where betting is carried on in the streets as it is in Watford, and it is gradually on the increase. All this is probably due to the size of the Town.

W. Wood Supt.

Lt. Col. Henry Daniell to Superintendent Wood on 26th May 1902.

Street Betting.
You will give instructions for the Police to make notes of any cases they may observe, between now and the 10th June, when you will send in all reports, ready for the information of the Standing Joint Committee.

By Order, Chief Clerk.

Letter to Chief Constable dated May 29th 1902 from Watford and District Free Church Council's Hon. Secretary Horace A Hunt 15, Westland Road, Watford.

Dear Sir,
The above Council view with alarm the increased prevalency of street betting in Watford and many complaints have been made by tradesmen and other reputable inhabitants of the nuisance caused thereby; and finding that the Police have no power to Interfere, The Council would respectfully

urge on you the necessity of something being done in this direction.

If you could see your way after due inquiry to advise the County Council to pass Bye Laws empowering the Police to take action, this in the opinion of the Council, would meet the difficulty, and bring about an abatement of the evil.

Trusting the humble application will receive your kind attention.

I remain Dear Sir
(On behalf of the Churches of Watford)
Yours Sincerely
Horace A Hunt.

From Lt. Col. Henry Daniell to the Reverend Horace A Hunt on 30.5.1902.

Dear Sir,

Your letter of 29th.
The subject of Street Betting in Watford has been brought under my notice by the Superintendent of Police.

The matter is being watched, and I must be able to have sufficient data to move the County Council to pass a Bye Law dealing with the subject at their next meeting.

Henry Daniell

Future Chief Constable

George Thomas Knight joined the Force on 24th August 1896, a baker by proffession. Earned 22/9d per week and was to rise through the ranks to become Chief Constable in 1928. He retired in 1939, and died 2 years later in 1941.

St. Albans Rd Police Station, Watford, completed 1896 at a cost of £3,143. Photograph from the Watford Observer, 1949

Watford Christmas Boxes - 1897

In 1897, the Deputy Chief Constable of the Herts. County Constabulary was Captain Wymer, the Superintendent of Watford. The Christmas Box affair led to his resignation. In the archives held at Police Headquarters, the original reports, letters and much of the documentation of this event are still kept, some of which are produced here.

Hatfield 4th January 1898

To: Superintendent 'C' Division and Deputy Chief Constable

It has been reported to me that a Constable stationed at Watford called at the residence of a Mr. Moore in Watford and asked for a Xmas Box. It is further stated that this Constable had a book with him, in which apparently the names of donors and perhaps the amount subscribed was entered. This is absolutely against existing orders. You will please make full enquiry and send me a detailed report showing who asked for Xmas boxes, who received or participated in any such money, and the book above mentioned should be forwarded to

Henry Daniell
Chief Constable.
5th January 1898.

Sir,
Replying to your letter of 4.1.98, the first Christmas that I was in charge of this Division, enquiry was made of me whether I had any objection to the men receiving Christmas Boxes. I asked for particulars and was informed that in connection with the safeguarding of empty houses and duty of this description, it had been the custom to send donations or gratuities to the Police Station but that it sometimes happened that individual Constables received money and retained it. I enquired what had been the custom before I came and was told that such monies had been received and collected and divided among the Constables in the Town. I said that I was prepared to sanction what had been previously authorised by my predecessors, at the same time any money received must be spontaneously given as I could not allow any asking, and any such monies must be equally divided and I should expect no man to withhold any money from such division, this was virtually what had always been done before. I replied in the same terms to the enquiry the following year.

This year Sergeants 82 Draper and 52 Fisher made the same enquiry and I replied in substance the same as before, one remark I made and that was, there must be no asking. It is I believe a fact that some of the most prominent residents and tradespeople in the town have been in the habit for many years of giving money to the Police.

In the present instance, the same post that brought your memorandum brought a letter from Mr. Moore asking whether the Constables were allowed to ask for Christmas boxes, I may at once say this is a thing I absolutely forbid.

Sergeants Draper and Fisher have both been questioned by me and positively deny that they have asked any person for a Christmas box. The money that has been received by them has not yet been divided.

I attach their reports together with one by Inspector Turner and the book to which you make reference.

I have the honour to be,
Sir,
Your obedient servant,
R. Wymer Capt.
Deputy Chief Constable.

Occurrence Reports Dated 5.1.98

Sir,
I have the honour to report that with reference to the Christmas boxes received by Sergeants Draper and Fisher, this has I believe been the custom for some years. I know of my own knowledge that it was done last year and that the money was shared with every man in the town. I believe that the practice has met with general public approval.

I am Sir,

Your obedient servant.

J. Turner Inspector.

Sir,
I have the honour to report that with reference to my receiving some money for Christmas Boxes I beg to state that it has been the custom for the last 9 or 10 years for several gentlemen to send some money to the Police Station at Christmas time, and divide the amount equally amongst the men. I have received some this year in the same way, but have not asked anybody to give us any.

W. J. Draper Sergeant 82

Sir,
I have the honour to report that I have received Christmas Boxes from various persons in the Town of Watford find it was the practice for years and put the amounts received in a book. I have never ask for any. I was passing Westfield, Watford Road, Watford about a week agoe, and saw two servants standing their, one of them said to me when are you coming for Christmas box and said the gentleman was not at house and said call in the evening and I will get it for you. I dont know Mr. Moore and have not received any money from him.

James Fisher Sergeant 52

Capt. Wymer 6th January 98

The receiving of money whether in the form of Christmas Boxes or otherwise is strictly in opposition to Standing Order No 5 dated 13th December 1880, and I doubt if any Standing Order in existence is better known to every officer or man of this force.

It appears from your letter under reply that you were asked by the men the first Christmas you were on duty at Watford if you had "any objection to the men receiving Christmas Boxes."

If you had any doubt, though I cannot see where any such doubt can come in, as to S.O. No 5 of 1880 referring to Christmas Boxes, the matter should have been referred to me. But you conceived it to be your duty to decide this question for yourself, and to allow a matter, which at the onset, was to my mind most prejudicial to the morale and discipline of the Force to grow into really large and important dimensions, instead of putting a stop to it at once or giving me the opportunity of doing so.

That the custom existed before you took charge at Watford is no excuse whatever.

You say that the asking for Christmas Boxes by the men is entirely against your instructions.

A perusal of the book which accompanies your report shows clearly that some of the men have called on various people, and there and then entered the names of the donors in this book.

From the book and scraps of paper accompanying it, I cannot arrive at any certain conclusion as to the amount of money received by the Watford Police for Christmas Boxes this year. Please ascertain and inform me of the exact amount received by the Officer who acts as Treasurer for this most unauthorised fund, and inform him that the money is not to be dealt with by him in any manner whatsoever until I have arrived at a final decision on the matter.

Henry Daniell
Chief Constable of Herts.

Pc 12 Brown of "R" Division received a telephone call at 1235 p.m. on 10th January 1898 at Headquarters from Capt. Wymer for the Chief Constable stating " Referring to your letter, the amount received is £26."

Capt. Wymer DCC and Supt. C Division. 13th January 1898

I have now received categorical replies from all Divisions of this County, and the Superintendents of A. B. D. E. and R. Divisions are perfectly unanimous as to there being no system of applying for or receiving Christmas Boxes among the men of those Divisions. Some of the men have received Christmas Boxes, but this has happened in comparatively few instances, and in no case with the knowledge, sanction or approval of the Superintendent.

In your Division, application for Christmas Boxes has been made on an organised system, and I cannot meet the case as regards the men, with the severity it deserves, in as much as they came to you the first Christmas you were in Watford and asked your permission to receive Christmas Boxes. You state that you by no means gave permission to the men to ask for Christmas Boxes, but this action was the immediate result of your acting in defiance of a Standing Order from this Office.

The matter in your Division, has assumed the dimension of a grave scandal and must inevitably reflect on the Police as a body and on my administration of the Force. It is a scandal which cannot be concealed or kept quiet, inasmuch as I feel it my duty to offer to those donors of Christmas Boxes to the Watford men, whom I can trace, the option of receiving back their donations. This, of itself must render your position, as a Superintendent of this force untenable.

Furthermore, the matter was brought to my notice by the Chairman of the Standing Joint Committee, who looks upon the matter in a most serious light.

It is now my duty to request you to submit to me your resignation of your position in this Force, which must take effect from midnight on Wednesday the 16th February 1898, on which day your name will be struck off the Roll of this Force.

You will be granted 21 days Leave of Absence on the 27th January 1898 and will give over charge of your office to the officer directed to relieve you, on the afternoon of Wednesday 26th January 1898.

Henry Daniell
Chief Constable.

15.1.98.

Sir,
In reply to your letter of 13th January 1898, the notice of the action you propose to take is sprung upon me so suddenly that you have of course precluded my seeking advice as to the steps I should take, and I can in the absence of such advice only adopt the course that my duty indicates viz. to avoid in the most emphatic manner concurring in any way in the course you have taken. I must disassociate myself entirely from particip-ation in this action, and I must decline to submit my resignation or in any action whatsoever to hand over charge of my Division to another, and I most entirely protest against the action you announce it is

your intention to take as being absolutely unjustifiable. I shall seek the verdict of public opinion and you will act entirely on your own responsibility unaided by me.

The statement in your letter I deny, and I contend that the matter so far as I am concerned (and with this only do I now deal) is misrepresented.

R. Wymer Capt.

DCC of Herts.

Captain Wymer was then informed by the Chief Constable that if he did not resign then he would act by the powers invested in him by Act of Parliament. Capt. Wymer replied by asking for an interview with the Chief Constable on 19.1.1898.

Capt. Wymer 20.1.1898

I am in receipt of your letter of yesterday.

I must decline to grant you an interview and until your letter of the 15th January, is withdrawn without further delay or if you attempt at entering into further correspondence with me, you will be summarily suspended from your duty and the option offered you of resigning your position in the Force, will be withdrawn and your name will be struck of the Rolls of the Force.

Your letter to me on this subject cannot be treated by me as private.

Henry Daniell

Chief Constable.

The Chief Constable received on 20th January 1898 a letter from Charles Longmore the Chief Clerk stating that the Chief Constable has the power to dismiss any officer for breaking a standing order provided there was evidence that he had done so.

On the 21st January 1898, the Chief Constable received a letter from Capt. Wyman.

Sir,
I beg herewith to tender my resignation of my appointment in the Herts Constabulary as from the 16th February 1898.

Reg Wymer Capt.

DCC of Herts.

Subsequently, for matters of a "personal nature" Captain Wymer asked that his resignation be postponed until 23rd March.

The Chief Constable refused to accede to this request and issued a General Order announcing the Captains resignation on 22.1.1898

Various letters from local residents were sent to the Chief Constable pleading on Capt. Wymers part for him to reconsider the matter, all of which were dismissed out of hand by him.

On 24.1.1898, Capt. Wymer wrote as follows.

Sir,
In stating as a reason for fixing my date of resignation as the 23rd March 1898, I asked for an interview with you, which has been refused. The reason is, you are aware that I am a candidate for two vacancies in the Service very shortly available, my leaving the Force at the date you quote renders me ineligible and would compel me to withdraw my candidature and would deprive me of all prospective means of salary. My further reason to postpone my resignation is that severe illness in the house renders it, so far as can at present be judged, most doubtful that I should be able to vacate this house on the date you have specified.

R.Wymer

Capt DCC Herts.

The Chief Constable further wrote on 26th January.

I am in receipt of your letters of yesterday's date. General Order 1 of 1898 cannot be altered. Under no circumstances can I consent to allow you to perform any duties in connection with this Force after today. Your appointment as Deputy Chief Cpnstable ceases on your being relieved this day of your duties as Superintendent. Your second letter of the 24th is receiving consideration.

Henry Daniell

Chief Constable.

General Order 2 of 1898.

Superintendent Wood will take charge of the C Division from Capt. Wymer tomorrow the 26th January 1898. Superintendent Wm. Reynolds Chief Clerk will accompany Superintendent Wood in order to go through the books and accounts, and verify the County property in Capt. Wymer's charge.

Henry Daniell Lt. Col.

Chief Constable of Herts.

General Order 3 of 1898.

The sum of £26 having been collected by the Police in Watford in a most improper manner and in direct violation of the Orders of this Force for the purpose of division among the Constables stationed in Watford, Superintendent Wood is directed to trace out as far as he possibly can, the subscribers to this fund, and to offer to each of them a refund of the amount subscribed by him.

Should the subscriber decline to receive back the amount of his subscription, he will be informed that the money will be credited to a fund in the Chief Constable's charge, for rendering assistance to Constables and their families in time of trouble and distress caused by prolonged and expensive illness.

The action of the Inspector, Sergeants and Constables who are concerned directly or indirectly in the creation or collection of this fund will be dealt with later on.

At present the Chief Constable's great desire is to get this money restored to the donors, and to remove from any portion of this Force the odium of begging for money, as far as it is now possible to do so.

Henry Daniell

Lt. Col. Chief Constable of

Herts.

Chief Constable's Memorandum to Supt. Wood, dated 26.1.98.

On taking charge of the "C" Division today, the door leading from the office at Watford, to the Superintendents quarters is to be locked, and the key retained in your possession to prevent access from the Superintendent's Quarters to the Police Station.

Henry Daniell.

On 27.1.1898 An Occurrence Report was submitted to the Chief Constable from Inspector Turner.

Sir,

I have the honour to report that referring to the money collected by the Police at Watford during the past Christmas, I was under the impression that I was in no way to blame, and in that I think you will agree when you know the circumstances, for I find to my surprise that I am mentioned in a General Order, as having to receive punishment. The matter was entirely arranged by Capt. Wymer; Sergeant Draper and Sergeant Fisher were called into the office and received their instructions from him, not in my presence or hearing, and not with my approval. It was certainly done with my knowledge, but I did not consider that I had any right to interfere with an arrangement made by the DCC and I assisted in no way whatever, with one exception, that one subscription of 10/- was handed to me by Mr. Harry Camp, Rate Collector of Market Street, which I at once handed over to Sergeant Fisher.

Under these circumstances Sir, I hope you will exonerate me from blame, and allow me to tell my wife so at once, as she as well as I, are greatly upset about it. She has a weak heart, and I am afraid it may turn serious with her. We have only recently moved into this station, and have worked hard and spent a lot of money to get it into order, and we should feel it exceedingly hard, if again called upon to break up our home.

I have also just recently apprenticed my boy in the Town. Hoping to receive an early favourable reply in order that I may ease my Wife's mind.

J. Turner Insp.

On 3.2.1898 Superintendent Wood submitted his final Report to the Chief Constable.

Sir,
I beg to report that in accordance with your instructions, I have seen those who gave money to the Police as Christmas Boxes and offered to return the money to them. I explained to the subscribers that it was entirely against your orders for the Police to go round collecting in this manner and that you were most anxious to return the money.

I herewith enclose receipts value £5.11s.6d from those who accepted the money. I mentioned to the gentlemen who did not desire to have the money returned that you intended to use it for the benefit of Constables in case of sickness etc, and they expressed the desire that you should do so, several of the tradesmen informed me that for a number of years they had given something at Christmas to the Police.

I have not received a single complaint against any member of the Force for being in any way "forward" or "pressing" for a Christmas box. The usual practice has been for a Sergeant and a Constable, or two Sergeants to go round and collect, and the shopkeeper, or whoever it might be knew what they had called for, and gave them a Christmas box, without the Police directly asking for one.

Sergeant 52 Fisher states he called on Mr. Moore, at his residence "Westfield", Watford on two occasions, the first time Mr. Moore was out, the second time he called he was informed by the servants that Mr. Moore did not give anything; Mr. Moore had not previously subscribed. The other officers state that they did not look out for new subscribers, and that they only accepted what was given them, they are all exceedingly sorry that they have disobeyed your orders, and state that they will never do such a thing again.

I am pleased to report that the Sergeants have most willingly shown me where they got subscriptions from and thus enabled me to offer the money back to the subscribers. Balance £20.8s.6d herewith returned.

W. Wood Superintendent.

Of the money returned, several local and well known names appear on the receipts as below.

J. Longman Sedgewick Solicitors

E.M. and M.J. Chater

Chas H Peacock

Broad Riggall Solicitors.

On the 7th February 1898, the Chief Constable wrote a letter to Supt. Wood some of which appeared as a subsequent Standing Order.

Supt. "C" Division.

All the Officers and Constables stationed at Watford are aware from the point of view of the Secretary of State in the Home Department, with whose opinion every Chief Officer of Police must be in absolute concord, a very grave breach of the Regulations governing the Police has been committed by the local Police of Watford, in going round to private residences and places of business and trade collecting Christmas Boxes. Nothing can be more destructive to the morale and discipline of the Force. How would it be, if a Constable in the witness box were asked in cross examination "Did you go to the plaintiff's (or defendant's) house for a Christmas Box?"

Answer "Yes"

"Did he give you one?"

Answer "No"

Would not the counsel immediately make a point that the Police were against his client on account of having been refused a Christmas Box?

The men considered they had the permission of their Superintendent, and their fault is not therefore, so grave as it otherwise would have been.

They have also as far as possible atoned for their fault by giving Supt. Wood all information, to enable him to offer a return of their donations to the givers of money.

The Chief Constable will now consider the matter closed. Donors of £5.11.6 have taken back their money. Donors of £20.8.6. have declined to receive back their money, but have agreed to it being credited to the Chief Constable's Fund for assistance to men of the Force or their families in times of distress caused by prolonged and expensive illness.

This Order is to be read to every man of the Force.

Lt. Colonel Henry Daniell
Chief Constable of Herts.

Capt. Wymer, his extension of service refused asked on 8th February for an extension of stay at Watford. Once again the Chief Constable refused this application.

The Chairman of the Standing Joint Committee wrote congratulating the Chief Constable on his speedy resolution of the situation.

The final letter came from the Reverend R. Lee James of Watford Vicarage to Lt. Colonel Daniell on 5.3.1898.

My Dear Sir,
I have taken the advice of one or two of my principal parishioners about writing to you and on their advice I think it only right to inform you that there is in the mind of many of us a doubt as to whether all the facts relating to the dismissal of Captain Wymer have been fairly and rightly laid before you.

With the exception of two I believe all the Magistrates have testified their entire satisfaction in the way of his performance of his duties and your own previous and most valued testimonial makes us feel that there is something very wrong in the way in which this man has been brought to your notice, and we feel that the punishment dealt out bears no proportion to the apparent offence, and the way in which he was dealt was most cruel and injurious to his prospects. I think I ought to tell you that this feeling is deep and widespread throughout Watford.

Yours faithfully

Rev.d M. Lee James.

The Chief Constable's reply was blunt.

Dear Sir,
I acknowledge receipt of your letter of yesterday.

I alone am responsible to the Government and to the Ratepayers of this County for the Discipline and efficiency of the Police Force entrusted to my control and am necessarily more fully acquainted with all the circumstances connected with Capt. Wymer's conduct of his duties as Superintendent of a Division, than any private individual can be.

Under these circumstances, you will not think me discourteous in saying that it is impossible for me to discuss the matter of Captain Wymer's leaving the Force, with you or any other private gentleman interested in Captain Wymer.

Henry Daniell., Lt. Colonel

Chief Constable.

So, ended the biggest scandal to beset Policing in Hertfordshire and certainly in Watford. Once again, the Chief Constable already with a reputation as a strict disciplinarian had shown that he would not tolerate disobedience to his Orders, but also showed that he was fair, in not punishing any of the other participants in the matter, and of his formation of the "Hardship Fund."

Extra Leave - 1897

During the 60th year of Queen Victoria's reign, 3 extra days of annual leave were granted. This brought the annual leave entitlement up to 1 week per year. In addition to this Officers were granted one rest day per calendar month (instead of one every three months), but this day did no apply in the month in which the annual leave was taken.

Superintendent Wood, appointed 'C' Division 1898

STANDING ORDERS
1st January 1898

During the 1800s and early 1900s, life was hard, much more than we know it today, the constables life was no exception to this. Officers had to live by a strict code of conduct and work very long hours. Even so, there was no lacking in new recruits. At least the constables had a secure job and regular wage. The below is a summary of some of the rules that the constables had to live by. It was issued in the form of a book of framed orders.

The order book issued to each officer in the Force is summarised.

Disregard of a Standing Order may be met by the Chief Constable in the following manner:-

1. The offender may be fined an amount not exceeding one week's pay, OR

2. May be reduced in rank, grade, or class, OR

3. May be suspended from duty, with entire loss of pay, OR

4. May be disharged from the Force, OR

5. May be dismissed the Service.

With or without prosecution for neglect or violation of duty.

Constables who are guilty of neglect or violation of duty are, on conviction, liable to a penalty of £10, or the offender may be imprisoned for one calendar month.

REGULATIONS

1. BICYCLES
Subject to the following regulations, an allowance of three pence per hour, not exceeding two shillings for a day, is sanctioned to Constables using their own Bicycles on the public service.

These Bicycles may be used for any specific errand, which demands speed, and where the use of the Bicycle will save time or money.

1st. In the abscence of the Constable from his station, and

2ndly. In reaching the scene of an offence where the Constable's presence is required, with rapidity.

3rdly. In the pursuit of an offender for the purposes of apprehension.

4thly. When railway fare or horse hire will be saved.

Every application for Bicycle allowance must show, clearly, the object with which the Bicycle was taken out, distance travelled, and time occupied.

Under no circumstance is a Bicycle to be taken out for any purpose after one hour after sunset, or until an hour before sunrise.

It must be distinctly understood that no Constable is allowed to leave the limits of his Station on a Bicycle during his hours of recreation without the permission, previously obtained, of his Superior Officer.

2. CYCLISTS
The Chief Constable, from general observation, is of the opinion that the control exercised by the Police over cyclists riding at such a rate of speed as to constitute a danger to the public, is not as strict as it might be under the existing law.

Every endeavour should be made to stop cyclists coming down a hill with one or more corners on it at a high rate of speed, and without sounding their bell before turning the corner, or riding at a high rate of speed through a town or village.

Any accident occurring to a person through a cycle collision is to be the subject of a Police (not private) prosecution, if possible, and the occurrence of every such accident is to reported in detail to this office by telephone.

(It should perhaps be noted here that Lt. Col. Henry Daniell the Chief Constable was extremely suspicious and noted with concern the development of transport. He considered bicycles to be extremely dangerous hence, the extraordinarily high allowance for their use.)

6. LICENSED HOUSES
No Constable is to enter a Public House, except on duty, or for the purpose of needful refreshment when absent at some miles distance from his station.

In these circumstances, a Police Officer may

enter and obtain the meal he requires, but under no circumstances is his stay to exceed half-an-hour.

9. CORONERS
The telephone is open at the under mentioned towns where Coroners reside. Hertford, Hatfield, Hitchin, Hemel Hempstead, Royston, Bishop's Stortford, and Watford.

Reports of deaths to Coroners should be made by Constables going to the nearest Telephone Station (if nearer than the Coroners residence) to take the Coroners instruction. The Constable in charge of the case should remain at the Telephone Station until he has received the Coroners Instruction, or is informed at about what hour he should return for instructions should the Coroner be out.

The Chief Constable finds it necessary to remind all Officers that the Constable in charge of the case becomes a Coroner's Officer and it is his duty to preserve order and prevent noise or conversation at an Inquest, that is likely to distract a Jury from the business for which they are empanneled.

The Coroner's Officer will attend smartly to his duty, and to the business of the Court. He will not sit down in Court without the permission of the Coroner. All Police Officers attending a Coroner's Court as Witnesses, or otherwise on business, are to remain standing until, or unless the Coroner gives them permission to take a seat.

13. DIVINE SERVICE
Every man, unless prevented by duty, shall attend Divine Service once on Sunday. When attending alone, they are to wear their uniform. Married men of the Force accompanying their Wives or Families are permitted to wear plain clothes. The cause of prevention from attending Divine Service will, be entered in the Weekly Journal.

14. HAIR AND BEARDS
In order to improve the appearance of the Officers and men of this Force, it appears necessary to make some regulations as to the manner in which members of the Force wear their hair and beards.

The hair of the head is to be kept short. Every man must have his hair cut once a month. Men may either shave or not shave, but if a man wishes to wear a beard he must wear a moustache also, and his face must not be touched by a razor. The beard must be trimmed close to the cheeks and cut to a point below the chin.

Men who shave may wear a moustache only, and shave the cheeks and chin clean, or they may wear a moustache and whiskers. In this case the whiskers must be cut short, and must not come lower than on a level with the mouth, and a space of an inch must be shaved clean between the whiskers and moustache.

15. EQUIPMENT
The use of walking sticks by men on duty during the day is prohibited.

Walking sticks may be carried at night.

16. DRESS
Police Officers in plain clothes, even when leaving their quarters not on duty, must be properly dressed and wear a collar and necktie.

This order has no reference to Officers who may assume any tradesman's or labourer's dress for the purpose of detecting an offender.

Riding Boots supplied for the use of Mounted Constables must be kept in repair at the Constable's own expense.

Sergeants and Constables will wear their Great Coats buttoned on the Right or Left sides, week and week about, each week to commence on Sunday. Coats will be buttoned on the left side during the week commencing on 1st January.

19. SMOKING
No member of the Force in uniform is allowed to smoke in public. This does not refer to railway carriages.

22. EQUIPMENT
It appears to be common practice for the Constables to use their Night Belts as a razor strop.

The appearance of a belt so used is unmistakeable.

At the periodical inspections of clothing and necessaries, the belts are to be taken off and inspected. Every belt found to have been so misused will be replaced by a new belt at the expense of the Constable.

26. DUTIES
On returning from night duty Constables are to remain at home for eight hours for rest and refreshment unless they are called away for duty. At the expiration of the eight hours off duty, Constables are to go out for three hours day duty, leaving word in their house in what direction they have gone. At the expiration of the three hours duty, Constables are to return to their quarters, and are off duty unless anything specially requires their attention, until it is time for them to go out on night duty.

27. INDECENT ADVERTISEMENTS
Constables are warned to destroy notices posted on walls, gates, &c., containing indecent medical advertisements and to rub out any obscene or indecent words they may find chalked up in any place on their respective beats.

33. DUTIES
There appears to be some idea among the Constables of this Force that they are not expected to do more than 9 hours' duty in the 24 hours.

This is entirely incorrect. It is true that a Constable's ordinary night duty is 6 hours and his day duty 3 hours on his beat, besides the hours that may be occupied in visiting ratepayers who may have left word that they wish to see him, or in serving Summonses and executing Warrants, or any such duty as ordinarily devolves on a County Constable.

But every man is expected to do as many hours as his Superintendent or Inspector may direct at their discretion.

Any man reported to be constantly grumbling at his hours of duty, will be recommended to resign the service.

34. DUTIES
Every statement of any sort, having reference to the charge, made by a prisoner, is to be taken down in the prisoner's own words, in the Officers notebook, and the hour, date, and place of the statement being made is also to be entered in the notebook.

The statement is afterwards to be copied out for or by the Superior Officer in charge of the case. The copy is to be given to the person who conducts the prosecution before the Justices, and is to attached to the depositions.

Under no circumstances is a prisoner in the custody of the Police to be called on to sign any statement made by him.

39. DUTIES
The Chief Constable has no objection to Constables on rural stations being accom-

panied by a dog when out on duty.

But a Constable so accompanied must always carry a string in his pocket and must never enter any house or enclosed land without having his dog on a string.

49. CHARGE SHEETS
At all Police Stations where a prisoner is brought in, a Charge Sheet is to be on the table or be otherwise available. The Constable bringing in the prisoner is immediately to fill in the Charge Sheet to the best of his ability (should no Superior Officer or Clerk be present). The Superintendent or Inspector will, when the case comes under his notice amend the Charge Sheet, if necessary, on a fresh sheet, instructing the Constable, should he have made omissions or mistakes. These original Charge Sheets are all to be filed in the Superintendents Office, where they will be inspected by the Chief Constable, who will then be able to judge of the ability of each Constable bringing in a charge.

52. EVIDENCE
All Police Officers are to be informed that it is not their duty to give up the name of an informant from whom they have obtained information. Should a lawyer, or the Plaintiff seek, in examination or cross-examination, to elicit the source of information received by the Police, the officer is to refuse to reply to the question, and may quote this order as his authority for such refusal.

53. EVIDENCE
The Chief Constable has noticed the demeanour of some Constables in the witness box as being highly incorrect.

Officers of all ranks are ordered to stand to attention in the witness box, right hand ungloved, and the glove passed neatly under the waist belt on the right hand side.

When giving evidence, Officers are not to gesticulate or point in any direction. Evidence is to be given by word of mouth only, and not with the assistance of the arms or legs.

54. ANNUAL LEAVE

Superintendents are entitled to 21 days

Inspectors 14 days

Sergeants 10 days

Constables 7 days

Two extra days are allowed to officers travelling to Scotland or Ireland on Annual Leave.

Officers of all ranks are entitled to 24 hours off once in every calendar month provided this can be granted without detriment to the public service. 24 hours leave cannot be granted until the expiration of 28 days duty from the previous leave (included annual leave). Annual leave, stops the 24 hours leave for the month in which the annual leave is taken.

59. MARRIAGE
No Constable will be allowed to marry, without signing a Declaration that he is free from all debt, and is possessed of furniture to the value of £20, or the sum of £20 cash.

83. REVOLVERS
Revolvers are only to be issued to Police who desire to have them when employed on Night Duty, and who can, in the opinion of his Superintendent, be trusted to use them with discretion.

Six rounds of ammunition per revolver may be used annually for practice.

85. TELEPHONE
The Force is now in Telephonic communic-

ation with London and other parts of England where the telephone has been established.

The Herts Constabulary Telephonic number is 38 Watford Exchange.

IN THESE ORDERS, THE DESIGNATION "CONSTABLE" REFERS TO EVERY MEMBER OF THE FORCE.

LIEUT.- COLONEL,
HENRY DANIELL
CHIEF CONSTABLE OF
HERTS.

Pocket Books - 1898

Pocket books issued to the Police, previously the officers had to supply their own.

Telephones - 1898

22nd April 1898, telephonic communication established between Watford King Street and St. Albans Rd Police Stations.

Private Motor Car - 1898

First motor car in the County, a Daimler capable of 16 m.p.h. appears at Watford.

The Murder of Caroline Ansell

On March 9th 1899, a parcel was delivered to Caroline Ansell, aged 26, a patient for the previous four years at Leavesden Hospital. In accordance with the regulations, the parcel was opened by Charge Nurse Alice Felmingham, who found it to contain a small flat sandwich type cake with a yellow filling. The cake was given to Caroline, who the next day ate half herself, but shared the remainder with four fellow inmates. One complained immediately that the cake had tasted bitter and spat out her mouthful and was then sick. The others, experienced violent stomach cramps and were also observed to have vomited several times. The following day, though, all appeared to have recovered and ate the Sunday lunch. Two days later, Caroline became seriously ill and was transferred to the hospital infirmary suffering from severe abdominal pain. She later slipped into a coma and died. The Hospital's Medical Superintendent Henry Elkins and his deputy Dr. Cameron Blair both felt that Caroline had probably suffered from peritonitis. On hearing from the ward staff how others had experienced the same early symptoms after eating the cake, the doctors approached Caroline's family for their permission to have a post mortem examination performed. This was refused. The Doctors had though reported the death to the Watford Coroner who instructed an independent doctor to carry out a post mortem examination. His findings were that she had died of phosphorous poisoning, a fact that was later confirmed by a Home Office Pathologist. Dr. Thomas Stevenson stated that phosphorous was a strong irritant poison which when first taken would produce sickness, nausea and internal irritation. The patient would appear to recover after about 24 hours and appear well for two to three days. During this time, however, the poison would be attacking the kidneys and liver causing eventual severe pain and collapse.

Superintendent William Wood was in charge of the Police enquiry, and he interviewed the staff at the Hospital. From them. he elicited several strange circumstances. A month previously, Caroline had received another parcel containing tea and sugar. The tea was made the following day but tasted so bitter that it was all thrown away. At about the same time, Nurse Felmingham had found Caroline crying over a letter she had received purportedly from a cousin, telling her that her parents had died. This was found to have been untrue. Police Constable Tom Piggott, carried out a search on the asylum rubbish tip and found the brown paper wrapper in which the cake had arrived. The wrapper bore a W.C.1. postmark - the same postal area as the Ansell's home in Tankerton Street, London.

The enquiry as to who had sent the parcel was focused on Caroline's family and her sister Mary was quietly looked at. Enquiries revealed that she had been employed as a servant to a Mr and Mrs Maloney, who lived in the same area in Coram Street. In September 1898, roughly six months before the murder it was established that Mary had insured her sisters life for £22.10.6d. with the Royal London Friendly Society saying that Caroline was a general servant at Leavesden Asylum and was in good health. No checks were made as to the truth of her statement and the policy had been granted. Since the policy had only been in effect for six months, only half of the benefit was payable on Caroline's death. On interviewing Mrs Margaret Maloney, it was found that Mary and her boyfriend had been planning to marry in the easter, but that the boyfriend had cancelled the wedding until he had sufficient money to keep them both. She also stated that Mary had lived in the kitchen whilst working for them. The kitchen was searched and on a shelf in the pantry, a small jar of phosphorous paste was found. The paste was a rat poison and found available in hardware shops. In a nearby hardware shop, the owner recalled that in February or March, Mary Ansell had bought three or four jars of the poison. Mrs Maloney stated that she had never instructed Mary to purchase rat poison. Superintendent Wood purchased a couple of jars which were then sent for analysis. Each jar was found to contain enough poison to kill three humans. On April 6th 1899, Mary Ansell was arrested and charged with murder. She protested her innocence saying "I am as innocent a girl as ever was born."

Mary Ansell was the only woman to be hanged at St Albans Goal, she would have been taken to the prison in a vehicle similar to the one shown above.

On June 29th she appeared at the Hertford Assizes before Mr. Justice Mathew. In her trial, the letter alleging the death of her parents supposedly from a cousin to Caroline, was proved by an expert to be in Mary's disguised handwriting. The evidence against Mary was damning, but her defence lawyer did little to try and disprove the case against her. The jury found her guilty. Mr. Justice Mathew put on his black cap and pronounced upon Mary Ansell the death sentence.

A campaign was immediately launched for her reprieve from the death sentence. The Daily Mail set out to establish some of the facts not covered by the defence during her trial, the question of Mary's own sanity. The paper claimed to have found cases of insanity on both sides of her family, stating that all the mother's sister had died insane, that the father's two sisters had died in an asylum and the fact that Mary's younger sister was also in an asylum for the insane. The paper stated "If Mary Ansell is not mad, then the laws of heredity have been almost miraculously suspended on her behalf."

An opinion was sought from the eminent Dr. Forbes Winslow who stated "I am of the opinion that she is a mental degenerate, and ought to be held irresponsible in the eyes of the law. I am further of the opinion that if the question of her insanity been raised at her trial, no jury could have convicted her upon the evidence which might have been adduced." The doctor was refused leave to examine her personally despite turning up at St. Albans gaol to do so. The chairman of the jury, Charles Cusworth of Bushey protested against the Home Secretary's refusal to grant a reprieve stating that had the jury heard the evidence of her possible insanity, then they would been unanimous in recommending a commutation of the death sentence. The Daily Mail received over 10,000 letters and telegrams protesting about the Home Secretary's refusal to reprieve Mary Ansell. The matter was raised in Parliament, and a deputation was made to Queen Victoria, who referred them back to the Home Secretary.

At eight o'clock on the Wednesday 19th July 1899 Mary Ansell dropped seven feet from the gallows. She died instantly. Two hours later an Inquest was held, and Mary was buried by tradition in a corner of the prison yard. In 1930, when the prison was purchased by the City Council for their Highways Department, Mary's remains together with those of the two men executed at St. Albans, were re-interred at the City Cemetery.

To each and every member of the Standing Joint Committee

Chief Constable's Office
Hatfield, May 1899

1. The County Constabulary Force has from time to time been increased, in accordance with my recommendations, but I cannot withhold my opinion that its existing strength is generally insufficient, especially in towns of over 2,000 of population, to afford the residents and ratepayers the Police protection they expect and have a right to demand.

9. The town of Watford contained in 1891, according to the Census Returns of that year, a population of 20,269. That population has now increased, I believe, to almost if not quite 30,000, while the town is daily being extended more into the country. It is a suburban residential town, and adjoins the Metropolitan Police District. The area of Urban District Council contains thirty one and a half miles of streets, courts, alleys and public paths. The Police in Watford are working in three shifts of 8 3/4, 9 and 9 1/2

Hertfordshire Police Cycle Corps (The Scorchers), Established by Colonel Daniell in 1899. The officer in uniform is Constable Beecroft.

hours, the last day shift overlapping the night shift, so as to have an extra Force of Police on duty during the last 2 1/2 or 3 hours of the licensed houses being open.

The town is at present divided into seven night beats, but as six of these beats take, on average, more than four hours to work once, it is obvious that they are too large.

Three additional beats are absolutely required, and an addition of 6 Constables is required to work these beats.

I was lately in Watford inspecting the night duties, and on that night, owing to absences caused by sickness or special duties, five Constables only were available to work the seven beats.

After the most careful consideration I beg respectfully to report that I consider an increase of one Inspector, six Sergeants, and thirty six Constables necessary for the efficient performance of the Police Duties of this County committed to my charge.

Henry Daniell., Chief Constable

Year	CC.	Supt	Insp	Sgts	PC's	Total
1888	1	5	6	15	119	146
1889	1	6	7	17	129	160 inc
1890	1	6	7	17	130	161 inc
1891	1	6	8	19	136	170 inc
1892	1	7	7	19	142	176 inc
1893	1	7	7	20	157	192 inc
1894	1	7	7	20	157	192
1895	1	7	7	23	154	192
1896	1	7	7	23	155	193 inc
1897	1	7	7	23	155	193
1898	1	6	8	23	167	205 inc
1899	1	6	8	23	167	205

Have a Peep - 19th October 1900

Superintendents are desired to make sure that every Constable on a Station, or visiting a Station for any purpose, has the opportunity of seeing any or every prisoner who may be under detention in the cells.

It will not be necessary to open the door of the cell and disturb the prisoner for this purpose, unless of course the prisoner's identification is required by any individual officer.

The Constables can see the prisoner through the eyehole, take notice of his appearance, and enter the same, with the date, in their note books, with a view to future recognition.

Henry Daniell
Chief Constable of Herts.

Court Reports

Watford Petty Sessions - 5th January 1901

Attempted Suicide

Henry Birch aged 21 a Labourer of 12 Fearnley Street, Watford, was charged with attempting to commit suicide. by cutting his throat with a razor on December 27th 1900. Police Sergeant Peck stated that about 10.15 p.m. on Thursday he went together with Police Sergeant Sullivan and Police Constable Debenham to 12 Fearnley Street. They went upstairs and found the prisoner in bed being held down by two neighbours; he had evidently been drinking and had some slight cuts in his throat. His mother handed the officer a razor which had some bloodstains on it and said in the defendants presence "He has been drinking all Christmas. He got up today at about 1 p.m., and went out returning at about 9 p.m. He then said he would go for a soldier and go to bed." She went upstairs shortly afterwards and found him on the bed with the razor beside him. Dr. Smith who examined the prisoner said that he had obviously been drinking and evidently did not know what had occurred. The doctor admitted to the court that it was possible the cuts had been made whilst the prisoner was shaving especially as he was in drink. Inspector Boutell said that Superintendent Wood wished him to inform the bench that when the prisoner was brought in he was soaked with drink and it was thought best to keep him custody so that all the drink could get out of him. The prisoner promised the bench that he would reform and to sign the pledge of abstinence and was thereupon discharged after the Chairman had censured him severely and observed that excessive drinking was a curse.

A Terrible Woman

Alice Gurney, 15 Shaftesbury Road, Watford was summoned for cruelty to children on

September 25th. Mr H. Morten Turner prosecuting, said that the case had been remanded since October 2nd and since that time, there had been three distinct offences and that he must ask for exemplary punishment. On November 25th at about 1.30 a.m., a policeman had found the defendants boy George lying in a passage at the side of the house, very cold and afraid to go in. Defendant was then drunk. On November 28th, the defendants husband was turned out of the house by the defendant, and the boy who was in bed with his clothes on was made to get up as she alleged his clothes were wet. The boys father took him to the police station. On december 22nd, a policeman found the boy in the road at midnight and that his mother was very drunk and violent. When Mr. Gurney gave evidence, his wife kept up a running fire of abuse at him. The defendant said that her husband was a brute to her and encouraged the boy in misconduct. The defendant, who was sentenced to one months hard labour in July 1899, for a similar offence, was sentenced to six months hard labour. Inspector Boutell, in reply to a question from the bench, said that Mr. Gurney was a steady, quiet, hardworking man. The Chairman said the defendant was devoid of all proper and right feeling either as a woman, a wife or a mother. This was one of the most helpless cases the bench had ever had before them he added. On being removed, the defendant fought savagely with the constables and caused great commotion in the Court.

Watford Petty Sessions - 12th January 1901

Larceny

William Gurney aged 12 of 1 Grove Circus, Watford was charged with larceny. Police Constable Pitcher deposed that several complaints had been made of milk jugs and milk cans being stolen from various streets. The defendant admitted stealing the milk jug produced on January 4th from 4 Estcourt Rd, Watford. It had been placed by the occupant Mrs Nichols on her doorstep for the milkman. The Constable found the jug at the defendants home address concealed in the water cistern. The defendant admitted several similar offences and stated he stole them to drink the milk. Superintendent Wood stated that in 1899 the boy had received six strokes for stealing money. The boy was sharp but had received no proper training. The Bench ordered the boy to be sent to a reformatory for three years.

Assualt

George Herbert Varney, 16 Cannon Road, Watford was charged with assault on his wife Emma Carra Varney who appeared with a badly bruised face. The Complainant said that the defendant had come home at 11.30 the previous night intoxicated and threw her on the ground out the house. He then blackened her eyes. He had ill treated her before but only when he was in drink. Police Constable Young said that when he arrived he saw the defendant knocking his wife about, she was shouting "Police, Murder". He saw him strike her heavily and tear her dress, he was obviously under the influence of drink. Superintendent Wood said that the defendant's conduct to his wife had been for a long time perfectly brutal.

The Chairman: "What work does he do?" Superintendent Wood: "None, he married this woman who had a little money, and who is most quiet and respectable. He is a worthless scamp."

The Bench sentenced the defendant to six weeks hard labour.

Watford Petty Sessions - 26th January 1901

Breach of the Peace

George Clark of Breakespeare Road, Abbots

Langley and Harry Shippin of Leavesden Asylum appeared before the Magistrates for Breach of the Peace on 14th January 1901. They both pleaded guilty and on the evidence of Police Sergeant Stoten were bound over to keep the peace for six months and were each ordered to pay the costs of 6/3d.

Unattended Horse

Sidney James Anderson of 45 St. James' Road. Watford was summonsed for a highway offence - leaving his horse unattended in the Rickmansworth Road, Watford on January 15th 1901 and pleading guilty was fined 5/- including costs. Police Sergeant Page proved the case.

Hooting and Yelling

Robert Dorrofield of Watford was summonsed for hooting and yelling on January 19th 1901 and pleaded guilty. Inspector Boutell said the defendant who was arm-in-arm with others in the High Street, Watford made a hideous noise and knocked people off the path. He abused a witness who has asked him to desist. He was fined £1.

Watford Petty Sessions - 29th January 1901

Death of Queen

The Chairman remarked on the nation's loss following the death of the Queen.

New Constable

John Kipping was sworn in as a new Police Constable.

Horse Cruelty

Joseph Chandler was charged with cruelty to a horse on January 21st and pleaded guilty stating that he did not realise the horses collar was rubbing. Inspector Street of the RSPCA, stated that he noticed the defendants bay mare was restless and when lifting her collar, he found a large raw wound. Fined £1 and costs.

Drunk

James Dow 17, St Francis Rd, Watford was summoned for being drunk and disorderly on January 24th, and pleading guilty was fined 6 shillings including costs.

Drunk

Edward Millar, 51 Ballard's Buildings, Watford was summoned for being drunk and disorderly on January 28th. Police Constable Webb said that at about 1.20 p.m.,he found in the Lower part of the High Street the defendant very drunk and noisy. He told him to go home quietly, the defendant replied he would go home when he liked. Fined 10/- including costs.

Drunk

Elizabeth Rapley of Church Street, Rickmansworth was charged with drunkenness on January 19th and pleaded guilty. Police Constable Herring said that the woman who was married was found so drunk that she could not speak and had to be carried home. A fine of 5/- was inflicted.

Drunk

Susan Sarah Bennett of Rickmansworth was summoned for being drunk and disorderly on January 26th. Inspector Turner said that at about 12 p.m., he was called to the defendants home. He found her drunk and shouting about in the street in an excited manner. She was threatening to drown herself and her children who were crying around her. The Officer put her into her home by force, but she came out again and he was obliged to take her into custody. Police Constable Herring corroborated the Inspectors evidence. The defendant said the evidence was quite false but was found guilty and fined 10/- including costs.

Dangerous Vagrant

Ernest John Gladman of Amersham, was charged with vagrancy and with an assault on police on January 24th. Police Constable Smart said that he and police constable Matthams had found the defendant and another man in a shed at Shepherds Farm, Mill End, Rickmansworth. Defendant attacked the witness with the butt end of a gun and his dog flew at the witness, who thereupon hit him upon the head with his walking stick and with the assistance of the other constable he was taken into custody. The other man escaped, but did not commit any assault. Superintendent Wood told the Court that the defendant had 10 convictions for poaching, one for assaulting police and two for obscene language. The bench sentenced Gladman to one months hard labour for vagrancy and three months hard labour for assaulting a police officer, to run consecutively.

Assualt

George Langham of Albert Street, Watford was summoned for an assault on Eliza Blanchard on January 26th. The Complainant said that she lived next door to the defendant. On Saturday at 8.45 p.m., she was in the Market place with her husband and a friend when the defendant came up and deliberately hit her in the mouth with his fist. Previously that evening she had had to inform the Police that he had been knocking his wife about. Rhoda Elizabeth Stamp who was with the witness corroborated her evidence. The defendant said that Blanchard ought to be standing where he was (laughter). He continued that it was he who was assaulted. The bench inflicted a fine of £1, including costs and he was bound over to keep the peace for six months. The Chairman told Langham that he had been guilty of a cowardly, unmanly and brutal action.

Watford Petty Sessions - 9th February 1901

Asleep in charge of Cart

John Battams of Piccotts End, Hemel Hempstead, was fined 10/- and costs for being asleep while in charge of a cart on January 27th in Watford. This was the 22nd time he had been up for a similar offence.

Playing Football

George Hutchings, Herbert Baker, George Smith and Ralph Carpenter, lads of Rickmansworth pleaded guilty to playing football on a highway on January 27th and on the evidence of Police Constable Spencer were dismissed with a caution.

Watford Petty Sessions - 16th February 1901

Furious Driving

Ernest Bates, 7 Red Lion Yard was summoned for furious driving on February 8. Police Constable Beecroft stated that at 4.45 p.m., he saw the defendant driving a pony attached to a coster cart. He was using the whip and making the pony go full gallop. When the witness called to him, he went faster and laughed at the officer. The horse was in a lather. When the defendant was seen later in the day he denied being there and refused to give his name and address until taken to the Police Station. He was fined 10/- including costs.

Collecting Alms

Harriet Kibble of 10 Tipple's Yard, High Street, Watford the wife of John Kibble a Private in the 4th Beds Militia currently serving in South Africa, was charged with fraudulently collecting alms on February 7th. Police Sergeant Sullivan deposed that on Thursday he received a complaint from Mr Rogers of Clarendon Road, respecting a woman who had called at his place at 2.15 that day and presented the subscription list now produced. The officer visited 10

Tipple's Yard the residence of Mr Harry Mead. There, he saw the defendant and asked her what her name was. She replied "Kibble". He asked her to see the paper on which the subscription list had been made. She turned round and threw herself down on a chair apparently in a fainting fit. He told her firmly that he would not have this nonsense. She then went to a cupboard and produced a list. He asked her if it was correct that her husband was in South Africa, she said "yes". He also asked her if it were true that her grandmother was dead and her reply was " Well no, but I had a telegram to say that she was not expected to live and I wanted money to go home and see her". She was taken to the Police Station where she admitted making up the subscription list and writing the telegram herself. She was then released, but following further complaint re-arrested. The court heard how she had obtained 11/8d from Canon Reith the Treasurer of the Watford Division of the Soldier's and Sailor's Families Association and saying that her grandmother had died and that her child lay ill both in Norfolk. Canon Reith stated that he had gone to her address only to find that she had not gone to Norfolk but was out with her young man. Miss Emma Burland of the Manor House deposed that she had given the defendant half a sovereign and asked her to send a postcard telling her how her child was when she got to Norfolk. Superintendent Wood said that it was true that she had been with her young man and that it appeared she was a thoroughly bad lot. The prisoner was sentenced to one months hard labour. The Chairman of the Bench mentioned that the prisoner had also tried to get money from him and another of the Magistrates on the Bench and had been guilty of a gross fraud which was calculated to prejudice genuine cases of want. (W.O. 1901)

Pay

On the 22nd March 1901, the Police Review carried the following anonymous letter from a Hertfordshire Officer, which on 30th March 1901 was reproduced in its entirety by the Watford Observer.

Sir,

Seeing that the pay received in other forces is much above that received by Constables of this force viz 21/7d per week. We in this County maintain that it is impossible for a man who is married to exist on same, hence the reason for cases of fowl stealing and money borrowing, which have occurred of late by officers of this force. We are a down trodden race, especially in this County. Not one seems able to pluck up courage and ask the Chief for an increase. They resign and get a situation at 30s per week, does anyone blame them? For they are hunted about from pillar to post every half hour. They do nine hours night duty and if we miss a point, probably fined one days pay, which means no food for us and ours for one day. Service in this force is below any other County, and I believe also the pay. Well, we are opening up the subject through this medium as it is not possible for us to communicate to other members on the subject except by this means, and we hope when the time comes we shall get a long looked for increase in pay and a substantial one. The only reason for this state of affairs is that officers who have a few years in will not move on as they are afraid of the pension and the younger ones are not capable. Well, let this letter be the means of the force waking up and combining for an increase in pay much needed by us to keep ourselves and family respectable.

Anon.

The pay amount quoted in the letter, was for officers at the time of joining, which rose to 27/5d per week after eight years service.

This figure was set in 1881. The letter appears to have had some effect, in 1901 although the starting salary remained the same, officers with eight years service were earning 29/2d per week. It would be another 16 years in 1917 before pay for the more senior Constables would move to 30/11d.

The letter, was of course anonymous for the simple reason that Lt.-Colonel's Standing Orders stated any officer who constantly complained would be dismissed.

Dismissal of Constable Herbert Axom

County Court,
Herbert Axom v. C.C. of Herts

Herbert Axom, brought an action for damages for wrongful dismissal from the Hertfordshire Constabulary, against the Chief Constable, Lieutenant Colonel Henry Daniell. A jury was sworn to try the case and there was a large attendance of Police Officers. The amount of damages claimed was £50.

Axom, joined the force on 12.7.1900. On 16.5.01, races were being held at Beech Bottom, Harpenden and Constables were drafted to the racecourse to keep order. Axom, with several others from Watford, went to Beech Bottom, leaving Watford at 8.15 a.m. At St. Albans, Axom with 9 or 10 other Constables, went to the London and North Western Hotel for a drink before commencing the long walk to the racecourse. Between them, the Constables had 5 quarts of beer, and stopped at another pub before reaching Beech Bottom. At the racecourse, was a tent for the officers in the charge of Superintendent John Reynolds from Hitchin. The names of the other Constables were called out, but not Axom, so he remained in the tent. After waiting for some time, he drew one of the two free pints of beer allowed to the Constables. Shortly afterwards, the Superintendent sent Axom to do duty on a certain part of the racecourse. After shifting him around the course several times, Superintendent Reynolds instructed Sergeant O'Connor to take Axom back to the tent saying that he was drunk.

The following day, Axom was called to see Superintendent Wood at Watford. He was given a phone message from the Chief Constable ordering him to go and fetch his clothes and give them in, which he did at 2.30 p.m. and received the balance of his pay. His clothes were taken and he was told by Superintendent Wood that he was no longer a member of the force. He was stopped 5/- from his pay for alterations to his uniform. On Sunday, he received an order to give an explanation of what had taken place, but as he had been dismissed, he refused to do so. He then received a letter to report for duty at 9.15 a.m. on Monday, but refused to do so as he had no uniform and could not obey the order. He received another note summonsing him to see the Chief Constable at the Superintendent's office in Watford. He went and the Chief Constable tried to persuade him to return to duty. He said he would not do so and the Chief Constable then told him that he was dismissed from the force. He was then paid for the Thursday and Friday of the week before, but not up to the Tuesday when the Chief Constable told him that he was being dismissed. It was held that this meant that he had been dismissed on the Friday and was therefore dismissed wrongfully as only the Chief Constable and not his servant, had the authority to dismiss him. The court therefore awarded him £50 damages. (W.O. 20.7.01)

Chief Constables letter to all registered Car Owners

3rd December 1901

The Chief Constable desires to inform owners and drivers of Motor Cars in the County of Hertford that constant complaints are made to him of the alarm and danger to the public caused by the reckless driving of some of these vehicles.

The Chief Constable reminds owners and drivers that the speed at which a Motor Car may be driven on a highway is limited by law to twelve miles an hour. It by no means follows that this speed may be sustained when Motor Cars are passing or meeting other vehicles or horses, or when passing through towns, villages, or other inhabited places. On each of these occasions it is incumbenton the drivers of Motor Cars to reduce their speed to such a pace as would be safe and reasonable were the vehicle drawn by a horse instead of mechanical power. Failure to observe this precaution will render the driver of a Motor Car liable to prosecution under Article IV., Sec. 1., of the Locomotives on Highways Act 1896.

Owners and drivers of Motor Cars are also reminded of the necessity of reducing the speed of the Car when passing cross-roads or turning corners, and on approaching such cross-roads or corners the horn or bell of the Motor Car should always be sounded, so as to give notice of the approach of the vehicle.

HENRY DANIELL, Lt.-Colonel,
Chief Constable of Herts.

Police escorting walkers through the town - circa 1900

The Watford Riot 1902

Thursday 26th June 1092, was to be the day of the Coronation of King Edward VII. Watford, in common with most other towns was planning to celebrate the event, with a series of festivities, including a huge bonfire. On the day set aside for the event however, the King was fighting for his life, and the people of Watford fighting to protect their homes and businesses from a mob of rampaging rioters.

The king, had just undergone an operation for appendicitis, a simple enough matter to-day, but one which in 1092 carried a very real and significant risk. Even penicillin of course was a drug of the future at that time. As a result, all local festivities were cancelled after a series of meetings under the chairmanship of the chairman of the Town Council Mr. Francis Fisher, a local butcher.

The 26th June dawned as a hot sultry midsummers day with few of the local people reporting for work. Instead the townsfolk gathered in the town discussing the latest bulletins on the King's health. Towards the end of the day the mood of the people began to change, egged on by some of the less salubrious characters who demanded compensation for the lack of festivities. It was not long before the blame was being laid squarely on Councillor Fishers shoulders.

At 2130 hrs, the elderly nightwatchman in charge of the town's bonfire found himself confronted with a large crowd of between 200 and 300 people intent on lighting the bonfire. The watchman tried to defend the bonfire, but after a beating and the promise that he would be sitting on the top after the fire was lit he made good his escape. Within minutes the bonfire was alight together with all nearby council fencing and the nightwatchman's hut!

The Town's Surveyor Mr. Waterhouse arrived and tried to reason with the crowd, for which he was pelted with stones and forced to seek refuge in a nearby cottage on which the crowd vented their fury breaking all it's windows. The mob by now armed with wooden clubs, metal piping and stones then made off to the Town to "get" Fisher.

The situation was now one that the Chief of Watford Police Superintendent Wood was totally unable to contain, with his limited resources and manpower. This was exacerbated by the fact that of his total strength of 20 officers, half had been despatched to Hemel Hempstead to deal with sporadic outbreaks of violence there. He had at his command the services of an Inspector, a Sergeant and a handful of mounted and footpatrol officers. As Supt Wood frantically phoned round neighbouring forces for assistance (and you thought mutual aid was a new idea?), the mob started to wreak havoc in the town with the centre of their attraction Councillor Fisher's Butchery, and three other shops, two drapery stores and a shoe shop which belonged to another member of the Coronation Committee George Longley.

Francis Fisher, had however been forewarned and had taken precautions to barricade himself and his staff in the shop. Fisher and his staff put up a stout resistance to the mob, despite the flailing clubs which broke his windows and then pulled down his shutters onto the hands of some of the leading rioters. This action however sparked off the rumour within the crowd that he was using Meat Cleavers to chop off the fingers of those that were trying to gain entry which further inflamed the crowd. Fisher and his staff beat a hasty retreat. The crowd gained entry to his premises and then tried to set fire to them, an action quickly forestalled by the arrival of the Fire Brigade despite various attempts made to cut their water

Convicted rioters being marched through the town as an example to others

hoses.

George Longley on the other hand put up no resistance to the violence and subsequent pillaging of his stores, but did take very careful note of the faces of those involved.

By 2330 hrs Supt Wood was still awaiting his much needed reinforcements, so he took the step of asking for civilian volunteers, however, in order to have the authority to do this, the Riot Act had to be read. This task fell to a local Magistrate W. T. Coles, who read the following:

"Our Sovereign Lord the King chargeth and commandeth all persons being assembled immediately to disperse themselves and peaceably to depart to the habitations or to their lawful business upon the pains contained in the Act, made in the first year of King George (1714) for preventing tumultuous and riotous assemblies. GOD SAVE THE KING."

This was done in the market place by the brave Mr. Coles whilst dodging various missiles thrown at him by the crowd.

This, gave Supt Wood the authority he needed and 200 men out of 500 volunteers who had been watching the disorder with growing shame and anger were hastily recruited, sworn and issued with staves and truncheons. They were then divided into squads each led by a uniformed officer. There then folowed a series of baton charges into the crowd, resulting in several split heads and the arrest of 35 people, including 8 women and some of the ringleaders. Order in the town was restored by 0300 hrs. Due to the lack of space at the Police station, the arrested were taken to St. Albans Gaol to await their court appearances.

Incredibly, despite the extreme violence, there were no fatalities or critically injured. Inspector Boutell, a Sergeant and three constables though all received nasty head wounds though none was off duty for more than a few days.

Boarded up shops at Langley after the Riot - Photograph from the Book of Watford (J.B.Nunn)

Friday morning saw the people emerge to the streets covered with debris of broken glass, stones, wood and the occasional pool of blood. The volunteer specials after a short rest break then commenced the clearing up operations, which encountered some sporadic stoning, but no repetition of the violence of the night before. By this time the Control of the town had passed to the Hertfordshire Constabulary Chief Constable Colonel Henry Daniell, ably assisted by the Deputy Chief Constable John Reynolds (any relation guv?)

Rioters being taken away to St Albans Goal

John Reynolds, was a strict disciplinarian, an autocratic but highly popular man who served for 51 years with the force. He organised the merciless search of the Town's slums in the Ballards Buildings and Red Lion yard, resulting in more arrests and a large proportion of the stolen property being recovered. Whilst all this was going on though, he had also taken the precaution of employing several of the Town carpenters turning out dozens of new truncheons on their lathes!

Later that day, the arrested were brought before the court although luckily for them, none were charged with offences under the Riot Act, which carried a maximum sentence of penal servitude for life. The charges ranged from assaults and larcencies to attempted arson. A total of 54 persons including the 8 women were subsequently found guilty and received sentences from fines or fourteen day's imprisonment to 10 months hard labour. On the day when the ringleaders were in court and the heavier sentences passed, Mr. Reynolds took the accused on a humiliating walk through the town handcuffed together in pairs and surrounded by Police. The Watford Observer reported this as follows:

"As they left, they affected an air of bravado, but as the last house passed them by, their faces changed and more than one was seen to be crying."

As the Riot Act had been read, all the victims were entitled to compensation from the Town Hall, a bill that exceeded £2,000. The 200 special constables were each presented with their truncheons as a momento of their service to the Town.

Retirement Inspector Boutell

After serving for 26 years in the Hertfordshire Constabulary, Inspector Boutell retired last week. For the past three years he had been the right hand man of Superintendent Wood. During his quarter of a century of service, the Inspector has seen many changes, the uniform included, his first uniform consisted of a high beaver hat, and long frock coat. Each man was allowed night and day to carry a walking stick and a Constable could wear a long beard if he chose. The present helmets were introduced when the present Chief Constable Lt.-Col. Daniell was appointed. His successor will be Inspector Draper. (W.O. 1902)

Organ Playing

Giacomo Grimaldi of Days Lodging House was summonsed for playing an organ after being requested to desist. When spoken to by Police he replied "Me no speak English." He was fined £1. (W.O. 1902)

Animal Contract

I Mary Lane of The Kings Arms, Watford in the County Hertford hereby agree, for the consideration hereinafter mentioned, to receive from the Police Authorities at Watford, in the "C" Division of the Hertfordshire Constabulary, any such animals specified in the schedule hereto which may be found by, or may otherwise come into the possession of the Police, and I hereby undertake to provide such animals during their confinement with a sufficient quantity of fit and wholesome food and water, and to hold myself responsible for their proper care and safe custody; and further that no such animals shall be given up to any persons except in the presence, and by the direction of a Police Officer duly authorised to give permission for the restoration of the same to the owner or his agent. In Consideration whereof I hereby agree to accept the sums specified in the schedule in full satisfaction of any claim I may have for the keep and care of such animals as aforesaid.

The Schedule above Referred to

Cattle, Horses, Mules and Asses..per head 2s 0d per day or any part thereof.

Goats, Sheep, and Pigs per score or any part of a score above 9 5s 0d. per day or any part thereof

Goats, Sheep and Pigs per score or any part of a score above 9, after first day 7s 6d per day or any part thereof

Goats, Sheep and Pigs, if less than 10, first and each succeeding day, per head 6d per day or any part thereof

Goats, Sheep and Pigs and number up to 9 over each complete score, per head 6d per day or any part thereof

Dogs or Poultry each 6d per day or any part thereof

The day will be counted as 24 hours from the time the animal is placed in the Greenyard.

As witness my hand this 10th day of July One thousand, nine hundred and five.

Signed by the said Mary Lane
in the presence of W.Wood Supt

Speed Checks

Chief Constable orders measures to be taken to deter or catch speeding car drivers. Special instructions issued with measured distance checks carried out by four Constables, the officer taking the time check to be in plain clothes.

Daily Mirror cartoon - 1905

Blood Hounds

As an experimental measure, sucessful use was made of Major Richardsons bloodhounds in the detection of crime.

Bloodhounds - 1908

New Chief Clerk

In 1909, following the Retirement of the Chief Clerk, the Chief Constable appointed Captain Unett, to the post, a decision that caused a good deal of unrest within Police Forces throughout the Country, even moving the Editor of the Police Review to write to the Secretary of State for the Home Department, the Rt. Hon. Herbert J. Gladstone, M.P. The letter was dated 10th November 1909.

Sir,

Your attention has already been directed by Sir Charles Schwann, Bart.,M.P., to the recent appointment by the Watch Committee of the Borough of Bolton, contrary to its local regulations, of a clerk (previously employed in the office of the magistrate's clerk) to the post of Police Inspector, to act as Chief Clerk of the Force.

I now beg leave also to direct your attention to a similar occurrence in the County of Hertford, where the Chief Constable, Liet-Colonel H.S. Daniell, has filled the vacancy in the Chief Clerkship of the Force, caused by the retirement of a Superintendent, by the appointment of a Captain Unett, an Officer of the Army, without any previous Police experience.

Both these appointments have caused strong feelings of resentment in the minds of the members of the respective Forces, not only those considering themselves eligible for the positions, but also those below them who are qualified to rise to the posts that would be thus vacated. Beyond the Forces themselves, the consternation is widespread amongst the police of the United Kingdom.

It is not admitted that within the forces named there were no officers waiting promotion, admirably qualified for these posts; but if judged otherwise, there are thousands of highly qualified men in other forces awaiting promotion, who would become eager applicants for the appointments.

You are aware, Sir, that the disciplinary conditions of the Police Service are such as to prevent constables from themselves representing to you or to the local authorities, their deep sense of this grievance.

If, however, such a practice of individual patronage is to become prevalent with the police, it will lead to very serious discontent and dissaffection; it will prevent worthy and eligible men from joining the service; and it will destroy confidence in the pledges of the local authorities, held out to the men when they are enlisting, that they would have every opportunity of rising by meritorious conduct and ability.

I assure you, Sir, that practically the whole service affected are anxiously hoping that you may be able to promote or assist some measure, or to give some expression of opinion that may be calculated to prevent a recurrence of similar transactions.

Your obedient servant,
JOHN KEMPSTER.
Editor of the Police Review.

The Editor received the following reply dated 17th November 1909.

Sir,
I have laid before the Secretary of State your letter of November 10, respecting certain recent appointments in the Police Forces, and I am Directed by him to say that he is not responsible for appointments, in the Police Forces, and in his opinion no good purpose would be served by intervention on his part in the matter.

W.P. BYRNE.

Rest Days 1910

The Police (Weekly Rest Day) Act was passed, requiring every Constable below the rank of Inspector to be allowed 52 Rest days in the year, on which he was not required to carry out Police duties. The Act gave 4 years grace in which to phase the rest days in.

Police Concert

Under the patronage of the Watford Magistrates Bench, a concert was put on at the Town Hall by Police Officers and their families in aid of the Watford Police Court Poor Box. The Officers performed various songs and recitals. (W.O. 5.1.1911)

Ambulance

Superintendent Wood of the Watford Police announced that £85 had been raised by the Police concert and offered a hose drawn ambulance be offered to the Watford District Hospital as a Coronation gift from the Watford Division of the Hertfordshire Constabulary to be paid for out of the Poor Box Fund. (W.O. 17.1.1911)

On 23rd March 1911, the presentation of the ambulance was made to the Hospital at Clarendon Hall.

Public Houses

Superintendent Wood of the Hertfordshire Constabulary reported to the Licensing

Magistrates the existence of 97 Fully Licensed Public Houses, 46 Beer Houses for consumption 'off' the premises and 15 licences to grocers to sell alcohol. (W.O. 10.21911)

Murder of Rose Gurney

The Cock Public House (1991)

On July 16th 1911, Charles Coleman was arrested by Constable Clark at the Cock Public House, Sarratt, on suspicion of the murder of Mrs Rose Gurney. It is reported that as the Constable entered the Public House, Coleman leaned on the bar, quietly finished his beer and said "If I had known you were coming, I would have put my head under a train". Coleman, was the last man to be hanged at St. Albans Gaol on 21.12.11.

Superintendent Wood Deputy Chief Constable

During the past week, Superintendent Wood of Watford has received many congratulations on the fact that he has been appointed Deputy Chief Constable of Hertfordshire in succession to Supt. John Reynolds of Hitchin. Supt. Wood, who is the eldest son of the late Mr Charles Wood, farmer, of Burnside, Adney, Aberdeenshire, joined the Police Force at Reigate Borough in 1880. After 4 years service in the Surrey Constabulary, he became a Sergeant in the Borough Force at Hertford, where he remained for 5 years. He gained promotion rapidly and after a term as Inspector at Buntingford and Ware, he was Supt. at Ware for 3 years. He succeeded Captain Wymer as Supt. at Watford, where he has been in charge of the town's police for nearly 14 years. Altogether, he has seen 31 years service and is the senior Superintendent in the County. Soon after he had taken up his duties at Watford, Supt. Wood did a real service to the community by clearing out of the district men who were engaged on the nefarious traffic of obscene literature. Since Mr. Wood has been in Watford, the force under him has doubled in number owing of course to the increase in the population. Scores of young constables have received their training under him and many owe their after success to his careful inculcation of the principles which go to the making of a good police officer. In the cause of charity, as represented by the Police Poor Box, Mr. Wood has for some years arranged police concerts on a large scale and so much have his efforts been appreciated that he was able recently to present the district hospital with a bus ambulance which cost over £100. Each year too, a cricket match with St. Albans police contributes materially to the funds of the police orphanage. The inhabitants of Watford will be pleased to hear that Supt. Wood remains in the town.

The great efficiency and admirable tact with which he has always carried out his public duties, combined with his high personal character, have won for him universal esteem.

Miners Strike

Mutual assistance was again rendered in 1911, when police came under pressure from a series of Nationwide strikes. Hertfordshire Constabulary sent 30 men to assist at the Gilfach Goch colliery in South Wales.

Hertfordshire Police detatchment on duty at the Gilfach Goch Pit,
Photograph from The Story of the Hertfordshire Police.

Constable James Woolnough on duty at the pit.

Watford Police F.C. 1912 - 1913

P.C. 108 Killeen P.C. 237 Gristwood *(Sub Captain)* P.C. 183 Vickers *(Captain)*

P.C. 97 Baker P.C. 30 Ward P.C. 75 Cobb P.C. 56 Cooper P.C. 111 Sweetlatic P.C. 258 Wicks

P.C. 132 James *(Secretary)* P.C. 60 Smith P.C. 277 Crew Supt (DCC) Wood *(Treasurer)* P.C. 281 Gillett P.S. 51 West

Death of Constable Peddle

The funeral of Mr. Alfred Peddle of Laurel Villas, Mill End, Rickmansworth, took place at Rickmansworth Cemetery on Tuesday. Mr. Peddle who was 78 years, was born in the village and was formerly the village constable having succeeded Mr. H. Ryder who still resides in Mill End. (W. O. 18th May 1912)

Police Strength

Today the Police Force in Watford consists of Superintendent Wood, the Deputy Chief Constable of Hertfordshire, Inspector Decimus Domoney of St. Albans Rd. Police Station, Inspector Patrick O'Connor of King Street Police Station, 7 Police Sergeants, 1 Detective Sergeant, 63 Police Constables and 1 Detective Constable. (WO 2.2.1913)

My memories 1914

On the 25th March 1948, a letter was received by the Chief Constable from retired Constable Albert Aldridge of Stanmore Rd, Watford, recollecting incidents that had occurred during his service with the Hertfordshire Constabulary. The earliest incident he recalled was from 1893 at Royston, but he went on to recall the following incident.

During the 1914-1918 war, on a date I can't remember, I was on duty just after midnight in St.Albans Road, Watford, when I saw a man standing outside Christ Church looking up at the window. I asked him what he was doing, and he replied " I was going in here if you hadn't come along, I have been in one church tonight, I done a lot of damage, I would have set fire to the church if I had had any matches".

I took him to St.Albans Road Police Station. I then visited St.George's church where I saw a window broken. I fetched the curate and together we went to the church. In the vestry, we found every surplice and cassock had been torn up and thrown in a heap in the centre of the room. In the church the back of the organ and part of the inside had been pulled out. Damage of £30 had been done.

I charged the man with breaking in and doing damage, he admitted it and he said "I have just done 3 years for breaking into a church at Norwich and I expect I shall get 3 years for this job".

He was committed for trial at the Quarter Sessions where he received 3 years penal servitude.

The first Hertfordshire police car (1914), a two seater Swift. The driver is Superintendent Reed.

Photograph from The Story of the Hertfordshire Police

First Police Vehicles

The first motor vehicle allocated for use by the Hertford County Constabulary was in 1914, when a "Swift" cycle car Index Number AR 4364 was purchased for £119. This vehicle was used by Superintendent George Reed of Hitchin, and was sold in 1922 for £61 to Mr. East of Bishop's Stortford.

In 1915, a similar car was purchased, which was also sold in 1922. The two vehicles were replaced by an "Overland" costing £287.5s, and a "Ford" costing £105.

The first recorded use of motorcycles within the Force is in 1920, when two "Triumphs" were lent by the Government for use in connection with strikes. In 1921, these were purchased from the Government for £50 each.

Christmas Eve, 1914, Queens Road, Watford (outside the old Boots).

Photograph from the Book of Watford

Special Constables

The Special Constables Act of 1914 empowered that during the Great War, constables might be appointed under the Special Constables Act 1831, although a tumult, riot or felony had not taken place or was not immediately apprehended. This was followed by the Special Constables Order 1914 which authorised the formation of a permanent special constabulary reserve and set out working regulations, conditions of appointment, resignation and discharge and also that steps be taken to see that their duties were efficiently discharged.

Control of Rats and House Sparrows

During the two World Wars, the Governments were very concerned with the preservation of food supply, as by prevention of waste, less money needed to be expended for the import of food and the obvious risk of getting shipping bast the enemy. In order to try and prevent waste, pests needed to be culled. This gave rise to correspondence initially from the Home Office and then to Superintendents from the Chief Constable.

The Under Secretary of State.
Home Office
6th June 1917.

Sir,

In view of the Importance of taking all practicable measures at the present time for protecting the National food supply, the Board of Agriculture have recommended that certain measures be taken for the destruction of rats and house sparrows.

The Board of Agriculture, issued a leaflet detailing the following rewards to be made:

Rats tails 1/- per dozen.

Heads of unfledged house sparrows 2d per dozen.

Heads of fully fledged house sparrows 3d per dozen.

House sparrows eggs 1d per dozen.

The leaflet also encouraged the setting up of Sparrow and Rat Clubs to encourage the population in the destruction of the pests.

The Chief Constable sent copies of the leaflet to all Divisions and asked for a report in the returns and payments made.

The reply from "C" Division.

195 Rats tails

248 Fledged house sparrows

154 Unfledged house sparrows

252 Sparrows eggs.

In addition, Abbots Langley had set up its own Sparrow and Rat Club making payments at the nationally advertised figure, and additionally offered prizes of 10/-, 6/-, and 3/- for the best individual returns each month.

Police Sergeant 181 James Woodward, stationed at North Watford Police Station, made enquiries of local land owners and found that Mr. Hollins, Bailiff to the Hon. A.H. Hibbert of Munden, paid 2d per rat tail.

At Rickmansworth, The Rickmansworth Welfare Committee ran a Club offering the following payments:

Sparrows 6d per dozen

Sparrows eggs 3d per score

Rats tails 2/- per dozen

Mice tails 3d per dozen.

This Club had regular collectors, Samuel Young of Woodcote Farm, West Hyde, R. Ayre of Shepherds Farm, Mill End, E. Dickens of Croxley Green, W.E. Franklin of Parsonage Farm, Rickmansworth, H. Giles of Stockers Farm, Rickmansworth and R.J. Dickens of Moor Farm, Rickmansworth.

The total Divisional returns for a three week period added up to:

6,181 Rat tails

4,193 Sparrows

7,431 Eggs.

Payment, was made from the Police, who submitted accounts which were then sent to the Board of Agriculture and re-imbursed. Rural beat officers, were expected to make payments from their own pocket and submit claims to the Superintendent weekly, when they would get re-imbursed on supply of the evidence. This could sometimes lead to hardship especially towards the ends of a week when money was tight in the household. As in many other forms of Police duty, Officers wives were expected to make these payments when their husbands were out on duty and also to complete the necessary paperwork and count the spoils. Most returns appeared to be made as farm workers returned to their homes after a day in the fields at about 7 p.m., roughly the same time as the hungry officers returned from their tour of 8 hours duty, thereby often finding the Officers wives in the kitchen preparing their husbands meal, and having to interrupt this event to count Rats Tails or the heads of sparrows!!

Good Conduct Badge

A Good Conduct Badge has been awarded to the undermentioned Sergeant:-

PS 134 Hunt J. of "C" Division,
Second Class Good Conduct Badge.

The award is dated from 24th February 1918, and carries with it 1d. per day Good Conduct Pay. (G.O. No.31 1918)

FUEL COAL FOR YEAR

1st July 1918 to 30th June 1919

Coal will be supplied to the undermentioned stations as follows:-

"C" Division.

Watford including Station House, 35 tons delivered to Watford Railway Station.

St.Albans Road, 18 Tons delivered to Watford Railway Station.

Rickmansworth, 12 Tons delivered to Rickmansworth Railway Station.

The Coal will be supplied by Bestwood Coal & Iron Ltd.

Tenders

Tenders to cart Coal from the Railway Stations to Police Stations have been accepted in accordance to the Schedule attached hereto.

Superintendents will notify the persons concerned and arrange for the cartage when necessary.

"C" Division.
To Watford (King Street & St.Albans Rd), Contractor A.Saunders at 4/- per ton.

To Rickmansworth, Contractor J.Atkins at 2/- per ton and Weigh Tickets extra. (G.O. No.56 1918)

Obituary

The Chief Constable regrets to announce that:-

No 1281 Lance Corporal William James Walton Kendall, 3rd Battalion, Grenadier Guards was killed in action on 25th September 1918.

Ex-Police Constable Kendall 129 of "C" Division, stationed at Watford, joined the Hertford County Constabulary on 27th October 1910, and was recalled to the Colours on 4th August 1914.

Protection of Crops

At a meeting of the Hertfordshire County Council held on November 11th 1918, it was resolved that the rewards for the destruction of rats and sparrows should be increased.

As of 1st December 1918, the following rates will apply.

Rat Tails 1/6d per dozen.

Heads of fully fledged house sparrows 6d per dozen.

Heads of unfledged house sparrows 3d per dozen.

Eggs of house sparrows 1d per dozen.

Posters showing the new scale of payments were forwarded at the same time of the Order for display throughout the respective Divisions.

Pay of the Force

On 19th November 1918, the Secretary of State signified his approval to the following scales of pay, with a bonus of 7/- per week added for all ranks, for the Hertford County Constabulary, with effect from 1st July 1918, inclusive:-

CONSTABLES

On appointment £112.2.2d p.a.

Third Class

After 1 year service £114.14.3d p.a.
After 2 years service £117. 6.5d p.a.

Second Class

After 3 years service £119.18.7d p.a.
After 4 years service £122.10.9d p.a.

First Class

After 5 years servive £125.2.10d p.a.
After 6 years service £127.15.0d p.a.
After 7 years service £130. 7.2d p.a.
After 8 years service £132.19.3d p.a.

After 15 years service £135.11.5d p.a.

After 20 years service £138. 3.7d p.a.

The advances in scale at 15 and 20 years service respectively are to be granted subject to the following conditions:-

That after 15 years service, with the last 5 years free from misconduct entry, there be paid to Constables 1/- per week extra, and after 20 years service with the last 5 years free from misconduct entry, an additional 1/- a week extra, provided that if there has not been 5 years freedom from misconduct at the expiration of 15 years service the extra 1/- per week may be witheld until such 5 years freedom from misconduct has accrued, and the second 1/- per week until another five years freedom from misconduct has accrued.

SERGEANTS

On appointment £146.00.0d p.a.

After 1 year in rank £148.12.2d p.a.

After 2 years in rank £151. 4.3d p.a.

After 3 years in rank £153.16.5d p.a.

After 4 years in rank £156. 8.7d p.a.

The "Merit Pay" for Constables and Sergeants is confined to those Constables and Sergeants to whom it has already been awarded.

INSPECTORS

On appointment £177.18. 9d p.a.

After 1 year in rank £182.10. 0d p.a.

After 2 years in rank £187. 1. 3d p.a.

After 3 years in rank £191.12. 6d p.a.

After 4 years in rank £197.14. 2d p.a.

After 5 years £203.15.10d p.a.

SUPERINTENDENTS

Second Class

On appointment £235.14. 7d p.a.

After 1 year in rank £246.07. 6d p.a.

After 2 years in rank £257.00. 5d p.a.

After 4 years in rank £267.13. 4d p.a.

After 6 years in rank £278.06. 3d p.a.

After 8 years in rank £288.19. 2d p.a.

First Class

On appointment £295.00.10d p.a.

After 2 years £302.12.11d p.a.

After 4 years in rank £311.15. 5d p.a.

The First Class is limited to a number not more than five. Appointments will be made by selection.

DEPUTY CHIEF CONSTABLE

In addition to pay as an ordinary Superintendent:

On appointment £ 40

After 2 years in rank £ 60

After 4 years in rank £ 80

After 6 years in rank £100

No advance in the scale of pay of any rank will be considered to be automatic, nor can it be claimed as a right - the increase being subject to its being merited by attention to duty, good conduct, efficiency and to the approval of the Chief Constable.

The scale of pay will be brought into operation forthwith and the payments due in respect of the retrospective period from 1st July last, will be made on the paysheets for month ending 4th December 1918.

From the 5th December 1918 advancement of pay will be increased from 20/- to 30/- per week for each Constable and Sergeant.

OBITUARY.

The Chief Constable regrets to announce that Lieutenant Colonel Henry Smith Daniell formerly Chief Constable of the County of Hertford died on 15th December 1918.

Lt. Colonel Henry Smith-Daniell

The Funeral will take place on Thursday 19th December 1918. The funeral cortege will leave Sele Grange, Hertford, at 1.45 p.m. and proceed to St. Andrew's Church, Hertford, where a funeral service will be held at 2 p.m. The body will then be conveyed to the Cemetery, Hatfield for interment at 3 p.m.

Police arrangements at Hertford

The Superintendents of the Force will act as Pall Bearers and will be under the charge of Supt. Wood, DCC. The Pall Bearers will parade at Hertford Police Station at 1.30 p.m., and proceed direct to Sele Grange and march on either side of the hearse to St. Andrew's Church.

The order of the Funeral procession will be:

1. Hearse with pall bearers.

2. Mourners.

3. Chief Constable.

4. Funeral Party of Police. This will consist of 1 Inspector, 5 Sergeants, and 34 Constables.

This party will march 4 deep with 3 paces between each rank. The funeral cortege will halt 50 yards from the entrance of St. Andrew's Church whilst the Funeral Party will proceed to line each side of the footway from the Churchyard Gate to the Church door, facing inwards and spaced at regular intervals.

When the Service is concluded the funeral party will leave the Church in advance of the body and mourners and will take up their former positions until the funeral cortege has left for Hatfield.

Immediately the funeral cortege has departed the funeral party will be dismissed and every man will return to his respective station.

The Pall bearer party will proceed to Hatfield by motor car which will be provided.

Police Arrangements at Hatfield

"C" Division will provide 2 Inspectors, 2 Sergeants, and 18 Constables, out of a total of 3 Inspectors, 10 Sergeants, and 62 Constables.

On arrival at Hatfield, the funeral cortege will halt at the Constabulary Headquarters. The Pall bearers will take up position on each side of the hearse and the cortege will march of as before.

At the Cemetery, the cortege will halt outside, whilst the funeral party will proceed:-

1. A detachment of 30 men to form 3 sides of a hollow square round the grave side, the men will be spaced at regular intervals and ample room will be left for clergy and mourners.

2. The remainder of the funeral party will line the Cemetery carriageway from the entrance gate to the grave, a distance of approximately 80 yards. The party will be evenly spaced and face inwards.

When the mourners and the Chief Constable have passed the funeral party will fall in and proceed to the grave side forming up in the rear of the mourners but so as not to impede their departure.

After the mourners have departed the funeral party will be formed up, marched to Headquarters and dismissed, every man to return to his station direct.

Preference will be given on the selection of men to volunteers and those who formerly served under Lt. Col. Daniell.

Claims for travelling and subsistence allowances will be paid from Police Funds in the usual way.

Commendation

Samuel Williams alias Allworthy was convicted at the Watford Petty Sessions on 24th December 1918 and committed for three months Hard Labour for cycle stealing at Watford on 17th December 1918.

The action in the case of Police Constable 185 Arthur Goodship of Watford, has been brought to the notice of the Chief Constable. The thief is reported to be an expert cycle thief and a member of a gang living at Bethnal Green, London. His detection and apprehension with the stolen property in his possession was due entirely to the manner in which Police Constable Goodship exercised his powers of observation whilst on patrol duty.

Bi Cycle Allowance

CYCLE PATROLS- Inspectors and Sergeants 1/6d per week each, Constables 1/- per week each.

OTHER CYCLISTS- $^1/_2$d per mile (not exceeding 2/- per day).

The following officers are entitled to the Cycle Patrol Allowance.

PS 98 Berry W.J. Watford
PS 181 Woodwards Watford
Insp Smith S.C. Rickmansworth
PS 196 Mead J.E. Rickmansworth
PC 61 Stevens W.R. Bedmond
PC 94 Clark J. Mill End
PC 220 Ephithite H. Eastbury.

Commendation

The conduct of Police Constables Charles James Hodgskins 293 "C" Division and Alfred Madgwick 186 "C" Division in stopping a runaway horse at Watford on 15th January 1919, has been brought to the notice of the Chief Constable.

The statements of the witnesses show that the Police Constables acted with promptitude, and that at the risk of personal injury, prevented what might have been a serious accident.

Police Constables Hodgskins and Madgwick are hereby commended and the Chief Constable directs that appropriate entries shall be made on the Constables record sheets.

General Instruction and Drill

Superintendents are hereby empowered to cause an examination of all Constables in their respective Divisions in drill. If certified as efficient a Constable will in future only be required to drill once in every three months. The time previously occupied in this manner should be taken advantage of in providing instruction in police duty, ju-jitsu and physical exercises. The work should be made interesting and instructive.

Superintendents will select suitable officers to act as permanent Divisional or Sectional Instructors. Arrangements will be made for the attendance of an Instructor from Headquarters occasionally.

Detection of Crime

For the forthcoming Herts Quarter Sessions, there are only three cases from Watford, none of them singular or symptomatic of the class of crime which elsewhere is giving cause for grave concern. A great deal of Watford's immunity from serious offences against Society may reasonably be attributed to the efficiency of the local police force under Deputy Chief Constable Wood. The fact that Watford is so near the Metropolis and that it is easy for gangs of thieves and criminals in London to make flying visits to the town adds to the problems faced by the Hertfordshire Police.

In unravelling mysteries of the higher class of crime which have occurred in West Hertfordshire, Superintendent Wood has a record calculated to give criminals pause. He took control of the Bricket Wood Crime. He brought home "the poison by post" murder to Mary Ansell and sent her to the gallows. In a shooting case it was through his vigilance that the victim's body was exhumed and the man arrested, on whom the death sentence was passed; and more recently he had a Rickmansworth murderer in custody within 24 hours of his foul deed. As a matter of fact, only three criminals have been sentenced to death in the County during the last 30 years, and all three went to the bar of Justices through the instrumentality of the head of the Watford Police.

Colonel Law at the wheel of his 1919 two seater Calcott, index AR3333

(Chief Constable 1911-1928)

Discipline

On the 24th of October 1920, it was alleged that Pc 59 R.Fordham "Did make a certain noise with his mouth with intent to insult one Thomas Walker of Watford in the High Street, Watford"

This case was not substantiated as "the said Thos Walker was apparently the worse for drink and believed to be very hostile to Police."

On the 21st of December 1920, Pc 61 R.Burgess was disciplined and cautioned on a charge " Did fail to report to his Sergeant the report of an alleged larceny-Tame Rabbit and to make enquiries regarding same."

Hertfordshire Police Sports Day 1921

A BRILLIANT EFFORT

St.Albans was the scene of a striking effort on the part of the Police of the County yesterday, when a fine programme of sports was given to the large crowd of spectators at Clarence Park. The first gala day of the kind arranged by the Police in Hertfordshire, this had the advantage of ideal weather conditions, a specially gratifying fact in view of the consideration that practically all tickets were sold before the day of the sports.

It has not yet been officially decided whether these sports are to be an annual event, but they were attended with such a measure of success yesterday and were generally so well appreciated by the spectators, who assembled in considerable numbers, that it is quite likely the function will be repeated in future years.

The events, were extremely varied in nature with Police only races, handicap races, open races, obstacle events, fun races and events for children.

Some of "C" Divisions successes are detailed below.

Tug of War, here, "C" Division received a bye in the first round, beat "A" Division in the second round and triumphed in the final by beating "E" Division.

One Mile Walking Handicap- 1st Pc F.Webb (Bedmond) 70 yard start, 2nd Pc A.Mansfield (Watford) 20 yard start. Winners Time 8 minutes and 20 seconds.

One Mile Flat Handicap- 1st Pc H.A.Goodson (Watford) 10 yard start.

880 yards 1st Pc H.A.Goodson (Watford)

Treacle and Bun Race- 1st Pc R.H.Wigg (Hatfield), 2nd Pc A.Smith (Watford), 3rd Pc G.Sermons (Watford).

4 Legged Race- 1st Pc's W.J.Ward, H.W.Thorpe and Sgt A.C.Sampson.

2nd Pc's A.Camp, W.Nottage and J.Berry.

Thief Race- 1st Pc's White and Goodson.

The latter was unfortunately not one of the more exciting events as it will no doubt be on future occasions, the thief in this case being no match for his pursuer, being caught in about ten seconds.

The youngest competitor in the Sports was little Miss Skeggs aged 4 years and 4 months who with a 34 yard start came in second in the 80 yards race, toddling up to the winning post with mighty determination and thereby winning a tennis racket, which she probably found very difficult to carry away!!

The prizes were distributed by the Marchioness of Salisbury. (Hertfordshire Record August 19th 1921)

Shopbreaking

Between 30.12.22 and 1.1.23, a shopbreaking occurred at a Lock up shop at 116A High Street, Watford. The offender Archibald Charles Henry Fox aged 35 scaled a side gate, scaled a 6 foot high fence, broke a pane of glass on the ground floor at the rear and reached in and unfastened a catch. He stole two one pound Treasury notes and 11/- in silver and copper. On 18.1.23 Fox appeared at Luton Boro. and received 6 months imprisonment.

Equipped for Crime

On 13.1.23 Stephen Brown alias Arthur Jackson was found in possession of housebreaking implements at night by Constable 338 Prentice and dealt with at Hertford Assizes on 13.2.23 and sentenced to 12 months imprisonment.

Theft of Duck

On 25.11.23 Sidney Phipps of 71 Church Lane, Rickmansworth reported the Theft of a white Aylesbury Duck valued at 8/- from an open shed at his allotment. Alfred Peak, aged 10 years was arrested for this offence and received 12 months probation on 4.12.23 at Watford Petty Sessions.

Assualt

On 13.10.23 Sam Quarterman aged 51 years returned home allegedly under the influence of drink, had words with his wife and then

Assisting the county surveyor's staff to lay some of the first white lines, in Watford, 1921. Photograph from the Story of Hertfordshire Police

struck her on the head with a length of chain. On 30.10.23 he was sentenced to 12 months imprisonment for Assault occasioning bodily harm.

Shoplifting

On 1.1.24 Harold Christie of 186 High Street, Watford saw at 2 p.m. a young boy steal a packet of cigarettes and a box of matches valued at 7 $^{1}/_{2}$d, the boy Bertie Pearce was apprehended but Mr.Christie withdrew his complaint on hearing that the boy was to be thrashed by his parents.

Theft of Cycle

At 5.15 p.m. on 5.4.24, Jack Harris of 141 Sparrows Herne, Bushey, had his cycle stolen from outside the Football Ground. The cycle was valued at £9. Charles Wood aged 22 years was arrested and subsequently found guilty on 16.4.24 and sentenced to six months imprisonment.

Theft of Tyre

On 11.4.24, Claude Buxton of 9 Carey Place, Watford reported the theft of a tyre and tube valued at £1, from his motor car standing in a private yard in King St. The crime remains undetected.

Theft of Coats

On 29.3.24 a Simple Larceny of a parcel of 7 coats, stolen from a LM and S Railway Train at Garston valued at £14 was reported. Charles William James Woods aged 28 years was arrested for the offence and on 15.4.24 was sentenced to 6 months hard labour.

Theft of Cash

On 30.4.24 an offence of simple larceny by trick was committed when Minnie Brooks of 48 Nascot Street, Watford received a telegram asking for £2. The telegram purported to be from her son. Cash was wired to Bournemouth where it was signed for. Frederick Goat, aged 25 years was arrested for this offence in Portsmouth and subsequently on 20.5.24 appeared at Watford Petty Sessions and received 1 years Probation.

Theft of Sheets

On 31.7.24 between 1000 and 1230 hours at 29 Salisbury Road, Watford, a pair of unbleached sheets value 16/- was stolen by Harry Chance aged 24 years a lodger at that address after he was turned out for being undesirable. On 5.8.24 he appeared before the St.Albans Quarter Sessions and was sentenced to 3 months imprisonment.

Russeling

On 16.9.24 Thomas Simmons of 28 Market Street, Watford reported that he had a bay mare stolen from the stables at Percy Road, Watford. The mare being valued at £23. Thos. Clifford aged 32 was arrested and sentenced to 15 months hard labour.

Carnal Knowledge

On 8.12.24, a man aged 59 years, and a musician was arrested for having had carnal knowledge of his daughter aged 19 years at Watford. On 17.12.24 he appeared at the Watford Petty Sessions and was committed to the Herts. Assizes on 16.2.25 where he was found guilty and sentenced to three years penal servitude.

Theft of Mole Traps

At 1130 a.m. on 1st March 1925, Albert Webb aged 19 years and Leonard George Sweeting aged 18 years were both arrested for stealing 9 mole traps valued at 9/- from a meadow in Loudwater Farm, Rickmansworth. They were both fined £1.

Store Breaking

On 29th March 1925, at Watford Co-op Stores, Queens Rd, Watford at 1210 a.m., Constable 123 Bone found Leonard John Austin in the basement of the store, he having broken in through a skylight. Austin was charged with the Theft of a jam sandwich and a candle, valued in total at 6d. He was on 7.4.25 sentenced to 3 months Borstal.

Unlawful Wounding

On 8.4.25 Robert Rayns a commercial traveller of Watford, was hit by a brick thrown at him whilst motorcycling along St.Albans Rd, Watford. Alexander Darrock aged 56 years was arrested and charged with unlawful wounding. He was sentenced on 30.6.25 to 3 months imprisonment.

Indecent Assualt

On 24.4.25 a girl aged 6 years of Benskin Road, Watford was indecently assaulted in a chicken house at the rear of her home by a boy aged 11 years. At the Watford Petty Sessions, the boy was sent to an Industrial School until he was 16 years.

Theft of Ladder

On 21.5.25 an offence of simple larceny of a ladder was reported to Police by Frank Saunders of 229 Gammons Lane, Watford. Following Police enquiries, the ladder was found to have been sold accidentally at an Auction sale held on those premises the previous day.

Theft of Horse Braces

On 17.4.25 the simple larceny of two pairs of horse brasses valued at 10/- from stables at Bedmond Hall Farm, was reported by Frederick Pedder of Toms Lane, Bedmond and David Bennett of High Street, Bedmond. Herbert George Botwright aged 16 years was placed on 12 months probation for this offence when he appeared before the Watford Petty Sessions on 5.5.25.

Shop Breaking

At 1140 a.m. on 14.6.25 Sergeant 158 Roddis found two shops in Station Approach, Chorleywood had been broken into and a quantity of cigarettes and tobacco stolen from one and chocolates from the other. Outside the premises, the officer found freshly cut ham and beef sandwiches. The official Crime Report states "A picnic or cycling party are suspected as being responsible".

Handbags Stolen

On 9.6.25 Muriel Dean of Beech Road, Watford, Winnie Bishop of 'Orendon', Rickmansworth Rd, Watford and Nellie Lyon of 181 Chester Rd, Watford all had handbags stolen from perambulators in Woolworths and the Market Place, Watford, by James Williams aged 52 years who was arrested and charged with the offences. On 30.6.25, he appeared at the St.Albans Quarter Sessions and was sentenced to 18 months Hard Labour.

Attempted Suicide

Attempted Suicide, was extremely prevalent in 1925, with no fewer than 7 cases being recorded in a 4 month period.

On 5.6.25 a woman aged 19 years of Breakespeare Rd, Abbots Langley was found by Constable 148 Huggins lying in a field at Hazelgrove Farm, Abbots Langley. She had a hankerchief tied tightly around her neck and admitted that she had tried to take her own life. She was bound over in the sum of £10 and sent to a home for 3 years when she appeared at the Watford Petty Sessions on 30.6.25.

On 15.9.25, a man from Mill End, Rickmansworth attempted suicide by drowning in the Grand Junction Canal, Rickmansworth. No criminal proceedings were taken against him following assurances by his wife that she was willing to look after him.

A man aged 44, a labourer lodging at The Green Man Public House, Bedmond threatened to drown himself, but was removed to the Watford Poor Law Institution by Pc 312 Cattermole in September 1925.

Theft of Architrave

On 29.6.25 at 1 p.m., Arthur Mullett was arrested by Pc 208 Lawrence for being in possession of 3 pieces of Architrave mouldings value 9d, the property of Clifford and Gough of 96, Estcourt Rd, Watford from a house in the course of erection at Ashlands, Watford. The case did not proceed to court, as the Magistrates' Clerk refused to grant process of a summons.

Theft of Emerald Tie Pin

Between 6 p.m. on 25.5.25 and 1220 a.m. on 26.5.25, a diamond and emerald tie pin valued at £106 was stolen from a drawer in a dressing room at Russells, Watford. The pin being the property of the resident, His Highness The Maharajah of Baroda. The crime was not detected.

Fatal Accident

On 6th August 1925, Joseph Gregory Darey aged 47 years of Kings Langley, was knocked down and fatally injured in a vehicle whilst wheeling his bicycle on the Watford to Kings Langley Road in the Parish of Abbots Langley. On 1.9.25 George Elijah Harvey aged 36 years appeared at the Watford Petty Sessions on a charge of manslaughter, the case against him was dismissed.

Stealing Dead Fowl

On 16.11.25 Harry Wraight aged 56 years was arrested for stealing one "dead fowl" fro J.Sainsbury Ltd, The Parade, Watford valued at 6/10d. On 17.11.25 he appeared before the Watford Petty Sessions and received 1 months Hard Labour for Simple Larceny.

His wife, Grace Wraight who was with him at the time of his arrest was found at that time to be in possession of one pair of Gents Boots valued at 12/9d, the property of Freeman, Hardy and Willis, of 99 The High Street, Watford. On 17.11.25 she too was sentenced but to 14 days Hard Labour for simple larceny.

Theft of False Teeth

On 24.11.25 Alfred George Catesby of Jersey Lodge, Rickmansworth Rd, Watford reported the breaking into of his house and the larceny of two sets of false teeth valued at 15/-. Sergeant 289 Springett investigated the case, which remains undetected despite the fact that the Sergeant circulated the description of both the crime and the teeth to the 'Metro Information List 2' of 30.11.25, and the 'Police Gazette', Case 39 of the same date and also local circulations C1717 and C1718.

Burglary

At midnight on 11.12.25, Police on routine beat patrol disturbed burglars at the home of Mrs Kathleen Forsyth, Newlands, Cassiobury Park, after they had gained entry and stolen property to the value of £138.8.2d in clothing and jewellery. £64.12.2d was recovered at the scene of the crime. Charles Robertson made good his escape and was subsequently arrested by Bucks Police and sentenced to 5 years penal servitude at the Herts Assizes. Harry Ruston aged 30 years was sentenced to 2 years Hard Labour for his part in the burglary.

Assualt on Police

At midnight on 18.12.25, Constable 224 Hubert Wm Akers stationed at Watford, was seriously assaulted by a man and a woman whom he found in a lorry standing at the rear of shop premises in the High Street, Watford. The Constable received injuries to Head, Face and Body and was removed to Hospital and detained. George Albert Thompson aged 26 years, and Agnes Thompson were arrested and at St.Albans Quarter Sessions of 5.1.26 were both found guilty of causing Grievious Bodily Harm. George received a sentence of 4 months Hard Labour, and Agnes 3 months Hard Labour.

Designation of the Force

The proper designation of the Force is "Hertford County Constabulary".

It has been noted on various occasions, especially in connection with matters of Sports, that Divisions have been referred to in newspaper reports and on posters adverti-sing events as "The Ware Police", "Hertford Police", "Watford Police" and so on. This practice will be discontinued and the proper designation used, viz:-

"The Hertford County Constabulary, Blank Division", or "The County Police, Bishops Stortford Division".

Police keeping a watchful eye - *General Strike 1926*

There will be no objection to the name of the Division as well as the identifying letter, A, B, C, etc, being used, viz:-"A" or Bishops Stortford Division".

Superintendents should endeavour to have newspaper reports and posters correctly made out by those responsible.

Commendation

The conduct of Police Constable Frederick William Charles Dunsby, 231 "C" Division, in effecting the arrest at Watford of three men of the tramp class, who were subsequently charged with and found guilty of larceny from the Kensington Gardens Tea Rooms, London, has been brought to the notice of the Chief Constable.

The reports show that the Constable was observant, attentive to his duties, and exercised the powers of search and arrest upon reasonable suspicion.

The Chief Constable commends Constable Dunsby and orders that an appropriate entry shall be made upon his record of service.

Commendation

At Watford on the 25th July 1927, at 1.15 a.m., Constable 134 Gay "C" Division, apprehended a man named Joseph Worthy who was acting suspiciously.

At Watford Petty Sessions on 26th July, the Justices did not convict, but the Chairman, Henry Brown Esq, commended Constable Gay for his action. The reports in this case show that although the charge of being in possession of housebreaking implements by night was not substantiated, the Constable acted properly in arresting the man on reasonable suspicion.

The Chief Constable hereby endorses the commendation of the Justices and directs that an appropriate entry shall be made on the Constable's record of service.

POLICE FEDERATION.

Constables Branch Board Meeting held at Constabulary Headquarters Friday 28th January 1927.

SICKNESS

That the Chief Constable's attention be drawn to the fact that certain members of the Force whilst on strike duty at Ilkeston, Derbyshire, were poisoned by food supplied through the Derbyshire Police Authority which necessitated their being placed on the Sick List through no fault of their own, and whilst so sick were put under stoppages of pay.

Chief Constables Note.

Under the proviso to Police Regulation No 89, the circumstances under which various members of this Force performing duty in Derbyshire, were placed on the Sick List through eating food which was supplied to them on behalf of the Derbyshire Police Authority, has been referred to the Staff Surgeon, who recommends that in the following cases, the sickness be treated as an injury received on duty, viz:-

Police Constable 104 Snoxell B Division
Police Constable 179 Smith B Division
Police Constable 9 Emery B Division
Police Constable 329 Smith C Division
Police Constable 59 Fordham D Division
Police Constable 15 Geary E Division
Police Constable 320 Collett E Division
Police Constable 137 Dowty E Division
Police Constable 61 Burgess E Division
Police Constable 106 Radford E Division

The Chief Constable approves the recommendation of the Staff Surgeon and directs that where stoppages have been made from the pay during the sickness of the Constables named above, that an appropriate refund shall be made.

Discipline

Probationer Constable Edwin George Bailey 21 "C" Division.

Being late for duty in that he at Watford on Sunday 4th December 1927, having been ordered to parade for duty at 2345 hours, did without reasonable excuse fail to parade until 2400 hours that is 15 minutes late.

Found guilty. The Constables appointment is thereby not confirmed and his services will be dispensed with as from Wednesday 21st December 1927.

Regulation of Traffic

Police on duty at Traffic points are to regulate the flow of vehicles, assist pedestrians and generally to carry out such duties as are necessary to prevent danger, facilitate progress and to enforce the provisions of the law.

When vehicles are to be stopped the Police are to give warning to drivers so that they do not have to pull up quickly. Vehicles are not to be allowed to remain in crossings and when vehicular traffic is held up, it must be stopped so that pedestrians wishing to cross the road may do so in safety. Heavily laden vehicles, more particularly those drawn by horses, should not, as a rule, be stopped, especially when the point is approached by an up or down gradient.

Where both a motor and horse drawn vehicle are likely to arrive at a traffic control point at approximately the same moment, and circumstances permit, priority should always be given to the horse drawn vehicle. Traffic must not be held up too long, a minute or a minute and a half should generally suffice.

Police should not seize the bridles of horses, except when necessary to arrest an offender, or to prevent an accident. The precise point at which a Constable stands is immaterial provided that he has a good view in all directions, and can be clearly seen.

The order then goes on to describe in great detail the exact positions of the Constables hands etc, whilst making signals and also those that should be made by drivers to signify to the Officer they wish to go.

Horse drawn users are advised to make the following signals:

I am going to stop.

Raise the whip vertically with the arm extended above the right shoulder.

I am going to turn.

Rotate the whip above the head, then incline the whip to the right or the left to show the direction in which the turn is to be made.

The drivers of horse drawn vehicles using these signals should be careful to keep the whip clear of other traffic.

It is most desirable that careful instruction be given in the correct method of Officers giving these signals, with actual demonstration of the signals and followed up by careful supervision. Any faults should be corrected and Divisional Superintendents will arrange for instruction on the traffic signals to be given at the monthly instruction classes.

(S. O. No 154, 1928)

Saluting

It has come to the knowledge of the Chief Constable that there is a certain amount of slackness in some Divisions in saluting Magistrates. When a Constable sees a lady or gentleman they know to be a magistrate a salute will be given in the proper manner. Whenever there is any doubt in the mind of a Constable whether a certain lady or gentleman is or is not a Justice of the Peace, the salute should always be given.

The efficiency of the Constabulary Force is often judged in the estimation of the public by the cordiality which it extends to members of the public, and persons of consequence should always be saluted as an act of courtesy. (G. O. No. 102, 1928)

Connendation

At the Herts Quarter Sessions, held at St.Albans on 3rd April 1928, the Chairman E.A. Mitchell-Innes, Esq, K.C., commended Constable 326 Arthur George Bishop "D" Division, for great intelligence shewn in the investigation of a case of warehousebreaking and larceny at Hemel Hempstead on the night of 6/7th March 1928, and presentation of the case against George William Hazell and William Thomas Hollick.

The Chief Constable directs that an appropriate entry shall be made on the Constable's record of service. (G. O. No. 46, 1928)

Police Cottage Cesspools

The occupier of every County owned cottage which is provided with a cesspool will inspect the cesspool on the last day of each month. A report will be submitted to the Divisional Superintendent on the first day of each month showing whether or not the cesspool and drainage system is in proper working order.

A summary of the Inspection reports will be rendered to Headquarters by Divisional Superintendents on the third day of each month. (G.O. No. 114, 1928)

Obituary 10th November 1928.

The Deputy Chief Constable regrets to announce that Lieut. Colonel Alfred Letchworth Law, Chief Constable of Hertfordshire, died on 8th November 1928, after a prolonged illness, unselfishly and bravely borne.

Chief Constable
Lt. Col. Alfred Letchworth Law

Funeral.

The funeral of the late Lieut. Colonel Alfred Letchworth Law will take place on Tuesday 13th November 1928 at Hertingfordbury Church, near Hertford.

The funeral cortege will leave the Dell, Hertingfordbury, at 2.45 p.m., and the funeral service will be held in Hertingfordbury Church at 3.pm.

Order of Funeral Procession.

1. Military Escort,
   1 Officer,
   50 other ranks.
2. Firing Party,
   2 N.C.O's,
   12 Privates,
   1 Bugler.
3. Gun Carriage conveying coffin.
4. Chief Mourners.
5. Personal servants.
6. Members of the Hertford County Constabulary in uniform.
7. Special Constables in uniform.
8. Other mourners not in uniform.

Pall bearers.
The Superintendents of the Force will act as Pall Bearers, and will march on each side of the gun carriage from "The Dell" to Hertingfordbury Church.

Superintendent B Division will detail 3 Sergeants and 18 Constables for Traffic duty in Hertingfordbury and vicinity.
(G.O. No. 142, 1928)

Manner of giving Evidence

Before entering the Witness Box the right hand glove will be removed. When a Constable has entered the Witness Box he will stand to attention.

On no account are Constables to take up the Testament and swear themselves after the fashion prevalent in the Metropolitan Police Courts. Constables will await the order of the Chairman or Clerk to the Court before taking the oath. When the time has arrived for the administration of the oath, the Testament will be taken in the right hand and raised in front of and in line with the top of the head. In reading or repeating the oath the Constable must speak slowly and distinctly and with due regard to the solemnity of the occasion. When the oath has been taken the Testament will be placed on the Witness Stand and the Constable will remain at attention until asked by the Clerk of the Court to give his name and rank. These particulars will be given in the following manner:-

Herbert Brown. Constable 401, stationed at Blank.

The evidence will be given slowly and clearly with the facts in the proper sequence and with impartiality.

Abbreviations, such as:

P.C. for Police Constable, P.S. for Police Sergeant, P.H. for Public House, B.H. for Beer House, Via for route, Inst. for present month, and Ult. for past month will not be used.

After having given evidence in chief the Constable may assume the stand at ease position, always coming to attention when spoken to or when speaking. The Constable is permitted to refresh his memory by reference to entries or memoranda made in his official pocket book at the time of the occurrence or as soon as practicable afterwards.

The oaths of the Petty Sessions, Quarter Sessions and Assizes of both Felonies and misdemeanours, and the oath of an Inquest are to be learned by heart by every Constable. Superintendents will satisfy themselves from time to time that all members of their Divisions have the necessary knowledge.

(G.O. No. 30, 1929)

'C' Division Circa 1929

WATFORD PROPRIETORS: THE WATFORD SUPER CINEMA, LIMITED.
PHONE 855 *Manager:* HUGH D. WILSON PHONE 855

WEEK, MONDAY, 21st, to SATURDAY, 26th OCT.

A Special Paramount Talkie

Tingling, Thrilling Mystery!

A MALCOLM ST. CLAIR Production..
ADAPTED BY ALBERT SHELBY LEVINO
FROM THE NOVEL BY S. S. VAN DINE
SCREENPLAY BY FLORENCE RYERSON
B.P. SCHULBERG GENERAL MANAGER WEST COAST PRODUCTIONS
PRESENTED BY ADOLPH ZUKOR AND JESSE L. LASKY

Was it robbery? Fear? Revenge? What caused the sensational crime, "The Canary Murder Case." See the picture made from S.S. Van Dine's best-selling novel.

ALSO

RICHARD BARTHELMESS
in SCARLET SEAS *(Silent)*

One of the most stirring Sea Stories ever filmed.

The Super Orchestra Plays Afternoons and Evenings

Continuous 2.30 to 10.30. Doors Open 2. PRICES: 6d. to 2/4.

During the week commencing Monday 21st October 1929, The Watford Super Cinema were showing A Special Paramount Talkie "The Canary Murder Case" The poster shown to the left advertised the forthcoming feature.

However this modern film was not to everybodies liking and Miss H.L. Edwards of "The Corner, Cassio Road, wrote to the then Superintendent of Police Superintendent Maskell. Complaining that "It is very unpleasant in character and I do not think it tends towards the moral tone either of this town or any other. It is very bad for boys and girls and myself to see. Can it be removed?"

Superintendent Maskell had to refer the matter the Chief Constable George Knight, in his letter he stated that "The poster had been seen by the Board of Film Censors and passed."

Needless to say no police action was taken, regarding the poster, and one of Watford's first talking picture shows was allowed to be advertised as the makers had intended.

Duties of Police Inspectors 1929

In 1929, the Chief Constable, ordered a review to be made of the duties of the rank of Inspector throughout the Force. Superintendent Maskell at Watford devised the new 'Job Description' for Inspectors serving in "C" Division.

Residence

The Inspectors of the "C" or Watford Division will reside as under:-Watford No. 1 Section - King Street Police Station.

Watford No. 2 Section - St. Albans Rd Police Station.

Sections in Charge of

Watford No. 1 Section-That portion of the Borough of Watford that lies South of St. Johns Road, St. Albans Rd and Rickmansworth, also Watford Heath and Eastbury.

Watford No. 2 Section-That portion of the Borough of Watford that lies North of St. Johns Rd, St. Albans Rd and Rickmansworth Road and the Parishes of Abbots Langley, Bedmond, also Rickmansworth Urban, Mill End, West Hyde, Chorleywood, Sarratt and Batchworth.

Duties

The Divisional Superintendent will arrange that each Inspector shall obtain full knowledge of all parts of the Division, also the working of the Divisional Office in order that he may, if and when required, take charge and act as Superintendent. The Inspector will arrange the duties of the Sergeants and Constables in his Section, subject to the approval of the Superintendent, in order that the best possible protection is afforded both by day and night. He must make a daily survey of his section, noting Police Sergeants and Constables who are Rest Day or required for duty elsewhere, in order that the duties of the sergeants and constables remaining are utilised to the best advantage. Each police sergeant and constable should understand and appreciate his duties and responsibilities especially in regard to the prevention and detection of crime, and with this end in view the Inspector will instruct all members of his section in the powers conferred on them by law under the -Vagrancy Acts

Pedlars Act

Town Police Clauses Act

Each member of the Division should be encouraged to exercise his power of arrest on reasonable suspicion that a felony has been committed.

Crime

On the report of a crime being received, the Inspector will at once detail a constable to attend to and make the necessary enquiries, the Inspector will inform the Superintendent giving all the particulars available, and saying what action he is taking. The Inspector should make a careful study of the crime committed in his section in order to ascertain if it is the work of:-

1. Local thieves,

2. Vagrants passing through,

3. Organised Crime by persons living some distance away.

In the first place the public should be encouraged to give information when stolen property is offered for sale, or when known thieves are seen acting under suspicious circumstances.

Vagrants - In this County, there is a way ticket system in force therefore there is no excuse for begging and the Vagrancy Acts regarding begging, sleeping out and loitering with intent should be strictly enforced.

Organised Crime -Experience shows that many of this class of offence (house and shopbreaking) are committed by persons with motor cars which in some cases are stolen. ALL motor cars seen out at night after 12 midnight should be stopped, names and addresses of drivers and occupants taken, licences should be examined and particulars noted. If the constable has reasonable suspicion that a felony has been committed he should take the people with the motor car to the Police Station where the case will be investigated by the Officer in charge of the police station. Other forms of transport may be used such as lorries, omnibuses, road coaches, horses and carts and especially pedal cycles. Any person seen acting suspiciously whilst in charge or accompanying one of these vehicles should be questioned and his bona fides established. The Inspector should also arrange for a constable to be on duty at principal railway stations when the last two or three trains arrive at night to note what persons come off, and, where possible, the same constable should be at that railway station when the first two or three trains leave in the morning.

Reports

The reports submitted to the Inspector will be examined by him and he will see that they are written grammatically and concisely, before being submitted to the Superintendent. Special care must be taken in instructing Police Sergeants and constables in taking statements from witnesses in order that essential points are not overlooked. The Inspector will give his recommendation of the action to be taken and if proceedings are recommended the Inspector will quote the Act and Section or Byelaw.

Discipline

Every act of irregularity, neglect of duty, breach of discipline, slovenliness of person, or carelessness on the part of any Police Sergeant or constable coming to his notice must be reported to the Superintendent immediately. A certificate will be rendered weekly to the Superintendent that discipline has been maintained.

Books and Records

All books and records kept at Sectional Police Stations will be examined by the Inspector weekly who will see that they are kept in accordance with the Chief Constable's Orders. All books will be initialled and dated each time they are inspected. The pocket books and journals of the Police Sergeants and constables under his command will be examined and initialled by the Inspector in accordance with Force Orders.

Returns

It is the Inspector's duty to see that all returns required from himself and the police sergeants and constables in his section are submitted in accordance with the Chief Constable's Orders and the Orders given by the Divisional Superintendent.

Police Stations and Cottages

The Inspector will examine all Police Stations and Police Cottages in his section to see that they are kept clean and tidy, special attention must be paid to notice boards and in rural constables stations, to the approach to the cottage and garden. The Inspector will report on 31st March, 30th June, 30th September and 31st December, showing the results of the Inspection and if repairs are required, and whether such repairs are due to fair wear and tear or otherwise.

Uniform and Equipment

The Inspectors will see that the uniform clothing held in charge by the police sergeants and constables is cared for properly and only worn in accordance with the Chief Constable's Orders. Any infringement of the Orders or damage to clothing or equipment must be reported to the Superintendent immediately.

Knowledge of Men in Section

The Inspector will keep a record showing the following particulars regarding the Police Sergeants and constables in his section:- Name, age, length of service in Force, length of service at Station, married or single, number of children, education, ability, home attributes, and any other matters of interest.

Pay

The Inspector will certify that each Police Sergeant and Constable has received his pay by Friday in each week. If every member of these ranks has not received his pay on the date stated the reason will be given.

Sick List

The Inspector will arrange that all Police Sergeants and constables who are on the sick list in their cottages are visited weekly (except those suffering from an infectious disease, or when the doctor attending does not allow them to be visited) and that the men receive the pay and allowances due to them. A certificate will be rendered each Saturday to the Divisional Superintendent showing whether this Order has been complied with or explaining any case of non-compliance.

Drill and Instruction Classes

The Inspector will attend drill and instruction classes in order to advise and assist the police sergeants who are instructing or drilling. A rota of instruction classes will be prepared by the Superintendent and each police sergeant and Inspector will be given a subject for instruction in order that the lecturer can look up the subject and prepare his lecture.

Forthcoming Events

All forthcoming events will be reported to the Superintendent as soon as knowledge reaches the Inspector. The report must show whether or not extra Police will be required to deal with the event.

Dangerous Drugs

Inspections under the Dangerous Drugs Acts and Regulations will be carried out by Inspectors who will examine the registers and record of stock required to be kept by chemists and will report the results of his visits to the Superintendent. The Inspections are to be made quarterly and while he is carrying them out, the Inspector will wear plain clothes.

General

The foregoing instructions are not intended to be a complete list of the Inspectors duties, but to guide him in the more important matters which it is his duty to supervise and instruct the police sergeants and constables in his section. He will also be expected to take an intelligent interest in all matters connected with the working of the Force and to suggest to the Superintendent any improvements which may occur to him.

Discipline

On 4th July 1931 P.C. 195 Leonard Brown was fined 7/6d for Discreditable Conduct, "In that he did act in a manner likely to bring discredit on the reputation of the Hertford County Constabulary viz 'did smoke whilst on duty'."

ROWDY SCENES IN WATFORD STREETS.

Between the two world wars, a retraining centre for redundant Welsh miners was set up by the Government in Callowland, Watford. The setting up of the centre, occasioned much friction between the trainees and the young men of Watford, most of whom were also desperately looking for work. A young local lad was quoted as saying "When the Welshmen go we shall get jobs, why should they be trained for other work while we have to stay on the dole?" This would seem to have been the feelings of the majority. The feud began to grow. There were reports of fights between the two factions in various parts of the town. Rumours were spread, most patently untrue, but the tension grew. In January 1930, the rumours stated that a Watford lad had been set upon by the Welshmen and left in the street injured. This inflamed the locals and they banded together into gangs looking for the Welsh to avenge the attack. A week after the rumours started, two Welshmen were ducked in the pond. Three days later, things came to a head. Groups of locals roamed the High Street, there were odd fights, a shop window was broken, but the Police kept the youths moving and they moved into St. Albans Rd. There was a report of a fight in Clarendon Rd where a man was said to have been kicked as he lay on the ground. A Welshman was chased through the Churchyard, another suffered head injuries. The Welsh were later to state the odds were a hundred to six against them. The youths ambushed the six Welshmen and one James Rose was seriously assaulted, three men were arrested, Albert Grange, Frederick Stevens and George Plant, it was alleged that they had chased Rose, and when they caught him he was thrown to the ground and kicked about the head to the cries from the crowd of "Kill him". The three were all convicted of assault and sentenced to a term of hard labour.

On the evenings after this assault, extra Police were drafted in from throughout the County, allowing patrols of two's and three's, the Railway stations were placed under guard in case other gangs from nearby towns arrived for what was being described locally as "The Battle of Watford", but the battle never materialised. Although there were groups of youths congregating in the Town Centre the Police kept them moving and thereby broke up the impetus towards trouble. The situation gradually calmed down and there were no further problems.

Sergeant Herbert Allen Badcock appointed 1899 - Retired 1931

Merchant Taylor's School - Laying of Foundation Stone.

Their Royal Highnesses the Duke and Duchess of York will lay the foundation stone of the new building of Merchant Taylors' School at Sandy Lodge, Moor Park, Rickmansworth on the afternoon of Thursday 11th June 1931.

The detachment of the Hertford County Constabulary on duty will be under the command of Supt. E. Maskell "C" Division.

Out of the 28 officers on duty, "C" Division provided the following:-1 Superintendent, 1 Inspector, 2 Sergeants and 6 Constables.

The Hertfordshire (Good Rule and Government) Bye Laws 1930

1.) No person shall, with intent to cause any annoyance or inconvenience to any person in any place of entertainment to which the public are admitted with or without payment of money, throw or let off any firework, stink bomb, or similar article or squirt, spray or otherwise throw or scatter any offensive liquid, powder or substance in any such place aforesaid.

2.) Any person offending against the bye law shall be liable to a penalty not exceeding £5.

Telephone Directory - 1931

Watford King Street . Watford 38
Rickmansworth . Rickmansworth 163
Eastbury . Northwood 498
Chorleywood (Solesbridge Lane)
Chorleywood 224
Chorleywood (Capel Hamlet)
Chorleywood 320
Garston . Watford 121

Police Vehicles

The following vehicles were used as Police Vehicles in 1931.

Motor-cycle patrol in the St Albans district

Morris Oxford Six
Morris Isis
BSA Combination
BSA Solo
Invicta car
Morris Oxford Four

The first Hertfordshire Police traffic car, Morris saloon, index UR4197, with Constable Reginald Burgess

Use of Telephones

Telephone instruments are provided at Police Stations primarily to enable the public to communicate with the Police, and for the use of the Police on matters of urgency.

Superintendents will take steps to ensure that telephone calls are not made by Police unless there are grounds of urgency or a saving of expense will be affected.

Records of all calls made by the Police will be kept and forwarded to HQ together with the account for that particular installation at the end of each quarter. (S.O. No. 163, 1931)

Quarter Sessions Commendation

At the Quarter Sessions held at Hertford on Monday 4th January 1932, the Chairman, Sir Joseph Priestley K.C., said:-

"There is one thing I should like to say, Mr. Chief Constable, and that is that knowing as I do from reading the depositions so very closely as I had to in this case to discover the facts, this was one of the smartest pieces of detective work that I have known for a very long time. Shortly it was this, that because Johnson stated to the Police Officer when the motor accident occurred that he was with a man called Brown, and that he, Brown, was looking for some goods that he had buried, the Police Officer immediately put two and two together and thought it must be the man Brown who was in the habit of burying treasure which he had stolen. Thereupon they took Johnson to Harringay and went round to where Johnson supposed the house was where he with Brown had lived, and went inside and found the stolen goods there. After that they waited outside till Brown appeared that same evening when he was arrested. It was one of the smartest pieces of work that I have heard of for a very long time. I commend the officers for your proper consideration."

The officers concerned in the case were Inspectors' Bateman "C" Division and Camp "R" Division, Constables 317 White and 187 Farrow "C" Division. (Previously on 24.11.31 at the Watford Petty Sessions, the Chairman Henry Brown Esq., J.P. commended Constable Farrow for his action in arresting George Johnson on a charge of stealing a motor car from Piccadilly.)

The Chief Constable has much pleasure in endorsing the commendation. The action of the Police in this case resulted in the recovery of the whole of the stolen property to the value of £166, and also in the prisoner Brown being sentenced to 4 years Penal Servitude, and 5 years Preventive Detention.

(G.O. No.5, 1932)

Federation Meeting

At a meeting of the Constables Branch Board on 5.2.32, the following questions were tabled to the Chief Constable.

1. That the Chief Constable be asked that owing to the inconvenience caused to members of the motor patrol, in that their duties are not rostered in many instances until after the officers have booked off duty for the day, and which necessitates them attending the Police Station again to find out the times of their duty the following day, if the duties were arranged earlier, this inconvenience would be avoided.

The Chief Constable replied.

The Chief Constable understands that in each Division it is the practice except where the exigencies of the Service render such a course impracticable, for all rosters of motor patrol duties to be posted not later than 6 p.m. on the day preceeding that on which the duty is to be performed. This practice appears to be reasonable and equitable and has the approval of the Chief Constable.

2. That in view of Regulation 73 (3) IV of the Police Regulations of October 1st 1931, the Chief Constable is respectfully asked to consider the desireability of discontinuing the practice of officers being detailed to act as Stave Bearers to the Mayor and we consider this duty to be contrary to the present state of economy and to the efficiency of the Police Force.

The Chief Constable replied.

The Chief Constable has satisfied himself that no member of the Hertford County Constabulary is required to act as "Mayor's Attendant" as defined by the Police Regulations. (S.O. No. 30, 1932)

Hertfordshire (Good Rule and Management) Bye Laws 1931

1. No person shall in any street or public place, or in or in connection with any shop, business premises, or in any place which adjoins or is near to any street or public place, and to which the public are admitted, operate or cause or suffer to be operated, any wireless, loudspeaker, gramophone, amplifier or similar instrument, in such a manner as to cause annoyance to, or disturbance of occupants or inmates of any premises, or passengers.

2. Any person offending against the foregoing bye law shall be liable to a fine not exceeding £5. (S.O. No.38, 1932)

'C' or Watford Division Tug of War Team 1933
Winners Inter-Divisional Challenge Cup

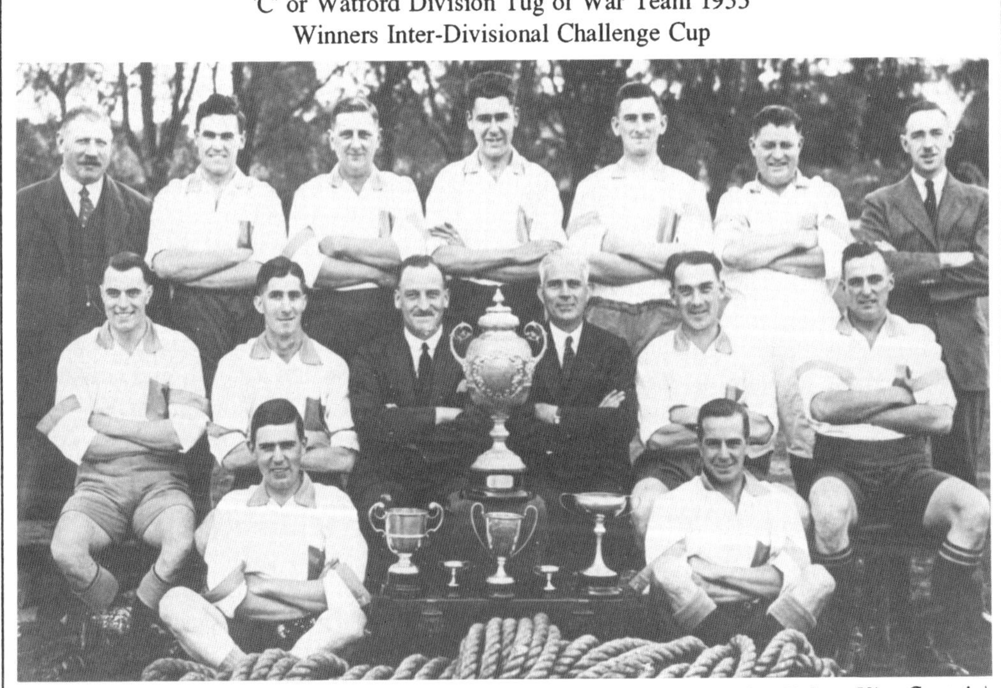

Sgt Emerton (Captain), Constables Philp, Hilton, Newlyn, Gray, Sgt Darton, Sgt Bishop (Vice-Captain)
Constables Oakley, Frewin, Supt. Sharp, Insp. Batchelor, Constables Dennis, Gay
Constables Dale, Goddard

No Sale

It has been agreed with the Secretary of State that in future no member of a Police Force will offer entertainment tickets for sale to motorists. No member of the Hertford County Constabulary will, therefore, stop any motorist on the highway for the purpose of endeavouring to effect the sale of tickets for the Hertfordshire Police Sports, or other entertainment in connection with the Police Force. (S.O. No. 77, 1932)

Commendation

At the Hertford County Petty Sessions held on Saturday 9th December 1933, the Chairman Major Barber, O.B.E., commended Constables 100 Martin and 163 Heath, "C" Division, stations Watford, for their action whilst on motor patrol, in apprehending Kenneth Ivor St. Clair Shorter and Robert Melvin on charges of stealing a motor car from Scotland and 21 fowls from Chapmore End, Ware, during the night of 3/4 th December 1933.

The reports in the case show the Constables were alert and attentive to their duty and acted with intelligence.

The Chief Constable has pleasure in endorsing the commendation and directs that an appropriate entry be made on the Officer's records of service. (G.O. No.143, 1933)

Discipline

Police Sergeant 96 Joseph Wallen "C" Division.

Neglect of duty:- Did, without good and sufficient cause, fail to attend the scene of alleged suicide reported to him at Watford on 4th March 1933.

Found Guilty and Reprimanded.
(G.O. No.29, 1933)

Federation Meeting

Constable's Branch Board Meeting held at Constabulary Headquarters, Hatfield, on 27th July 1934.

1. That the Chief Constable be respectfully asked to grant permission to the Motor Patrol Drivers to wear serge trousers in the Summer period, instead of breeches and gaiters, as these are very hot and uncomfortable during the hot weather, also a different type of cap with a larger peak, as the drivers complain of the sun getting in their eyes while driving.

Chief Constable's Note.

The Chief Constable has no objection to Motor Patrol Drivers wearing serge trousers during exceptionally hot weather, but breeches and gaiters will be worn normally.

Larger peaks to caps will be provided as and when new caps are issued.

2. That the Chief Constable be respectfully asked if the practice of calling upon the wife of any Police Officer, to search, and attend to female prisoners, can be abolished.

Chief Constable's Note.

The number of female prisoners detained in Police Stations of the various Divisions during the three years ended 31st July 1934, was:-

"A" Division	19
"B" Division	28
"D" Division	15
"E" Division	16

"C" Division not included since Women Constables are stationed there.

Having regard to the small number of prisoners, the Chief Constable cannot believe or ascertain that any hardship is occasioned by the present system. (G.O. No.100, 1934)

Discipline

On 26th January 1934.

Constable Frederick George Abbot Goddard 25 "C" Division.

Neglect of Duty.

1. Did fail without good and sufficient cause to work his beat in accordance with Orders.

2. Did without good and sufficient cause, leave his beat without permission or authority of a superior officer.

3. Did idle and gossip on duty at Watford on the 21st January 1934.

Found Guilty on all three charges and reduced two grades of pay, i.e., 4/- per week for six months from 26th January 1934 inclusive. (G.O. No.10, 1934)

Commendation

At the Herts Quarter Sessions, St. Albans, on 5th February 1934, Harold Sidney Greening and Jesse Gladstone Reeves were indicted on a charge of larceny of wireless parts at Watford during 1933.

At the conclusion of the case, His Honour Judge Sturges, K.C., commended Constable 132 Pomfrey "C" Division. for the manner in which he gave his evidence, remarking that he had given his evidence very well in a difficult case.

The Chief Constable has pleasure in endorsing the commendation and directs that an appropriate entry be made on his record of service. (G.O. No.13, 1934)

Commendation

By the Commissioner of Assize, Samuel Lowry Porter, Esq., K.C., at Herts Assizes on 18th June 1934.

Constable 352 Farnsworth, "C" Division, stationed at Chorleywood for his courage in attempting to arrest Victor Hugo on a charge of Housebreaking at Chorleywood, after he had been seriously assaulted by being struck with a jemmy.

The Commissioner remarked that Constable Farnsworth acted in a manner of which the Hertfordshire Police might well be proud.

The Chief Constable endorses the commendation and directs that an appropriate entry be made on the Constable's record of service.

Commendation

By A.W. Wiggs Esq, J.P., at Watford Petty Sessions on 11th December 1934.

Constable 132 William Pomfrey "C" Division, stationed at Watford, for his action in arresting Taliesin Evans on a charge of attempted murder at Watford.

The reports show that Constable Pomfrey acted with courage and intelligence, and the Chief Constable has pleasure in endorsing the commendation and directs that an appropriate entry be made on Constable Pomfrey's record of service.

Federation Meeting

Meeting of the Constable's Branch Board at Constabulary Headquarters on 25th January 1935.

Tours of Duty

That the Chief Constable's attention be respectfully drawn to the unsatisfactory position in which Officers of the "C" Division are placed, in that tours of duty are

Train Crash, (at the rear of the Railway Arms Pub) Lower Road, Kings Langley, 1935.

altered after the Officers have booked off duty for that day, that they have not been informed personally, and have been informed that they should attend their Sectional Station each night to ascertain what duty they are required to perform the next day, and we respectfully ask for this procedure to be altered owing to the interference that is caused to Officers who are on Rest Day etc.

Chief Constable's Note.

The Chief Constable has made enquiry in this matter, but has been unable to confirm that this is the practice in "C" Division. (G.O. No.29, 1935)

Commendation

At Watford Petty Sessions by Frederick Martin Esq., on 18th June 1935.

Constable 246 Gray, stationed at Croxley Green and Constable 25 Goddard stationed at Watford, for their action in arresting William Surridge and Harold Shaw, on a charge of stealing lead from a building in the course of erection.

The reports in this case show that Constable Gray acted intelligently and courageously, and Constable Goddard was alert and attentive to duty.

The Chief Constable has pleasure in endorsing the commendations and directs that appropriate entries be made on the two Constables' records of service. (G.O. No.83, 1935)

Obituary

The Chief Constable regrets to announce that Constable William Pomfrey, 132 "C" Division, died on 12th July 1935.
(G.O. No.91, 1935)

DEATH OF A WATFORD POLICEMAN

WATFORD OBSERVER

In the death of Police Constable Pomfrey aged 32, the Watford Division of the Hertfordshire Constabulary has lost a popular and able officer. He was admitted to the Peace Memorial Hospital a few weeks ago and passed away on Friday night the 12th July 1935, from meningitis. He joined the Herts. Constabulary in 1927, and was first stationed at Hitchin. He came to Watford the following year and has remained on the plain clothes staff here since. He received several commendations from the Watford Bench for bravery and smartness. Amongst the recent cases in which he had distinguished himself were the North Watford manslaughter case in which he succeeded in arresting Leslie David Harding, who is now serving sentence and the arrest on the live rails at Watford of the Irish Labourer who was accused of the attempted murder of his wife.

Police Constable Pomfrey was a good footballer, being centre half in his Division's team. He was also a smart boxer. The funeral service was held at St. James's Church, Watford on Tuesday 16th July, and the procession to the Vicarage Rd, Cemetery was headed by a contingent of police representing all the divisions in the County under Superintendent G. Sharp and Inspector Spicer, Sergeant Ellis and representatives of the "S" Division of the Metropolitan Police at Bushey were also present. Besides the immediate mourners those who attended included the Deputy Chief Constable (Supt. A.H. Randall) representing the Chief Constable (Mr G. Knight), ex-Superintendent King, and representatives of the County Constabulary Old Comrades Association, Mr. S.B. Manning (Chief Officer of the Watford Fire Brigade), Inspector Josling and a number of drivers and conductors of the old National Omnibus Company, of which Pc Pomfrey was at one time a conductor. Police Sergeant Bishop and Police Sergeant Mansfield with four other constables acted as pall bearers.

Conveyance of Prisoners

That the Chief Constable's attention be respectfully drawn to the fact that an officer of the "C" or Watford Division applying for a taxi fare for conveying a prisoner to the Remand Home, Battersea, this prisoner being one who had escaped from that Home previously, had been refused that application, and has been informed by the officer in charge of the office, that only taxi fares were paid for conveying prisoners to Pentonville Prison.

As there are no prisons specified in the Order 81/31 which governs the conveyance of prisoners, the Chief Constable is respectfully asked to give his ruling on this matter.

Chief Constables Note.

The Remand Home is not a prison. However, having regard to the character of the young person in this case, he is prepared to allow the charge of the conveyance by taxi cab on this occasion. In all future cases where a child or young person is to be conveyed to the Remand Home, the Divisional Superintendent will give instructions as to the route to be taken and the means of conveyance. (G.O. No.163, 1935)

Discipline

Constable 339 Thomas Oliver "C" Division.

Neglect of duty:- That is to say, did fail to make a necessary entry in the Guardroom Occurrence Book at King Street Police Station, Watford, of a report of a collision at Watford on Friday, 18th October, 1935.

Found Guilty and Reprimanded.

Hertfordshire County Council Act 1935

The Hertfordshire County Council Act of 1935 conferred upon Police the power to Stop, Search and take into custody any person who has in his possession or conveys in any manner anything which may be reasonably suspected of being stolen or unlawfully obtained.

The police fought long and hard to get this power, citing some of the reasons of the need for the powers the following cases.

On the 21st November 1932, Pc 68 Baker arrested Charles Medhurst, a labourer, of no fixed abode, who was in possession of a considerable quantity of clothing, in good condition, which he stated had been given to him by various persons, with whom he had casual employment. As it appeared impossible the clothing had been given to Medhurst, he was charged with stealing it from persons unknown, and at the same time great endeavour was made to trace the owners of the property. No further information was obtained and it could not be proved that Medhurst had stolen the property. On 29th November 1932, at Watford Petty Sessions the charges against him were dropped and consequently the clothing was returned to him.

On 15th June 1933, Pc 124 Dixon, arrested Ernest Beach, of Hayes, Middlesex, who was in possession of a Gents 'Royal Enfield' new bicycle. Beach produced what purported to be a receipt for the machine, but although the receipt was made out on the printed bill head of a firm at Hayes, it was written in a very illiterate style, in consequence of which, enquiries were made and the firm at Hayes denied the sale of the bicycle to Beach, but said he probably came into possession of one of their bill heads when he was in casual employment with them. Beach was charged with stealing the cycle from a person unknown, but as the owner could not be traced, he was discharged at the Watford Petty Sessions on 27th June 1933 and the cycle had to be returned to him.

On 9th December 1933, Pc 103 Shipgood arrested Molly Smith, age 56, of no fixed abode for being drunk and incapable on the public highway at Watford, she was in possession of a brand new pair of boy's boots, which she stated had been given her by some other person on the road. She was charged with stealing the boots from a person unknown, but as the owner could not be traced, the case against her was dismissed at Watford Petty Sessions on 12th December 1933 and the boots were returned to her.

On the 25th April 1935, at Croxley Green, a man named George Rhodes, of no fixed abode, sold 12 new good quality nickel plated dessert spoons in a cardboard box to a man for 1 shilling. Rhodes said he had found them on a dump in Portsmouth. From the appearance of the spoons and the box, this could not be correct and Rhodes was arrested. As the owner of the spoons could not be found, on 30th April 1935, the charge against Rhodes at the Watford Petty Sessions was dismissed.

One of the important constituents of the new power under Section 130 of the 1935 Act, was the fact that the onus of proof, lay with the defendant to prove that the items were not stolen. The power attracted a great deal of interest from other police forces in the country, and as late as 1948, the Rochdale Borough Police, wrote to the Chief Constable asking for details of the power in an effort to get the same powers conferred upon themselves.

His Late Majesty King George V.

As a mark of respect to his late Majesty, King George V, Superintendents and Inspectors of the Hertford County Constabulary, will wear a crepe armlet $3^{1}/_{4}$ inches wide, on the left sleeve of the great coat, or when that garment is not being worn, of the jacket, for a period of six months, ending 22nd July 1936. (G.O. No.9, 1936)

Proclamation of His Majesty King Edward VIII

Lieutenant Colonel W.H. Wild, D.S.O., High Sherriff of the County is charged with the proclamation in Hertfordshire and for this purpose will attend as follows:-

Friday 24th January 1936.

Town Hall,
Great Berkhamsted .... 1030 a.m.

Urban District Council Offices,
Rickmansworth .... 1145 a.m.

An escort of one Police Sergeant and 8 Police Constables will parade at the under-mentioned places at the time shown, where they will await the arrival of the High Sherriff and his party, and will then march in procession, four Constables on either side of the High Sherriff's cars to the place of proclamation, arriving at the time shown above.

St. Peter's Church,
Great Berkhamsted .... 1015 a.m.

The Picture House,
Rickmansworth .... 1130 a.m.

(The following day, the High Sherriff was to visit Hitchin, Letchworth, Bishops Stortford and Hoddesdon, where similar escorts were planned.)

The Divisional Superintendent concerned will be with the escort when the High Sherriff arrives and arrange for the order of procession.

Places of Proclamation

Superintendents will arrange for a suitable number of officers and men to be on duty at the place of proclamation in order that a clear space can be kept for the ceremony. He will also arrange for a suitable place to be kept for the High Sherriff's cars, so that after the ceremony they can return and pick up the High Sherriff and his party. (G.O. No.10, 1936)

Commendation
By the Chairman of Uxbridge Petty Sessions, on 20th December 1935.

Constable 151 Turner, "C" Division, stationed at Rickmansworth, for his action in arresting Alfred Lloyd and William Gillespie Kenny, at Mill End, Rickmansworth, on 5th December 1935, for robbery with violence at Harefield.

The reports in this case show that Constable Turner was alert and attentive to duty, and the Deputy Chief Constable has pleasure in endorsing the commendation and directs that an appropriate entry be made on Constable Turner's records of service. (G.O. No.12, 1936)

Discipline
Constable 219 John Boyle McDonald "C" Division.

1. Neglect of Duty:- That is to say did idle and gossip in St. Albans Road, Watford on Sunday 29th March 1936.

2. Failing to attend a Conference Point at Watford on Sunday 29th March 1936.

Found Guilty on both charges and reduced in pay from £4.6.0d to £4.4.0d per week for six months. (G.O. No.43, 1936)

Police Federation
Meeting of the Joint Branch Board, held at Constabulary Headquarters, 24th April 1936.

That the Chief Constable be respectfully asked if patrol cars can be fitted with two windscreen wipers (one for the observer) as at present he is useless as an observer when it is necessary for a windscreen wiper to be used.

Chief Constable's Note
This matter shall receive attention.

(G.O. No.70, 1936)

Police Federation
Joint Branch Board Meeting at Constabulary Headquarters on 16th October 1936.

That the Chief Constable's attention be respectfully drawn to a Divisional Order made in "C" or Watford Division, whereby officers are not allowed to leave their station without permission. It is respectfully pointed out that men who are stationed at Watford are prevented by the Order from taking a walk in the country, and we ask if the Chief Constable will give a ruling upon the matter.

Chief Constable's Note
The Divisional Instruction is based on the Standing Orders of the Force which are in accordance with the "Report of the Committee on the Police Service of England, Wales and Scotland" (Desborough Report).

The Chief Constable is unable to ascertain that any hardship is caused to members of the "C" or Watford Division, or that the Orders are improperly interpreted.

(G.O. No.130, 1936)

Discipline
Constable 234 George Halford Geary "C" Division.

Charge- Absent without leave from his station at Rickmansworth at 1145 p.m. on

2nd November 1936.

Found Guilty and fined 40/-

(G.O. No.135, 1936)

Discipline

Constable 264 Walter Ernest Rolph "C" Division.

Charge- Absent without leave from his station at Rickmansworth at 1145 p.m. on 2nd November 1936.

Found Guilty and Fined 40/-

(G.O. No.136, 1936)

Return of Found Property

At the Police Federation meeting of the Constable's Branch Board at Constabulary HQ, on 29th January 1937.

The Board asks that the Chief Constable's attention be drawn to the practice at present in operation of uniformed officers returning found property to finders. It is considered that the carrying of umbrellas, walking sticks etc., tends to lower the status of the Force, and we respectfully ask if this can be done by a plainclothes Constable".

The Chief Constable replied, " This matter is dealt with by Order 144 of 1926. The intention of the Order is that the property shall be claimed by the Finder. In cases where valuable property is concerned, the finder will be notified by the Superintendent that it is available for collection at a named Police Station. (G.O. No.33, 1937)

Coronation of their Majesties King George VI and Queen Elizabeth

The Chief Constable has much pleasure in announcing that the Standing Joint Committee has authorised the grant in 1937 to all members of the Hertford County Constabulary, in connection with the celebration of the Coronation, one day's leave with pay in addition to their ordinary leave and rest days. The Standing Joint Committee, in authorising this grant, have had regard to the fact that the Police will by the nature of their duty, be in the main, precluded from sharing in the benefit of the Public Holiday which has been appointed for Coronation Day (12th. May 1937) and that some addition to their normal duties may be expected both on that day and during the following fortnight. (G.O. No.50, 1937)

Cancelled Rest Days

Rest days will be cancelled for Tuesday 11th May and Wednesday 12th May 1937 for duty in connection with the Coronation Celebrations. (G.O. No.70, 1937)

Police Federation

Meeting of the Joint Branch Board at Constabulary HQ on 23rd April 1937.

The Board asks, "That the Chief Constables attention is brought to the procedure at present with regard to stray dogs brought to the home of an out-station Officer by a member of the public. The dogs are brought to his home at all times of the day, and often when he is out. At the majority of out-station cottages, there is no convenience whatever for taking in stray dogs, and when taken in, considerable damage is done, a mess made, and they are a danger to the children of the Constable. In most cases, they have to be placed in the Constable's garden.

The Chief Constable replied that when a dog was taken in, either he or if absent, his wife would telephone the Superintendent for instructions as to the dogs disposal. The

Superintendents will make provision to ensure that stray dogs are conveyed to the nearest Police Station with provision for the keeping of stray dogs. (G.O. No.83, 1937)

Pay of Superintendents and Inspectors

On and after 1st July 1937, the pay of Superintendents and Inspectors of the Hertford County Constabulary will be as follows:-

Superintendents

On appointment £430 per annum
After 1 year £447.10.0d per annum
After 2 years £465 per annum
After 3 years £482.10.0d per annum
After 4 years £500 per annum
* After 5 years £520 per annum
* After 6 years £540 per annum

* These scales apply only to the Superintendent and Chief Clerk at Headquarters, and the two Superintendents at the two larger Divisions. (This included Watford)

Inspectors

On appointment £320 per annum
After 1 year £330 per annum
After 2 years £340 per annum
After 3 years £350 per annum
After 4 years £360 per annum

(G.O. No.110, 1937)

Commendation

By the Chairman of the Herts Quarter Sessions, Sir Joseph Priestley, K.C., D.L., at the adjourned hearing at Hertford on 12th January 1937.

Sergeant 83 Paton and Constable 151 Turner, "C" Division, stationed at Rickmansworth and West Hyde respectively, for their action in arresting Jack Reeve, Percy Vickers and John William Edward Irving on a charge against the Larceny Act 1916, Section 16-Storebreaking-and Charles Edwin Chatwin, John William Canvin, George James Canvin and Edward Thomas Canvin, on a charge against the Larceny Act 1916, Section 33- Receiving Stolen Property.

Sir Joseph said, "Through the patience and perseverance of Sergeant Paton and Constable Turner, this very gross theft has been brought to justice."

The Chief Constable has pleasure in endorsing the Commendation and directs that appropriate entries be made on Sergeant Paton's and Constable Turner's records of service. (G.O. No.10, 1937)

Commendation

By the Chairman of Watford Petty Sessions, A.W. Wiggs, Esq., on 14th January 1937.

Constable 68 Baker, "C" Division, stationed at Watford, for his action in arresting Herbert Trumper on a charge against the Larceny Act 1916, Section 2 (Fowl Stealing).

The Chairman said. "The Bench wish to congratulate you very highly on the way you have taken this case in hand and arrested this man."

The Chief Constable has pleasure in endorsing the commendation and directs that an appropriate entry be made on Constable Baker's record of service. (G.O. No.11, 1937)

Appointment

Superintendent Abel Camp, "C" Division is appointed Deputy Chief Constable with effect from 19th February 1937, subject to the approval of the Standing Joint Committee which will be applied for on 2nd April 1937. (G.O. No.22, 1937)

Discipline

Probationer Constable 279 Bert John Heydon "C" Division.

1. Neglect of duty - Did fail to work his beat in accordance with orders by omitting to attend his 12.30 a.m. Conference Point at Watford, on 6th July 1938.

2. Discreditable Conduct - Did smoke whilst on uniform patrol duty at Watford on 6th July 1938 at 1.30 a.m.

Found Guilty to both Charges. Not likely to become an efficient and well conducted Constable. Services dispensed with as from 21st July 1938. (G.O. No.111, 1938)

Commendation

By the Chairman of the Watford Petty Sessions, David Blackley Esq., on 13th October 1938.

Constable 244 Dear, "C" Division, stationed at Watford for his action in affecting the arrest of Dennis Turner and Brian Irvin Bishop, on several charges of larceny from dwelling houses at Croxley Green.

The Chairman said, "The Officer in the case has done a smart piece of work, not the least valuable part of it is the opportunity it gives these lads to make good. He has probably been their best friend. It was a very fine piece of work and we feel the detection is worthy of commendation."

The Chief Constable has pleasure in endorsing the commendation and directs that an appropriate entry be made on the Constable's records of service. (G.O. No.167, 1938)

Commendation

By the Chairman of Watford Petty Sessions, David Blackley, Esq., on the 10th January 1939.

Constable 273 Hills, "C" Division, stationed at Watford, for his in arresting whilst off duty, George Stanley Blythe and Peter Nea on a charge of being found on enclosed premises under the Vagrancy Act 1824.

The Chairman said, "We appreciate the smart way in which your officer acted. It is proof that a policeman is never off duty. He gave his evidence very intelligently and we are satisfied it was true."

The Chief Constable has pleasure in endorsing the commendation and directs that an appropriate entry be made on the Constable's record of service. (G.O. No.9, 1939)

Commendation

On Saturday 9th December 1939, Constable 259 Cresswell, "C" Division, stationed at King Street, Watford, was driving the Police patrol car, when he saw a motor car being driven from St.Albans towards Rickmansworth in an erratic manner. Constable Cresswell, with some difficulty, stopped this vehicle and arrested the driver, William John Upson, who was later charged with being under the influence of drink whilst in charge of the motor vehicle and also with stealing the car. Percy George William Saunders, a passenger in the car was also arrested.

At watford Petty Sessions on 14th December 1939, the Chairman of the Bench, David Blackley, Esq, J.P., said at the conclusion of the case, " We feel that Pc Cresswell did a very good piece of work. It was very difficult. Under difficult circumstances he seems to have kept a clear head and avoided trouble which might easily have come. We appreciate his action and the way he carried out his work very much".

The Chief Constable has pleasure in endorsing the commendation and directs that an appropriate entry be made in the Constable's records of service. (G.O. No.243, 1939)

Fingerprintes

In accordance with the recommendation of the Departmental Committee on Detective Work and Procedure, it has been decided to keep at Headquarters a complete record of the fingerprints of each member of the Hertford County Constabulary.

Superintendents will arrange for all members of their respective Divisions to be fingerprinted as early as possible, and for the forms to be forwarded to Headquarters, for record purposes. (G.O. No.93, 1939)

Commendation

At Watford Petty Sessions on the 8th August 1939, the Chairman of the Bench A.W. Weeks Esq., J.P., commended Constable 151 Turner of "C" Division, stationed at Rickmansworth, for his action in effecting the arrest of John Henry Snelling, 7 Chambers Lane, Willesden, N.W.10, on a charge of being in possession of housebreaking implements by day and attempted housebreaking at Moor Park. A considerable quantity of stolen property was found at Snelling's address which connected him with ten cases of housebreaking in the County.

At the Conclusion of the case at the Petty Sessions, the Chairman said, "The Bench wish me to compliment you on the smart way you have dealt with this case and I hope our commendation will be sent to the Chief Constable. If it had not been for your smartness, the prisoner would not have been here today".

The Chief Constable endorses the commendation and directs that an appropriate entry be made in the Constable's records of service. (G.O. No.163, 1939)

Armistice Day

The Secretary of State has been approached by the British Legion on the question of allowing Police in uniform to wear a poppy on Armistice Day. The question has been considered on several occasions in the past but the view has been taken that it would not be appropriate to permit Police in uniform to wear any emblem. This year however, the Army Council have modified King's Regulations so as to permit the wearing of the Haig poppy by all ranks when on duty, provided that when so worn it is of reasonable dimensions and since similar action will be taken with regard to the other fighting Services, it is considered appropriate to give similar permission in the case of the Police.

This conclusion has been reached in view of the special significance of the Haig poppy and no similar relaxation will be made in the case of any other collection.

Superintendents will ensure that all members of their respective Divisions are aware of the above permission and that only poppies of resonable size are worn, in the left hand jacket pocket, and second or third buttonhole of the greatcoat. (G.O. No.186, 1939)

Discipline

War Reserve Constable 35 Herbert James Smith.

Neglect of duty

That is to say whilst on duty at a vulnerable point at the Electric Power Station, Cardiff Rd, Watford, was found asleep at 0515 hours on 23rd April 1940.

Found Guilty and Required to resign as an alternative to dismissal. (G.O. No.108, 1940)

Commendation

On Saturday 16th March 1940, Constable 45 West stationed at St.Albans Rd, Watford, received a report from a shopkeeper in Bedford Rd, Watford that just previously a small boy had entered his shop, rifled the till and had ridden away on a cycle.

The Constable made enquiries at 2 Middle Way, Watford, in order to interrogate Edmund Percy William Atkins, aged 9 years, but found that the boy was not at home. After searching the district, Constable West traced the boy and found in his possession the 10 £1 notes he had stolen from the shop.

At Watford Juvenile Court on the 19th April 1940, Atkins was ordered to be sent to an approved school for this offence.

The reports in the case show that the Constable diligently followed up the little information at his disposal, making good use of his knowledge of local juvenile thieves. The Chief Constable has much pleasure in commending Constable West on his perseverance and directs that an appropriate entry be made in the Constable's Record of Service. (G.O. No.88, 1940)

Dismissal

On 23rd March 1940, Police Constable 278 Hodgkins, "C" Division, was arrested and charged with one case of shopbreaking and one case of officebreaking at Watford between 30th January and 12th March 1940.

At the Herts. Quarter Sessions held at St.Albans on 1st April 1940, Constable Hodgkins was convicted and sentenced to 18 months imprisonment.

Constable Hodgkins is dismissed the service as from 23rd March 1940. (G.O. No.66, 1940)

Discipline

War Reserve Constable A.S.Ward, "C" Division

Discreditable Conduct

That is to say, whilst on duty at the Grid Electricity Station at Hollywell Farm, Watford, during the night of 1/2 April 1940, did write and exhibit indecent and obscene writings at the said Electricity Station.

Found Guilty and dismissed the Force. (G.O. No.64, 1940)

Parachute Landings

The Air Ministry, fear that with the extensive measures being taken to deal with the threat of an enemy parachute landing, there is a danger that Royal Air Force or Allied Airmen who may be in distress and forced to take to their parachutes may be attacked or not receive immediate aid that they need. The Air Ministry have therefore requested that the following points be brought to the notice of the members of the Force.

1. It must be borne in mind that parachutists may be divided into two classes: (a) those in distress and (b) armed invaders intent on destruction.

2. In cases of parachute descent through distress the aircraft from which the crews are escaping by parachute will probably be seen to crash in the vicinity.

3. As some aircraft of the R.A.F. now carry crews of six men it must not be assumed that because there are six parachutists coming down together they are necessarily enemies. Any number greater than six should be regarded as probably enemy.

4. Airmen landing by parachute in distress or crews of crashed aircraft may include British, Allied or enemy personnel, and immediate first aid should be rendered, if necessary in any such case. (G.O. No.143, 1940 - 5.6.40)

Dress and General Appearance

It has come to notice that Officers have been on duty in Police Stations in their shirt sleeves and without a collar and tie. General Order No 4 of 1927 is republished for the information of all members of the Force, and will be strictly complied with.

"When visiting the cottages of various members of the Force the Chief Constable that the door is answered sometimes by the Constable appearing in his shirt sleeves and without neckdress. The Chief Constable understands that in some cases the Constable may have been working in his garden or otherwise engaged in some form of manual labour, but he desires to impress on every member the individual responsibility for maintaining the credit of the Force to which he belongs. Except in cases of extreme urgency, where immediate action is demanded in the public interest, a Constable should always put on his coat and make himself presentable before answering the door, whether to the Chief Constable, a superior officer or a member of the public.

The Chief Constable regrets that he has also seen members of the Force unshaven quite late in the day. It appears to be thought by some members that the necessity for shaving arises only when about to go on duty. This view lowers the the dignity of the Force, the proper time for shaving and cleansing is immediately after arising from bed at whatever hour. It is hoped that further references to this subject will be unnecessary and that in future the upholding of the good name and dignity of the Force will be the first consideration of those members who hitherto appear to have failed to grasp the importance of a clean and well turned out appearance on all occasions.

The Chief Constable regrets also to have to place on record that he has seen instances where the provisions of Order 138 of 1925, regarding the prohibition of the wearing of part uniform and part plain clothes, have been disobeyed. When uniform trousers are worn, a uniform jacket must be worn also, and when other trousers are worn an ordinary jacket must be used and vice versa. (G.O. No.14, 1940)

Commendation

On Saturday 9th March 1940, Special Constable 260 William Sharman, stationed at Hemel Hempstead, was in Queen's Rd, Watford, when he saw a man come out of a tobacconist's shop, carrying a box under his arm.

This man when stopped by the proprietor of the shop, dropped the box and ran away. The Special Constable immediately mounted his cycle and followed the man, and after a chase which lasted some time, Special Constable Sharman succeeded in capturing him.

At Watford Petty Sessions, on the 14th March 1940, the thief William Slater, was convicted and sentenced to six months imprisonment. At the conclusion of the case, the Chairman, David Blackley, Esq, said to Special Constable Sharman, "You are new to the work but you seem to habe a flair for it. You were persistent and stuck it out and got your man. We feel it is up to us to say 'Thank You' ".

The Chief Constable has much pleasure in endorsing the commendation and directs that an appropriate entry be made in the Special Constable's Record of Service. (G.O. No.51, 1940)

Police Federation

Meeting of the Joint Branch Board at Constabulary HQ on 26.4.40.

Replacement of Uniform Boots

The Chief Constable stated that applications for the replacement of uniform boots are dealt with when supplies become available. All ranks will realise that owing to the necessity of supplying the fighting services, some delay must be occasioned in deliveries, but it is hoped that matters will improve. All members of the Force are in possession of 3 pairs of boots.

Housing Conditions

Responding to a complaint on the Standards of Police Housing, the Chief Constable commented, " It has always been the desire of the Chief Constable to see all members of the Force properly and correctly housed. The Chief Constable has no knowledge that any house occupied by a member of the Force has been condemned, but if one has, then if he is given all details he will make full enquiry. (G.O. No.118, 1940)

Commendation

On Friday 12th April 1940, as a result of extensive enquiries, Constable 190 Wright and Constable 323 Springham, "C" Division, stationed at Watford arrested Stanley Reginald Braithwaite, aged 18 years, Kenneth Leonard Bowden, aged 24 years and Ernest James Collins aged 25 years, all of Watford, for the larceny of two cycles at Watford.

Property subsequently found in their possession connected them with a shopbreaking in Market Street, Watford the same day, and further enquiries showed that they were responsible for 55 cases of larceny cycles and officebreaking.

At the Herts Quarter Sessions on 20th May 1940, Braithwaite was placed on probation for three years and Bowden and Collins were both sentenced to nine months imprisonment.

At the Conclusion of the case, Mr.Seaton prosecuting, said, addressing the Chairman Mr.G.B.McClure "I do not know whether you, Sir, have any views with regard to the conduct of the two Police Officers in the case. I understand it was due to very patient enquiry on their part that there were brought to justice these three men for stealing bicycles".

The Chairman said "I think the Police have behaved with great skill and patience in the matter. It is the view of the Court that they have acted very well indeed in the matter of getting this thing stopped so quickly".

The Chief Constable has much pleasure in endorsing the commendation and directs that appropriate entries be made in the Constables' Records of Service. (G.O. No.120, 1940)

Wireless Receivers in Road Vehicles

On the 29th May 1940, The Defence Regulations of 1939 were amended under Regulation 8, making the following an offence.

"No person shall use or have in his possession or under his control any wireless receiving apparatus installed in any road vehicle".

For the purpose of the Act, any wireless receiving apparatus shall, notwithstanding that it is not fixed in position, be deemed to be installed if it is in a vehicle in circumstances in which it can be used or readily adapted for use.

A press release to the public called on all persons having such equipment to take immediate steps to remove them including aerials, not later than on Sunday 2nd June 1940, whether the vehicle is at present in use or is laid up.

The Regulation gave Police the Power to disable and remove any such apparatus found.

Publication of Disturbing Rumours

A new Defence Regulation has been made in the following terms.

39BA. Any person who publishes any report or statement relating to matters connected with the war which is likely to cause alarm or despondency shall be liable on summary conviction to imprisonment for a term not exceeding 1 month or to a fine not exceeding £50 or to both such imprisonment and such fine.

A prosecution in respect of an offence against this regulation shall not be instituted by a Constable. (G.O. No.157, 1940)

Fire Precautions - Clearence of Lofts

Defence Regulation 27 (Para.2)-
Requires all occupiers of dwelling houses to clear and keep clear of all articles any loft which is not used or furnished for use for human habitation. The term dwelling house will include flats, hotels, other residential buildings and hospitals.

In the event of a fire due to an incendiary bomb in the roof of a dwelling house the extinction of the fire should not be impeded by the storage of articles, whether inflammable or not. Accordingly, the Order requires ALL articles to be removed and not merely those which are flammable.

Under the terms of the Order, the Local Authority is empowered to authorise any officer or servant of the Council to enter and inspect premises to which the Order applies for the purpose of seeing whether the Order has been complied with. (G.O. No.205, 1940)

Discreditable Conduct

War Reserve Constable 129 Floyd.

That is to say on 6th August 1940 was found asleep whilst on duty at the Grid Electricity Station, Hollywell Farm, Watford at 0315 hours.

Found Guilty and required to resign as an alternative to dismissal.

War Reserve Constable 28 John Edward Rogers.

That is to say on 25th July 1940 was found by Police Sergeant 36 Newnham to be sitting in a chair in the roadway adjoining Hollywell Farm Power Station, Watford, reading a newspaper and smoking a pipe at 1555 hours, wheras he should have been patrolling the Power Station in accordance with orders.

Found Guilty and required to resign as an alternative to dismissal.

Police Constable 285 Arthur Ronald Hendy

That is to say was found asleep on duty at King Street Police Station, Watford at 0420 hours on 17th August 1940.

Found Guilty and Severely Reprimanded. (G.O. No.241, 1940)

The Downfall of Constable Baulk

One order relates to the discipline of Police Constable 21 Douglas Victor Baulk. Constable Baulks personal file is still at HQ and shows he joined the force in 1927 and had one commendation for arresting and disarming a man armed with a knife. However, his early promise began to wane from the report made in 1932 by his Superintendent suggesting he be made up to a Constable 1st Class thereby warranting an extra 10 shs a week, in which he described him as a zealous and enthusiastic officer popular with his colleagues.

On 21.7.39 he was cautioned at a Disciplinary Hearing for failing to keep a point whilst on duty in D Division. He was also transferred to B Division.

In 1941, his pay was reduced from £4.10.0 to £4 per week for associating with undesirables and entering licensed premises other than in the execution of his duty.(This related to an off duty period).

He also appeared before a hearing on a charge that he was not at home whilst sick and had failed to notify the Chief Constable of his whereabouts. This related to his convalescence from appendicitis, when on reaching his home found his landlady to be suffering from influenza, so he went to his parents home in Hitchin. His explanation in this case was accepted and he was warned that in future he should get permission from the Chief Constable BEFORE acting.

The following report was submitted by Superintendent A. Saunders to the Chief Constable which resulted in Pc Baulks next Disciplinary Hearing.

Sir,
I respectfully report that at 0528 hrs on Saturday 19th April 1941, I entered Harpenden Police Station. I there saw the following officers:

1. Constable 301 Betts
2. Constable 21 Baulk
3. Constable 59 Barnard

Constable Betts was performing Station Reserve Duty.

Constable Baulk was seated at the table with his helmet off and talking to Constable Barnard who was leaning on the table.

I said to Constable Baulk " What are you doing here?" He said " I have just made a 5 o'clock point at Cooters End and have called in here. I have only been here a minute or so."

I said to the Constable " Get out on your beat."

On this date, the Constable was detailed for the following duty 0200-0600 hrs. With the following points to make.

0300 Ayres End Lane

0400 Harpendenbury

0515 Cooters End Lane (1 mile from Police Station)

Signed A.Saunders Superintendent

Subsequently, Constable Baulk appeared before the Chief Constable on the following Charges.

1. Neglect of duty.- that is to say did fail to work his beat in accordance with orders, that is to say did not attend at 0515 Conference Point at Cooters End Lane, Harpenden, on 19th April 1941 and remain there for 15 minutes.

2. Neglect of duty.- that is to say did idle

and gossip whilst on duty at Harpenden Police Station at 0528 hrs on 19th April 1941.

Plea- Not Guilty
Finding- Guilty

Award- Ordered to Resign as an alternative to dismissal.

Criminal Investigation Department

The Criminal Investigation Department of this County will consist of the following Officers :-

"R" Division.
Superintendent Reeves (In charge)
Sergeant 257 Elwell
(Photography and Records)
Constable 19 Harries

"A" Division.
Bishops Stortford
Acting Sergeant 31 Hall

"B" Division.
Hertford
Acting Sergeant 3 Armitage
Welwyn Garden City
Constable 103 Shipgood

"C" Division.
Watford
Inspector Calcutt
Sergeant 176 Murphy
Constable 151 Turner
Constable 18 Wood
Constable 74 Charles
Constable 244 Dear

"D" Division.
Hemel Hempstead
Sergeant 180 Flower
Constable 97 Kiteley

"E" Division.
Hitchin
Sergeant 252 Perkins
Constable 208 Lawrence
Letchworth
Constable 318 Yeates

(G.O. No.24 1941)

Use of Pilot Balloons at Night

Information has been recieved that small pilot balloons are being used by the Royal Air Force. These balloons carry small candle lanterns which at a distance of a few hundred feet look to the naked eye like a not very bright star, and are used for determining the height of clouds. The public may on seeing these lights report them as suspicious lights. This Information is published in order that all officers may be aware of these circumstances. The information must be treated as strictly confidential by all ranks. (S.O. No.78, 1941)

Crop Wastage

Defence Regulation 62 D. - provides that if the crop harvested from any agricultural land is damaged or goes to waste as the result of any failure or delay by the occupier of the land in taking such steps as are reasonable to keep the crop in good condition, the occupier shall be guilty of an offence and shall on summary conviction be liable to a fine not exceeding £50. (S.O. No.101, 1941)

Voluntary Exchange Between Forces

The Secretary of State has had under consideration the question of whether it is practicable to make arrangements to provide relief for members of the Police Forces in areas which have been subjected to heavy air raiding, where the strain of continued air attack may have an adverse effect upon the health of a proportion of the men. Where this produces actual illness the necessary medical treatment should of course be provided, but in the majority of cases all that is required is a change to a quieter environment.

There would as a rule, be no justification in giving men leave for this purpose, and the most practicable method of achieving the desired result would seem to be exchanges of men between forces in heavily bombed and quieter areas. A successful experiment of this kind has already been made by the Southampton and Exeter Police Authorities, and, since such a scheme not only gives forces in quiet areas an opportunity of helping others which are more heavily pressed, but may also provide valuable experience, the Home Secretary hopes that the Police Authorities will be prepared to co-operate in arrangements of this kind where they may be found necessary.

1. Only volunteers will be exchanged.

2. The period of exchange will be a matter of mutual arrangement, but ordinarily will not exceed a month.

(S.O. No.105, 1941)

Commendation

On 25.3.41 War Reserve Constable 34 Smith, saw Frank Mann a previously convicted felon acting in a suspicious manner in the High Street, Watford. He kept him under observation until he was satisfied that he was loitering for an unlawful purpose. He was thereupon arrested for 'Loitering with intent to commit a felony' under the Vagrancy Act of 1824. At the conclusion of the case at Watford Petty Sessions on 1.4.41, the Chairman W.A. Wiggs Esq. addressed the War Reserve Constable and said "My colleagues and I wish to commend you for the smart action you have taken, especially coming from a War Reserve, as we expect it from the Regular Police, your action was very highly commendable".

Enemy Aircraft Crashes

Officers are reminded of the importance of ensuring that the Police do all they can to prevent members of the public from taking away souvenirs from crashed enemy aircraft or tampering with them in any way. Cases have occurred recently in which instrument labels were removed before the arrival of the RAF Intelligence officer and valuable information was thereby lost. (S.O. No.115, 1941)

Safety precautions in the vicinity of an unexploded mine

Parachute mines are liable to detonate magnetically or through vibration. To obviate the former risk, small steel or iron tools, shovels, hammers, chisels, screwdrivers and steel helmets should not be brought within 4 or 5 yards of a mine. If a mine falls in water, it may become active as a magnetic mine.

The risk of detonation through vibration is a serious one. The explosion of a mine depends upon the action of a clock work fuse which may be interrupted when a mine is falling or as it comes to land. Very slight vibration may set the fuse going again. In this respect, mines differ fundamentally from bombs, and this fact accounts for the special precautions necessary in the case of mines and for the great importance of enforcing them strictly. It should be remembered that it is not sufficient to evacuate an area; all entrances to the cleared area must also be stopped with barriers and guards.

The explosive effect of mines is very much

greater than that of bombs. The blast of a mine may break windows up to a distance of 800 yards and has had marked effects at even greater distance. The risk of detonation of a mine is particularly great when the naval parties are dealing with it.

A parachute mine which has been rendered safe for transportation is still dangerous to handle and interference with it must be prevented. The mine may contain booby traps and contact with the Hexanite filling, parts of which may be on the mine case (and on parts of exploded mines) causes a painful skin disease (Dermatitis). (Note to cure Dermatitis apply UNNA paste, obtainable at all chemists.)

An explosion may be caused when the mine is burnt out or it may be necessary to explode the mine in situ (Counter mining). The choice of the method of disposal of an unexploded parachute mine rests with the Naval Officer in charge of disposal. He will inform a Senior Police Officer before burning out or countermining a mine.

The Police are responsible for enforcing safety precautions in the vicinity of all unexploded missiles, and assistance should be given to them wherever possible by the wardens service, who should if they arrive first on the scene take the necessary steps themselves to put the precautions into force.

The following rules for safety precautions in the case of unexploded parachute mines must be strictly observed.

1. All buildings including industrial premises within 400 yards of the mine must be evacuated, except that where the mine is masked by strong steel framed concrete buildings the distance may be reduced to 300 yds.

2. All traffic, including pedestrians, bicycles and horse drawn vehicles, must be stopped by a physical barrier at not less than 400 yds from the mine except where the mine is masked as at 1. where the distance is reduced to 300 yds as before.\

This rule applies also to Rail Traffic and to vehicles of the Armed Forces.

The Naval Officer in charge of the R.M.S. Party will always be prepared on his arrival, to consider whether in the special circumstances of the case, an exception can be made to this rule: but the Police should not, themselves, take the responsibility of allowing an exception. In particularly urgent cases, a telephone call can be put through to the Admiralty.

3. Fire fighting, rescue work and first aid will be allowed to continue where necessary within the area evacuated. The Naval Officer in charge of the R.M.S. party will decide after consultation with the responsible civil authorities whether in particular circumstances he will be justified attempting to render the mine safe. In no cases may fire pumps be operated within 200 yards of the mine while the naval party is at work.

4. No stakes are to be driven into the ground (e.g. for the purpose of making barriers) within 300 yds of a mine.

5. If a mine falls in water the water level must not be lowered without the approval of a naval officer of the R.M.S.

6. When a mine has been rendered safe for transportation, a barrier must be erected around it to prevent people touching it.

Commendation

On 11.4.41, Constable 151 Turner stationed at Watford was examining shop premises in the High Street, Watford when he found a man at the rear of a block of shops.

Not being satisfied with the mans explanation, the constable took him to Clarendon Rd Police Station, where he was found to be in possession of cigarrette lighters stolen on 2.4.41 from a shop in Watford.

At the Herts Quarter Sessions, Hertford on 19th May 1941, John Wright alias Blaney appeared on 4 charges of shop-breaking and larceny and was sentenced to 9 months hard labour.

The attention to property given by the constable and his zealous pursuit of his duty was primarily responsible for the satisfactory clearing up of these shop-breakings and the Chief Constable has pleasure in directing that an appropriate entry be made in Constable Turner's records of service. (S.O. No.154, 1941)

Commendation

On the 14th May 1941, a report was received at Rickmansworth Police Station that a bicycle had been stolen from Harefield, Middlesex in the Metropolitan Police District.

Five days later, Constable 239 Frewin, stationed at Rickmansworth, was on duty at West Hyde, when he saw a boy riding a bicycle which appeared to answer the description of the stolen machine. The boy gave a plausible reason for his possession of the cycle, but Constable Frewin. not being satisfied with his explanation, made further enquiries and found that the machine in question, was the stolen one.

At Uxbridge Juvenile Court on the 22nd May 1941, Ronald Harvey PEAKS was bound over in the sum of £1 and placed under the supervision of the Probation Officer for 12 months.

The zeal and praiseworthy action of the Constable has been brought to the notice of the Chief Constable by the Commissioner of Police of the Metropolis and an appropriate entry will be made in Constable Frewin's record of service. (G.O. No.194, 1941)

Employment of wives of police officers

The Secretary of State has considered the position of Police Officer's wives who have to register under the Registration for Employment Order. He has decided that there can be no exemption for Policemen's wives generally being exempted from the operation of the Order, but it is recognised that, particularly in rural districts, policemen's wives are often rendering a valuable service to the Police Force, and that in such cases it would not be in the Nation's interest that she should be required to take outside employment. In cases where the wife of a Police Officer has a specific obligation in connection with the Force, e.g. where she occupies a Police House which is also a Police Station and has to attend to Police matters in the absence of her husband, she should take with her to any selection interview a memorandum from the Chief Constable or a Senior Police Officer stating that it would be detrimental to the efficiency of the Force if she were required to gain employment. If this is done, no further steps will in the absence of special circumstances be taken to place her in employment. (G.O. No.218, 1941)

Incendiary Leaves

The Minister of Home Security reports that the enemy may use 'incendiary leaves' for the purpose of setting fire to woods and forests, heathlands, stubble and growing crops. Therefore all members of the Force should learn how to recognise these 'leaves', and how to render them harmless.

The leaves, are wet when dropped, and as soon as drying is completed, they burst into flame. The time of burning is from 8 to 10 minutes. If dropped at night, they do not ignite until the dew has evaporated the next morning. They may be in the form of a sandwich of celluloid wafers, with one or more holes in the centre or at the corners, while others may be in the form of a single celluloid wafer with a phosphorous disc fastened to it. The wafers may be 4" square, 4" x 1", 2" square or other shapes and sizes. Any such objects in fields should be regarded with suspicion and children especially should be warned against touching or moving them.

An individual leaf, can be easily extinguished, but large numbers may be dropped together, and the resultant fires may consequently prove difficult to control. It is therefore desirable that they should be detected early in the morning when they are still wet and removed to a place where they can burn harmlessly. They should not be touched with the bare hand. Farm workers and others who are about early in the morning should keep a sharp lookout for these leaves.

The leaves, can be kept under water with safety, and wetting will delay their bursting into flame. (G.O. No.240, 1941)

Commendation

At 2345 hours on the 23rd September 1941, Constable 193 Wood stationed at Watford, saw a youth at the side of the Gaumont Cinema, Watford. The youth was questioned and he produced a ration book in the name of McLennan, but the Constable was not satisfied as to his identity. He searched him and found in his possession two pairs of pliers, a spanner, three keys and an electric torch.

Constable Wood arrested the youth and it was found that his correct name was Norman Harry Price and that he had escaped from an Approved School. Price admitted two cases of Larceny from gas meters in this district and three cases of housebreaking in the Metropolitan Police District.

At Watford Juvenile Court on the 3rd October 1941, the Chairman A.W.Wiggs Esq, J.P., said to Constable Wood " I think you acted very intelligently indeed and I trust the Superintendent will pass this commendation of the Bench to the Chief Constable". (G.O. No.308, 1941)

Discreditable Conduct

Police Constable Frederick Henry Osborne 284 "C" Division

That is to say, did break open a wooden box by removing padlock, containing tools, the property of Constable 124 Dixon, and take there from a towing chain for the purpose of towing an abandoned car at Watford on 7th December 1941.

Found Guilty, Severely Reprimanded and taken off Motor Patrol and returned to Street Duty.

Police Constable Hubert Walter Dixon 124 "C" Division

Insubordinate Conduct

That is to say, did use obscene and insulting language to Constable 284 Osborne at Watford on 7th December 1941.

Found Guilty, Severely Reprimanded and

taken off Motor Patrol and returned to Street Duty. (G.O. No.386, 1941)

Tyres in Possession of Police

In the event of any rubber tyres or tubes coming into the possession of Police as found property, on the expiration of the appropriate period for retention, a report will be made to Headquarters, giving particulars of the tyres and tubes in hand, stating the size and make and whether new or part worn, in order that a report can be sent to the Ministry of Supply Rubber Control.

On receipt of this information, the Ministry will issue instructions for the tyres and tubes to be offered for sale at an agreed price to either a tyre manufacturer or an Authorised Tyre Depot. (G.O. No.149, 1942)

Commendation

At 1230 hours on the 30th May 1942 Police Constable 18 Woods was on duty in Moor Park, Rickmansworth, when he interrogated Clifford Woodward alias Pennell. Not being satisfied, he searched him and found in his possession a loaded revolver. Woodward was arrested and at Rickmansworth Police Station was further searched when sixty £1 notes were found in his possession.

On the 4th June 1942, Woodward appeared at the Watford Petty Sessions on three charges of housebreaking and larceny. At the conclusion of the case, the Chairman D.Blackley Esq, J.P., commended the Constable saying "I feel that I am doing the right thing in representing not only my feelings in the matter but that of my fellow Justices when we say that we consider that you have done good service in this case. It was a very smart piece of work and has been intelligently followed up."

At the Herts Assizes on the 17th June, Woodward was sentenced to three years penal servitude.

In this case, the Constable acted with initiative, intelligence, courage and devotion

Detective Couse, Wakefield, Yorks, 1942. Constable Shipgood 5th from left top row.

to duty, which ultimately resulted in 23 cases of housebreaking being cleared up, eight of which were in this Police District.

There is no doubt that Woodward was a persistent housebreaker and but for the timely arrest by the Constable, would still have been committing serious housebreaking offences. (G.O. No.164, 1942)

Commendation

On Wednesday 24th June 1942, Constable Wood stationed at Watford, was on duty in Clarendon Road, when he saw a man whose jacket appeared to be bulky. Constable Wood stopped this man and found him to be in possession of a lady's handbag, which was later found to have been stolen from the Town Hall. Watford.

The man was arrested and later identified as Walter Baldwin, and at Watford Petty Sessions on the 30th June 1942, he was sentenced to 6 months imprisonment for larceny. (G.O. No.182, 1942)

Commendation

On the 8th July 1942, Constable 238 Plested stationed at Watford stopped a man who was riding a pedal cycle which the Constable recognised as having been stolen from Watford on the 3rd July 1942.

The Constable interrogated the rider and in consequence of what he was told, he later arrested James Charles George Eldridge and Roy Sidney Dunn on charges of cyclestealing. At Watford Petty Sessions on the 14th July 1942, Eldridge was sentenced to two and two months imprisonment concurrently, and Dunn was sentenced to 1 months hard labour.

As a result of Constable Plested's powers of observation and attention to duty, 13 offences of cyclestealing were cleared up and 12 of the cycles recovered. (G.O. No.193, 1942)

Commendation

On Sunday 5th July 1942, Constable 18 Wood and Constable 143 Green, stationed at Watford, were on duty in the High Street, Watford, when they stopped and interrogated a man who refused to account for the sum of £107.10.0d which the Constable's found in his possession.

The man was arrested and later identified as as James Schofield alias Jack Blott, and the money was found to be the proceeds of a case of housebreaking at Watford on the 3/4th July 1942.

At the Herts. Quarter Sessions on the 10th August 1942, Schofield was sentenced to 12 months hard labour for receiving stolen property and at the conclusion of the case the Deputy Chairman, Sir Granville Ram, K.C.B., commended the Constables. (G.O. No.225, 1942)

American Coloured Troops

1. The American Troops who are now coming to this Country in increasing numbers include a certain proportion of coloured troops.

2. From reports which the Secretary of State has received from various parts of the country it appears that there is ground for thinking that difficulties may be caused by the presence among the civil population of coloured troops, and by their association both with other troops and with British women.

3. It is not the policy of His Majesty's Government that any discrimination as regards the treatment of coloured troops should be made by the British Authorities.

Superintendents will therefore ensure that the Police do not make any approach to the proprietors of public houses, restaurants, cinemas or other places of entertainment with a view to discriminating against coloured troops.

4. If the American Service authorities decide to put certain places out of bounds for their coloured troops, such prohibition can be effected only by means of an Order issued by the appropriate American Army and Naval authorities. The Police will not make themselves in any way responsible for the enforcement of such orders. (G.O. No.243, 1942)

Motor Vehicle Patrols

On 18th September 1942, an Indian motorcycle Registration Number GUC 19 was stationed at Watford Police Station. The Force had a fleet of 10 of these motorcycles, consecutively numbered from GUC 12 to GUC 21.

The vehicle at Watford, was authorised to be ridden by Pc 102 Street only.

MAXIMUM SPEED. A maximum speed of 35 miles per hour will be strictly adhered to unless a greater speed is required for the proper execution of duty.

MAINTENANCE. All parts on the vehicle which are fitted with grease nipples for use with with a grease gun will be greased weekly. All other moving parts such as brake rod connections etc will be oiled weekly. The Air cleaner will be inspected weekly and if necessary replenished with oil to the level indicated.

Spares and Accessories

Each vehicle will carry the following:

Two First Aid bandages
Two spare chain links
Two spare sparking plugs
Puncture Repair Outfit.

DRIVING. Accelerating gently, negotiating bends at reasonable speed, and careful application of the brakes are the governing factors in the life of the vehicle, tyres and all accessories. These facts will be borne in mind and only disregarded in extreme emergency.

IMMOBILISATION. The officer in charge of the vehicle will ensure that it is properly immobilised should it be necessary to leave the vehicle unattended. (G.O. No.251, 1942)

COMMENDATION

At 3.10 a.m. on the 17th December 1942, Police Sergeant 15 Geary and War Reserve Constable 167 Lilley stationed at Watford were patrolling Vicarage Road, Watford, when they observed an unusual light in the Sub Post Office.

The Officers stationed themselves at the Front and Rear of the shop respectively and almost immediately a man broke out of the premises by bursting through the plate glass window. The Sergeant closed with him but he broke away, and War Reserve Constable Lilley took up the chase and caught the man about 400 yards from the scene of the crime.

The man was later identified as Harold Walter Pearson and at Herts Quarter Sessions on 4.1.43, he was sentenced to 12 months imprisonment for burglary. (G.O No.14,1943)

OBITUARY

The Chief Constable regrets to inform all Ranks that Constable Arthur James Palmer 153 of "C" Division stationed at Eastbury died today 2nd February 1943 whilst serving in the Royal Artillery.

Venereal Diseases

A list of the treatment centres for Venereal Diseases in the Hertford County Constabulary District together with times for attendance are published for information.

WATFORD- Special Clinic at Shrodells Hospital, Vicarage Rd, Watford.

MEN	Tuesdays 5 - 7 p.m.
	Fridays 2 - 4 p.m.
WOMEN	Mondays 5 - 7 p.m.
	Fridays 10 - 12 noon

Superintendents will ensure that all members of their respective Divisions carry a note of addresses and times of attendance whilst on duty and should they be approached for this information it will be supplied, and recorded, but the names and addresses of persons enquiring will not be asked for. Superintendents will report giving details of the use made by members of the public of this means of obtaining information regarding treatment. (G.O. No.61,1943)

Auxilliary Police Association Meeting

Held: at Hatfield on 26th February 1943

1. Issue of Second Hand Boots- The Chief Constable stated that the issue of second hand boots was decided on only because he felt that these boots must not be wasted. This issue, had almost ceased and will only be made when absolutely unavoidable.

2. Issue of Batteries and Lamps- The Chief Constable intends to issue each Constable with an improvised dual purpose lamp as soon as possible as the original issue is now unobtainable. The greatest of economy is necessary in the use of batteries.

3. Facilities for preparing Tea etc. at some stations is stated to be inadequate- The Chief Constable states there have been some improvements recently, and this is a matter upon which the Chief Constable is most anxious that members are satisfied, but they must be prepared to put up with minor inconvenience in the interests of economy. Electricity must not be used when a coal fire is already in use. (G.O No.70,1943)

Barrage Balloons

The Public have been Informed to notify the Police if they see a grounded barrage balloon. If Police observe such a balloon they should-

1. Inform the nearest RAF station
2. Guard the balloon until the arrival of the RAF party
3. Prevent unauthorised persons from handling the balloon
4. Stop smoking and prohibit all naked lights in the vicinity.

The deflation of balloons is the responsibility of the RAF and must not be undertaken by members of the Police Force. It should be noted however that grounded balloons may become rent and partially deflated with a consequent escape of gas liable to combine with the air to form an explosive mixture.

Weights should be attached to the rope lines. In the case of a damaged balloon, sandbags, sand or earth should be placed on the balloon itself to stop the wind getting underneath it. (G.O. No.112, 1943)

Defence Regulation No.61

If without reasonable excuse, any person

1. tresspasses on any land in the United Kingdom which is being used for the purposes of allotments OR

2. tresspasses on any land in the United Kingdom on which any crop is growing and thereby damages that

Wings for Victory week, American servicemen and women in March-past at Watford, May 1943. Photograph from Book of Watford

crop or any part thereof;

That person shall be guilty of an offence against this Regulation and liable on summary conviction to a fine not exceeding £50. (G.O. No.140, 1943)

Commendation

On the 6th June 1943, the Metropolitan Police circulated the description of a soldier who was wanted for shooting a War Reserve Policeman and breaking and entering two houses at Mill Hill.

On the 7th June 1943, Police Sergeant 36 Newnham stationed at Watford, received a report from a boarding house keeper that a soldier had taken a room at her house and he purported to be attached to the Police.

Sergeant Newnham interrogated the soldier and from his description, he formed the opinion that he was the wanted mam. He arrested him and when in custody, he admitted responsibility for shooting the Policeman and the two cases of burglary. The soldier was found to be John Desmond Ware, and at the Central Criminal Court on 21st July 1943, he was sentenced to five years penal servitude.

The Commissioner of the Metropolis has expressed his appreciation of the valuable assistance rendered by Sergeant Newnham. (G.O. No.187, 1943)

Plain Clothes Allowance

Meeting of the Joint Branch Board held at Constabulary HQ, on the 29th October 1943.

The Federation requested that while Officers are on Annual Leave, that they be entitled to Plain Clothes and Detective Allowances.

The Chief Constable Noted, that this would be allowed. (G.O. No.274, 1943)

Grounded Barrage Balloons

A report has been received of an accident, which occurred recently when two small experimental barrage balloons, attached by some 2,000 feet of cable came to earth.

An Inspector of Police (accompanied by a Constable) examined the balloons and cables for the presence of any lethal device, but did not see one. He then proceeded to deflate one balloon by manipulation of the gas valve, but stopped doing this when the the balloon had been deflated to a height of about 2 feet from the ground. Warning bystanders to keep clear and not to smoke, and leaving one bystander with instructions not to allow interference, he left to attend to the other balloon a quarter of a mile away.

In spite of the warning, two members of the public (including the bystander to whom special instructions had been given) began to roll up the half deflated balloon from the nose and it is presumed that the friction on the fabric generated static electricity causing a spark, which ignited the hydrogen-air mixture in the balloon. Either the resulting explosion or the handling of the balloon detonated the lethal device which was in fact fitted and present. One of the men rolling the balloon was killed and five bystanders were injured.

Although the Police had duly observed their instructions in this case and cannot be held responsible for the accident, Superintendents will draw the attention of all members of the Force to this incident and to the great importance of preventing any unauthorised persons from handling grounded barrage balloons or their mooring cables. (G.O. No.297, 1943)

3rd Birthday of the Home Guard; March-past of the 10th Battalion, and part of the 7th, Wings for Victory Week, dias outside the Town Hall, Watford, 1943. Photograph from the Book of Watford

Commendation

At 1140 p.m. on 22nd January 1944, a Station Porter on the Metropolitan Railway Station, Croxley Green, was held up by a soldier at the point of a revolver and robbed of 18/6d in cash. After obtaining possession of the money the soldier struck the Porter with the revolver.

The Police were informed and it was ascertained that the soldier had concealed the lower part of his face with a khaki scarf.

Police Sergeant 100 Martin, stationed at Rickmansworth commenced enquiries and at 0025 hours on the 23rd January 1944, he saw a soldier on the Railway Station, Rickmansworth who was wearing a scarf similar to the one described by the Porter at Croxley Green.

The Soldier gave his name as John Grant and refused to be searched, but whilst being interrogated he was seen to try and dispose of a .32 "Smith and Wesson" revolver.

Grant later admitted the offence and at Herts Assizes on the 17th February 1944, he was sentenced to receive 12 strokes of the birch and 1 months imprisonment for robbery with violence.

The Acting Chief Constable commends Sergeant Martin for his initiative and attention to duty which resulted in a serious offence being detected and directs that an appropriate entry be made on the Sergeant's record of service. (G.O. No.44, 1944)

Cycle Stealing

Since January 1944, pedal cycles have been stolen in the various Divisions as under:-

"A"....... 62 Stolen.....17 Detected.

"B"....... 73 Stolen.....12 Detected.

"C".......119 Stolen.....11 Detected.

"D"....... 42 Stolen..... 5 Detected.

"E"....... 87 Stolen.....17 Detected.

Total.....383 Stolen.....62 Detected.

This leaves a Balance of 321 undetected cycle thefts.

In addition to this, 310 cycles have been stolen, later found abandoned, returned to their owners and accordingly recorded as "No Felony".

I am sure that all members of the Force will agree that this is a very serious matter and I should welcome any suggestions from any member of the Force to prevent and detect these offences.

Will any member of the Force who has a suggestion to offer please forward it through his Superintendent as soon as possible. (G.O. No.177, 1944)

Bombing of Police Headquarters

About 5 a.m. on Tuesday, 10th October 1944, a fly bomb exploded about 30 yards in the rear of Constabulary Headquarters at Hatfield. There were eight fatal and about 30 Serious casualties. Several Police Officers and members of their families sustained injuries, more or less severe. Amongst other property, the Police Headquarters suffered extensive damage and four Police cottages in St. Albans Rd were almost wrecked and the residential quarters in the Police Station Yard and the Police Cottages in Beaconsfield Road were considerably damaged.

It is very difficult for me to single out particular officers for commendation, but the work of Superintendent R.C. Offord, Police Sergeants 79 Sanbridge, 44 Oliver, 290 Gregory, 295 Winser and Police Constable 57 Pollard calls for particular mention and I am submitting a special report on their efforts to the Standing Joint Committee.

The excellent work performed by Inspectors Whittenham and Evans, Acting Police Sergeant 329 Paybody, and War Reserve Constable 88 Paine also calls for special mention and I have directed that appropriate entries be made on their records of service.

Every Police Officer, undeterred by his own anxiety for his personal affairs and family, displayed discipline and efficiency of the highest order and I pay a special tribute to the conduct and courage of their wives and families in their terrifying experience.

I cannot speak too highly of the splendid assistance rendered by the Special Constabulary under Superintendent Escombe and Inspector Lilburn. The Commandant arrived shortly after the incident and it was due to the valuable assistance rendered by the Special Constabulary that I was able to relieve some of the Regulars to attend to their own personal affairs.

Special praise is also due to all members of the Women's Auxilliary Police Corps of the Headquarters Staff who have carried out their work most efficiently under very trying and difficult conditions.

We are very much indebted to those police officers who were so soon on the scene and immediately rendered very valuable assistance in recovering and removing furniture and effects and I thank those members of the Force and their wives who so kindly offered accomodation and assistance to those who were temporarily homeless and I am very pleased to say that I have now found new Quarters for all those whose homes were destroyed or made uninhabitable.

Flying Bomb damage at Police Headquarters, Hatfield, 1944.
Photograph from the Story of Hertfordshire Police.

We are very grateful to those members of the Force, both Regular and War Reserve, who have been and are still working so very hard to make some of the houses habitable again and I ask them to accept our very sincere thanks.

On behalf of all the Police Officers and their families who have suffered injury and damage I tender our sincere thanks, and at the same time express our appreciation to those members of the Force who have rendered many acts of kindness which have gone a long way to alleviate a good deal of anxiety and hardship and I tender my special thanks to all those members of the Force who have been so kind and sympathetic towards my own family.

We have received considerable assistance from the Standing Joint Committee, the County Surveyor, the County Controller, the Hatfield Rural District Controller, the Women's Voluntary Service, Royal Air Force at Mill Green and others, and I have written and expressed our appreciation of the kind assistance given to us.

At an Emergency Meeting held on Friday 27th October 1944, Sir Will Spens, the Regional Commissioner for the Eastern Region, paid a special tribute to the work of the Hertford County Constabulary in this incident and particularly mentioned the efficient manner in which everything was carried out and said that what he admired most was the entire lack of fuss and show and I feel very proud to have had the honour to command the Force at this particular time. (G.O. No.253, 1944)

Signed A. CAMP.
Acting Chief Constable.

Abel Camp, M.B.E., D.C.M., M.M. Acting Chief Constable 1943-5. Photograph from the Story of Hertfordshire Police.

Mileage Allowance

Mileage allowances for cars up to 8 h.p will be $3^1/_2$d per mile.

Petrol will be issued Free on the following scales of allowance up to 8 h.p. 32 miles to the gallon. (G.O. No.3, 1945)

Promotion Exam

The Promotion exam will consist of 2 parts.

Part 1

Arithmetic	60 marks
Geography	60 marks
Writing,Spelling	60 marks
Puntuation & Composition & General Knowledge	60 marks
Intelligence, Principles of Local Government	60 marks
Reading	30 marks

Part 2

Criminal Law	100 marks
Evidence & Procedure	100 marks
Police Duties	100 marks
Local Bye Laws	50 marks

In order to pass, Qualification must be reached in both parts. For Part 1 this 165 marks out of 330 which must include a minimum each of 30 marks for Arithmetic,Spelling and Local Government. In Part 2, the qualification mark is 175 out of 350 with at least 50 for all subjects except bye laws which is 25.

Selected items from the North Watford Police Station Occurence Book

Larceny by Servant - 25.12.45

At 2150 hours on 24.12.45 PC 238 Plested arrested Alec Clay Tully of Hill Farm, Leavesden, aged 27 years, for stealing 3 sacks of barley to the value of £6.10.0. the property of his employer William Frederick Webber, Hill Farm, Leavesden between 20th and 24th December 1945.

ACTION TAKEN- Charge sheet and all Enquiries made and prisoner released on bail to appear at Watford Petty Sessions 3rd January 1946.

An additional note entered in red states- Sir, At Watford Petty Sessions on 3.1.46 Tully was sentenced to 6 weeks imprisonment.

Dog Destroyed Webber - 6.1.46

At 1100 hrs today Mr.Webber of Hill Farm, Leavesden reported to me at this station that he had that morning shot a dog belonging to Alec Clay Tully of Hill Farm, Leavesden.

Webber stated that he had seen the dog attacking fowls on his farm and had tried to catch it, but the dog had turned on him. He was unable to contact Mrs.Tully as she had gone away. Webber said he would inform Mrs.Tully when she did return. I informed him that a record would be made at this station.

Arthur Hendry PC 285

Sudden Death, Leach - 27.12.45

At 2137 hrs 26th Inst. a telephone message was received from Mr.Leach, Fern Way, Watford to the effect that he believed his wife had gassed herself.

ACTION TAKEN- I at once attended and saw the body of Doris Evelyn Leach aged 33 years lying on the floor of the kitchenette in front of the gas stove. The door of the gas stove was wide open and a gas poker had been connected to the gas tap by a rubber tube and was also inside the gas oven. All windows were secure and the ventilation stuffed with a duster, there was a strong smell of gas. Dr.Woods was in attendance and he pronounced life extinct. There were no signs of foul play and no marks on the body. All particulars obtained and Reports submitted in duplicate to Superintendent "C" Division and H.M.Coroner.

Meteorological Equipment Found - 14.1.46

At 1335 hours today, Inspector R.Neale of de Havillands Security Police reported to me that a parachute with a container attached had landed in a field at Hill Farm, Leavesden.

ACTION TAKEN- I at once attended and was handed a linen parachute to which was attached a container number D6559. A postcard had been attached to the container addressed to Senior Meteorological Officer, School of Artillery, Larkhill, Salisbury Plain. This postcard had been posted prior to my

Superintendent H. Smith (Superintendent Watford, 1946-1954)

arrival by Derek Banks, 8 Hill Terrace, Abbots Langley, who had first reached the container. Container now lodged at this station.

John Swain PC 14

Report of Accident - 18.1.46

At 2330 hrs Thursday 17th January 1946 a telephone message was received at this station from the ambulance station to the effect that they had been called to the Loco sheds, LMS Railway, St.Albans Road, Watford, where a man had fallen from a considerable height.

ACTION TAKEN- I attended and ascertained that whilst Harold White approximate age 44 years, of Railway Cottages, Kings Langley, was standing on top of the Water Tank of an engine filling same, and whilst pulling the chain of the tank, the chain broke, and he fell a distance of 15 feet to the ground between the engine and a brick wall, a space of 3 feet. White received injuries to his back and was conveyed to the Peace Memorial Hospital by Ambulance.

PC 63 W.C.LOWIN

The final entry in the occurrence book reads :- NORTH WATFORD STATION CLOSED AT 0600 HOURS ON 20.1.46.

ALL BUSINESS TRANSFERRED TO CLARENDON ROAD STATION.

Anti-Radar Strips

Strips of Stiff paper covered on one side with tin foil are dropped in loose bundles from aircraft to confuse radio-location apparatus from the ground. These strips separate in falling, so they may be found over a wide area. The standard German type is about 31 inches long and three-quarters of an inch wide, and is often sprayed with graphite over the tinfoil to remove the shiny appearance. Strips of British origin may also be found, varying in length from a few inches to several feet, and from one sixteenth to three inches in width. So far, they have not been coated with graphite so retaining their shiny appearance. (S.O. No.41, 1945)

Colonel Arthur Young. C.M.G.
Chief Constable 1945-1947

Breeches

The wearing of Breeches and leggings by officers on motor patrol duty will in future be confined to the drivers of motor-cycles. Whilst driving motor cars, the drivers will wear ordinary uniform trousers. (S.O. No.37, 1945)

New Standing Orders

This order, rescinded all existing Standing Orders and republished them in book form. However, the restriction forbidding members of the Force to enter licensed premises when off duty was rescinded with the following proviso.

This standing order rescinds all previous Standing Orders including those in relation to the use of Licensed premises by members of the Force. Now these restrictions whilst off duty no longer apply. The Chief Constable takes this opportunity of bringing to the notice of all ranks, that in the interests of the efficiency and reputation of the Force, it is necessary that this facility should be exercised both with discretion and moderation. Such forbearance is particularly necessary in country stations where an officer is well known and where over familiarity on his part with licensed premises is bound to result in loss of esteem and dignity. In absence of this rescinded order, the Chief Constable relies on the goodwill and discretion of all members of the Force to ensure that no embarrassment is occasioned. (S.O. No.109, 1945)

Commendation

On Wednesday 24th October 1945, Constable 333 Wornham, stationed at Watford, stopped a soldier in the High Street, Watford and questioned him. Suspecting that he was an absentee from his unit, the Constable ascertained his name was Ivor Lanagan and arrested him.

On the way to the Police Station, the soldier commenced to draw a firearm from his pocket. The Constable attempted to close with the man, but before he could do so, the soldier fired, but Wornham was able to avoid the shot by throwing himself to the ground.

Lanagan ran away but was later arrested in possession of a revolver and seven rounds of ammunition.

At the Cental Criminal Court on 10th December 1945, Lanagan was sentenced to 12 months imprisonment, on a charge of discharging a firearm with intent to resist arrest. (G.O. No.302, 1945)

Health of Officers

This regards the provisions made for the Health of officers and includes the following.

Masseur

A part time Masseur will be appointed by the Chief Constable upon the recommendation of the Staff Surgeon, to provide treatment to officers from the force suffering from lumbago, sciatica, rheumatism and similar ailments.

Artificial Sunshine Lamp

An ultra-violet or 'artificial sunshine' lamp has also been installed at the Chief Constables Office and is available for all members of the force. Sun baths can be taken in accordance with instructions laid down by the Staff Surgeon. (G.O. No.36, 1946)

Commendation

On the 6th April 1946, Detective Constable 245 Martin was on duty in High Street, Watford, and at 2240 hours he saw two men, one of whom was carrying two suitcases. He became suspicious of the men, who later parted company, and Detective Constable Martin stopped and questioned the man who was carrying the suitcases. While he was being questioned, this man suddenly threw one of the cases at the officer and made off. Detective Constable Martin obtained assistance and later arrested the other man, John Morgan outside Watford High Street Railway Station.

Later, two cases of housebreaking at Croxley Green were reported to the Police and property found in the suitcases and in possession of Morgan was identified as that stolen from the two houses.

At Herts Quarter Sessions, Hertford on 20th May 1946, Morgan pleaded guilty to receiving and was sentenced to 21 months imprisonment.

The reports show that Detective Constable Martin was alert and attentive to duty and as a result of his action Morgan was committed and part of the stolen property recovered. (G.O. No.113, 1946)

Commendation

On Saturday the 20th April 1946, at 2150 hours, Police Sergeant Snoxell was on duty in St. Albans Rd, Watford, when he saw a man come from the entrance to a factory. The man saw the officer and turned back, but as his action appeared suspicious, Sergeant Snoxell followed him and overtook him in the factory yard, where the officer noticed that the man had something bulky concealed under his jacket. The man, Arthur William Ellement, 62 years, a carriage examiner, employed by the Londom, Midland and Scottish Railway, was searched and two parcels containing dress material were found concealed under his jacket.

Ellement was arrested and admitted stealing the property from his employers at Watford Junction Railway Station. Ellement's house was searched and further property stolen by him, to the value of £350 was recovered. Ellement's son Arthur William Ellement, aged 38 years, of the same address, was later charged with receiving property to the value of £150 which had been stolen by his father.

At Watford Petty Sessions on 23rd April 1946, Ellement Senior was sentenced to six months and six months imprisonment concurrent, and Ellement junior was fined £25 or three months imprisonment and was committed.

At the conclusion of the case the Chairman of the Court, Major Gordon Ross, J.P., said to Sergeant Snoxell, "The bench wish me to commend you on the astuteness you have shown in this case". (G.O. No.114, 1946)

Bread Rationing

1. Bread rationing will come into force on the 21st July 1946. Certain arrangements have been made whereby extra coupons are available for 'manual workers' in which category policemen are included for the above purpose.

2. Police Officers who will NOT be eligible for these extra coupons are:-(a) Those engaged on light or sedentary work, e.g. Clerks.

(b) Administrative or supervisory workers.

3. The Chief Constable is advised that, in general, the exceptions mentioned in paragraph 2 above are intended to apply to men or women who are to a great extent engaged on desk work. Patrol and C.I.D. Sergeants and Inspectors will, therefore, be entitled to the extra coupons.

4. Application must be made on Form BMW 2, a supply of which will be forwarded to Superintendents by the local office of the Ministry of Labour. Superintendents will ensure that these forms are distributed to Sections, completed by the men concerned and returned to them as soon as possible. The completed forms, together with Form BMW 3 (which Superintendents will use as a covering note) should be forwarded to the local office of the Ministry of Labour accompanied by a covering letter on official notepaper in a package clearly labelled "BMW" as early as possible, and in any case not later than the 13th July 1946.

5. New entrants to the Service and men who return from Training Schools should complete Form BMW 2 in the usual way.

6. If application forms are not received in the next few days, Superintendents should get in touch with the local office of the Ministry of Labour.

7. Any difficulties experienced in the above connection should be reported to the Chief Constable. (C.C.s Memo 3.7.46)

Commendation

On 2.6.46 a description was circulated of a man wanted for committing an offence of Buggery at Croxley Green.

On 5.6.46 PS 104 Snoxell stationed at Watford whilst on duty in St.Albans Rd, saw a man answering the description. He interrogated the suspect and not satisfied with the man, arrested him. He subsequently admitted the offence and on 24.7.46 he pleaded guilty and was placed on probation for 12 months.

This is a particularly vile type of offence and his continued liberty would have been a serious matter, therefore the Chief Constable commends him and directs that an appropriate entry be made on his record of service. (G.O. No.178, 1946)

Threshing Machines on Roads

The Motor Vehicles (Authorisation of Special Types) (Amendment) (No 2) Order 1946.

The above order which comes into force forthwith and will expire on 30.11.46 provides for the period of the present Grain Harvest Season only that combined reaping and threshing machines exceeding 10 feet but not 14 feet in total width may be used on roads subject to a speed limit of 4 m.p.h. The order also makes it obligatory for machines in excess of 10 feet wide to have 2 persons in addition to the driver present, one in front and one behind the machine to give warning to other traffic on the road. (G.O. No.179, 1946)

Granting of Visa's

The Home Secretary has notified that he has delegated to Passport Control the authority to grant visas for the U.K. to aliens of Europe and North Africa including those of enemy nationality who are in distressed circumstances as a result of war and who have relatives in this country able to provide for them.

If the Police become aware of reasons why an alien of enemy nationality who has recently arrived should not enjoy the exemption, a report in duplicate should be forwarded to Headquarters. (G.O. No.192, 1946)

Ascot Races

Ascot Races, will take place on Friday 27th and Saturday 28th September 1946. The contingent from this Force who will be responsible for the 10/- Ring will be made up as follows:-1 Inspector, 3 Sergeants and 25 Constables, which includes 1 Sergeant and 5 Constables from "C" Division. (S.O. No.202, 1946)

With Reference to Standing Order 202/46

Sleeping accommodation - Camp beds, palliases and blankets are provided but not sheets or pillows. Officers should take with them a shaving mirror.

A conveyance has been hired which will pick up men on 27.9.46 at Watford Police Station at 0900 hrs and Rickmansworth at 0915 hours. (S.O. No.222, 1946)

German Prisoners of War

German P.O.W.'s employed in Agricultural and Forestry work, are no longer being accompanied to and from work by guards. A limited number of prisoners are now employed on night shifts at gas works and brick kilns. On account of a shortage of manpower these men are now permitted to go to and from work without an escort. Camp leaders, clerks and other selected members of the camps are now to be permitted to take exercise outside the camps unescorted. This privilege is conditional on the concurrence of the Local Police and the good behaviour of the prisoners. (S.O. No.228, 1946)

Rent Allowance

	Married	Single
C/Supt. & Supt.	27/-	12/6
C/Insp. & Insp.	23/-	11/-
Sgts. & P.C.s	20/-	10/-

These rates are "Maximum Limit" Rates, so that officers who are in fact paying less than the amount provides will receive only the rent that they are paying. (S.O. No.229, 1946)

Road Safety.

Training Courses for Officers visiting Schools.

As a result of the Road Safety Training Couse held at HQ, the undermentioned officers have qualified to give talks to school children on Road Safety and to undertake the Inspection of cycles at schools.

PS 44 Oliver

PS 217 Foxon

(G.O. No.258, 1946)

Commendation

On Thursday 26th September 1946, Police Constable 175 Foxen was on duty in Hampermill Lane, Watford, and at 4 a.m. he stopped a man who was riding a cycle and who approached from the direction of Northwood. The cycle was a ladies model and in the basket at the front was a camera, which the man was able to describe correctly.

Police Constable Foxen then asked the man to produce his Identity Card and he replied, "I have not got it with me. I have been to see my girl and am returning to Watford." The Constable told the man that he was not satisfied with his explanation, whereupon the man pushed the officer away and attempted to mount the cycle. Constable Foxen arrested him and upon searching him found, amongst other property, a combined knuckle duster and dagger of the type used by Commando troops and five clothing coupon books in the name of Pratt, 50 Rofant Road, Northwood.

The man gave his name as Eric Lomas. He admitted being a deserter from the Army since July 1946, and also stated that he had broken into a house in Northwood.

Lomas was handed over to the Metropolitan Police and upon his committal for trial at Uxbridge Magistrates' Court on two charges of burglary and one charge of possessing housebreaking implements by night, the Chairman of the Magistrates said to Constable Foxen, "We wish to commend you for your smartness."

At Middlesex Sessions on the 7th November 1946, Eric Lomas was sentenced to 4 & 4 years penal servitude concurrent for burglary (2 cases). He admitted and had taken into consideration 47 other offences of burglary, housebreaking and receiving. (G.O. No.293, 1946)

Commendation

On Sunday 29th September 1946, Police Constable 183 Elfleet was on duty at Watford. At 5.50 a.m. he saw a youth sitting on a bale of newspapers near Watford Junction Railway Station. The Constable interrogated the youth regarding his prescence in Watford and not being satisfied with his explanation, searched him and found in his possession nine clothing books bearing names and addresses of persons residing in Kew, Surrey and Preston, Lancs.

The youth gave his name as Leonard Leon and he was told by the Constable that he would be detained pending further enquiries. Leon then asked the Constable if he could collect 2 suitcases which he had deposited at the station. He was allowed to collect the cases and when these were searched, property was found which proved to be the proceeds of burglary at 49 Sutton Rd, Watford, on the night of 28/29th September 1946.

Other property in his possession, connected Leon with cases of burglary at Kew and Preston. He was found to be an escapee from Latchmore Borstal Institution, Richmond.

At Herts Quarter Sessions, Hertford, on 25th November 1946, Leon was indicted for burglary and found guilty. He was sentenced to one months imprisonment and ordered to be returned to a Borstal Institution. Three cases of Burglary and one of attempted housebreaking were taken into consideration when sentence was passed. (G.O. No.295, 1946)

Commendation

Between 6 p.m. and 9 p.m. 14th January 1947, an Austin motor car was stolen from South Harrow. At 9.10 p.m. Police Constable 174 Saunders received the report of the vehicle and information that it was believed to contain a soldier and two civilians, and was travelling towards Watford. The Constable went to a point near Watford Town Hall with the object of stopping the car in question.

At 9.20 p.m. he saw a soldier and two civilians walking towards him from the direction of Rickmansworth. The officer stopped the men and asked from where they

Hertfordshire Police, Mutual Association, Annual General Meeting, Circa 1947.

had come. One of the men said, "Just down the road. We want to get back to Greenford". The two civilians could not produce Identity Cards. The soldier produced an Army Pay Book and Leave Pass which were in order. Constable Saunders was not satisfied and arrested the men on suspicion of having stolen a motor car. They were taken to Watford Police Station where they were searched and were found to be in possession of a car clock, set of spanners and a toy pistol. They eventually admitted taking the car and stealing the clock and spanners from it. The car was later found abandoned in Watford.

At Middlesex Sessions on 6th March 1947 John Scrowther, 17 years, Cyril Garvey, 17 years, and Robert Yates, soldier, all of Greenford appeared before A. Capewell, Esq., K.C., charged with being concerned together in taking the motor car without the owner's consent, stealing the clock and spanners from the car and at the time of their apprehension for these offences having in their possession an imitation firearm. They pleaded guilty to all counts and were each bound over in the sum of £5 for two years.

The reports show that Constable Saunders was alert and attentive to duty, especially as the men were not found in possession of the motor car. The Chief Constable has much pleasure in commending him and directs that an appropriate entry be made on his record of service. (G.O. No.85, 1947)

Drill and Instruction Parades

Police Federation Joint Branch Meeting 6.6.47.

That the Chief Constables attention be drawn to the fact that monthly drill and Instruction parades are still being held in the "C" or Watford Division.

We respectfully ask that the Chief Constable issues instructions to abolish this procedure as we are of the opinion that training is now given at Pendley Manor on Refresher Courses.

The Chief Constable replied.

It has not yet been possible to hold all necessary courses at Pendley Manor, and in view of the manpower shortages it is doubtful that they will become a regular feature for some considerable time. Monthly instructions are necessary to provide opportunity for up to date discussion and explanation of current Police Matters. (G.O. No.169, 1947)

Lt. Colonel A.F. Wilcox., C.B.E.
Chief Constable 1947-1969

Infanticide

In August 1947, a 25year old, domestic servant living in Northwood, killed her baby son aged 1 month and threw his body into the Grand Union Canal at Watford. At the Hertfordshire Assizes in November 1947, she was found not guilty of Murder but

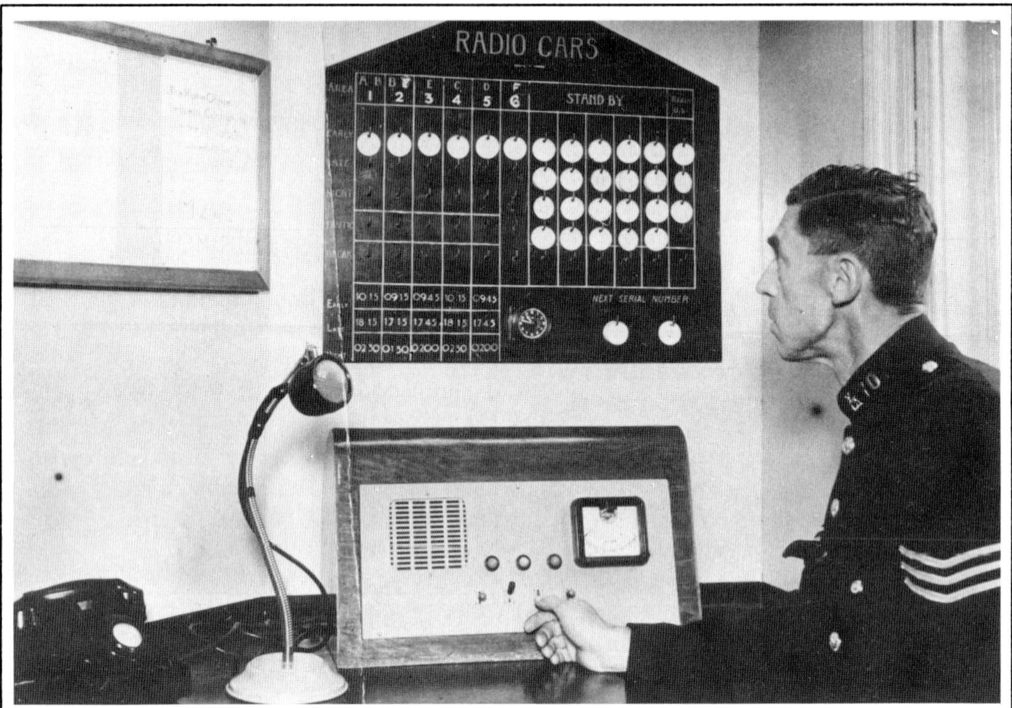

Radio Control room at Hatfield (Approx 1947), Controller Sergeant Pryce.

Radio Car (Approx 1947). Constables Sharkey and Rowe

guilty of infanticide and sentenced to 3 years penal servitude.

Poison Gas

In August 1947, John Grieves, aged 53 years, a gardener living in Garston, knocked his wife unconscious and then severed the gas pipe at their house with a bread knife. Both died from coal gas poisoning.

D.C. Halsey dusting for fingerprints, Circa 1947

Photography

The Force photography department took delivery of a Morris 12 h.p. van, fitted out as a mobile dark room.

Criminal Investigation Department 1947

The following officers were trained and serving in the C.I.D. in "C" Division in 1947.

Inspector Oliver
Inspector Dear
Sgt Murphy
Sgt Conway
Sgt Gray
Pc Wright
Pc Pegg
Pc Shipgood
Pc Martin
Pc Charles
Pc Pearce

Women Police - 18th March 1948.

As from today, Regular Police Women in this Force will be allocated numbers.

The following numbers are now allocated to personnel already serving and further consecutive numbers will be allotted to new entrants.

WPS GOTT 1
WPC CARR 2
WPS JOHNSON. A 3
WPC LEE 4
WPS JOHNSOM. M 5
WPC BELL 6
WPC FINDLAY 7
WPC FOGG 8
WPC FLEMING 9
WPC HORTON 10
WPC PICTON 11
WPC NIVEN 12
WPC STREBBEDS 13
WPC WYND 14

Robbery

1950, Leonard Platten and George Saunders, aged 19 and 20 years respectively, obtained a lift in a motor car travelling from Watford towards Aylesbury. They held up the driver with a revolver and demanded money from him. Both were caught and upon conviction were sentenced to Borstal training.

More Police

On the 5th June 1950, the Standing Joint Committee approved an increase in the Force Establishment of 207 Officers. Woman Police Officers accounted for 25 of this figure, comprising one Inspector, 3 Sergeants and 21 Constables. A total of 133 Civilians were also employed by the Force.

Nylon Smuggling in Watford

Large-scale smuggling and evasion of import and export prohibitions on nylon stockings and currency were revealed in a case, which sounded something like an American gangster thriller, to Watford Magistrates Court on Tuesday. There were seven charges preferred against an American citizen, and an Englishman was sent to prison for carrying nylons with intent to evade Customs Duty.

T.C. Fry, Jun., the American, of Sandringham Road, Watford, was charged with dealing in nine dozen pairs of nylons with intent to evade duty in April; dealing in 108 pairs of nylons with intent to evade duty in April; dealing with in nylons at Brize Norton, Oxfordshire, with intent to defraud duty for 72 pairs between February and April; dealing in 72 pairs of nylons with intent to evade import prohibition; attempting at Ruislip to evade duty on 120 pairs of nylons with intent to evade the import prohibitions; and in March, contrary to export prohibitions, sending 35 £1 notes out of the country.

Fry pleaded guilty to all charges. He was represented by Mr. Donaldson

(W.O. June 1951)

1st Teleprinter

First teleprinter installed at Watford Police Station in 1951.

Long Service Awards

Fifteen Watford police officers each with at least 22 years' service, have qualified for the new long service and good conduct medal. They are, left to right: (standing) Constables W. Aldridge and L. Scott, Det Sgt A. Rogers, Det Insp E. Flower, Det Sgt P. Gray, Constables W. Frewin, G. Cross and W. Lowin; (sitting) Sergeants W. Butterfield and H. Dennis, Insp A. Bishop, C.Supt H. Smith, Insp K. Couper, W. Sgt M. Johnson, and Sgt F. Foxon.

The New Rickmansworth Police Station 1952

The following article, is adapted from "The Architect and Building News" Volume 201 of April 24th 1952.

The new Sub-Divisional Station, was the first of a programme of post-war stations planned to provide improved accomodation for a modern Police Force, committed to greater responsibilities by the increasing population in many parts of Hertfordshire.

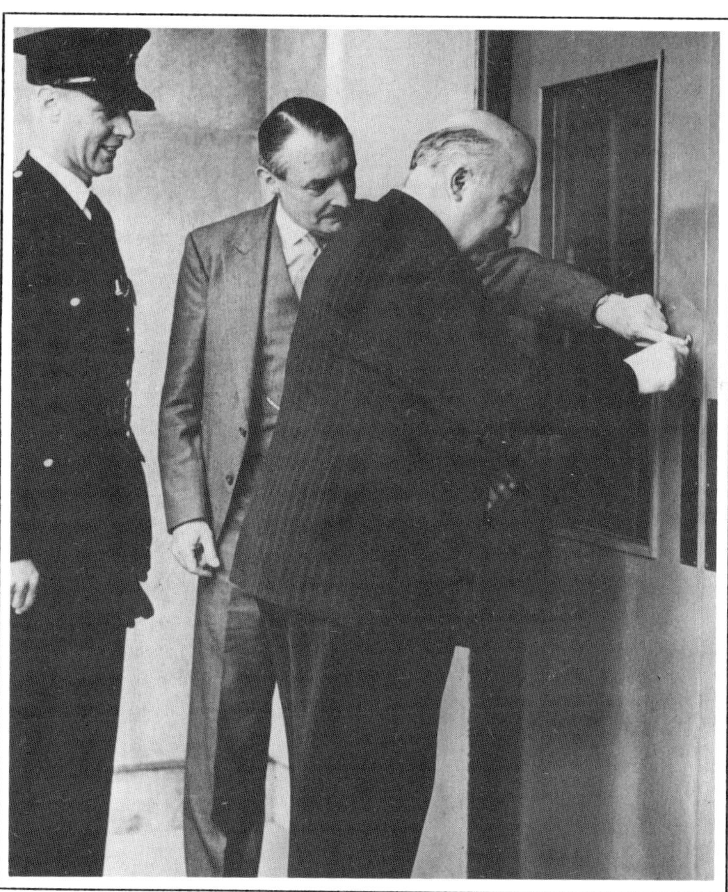

The Station, which was opened by the Home Secretary Sir David Maxwell Fyfe, on April 17th 1952, was designed in consultation with the Chief Constable. The main requirements were as follows:-

(a) Office accomodation giving maximum flexibility of space within external walls. With separate entrances for Public and Police.

(b) Cell areas inaccessible to the public and with a rear entrance.

(c) Recreation and Refreshment Rooms.

Garaging for four wireless cars and one van was also required.

On completion, the staffing consisted of 1 Inspector, 4 Sergeants, 20 Constables, 3 Detectives, 2 Policewomen and Special Constables, in order to serve a population of 30,000. A considerable amount of research into the exact requirements of the Police was necessary as little data existed and it was felt that many existing Stations followed too much of an established Police Station plan and facade treatment that were not necessarily suitable or expressive of the Police Force as it was in 1952. The contract price was £36,998 (3s8d per cubic foot).

Site and Planning

The open corner site of one acre at the junctions of the Uxbridge, Rectory, Ebury Roads and the High Street was central and gave quick access for patrol cars to all the main roads leading to the North-West, North-East and South. At the time of building, the proposed Rickmansworth Bye-pass had not been constructed but when finished it reduced the site are to 0.65 of an acre and thereby greatly influenced the finished design of the Station.

Guard of Honour

Foundations and Structure

Sub-soil investigations carried out from trial holes showed a water table level of 7-8 feet down, so specially designed piles were made through a good 9-10 foot deep ballast. 25 piles a day were bored and concreted, The first barrow loads of concrete were poured dry where the bottoms of the piles were below water level.

The steel frame consists of stanchions formed from two 6in x 3in channel sections welded together. Due to a national scarcity of bricks, research was encouraged into the use of light panel walls between the stanchions. This was achieved by using extruded aluminium window sections fixed directly to the stanchions. Insulation was then added to the internal walls. The first floor and roof are constructed from 6in precast concrete beams. The roof finish was 3 ply felt on 1 inch vermiculite screed. All ceilings were suspended and room partitions can be moved

Sir David Maxwell Fyfe Q.C. M.P. (Home Secretary), Inspector W. Oliver (I/C Rickmansworth), Assistant Chief Constable A. Camp Esq. M.B.E. D.C.M. M.M.

with the minimum of trouble on a 3ft 4 in grid to then line up with external windows.

Cell Block

This was required to be on the ground floor, and Home Office regulations laid down the wall thicknesses and sizes etc. An attempt has been made to emphasize the character of the block by means of deep corridor window sub-frame reveals and the use of pavement lights in the roof over the cells. The cells are naturally ventilated with built in bunks over a central heating coil. The walls were plastered and painted.

The Opening

On the day of the opening of the Police Station, certain invited guests were supplied with a luncheon at the Crown Hotel Garston. (A memo from the Chief Constable to the Clerk of the Standing Joint Committee asking for light refreshments at a cost of 1/-d per head and promising that not more than £5 will be spent has been found at HQ Archives.) The Guest List included the following, The Lord Farrar(Chairman-Standing Joint Committee), The Viscount Hampden(Lord Lieutenant), Mr.Maynard(High Sheriff), Colonel Halland(HMI), Sir Harold Williams(Chairman of County Council), Mr C.H.Aslin(Architect) and the Chief Constable Lt.Colonel A.F.Wilcox and the Divisional Superintendent at Watford H.Smith.

The New Station although generally applauded by both National and Local Press, was not without its' critics. The following article reproduced in its' entirety appeared as the Editorial comment in the Watford Observer of 25.4.52.

A worrying thought

Despite the strong defence submitted by Sir David Maxwell Fyfe on Thursday, many years will pass before the majority of Rickmansworth and Chorleywood residents approve of the external appearance of their new Police Station whatever may be their views on the interior.

We have been told that the shape of the building-likened by one local Councillor to "three match-boxes stuck together" was determined "by Police requirements, rather than a preconceived idea of what a Police Station should look like." Of that, there can be little criticism, for usefulness must come before looks.

The worrying thought for the residents of this country district is that the building is a County Development, approved by the men who will be responsible for a great deal of the development which is to take place in Rickmansworth, and more especially in Chorleywood in the next few years.

Assurances have been given in the past by the County Council and the local Councils concerned that everything possible will be done to ensure that development does not clash in any way with local amenities.

The new Police Station has been completed since those assurances were given. The local residents concern would appear to be justified.

There can be no criticism of the interior of the building. Those who cry "Extravagant luxury" do so without consideration, and without thought for the men and women who work and play within those glass walls.

One of W.S.Gilbert's most famous couplets ran "When constabulary duty's to be done, a policeman's lot is not a happy one." There can be no denying the truth of that statement, humorous though it may be in its context.

When that constabulary duty is over, or when it takes the man or woman concerned into the Station, no right thinking person will grudge any reasonable comfort or recreation facilities that can be provided.

W.P.C. Rafter on traffic duty. April 1953 - Photograph from the Book of Watford

Watford's Transport Section 1953
P.C.s 64 Sadler, 233 White, R. Yates, 260 Aldridge, Dumpleton, Innes, C.Supt H. Smith, Sgt Foxon, P.C. Rowe, Cadet J. Ellis, P.C. A. Hughes. Photograph G.Rowe

Oxhey Police Station Opened

Oxhey Police Station opened 31.1.53 by Lord Chief Justice of England Lord Goddard. Also present Lord Lieutenant of the County the Honourable David Bowes-Lyon.

Parcel Bullet at Watford

On May 25th 1953, at Watford, a man received a parcel through the post. On removing the wrapping, he found a trinket box. He had a little difficulty opening the box and turned it to one side in order to get a better purchase. As the lid opened, an explosion occurred and a bullet was projected from the box. The bullet missed him, but embedded itself in the wall behind him. The man's wife was standing beside him at the time, and it appears that the bullet passed between them. The box was sent of for forensic examination.

A ballistics expert commented after examining the box. "It is a cleverly designed and lethal weapon", the box was capable of discharging a .45 bullet to penetrate a $1^1/_2$ in. wooden plank and embed itself into a second plank of the same thickness.

It was obvious from the start of this enquiry, that the man had made enemies in the past and following skillful questioning, it was found that he had broken off an engagement with another woman prior to marrying his wife. His previous girlfriend was traced and it was found had also remarried to a precision instrument maker. The instrument maker was arrested and interviewed and admitted the offence stating that he had been consumed by jealousy after his wife had admitted that she had slept with her previous fiance. He had planned his revenge and on the day of the incident even bought an evening newspaper expecting to read of his success. He subsequently appeared at the Central Criminal Court and was sentenced to two years imprisonment.

Royal Review of Police at Hyde Park 14th Juky 1954. Hertfordshire Constabulary were represented by a detatchment of 71 officers commanded by the Chief Constable.

Aircraft Crash

On 5th September 1954 a Miles Magister aircraft made a forced landing at Maple Cross, Rickmansworth after suffering from engine failure. The pilot, sustained slight injuries.

No Sleigh for Santa

The Watford Police Sports and Social Club Christmas Party was held at the end of the year. There is none of the old fashioned nonsense of Santa Claus arriving on a sleigh drawn by reindeer at their Christmas parties, last year the revered old gentleman arrived on the back of a police motorcycle, but this year he became even more up to date and arrived by tube - not the underground variety but of the cathode ray type. A giant television screen was built for the purpose and the children were invited to switch it on. As the switch was turned, sleighbell music was faded in and Santa (Police Constable I. Eames) appeared on the screen. The idea was for Santa to smash the screen and climb through it, bringing gifts for each of the 180 children present, but things did not go according to plan. So eager was he to join the children that he struck the screen with too much force and to the dismay of the hosts and the delight of the young guests, the whole front of the television set collapsed.

(W.O. January 1955)

Driving without due care

At Watford Magistrates Court in January 1955, Laurence Preston of Harrow, admitted driving a car without due care and attention on the arterial road at Hunton Bridge. He was fined £5. Chief Inspector Hickford said that Preston took too wide a turn and hit another car. The defendant told the court that when he saw the other car his foot slipped off the brake.

16th Annual Police Ball

The 16th Annual Police Ball was held at Watford Town Hall and was a complete 'Sell out'. Dancing was to the music of the Valetos. Various dignitaries including the Mayor, the Chairman of the Magistrates and the Watford Town Clerk were present with all proceeds going to Police Charities.

Snow problem

On 17.1.55, severe snow caused problems on the areas roads and during the night, police officers at Croxley Green took to shovelling the snow from Scots Hill and spreading grit on the road in an effort to keep the road passable. The following morning, three accidents occurred in the locality, fortunately without any injury. On 20.1.55, a Green Line coach ran into difficulty during a blizzard on Batchworth Hill, compounded when an American car tried to avoid the stuck bus and skidded, the two vehicles completely blocking the road in front of an ambulance with an emergency case aboard en-route to Mt. Vernon Hospital. The ambulance crew were preparing to carry their patient on a stretcher to the hospital, when some of the men who had been in the coach decided to try and clear the road by moving the coach, they succeeded by placing their overcoats under its rear wheels.

Royal Visit

11th March 1955, Queen visits Royal Masonic School for Girls at Rickmansworth.

Duke of Edinburgh Visits

On 4th November 1955, the Duke of Edinburgh opened the Woodside PLaying Fields at Leavesden.

Aircraft Crash

On 31.3.55 the pilot of an Auster aircraft, made a forced landing on the Orbital Road at West Hyde. The pilot was uninjured.

Police Houses

County Councillor Mrs R. Short had a tilt at the County Council at a meeting of the Watford Rural District Council on 1.3.55, when she commented on a letter from the Housing Committee. "I see the County Council Council are now coming cap in hand asking for new sites in Abbots Langley for police houses, yet I understand that there was a site in the High Street which would have been eminently suitable for this purpose, but which the County Council Planning Department decided would be more suitable for a garage. They sign away a site for a garage that no one wants and then come crying to us for a site for Police Houses," she said. The Committee decided to recommend that they could not assist in the matter.

W.O. March 1955

Assault

A fine of £2 was imposed at Watford Magistrates Court on 1.3.55 on Dudley Hodges of Fourth Avenue, Garston, for assaulting and beating his wife Rita Estelle Hodges of the same address. Both parties were also bound over to be of good behaviour for 12 months in the sum of £10. In the witness box Mrs. Hodges said that although a separation order had been obtained in July, she and her husband continued to live in the same house. She alleged her husband had struck her in the face after a difference over the electric iron. Hodges denied the offence and said that his wife "bumped her face against me during a scuffle."

Masked men burst into Oxhey 'Farmers bedroom

On 14.3.55 in the early hours of the morning, five masked men burst into the bedroom of Oxhey Dairy Farmer Sydney Brazier and threatened him and his wife with crowbars before escaping with £100. They gagged his wife with a pair of silk stockings, and ordered Mr Brazier to open his safe after taking £100 from his pockets. On going downstairs, Mr Brazier realised that the key to the safe was not on its hook and that his son had the key, the robbers did not believe him and were taking him back upstairs when he ran into a spare room and smashed a window before shouting out of the window for assistance. A policeman who lived in a nearby cottage was awoken by the shouts and the robbers ran off. Mr Brazier suffered cuts on his arms when breaking the window. A coalman who was arrested and charged with this offence was later found not guilty at the Hertfordshire Assizes in May.

Theft

Violet Rosina Blackwell aged 41, a mother of five children of Gammons Lane, Watford appeared before Watford Magistrates Court charged with Theft. Detective Constable Murray said that the accused woman was employed as a cleaner at the Tudor Arms Public House in Bushey Mill Lane, Watford, where her duties left her alone in the bars whilst the manager was upstairs. After suffering some losses of cigarettes, the manager became suspicious and kept a close watch on his stock. He found that in three days, 40, 60 and 40 cigarettes went missing. He informed the police. The constable kept observation in the cellar of the house looking through a mirror which was attached to the roof, he saw the accused take a green packet of cigarettes and secrete them under her clothes. The accused stated she stole them for her son who had little money. Sentencing her to two years probation, the Chairman of the Bench warned her that if she committed any further offence there was no doubt that she would go to prison.

Grevious Bodily Harm

Police Constable Richard Frost, who was bitten in the face whilst on duty at Watford on Bank Holiday 1.6.55, came from hospital to give evidence against four men in the dock at Watford Magistrates Court the following day. Two of the men, Jeremiah Casey, aged 28, of Kilburn and Patrick Greenan aged 27 and lodging in Percy Rd, Watford were charged with inflicting GBH on the constable, whilst Bernard Francis Hennelly aged 37 of Chalk Hill, Bushey and Joseph Durkin alias Flynn of Louvain Way, Garston were charged with obstructing the constable in the execution of his duty. Inspector Oliver said that on Monday afternoon, Police constable Frost and other officers brought Casey to the police station. He was struggling violently and had blood on his face. The constable had an open wound to the side of his face, his tie was torn, his collar off and his uniform bespattered with blood. The three other offenders were then seen walking down Clarendon Road and arrested. The Inspector said the four though not drunk were under the influence of alcohol. He added that the wound on the constable's face was a bite and had removed part of the skin which will probably need a skin graft. The officer had been placed on the sick list. Constable Frost then entered the court having come directly from Hospital with a large dressing on his face. The officer said that he had seen about ten men shouting on the footpath outside the Rose and Crown Public House. He told the men to move along, but Casey tried to hit him. The officer drew his truncheon, but a pair of hands came from behind him and took the truncheon. Casey then bit the officer in the face. He tried to get Casey, but the others prevented him, he managed to break free from them and pulled Casey to the ground, but he got up and ran off, but was arrested by two other officers. The prisoners were all remanded for one week. At the resumed hearing, Casey pleaded guilty to assaulting the officer by biting him and was sentenced to prison for six months. The Chairman told him that his crime was a foul, vicious and a disgusting one. Greenan, was found not guilty of GBH, but guilty of assaulting the officer and fined £10 and bound over to keep the peace for 12 months in the sum of £10. Hennelly and Durkin were both found guilty of obstructing the officer and fined £3 each and also bound over to be of good behaviour for 12 months in the sum of £10. The Chairman Mr. Gordon Ross, after announcing the penalties said "The Court would like to commend Police Constable Frost for his courageous conduct."

The Constable who still has a large scar on his cheek has been on the sick list since the incident.

W.O. June 1955

Red Light

Driving his car in Watford on April 30th, Donald Higgins aged 24 of Hamilton Rd, Hunton Bridge, saw his mother on a bus and was distracted from his driving, as a result he went past a red traffic signal. At Watford Court, he was fined 30/-.

No Brakes

For using a motor lorry in Watford Road, Croxley Green, when the braking system was not in good working order and there was no warning instrument on the vehicle, William Robert Stanley Wilson aged 40 of Phillimore Place, Radlett, was fined a total of £2 at Watford Magistrates Court. Police Constable G. Jones said that when the hand brake was applied the vehicle could still be pushed by hand and the horn was not working. For permitting the above two offences, Carmac Plant Hire (Oxhey), were fined £5 and £2 respectively. The company was fined a further £1 with 3/6d costs for using the vehicle with no road fund licence in force. Mr Fletcher for the company said a cheque had been made out for the road fund licence but had not yet been posted at the time of the offence.

Obscene Calls

A young man said to have a grammar school education and to be employed as a research chemist pleaded guilty at Watford Magistrates Court on 2.6.55 to four charges of sending obscene messages by telephone and a fifth, arising out of the others of fraudulently consuming electricity belonging to HM Postmaster General. The man who asked for other similar offences to be taken into consideration was William Stewart Reich aged 23 of Carpenders Avenue, Oxhey. He was fined a total of £25. Detective Sergeant How, told the court that on different dates in April and May, young women operators at Watford Telephone Exchange received obscene messages. On May 10th, he went to a telephone kiosk at Garston and found the defendant using the telephone. Reich said "Please officer give me a chance. I know that I have been an utter fool. I am finished if this gets out, I have no wish to repeat the things I said to the girl operators as I realise now that they were horrible. I am utterly ashamed of myself and wish to apologise to all concerned." A probation officer said that Reich was a single man and had been engaged to be married for the last 18 months and was the son of a retired schoolmaster. He added " The offences seem completely at variance with his background and character."

Driving without Care

A young Oxhey police constable Ronald Newman, was summoned before the magistrates for an offence of driving without due care and attention, following an accident that had occurred at the junction of Prestwick Rd and Little Oxhey Lane on April 23rd. The Officer stated that he had been slowing up before the junction to allow a taxi to pass before he made a turn when suddenly a man who he had since been unable to trace ran into the road on his nearside and caused him to swerve to his right and collide with the taxi in his police car. The chairman said that there had to be some doubt that this was a careless action and therefore the case was dismissed.

Assualt on Woman Constable

A woman police officer told Watford Magistrates Court on Tuesday 28th June 1955 how she tried to break up a fight between two men and was struck a blow in her face which fractured her nose. Henry Smith aged 39 of Church Lane, Mill End, Rickmansworth pleaded guilty to acting in a manner whereby a breach of the peace was likely to be occasioned, but not guilty to a charge of malicious and unlawful wounding. WPC Mary Elizabeth Clarke told the court that at 10.50 p.m. on Saturday 18th June 1955 she was in Market Street, Watford. She had occasion to intervene when a woman caused a disturbance in a bus queue. Whilst she was thus engaged, she heard a scuffle and saw two men fighting. She made several attempts to stop them, but they kept on fighting. She saw one of them, Smith had his arms around the other and as she tried to part them, Smith lifted his right arm and deliberately swung it at me, giving me a severe blow to the face. Smith had been drinking. Smith claimed that he had been taunted in the queue and had lost his temper and that he had come to blows with his tormentor. He did not remember a police woman intervening and he did not mean to hit her, all his blows were aimed at the man he was fighting. The Bench found Smith guilty and the Chairman said "It is our duty to protect police officers both men and women from persons like yourself, and we will not allow these assaults to be committed with impunity." A woman left the court sobbing as Smith was sentenced to 3 months imprisonment and bound over to be of good behaviour for twelve months.

North Watford Police Station

At a meeting of the Herts County Council on 4th August 1955, the report of the Standing Joint Committee stated that the Home Office have allocated June 1956 for the starting of a project to build a Police Station at North Watford. The site is to be part of the playing fields of the Leavesden Green Junior Mixed School, fronting onto the North Orbital Road, Watford. A total of £26,650 has been set aside in the budget for the development.

No new Yard

At the same meeting, a proposal to resurface the Police Station and Court House Yard, Clarendon Rd, Watford, was criticised by Mr. Fairfield. It was proposed to resurface the yard and carry out repairs to the gulleys etc., at an estimated cost of £600, less 20% which would be charged to the Magistrates Court Committee. Mr. Fairfield stated that he had "particular experience of the yard in question, while its surface was rough, it was better than a number of the roads in the area" he said. "It would seem to have a considerable amount of wear left in it," he added. The Chairman said the Standing Joint Committee had been advised by experts that the work needed doing and rejected Mr. Fairfield motion, but said he was prepared to ask the Standing Joint Committee to reconsider the matter at their next meeting.

Stealing Cycle

Dennis Gerald Appleton pleaded guilty at Watford Magistrates Court on 13.9.55 to stealing a bicycle from outside a Watford Store. Appleton, said to be sleeping rough and in hostels in Watford, told the court he had taken the cycle to get to London. He admitted 5 previous convictions and that in June he had been placed on probation for theft. He was sentenced one month's imprisonment for breach of his probation and two months consecutively for the theft of the cycle.

(W.O. September 1955)

Defective Steering

George Edward Hackett, appeared before Watford Magistrates Court in October 1955 and was fined £4 for using a car at Watford with defective steering and with brakes not in efficient working order.

Pithe Helmets

Before stepping into the witness box at Watford Magistrates Court on Tuesday 25.10.55, Police Constable Jesse Page, deposited a policeman's helmet and a pith sun helmet on the Clerk's table. In Gaddesden Crescent, Garston, he had seen a van loaded with old police helmets and solar topees, which were being given to children in exchange for rags. He had recovered the exhibits from two of the children. Watford Borough Councillor Thomas Johnson of Gaddesden Crescent, told the court that he was called by one of his sons to see "the man with a funny hat". He looked out of the window and saw the man giving helmets to young children in exchange for rags. The councillor took the number of the van and called the Police. An eight year old girl confided to the magistrates that she and a friend had given the man a coat each and a little boy had given him some rags. The two girls each received a helmet and the boy a topee. Police Constable Page told the court that he had told the van man that "it was against the law to give a child under 14 years of age an article in exchange for the rags and old clothes he was collecting." The reply was "On my life I did not know it was an offence." But the bench proved it was by fining William Ernest Proctor £3 on three charges.

(W.O. October 1955)

New By-Pass (M1) - proposed

Cyclists and pedestrians not allowed. Motor vehicles only. Your speed? Don't dawdle - this road is designed for the 75 miles per hour man. These are all features of the exciting St. Albans bypass, one of the schemes in an expanded road programme announced by the Minister of Transport. In the next few weeks, the Minister is expected to advertise details of the new road, which forms the Southern part of London to Yorkshire Road. Overall the road will be 16 miles in length between Luton and Berrygrove, Watford, and will bypass Watford, St. Albans, Hemel Hempstead, Redbourn and Harpenden.

(The Road is now better known as the M.1 Motorway Junctions 5 to 10.)

W.O. November 1955

Forced Landings

On 11.3.56 a Miles Gemini aircraft made a forced landing on Oxhey Golf Course, causing slight injuries to three passengers.

On 27.7.56 the pilot of a Miles Messenger aircraft made a forced landing in a field near Rose Acre Farm, Bedmond. The pilot was uninjured and the plane undamaged.

Teddy Boys

Three persons were arrested for assault on Police and breaches of the peace following a disturbance by Teddy boys at a Watford performance of "Rock around the Clock".

Cycle Proficiency

On the 16th July 1956, the 2,000th Child in Watford, successfully passed the Cycling Proficiency Test trained by Police Officers.

Chief Constables Review

In the 1957 Annual Report, the Chief Constable A.F. Wilcox wrote the following Review of the year.

During the year crime rose by 13%, an increase only partly attributable to the growth of the population of the County. Much of the crime, it is true, is of a petty nature, but it is disquieting to note that so many of the offenders are children under 17 or youths between 17 and 21. It cannot be said that these youngsters who break into shops and houses or steal from large stores or unattended cars are in want. The school children are usually provided with substantial sums of pocket money; and often enough youths of 19 or 20 brought before the courts on charges of housebreaking are in regular employment earning £8 to £12 a week. It must be a matter of concern to those responsible for bringing up children that during 1957 one child in eighty, between the ages of 8 and 17, was caught committing some form of crime.

The number of vehicles on the roads in this country is growing at the rate of half a million a year. In Hertfordshire, as elsewhere, the problem of providing garages or parking spaces is growing more acute. The time is coming when every other family will own a car and few will have a garage in which to keep it. It is to be hoped that provision will be made in development plans for an adequate number of garages, or at least for the construction of parking lots off the highway. The nuisance caused by leaving cars in roadways or on grass verges all night, sometimes without lights, has led to a large number of complaints from residents. Warnings by the Police have not always been effective and many prosecutions for obstruction and leaving vehicles unlighted have been brought.

Towards the end of the year the new procedure under the Magistrates Courts Act 1957, was introduced. More than 80% of the defendants in minor traffic cases have chosen to plead guilty by letter, thus dispensing with the necessity of calling witnesses. The new scheme has worked very smoothly and has resulted in a saving of time and money.

Throughout the year all ranks of the regular police and the Special Constabulary have carried out the duties required of them in a loyal and steadfast spirit.

A.F. Wilcox,

Chief Constable of Hertfordshire

Emergency Landing

On 21.6.57, an R.A.F. De Havilland Devon Aircraft made an emergency landing at Leavesden aerodrome, resulting in damage only.

On 16.12.57, a De Havilland Dove aircraft undershot the runway at Leavesden, also resulting in damage only.

Police Dogs

Police dogs, attended 367 Incidents in the year, resulting in the tracing of 73 persons, and in 19 articles of stolen property recovered where the offenders were not traced. This was achieved with just two dogs for most of the year, although a third dog was operational after training towards the end of the year.

Wheeling Good

Following training for cycle proficiency tests, 7 teams from Hertfordshire entered the National Annual Cycling Festival Competition at Crystal Palace on 10th August 1957. Watford came second and Rickmansworth 4th out of a total of 40 teams. All training of the teams was carried out by Police Officers. A total of 42 Officers are now trained in Road Safety work.

Under Strength

In his annual report of the year, the Chief Constable commented on the manpower problems of the Force.

At the present time, the Force is 20% below strength. It will be many years before the force can be brought up to strength. At present, a good deal of overtime has to be worked and it is still impossible to grant the third rest day a fortnight introduced by Police Regulations in 1955.

Shot Dead

On 16th November 1958, a party of seven youths and two girls were shooting vermin in Tunnel Woods, Watford, and when returning home one of the youths, aged 16 years, pointed his gun at one of the girls and pulled the trigger thinking the gun was not loaded. The girl received a wound in the mouth and upon arrival at hospital was found to be dead. The youth pleaded guilty to manslaughter at Hertfordshire Assizes, and was placed on probation for three years with a condition not to possess or use firearms.

Brawls

During the year, there has been a noticeable increase in the number of fights and brawls taking place in the streets. Assaults arising out of quarrels among men the worse for drink account for a proportion of these offences of violence.

Retirement

During the year, Chief Superintendent Smith retired after 39 years service.

40 M.P.H.

On 15.3.58, a 40 m.p.h. speed limit was introduced on the A41 at Watford.

Congested Traffic

Congestion of traffic in Rickmansworth High Street, calls for almost constant supervision. It is hoped that in 1959, a scheme will be introduced to improve the circulation of traffic.

Aircrash

22.3.58, a Moth Major aircraft crashed in a field at Mill End, Rickmansworth resulting in slight injury.

Forced Landing

17.11.58 a Danish passenger aircraft made a forced landing at West Hyde resulting in damage only.

Police Pillar Boxes

A revision of the Police pillar system is in hand at Watford. New pillars are to come into operation when North Watford Police Station is opened.

New Aerial Site

It is necessary to move the wireless masts from Leverstock Green in Hemel Hempstead, because the ground is now required by the Hemel Hempstead Development Corporation. Difficulty has been experienced in finding a new site but there are now prospects of acquiring a suitable piece of land in Bedmond.

Rubber Cosh

On the 13th November 1958, at Abbots Langley, a youth was assaulted by a man using a rubber cosh. The youth received a fractured cheek bone.

On the 19th November 1958, a Police Sergeant saw a number of youths near the scene and they were seen to throw a cosh over a garden wall on his approach. Enquiries showed that the offence of Wounding was an act of retaliation for past insults, and that a further assault had been planned for the night of the 19th November 1958.

At the Hertfordshire Quarter Sessions on the 10th February 1959, the leader of the youths responsible for the assault was sent to Borstal and the others involved were Fined and Bound Over to Keep the Peace.

County.

1. A412 St. Albans Road, Town Hall to Dome Roundabout, 59 recorded injury accidents.

2. A411 High Street, Watford from Benskins Brewery to Town Hall, 42 recorded injury accidents.

3. A41 North Western Avenue, Watford from Dome Roundabout to junction with A411 (now Hunton Bridge Roundabout), 31 recorded injury accidents.

Ring Road

A new traffic circulatory system was introduced in Rickmansworth Town Centre, creating a one way system to try and reduce traffic flow problems.

Black Spots

In 1959 a survey showed that Watford, had the 3 worst accident black spots in the

M1 Opened

M1 Motorway was opened to traffic on the 2nd November apart from the final two and a half miles from Bricket Wood to Aldenham, which opened on 21st December. The flow of traffic exceeds 14,000 vehicles a day. The opening of the motorway has already seen a 33% drop in the number of accidents on Hertfordshires Trunk Roads.

Aircraft Crashes on Motorway

On 7th July 1959, a de Havilland Dragon Rapide aircraft, attempting to land on the new unfinished M1 Motorway crashed and burst into flames. One passenger was killed, the pilot and three other passengers were injured.

Fireworks

On the 5th November 1958, Terry Shinross, whilst attending a firework display at Oxhey, accidentally ignited a firework which set fire to his clothing. Sidney Searle, aged 15 years, of 50 Woodhall Lane, South Oxhey, removed a firework from the boys pocket and extinguished the flames, an act which subsequently resulted in him being awarded a Certificate from the Society for the Protection of Life from Fire recommended by the Chief Constable.

Rescued

Testimonials on parchment from the Royal Humane Society were awarded following the recommendation of the Chief Constable to Denis Wretham, aged 14 years, Brian Wretham, aged 16 years, both of 9 Winchfield Way, Rickmansworth and Keith Bunker, aged 15 years of 10 Winchfield Way, Rickmansworth for their act of rescuing from the River Colne at Rickmansworth, Lawrence Edscar, John and Barbara Pink and Sheila Moorby.

On the 23rd August 1959, Ian Dunford aged 21 years was rescued from drowning in the Bury Lake, The Aquadrome, Rickmansworth. He was also subsequently resuscitated, resulting in rewards from the Royal Humane Society to Sergeant Eric Noakes of the Metropolitan Police (Testimonial and Resuscitation Certificate), Frederick Jay, aged 23 years of Burnt Oak (Testimonial), and Mrs Kaye Harrold, of Northolt (Resuscitation certificate).

Police Pillar Boxes

The new Police Pillar system at North Watford was brought into operation, connected to the new operational Police Station. The new Station was opened officially on 29.4.59.

Road Safety - 1960

A demonstration of the importance and relative safety of Motorway travel compared to other Trunk roads becomes apparent at the end of the first year of the M1.

The M1 and A1 in Hertfordshire, both total 17 miles in length, a direct comparison in road traffic accidents shows clearly the safety of motorway travel.

6 killed on M1, 92 injured.

13 killed on A1, 261 injured.

Traffic control at the Whitsun Carnival 1960

Watford's One Way System
Work commences on one way system in Watford Town Centre in 1961.

Visit by Princess Alexandra
On the 1st July 1961 Princess Alexandra attended the Sports Day at Rickmansworth Masonic School for Girls.

New Mast
On 21st July 1961, the new Police wireless station at Bedmond, came into operation, greatly improving signal strength throughout the County.

Pay by Cheque
Methods of pay to Police Officers changed from fortnightly cash or cheque to a monthly cheque only.

Recruiting
Recruiting is still a problem, with the Force 25% below its authorised strength of 899 Officers.

M1 Safe
The safety of the new motorway the M1 is still obvious in comparison to the A1:

M1, 4 fatalities and 126 injured.

A1, 18 fatalities and 293 injured.

Black Spots
Accident statistics in "C" Division still a cause for serious concern, with 8 black spots out of the designated 19 in the County.

Retirement
The Assistant Chief Constable Abel Camp, M.B.E., D.C.M., M.M., retired after 42 years service with the Force. Mr Camp joined the Force in January 1919, after serving with the Royal Artillery during the 1914-18 war in which he was awarded the D.C.M. and M.M. He was appointed Deputy Chief Constable in 1937, and between 1943 and 1945 he took charge of the Force in the absence of the Chief Constable. In 1945, he was awarded the M.B.E., and in 1949 the King's Police Medal. Mr Camp was a previous Superintendent at Watford. He has been replaced by the appointment of Mr C.H. Cooksley on 1.11.61. Mr Cooksley has served as a Chief Superintendent in the Nottinghamshire Constabulary, although latterly he has been a Director of Studies at the Police College.

Neighbourhood Policeman
Experimental "Neighbourhood Policing" started at Stevenage and other Divisions.

School Crossings
School crossing patrols are introduced throughout the County.

Aircraft Crash
On 25.3.62, a Currie Wot biplane, crashed at Sarratt, resulting in damage only.

One Way Opened
On the 20th May 1962, the long awaited one way system was opened at Watford. The

new system incorporated new no waiting regulations. Conditions in the town showed an immediate improvement, with the previous obstructions cleared and traffic movement speeded up. The accident rate for the new system showed 251 recorded accidents since its inception to the end of year, identical to the figures in 1961 for the same dates. However, there was a significant increase in the number of accidents in the first 8 weeks before the public had become familiar with the new system, subsequent to this, there has been a gradual reduction in the number of accidents.

Scenes of Crime

42 Officers of the Force trained in basic Scenes of Crime work.

Train Crash

During the morning of Tuesday 16.10.62, an electric train travelling from Watford to Euston ran into the rear of another electric train which had been stationary between Watford Junction and High Street Stations. Five persons were slightly injured, and two were taken to Hospital with serious injuries.

Death of Retired Officer

Ex-Sergeant J. Snoxell, died on 12.8.62, aged 62 years, following his retirement on 12.8.50 after having served for many years in "C" Division.

Police Five

In December 1963, the ITV programme "Police 5", featured a photograph of a Chippendale mirror valued at £440, which had been stolen during a burglary at Moor Park. On the following day, an antiques dealer in Hanwell, Middlesex, telephoned to say that he had recently purchased the mirror. His information, led to the capture of the thief.

Crime Prevention

The Force appointed a Chief Inspector to co-ordinate its Crime Prevention Drive. Training courses were arranged throughout the year and 18 officers are now trained in basic Crime Prevention techniques.

Court Ushers

Civilian Court Ushers were appointed to Watford Magistrates Court, thereby releasing Police Officers for operational tasks.

Extension to North Watford Station

Approval was given to a planning application for an extension to North Watford Police Station to form the first of the new Police Traffic Bases in the County. Work is expected to commence in March 1964 and take 12 months to complete.

Women C.I.D.

The Force appoints two Women Police Officers to the C.I.D. as an experiment, which is seen to be successful.

Traffic Wardens

Traffic Wardens are appointed to St. Albans as an experiment, resulting in 1,935 tickets being issued in the first year.

Drugs

17 prosecutions were made for illegal possessions of drugs in the County.

Rest Days

In 1955, under Police Regulations, Police Officers became entitled to three Rest days every fortnight. In September 1964, despite the shortages in the Force the Chief Constable accepted that he could no longer justify not implementing this right and accordingly allowed granted a third day as a rest day.

Neighbours Policemen

"Neighbourhood Policing" was extended to

Watford and Rickmansworth.

Court Duty
The Court Officer at Watford Juvenile Court was given over to a Woman Police Sergeant for the first time.

Police Matron
In October, a Police Matron was appointed to Watford thus relieving Women Police Officers of the need to attend to female prisoners.

Best Garden
Following his retirement as Chairman of the Watford Bench of Magistrates in November 1963, Mr Gordon Ross, M.C., J.P., gave a cup to be presented to the winner of an annual competition for the best kept garden of a police house in the Watford Division. The first competition was judged on 27th July 1964, and was won by Inspector Mead.

Retirement
Chief Superintendent E.J. Player formerly C/Supt. "C" Division retired after 33 years service on 31.6.64.

Whitsun Carnival
On 7th June 1965, 27,000 people attended the annual Watford Borough Whitsun Carnival in Cassiobury Park, Watford.

March Past
On 3.7.65 HM Queen Mother took the salute at the march past of the men and cadets of the 1st Battalion the Bedfordshire and Hertfordshire Regiment (TA), at Watford Town Hall.

School Sports
On the 16th and 17th of July, the English School Sports Championships were held at Woodside Stadium, Watford. On both days, over 15,000 spectators attended.

Regional Crime Squad
At the end of 1964 a Regional Crime Squad was formed, with Headquarters at Welwyn Garden City and a branch office at Rickmansworth. The formation of the squad, is of an experimental nature and will be assessed at the end of 2 years. The function of the squad, is co-operation between the neighbouring forces to target and deal with criminals who deal in high class serious crime across County Boundaries.

Crime Prevention
A Crime Prevention Officer was appointed to act in each Division.

Accidents Reduced
"C" Division has only 2 out of the 18 in the County of Accident black spots, and these are in 9th and 10th places.

Radr speedguns
The Force purchases Radar speedguns, which are used to detect 1,621 offences within the year.

Photocopiers
Each Divisional station receives a photocopier.

Traffic Base
The Traffic Base at North Watford Police Station is completed and becomes operational.

New Headquarters
Work commences on the new Police Headquarters at Welwyn Garden City.

Anthrax
1 case of anthrax and 7 of fowl pest reported to Police under the Diseases of Animals Act.

1966

Burglar Alarms
Total number of burglar alarms fitted in the County is 590. One activation which lead to the arrest of the offender resulted in him admitting over 50 Burglaries.

Police Dogs
Police Dog Section make 45 arrests, find 6 missing persons and recovered 16 items of stolen property.

Temporary Speed Limit
The temporary 70 m.p.h. speed restriction is put into force on unrestricted roads in the County. It is difficult to assess the effect of the speed limit on the prevention of accidents generally, but comparable figures in 1965 and 1966 show that injury accidents have been reduced from 153 to 97 and fatalities from 11 to eight on the M1 and M10 Motorways. It is probable however that another factor contributing to this reduction was the banning of lorries from the outside lane of the motorways.

Traffic Wardens
2 Senior and 23 Traffic Wardens appointed to Watford.

1967

Police Committee
At a meeting of the Police Committee on 6th January 1967 the Chief Constable reported the following:

ESTABLISHMENT

	Authorised	Actual	Vacancies
Men	1,323	913	410
Women	76	46	30
Total	1,399	959	440

Drug Squad
A Drugs Squad was formed on 1st January 1967, with a strength of one Detective Sergeant, one Detective Constable and one Woman Detective Constable. They will be based at Headquarters. 26 persons were prosecuted in 1965 for illegal possession of drugs, the figures for 1966 show a sharp rise.

Tactical Patrol Group
The Force formed a Tactical Patrol Group on 1.10.65 to enable a reserve of officers to deal with public order and other responsibilities where required. The group consists of one Inspector, one Sergeant and 10 Constables. In 1966, the Group were responsible for 104 Arrests.

Budget
The Chief Constable asked for permission of the Police Committee for:

1. To set up an underwater search team at a cost of £1,135 for equipment.

2. To obtain a tape recorder in order to arrange a taped record of all messages on both wireless and telephones into the control room, at a cost of £3,198.

3. For the purchase of 7 postal franking machines at a cost of £522.1 shilling.

4. Replacement of accident damaged vehicles:

(a) Austin A60 by a Ford GT Cortina, cost £752.

(b) Austin Mini van by a Bedford 6 cwt van, cost £413.

He also informed the Committee that the planning application for a Neighbourhood Office and Garage at 74 Sandringham Road, Watford had been granted.

Whitsun Carnival

On 15.5.67 24,000 people attended the Whitsun carnival at Cassiobury Park.

Beat Patrol motor cyclist riding a Velocette fitted with two-way radio 1967. Photograph from history of Hertfordshire Constabulary 1969

Rural Beats

On 1st April 1967 a Rural Beat experimental scheme was introduced in Chorleywood. Four Bedford vans were purchased for use by Rickmansworth rural officers.

Unit Beat Policing

In St. Albans, unit beat policing was introduced using new personal radios. Phase II of the system will see Watford moving to unit beat patrol.

Male Hostels

A house was purchased by the Police and converted into accommodation for 3 single male officers.

Robbery

A gang of six men at Watford, climbed through the first floor window of a printing company and attacked a wages clerk and security officer working in a locked room. The gang tied up the employees and escaped with £10,000 in cash. Eventually, one of the gang was traced to Huntingdon, arrested, convicted and sentenced to 5 years imprisonment.

Assualt on Police

A total of 82 prosecutions were brought for assault on Police during the year. A number of officers were assaulted whilst questioning suspects. On one occasion at Moor Park, a detective officer was interrogating the occupants of a suspicious car, when the vehicle was suddenly driven at him. He threw himself on to the bonnet and was carried for over a mile before the vehicle stopped. The occupants were arrested. For his bravery, Constable Lee, a member of the Buckinghamshire Constabulary attached to the Regional Crime Squad, received the queen's commendation.

Drugs

In the first year of operation the Drugs Squad made 89 arrests for illegal possession of drugs. Two persons in the County died through drugs overdoses.

Breath Tests

On the 9th October 1967, the Alcotest Breath test was introduced. 101 Breath tests were administered before the end of the year, 26 of which were positive. Five persons were prosecuted for refusing to take the test. The average alcohol content of those found positive was 163 mg/100ml in blood (legal limit 80 mg/100 ml).

Queen's Commendation

The Queen's Commendation for Brave Conduct was awarded to Sergeant G.F. Thompson and Mr P.C. Gurney for tackling a man armed with an automatic pistol who was creating a disturbance in a Watford Dance Hall. In the course of the struggle to effect the arrest, Sergeant Thompson sustained cuts and bruises and a broken finger. The awards were presented on 26.4.67 by the Lord Lieutenant Major-General Sir George Burns, K.C.V.O., C.B., D.S.O., O.B.E., M.C. on behalf of her Majesty.

New Headquarters

The new Police Headquarters set in a site of 30 Acres becomes operational. Phase II of the building programme for a Training Bloc is to be built in 1969-1970.

Deaths

The following ex-"C" Division Officers died during the year.

Supt H. Batchelor aged 75 years on 6.1.67. Retired 31.12.38.

PS Springett aged 74 years on 19.6.67. Retired 4.8.38.

Information Room at the new police headquarters (1968)
Photograph from History of the Hertfordshire Constabulary

Retirement

Chief Superintendent Dear Retired during the year after 35 years service to the Force.

Motorway Phones

Motorway phones now fitted to the A1(M).

1968

Murder

The body of a young Indian woman was found strangled in bed at her home in Watford. Protracted enquiries made by a team of 50 Officers resulted in the arrest after six weeks, of a man of Pakistanian origin, who was subsequently charged with murder. On the same day, also in Watford, a Nigerian man and his wife were attacked by a man with a knife. The husband, received fatal injuries, but the wife survived. A fellow Nigerian was arrested and found guilty of manslaughter. He was committed to Broadmoor.

Manslaughter
A Watford man, had petrol thrown over him by his wife, who then ignited the petrol. The man died from his burns. His wife was found guilty of manslaughter and was ordered to be confined to a mental institution.

Robbery
Six or seven men, using stolen cars, rammed a security vehicle in Watford. They attacked the three guards with ammonia and shot at, but missed, a woman witness standing nearby. The robbers made off with over £6,000. One of the gang was later arrested and sentenced to 12 years imprisonment.

Stolen Furs
Furs valued at £3,000 were stolen from a Watford shop, when thieves pushed a tree branch through the bars of a rear window and dragged the racks on which the furs were stored within their reach. By carefully pulling the furs through the window bars, the burglar alarm was not activated.

Assualts
86 people were prosecuted for assaults on Police. At Watford Police Station, a Sergeant was attacked by a detained drug addict and was badly cut on his hand.

A Constable questioning two youths late at night at Moor Park was suddenly and violently attacked. The youths escaped leaving the officer with cuts to his head and face.

Dual Carriageway Complete
The A405 Dual Carriageway in Garston was completed.

Shotguns Registered
On the 1st May 1968, all holders of shotguns were required to register the weapons with the Police. As a result, 9,643 Certificates were issued. Extra clerical staff had to be employed to ease the burden of this work.

Assistant Chief Constable
In 1968, the strength of the Force justified the appointment of an additional Assistant Chief Constable. Accordingly, the Police Committee appointed to the post Mr. Ivor Jones, who had served for 33 years in the Metropolitan Police Force. Mr Jones took up his duties on 1st January 1968, but on the 29th January, he had a sudden heart attack at Police Headquarters and collapsed and died within a few minutes. He left a widow and two sons.

Mr Leonard Sample, then serving in the Essex Constabulary, took up the appointment of ACC on 1st April 1968.

Death
The Retired Deputy Chief Constable Abel Camp, aged 72 died on 1.3.68.

1969

Train Derailed
On the 8th August 1969, an express train travelling from Glasgow to London was derailed in the Watford tunnel. A number of passengers were slightly injured but did not need hospital tratment. All passengers were conveyed from the scene to Watford Junc-

tion Station for onward journeys.

Annual Report

Foreword to the Annual Report into the year 1969 by the Chief Constable R.N. Buxton.

It is not the usual practice to include a foreword to the Annual Report, but there are special reasons why one is appropriate for 1969.

Firstly, the year saw the retirement of Mr. A.F. Wilcox, C.B.E., Q.P.M., who was appointed Chief Constable of Hertfordshire in 1947, prior to which he had served at Bristol, in the Metropolitan Police and for a short while as Assistant Chief Constable of Buckinghamshire. During his period of 22 years as Chief Constable, the population of the County Police District rose by 300,000; the establishment of the Force increased from 613 to 1,400, and there was a rapid expansion of the Police Cadet Corps and civilian staff. In addition, traffic wardens were introduced to deal with parked vehicles and other forms of traffic control. The fleet of vehicles grew from 58 in 1947 to 270 in 1969 and many items of equipment in both the operational and administrative fields were introduced. The network of telephone lines and teleprinters was extended and sophisticated systems of radio communications brought into use. The programme of station building was stepped up and in 1967 the new County Police Headquarters at Stanborough Rd, Welwyn Garden City, was opened. At the end of the Second World War, the Police Authority owned or rented 274 police houses or quarters. By 1969, 771 new houses had been built and a start made on providing hostels and quarters for single men and women.

These achievements under Mr. Wilcox's command reflect his foresight and energy and the Force is grateful for his leadership over such a lengthy period.

A second good reason for a foreword is that at a time when crime is mounting, and when there is danger of violence, protest and public disorder becoming accepted features of everyday life, the Police Service has become the focus of attention in the Press, radio and television. Much has been written and said about morale and the effectiveness of the Police in what is now regarded as the "permissive" society. One cannot speak for the whole of the service but it is only right to recognize that the police in Hertfordshire although severely undermanned, have continued with great loyalty to preserve a high degree of law and order. The detection rate for crime has been maintained, the number of arrests and the total number of offenders brought before the courts has increased, and there is no falling away of the eagerness to serve the public.

It is true to say, however, that there is a great deal of disappointment and anxiety felt in the force by the pay situation, by the delay in the settlement of the increase in rent allowance, by the failure to gain an undermanning allowance and by fears about the proposed earnings related States pension scheme. All these, of course, are dependent upon National, not local, dictates. Nevertheless, despite these disappointments, the morale of the Force is surprisingly high.

Assaults on Police remain an area for concern, at Watford a Constable found two men in a van containing stolen property. The officer was butted in the face and received a broken nose and lacerations. The two men were later dealt with at Quarter sessions, and both received 6 months imprisonment.

Offences concerning the abuse of methadone, a drug used in the withdrawal of addicts from Heroin, increased considerably

Hertfordshire Police at the scene of an accident

Police accident tender fitted with two-way radio and carrying walkie-talkie pack sets and accident equipment, 1969.
Photograph from History of the Hertfordshire Constabulary 1969

over previous years as it is now more easily obtainable by illegal means. An example of the tragic consequences of this practice, occurred at Watford when a 16 year old boy was supplied with methadone tablets by a registered addict. The boy took the tablets orally and later died in hospital. The supplier of the drug was prosecuted and sentenced to 3 years imprisonment at Hertfordshire Quarter Sessions in July.

At the end of the year, the Force was 306 men and 28 women short of its established strength of 1400 Officers.

1970

34,000 Crowds at Watford

The Watford Football Club had a successful run in the F.A. Cup when the team reached the semi-final. Large crowds attended several home games. The most notable of which were Stoke City 24,000, Gillingham 20,000, and Liverpool 34,000.

Robbery

In March 1970, three employees were leaving a Watford Department store when they were confronted by four masked men carrying firearms. They were forced to return to the store and to disconnect the alarm system. With the keys taken from one of the employees, the safe was opened and £4,900 in cash was stolen. All the employees were then bound and left on the premises whilst the offenders escaped in a motor van. Despite extensive enquiries the crime remains unsolved.

Armed Robbery

In April 1970, an armed robbery occurred at a Watford bank. Members of a security firm were delivering money to the premises when they were set upon by armed criminals wearing stocking masks. One of the guards was shot and severely injured and the sum of £20,000 stolen. About two weeks later a man was arrested and charged with being concerned in the robbery. At the Hertfordshire Assizes he was sentenced to imprisonment for a period of 12 years.

Smoke Screen

An example of equipment specially designed to combat crime was successfully used occurred in September. A woman cashier in Watford was walking to the bank with the previous day's takings when she was attacked by three men. She was carrying £1,862 in a specially made security bag which was strapped to her wrist. The bag was snatched from her but this action activated a mechanism causing the emission of thick smoke and dye. The thieves escaped in a car but experienced difficulty with the security bag which continued to emit smoke and they were forced to transfer the bag from the interior of the car to the boot. As a result of this delay their escape route was cut by the police who set up road checks on the outskirts of Watford. Within 25 minutes of the robbery, three men were arrested in possession of the stolen money. They appeared at Hertfordshire Assizes and were sentenced to 18 months imprisonment, Borstal training, and a suspended prison sentence respectively.

Fraud Squad

1970 saw the formation of a Fraud Squad in Hertfordshire. In the first year they investigated 34 cases.

Fraud

A Watford Insurance broker submitted fraudulent hire purchase documents respecting non-existent motor cars to three finance companies and thereby defrauded them of £24,000. He subsequently appeared before the Hertfordshire Quarter Sessions and was sentenced to 18 months imprisonment. His five lesser accomplices received sentences ranging from fines to an absolute discharge (with 50 guineas costs).

Fingerprints
A new method of preserving fingerprints found at scenes of crime was brought into use towards the end of the year. This consists of developing the latent impression with powder and "lifting" the print by the use of transparent adhesive tape. This obviates the necessity to photograph marks and additionally, reduces the need to remove and store bulky articles for examination.

Scenes of Crime Inspector
A Detective Inspector was appointed in charge of the Scenes of Crime Department. This was placed on a proper footing with two full time detective constables at each division as SOCO's.

Cannabis Plants
A Watford resident, was found to have successfully grown 12 Cannabis Sativa plants 8 feet tall in his garden. He was prosecuted and fined £50.

Crime Prevention Panel
In 1970, a Crime Prevention Panel was formed in Watford.

Fog
On the 12th March 1970, 24 accidents occurred in fog conditions on the M1. 87 vehicles were known to have been involved. One person was killed and 10 were injured. The first accident occurred at 8 a.m. on the southbound carriageway of the two lane section near the A 405 junction. A further 8 accidents followed and by 9.15 a.m., it was necessary to divert southbound traffic from the M1 to the M10. Further accidents occurred further North at Hemel Hempstead, and it was eventually necessary to close the motorway at Luton until all wrecked vehicles could be removed. The motorway was re-opened at 12.21 p.m. As a result of these accidents, 23 persons were prosecuted for careless driving of which 20 were convicted. Two were dismissed and the third has not proceeded due to the injuries sustained by the defendant.

Acid Spillage
On the 14th December 1970, following a series of minor accidents in fog on the two lane section of the M1 near the junction with the A 405, an articulated tanker lorry containing 2,000 gallons of hydrochloric acid overturned and completely blocked the southbound carriageway and hard shoulder. Traffic was diverted onto the M10 at 10.02 a.m. and the diversion was not lifted until 3.35 p.m.

New Roundabouts
Two new Roundabouts were completed at Two Bridges, resulting in better traffic flow.

Visit to Mainz
Constable Maxwell, the "C" Division Road Safety Officer and 8 members of the local Junior Accident Prevention Council visited the twin towns to Watford, Mainz, West Germany and Nanterre, France. In both towns, demonstrations of British methods of teaching Road Safety were given to members of the public and the events were widely covered by the press and local radio and T.V. stations.

VHF Radio
The main scheme VHF radios now linked to the Metropolitan Police and neighbouring police forces.

Emergency Phones
All emergency telephones on M1, M10, and

A 1(M) now switched directly to Headquarters rather than to Hemel Hempstead as before. All '999' calls also switched through to HQ rather than Divisional Stations.

Gas Emergency

In May 1970, three youths, who were later reported for wilful damage, interfered with the mechanism of a small roadside gas regulator causing a severe rise in mains pressure in the Abbots Langley, Kings Langley, Leavesden and Garston areas. The neighbouring areas of Chipperfiel and Bovingdon were also affected. The build up of pressure caused several fractures in the mains, major leaks at Abbots Langley, and explosions and damage occurred in several dwelling and business premises. Five persons were injured but were discharged from hospital after emergency treatment. The Police, Fire and Ambulance Services treated the incident as a full-scale emergency. Overall evacuation of the area was considered a possibility but a reduction of mains pressure by the Gas Board made this unnecessary. Nevertheless, over 100 Police Officers were involved in warning householders of the dangers until appliances had been inspected by Gas Board Officials. About 100 Gas Board fitters worked throughout the night and the following day until every house had been visited and appliances checked.

Double Glazing at Rickmansworth

Major structural alterations were carried out at Rickmansworth Police Station, installing double glazing and the addition of new offices making use of space in the entrance hall.

Robbery

A nasty robbery concerned the waylaying of pedestrians going about their lawful business in July 1971, at Watford, when four men were attacked one after the other by a 30 year old man and a 16 year old youth without any provocation whatsoever. The first incident involved a 64 year old man who was kicked unconscious and received a broken leg and lacerations which required 20 stitches. A 32 year old man was robbed of £32 and received a broken nose and severe lacerations. A third man was attacked with a razor and a fourth slashed with a metal object. Following intensive police enquiries, both offenders were arrested 5 days later and at the Central Criminal Court, on charges of robbery and unlawful wounding, the older assailant was sentenced to 6 months imprisonment on each count (concurrent) and the 16 year old youth was sent for Borstal training.

Armed Robbery

Two men attacked a jeweller's shop at Watford and threatened the manager and his staff with a shotgun. Cash and property to the value of £6,745 were stolen. Two men were arrested and were sentenced to 4 and 5 years' imprisonment respectively.

Attempted Murder

In July 1971, a 6 year old girl was left to play for a short while in a public park at Oxhey. Following a search, she was found in a semi-conscious condition in a nearby copse suffering from 8 stab wounds. Her condition for a time was critical but she subsequently recovered and her assailant, a 17 year old local youth, was traced and charged with attempted murder. At the Central Criminal Court in November he was sentenced to 5 years imprisonment.

Didn't like breath Test

A motorist attacked a Police Constable in Watford who had asked him to take a breath test. The officer was butted in the face causing a wound that required 15 stitches.

As a result, he was off duty for seven days. The man was charged with unlawful wounding and at the Hertfordshire Quarter Sessions he was sentenced to 9 months imprisonment suspended for 2 years.

Community Relations

At Watford, a senior police officer was appointed as part time Community Relations Officer and co-opted onto the Advisory Commission on Immigration, but without voting rights.

Process Servers

The force employed 6 civilian process servers/fines enforcement officers on a shared cost basis with the Magistrates Courts. One officer was posted to each division. In the first two months of operation, they dealt with over 500 Warrants and 600 Summonses.

Black Spots

Out of 12 designated Accident black spots in the County, 5 were in "C" Division.

The worst black spot in the County was the A 412 Town Hall to Gammons Lane, Watford which saw 37 recorded injury accidents.

Also included were the B 4542 Oxhey Woods House to Lytham Ave, Oxhey, A 4145 Railway Bridge to Kelmscott Crescent, Watford, A 412 Gammons Lane to Sheepcot Lane, Watford, and the A 405 Trevellance Way to M1 at Waterdale.

Operations Room

The new operations room at County Police Headquarters became fully operational.

Telephone Exchange

North Watford Police Station receives its own telephone exchange.

Incident Room

A new Incident Room is set up at Rickmansworth Police Station with 4 telephone links.

Mobile Police Station

A new Mobile Police Station is purchased by the Force to replace the original one (purchased in 1951). The new vehicle is capable of dealing with both VHF and UHF radios, in its own control room. The vehicle has its own telephone exchange with two public exchange phone lines. It is equipped with flashing blue lights and has an public enquiry area and a conference room. The now obsolete vehicle is retained by the force for use as an exhibition unit for road safety or crime prevention and as a mobile canteen.

Nosy Dog

Following a report of a burglary at Rickmansworth, a dog handler was en route to the scene when he saw two men who answered the description of the offenders. He arrested one man, but the other ran off. The dog handler called for assistance, handed his prisoner over to the other officers and set off with his dog in pursuit of the second man. The dog tracked for half a mile and caught up with the man who was also arrested.

Clever Graduate

The first University graduate accepted to the Force under the graduate entry scheme was Constable A. Mansell who was appointed on 30.9.71 and posted to Watford Division.

Women Cadets

In September 1971, the first 10 girl cadets were appointed after the Home Office granted an establishment figure of 10 female cadets. In addition, there are 120 Male cadets in the Force.

Increase in Crime

1972, showed what initially appears to be a huge increase in crime of 2,296 more crimes than in 1971. 1,018 of these are however due to a change in the reporting of cases of criminal damage. Previous to January, criminal damage under £100 was not recorded as a crime.

The detection rate for crime reached 53% the highest ever rate for the County.

Aggravated Burglary

A private house in Moor Park was forcibly entered by three men. The occupants, were threatened with violence and jewellery and cash was stolen. When Police were notified, an immediate investigation was mounted and, while this was still under way, an alarm call was received from a house in Rickmansworth. Police officers attended and after a short chase a man was arrested. Following further investigation, a second man was also arrested in connection with the two offences.

Central Intelligence

Criminals, have no respect for boundaries, and the Criminal Intelligence Section (CIS), based at Headquarters, provides valuable information by identifying patterns of crime which are not restricted to a particular area. An example of the co-operation that exists between this department, Scenes of Crime Officers (SOCO) and other branches of the Force is illustrated by the investigation into an offence of burglary which occurred in June 1972, at Moor Park. Following several burglaries in the area, the CIS, forwarded the index numbers of certain vehicles and a member of the Tactical Patrol Group who was engaged on observation duties saw one of the suspect vehicles parked unattended. Shortly afterwards, a burglary was reported in the area and the owner of the vehicle was seen but he denied the offence. However, SOCO found glass fragments in the suspects possession, which the Forensic Science Laboratory matched with broken glass found at the scene of the crime. In addition, tools found in the suspects possession bore paint scrapings which linked him with another offence that had occurred in the Metropolitan Police District. At his appearance at St. Albans Crown Court in November, the offender was sentenced to 6 years imprisonment.

Arson

During a night in December 1972, a timber merchant's premises at Rickmansworth was set on fire by intruders. Damage to an approximate value of £48,444 was caused and two 14 year old offenders were arrested and charged with the offence.

Drugs Dog

The Dog Section, had available for the first time a golden Labrador 'Buck' handled by Pc Flint, trained to detect cannabis. In the first year, 'Buck' was involved in 42 searches, finding 17 items of drugs resulting in 19 Arrests.

Dog Trials

The Police Dog Section holds its first Police Dog Trial which is now an annual event.

Deeper Accident Investigation

The Traffic Management and Accident Prevention Department, took on a new role with officers trained in Deeper Accident Investigation, to provide a detailed and thorough investigation into the causes of serious accidents.

Gas Explosion

On 30th January 1972, an explosion occurred in a block of flats in Croxley Green, causing the death of one man and injuring several other persons. The explosion was believed to have been caused by a build up of gas and one end of the block of flats was severely damaged.

Fire
On the 19th March 1972, a house at Scotts Hill, Rickmansworth, was gutted by fire. The A 412 road was closed and traffic was diverted for two hours.

Found after Search
In September 1972, an 83 year old woman was reported missing from her home near Watford. A police search was mounted, involving over 60 officers, and the team was successful in finding the woman the following day lying in woodland some miles from her home and suffering from exposure.

Plan Drawers
The Force now has 3 Sergeants and 7 Constables fully trained as Plan Drawers.

Modernising Watford Station
Planning was started for the modernisation of the Sub-divisional station at Watford and the building of a new Divisional Administration block to include hostels for single officers.

First Chaplain
The Force appoints its first Chaplain.

Welfare Officer
The Force also appoints a full time Welfare Officer.

More Policemen Needed
Between 1969 and 1973, the actual strength of the Force has increased from 1,066 to 1,262 officers. This is still short of the authorised establishment of 1,400, which was fixed in 1965 for the needs of that year. The authorised establishment has now been increased to 1,472 but this is only a first phase in that in 1972, the Police Committee agreed that an establishment of 1,642 officers was required for adequate coverage of the County Police District. This means, that in reality, there is a deficiency of some 400 men and women for the needs of 1974.

Airship at Leavesden
On 22.6.73 to 30.6.73, the Airship "Europa" was moored at Leavesden aerodrome, which generated large numbers of sightseers to the aerodrome and its surrounding roads.

Murder
In February 1973, a woman was charged with murder after her husband was found dead from stab wounds at South Oxhey. At her trial at St. Albans Crown Court in June, her plea of self defence was accepted by the jury and she was acquitted.

Mugging
In the early hours of the morning of 28th January 1973, an 18 year old youth was attacked by a gang of youths in a Watford Street and robbed of his coat and its contents. In the attack, a serious head injury was sustained. However, police obtained a good description of the youths and their vehicles. A few days later, the suspected vehicles were sighted in Watford and followed to an M1 service station by a Hertfordshire Officer. There, with the aid of the Metropolitan Police, a number of youths were arrested. At the St. Albans Crown Court, one youth was sent to Borstal, two to Detention Centres and six others were fined between £10 and £50.

Armed Robbery
On the 18th February 1973, a cinema manager was held up and robbed of £60 by two men, one of whom fired a pistol at the manager's assistant who came to his aid. A few days later, 2 men armed with pistols

attacked a Watford man at his home. The householder was shot in the leg after which he and his family were tied up and the telephone wires were ripped out. The intruders then made off after stealing £600. Both of these offences were linked balistically, and as a result of widespread police enquiries, two men subsequently appeared before St. Albans Crown Court, where one was sent to prison for 10 years, and the other for 5 years. In June 1974, in the presence of the Chairman of the County Council and members of the Police Committee at North Watford Police Station, the Chief Constable presented a Certificate of Commendation to Geoffrey Lycester Antrobus of Watford for the courage he displayed when he went to the aid of the cinema manager, during the course of which, he was in grave danger from shots fired from a .22 pistol.

Burglary

In the early hours of a Monday morning in October 1973, two uniformed officers on patrol in Watford Road, Croxley Green, Rickmansworth, saw a 34 year old London man walking along the road and found him to be in possession of a record player and a silver cigarette case. Upon a further search of the suspect, they found a pair of gloves, torch, a punch, a length of wire, sellotape, a knife and a screwdriver. The man subsequently appeared at St. Albans Crown Court on three charges of burglary with over 100 cases taken into consideration. He was sentenced to a total of 7 years imprisonment.

Affray

In March 1973, 32 arrests were made at Watford following a fight in a ballroom involving local youths and others from North London. A more serious affray took place in Watford in September, when two groups of youths clashed after late-night parties. Some armed themselves with bread knives and one youth was stabbed in the stomach. On seeking refuge by forcing his way into a private dwelling house he was pursued by his attackers. Six men were arrested and as well as the knives, a pickaxe handle, a broom and a builders shovel were taken from them. Another affray also took place at a public house in Watford, in November, where six coloured men were arrested following a fight in which a man received stab wounds to the stomach.

Damage to School

Two 14 year old boys in Watford were made subject of supervision orders, fined and ordered to pay compensation after they had caused over £1,000 worth of damage to a Watford School.

Fuel Shortage

The fuel shortage which occurred towards the end of the year inevitably led to thefts of petrol and diesel oil. At Watford, in late December, 500 gallons of diesel valued at £300 was stolen from a tank. The thieves lifted the inspection cover, drew off the fuel and then refilled the tank with water so that the fuel gauge was unaffected.

Dirty Books

Early in the year, Metropolitan and Hertfordshire Officers searched a warehouse in Watford and seized large stocks of pornographic magazines. Later in the year, a further combined search resulted in large quantities of magazines, books and films being seized from various other addresses in Watford. Ten people were charged with offences under the Obscene Publications Act.

Hostages

Three Pakistani youths, masked and armed with knives, acid and what were later discovered to be toy pistols, entered the Indian High Commission Offices in Aldwych, London and took hostages. Metropolitan officers attended and two of the youths both aged 19 years, were shot and killed. The third youth, aged 15 years, was arrested. At the time, all three were resident in the Watford area, the two older youths being employed in Rickmansworth while the 15 year old attended a secondary modern school in Watford. Hertfordshire Special Branch Officers helped members of the Metropolitan Police in extensive follow-up enquiries in the County Police District to establish the background to this incident and to trace the source of the weapons.

Overdoses

6 Drug addicts in the County died from accidental over dosage of drugs.

Reducing Speed

On 28th August 1973, the Transport and Road Research Laboratory laid transverse yellow lines with gradual diminishing distances between them over a distance of 405 metres on the eastbound carriageway of the A405 west of the A6 junction (London Colney Roundabout). It is hoped that the lines will be effective in reducing approach speeds to the roundabout and thereby prevent accidents.

Traffic Administartion

On the 10th September 1973, a Traffic Administration Unit was set up at the North Watford Traffic Base to deal with the Administration of traffic related offences and accidents.

Flick Knife

At Watford, following a call by detective officers, a dog and handler attended an incident requiring the arrest of a man armed with a flick knife who was wanted for assault on Police and other offences. On being confronted by the dog, the man, who was known to have a violent disposition, threw the weapon away and allowed himself to be detained.

Drugs Dog

Constable John Flint with "Buck" the Golden Labrador drug dog continued to provide support in the detection of drug offences. In the first full year of operation the dog was used in 92 searches, finding 31 items of drugs and contributing to the arrest of 48 persons suspected of drug offences.

Home made Bomb

On a Saturday evening in March 1973, a group of youngsters had a very lucky escape. Following a loud explosion, Police and firemen went to a playing field near Bedmond School and found that boys aged between 14 and 15 years had been experimenting with a mixture consisting of weedkiller and other substances. The youths were unharmed, but a woman living nearby required hospital treatment for shock. Following an investigation, court proceedings were not considered necessary but the boys were warned of the likely consequences of repeating the experiment.

Fatal Accident

On the 10th September 1973, Constable C. Roddis was killed on duty when the motor cycle he was riding was in collision with a heavy goods vehicle. He was not married. He joined the Force in 1961, and was stationed at the North Watford Traffic Base.

Women Traffic Cops

During the year, the first two Women Police Officers, joined the Traffic Department, two joined the Tactical Patrol Group and the first Woman Detective Sergeant was appointed.

Going for Gold

JUDO- Woman Constable S.A. Evans was

awarded an Individual Gold Medal in the Northern Home Counties Judo Championships held in May. As a member of a civilian team, she also won a silver medal in the team event.

Pop Concert

On 5th May 1974, a 'Pop' Concert was held at Watford Football Ground. Various well known artists performed, and the attendance was in excess in 30,000. The event passed off without untoward incident. The Policing of this event was to become extremely beneficial later in the year when the first Knebworth Pop Concert was held.

Fatal Fight

A large number of youths were involved in a brawl at a North Watford social Club in February, which culminated in the death of one of them from head injuries. Two men in their twenties subsequently appeared at St. Albans Crown Court charged with manslaughter. Both were acquitted on the substantial charge, but one was found guilty of causing actual bodily harm and was sentenced to 9 months imprisonment suspended for 2 years.

Robbery

In January, a shop manager was attacked by 4 men as he was locking up his premises in Watford. After assaulting him with a piece of metal piping and demanding money, the men escaped empty handed.

Robbery

In February, a sub-postmaster, was attacked by 3 men as he was leaving his Oxhey premises. The victim, was taken to the back of the premises, tied up with wire and robbed of his safe keys. The men then made off with cash and securities worth £9,000.

Robbery

An arrest was made in connection with a robbery at a sub-post office at North Watford in October, where £735 was stolen after the sub-postmaster had been struck with an iron bar and his wife threatened with an imitation firearm.

Robbery

A shop employee and his 15 year old son were taking cash to a night safe at Watford, when they were attacked and robbed of £165 by 3 coloured men.

Arson

Two teenage girls were dealt with at Watford Juvenile Court in November, after being found guilty of arson. Damage exceeding £12,000 was caused in an attack on premises in Rickmansworth. The two girls were arrested by a patrolling Police Sergeant, who saw smoke coming out of the building as the two girls were leaving it.

Fights

At a Watford dance hall in February, a fight occurred between 2 rival groups and one youth was slashed with a razor blade. After Police intervention, 5 persons were arrested. at another incident in Watford, during an attempt by one group of youths to goad another group into a fight, it was alleged that a shotgun was discharged.

Assualt on Police

Two Watford Officers were placed on the sick list, as a result of an attack on them where one officer received a broken wrist and the other a broken nose and rib. Another Watford officer received a fractured hand when assaulted whilst making an arrest.

A Constable at Watford was assaulted by a motorist who drove at him. The officer was forced to cling onto the bonnet of the car. The officer was commended by the Judge at the drivers trial which resulted in an 18 month prison sentence.

Stone Throwing

Three teenage youths caused £2,000 worth of damage in Watford, when after leaving a party they drove through the town, stopping only to throw stones at private dwelling houses and telephone kiosks. At St. Albans Crown Court, one of the youths was sent for 6 months to a detention centre, the other defendants were all given 6 month suspended sentences. All were banned from driving for one year in respect of driving offences and they were ordered to pay over £900 compensation between them.

Rape

At Watford, late one evening in February, a woman accepted a lift from a passing van driver. He took her to an isolated spot where he raped her under threat of violence with a hammer. The woman gave a good description of her attacker to Police, and also described his vehicle and a builder's hut near the scene of the offence. The following day teams of officers operating from an Incident Room at Watford set out to search building sites for the described builder's hut. Near the new Watford by pass (A405T Maple Cross to Hunton Bridge-now part of the M25), officers recovered an earring belonging to the victim which had torn off in the attack. Further enquiries took them to a depot in Chorleywood, where a man answering the description was seen. He was arrested and subsequently admitted responsibility for the offence. In July, at his trial he was sentenced to 18 months imprisonment.

Crime Prevention

The Crime Prevention Office is augmented by a Constable to work with the Sergeant.

Speeding

The Force purchase 5 VASCAR sets (Visual Average Speed Computer and Recorders), for fitting in Traffic cars.

Traffic Officers

All three traffic bases now have Policewomen attached to them.

Police Vehicles

The Police purchase 6 Ford Escort cars for use jointly by the Divisional Coroners Officers and the Women Police.

Police National Computer

The Police National Computer (PNC) becomes operational at HQ on 29.7.74. Between then and the end of the year, Police recovered a total of 843 stolen cars compared to 196 in the comparable period in 1973.

Stolen Car

In November, a Watford Policeman radioed details of a car he was following to HQ, for a check on PNC. The enquiry showed that the vehicle had been stolen from Bletchley a few days previously. Within one minute of making the enquiry, the car was stopped and four persons arrested.

Telephone Exchanges

New telephone exchanges were installed at Rickmansworth, Oxhey and North Watford to give direct dialling facilities and improved internal dialling facilities within "C" Division.

Dog Track

Following a burglary at Langleybury Cricket Club, a dog and its handler located and followed a track onto the A41 and into a pedestrian subway where the dog found a broken beer bottle. The bottle was handed to a SOCO, and from a fingerprint developed a local criminal was arrested who admitted the offence and implicated an accomplice.

Equal Pay

On the 1st September 1974, Women Police Officers received the same pay as their male counterparts.

Fatal Accident

On 9th November 1974, Traffic Warden Mrs J.M. Liberty received fatal injuries when she was involved in a road traffic accident whilst off duty. She was appointed in 1968 and was stationed at Watford.

Rail Crash, Water Lane, Watford, 23rd January 1975

WATER LANE RAIL CRASH

At 10.28 p.m. on Thursday 23rd January 1975, on the London to Glasgow Railway Line at Water Lane, Watford an express passenger train became derailed and encroached on the 'down fast' line. A second passenger train travelling north, at speed, collided with the derailed engine. The locomotive and leading brake van of the Glasgow bound train became detached and plunged down a 40 foot embankment, whilst the remainder of the train - 3 sleeper coaches, 8 passenger coaches, and a parcel van - came to rest with 2 of the coaches leaning at a dangerous angle to the embankment. Of the 300 persons on the trains, the driver of one was killed and 11 passengers were injured but only one seriously. Following the initial alarm, full major incident procedure was carried out. All unassigned mobile patrols were sent and additional police personnel were despatched from neighbouring divisions. A police incident post was set up at the scene and liaison was effected with the fire and ambulance services. Incident control was established at Watford Central Police Station together with a casualty bureau to deal with enquiries from the public and the media. Due to damage to overhead cables, passengers had to be contained within the carriages and reassured until the power shut-off had been confirmed. Traffic diversions were put into operation to facilitate the passage of emergency services vehicles. Security of trains and property were relinquished to the British Transport Police at 11.45 p.m., with Hertfordshire Officers retaining control of the area to prevent unauthorised access. The incident post at the scene was closed at 3.45 a.m. on 24th January, but a small contingent of officers maintained security until handing over to the British Transport Police at 10 a.m. Sightseers caused a great deal of traffic congestion and attention had to be given to the area by Police and traffic wardens until dusk on the 24th January, and during daylight hours for the next two days. The removal of the rolling stock also required police supervision. The incident control post at Watford Central Police Station closed at 10 a.m. on the 24th January, but due to enquiries from a wide area, the casualty bureau remained in operation until 1 p.m. on Saturday 25th January, by which time over 400 enquiries had been dealt with. A total of 82 officers were engaged in the initial phase of the operation and additional help was provided by the Metropolitan Police and the Special Constabulary. Taking into account the number of passengers carried and the circumstances of the accident, it was extremely fortunate that casualties were not a great deal higher.

Carnival

On 26th May 1975, the Watford and District Carnival procession culminated with various activities in Cassiobury Park. About 30,000 people lined the route and a further 18,000 gathered in the park.

Merchant Taylors

On the 10th November, Her Majesty Queen Elizabeth the Queen Mother, accompanied by the Archbishop of Canterbury, opened an extension building at Merchant Taylor's School in Moor Park.

Increase in Crime

Crime figures show a 22% increase in recorded crime to 30,431 offences. The highest single rise in the History of the Force.

Manslaughter

In April, Police were called to an address at Watford where they found the body of a woman who had been struck over the head with a blunt instrument. Subsequently, the deceased's 15 year old son was arrested and charged with murder. At his trial in October, he was convicted of manslaughter and made the subject of a Hospital order. The investigation only occupied 6 Police Officers and 360 hours of Police time.

Attempted Robbery

In January, a youth entered a sub-post office in Abbots Langley, and struck the sub-postmaster's wife over the head with an air pistol but ran off empty handed when other members of staff raised the alarm. He later gave himself up and at St. Albans Crown Court, he was sentenced to 4 years imprisonment.

Burglar Caught

The initiative shown by a uniformed officer on foot patrol, followed by good detective work and interrogation by a C.I.D. colleague, resulted in the appearance of a youth at St. Albans Crown Court in March, where he received a three year prison sentence for burglary and 197 similar offences were taken into consideration. The officer, was in Watford High Street, when he recognised a youth who had previously given false information about his identity. The officer arrested the youth on suspicion of theft, and protracted enquiries revealed his responsibility for the series of offences.

Burglaries

The latter part of the year, saw a spate of burglaries involving the theft of foodstuffs. In November, thieves broke into a garage at Rickmansworth and stole chickens, salmon, mackerel and teabags worth a total of £1,000, while selected cuts of meat worth £1,700 were stolen from a Watford butchers also in November after padlocks had been cut away from deep freezers.

Smash and Grab

Two men were sentenced to 4 years and nine months imprisonment respectively at St. Albans Crown Court for their part in a 'smash and grab' raid on a jewellers in Watford where they had netted £1,250 in jewellery.

Theft

An audacious walk in theft at Watford occurred when a man dressed as a Security guard succeeded in entering a shop where unsuspecting staff handed him £3,500 in cash and cheques.

Very Suspicious

In April, a uniformed constable on duty in the foyer of Watford Magistrates Court saw a man who was known to him, wearing an expensive looking pendant and a ring. The officer immediately reported the matter and enquiries were commenced. A search warrant was obtained and the suspect's house was searched, together with another house at Garston where jewellery, cosmetics and travellers cheques worth £14,000 were recovered. The property was the proceeds of a theft the previous day from a vehicle parked near Picadilly Underground Station, and from a number of theft's and burglaries committed in the Watford area. Two men appeared at St. Albans Crown Court in July when one was sentenced to 3 years imprisonment for theft offences, and the other was fined £200 for handling stolen property.

Stolen Lorries

A lorry was stolen from a locked yard at Watford, when thieves forced a padlock on the gates, was later recovered minus its load of metal alloy worth £3,000. Two lorries loaded with fencing material valued at £8,500 were stolen from a yard at Croxley Green. A lorry with £4,000 of timber was stolen from Rickmansworth and recovered minus the load.

Drugs Investigations

The merging of the Drugs Squad into the Central Detective Unit (CDU), has enabled a greater concentration of effort into the actions of illegal manufacturers and dealers rather than casual users. A particularly successful operation occurred when following the receipt of information by Hertfordshire Officers, the CDU, the Metropolitan Police Drugs Squad and the Regional Crime Squad (RCS) executed a search warrant at a pharmacy in Borehamwood in April. Five pounds of amphetamine sulphate, together with quantities of opium, L.S.D., and cannabis, the black market value of which was estimated to be in excess of £180,000, was recovered. Four persons subsequently appeared in court where severe penalties were imposed.

Coroners

The Watford and St. Albans Coroners Districts were combined under one Coroner following the appointment of Dr. Arnold Henry Mendoza.

Unknown reason for Death

In the early hours of a May morning, a man was found dead in the driveway of a house in Chorleywood with injuries to his face and skull. An incident room was set up at Rickmansworth Police Station, where despite having a team of 25 officers and spending 3,900 hours of police time investigating the circumstances, it was not possible to establish with certainty how the deceased had met his death. At the subsequent Inquest, the Jury recorded an Open verdict.

New Radios
The Police take delivery of new 3 channel radio units first installed in Hemel Hempstead.

New Teleprinters
The force changes its teleprinters and also changes to using rolls of paper in the new teleprinters.

TPG
The Tactical Patrol Group (TPG) expands from two to three units.

Burglaries
Two members of the Tactical Group, answered an alarm call to a Watford factory and arrested a man for burglary. A second man was arrested later and both admitted a number of breaking offences in the Watford area. Three other arrests followed and property valued at over £2,500 was recovered. During the follow up enquiries into these crimes, another man was arrested for theft of jewellery, foreign currency and travellers cheques valued at £15,000. A further charge of handling stolen property was proffered against against a seventh man and property valued at over £14,000 was recovered from him.

Less Hours
The police working week was reduced from 44 hours to 42 hours.

Women Police.
The seeds of a Policewomen's Branch in the Force was sown in 1928 with the appointment of the first two women constables. From that time women police had a special responsibility for work with women and children, but in more recent years their duties have diversified to a point that they are now engaged in all aspects of Police work. The implementation of the Sex Discrimination Act on 29th December 1975, closed a chapter in the history of the Police, as on that date the Women Police Branch ceased to exist and the strength of policewomen was absorbed into the overall establishment.

On 27.7.75 Woman Detective Constable Margaret Kenning died after a short period in Hospital. The constable joined the Force on 12.11.66 and was stationed at Watford.

Lottery
The Hertfordshire Police start a lottery for staff. The first month realises £855.20p in prizes.

Shoot Out
In August 1976, at Abbots Langley, following a dispute over a gambling debt, a 30 year old man fired an automatic pistol and seriously injured another man. The assailant then turned the gun on himself causing head injuries which proved fatal.

Kidnapping
In March 1976, two men broke into a house in Garston and when the 40 year old male occupier returned they assaulted and robbed him. The offenders then abducted the occupier and stole his car. For several hours they drove around the Watford area with their victim until the car was stopped by Police Officers and the full circumstances revealed. The offenders subsequently appeared at St. Albans Crown Court where they were each

sentenced to 5 years imprisonment for robbery and other serious offences.

Robbery
At Watford in September, security guards who were in the process of carrying cash from a bank were attacked and robbed of £20,000 by two men in possession of a sawn-off shotgun. During their escape from the scene in a stolen car the men discharged the shotgun but fortunately no injury was caused.

Jewel Robbery
In December, three men entered a jeweller's premises at Rickmansworth where they assaulted the proprietor, tied him up, and stole jewellery to the value of £17,000. The CDU commenced an investigation with local officers and as a result of intelligence the suspects were identified and the property recovered from a London address. A total of 4 men were arrested and charged in connection with the offence.

Football Hooligans
Football hooliganism, in the main at Watford was repeated during the year. In March, when a large contingent of supporters attended from Northampton, a number of disturbances took place resulting in 35 persons being arrested for a variety of offences.

Rear of Watford Police Station, Shady Lane, Circa 1976.

Later in the year, when Watford played Luton Town in a local 'derby' game, trouble was anticipated. The regular allocation of Police strength was augmented to 63 officers and there is no doubt that this had a preventative effect. Nevertheless there were a number of incidents centred on public houses in the vicinity of the ground and during and after the match 5 arrests were made for offences against the Public Order Act, and one for throwing a stone through the window of a coach carrying Luton supporters.

Taking Cars
In January 1976, a uniformed constable found three boys aged 14 to 16 years asleep

Fatal Accident

On the morning of the 10th June 1976, a fatal accident occurred on the two lane section of the southbound carriageway of the M1 motorway when the front offside tyre burst on a lorry travelling in the offside lane and caused the driver to lose control. The lorry swerved across the left hand lane and hard shoulder, ploughed through a crash barrier and bridge parapet and fell some 22 feet landing upside down in Bedmond Lane. Laden with 8 tree trunks the gross weight of lorry and load was 20 tons and it was necessary for special equipment to be brought in to effect temporary repairs to the bridge and while this was being done, to divert southbound traffic on the motorway. At 3.30 p.m. it was possible to open one lane to traffic and at 5.15 p.m., the motorway was re-opened.

in a car at Watford and discovered they had taken the car without the owner's permission. The juveniles subsequently admitted being responsible for 25 offences including burglary, theft, handling of stolen property and the unlawful taking of motor vehicles. A similar case occurred at Bedmond in June, when two 14 year old boys were seen by police officers carrying property along a country lane. The boys ran off when approached by the officers, but were all arrested shortly afterwards. Following interview, a 16 year old boy was also arrested and they were all subsequently dealt with at Watford Juvenile Court for a total of 51 offences including burglary, theft, handling stolen property, the unlawful taking of 30 motor vehicles and driving under age.

Forensic Detection

Minute particles play an important part in the forensic detection of crime as when in the early hours of a January morning police officers on patrol at Rickmansworth disturbed two men in the act of removing a large quantity of musical records from premises they had just entered. When challenged the men ran off but one was apprehended almost immediately and the other some hours later. Tiny glass splinters and chips of paint which had become detached from the glass door of the attacked premises were carefully collected by a SOCO and taken to the Forensic Science Laboratory, together with the clothing worn by both men. This evidence connected them with the scene of the crime and subsequently they were convicted at the Crown Court. One man was sentenced to 2 year's imprisonment and ordered to pay £165 compensation and the other to 12 months imprisonment.

Weighing of Vehicles

In April, all patrol Sergeants in the Traffic Department became authorised under Section 160 of the Road Traffic Act 1960 in the weighing of vehicles. As a result, 232 Vehicles were weighed of which 78 were found to be over weight.

A405T

On 26.2.76, the A405T Hunton Bridge to Maple Cross Road was opened (now incorporated in the M25).

A405

The final part of the dual carriageway at Garston of the A405 was opened on 21.7.76. Work continued however on the new A405 Junction with the A41 and the dual carriageway of the A41 due for completion in 1977.

Central Ticket Office

Following a detailed study, it was decided to set up a Central Ticket Office, for the administration of parking tickets throughout the County. Due to problems of space, room for the office was found at Bayley Hall in Hertford. The office started operationally on 1.1.77.

PNC

The new PNC, continues to be a useful tool in policing, although at present it can only be used for vehicle checks. The new Criminal record facility is expected to become available in Spring 1977.

Vehicle Check

A Dog handler on patrol in Watford early in December saw a Ford Corsair being driven through the Town Centre. He checked the vehicles registration number with the PNC unit at Headquarters over his vehicle radio, which revealed that the car had been stolen from Wembley just 8 minutes earlier. The vehicle was stopped and its three occupants arrested.

During 1976 3 Police vehicles were damage whilst stationary on hard shoulders clearly demonstrating that even plainly visible police markings do not render such vehicles immune.

Computers

Following Home Office recommendation, the Force agree to look into the purchase of a "Command and Control" computer system, to be based in the Force Control Room and computerise all ongoing incidents.

Bedmond Mast Down

During severe gales in January, the Force Radio Mast at Bedmond blew down seriously disrupting radio reception. Arrangements were made to install an aerial on the nearby Post Office Mast immediately, which although it resulted in a loss of signal strength was sufficient for operational needs. Work commenced on the building of a new mast which should become operational in 1977. While work is commencing, advantage was taken of the situation to cater for a third radio channel, and in preparation, all vehicle and mobile radios have been re-crystalled to accept the new channel.

Sniffed Out

At Watford, a dog handler was sent an alarm call and the dog was released in the courtyard of a nursery school. The dog quickly located a person hiding in a covered slide in the yard. A track was then found at the point of entry to the premises and followed for a short distance to a point where a second youth was found hiding in dense shrubbery. Both were charged with burglary and also taking a conveyance without the owner's consent.

Storms

During the night of 1st and 2nd of January 1976, a great deal of storm damage was caused throughout the County. A large number of trees were blown across roads, power lines and telephone cables were brought down and considerable repairs to private dwellings and business premises were needed. All available Police Units were fully committed during a period of intense activity from early evening until the early hours of the morning.

Train De-Railed

Early in the morning of 26th May, a train was derailed at Watford Junction Station, due to a trolley being left on the line. An engine travelling from Tring to Euston on an adjacent line collided with the derailed train and moved it some 100 yards. A British Rail Accident Unit and 12 Hertfordshire Officers were in attendance at the scene for 4 hours.

Posting closed notices at the Shady Lane Police Station, 1977.

Chief Constable Retires

Raymond Naylor Buxton Esq., O.B.E., B.E.M., Q.P.M., Retired as Chief Constable on 31.10.77, having been Chief Constable since 1.9.69. He started his Police career With Staffordshire in 1936.

New Station

In the summer, work commenced on the construction of the new Divisional Police Station at Watford on the site of the old police station in Shady Lane and also the improvement of the existing sub-divisional station on the same site. There has been a pressing need for some time for the new premises to relieve overcrowding and improve the totally inadequate facilities provided by the old buildings. The construction work is on schedule and should be completed early in 1979 but until then all policing in the area is carried out from a temporary police station located in redundant school premises at Addiscombe Road, Watford. This project provided a suitable opportunity to review the layout, organisation, and function of the communications/station duty complex, with the object of making the most efficient and economic use of both manpower and equipment, while at the same time providing the best possible working conditions for staff. In the planning of the new complex at Watford, advice has been sought from the Police Scientific Development Branch at the Home Office and Senior Officers of the Force have visited other police stations in the Country to observe different systems in operation.

Petrol Spillage

At 0700 hours on Friday 28th October 1977, on the A405T at Hunton Bridge roundabout, the driver of a Leyland articulated petrol tanker lost control of the vehicle which turned over. The driver, escaped with minor injuries but 5,000 gallons of petrol was discharged on to the road and surrounding area. Due to the high explosion risk, widespread traffic diversions were put into immediate effect, and the whole of the roundabout was sealed off. Most of the petrol, ran along gutters and then via storm drains into the River Gade where it was dealt with by Thames Water Authority. The recovery and removal of the tanker took 7 hours, during which time severe traffic congestion was experienced on most main roads in the area.

Chemical Spillage

On the morning of 22nd October 1977, a report was received of a spillage of a cyanide solution resulting in a concentration of cyanide fumes in the premises of Dawsquare Limited, Rembrandt House, Whippendell Road, Watford. It was necessary to evacuate the whole of the premises and those houses downwind of the scene. Members of the Fire Service, equipped with breathing apparatus entered the premises and dealt with the incident. Fortunately it was possible to complete the whole incident in little over an hour.

PNC Used

In April, a bystander observed a man stealing property from a car in Watford. He was unable to remember full details of the registration number of the vehicle used by the thief, but use was made of the descriptive search facility of the PNC, which provided details of 3 owners. The first owner interviewed admitted the offence, and 10 others.

Royal review of force - 6th May 1977 at Peel Centre

Football Hooligans

On 22nd January 1977, officers were engaged on duty at Watford in connection with the home football match against Southend United. A number of disturbances occurred, before, during and after the game resulting in the arrest of 18 persons for breaches of public order.

Robbery

On 22nd September 1977, an armed robbery took place in the grounds of Leavesden Hospital, Watford where £15,000 was stolen. The tactical patrol group (TPG), were called upon to assist C.I.D. officers in large scale enquiries. During the course of these enquiries, officers gained information which resulted in the recovery of the vehicle used in the robbery and the location of a house in which one of the offenders was arrested. A sawn off shotgun, a revolver and part of the proceeds of the robbery were also recovered. Subsequent enquiries by detective officers led to the arrest of 5 men and the recovery of almost £10,000.

Protective Equipment

During the year, the Force purchased new equipment. Nine lightweight bullet proof vests, twenty-one protective shields for use in public order situations and fifty reinforced uniform helmets.

Having a Party

In May 1977, a party at a house in Rickmansworth turned into a near riot when numerous teenagers spilled out of the house into the road outside and began fighting. Many officers were called to the incident which resulted in a young man receiving very serious head injuries. Two persons were charged with causing grievous bodily harm and 6 other persons were charged with criminal damage and public order offences.

Robbery

In July, a robbery took place at Watford, when two 19 year old girls left a discotheque late one evening and went to their car which was parked nearby. As they were about to enter the vehicle they were threatened by a man who forced them to drive towards London. At an isolated location, he stole £2 from them and indecently assaulted them both. A man was arrested and on his appearance before the Crown Court he was sentenced to two years imprisonment suspended for two years.

Going to Rob

A man was dealt with at court for going equipped at Watford, when one evening in February he was arrested in St. Albans Road, Watford wearing a stocking mask and armed with a starting pistol. He admitted he was on his way to rob a restaurant.

40 Hours

On 1.11.78, the Force working week is changed from 42 hours to 40 hours.

Sniffed Out

A dog and its handler were called to the scene of a burglary at Watford, one man had already been arrested, but his accomplices had made off. The handler commenced his search and the dog found a track to a nearby copse before indicating to his handler a man hiding under a bush. The man was arrested and the handler returned to the scene, where the dog picked up another track which it followed to the rear of the premises, across scrubland to a river, where the third man was found lying in the water.

Fire Brigade Industrial Dispute

From 13th November 1977 to 17th January 1978, during the national withdrawal of labour by some members of the Fire Brigade's Union, 11 "Green Goddess" emer-

On 28th June 1978 Her Royal Highness, The Princess Anne, visited 'Baileys Night Club' (now Paradise Lost), Watford. Picture shows W.P.C. Melanie Jay presenting a bouquet.

gency fire appliances and 133 servicemen were deployed in the Hertfordshire Police District for fire fighting duties. 25 Hertfordshire Police Officers per day were employed as liaison officers to the Service Units and attended just under 500 fire calls with the Service Fire Crews. Although picket lines were formed at various fire stations throughout the County, the reasonable attitude of the pickets caused no Police difficulties. There was one visitation by 'Flying Pickets' from Essex and London to some of the stations but this was contained by Police.

Toxic Leak

At mid day on 16th March 1978, a tanker carrying toxic materials developed a leak whilst travelling north on the M1 Motorway. The vehicle stopped near the Meriden Housing Estate, North Watford, where toxic fumes threatened the occupants of houses situated close to the motorway. Some 70 persons were evacuated by Police and Ambulance personnel to the Meriden Community Centre as a precautionary measure. All residents on the estate were warned of the potential danger, and the area was sealed off until declared safe by the Fire Brigade at 2.15 p.m. During this period all northbound traffic was diverted from the motorway.

Armed Robbery

On 24th August 1978, in the morning, four security guards at a Watford Bank were confronted by three robbers armed with shotguns. They stole more than £50,000. Despite an incident room being set up and over 3,000 man hours being expended the offence remained undetected at the end of 1978.

Aggravated Burglary

During the early hours of 8th February 1978, four men forced an entry to a house in Garston, where an 89 year old widower was asleep upstairs. He was tied up and assaulted and £1,400 in cash and a platinum ring were stolen. One offender has been sentenced to 4 years imprisonment for the robbery and two other men have as a result of enquiries into this offence been convicted and received suspended prison sentences for obtaining money by criminal deception.

Rape

On the night of 21st/22nd April 1978, at Garston, a 19 year old girl was alone in bed at her parent's ground floor flat when a youth aged 16 years, who lived nearby, gained entry to the flat by means of an insecure window. He raped the girl and committed other indecent acts towards her and then left. Police enquiries led to his arrest and at St. Albans Crown Court he was convicted and sentenced to four years imprisonment.

New Helmets

1978 Saw the introduction of a new style helmet with reinforced protection and a new all chrome crest on the front.

New reinforced hats were also issued to Women Police Constables for use in public order situations. Normal hostess type hat remains their normal uniform.

Rape

On 24th August, a 14 year old girl was alone in her parents home at Bedmond, when she answered a knock on the door. A man at the door made an excuse and left, a short while later she answered another knock on the door, and on opening the door the same man bundled her back into the house, where the same man raped her and committed other indecent acts towards her. Her assailant stole cash and jewellery valued at £2,000. After protracted enquiries, a 26 year old man was arrested for this offence.

Fire

In April, rubbish that had been left on a first floor landing in a Watford shop was set alight, resulting in serious damage to the building and the stock in the shop, amounting to £14,000.

1978 Also saw the introduction of Riot Shields and riot training. In response to outbreaks of violence in other parts of the country

Stolen Cheque

In January at Watford, an off duty Detective Sergeant saw a local criminal about to purchase goods with a stolen cheque. As a result of preliminary enquiries, it became necessary to set up an incident room to investigate the offences. A total of 15 persons were arrested and charged with theft and criminal deception for 1,894 offences, involving 143 stolen cheque books and 290 offences concerning credit cards. The monetary value of the offences disclosed came to £73,027.

Burglary

In January 1978, a burglary occurred at a Club in Watford. Cigarettes, spirits, and silverware to the value of £800 were stolen. The SOCO who attended noticed blood at the point of entry and sent a sample to the Forensic Laboratory. After examination, scientists were able to say that the blood group had never been found in the indigenous white population of this country, but occurred in 1 : 1000 of the negroid population. The information was given to the officer investigating the offence. A man who had been a suspect was arrested and subsequently admitted the offence.

Drugs

In June 1978, a warrant was executed at a private house in Watford. In the loft of the house, they discovered Cannabis Plants growing in a home made propagation installation, which included electric lights fitted with a timer, light/heat reflectors and an automatic watering device.

New Station Complete

The construction of the new Divisional Police Headquarters and renovation of the sub-divisional police station at Watford was completed on

schedule at the beginning of the year. The move from the temporary accommodation at Addiscombe Road School back to the Shady Lane site took place on Sunday, 11th February 1979. The building was officially opened on 14th June by Lord Lieutenant, Major General Sir George Burns, K.C.V.O., C.B., D.S.O., O.B.E., M.C., who also unveiled a plaque in the new building.

Major Incident Exercise

A practical major incident exercise was held for the emergency services on 14th October 1979, at the National Coal Board Depot, Garston. The participants were presented with a simulated explosion and fire in an inflammable spirit storage tank, together with a collision between a goods train and a double decker bus on an unmanned rail crossing, resulting in eight persons killed and 30 injured. The comments of observers from the emergency services, voluntary organisations and District Councils, together with those of key participants, were presented to a post exercise debriefing at Shrodells Wing of Watford General Hospital.

Four Arrested

Following a report of suspects on warehouse premises at Watford, a search was carried out by a dog handler with his dog. The dog indicated that persons were present in a locked room, and after the door was forced open four youth were arrested.

Ambulance Dispute

On Saturday 17th March 1979, during the one day national withdrawal of labour by some members of the Ambulance Service, seven police transit vans were equipped with stretchers, pillows and additional First Aid equipment and strategically deployed throughout the County, with the exception of the Stevenage and Hertford Divisions, where normal ambulance services were in operation. At 4 a.m., military aid in the form of 10 Army Ambulances, each crewed by a driver and a medical orderly were deployed in the affected area. The Police Vans were stood down but held in reserve. As in the Fire Service dispute of 1978, a police car and driver were assigned as guides to each operational military ambulance. During the day, 50 calls requiring an ambulance were made, ranging from Road Accidents to Maternity cases. Only one Police Van was used to convey an elderly lady suffering from a fractured hip from her home to hospital.

Party Piece

Following a private party held at Carpenders Park, Watford in June 1979, a fight took place between approximately 50 of the departing guests. They armed themselves with gardening tools, a sheath knife and an iron bar and many injuries were sustained. Five men were arrested and charged with a variety of offences.

Nosy

In April 1979, during an argument at a Watford Club, two men started to fight, a 26 year old later had treatment at hospital after part of his nose was bitten off. His assailant, was arrested and charged with causing grievous bodily harm.

Arson

In August 1979, an infants school at North Watford was entered. Inflammable material readily to hand within the building was ignited and extensive damage to the value of £120,000 was caused. Two 18 year old youths were arrested for the offence.

Assualted Police Officer

A Serious Assault on Police occurred in April 1979, when Police attended a disturbance at a North Watford Social Club. On arrival, police tried to stop the fighting. One officer, was punched and kicked receiving injuries to his spine and was off duty for 10 weeks. Another officer was punched and butted in the face causing bruising and cuts which required stitches. He was off duty for 10 days.

Aggravated Burglary

At Watford, during May 1979, an 85 year old man was at his home asleep when an intruder entered his house. The old man disturbed the intruder and he was struck about the head several times. Injuries which required hospital treatment were caused. The intruder fled having ransacked cupboards in several rooms. The house was searched by a SOCO who found fingerprints on containers that it was believed had been handled by the intruder. The marks found, were searched at HQ Fingerprint Bureau and as a result a 19 year old was identified by his fingerprints. He was arrested and admitted the offence of burglary and causing grievous bodily harm, and at his trial, a further 10 offences were taken into consideration.

Radio Base Station

In 1980, a new UHF Radio Base Station is sited on the roof of the YMCA building at Watford to improve radio transmission in the Division.

The Force switches to Burndept single unit radios which are being phased into operation instead of the previous Pye two piece sets.

Football Arrests

On February 9th 1980, Watford Football Club played Chelsea at Vicarage Road before a crowd of 25,000. A total of 52 persons were arrested in and around the ground for offences of Assault on Police, Threatening behaviour, Criminal Damage and Drunkenness. No police officer was seriously injured as a result of these assaults, but one officer sustained torn arm ligaments when a barrier collapsed. Of those arrested, 48 were Chelsea supporters. At the Arsenal match in March, a total of 23 persons were ejected from the ground and 21 arrested for offences of Assault on Police, Burglary, Criminal Damage and Public Order Offences. Six Police Officers were slightly injured but none required hospital treatment.

Stabbing

A stabbing took place in the carriage of a Glasgow to Euston train as it passed through Watford on the evening of Monday 31st March 1980. A 45 year old man, without apparent reason, stabbed a 31 year old male passenger several times about the body. On his appearance before the Crown Court on a charge of attempted murder, he was convicted and ordered to be detained without limitation of time under the provisions of the Mental Health Act 1959.

Grevious Bodily Harm

In early October 1980, a 14 year old Rickmansworth Schoolgirl was attacked in the street as she walked home one night. Her injuries included a fractured skull, severe lacerations and multiple bruising. Police enquiries led to the arrest of a 29 year old man, previously unknown to the victim who was charged with the offence of causing grievous bodily harm.

Arson

In February 1980, inflammable materials inside a Rickmansworth factory was set on fire and damage to the value of £60,000 was caused. An ex-employee, aged 25 years, was charged with the offence and ultimately sentenced to 4 years imprisonment.

Riot Helmets

Force purchases 60 ACPO approved NATO style helmets and fire resistant overalls for public order situations.

Grevious Bodily Harm

In February 1981, a 43 year old man demanded to take part in a game of cards being played at a club in Oxhey. Having been refused, he later followed one of the players, a man of 63 years into the toilets where he repeatedly punched him in the face. As a result of the assault his victim spent 8 days in Hospital, a further 12 days off work and has a permanent impairment of vision in one eye. At the Crown Court in July, his assailant was sentenced to 12 months imprisonment.

Robbery

On the evening of Friday 8th May 1981, two men aged 19 and 22 years burst into a small corner shop in Watford for the purpose of rifling the till. Once inside, they were confronted by the 46 year old shopkeeper who, in a violent struggle, sustained stab wounds, lacerations and head injuries. He spent 7 days in hospital, 2 of them in intensive care. Though charged with attempted murder the two assailants were ultimately convicted at Crown Court for robbery and inflicting grievous bodily harm. Each was sentenced to a total of 4 years imprisonment.

Double Murder

The village of Bedmond, was the scene of a double murder on the evening of 23rd September, when two infants aged three months and five years died with their Japanese mother in a blazing car. Medical and Forensic evidence enabled the police to establish that the mother had committed suicide. At a Coroners Inquest, it was found that the mother had committed suicide and that the two children had been unlawfully killed.

Golf

On 24th to 27th September 1981, The Bob Hope Golf Classic was held at Moor Park Golf Club, Rickmansworth, and attracted a crowd of over 80,000. Ex-President Gerald Ford of the United States of America was one of the Contestants.

Arson

One of the major fires in the County, gutted a two storey office block and a shed on the construction site of the new hospital at Shrodells, Watford. Damage amounted to £100,000. The fire was caused by a 27 year old man who deliberately set the premises alight with the aid of paint thinners. At St. Albans Crown Court in October he pleaded guilty to the offence and after the disclosure of a previous conviction for arson, was sentenced to life imprisonment.

Fatal Accident

In October 1981, an accident occurred on the A 405(T) (now M.25), near Hunton Bridge, when an articulated lorry collided with a pedal cycle travelling in the same direction. The male rider of the cycle, who had been riding on the hardshoulder, deviated into the nearside traffic lane and was killed instantly.

Chiltern Radio

October 1981 Chiltern Radio 'on air'. New liaisons were formed between the new radio station and the police.

Murder

On the 9th October, the body of a 12 year old girl was discovered on the ground seven storeys below her bedroom in a block of flats at Oxhey. Following Police enquiries and a post mortem examination, a 35 year old man was arrested for killing her.

Murder

In the course of being robbed on 12th October 1981, a 50 year old man was stabbed to death in public toilets in the underpass near the Town Hall, Watford. Two men aged 19 and a girl of 15 were later arrested. The men were charged with murder and robbery, the girl with complicity in the robbery. Photograph show police dog and handler searching at the scene (courtesy of Watford Observer)

Royal Visit

On the 11th December 1981, Her Majesty the Queen visited Parmiters School, High Elms Lane, Garston to open newly constructed buildings.

Road Works

Work has continued throughout 1981, on the project to widen the M.1 motorway between junctions 5 and 8 (Watford to Hemel Hempstead). The work should be completed in 1983, thus relieving some of the congestion that has occurred especially during peak periods for quite a number of years. Since work commenced, it has been possible to maintain a minimum of two lanes in each direction during daylight hours. The motorway has been closed at nights, with diversions put into force, the closure being lifted in time for the morning peak periods.

Suicide

A 41 year old research chemist went missing from his home in Rickmansworth and as he was in a depressed state and had easy access to drugs, there were fears for his safety. Although there was no indication as to his whereabouts, enquiries were made and a search of local woodland was mounted. The search was extended the following day and the man was eventually found dead by Hertfordshire Officers in woodland in the Thames Valley Police District, having committed suicide.

1981 RIOTS

Following the Brixton Riots, a 28 day prohibition order on political marches and demonstrations in London was made. Intelligence was received to the effect that the National Front were organising a march somewhere in the Home Counties on Saturday 25th April 1981. In common with neighbouring forces a contingency plan was made and Rest Days cancelled for all officers up to the rank of Inspector. On the morning of the 25th, it was announced the march would take place at Watford. Between 2.45 p.m. and 3.15 p.m., some 450 National Front supporters assembled at Bushey and Oxhey Railway Station. A written notice under Section 3 of the Public Order Act 1936 was served on the leaders of the march prescribing the route to be taken. This was to avoid the main shopping centre and the areas inhabited by immigrant communities. Officers were deployed along the route. The march went off peacefully with only two arrests, one for obstruction of an officer, and one for stone throwing. The Police operation involved a total of 595 Hertfordshire Officers and 409 Officers from Thames Valley, Bedfordshire, Essex and the Metropolitan Police under the command of the Assistant Chief Constable T.J. Jones.

Subsequently, the Watford Anti-Racism Committee organised a counter demonstration and march at Watford on 2nd May 1981. The route was agreed between the organisers and the Police and at 3.15 p.m., some 500 marchers moved off from Bushey and Oxhey Railway Station. The march took place without incident and dispersed from an open air meeting held near Watford Town Hall. A total of 395 Hertfordshire Officers were engaged on the operation.

Photograph from the Watford Observer

Photograph from the Watford Observer

Hertfordshire, did not entirely escape the widespread outbreaks of public disorder which occurred mainly in the inner city areas in the country. Following the July outbreaks of public disorder, it was deemed necessary to arrange for reserves of manpower to be available to deal with any incidents within Hertfordshire and to be available to assist neighbouring forces if necessary. From the 10th July, officers duty hours were increased to 12 hours to provide additional manpower at those times when the risks of disorder were considered greatest. Damage was caused on various nights in St. Albans, Hitchin, Stevenage and Hatfield. Over 40 persons were arrested for offences ranging from arson, criminal damage, possession of offensive weapons, assaults on police, burglary and public order offences. The outbreaks of public disorder in the County were without exception all contained rapidly by the Police. All the persons arrested were white local residents whose activities seem to have been motivated by a desire to imitate what was happening elsewhere.

Tennis Winners

Herts win Regional Team Competition for the 8th successive year at Tennis, the longest consecutive number of wins since the competition started in 1949. The team remain undefeated since 1974.

Headquarters Extension

It is hoped that work will commence on the new extension to Police Headquarters in 1984, with completion scheduled for December 1985. It is further hoped that the installation of the Command and Control Computer will be made into the new operations room early in 1986 together with a new computerised telephone system. The design and thought behind the Command and Control system will include the setting up of smaller Divisional Control Rooms.

A handler and his dog were called were assigned to a report of intruders on premises at Leavesden. On his arrival, they found a police officer who had sustained serious head injuries and a man armed with an iron bar was seen running away. The dog was released and after evading blows from the iron bar detained the man who as a result received injuries to his left arm and shoulder.[1]

Chief Superintendent M.G. Webber was awarded the Queen's Police Medal.

Grevious Bodily Harm

In Watford, a serious assault occurred when a young man left a discotheque following an argument with another. Three youths, one armed with a plank of wood, confronted the man outside and beat him to the ground. Whilst he was in the position and unable to defend himself, the youths simultaneously kicked him in the face causing serious eye injuries. All three youths were arrested.

At Rickmansworth, a youth was sitting on a wall adjacent to a public house talking with friends, when a group of youths approached. One of this group, without provocation, kicked the youth on the wall in the face, causing cuts and broken teeth which subsequently required complicated and protracted dental surgery in Hospital. The offender was arrested.

Golf

On the 23rd to 26th September 1982, the Bob Hope Golf Classic again took place at Moor Park Golf Course attracting crowds of 66,000.

Grevious Bodily Harm

One evening in March 1982, an argument over a girl broke out between two youths aged 17 and 18 in a village club near Rickmansworth. Later that night, one waylaid the other with a length of metal tubing, bruising him severely across his arms and back and inflicting an injury on his chin which required 5 stitches. At Watford Magistrates Court in May, the offender was fined £150 for unlawful wounding, £150 for possession of an offensive weapon and ordered to pay £200 compensation to his victim.

Assualt

On the evening of Saturday 25th April 1982, four youths at Croxley Green were confronted in the street by others, one of whom tried to provoke them into fighting. When the youths refused to be drawn into a fight, one received violent kicks in the face and body. His resultant injuries included widespread bruising and a cut lip which required stitches. In addition, most of his teeth had to be sewn back into position and supported for several weeks by a brace. As a result of the attack the youth was unable to eat solid food for two weeks and was unfit for work for six. His 16 year old assailant appeared before Watford Juvenile Court in June and was fined £75 and ordered to pay his victim

£50 compensation.

Robbery

Late in the evening of Friday 3rd September 1982, a 56 year old man was beaten unconscious and robbed of £2 in a footway known locally as 'Cut Throat Alley', off Queens Road, Watford. In the attack, he sustained three wounds and numerous contusions and lacerations to the head and in addition, many facial fractures requiring surgery which kept him in hospital for two weeks. Following enquiries from a Watford Incident Room, a 21 year old man was arrested for the offence on 8th September. He was eventually charged with 2 offences of robbery, one assault with intent to rob, one offence of theft and four cases of inflicting grievous bodily harm.

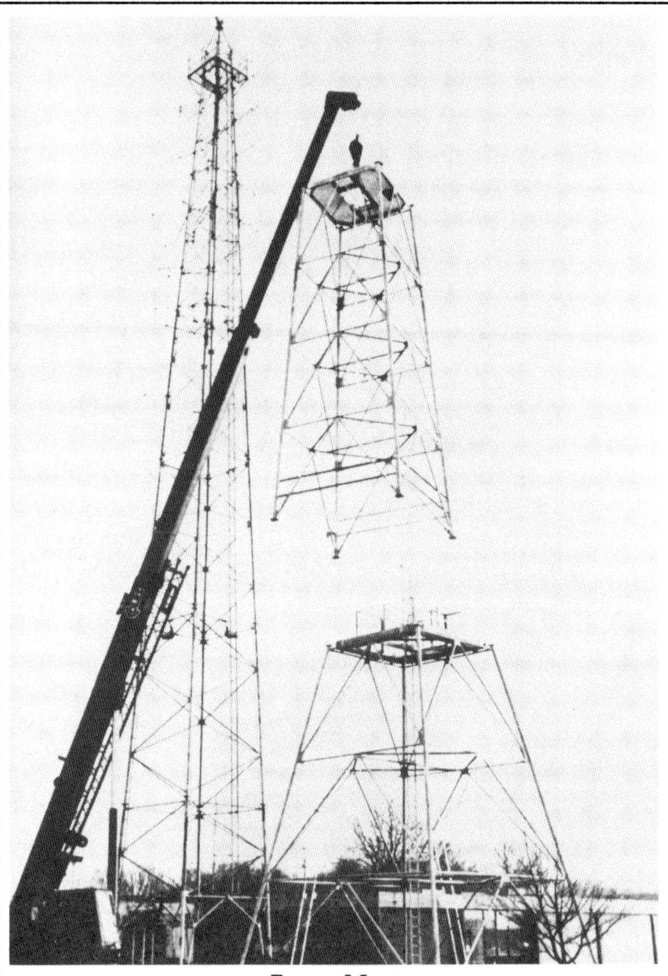

Rusty Mast

In January 1983, it was discovered that the tubular steel VHF radio tower at Police HQ was badly affected by rusting with a consequent reduction in the strength and safety margins of the mast. The County Architect and Home Office recommended that the tower should be replaced. Work commenced on 1st October.

Burglaries

During the summer months of 1982, a series of burglaries were committed on an Industrial Estate at Watford. In almost every case, the intruder entered the factory by way of a skylight and at several of the premises, SOCO found and preserved shoe sole impressions. The eventual discovery of a fingerprint led to the arrest of a man for that offence, but subsequently, forensic scientists were able to match his footwear with all the preserved shoe impressions found at the different premises. When confronted with this evidence, the offender admitted to 13 Burglaries and at Crown Court was sentenced to Borstal training.

Tennis

In 1983, Herts again win Regional Tennis Team Competition for 9th successive year.

Cart Racing

On Sunday 6th March 1983, 100 itinerant travellers with 25 vehicles and two horse boxes gathered beside the A 405(T) with the intention of closing the road to traffic whilst they staged a hose race on the highway. They were persuaded to move to Chorleywood Common while a more suitable location was found. In the meantime, contingency plans to reinforce local officers with officers from other divisions were implemented and finally faced with a refusal to allow the race on the public roads, the gypsies moved off.

Cock Fighting

On Saturday 2nd April, divisional officers and officers from all three Tactical Patrol Groups (including those based at Watford), together with senior officers of the RSPCA, executed warrants at premise at Temple End near Hitchin. At the time of entry, a cock fight was in progress and evidence was found of other fights having taken place and of the previous use of the premises as a cock pit. Eleven persons were arrested and subsequently appeared at Hitchin Magistrates Court in connection with offences of cruelty to animals and specific offences relating to cock fighting. This was the first successful prosecution in the Country concerning cock fighting since 1956 and substantial fines were imposed by the court on this occasion.

Fighting

During the early hours of a December morning in 1983, a serious disturbance broke out following an engagement party in Bedmond. Some 15 - 20 young people were involved in the fighting, which resulted in one man receiving an eye injury. Three men were arrested and charged with inflicting grievous bodily harm. They later appeared at Watford Magistrates Court where two were fined £250 plus £40 costs. The case against the third man was dismissed.

Double Murder

A double murder was recorded in Watford on 16th June 1983. At 12.50 a.m. that day, two patrolling officers accompanied an Asian man home after finding him wandering bloodstained in the street. In his house, they discovered two women aged 52 and 20 dead with multiple head injuries. The man was arrested and charged with both murders.

Assualt on Tramp

An assault resulting in appalling injuries was committed at Watford on 5th March 1983. During the night, a vagrant asleep in a derelict house was permanently blinded by another vagrant who gouged his eyes with his thumbs, and afterwards because of the severity of the wounds, one of the victim's eyes had to be removed surgically. In September, at St. Albans Crown Court, the offender was sentenced to 4 years imprisonment.

Kicking

Another serious assault was committed at a Watford college disco in June, when a 19 year old youth accused another youth of trying to 'stare him out'. When this was denied, he knocked the youth to the ground and repeatedly kicked him about the head. In dealing with the assailant in September for inflicting GBH, Watford Magistrates imposed a four month suspended sentence, and additionally ordered him to pay £26 costs and £100 compensation to his victim for the suffering caused by his injuries which included extensive bruising to both the head and body, numerous gashes to his head and face that required 14 stitches and a number of broken and loosened teeth which prevented him eating solid food for four days.

Police Dog Trials

The 12th Annual Hertfordshire Police Dog Trials were held in September and the awards were presented by Mrs A.J. Hughes, wife of the Chairman of the Police Committee. Constable McIver with Digby was the overall winner and received the Burns Trophy, the Harast Trophy for tracking and the Cain trophy for the best novice dog. Constable Ritchie with Bill gained second place and the Thessalus Trophy for obedience. Constable Collier gained third place and Gilpa Shield for searching. Constable Froy with Bodie was awarded the Mindale Shield for Criminal Work. Constable McNeil and Zimba were awarded the Superintendent's Association Cup for the Police Problem, and Constable Bain the Best Operational Dog Trophy.

Cop-A-Card

At the end of September, a public relations/ crime prevention competition called "Cop-a-Card" was launched in co-operation with the Eastern Region of the Post Office. This lasted for one month, and was aimed at children between 4 and 16 years of age who were encouraged to collect a set of 12 crime prevention cards which they could obtain one at a time by approaching uniformed police officers, either in the street or at police stations. The first youngster to return a complete a complete set of 12 cards was awarded a prize of a home computer. Twenty youngsters received runners-up prizes of a pocket calculator and a further 100 were awarded consolation prizes in the form of sets of postage stamps. In total some 470,000 cards were issued by police officers in the competition and 7,000 complete sets were returned. All the young people returning complete sets duly received a certificate jointly signed by the Chief Constable and the head of the Eastern Postal Region.

Neighbourhood Watch

On 4th October 1983, a public meeting was held at Moor Park for the purpose of organising a Neighbourhood Watch Scheme for the locality. The meeting was attended

by approximately 350 people who were addressed by their Member of Parliament, Mr. Richard Page, two members of the local resident's association and the Force crime prevention officer. There was unanimous support for the venture which was put into immediate effect and at the end of the year, 600 different households were actively participating in it.

Breath Test Machines

As a result of the introduction of the Transport Act 1981, a number of major changes were made in the law relating to drink/driving. One such change, allowed for the introduction of substantive breath testing devices, and in the Force, 11 Lion Intoximeter 3000 machines were purchased and installed at police stations throughout the County in April. The prescribed limit for alcohol in the breath is 35 microgrammes in 100 millilitres of breath. The legal limit for blood is 80 milligrams in 100 millilitres of blood, and for urine 107 milligrams of alcohol in 100 millilitres of urine.

Rape

In March 1985, a 17 year old girl, walking home in watford one evening, was accosted by two youths. They dragged her into an outbuilding of a school and tied her up by placing brown adhesive tape over her mouth. She was then raped by one of the offenders, both of whom later made off. SOCO's carefully examined the scene and recovered the tape amongst other evidence. This tape was submitted to the Fingerprint Bureau where it was treated with various chemicals to reveal fingerprints. Using a special lamp, these fingerprints were photographed, and following a search the fingerprint was positively identified and the offenders were arrested. They were both convicted at St. Albans Crown Court, one was sentenced to 5 years at a detention centre and the rapist to 8 years youth custody.

Stabbing

In the early hours of 27th December 1985, following a private party at a house in Bedmond Green, a girl was attacked by a youth, who held a knife to her throat. The police, including a dog handler Pc Donald MacLeod attended. Police dog Harvey tracked away from the scene following the offender across fields. When adjacent to some bushes, the dog handler was attacked and stabbed in the chest with a knife puncturing a lung. An accompanying police officer was also assaulted in the struggle to detain the offender who was later charged with attempted murder and other offences. In 1986 Pc Mcleod was awarded a High Commendation for his courage and determination despite serious stab wounds for his part in arresting a very dangerous man.

Drugs Factory

Following information that supplies of amphetamine sulphate in the Stevenage area were originating from the west of the country, a special operation was set up by the Drugs Squad. Their enquiries revealed that persons from the Watford area were purchasing precursor chemicals from pharmaceutical companies and this was believed to be bound for an illicit amphetamine factory. It also emerged that persons from London were engaged in this operation and following various enquiries, warrants were executed at various addresses where glassware, chemicals and amphetamine sulphate were seized. The culprits, were arrested and charged with the offences.

Fatal Accident

In September 1985, a motorcyclist riding along Rectory Road, Rickmansworth, hit a part of a house brick lying in the carriageway. The rider was thrown from his vehicle and received fatal injuries when he struck a road sign.

N.U.M. Dispute.

During the early weeks of the year, the Hertfordshire Constabulary continued to supply mutual aid to the Chief Constables of Nottinghamshire and Derbyshire in connection with the N.U.M. Dispute. The participation of the Force ended on 8th February 1985, as the tension in the aided areas decreased.

The total cost of the aid supplied during the year long dispute amounted to £2,195,846, with a further cost of £578,982 being incurred within the county where personnel worked long hours to cover the absence of their colleagues. A total of 42,147 man days of aid were provided from this Force and the impact on policing arrangements within Hertfordshire necessitated the working by officers of 60,430 hours overtime.

Tennis Again

Herts win Regional Team Tennis Competition for 10th successive season and extend their unbeaten run since 1974.

1974, Chief Constable Trefor Morris is awarded the Q.P.M.

High Commendation

A High Commendation is awarded to Inspector Phillip Andrews and Woman Constable Joanne Conner, who placed themselves in great danger in rescuing a man from a blazing house.

Probationer Training

The most important time for a newly appointed constable is those first two to three months when he or she arrives at a police station after training school. There is much to be learnt including local procedures, and how to deal with incidents and members of the public with whom they come into contact on the street. In an effort to give them the right guidance and training, all probationer constables posted to "C" Division now spend their first 10 weeks working with experienced tutor constables at Watford Central Police Station. Much of their time is spent working in the busy town centre accompanied by their tutors in an attempt to get them involved in as many aspects of police work as possible. They are constantly advised and counselled with the result that confidence is gained much quicker. Because of this concentrated training by dedicated officers, when a recruit joins a shift after the ten weeks, he or she is better able to perform the job required than in the past.

Attempted Murder

During the early hours of Monday 6th January 1986, an 18 year old girl was walking home along Cow Lane at Garston when she was accosted by a man who insisted on walking beside her for a distance of about half a mile. When they reached a point near a school, the man produced a knife and threatened the girl, forcing her into the school grounds where he attacked her with the knife, causing very serious injuries to her throat and various other parts of her body. The girl was later discovered in a semi-conscious state by her brother who had gone to look for her. An incident room was set up under the command of a Detective Superintendent and a 32 year old man was arrested and charged with attempted murder. At St. Albans Crown Court, he was sentenced to 12 years imprisonment.

Assualt on Police

At 0130 hours on Sunday 6th April 1986, Constable Grover of the Dog Section was moving a group of youths along Garsmouth Way, Garston, after arresting a man. The group surrounded Constable Grover and another officer and Constable Grover was struck in the face and kicked about the head and body. He received bruising and swelling to nose, forehead, chin, neck and legs.

Divisional Resource Unit

In April, the Divisional Resource Unit (DRU), is started at Watford. Effectively bringing several separate departments the Crime Prevention Dept, Juvenile Liaison, Coroners Officer and Collator under the control of an Inspector and C/Insp. The Tactical Patrol Group were renamed as the Divisional Support Unit and together with the new Divisional Control Room also came under the auspices of the new department together with two new posts a Research Officer and Field Intelligence Officer. The new unit also took over control of the Special Constables. The DRU, has continued to expand over the years with support by two Clerical Officers and the addition in 1990 of a Divisional Training Officer. The unit, also has the responsibility of managing the operational policing at Watford Football Ground.

Neighbourhood Watch catch Burglars

In July 1986, the Co-ordinator of a neighbourhood watch scheme in Northwood, noticed a group of three people acting suspiciously and he noted the registration number of their car. Two dwelling house burglaries were later reported in the same vicinity, and on following the information received, a man was arrested and some of the stolen property recovered.

Football Friends

"C" Division, run the "Football Friends" project, which took place throughout the school summer holidays and involved over 600 boys and girls aged between 9 and 16 years. All neighbourhood beat officers and Area Inspectors were involved in the organisation of the project which consisted of mixed teams competing in play-offs at various grounds in Watford, with the semi finals and final being staged at the Watford Football Ground. A total of 207 football matches were played before several hundred spectators. The final took place prior to the

Watford v West Ham match in front of 17,000 spectators.

Computerised Control Room

On 25.1.87, the Watford Divisional Operations Room (DOR) using the Command and Control Computer goes 'live'.

As an enhancement to the Command and Control system, the force issued a contract for vehicle encoders. These units, will allow car crews to update their duty status i.e. availability for assignment, or their current location, on the computer at the press of a few buttons and without the need to actually talk to the Control Room Staff. The technology for this system, is not new but has been developed by the Force to allow vehicle occupants to type entire messages such as requests for vehicle checks, results of assignments etc, and will allow HQ or other units to respond similarly. The advantage of the system is the security of the system and as it is much quicker than the voice, it will allow the radio channels to be used for urgent messages without the fear of the airwaves being busy.

Murder

On 27th February 1987, Richard Clements, a 31 year old man who lived in Hemel Hempstead, was reported missing by his parents. On the 1st March, his body was discovered in a lock up garage beneath a pile of rubbish. Death had resulted from head injuries. A local man was arrested and charged with his murder.

Murder

On the 15th May 1987, an incident took place in Market Street, Watford, involving four football supporters from Coventry who had travelled to the area to support their team in the F.A. Cup Final at Wembley. During a fight that ensued between them and local youths, Terence Shepherd aged 24 years was stabbed in the chest. The four men were arrested and one was subsequently charged with murder.

Fatal Accident

In August 1987, a horrific accident occurred on the M.1 Motorway in which four young men aged 17 and 18, were tragically killed when the hired car in which they travelling left the motorway and rolled over several times before coming to rest in a field. An investigation was set up and it was discovered from analysis of the scene by officers from the Deeper Accident Investigation team that the car had been travelling at a speed well in excess of 100 m.p.h. at the time of the accident. A design fault in the car's anti-lock braking system was also discovered by a vehicle examiner, although this had no affect on the accident. As a result of further police enquiries into this accident, a large hoard of video recorders stolen by means of burglaries in the Southall area of London were recovered in a hotel room in London.

Burlar Caught

During the night of 4th September 1987, Watford College was forcibly entered and the padlocks to cupboards broken open. Property including a video recorder and computer equipment was stolen. The following night, the same premises were entered again via another route which activated the alarm. A 19 year old youth was arrested on the premises in possession of stolen property. The youth denied any knowledge of the previous burglary. Padlocks obtained from the earlier burglary were submitted to the Forensic Science Laboratory together with Mole Grips found in the youths possession. Following examination, a Forensic scientist stated categorically that the padlocks had been broken using the mole

Some of the burglary tools and stolen goods coming into Police possession in 1987.

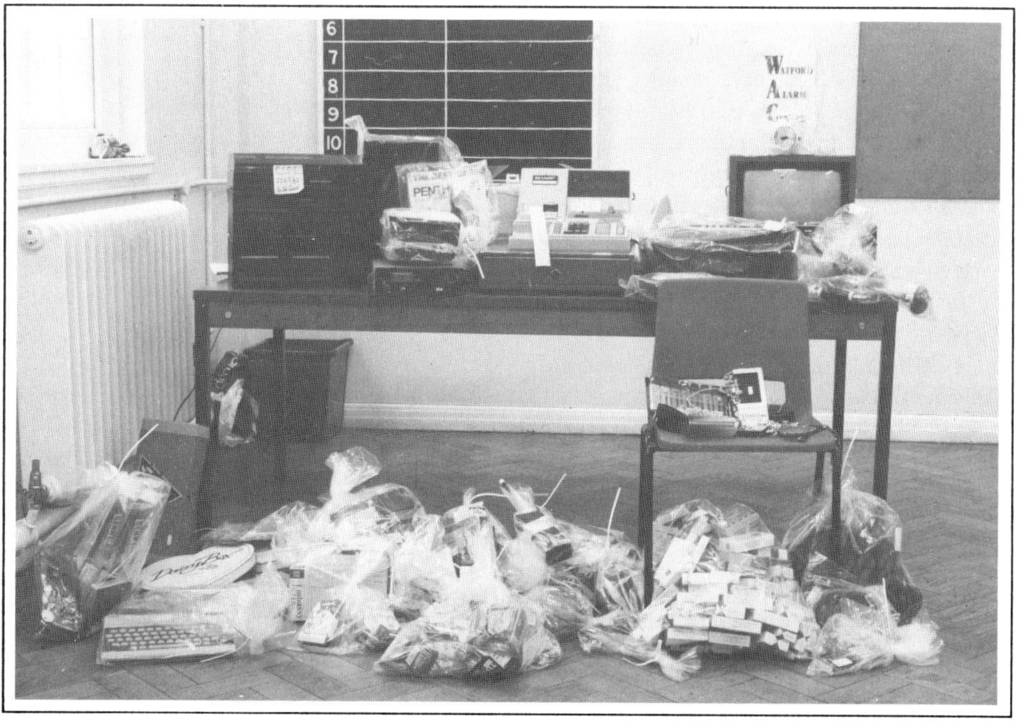

grips. The youth appeared at Watford Magistrates Court on the 26th October charged with two offences of burglary. Although he pleaded not guilty, the evidence against him was overwhelming and following his conviction he was sentenced to two years probation and ordered to pay £15 costs.

Burglars

On the evening of 10th September 1987, two men from the Notting Hill area of London, were stopped by police in Rickmansworth as they drove through the town. A search of their motor car revealed items of jewellery and radios which were later found to have been stolen by means of burglary. A search of their homes revealed many further items of property which had been stolen in the course of a series of burglaries in the Metropolitan Police District.

Murder

On Friday 13th November 1987, the body of a 57 year old man Kenneth Forrester, was found in the basement of a derelict shop in Queens Road, Watford. Forrester had suffered multiple injuries and his body was covered in paint. A murder investigation was commenced and three men were later arrested in connection with the case. One was charged with murder and the other two for assisting in the disposal of his body. The charge of murder was dismissed at Crown Court but all three were convicted of disposing of the body.

Burglary

A dog handler with his dog attended a burglary at a Watford Department Store, they followed a track from the store on a hard surface for half a mile. Several items of stolen property were found on the track which eventually led to a house. Enquiries within, led to three persons being arrested and property valued at £6,000 being recovered.

Fastfoto

In November 1986, a 'Fastfoto' system or P.R.O.D. as it has become known was installed at HQ. The system was designed to store electronic images - or 'photographs' and is capable of storing vast amounts of data and processing it at a very high transmission speed. The system is used with video cameras at thirteen locations within the County to photograph prisoners in police custody. On a regular basis the video cassettes are taken to HQ and processed onto an optical disk. The technology of the system allows recall of a single record in under one second. Additionally, it is possible to search the system by description, e.g. by entering a description, the computer can search and list all given possibles within the database of known local criminals.

New Pocket Radios

The Force purchases new UHF Radio's. The new radios with a remote microphone can be easily re-channelled to give access via the divisional control room equipment to all police forces in the U.K. Thus, allowing for the first time officers of Herts to communicate directly with officers from a neighbouring force without the delay experienced in the past of relaying messages via control rooms.

Football Friends

The Football Friends Scheme started in 1986 at Watford is extended in 1987 to take in the Dacorum and Three Rivers areas. Over 800 boys and girls take part in 229 games. Neighbourhood Officers supervised games taking place in various local parks and recreational grounds and in some cases 'managed' their local teams. All children participating received specially struck commemorative medals provided by the local Chambers of Commerce and Watford Football Club gave complimentary tickets to view a first team game at Watford. As a community exercise, the scheme again proved popular with those involved, players, parents and spectators alike with the added bonus to neighbourhood officers of being able to break down barriers that previously existed in police - community relations.

High Commendation

At about 1 a.m., on 16th October 1988, Special Constable Atkins and Constable Dent, were on patrol in the Parade, Watford. Both officers heard a gunshot and saw a man lying injured on the ground. Special Constable Atkins ran in the direction the shot had come from and his attention was alerted by the sound of a car engine. He saw a vehicle drive towards him with the passenger door open and noticed a man run alongside and get in. The officer called out to the driver to stop, which he failed to do and as the vehicle sped past him, the officer struck the windscreen and roof with his truncheon. The vehicle made off, but the officer was still able to note part of its registration number. The actions of Special Atkins were courageous and without regard for his own safety. As a result of his fortitude, quick thinking and keen observation, a man was later arrested.

The Chief Constable awarded a Commendation to Constable Dent for his actions in trying to prevent the vehicle getting away, and a High Commendation to Special Constable Atkins, the first time the higher award has ever been made to an officer from the Special Constabulary.

Murder

On 31st December 1988, a patient at Leavesden Hospital was found dead in the hospital grounds. A post mortem revealed the cause of death to be due to strangulation and consequently a murder enquiry was commenced. A 32 year old patient of the hospital was arrested and charged with murder. Following his trial at St. Albans Court, his plea of guilty to Manslaughter was accepted and he was committed under a Hospital Order to a mental institution at Rampton.

Shot

In February 1989, a young man was standing in a queue waiting to be served at a mobile burger bar in Oxhey, when he felt something hit his leg. On closer inspection, he realised that he had been shot by an air pellet. He subsequently received medical attention to remove the pellet. A month later, a search of an address in Oxhey revealed an air gun and pellets. These items were submitted to the Forensic Science Laboratory and following tests, the scientists were satisfied that the air pellet removed from the young man had been fired from the gun found. The owner of the gun was charged with causing GBH.

Deeper Accident Investigation

The Deeper Accident Investigation Unit were called to investigate an accident that occurred in Langley Road, Watford involving a single high powered motorcycle. Following the finding of scrape marks on the road the officer was able to calculate that the speed of the motorcycle was between 78 and 81 m.p.h. when the rider lost control and crashed.

Major Incident Exercise

A full scale practical major disaster exercise was staged at Watford to test various parts of the emergency services and other organisations that would be required in a real incident. The planning for the operation took almost a year and was code-named Oper-

President Gorbachev Visits

On the 6th April 1989, President Gorbachev of the USSR visited the Watford Business Park. Photographs from the Watford Observer.

ation Sleeper. The scenario, was a collision between a passenger train and a goods train in the Watford Tunnel. Over 150 volunteers, aged between 9-70 years, posed as passengers, with several injured, trapped or dead. Access to the scene was down a steep embankment and a touch of realism was added by the fact that it rained heavily making the task of rescue still more difficult. The exercise was a success and as is usual in these exercises various areas were earmarked for changes in written procedure for dealing with any future major incidents.

Dog Tracks

A dog and a handler attended a report of an armed robbery at a petrol station in Watford involving two men armed with a gun. A track was located away from the premises into a nearby sports ground. The police dog found a holdall containing clothes hidden in bushes. The discovery was passed to patrolling units, one of whom had previously seen two men jogging. As a result the addresses of the two joggers were checked and searched, resulting in property from the robbery being found under a bed. Both men were arrested. The dog continued to search the sports ground, and found an imitation firearm in a carrier bag partially submerged in an adjoining river.

Stuck to the Scent

A burglary, occurred at Chorleywood and some distance away, a stolen car which was believed to have been used by the offenders was discovered. A dog and handler commenced a search and located a track away from the vehicle, which was followed for approximately 2 miles across country during which time, the dog had to overcome a series of obstacles and distractions which included being attacked by a herd of bullocks and having to negotiate a section of the M.25 Motorway. The dog persevered and three persons were found hiding in a nearby field and arrested.

Sniffed out

A drug dog and handler were called to assist Drugs Squad Officers at an address in Watford. Whilst carrying out a search of the garden, the dog indicated the presence of drugs in a flower bed. A search found a two kilo block of cannabis buried 6 inches below the surface of the flower bed.

Helicopter Crash

On Sunday 5th November 1989, a small Robinson 22 Helicopter was on a practice flight at 1,500 feet over Sarratt when its engine failed. The machine crashed into a field and was extensively damaged. The pilot escaped without injury, but a passenger received a broken leg.

Ambulance Dispute

On 19th November 1989, Hertfordshire was the first area outside London to be affected by the Ambulance dispute. Following a request from the Chief Ambulance Officer, an operation was mounted to enable both the Police and the Army to provide an emergency ambulance service. Nine Police vans were converted for this purpose and posted to strategic points. Nine Army Field Ambulances, together with over 60 military personnel were located in various police buildings. All army ambulances were escorted by a police vehicle when attending an emergency. Between 19th November and the end of 1989, a total of 2,141 calls had been made by Police Vans and 2,710 by Army Ambulances.

Fighting

During the late evening of 27th May 1989, a party was being held in a basement flat in Gladstone Rd, Watford. Two hundred people

Members of the Hertfordshire Constabularies motor cycle display team, at the force motor cycle safety day, 1989.

were in attendance when a large scale fight broke out and spilled out onto the street. Police were called and on their arrival, were confronted with about 70 persons fighting. Re-inforcements from 4 divisions were summoned and order was restored. Eight persons were arrested for offences ranging from public order to drugs.

Acid Party

During the night of Saturday 2nd and Sunday 3rd September 1989, a very large number of young people attended a "pay party" held at Stockers Farm, Rickmansworth. Police endeavoured to stop the party, fearful of possible danger, disorder and public nuisance, but the large numbers already in attendance made this impossible. During the course of the event 13 persons were arrested for drug related offences and several other persons were processed for offences connected with the organisation of the party.

Crime Computer

Early in 1989, the Force took delivery of a new Crime Reporting System. The system was developed and in place by the end of the year at all Divisions. The system allows for fast searches for stolen property and management of crime and statistics. A crime bureau has been established at HQ for the inputting of data on a 24 hour basis.

Computerised Petrol Pumps

During the latter half of the year all petrol pumps at Divisional Stations were computerised with a fuel management system which improves pump security as well as enabling checks to be made on fuel issues to even a particular vehicle and checked against the vehicle mileage to monitor m.p.g. figures, as well as cutting the paperflow and administration time previously taken to manage the system.

The Memoirs of Inspector Arthur Bishop 1921 - 1954

The personal memoirs of Arthur Bishop appointed 14.3.21, and retired as an Inspector in 1954, (Now deceased). Our grateful thanks to his wife and family for making his memoirs available to us.

I joined the Hertfordshire Constabulary on the 14th March 1921. I was then 20 years of age. After about four months of training, I was posted to Bishop's Stortford where I served as a uniformed Constable for four years.

After about six months at Bishop's Stortford I was called upon to deal with my first body. I was patrolling my beat on a lovely Summer's evening, and feeling very proud of myself, when an elderly woman came from a house, obviously very distressed. She beckoned me and all I could get from her was "Upstairs, back room". When I entered the room I saw the body of a young woman, partly dressed, lying in a pool of blood, she was quite dead with a bullet wound in the region of her heart. A Webley revolver was by her side. This was a case of suicide. There was a history of depression, and her husband, who had been an Officer in the Army, foolishly left his revolver and some ammunition in an unlocked box under the bed. This case shook me rather at the time, but I think it was really a blessing in disguise as I was never afraid of a body after that.

Another very sad case which I had was that of a man who had been badly wounded in World War 1; he was always in pain and one day, in desperation, he purchased and drank half a bottle of spirits of Salt. He did this by the side of a river. Another Constable and I were called there. We got an antidote from a chemist and made him swallow it and he was taken to hospital, but it was too late. I stayed with him and he clung to me until he died in agony.

At this time, Bishop's Stortford was a fairly quiet town and nothing very sensational occurred. On 21st April 1923 I was married. We first lived in unfurnished rooms and were later allotted a Police Cottage. Police housing in those days was very poor, for instance in the cottage which we were allotted there was no bathroom, no electricity and no gas in the front room. About this time, I began to study hard for the promotion examination for promotion to Sergeant, and here I must pay tribute to my good wife who assisted me greatly by asking me questions from my books to see whether I knew the right answers. The examination was held early in the year 1925 and lasted from 9 a.m. to 7 p.m. The result was published about three weeks later and to my delight I saw that I had passed. The fact that one has passed the exam does not mean that he will be promoted, sometimes you may have to wait years as vacancies are very few as only a limited number of each rank is authorised in each force.

New recruits 1921, Constable Bishop, 2nd from right back row.

Shortly after passing the exam I was transferred to Hemel Hempstead to become the C.I.D. officer there. At this time, there was only one C.I.D. officer in each Division, except at Watford, where there was a Sergeant and two Detective Constables.

Hemel Hempstead Division at that time consisted of Hemel Hempstead, Harpenden, Berkhamsted, Tring and the surrounding villages. I was kept pretty busy and used to travel around on a motor cycle. I remained at Hemel Hempstead until August 1932 when I was promoted to Detective Sergeant and transferred to Watford in charge of the C.I.D.

Whilst at Hemel Hempstead, I had many interesting cases, including a murder at Tring. The victim of the murder was a woman of about 40 years of age. She was found having been battered to death, lying on a scullery floor and covered with a sheet, she had terrible head injuries. She was separated from her husband, who lived in another part of the town. It was known that he was of very low intellect so the local Sergeant and I decided to go and interview him. When we got to his cottage, we found all the outer doors locked and he looked through the window by the side of the back door. By the way, he was very deaf. We shouted to him to open the door, but he refused to do so until we threatened to break in. He then opened the door and attacked us. We had quite a struggle with him and decided to arrest him on suspicion. We later found witnesses who had seen him near and hurrying away from the house where his wife lived. Upon examining his clothing, we saw what we thought were bloodstains. We made him change into another suit and the same day I took the suit to Doctor Roche Lynch, the Home Office Analyst, at St. Mary's Hospital, Paddington.

Dr. Lynch found seventeen bloodstains on the suit, jacket, trousers and waistcoat. The man was then charged with the murder which he denied. Despite the fact that this was the most serious charge of all - Murder, there was an amusing incident at Berkhamsted Court when the case was opened. The prisoner, was allowed to sit with his brother. I gave evidence of arrest and produced the suit of clothes he was wearing at the time of arrest. At every place where he had found bloodstains, Dr. Lynch had cut away about a square inch of cloth, so you can imagine that the suit looked a bit of a wreck. I was just saying "When arrested, the prisoner was wearing this suit of clothes" which I held up for the Magistrates to see, when the prisoner clutched his bother's arm and in a loud voice shouted "Alf, just look at my bloody suit". I think he was more concerned about his suit than the charge of murder.

At his trial at the Herts Assizes, he was found "Guilty but Insane" and was sent to Broadmoor.

Another amusing incident occurred at Hemel Hempstead. I had in custody for housebreaking, two old clients of mine named Arthur and Henry. I went to Arthur's cell to see him about something and as I left I heard this shouted conversation between them - Henry to Arthur- "Who was that", reply "Old Bish", Henry- "What did he want?", reply, "Just fishing", Henry- "Be careful what you say, Old Bish is a nice bloke but he's a cunning bastard". They do say that listeners never hear any good of themselves.

Another case, where I got a ticking off from my Superintendent, was as follows:- One afternoon, I was at Berkhamsted Police Station when a telephone message was received that a man's blue Melton overcoat had been stolen from outside a shop at Apsley End and that a tramp was suspected. I mounted my motorcycle and when about a mile out of Berkhamsted I saw a tall chap wearing a fawn raincoat walking towards me along the footpath and as he walked, I could see something blue showing underneath. I stopped him and found he was wearing the stolen blue overcoat underneath the raincoat. I took him on the back of my motorcycle to Hemel Hempstead Police Station where he was charged. I took his fingerprints and sent them to Scotland Yard to see whether anything was known about him, meanwhile he was remanded in custody for a week. A few days later, the Supt' sent for me and said "Bishop, the other day you arrested a man for stealing a coat and brought him four miles on your motorcycle didn't you" I said "That's right Sir" whereupon he said "Well, look at this" and handed me a list of the convictions against the man received from Scotland Yard. There were thirteen convictions, nine of which were for ASSAULT ON POLICE. The Supt' said to me "You'll catch such a packet one of these days my lad". I said "Ah well Sir, All'bs well that ends well" and as I left his office I heard him say to the Station Sergeant "That young devil never sees any fear".

At about this time,, I began to take a great interest in fingerprints, realising that in cases of Burglary, Housebreaking etc., fingerprints were probably the only clue to the identity of the offender(s). During the year 1927, I had a remarkable run of success, seven cases of housebreaking detected through finger prints found at the scenes of the crimes, and during one of my frequent visits to the Fingerprint Bureau at New Scotland Yard I was called to the office of the Chief Superintendent in charge who personally congratulated me.

The Portman Jewell Case

A big case in which I played a part whilst at Hemel Hempstead, became known as "The Portman Jewel Case".

One Friday afternoon, Lady Portman was being driven by her chauffeur from London to Oxfordshire, via Kings Langley. She had with her, her jewellery, valued at over £10,000, in a jewel case at her feet on the floor. She was of course sitting in the back seat. After passing through Kings Langley, her car was overtaken by an open Sports Car containing four men. This car pulled across her car, forcing her driver to stop. One of the men then opened the rear door of Lady Portman's car and snatched the jewel case, meanwhile the bandits car had turned round and they made off towards London as fast as they could. Lady Portman reported the matter at Watford Police Station.

It so happened that that afternoon, Police Constables 297 Kempthorne and 339 Oliver who were on duty in Watford High Street, saw the four men travelling towards London and did not like the look of them, so much so, that they took the Registration Number and description of the car. This was before the Theft was actually reported. I was given the Registration number of the car and upon ringing up the Registration Authority I learned that the owner was a man named Isaac Bear of Portsdown Road, Maida Vale. I at once went there and saw the motor car which was thought to have been concerned, standing outside the house. I interviewed Bear, and he denied that the car had been anywhere near Watford or Kings Langley that afternoon. When asked to account for his movements he said he had taken his wife and child to the zoo at Regents Park, leaving his car there, and that his car was there when he came from the zoo. I searched his flat but failed to find anything. I did not believe his story and arrested him for being concerned in the robbery. He was brought before an Occasional Court on the Saturday morning

and was remanded until the following Wednesday. We decided to keep him in the cells at Hemel Hempstead instead of remanding him to Prison.

On the Sunday morning, he asked whether he could see his wife, here I had a brain wave, so said "Yes". I telephoned his wife and when she arrived I saw her first. She wanted to know what it was all about and I explained it to her. I also told her that I was certain that her husband was shielding the gang and that unless he was prepared to talk I was afraid he would have to "Carry the Can" for the others, whereupon she said "You fetch him out here, I'll make him talk", I brought him out and she at once said to him "Issy, you tell this Officer the whole truth", he said "Alright, if you want me to". I then took from him a statement (Yards of it), in which he gave the fullest details of the robbery, and it made very interesting reading indeed.

He said he had been approached by the gang who asked him if he would loan them his car "to do a little job", and they told him what it was. Bear said that Lady Portman's Chauffeur was involved in the plot, which I suspected, owing to the fact that the man who opened the door of Lady Portman's car knew just where to look for the jewel case, at Lady Portman's feet; moreover, although Lady Portman gave a fairly good description of the men, her Chauffeur said he could not, and that he had'nt managed to get the index number of the bandits car.

After Bear had made his statement I went to London and arrested Lady Portman's Chauffeur, a man named Carter. He crumpled up immediately, and admitted supplying the information to the gang as to the fact that they were making the journey and that Lady Portman always took her jewellery with her.

We then went on to arrest four other members of the gang and all (except Bear

Editors Note: The officers envolved in The Portman Case were commended for their actions, below is a copy of the commendation

Commendation

At the Hertfordshire Assizes on Thursday 23rd June 1932, 4 men were convicted with being concerned with stealing and conspiring to receive jewels to the value of £9338, the property of the Dowager Viscountess Portman, at Kings Langley, on the 29th April 1932.

At the conclusion of the case, the Judge, The Honourable Sir Raynor Goddard commended Constables 297 Kempthorne and 339 Oliver, "C" Division, for their vigilance, and Inspector Camp "R" Division, and Constable 326 Bishop, "D" Division, for their skill in investigating the case.

The detection of the offenders in this case, was primarily due to the acumen and observation of Constables 297 Kempthorne and 339 Oliver, who noted the number and description of a motor car used by the prisoners before any report was made to the Police.

The Chief Constable is very pleased with the action of the two Constables, and also with the work of all the other Officers concerned in the case, and has much pleasure in endorsing the commendation of H.M. Judge. He directs that an appropriate entry shall be made on the records of Service of each officer concerned.

who turned King's Evidence), were sentenced to long terms of imprisonment. We never found any of the stolen jewellery. They just would not tell us what they did with it, presumably they had a receiver whom they wouldn't "Shop".

About this period, there was not so much violence as there is today (early 1960's), but I had three rather bad cases which I will give the bare details of.

The first, was that of a young girl who was waylaid late at night on her way home. She was a nice decent girl and the young man who attacked her practically ripped all her clothes off her. No doubt his intention was to rape the girl, but she put up a terrific fight and he didn't succeed. When he heard someone coming he ran off. The girl kept her head and when I interviewed her she was able to give me a very good description of her attacker, whom I arrested the same day. He was 23 years of age. He admitted the offence and after some time, he was sent to prison for nine months.

The second case was that of an old lady, over 80 years, who was on her way home from church one Sunday evening. At a lonely part of the road a man came from behind and cracked her on the head with a pint beer bottle and snatched her handbag. Her condition was critical for some days. After a few days, I managed to trace her attacker who was sentenced to two months (a ridiculous sentence).

The other case was at Berkhamsted, on a man who was also nearly 80 years of age and who kept a small shop. One afternoon a young man went to the shop and asked for something. As the old man bent down under the counter he was struck on the head with an iron bar and the money was taken from the till. I succeeded in finding his attacker who was sent to prison for nine months.

In August 1932, I moved to Watford on my promotion to Detective Sergeant in charge of the C.I.D. (myself and two Constables). I found plenty of work to do. The first big case was another murder. This was a woman of 35 whose body was found, about six weeks after she had been killed, lying on a divan in a flat in St. Albans Rd, Watford. She had head wounds. This is the story leading up to the crime:-

The murdered woman, who was seperated from her husband, ran a Secretarial Bureau in Watford, teaching persons office routine, shorthand and typing etc. A young man who had been injured in a road accident, and who had received a sum of money by way of compensation, went to her for lessons, he was only 21 years of age. She persuaded him to become her partner in the business and he handed over his money. Their association ripened (as they say) and he went to live with her.

After the finding of her body we knew at once who we were looking for and the young man was found sitting on a seat in Cassiobury Park. When arrested he made a long statement in which he said that the business venture was a failure and that one evening he and the woman were talking about it, when she told him she was giving up the tenancy of the flat and moving out. He said that he said to her, "What about me?" and that she replied that he could do what he liked and that she could always get a job with her qualifications. He said that he then called her a rotten cheat, whereupon, she struck him across the face. He picked up a large spanner which was lying near and struck her on the head with it. He said that she did'nt move after he had struck her and he then panicked. This may or not have been true, anyway, at his trial at the Old Bailey he was found 'Not Guilty' of Murder but guilty of Manslaughter and was sentenced to 5 years imprisonment. About 12 years later he killed another woman and then committed suicide.

I also had two very big fraud cases, one of which I was investigating for seven months. I found that 51 firms had been defrauded of goods worth thousands of pounds, and the work involved was enormous. I got the gang of three eventually and they received long terms of imprisonment. At the Court I received a very nice commendation for my work. At the end of the case I measured the file of correspondence in the case and it was exactly 24 inches thick.

The other case, was one of a bogus insurance company. Two men set up an office in Watford and set up as the Monarch Insurance Company, the purpose of the company, was to insure persons against their doctor's bills. Persons were induced to invest money in the company, which never went into operation and the money was just pocketed. When I had sorted it out, one man went to prison for 3 years and the other for 12 months.

I think my best case was one of burglary and rape at Watford. At about 1 a.m. one night, a woman of about 40 years, ran across the St.Albans Rd to a Police Sergeant and Constable, she was in her night attire. She alleged that a man had broken into her flat, which was above an Estate Office, had stolen some jewellery and raped her. When they asked her where her husband was she said he was on night work. I am afraid that my colleagues at once jumped to the conclusion that she had been misbehaving herself and was trying to 'cover up'. A search was made of the district, but no trace of the man was found.

I was later called to the scene. The woman and her husband were Americans and he was an engineer. They had two children who were away at a Boarding School. I questioned the woman closely and examined the premises. There was a leanto building and drain pipe below the window and I could see that it would be quite easy for a person to climb up, which she said he had done. As a result of my questioning, I felt sure that the woman was telling the truth. When I asked her why she submitted to the man she said that he had seized her by the neck and that she felt quite certain that he would have strangled her had she resisted further, also that she thought of her husband and her children. Whilst talking to the woman, I noticed a small clock standing on the window sill, it was not in the centre where one would have expected it to have been, and in reply to my question, the woman told me that the man must have moved it to one side when he came through the window. I examined the clock carefully and saw what I thought was a thumb print on the glass. I removed the glass and with some white powder brought up the print which I could then see was a very good one. The same day I took the glass to the Finger Print Bureau at New Scotland Yard, where they promised to make a search for me.

I returned to Watford and commenced house to house enquiry in the vicinity of the Crime. At this time, there was a Government Training Centre in Sandown Rd, Watford, and lots of people took in lodgers who were attending the centre. They came from all over the country, and my enquiry was to see whether by any chance any lodger was out at the time of the offence. I was rewarded for my efforts, nearly a week later I called at a house nearly half a mile from the scene of the crime and the woman there told me she had a lodger who didn't come home until the early hours on the night of the offence. She said he was at the Government Training Centre and was able to give me his name.

I went to the centre and saw from his record cards that he had come from Sunderland. I telephoned Sunderland Police asking them if they had any record of him. They replied that he had four convictions for stealing and they gave me his Criminal Record Office number, from which I knew Scotland Yard would have his fingerprints. I rang up the Yard and asked them to make comparison with his prints and the print on the piece of glass I had taken there. They said they would do so at once and ring me back. About a quarter of an hour later Inspector Rapley phoned me and said that the impression on the piece of glass was identical with the man's left thumb print and that they were prepared to prove it.

I then went back to the centre and arrested the man. He was about 25 years old and a proper tough, I could see what the woman meant about being unable to resist him. A thorough search was made of his room and behind the draught plate of the fireplace we found most of the stolen jewellery tied in a handkerchief. He was charged with both Burglary and Rape and at the Old Bailey he was sentenced to 5 years imprisonment. At the end of the case the Judge called me forward and warmly commended me for my work. There was an amusing sequel to the case, for her future protection the woman's husband bought her a pedigree Alsation dog, and had it registered as "Sergeant Bishop", in my honour.

> Editor's Note:
> On the 12th September 1933, the defendant in this case was sentenced to 5 years penal servitude. Inspector Bishop was awarded a Judges commendation, for his detective work

After this, I had a rather pathetic case of "Concealment of Birth". One day I received a report from a woman that she had a girl lodger whom she suspected had given birth to a child. I called at the house and was shown to the girl's bedroom. She was 23 years of age. She was in bed and was evidently very distressed. I spoke to her as gently as I could and said "Mary, I am a Detective Sergeant, I have reason to believe that you have recently had a baby, would you care to tell me all about it?" She said "Yes".

I said "What have you done with it?"

She replied "It's in that first long drawer".

Close to where I was sitting, I opened a drawer and found the body of a female child wrapped in newspaper. I took the body in a suitcase to the mortuary, where a Post Mortem examination showed that it died from "Inattention at Birth". There was no evidence of any violence having been used. When the girl had recovered, a few days later I had to arrest her and charge her with Concealment of Birth. The Court was very lenient, placing her on probation for two years. I felt very sorry for her, I don't think she was a bad girl, just a silly girl who had been led astray.

After this, there were three more murders, the first being at a house in Harwoods Rd, Watford, occupied by a spinster of 76 years. She lived in the downstairs rooms and sub-let the upper rooms to a man aged about 50 years, his wife and their two teenage daughters. One Saturday morning, (which should have been my day off), the old lady was found lying across her bed in the front downstairs room, her clothes were disarran-

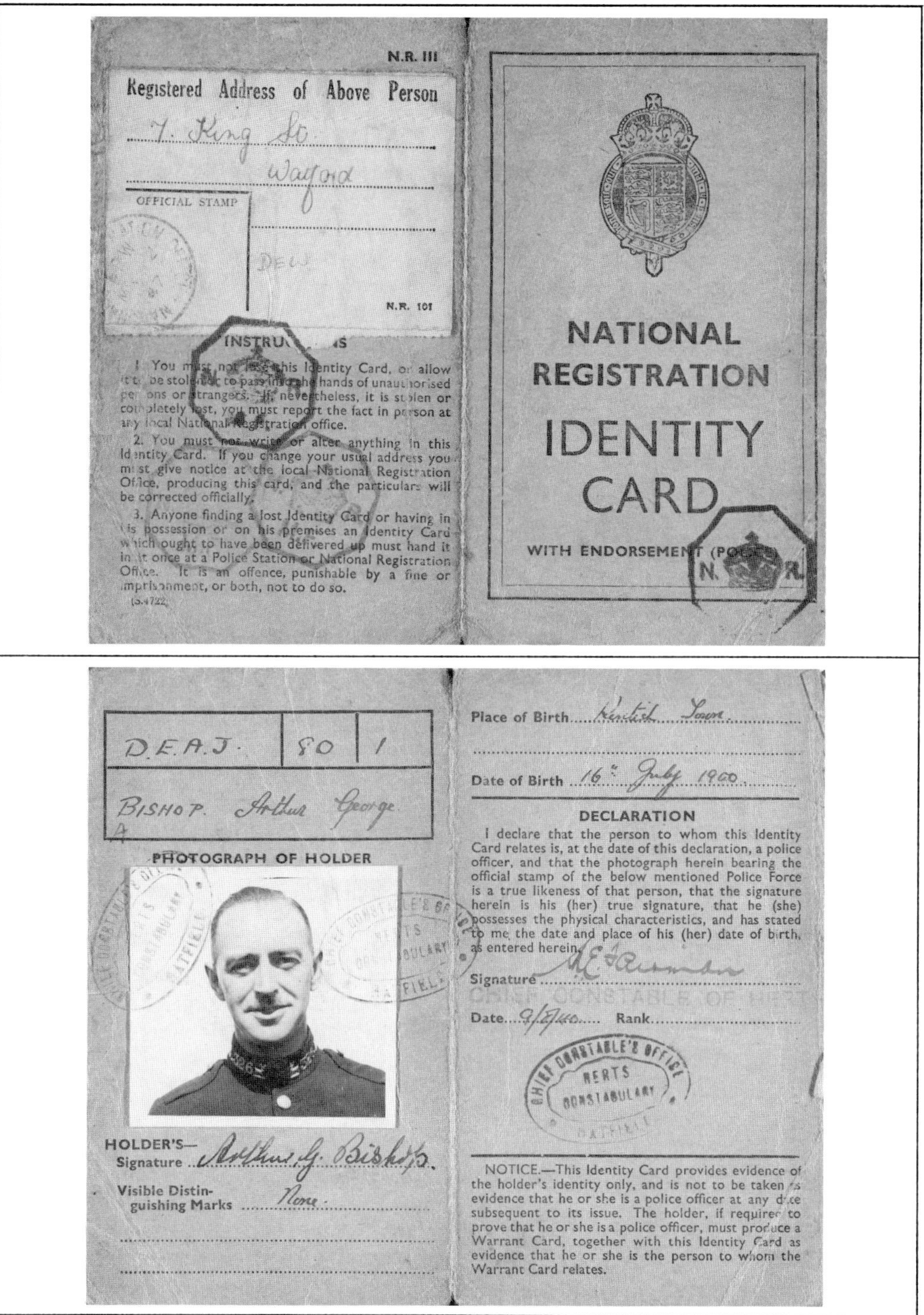

N.R. III

Registered Address of Above Person

7. King St.

Watford

OFFICIAL STAMP

DEW

N.R. 101

INSTRUCTIONS

1. You must not lose this Identity Card, or allow it to be stolen or to pass into the hands of unauthorised persons or strangers. If, nevertheless, it is stolen or completely lost, you must report the fact in person at any local National Registration office.

2. You must not write on or alter anything in this Identity Card. If you change your usual address you must give notice at the local National Registration Office, producing this card, and the particulars will be corrected officially.

3. Anyone finding a lost Identity Card or having in his possession or on his premises an Identity Card which ought to have been delivered up must hand it in at once at a Police Station or National Registration Office. It is an offence, punishable by a fine or imprisonment, or both, not to do so.

(S.4722)

NATIONAL REGISTRATION

IDENTITY CARD

WITH ENDORSEMENT (POLICE)

N. R.

D.E.A.J.	80	1
BISHOP. Arthur George 4		

PHOTOGRAPH OF HOLDER

HOLDER'S— Signature Arthur G. Bishop.

Visible Distinguishing Marks None.

Place of Birth Kentish Town

Date of Birth 16th July 1900

DECLARATION

I declare that the person to whom this Identity Card relates is, at the date of this declaration, a police officer, and that the photograph herein bearing the official stamp of the below mentioned Police Force is a true likeness of that person, that the signature herein is his (her) true signature, that he (she) possesses the physical characteristics, and has stated to me the date and place of his (her) date of birth, as entered herein.

Signature M.E. Alexander

CHIEF CONSTABLE OF HERTS

Date 9/2/40 Rank

CHIEF CONSTABLE'S OFFICE HERTS CONSTABULARY HATFIELD

NOTICE.—This Identity Card provides evidence of the holder's identity only, and is not to be taken as evidence that he or she is a police officer at any date subsequent to its issue. The holder, if required to prove that he or she is a police officer, must produce a Warrant Card, together with this Identity Card as evidence that he or she is the person to whom the Warrant Card relates.

Warrant card and National identity card - Arthur Bishop - 1940 ged and she had been raped, her death being due to shock. Enquiries revealed that the old lady was known to possess some rings and other jewellery, none of which could be found. It was also ascertained that the man living above was missing and that he was a confirmed drunkard. I searched the rooms occupied by the family, and never have I seen a family living under such filthy conditions. For instance the bed of the man and his wife had the springs all broken and the bed was supported by dozens of pairs of old boots and shoes, between which were cobwebs. The linen, was absolutely filthy. There were scores of old newspapers stacked against the wall.

Enquiries were made at all Public Houses, Pawnshops and Jewellers and most of the jewellery was recovered, having been sold by the man. A day or two later he was spotted by a Constable in Watford High Street and brought in. He was eventually committed to the Old Bailey where the charge was reduced to Manslaughter and he was sentenced to 15 years imprisonment.

The next murder was a really shocking business. A young married man living near Sarratt, came home one night the worse for drink and after a quarrel with his wife, he stabbed his two young children to death, stabbed his wife (who later recovered) and then stabbed himself. When he had sufficiently recovered, he was charged with the Murder of the two children and the attempted murder of his wife. At his trial at the Herts Assizes, he was found guilty but insane and sent to Broadmoor Criminal Lunatic Asylum. He was only 23 years of age.

The other case, was of an entirely different nature. One morning, the body of a well dressed man of about 45 years, was found just inside the gateway of a field, near Cell Barnes, St. Albans. I was sent over to assist. He had been shot with a revolver several times in the chest. There was nothing on him to identify him. After he had been seen by a Doctor and the usual photographs taken, the body was removed to the mortuary, where we sat him up, fixed his eyes with glue in the open position and had him photographed. We gave copies of the photo to the press and that evening his photo appeared in the evening papers with a request for anyone who recognised him to come forward, which several persons did. He was identified as a man with a very bad record so far as women and girls were concerned, he apparently got hold of young girls, induced them to become prostitutes and lived on the bulk of their earnings. It was also established that he was murdered in his flat in London and the body brought out from London by car and dumped near St. Albans. The Yard then took over, but I continued to work with them for about a fortnight, dealing with the Hertfordshire end of the enquiry. The murderer, a young man, was eventually traced to France and dealt with there. Apparently, he was trying to protect the girls and got away with imprisonment. I think this was a just result as no doubt the man had been living a life of luxury at the expense of these foolish young girls.

Before I move away from Watford, I must mention a very interesting case I had. For over a period of two years a number of Mansions all over the Southern part of the Country had been burgled and valuable silver, antiques and jewellery stolen.

One night, Langleybury, which was then a mansion, was broken into. Upon investigating I found on a black tin box which had been forced open, several finger impressions, and it appeared that the tip of one finger was missing. I at once took the box to the Fingerprint Bureau at New Scotland Yard where it was found that the prints were identical with a man named Anthony St. George. Upon making enquiries there was reason to believe that St.George was identical with a man going under the name of Arthur Hazel. I obtained the Index number of Hazel's car which was circulated throughout the country. Two days later a smart young PC was on duty in Rickmansworth when he saw the car outside a hairdresser's. He waited until the man came out, asked if his name was Hazel, which the man admitted, and then arrested him. When I saw him and told him that I had found his finger impressions he at once admitted it. He also admitted about 30 other offences. The value of property stolen altogether ran into thousands of pounds. There was an amusing incident while I was interviewing him. I was looking up cases in the 'Police Gazette' which I thought he might have committed, when I came upon particulars of a big job at Sherborne, Dorset. I said to him "Now this looks like one of yours Tony" and read out the particulars. He said "Yes, I did that, it was Lord Sherborne's residence, and by the way here's his tie pin". He then turned back one of the lapels of his jacket and pulled out the pin, a magnificent thing of gold and diamonds worth about £250. Here was a lesson on searching prisoners. On his arrest, he had been searched. He got 5 years.

One other exciting incident occurred before I left Watford, one day I went to arrest a man for blackmail. He had rooms over a shop in Market, Street, Watford. When I told him that I was taking him into custody, he seized a carving knife, but I twisted his arm and he dropped it. He got 12 months at the Old Bailey for blackmail. I didn't mention the knife incident, as I didn't want to rub it in.

I was then transferred back into uniformed duties to Baldock. This was a common practice in the County Forces, the object being to afford opportunity to as many men as possible in both branches of the Service.

Baldock, was a Sergeant's Section. I had three Constables in Baldock and I had three villages to supervise with a Constable in

Emergency repairs to traffic lights - Baldock 1937

each village. The section included six miles of the Great North Road and four miles of the Cambridge Road. Fatal accidents were numerous, mainly due to speed. In one case, we had five persons killed at once and in another four. There was very little crime there but quite a lot of hooliganism at week ends. At that time, there were no pubs in Letchworth (only two miles away), but there were 18 in Baldock and at weekends, they used to come in their hundreds, but we managed to keep them under control.

Bomb Course - Norfolk 1940

When the war broke out in September 1939, I was sent on an Army Bombing Course at Bury St. Edmunds and qualified as a Bomb Reconnaissance Officer. I returned to Baldock and after that I had to investigate reports of unexploded bombs and report to the bomb disposal squad. In addition to my other duties, I was also given the job of instructing the Women Police and Special Constables of the Division in First Aid and Ju Jitsu, so I was kept pretty busy. There was a Bomber Training Station just outside Baldock and the crashes were numerous. One night there was a mid air collision between a German bomber and one of ours. I had 11 bodies to deal with. It was a gruesome job. One of the Germans was wearing the Iron Cross.

I had one case of Manslaughter (Motor Vehicle) at Baldock. This was a very callous business. Late one Saturday night an 18 year old lad was cycling home from work along the Royston Road, when he was run down and killed by a motor car. The motorist had apparently thrown the boy's body in a ditch and his bicycle over a hedge. When I got there, I found pieces of the poor lad's skull all over the road. It was apparent, that the vehicle concerned must have been heavily splashed with blood so a telephone message was sent to all forces, asking for enquiries at all garages and hotels etc. to try and trace the car. Two days later, a message was received from the Police at Huntingdon that they had found a car, heavily bloodstained, in a Hotel yard there. I went there at once and saw bloodstains and human hairs adhering to the bonnet and windscreen. I had the car towed to Baldock, where it was later examined by a Serologist (a doctor who specialises in Blood etc). The doctor found that the blood was of the same group as that of the deceased lad and that the hair was of the same texture. By the length of the splashes he also said that in his opinion at the time of impact, the car was travelling at at least 60 m.p.h. I ascertained that the registered owner of the car was a Pilot Officer of the R.A.F. (incidentally he was the son of a well known Baronet, whose name it would not be fair of me to disclose). The Pilot Officer was stationed at an aerodrome near Huntingdon, and I went there to interview him. He admitted being the owner of the car and that he had travelled along that road on the night in question. I told him what I had found and asked if he had any explanation to offer. He denied all knowledge of the matter. I asked him how he accounted for the blood and hairs on his car and he replied "Oh, I thought I had killed a rabbit or something". At the Inquest, the Jury returned a verdict of "Manslaughter" against him, and I then arrested and charged him with the offence. He was committed for trial at the Herts Assizes, where he was sentenced to four months imprisonment and disqualified from driving for 5 years. About two years later, he was in trouble again, found driving whilst disqualified at Kingston, and I had to attend Court there to prove the disqualification. He was a wild and irresponsible type of person and he nearly broke his father's heart. I met his father, who was altogether different, he was a very kindly old gentleman and I felt very sorry for him.

On the 1st August 1942, I was promoted to Inspector and transferred to Hoddesdon. I was the only Inspector in the Hertford Division, and used to take charge of the Division in the absence of the Superintendent. The Division, consisted of Hertford, Hatfield, Welwyn, Welwyn Garden City, Hoddesdon and a few villages. The adjoining Division was the Bishop's Stortford Division, consisting of Bishop's Stortford and Ware etc. Soon after I arrived, the Inspector at Ware was taken ill and unfortunately died and for a long time, I was the only Inspector of the two Divisions, which kept me very busy.

Military Parade - Hoddesdon 1942

There was a fair bit of crime. There was a epidemic of fowl stealing at Ware and Hertford, but after a while we managed to get the gang and clear it up. There was also a run of housebreaking at Welwyn Garden City, eventually we got the gang (five youths), who cleared up 26 cases.

I was now riding a motor cycle again. One morning I was at Hertford Police Station,

when a message came through to the effect that a prisoner had just escaped from the cell yard at Ware Police Station; noting his description, I mounted my motor cycle and proceeded towards Ware, when halfway I saw a young man of the description given, walking along the footpath towards me. I stopped, jumped off and grabbed him, but he gave me no trouble. I put him on the pillion seat, jumped on and took him back to Ware Police Station.

My most thrilling moment however was the arrest of another escaped prisoner. A young man, one of those I had had for fowl stealing, was charged at the Hatfield Court with housebreaking and was remanded to prison. On the way to prison, he escaped. The Acting Chief Constable phoned me and told me that I had got to get him. I thought this was rather a tall order. I made enquiries and learned that he had a friend at Stepney, so to Stepney I went. Only to find that the house where the friend was said to be living, had been bombed to the ground, however, I decided to spend a little time at Stepney looking around. One afternoon, to my great delight, I spotted the man I wanted walking in Stepney High Street on the other side of the road. I crossed over behind him, caught up with him and grabbed him. I bet he was surprised when he saw who it was for he hated me like poison. I didn't exactly love him either. Two Metropolitan Detectives came over to see what it was all about, they had a car and took us to Leman Street Police Station, from where I took the prisoner to Wormwood Scrubs Prison.

Shortly after this I was transferred back to Watford, this caused quite a family upheaval. At this time, Joyce (our eldest girl), was working for the then Tottenham Gas Co., my Son was working at a local Engineering Works, and Joan was attending Ware Grammar School. Things sorted themselves out, Joyce got a transfer to the Watford Co., Joan to the Watford Grammar School and after a short time my Son got fixed up with an Engineering firm in Watford.

The frustrating thing was that when I had only been back in Watford about 12 months, the Chief sent for me and told me he was promoting me to Chief Inspector. I respectfully declined, as it would have meant moving again, to Hitchin, and upsetting my family again. The Chief was quite understanding when I explained the position, and said that I could stay at Watford for the rest of my service, which I did.

I did quite a lot of court work, and in addition to my other duties, took over the training of the Special Constabulary.

I hadn't been back at Watford for long before things started happening again. The first was a murder charge against a girl of 24 who had an illegitimate baby. When it was about a month old she took it to the canal

Garden of Rest - Watford 1952

near the Golf Links at Watford, killed it by bashing its head against the wall of a bridge and then threw the body into the canal, where it was found one Sunday evening. I was called there, removed the body from the canal and took it to Shrodells Mortuary. I communicated with Professor Camps, who arrived at midnight and made an examination. With the assistance of the Women Police, enquiries were made of all Doctors, Hospitals, Midwives and Maternity Homes and after a few days we were able to narrow our enquiries and I interviewed a girl who admitted that she was the mother of the child and that she had committed the offence. This was not an ordinary case of a girl finding herself in trouble, as I found out that she had two other children who were in a Home. At the Herts. Assizes, the charge was reduced to Infanticide (a special provision for any woman thought not to have fully recovered from giving birth), and she was sentenced to four years imprisonment. I am afraid she was a bad lot as she showed not the slightest remorse.

Another case which happened on the Harebreaks Estate, Watford, was entirely different. The family consisted of husband and wife, two teenage daughters and a small son. They lived a very rough life due to excessive drinking on the part of the husband. He was a brute of a man and when in drink became very violent, knocking his wife about and smashing up what little furniture there was in the house. One Saturday night, he came home drunk and chased the girls from the room and as they ran upstairs, he shouted that he was going to sharpen his knife and was coming to kill them. As he started to come up the stairs, the eldest girl (aged 19 years) in desperation picked up an Aspidistra Plant, which stood in a pot at the top of the stairs, and threw it at him. It struck his head and he fell back dead. When I got there he was quite dead at the bottom of the stairs and the Aspidistra leaves appeared to be sticking from his ears. The body was removed to the Mortuary, where a post mortem examination was made by Proffessor Keith Simpson who found that the cause of death was asphyxia. The blow on the head caused the man to vomit and as he couldn't expel it, he had choked.

After the post mortem I had instructions to arrest the girl and charge her with murder. This was reduced to manslaughter at her trial and when all the facts were made known she was acquitted, which I thought was only right.

There was another murder at Garston, but this was a straightforward affair - a man stabbed his wife to death and then committed suicide by gassing himself.

My last really interesting case was at Parkside Drive, Watford. One evening a man returned home from business and found his wife, little daughter and the wife's mother all lying on the kitchen floor, all had vomitted. The wife's mother and the little girl were dead and the wife unconscious.

It was at first thought that it was a case of food poisoning. I called in Proffessor Keith Simpson who established that it was Carbon Monoxide poisoning from the Ideal boiler in the kitchen. The explanation was quite simple, the boiler had been made up and some cotton wool dressings had been placed on top with the result that instead of the fumes going up the chimney they had escaped into the room. I am pleased to say that the wife recovered.

I now come to the end of my stories. I began to feel the strain, particularly of night work after 33 years of hard going, so I decided to retire.

Inspector Bishop receiving his retirement gift from Special Superintendent C.E. Ashby and Chief Superintendent H. Smith

Looking back I can honestly say that I enjoyed my service in the Police; there were times when things were pretty grim, but all in all it was a good life.

I would never hesitate to recommend the Force as a Career to any suitable young man or woman, but to get on, he or she must be prepared to work, and work hard.

Women's Police Department

The appointment of Women Police Officers, will always be a landmark in the history of the Hertfordshire Constabulary, there had been a deep reluctance to admit women into the male domain of keeping law and order. The constabulary had the services of the wives of police officers and saw no useful purpose in employing female officers. In 1928 they finally relented and 2 sisters were appointed Margaret and Annie Johnson. One can hold nothing but admiration for these two brave women, who had an extremely rough ride at the start of their careers. Upon being appointed the following order was issued:

Women Police - posting of

Women Police Constables Margaret Johnson and Annie Johnson having qualified by examination will be posted for duty on 7th December 1928, stationed at "C" or Watford Division, King Street Police Station.

The Women Police Constables will be available for duty in any part of the County where their services can be utilized in connection with any of the following offences:-

1. Indecent Assault.
2. Indecent exposure.
3. Rape and attempt to ravish.
4. Criminal Assault and all other offences under the Criminal Law Amendment Acts.
5. Bigamy.
6. Abortion.
7. Concealment of Birth.
8. Child murder.
9. Overlying of Children.
10. Taking information from female prisoners or witnesses in hospitals or other institutions.
11. Assisting in brothel cases.
12. Making enquiries as to the circumstances, etc., of female prisoners awaiting trial.
13. Other special cases or occurrences where their services would be desirable.

In all cases where reports under the headings shown are received by Divisional Superintendents an immediate report will be made to Headquarters in order that instructions may be given for one or more of the Women Police Constables to be detailed to undertake necessary enquiries in those cases where time permits and the Women Police Constables are not otherwise engaged.

Except when engaged on duties outside the "C" or Watford Division the Women Police Constables will act directly under the orders of the Superintendent "C" Division who will employ them at his discretion on the

This famous picture of a Woman Constable (Circa 1928), chasing illegal swimmers on the Serpentine, was used to advertise soap.

following duties in addition to those detailed above:-

1. Sudden death of infants.
2. Searching of, and attendance on women prisoners.
3. Escorting female prisoners.
4. Enquiries for Ministry of Pensions relating to behaviour of women pensioners.
5. Investigating cases of theft and malicious damage committed by Juveniles.
6. Keeping observation to detect pick-pockets, shoplifting and similar crimes.
7. Visiting premises licensed for music and dancing and/or under the Cinematograph Act as and when necessary.

The Women Police Constables may also be detailed for patrol duty when not required for other duties. When the Women Police Constables are detailed for patrol their duties will be confined to keeping observation on women, girls and children with a view to detecting and preventing cases of prostitution and/or molestation.

The Women Police Constables will report

Annie and Margaret Johnson
Hertfordshire Constabularies first policewomen - 1928

direct to the Divisional Superintendent in whichever Division they are engaged for the time being, and the Divisional Superintendent will instruct them on any points where advice is required.

Except where employed on special work the normal hours of duty of the Women Police Constables will be 8 hours per day in tours of not exceeding 4 hours each, arranged by the Superintendent of "C" Division.

Dated 30th November 1928

Uniforms

It was not until the 26th January 1929, were the ladies to be issued with uniforms.

Police Women - Regulations

Two years later, an amendment was made to the Police Women's regulations

A candidate for appointment as a Police Woman must be:-

1. Unmarried or a widow,
2. Not under 22 or over 35 years of age,
3. Not less in height than 5'4".

If a Police women's duties are wholly or mainly patrol duty, then the Police Authority may prescribe 7 hours as the normal duty period; where these duties are performed in one tour of duty, an interval of 30 minutes for refreshments shall be allowed.

PAY

On appointment 50/- per week.

After 1 year 52/- per week

After 2 years 54/- per week

Federation letter - 1934

That the Chief Constable be respectfully asked if the practice of calling upon the wife of any Police Officer, to search, and attend to female prisoners, can be abolished.

Chief Constable's Note.

The number of female prisoners detained in Police Stations of the various Divisions during the three years ended 31st July 1934, was:-

"A" Division 19

"B" Division 28

"D" Division 15

"E" Division 16

"C" Division not included since Women Constables are stationed there.

Having regard to the small number of prisoners, the Chief Constable cannot believe or ascertain that any hardship is occasioned by the present system.

Warrant Numbers Issued

On the 18th March 1948, there were still only 14 female officers in the force, and for the first time they were issued with Warrant Numbers.

WPS GOTT	1
WPC CARR	2
WPS JOHNSON. A	3
WPC LEE	4
WPS JOHNSON. M	5
WPC BELL	6
WPC FINDLAY	7
WPC FOGG	8
WPC FLEMING	9
WPC HORTON	10
WPC PICTON	11
WPC NIVEN	12
WPC STREBBEDS	13
WPC WYND	14

Police Womens Department (Circa 1958)

Assault on W.P.C.

A woman police officer told Watford Magistrates Court on Tuesday 28th June 1955 how she tried to break up a fight between two men and was struck a blow in her face which fractured her nose. Henry Smith aged 39 of Church Lane, Mill End, Rickmansworth pleaded guilty to acting in a manner whereby a breach of the peace was likely to be occasioned, but not guilty to a charge of malicious and unlawful wounding. WPC Mary Elizabeth Clarke told the court that at 10.50 p.m. on Saturday 18th June 1955 she was in Market Street, Watford. She had occasion to intervene when a woman caused a disturbance in a bus queue. Whilst she was thus engaged, she heard a scuffle and saw two men fighting. She made several attempts to stop them, but they kept on fighting. She saw one of them, Smith had his arms around the other and as she tried to part them, Smith lifted his right arm and deliberately swung it at me, giving me a severe blow to the face. Smith had been drinking. Smith claimed that he had been taunted in the queue and had lost his temper and that he had come to blows with his tormentor. He did not remember a police woman intervening and he did not mean to hit her, all his blows were aimed at the man he was fighting. The Bench found Smith guilty and the Chairman said "It is our duty to protect police officers both men and women from persons like yourself, and we will not allow these assaults to be committed with impunity." A woman left the court sobbing as Smith was sentenced to 3 months imprisonment and bound over to be of good behaviour for twelve months.

Matron

In October 1964, a Police Matron was appointed to Watford thus relieving Women Police Officers of the need to attend to female prisoners.

Equal Pay

On the 1st September 1974, Women Police Officers received the same pay as their male counterparts.

To celebrate 50 years of Policewomen in the Force, a reunion is held at HQ on Sunday 30th July 1978. The Guest of Honour was former Sergeant Annie Johnson, now Mrs. Baker. Photograph shows W.P.C. Loker presenting a bouquet to Mrs Baker.

25 Years of Service

by W.P.C. Ann Evans

I joined the Hertfordshire Constabulary in June 1966. Except for a short spell of night duty for the men and extra lectures on Children and young persons, and procedures in dealing with indecency offences for the women, the training school was the same for both men and women.

Having plodded through training school including the award of a bronze medallion and safety award for swimming (if you could struggle through a width of the swimming pool at the commencement of training, you had to take both). I was then posted to "C" Division at Watford Central Police Station and took up residence in the women police hostel, a terraced police house in Westland Road, Watford, shared by three policewomen. We were told at the time that it was to be pulled down the next year for the extension to the police station (this did'nt take place for several years). In those days, you were automatically posted to the Women Police Department because of your sex, and initially there was no other department open to you, even though it was considered a specialist department. At Watford, we had two sergeants and six policewomen. At North Watford, Rickmansworth and Oxhey, there was one policewoman and all of us were supervised by the two sergeants. The top ranks in the policewomens department were a Superintendent, a Chief Inspector and an Inspector all based at Headquarters, but who visited the various divisions from time to time.

The hours of duty worked by women police officers were 9-5pm and 3-11pm. We took it in turn to take call outs at night. Being woken in the middle of the night to go on duty whenever a W.P.C. was needed was no joke, especially when some sergeants forgot to look up to see who was on call and just sent an officer over to the hostel to "get a W.P.C.". I well remember being fast asleep on my rest day at about 4am, when there was a hammering on the front door. I knew that no-one in our hostel was on call, but the knocking persisted, so I got up like a bear with a sore head and opened the door to a stuttering young probationer. "What do you want?" I snorted. "We have got a woman to be searched" he said. "So what" I replied "I'm on rest day and nobody else here is on call". "But the sergeant says you must come" he said plaintively. I got dressed and went across to the sergeant and showed him the note on his desk telling him the W.P.C. on call. To be fair, this did not happen too often.

The main duties of the policewomen, consisted of anything to do with women, from rape to the taking of statements from women involved in road traffic accidents. We also dealt with missing person enquiries, as they often involved young girls staying out at night and having intercourse with men or youths. This could sometimes result in us being involved in bringing care proceedings, if the young person was seen to be beyond the control of their parents. Today of course this is dealt with by the Social Services. Shoplifters (and there were plenty of them), were another duty of the department varying from the old confused lady to those who made a living from it. I remember searching the room of a domestic at the Peace Memorial Hospital. I opened a cupboard and found it stocked from top to bottom with packets of tea and sugar. "What's this?" I asked. She replied "Oh, I drink a lot of tea." "All this amount" I said. "Well, I have a lot of friends" she replied. She also had numerous purses, hair slides and packets of buttons, all in their original packing. A veritable Aladdins cave. Obviously she was in need of psychiatric treatment.

When we had a series of indecent exposures or assaults in one area, a policewoman would team up with a C.I.D. Officer and take part in "observations". They would either walk around as a couple or the W.P.C. would act as a decoy (in plain clothes of course) whilst the Detective Constable would hide in the background ready to pounce if anything happened. Once, I was walking along a path near Bushey and Oxhey Railway Station. We had had a series of attacks on women, where they had been beaten with a stick. The path, had high fences, and although I had complete confidence in my partner, when I heard the sound of footsteps keeping pace with me a short distance behind, I literally felt the hair on the back of my neck stand on end. The man though overtook and passed me. It was not our culprit.

When I was at Watford, we had a very

enthusiastic Sergeant Jessie Bell. One evening, she took me round the licensed premises of Watford. We must have visited about 28 pubs. All had to be noted in my pocket book, giving the time and date we visited. My feet really ached when we got back to Watford Police Station. Unfortunately, Jessie was killed in a car crash a few years later, she was en route to her home in Southend with her 22 years long service and good conduct medal. I saw her the night before she left, she was so proud of her medal and was going to give it to her parents.

September each year was greeted with loathing by the Women's Police Department, as it was then that the Aliens Department went through their records and sent out sheaves of enquiries for updating or registrations. At that time, Watford had a considerable number of Aliens from Chinese and Italians to a large West Indian population. A letter, would be sent to each alien, with an envelope to return to the police, giving details of their present status. Of course, a lot of the letters were not returned and so we would have to visit the addresses with a duplicate to update the records. This meant a lot of footwork, as the only transport we had available to us were two motor scooters. Most of the aliens we visited, were very friendly and would continually offer us very sticky strong liqueurs which we would of course refuse. The Italians, were generally very voluble and excitable and many a time we would return to the station and started to 'talka with the Italiano accent' waving our arms and hands about, until we were brought back to earth by our colleagues. Eventually, the great pile of flimsy copies would decrease and the 'Great Alien Check' would be over for another year.

In those days, the Watford Central Police Station canteen was only open on weekdays at lunch time and for about one hour at breakfast time. When prisoners needed meals and during the afternoons, it was the lot of the WPC's to make the tea and meals for the prisoners. Two of us, would trudge across the yard with our petty cash box and open up the canteen. I was always a rebel and at one time when walking across the yard carrying the usual tea making equipment, I was met by the Chief Superintendent and other senior officers. "Ah" he said " You are going to make the tea, you don't mind do you?" "Yes" I said glowering over the petty cash box. He did not reply, I don't think he knew what to say. Another tea making ceremony was on football duty days when hordes of officers from all over the County descended on us.

At that time, Women Police Officers did not do football duty. However, one Saturday in December, Woman Sergeant Bell rang me at North Watford Police Station where I was then stationed. She told me I was to do football duty. "What making the tea?" I said in a disgusted tone, "No" she replied sharply " You are on duty in the ground". In due course, I found myself at Watford Football Ground. It was freezing cold. The outskirts of the pitch were covered in straw which I presume had previously covered the pitch to prevent the frost. Watford played Manchester United that day. I think they lost! All I knew was that I was frozen stiff! I have a pale complexion at the best of times, but when I returned to the station I think Sergeant Bell thought she was seeing a ghost! "Go inside and get some hot tea at once" she said. I think she rather regretted speaking sharply to me earlier.

The C.I.D., was the one department open to W.P.C.'s who showed an aptitude in this sphere. They dealt with most aspects of criminal investigation but again, specialised in serious crimes involving women such as rape. Many women officers did sterling work in the Regional Crime Squads. One of my colleagues was involved in the bringing to justice of the Kray brothers, before she had even finished her probationary 2 years with the police. She went on to become a first class C.I.D. officer.

The two motor scooters available to us for use were Vespa scooters and in order to ride them, we were sent on a two week course which ended with a test. I qualified to ride one and was soon buzzing around Watford on patrol and enquiries. In the last month of my probation, I was posted to North Watford Police Station an area which extended from Kings Langley to the Meriden Estate where it adjoined the Metropolitan Police District. I was the only W.P.C. at the station.

I enjoyed scooter riding and was shown the area by a P.C. on a Velocette motor cycle, which was the transport used then for covering the two beat areas of North Watford. This, was a very eventful journey as his motorcycle had a habit at times, of emitting great clouds of smoke. A voice from inside the cloud would say "We are going up here now." As we would both be enveloped in the smoke, it was sometimes difficult to see just where "Up Here" actually was! Still, we completed the journey without mishap. Many of the W.P.C.'s, did not like the scooters, and even though qualified to do so, would not ride them. As a result the garage staff at Headquarters came up with the (to them) brilliant idea of providing us with mopeds instead. These, were little more than glamorized pedal cycles with very hard seats. We had a one day initiation course with these machines, at the end of which everyone was walking with bow legs and a desire to sit on only the softest of chairs! After many protests, they padded the seats a little more, but they were always to be uncomfortable. They were also, not the easiest machines to start. If the mixture was not spot on, you ended up pedalling furiously for what seemed a very long time, much to the general amusement of the local 'yobs'. I had a really bad time one day, starting mine at North Watford Police Station, after having pedalled furiously around the yard three times, with no success, the Chief Inspector of the traffic

department (who were also based at North watford) came out and offered to help. After pedalling furiously around the yard for a fourth time without success and red in the face, with the perspiration dripping off he said "It's a bit of a beggar is'nt it?" About two years later the by now dusty and rusting mopeds were to everyone's relief, finally phased out.

Specialist courses for female officers were held at Chelmsford and every female officer went on one of these courses in their first years of their career. They were at that time and still are of a weeks duration. The course was enjoyable and it was interesting to meet W.P.C.'s of other forces to exchange ways of working, as these vary quite considerably from Force to Force. Sometimes, you were fortunate to meet friends from the initial training course. Firearms, although not used very often in those days, were being used and some women were trained in their use. Sadly this is coming more commonplace today as a sign of more violent times and several women are now trained in the use of firearms.

In 1975, the Women's Police Force became integrated with the men, which meant that they were paid equal money, and did the same duties. In Hertfordshire, women found themselves suddenly having to walk a beat alone on nights, a far cry from the 9-5 or 3-11, that they had worked before. Several officers were not happy and resigned, a pity as many of them were very good at the job they had been doing. Some forces, overcame this problem by forming a Social Services Liaision Department, ostensibly open to both sexes but in reality staffed by women officers, doing more or less the same duties as they had done before the amalgamation. Nowadays, Women who join the Force, do not expect to do anything different to their male colleagues. Most, would not like the service to return to the old days. Today, women are in all specialist departments and many are even trained in the Police Support Units, ready to face potential violent disorder against flying bricks or petrol bombs, standing beside and with their male colleagues. A sad but poignant reflection on the modern day, as we have to say farewell to the lost images of Jack Warners "Evening all" and the picture of a W.P.C. wiping away the tears of the lost child.

Watford and Rickmansworth Volunteer Cadets
By Constable Steve Hutchins

The Watford and Rickmansworth Volunteer Cadets, were formed in February 1988. It is one of two such groups in the county, the other being at Welwyn Garden City. It is an informal youth group hoping to break down barriers between local young people and the police. It is a nationally recognised means of promoting the police. Cadet groups exist in most UK police forces, many overseas forces and is particularly widespread in the USA. It is hoped that with the decreasing numbers of young people in the country, that each year the Cadet Corps will attract those who might be considering a police career, helping those who wish to join, and giving the police force an opportunity to evaluate potential recruits. The Corps is open to both sexes aged between 15 to 18 years.

The group is run by local members of the Hertfordshire Constabulary with other members of the force assisting in specialist areas, eg. Sailing and Climbing. At Watford the Cadets meet once a week at Watford Central Police Station for two hours, with occasional weekend activities.

Visits and various lectures are arranged throughout the year on the different departments of the police. These include Drugs, Firearms, Scenes of Crime, Dog Section, CID and Traffic. Activity evenings include Orienteering, Map Reading and First Aid. These weeks are alternated with sports including football, basketball and swimming at a local school.

The Cadet Corps also do community work with outside organisations with includes marshalling Watford Harriers races, helping at the Physically Handicapped and Able Bodied Youth Club and with various functions held at the Watford General Hospital, particularly the childrens Christmas party and Fun Runs.

The Cadets organise an activity holiday once a year for a week to Snowdonia in North Wales or Matlock, Derbyshire. These trips include abseiling, orienteering, caving, climbing, walking, canoeing and sailing. Twice a year the Cadets assist the Hertfordshire Education Foundation Sailing Centre on the Norfolk Broads. In early spring they help the Centre Warden float the boats and erect the tents ready for the new season. They return again in October when they sail and shut the Centre down for winter.

The Cadet Group is totally self-funding, and helps instil a community spirit amongst its members, whilst providing them with interesting and varied activities, giving those who are interested, an insight into the police force.

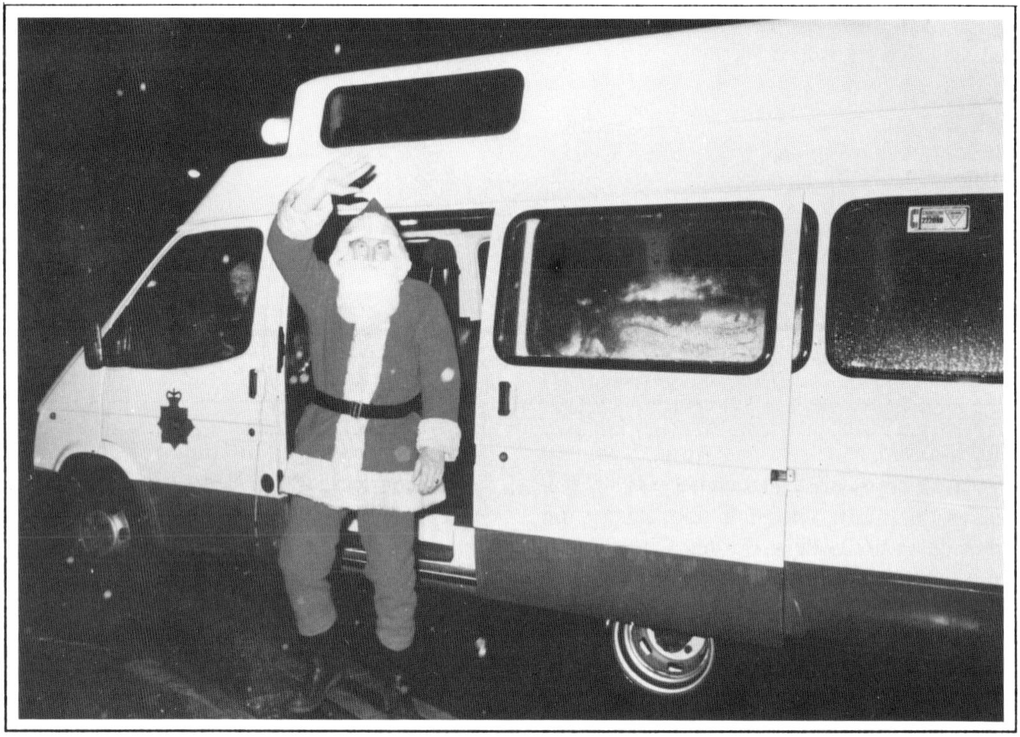

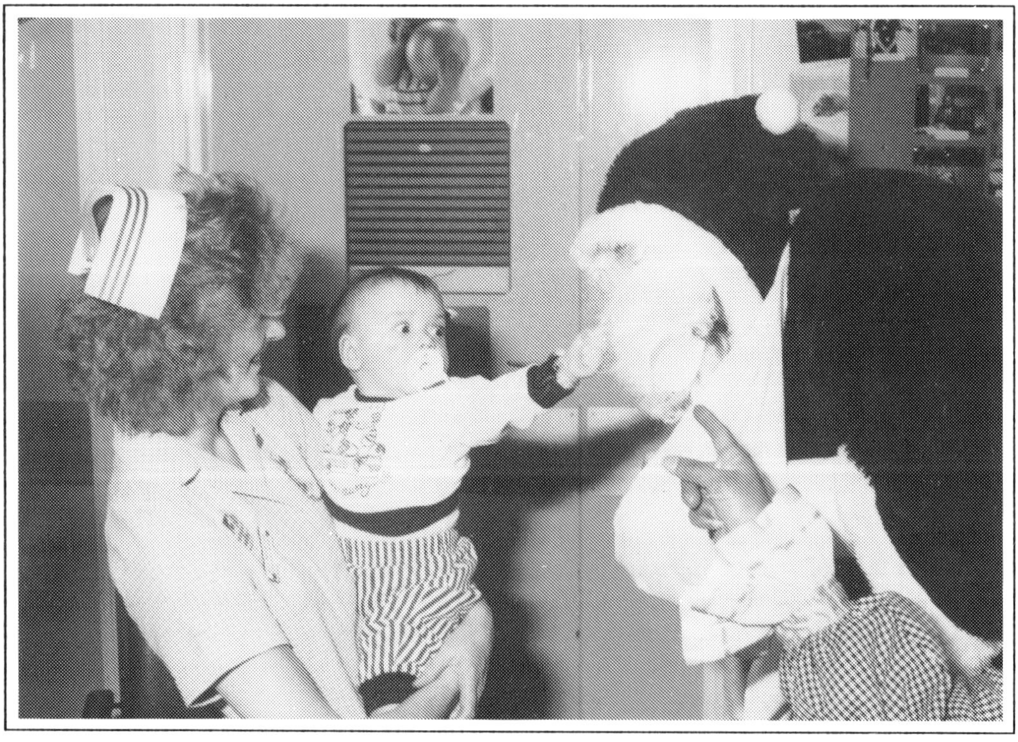

Policing Watford Football

By Inspector Barry Welch

Watford Football Club, has been playing Association football since 1886. It is a pity that the archives of the Hertfordshire Constabulary do not tell us very much about how we have policed football matches at watford in the distant past.

However, looking back through the club's history one is tempted to wonder if Watford's long-held reputation for having quiet, restrained spectators, has its rooted tradition in this 1904 regulation. Regulation 12 reads: "No public betting or unnecessary noise of any kind shall be permitted in any part of the ground."

Policing at the ground does have amusing moments, one long standing fan of the club "Harvey Ja˜quest" recollects: in 1912, that he had climbed over the fence to sneak into the ground without paying. Waiting for him on the other side was Police Sergeant Ginger Berry, who caught him and "gave me the biggest hiding of my life."

The 1923-24 season, seems to have been the first time that there had been a police presence in any number. When Watford played Newcastle United, five times cup finalists, 750 extra seats had to be erected, to help accomodate a record crowd attendance of 23,444. On duty at the match were one Sergeant and fifteen constables. Later in 1924, it was decided that one sergeant and four constables would be sufficient to police all first team games.

In 1933, the Watford public was censured for it's apathy and their apparent preference for criticising as opposed to encouraging the home team. A further indication of the codes and manners of the time, arose when the main stand exploded in uproar after a fan had rushed to the director's box and, as the Watford Observer put it, "made use of an objectionable sign."

The first signs of any sort of violence, came in the 1937-38 season when Watford played promotion rivals Queens Park Rangers. It was a spirited game watched by over 20,000, a small group of whom got got carried away and started to fight in the main stand.

For the most part though, a police presence at Watford football Stadium would hardly have been noticed until the 1960's. It was at about this time that the hooligan element in society, began to focus upon the football match as a source of captive audience to give vent to its potential for violent disorder.

Fortunately for the town of Watford, hooliganism has always been kept to a minimum, even when such anti-social behaviour was at its height during the late 70's and early 80's. This was in no small measure due to the success of team manager Graham Taylor with his continual emphasis on the team's friendly, family appeal which he projected and the creation of the first exclusive use Family Enclosure and Terrace at the ground. This policy, which built up a much respected relationship with the public, received widespread national acclaim from supporters and critics alike, flourished from his appointment in 1977 and has sustained and gathered strength to this day.

Coupled with this, has been the excellent working relationship between the club and the Watford police who, together, have worked hard in their endeavour to keep violence out of the stadium and off the streets at Watford on match days. So successful has been the liaison, that during the early and middle 1980's, Watford actually saw a decrease in the number of arrests (for criminal offences) and ejections (for breaches of ground rules) at a time when average attendances significantly increased. This proud boast could not be said of many other clubs in the Football League.

It must be stated that the good nature of the average Watford supporter has played a big role in achieving the reputation for which Watford is held in such high regard by the game in general. Graham Taylor, once put it like this "Herts people are not violent or particularly passionate. They like their football but are not passionate about it, which is not so bad because when you have passion, the next thing is violence".

It is precisely because the police have generally felt able to regard local supporters in this way, that they have been able to concentrate their efforts in looking after the problems which the less predictable visiting supporters may present. Over the last 20 years or so, a number of initiatives have been taken by the club and the police in conjunction with the local authority, British Rail and other organisations to bring about the more orderly control of football supporters. Some, have been taken as a direct result of local hooliganism problems and others have followed because of the tragic consequences of incidents such as the Bradford City fire and disasters at the Heysel stadium in Brussels and , more recently at the Hillsborough Stadium in Sheffield.

Watford

Where once it was the prime responsibility of police to concern themselves with the control of the rowdy element before, during and after the game, the emphasis now is more on the safety of all the football going public, the vast majority of which, are law-abiding. But, as we have seen, they can so easily end up the innocent victims of tragedy. Arguably, this is the priority for police and club officials at all football matches nowadays. It is for this reason that officers in the stadium now wear high visibility tabards, distinguishable from those worn by stewards, but adorned to promote the same effect, in that they are all instantly recognisable in an emergency. Both police and stewards receive training in awareness and recognition of crowd dynamics and signs of distress and know how to react to it.

Modern technology is used to great effect in monitoring the safety of the crowd, the prevention and detection of criminal acts and the control of loutishness and other forms of misbehaviour which can all to easily lead to total chaos or disorder if left unchecked.

Watford

Closed circuit television cameras around the stadium, with monitors and recording facilities installed in the police control room, located in one corner of the stadium, are of particular benefit. These are closely watched at all times by a trained officer who will report perceived problem areas to the Ground Commander (or police superintendent in charge of the operation). Through the radio controller in the same room, remedial action can be considered and initiated quickly using nearby officers, many of whom will be equipped with personal radio. As an aid to preventing crushing by too many fans concentrating in one area or pen, officers in the control room also have access to a computer terminal which registers the total number of people admitted through all the turnstiles in a given sector of the ground. When each nears its maximum capacity, an alarm sounds, enabling the closure of the area in time to prevent overcrowding.

A long established method of crowd control used at Watford is the segregation of rival fans. All visiting supporters are allocated a designated section of the stadium for standing and seated accommodation. An important function for officers on duty at the turnstiles is to be vigilant to prevent the infiltration of the home supporters terraces and stands by the visitors. Successful segregation works well to eliminate the chance of unnecessary confrontation which the hooligan with evil intent is all to eager to exploit.

Keeping the fans segregated is, in fact, the idea objective at all stages before, during and after the match, although outside the stadium, the task is obviously much more difficult, if not impossible to attain.

Where opposing fans have to share, even compete for, the same scarce parking facilities or, to commonly use the same public transport systems, it is virtually impossible to separate the two until they reach the confines of the stadium itself. Many are obliged to use the same streets and town centre car parks, often posing confrontational situations with shoppers and other road users, while making their way to the ground. To cope with this and to protect the non-football going public and, to minimise their inconvenience as far as possible, a number of the police squads have to be deployed along the various routes to the town centre, in the main shopping areas and along the approaches to the railway stations serving the town.

A very important facility, established in 1982 for the exclusive use of the visiting supporter, is the Stadium Halt. Passengers arriving by special chartered trains at Watford Junction, can be transferred to 'shuttle' trains and taken direct to the stadium, thereby avoiding the long trek through or round the town as well as areas of possible conflict. Officers of the British Transport Police help to monitor and control the behaviour of these travellers whilst on railway property. Liaison is developed between the two forces in the days leading up to the match and this is maintained on the match day itself.

Of course, drunkeness is one of the most obvious problems which has to be controlled. Too much drink is the chief reason for misbehaviour and acts of violence and crime, not only on Friday and Saturday evenings, but at many football matches. Since alcohol was effectively banned at designated sporting events by Act of Parliament in 1985, both at the stadium and on coaches and some trains carrying supporters to the game, the problem has somewhat diminished. Anyone who is drunk is now unlikely to get into the stadium unseen. Even if they do, they will soon come to notice and become subject to arrest and removal from the stadium.

Many of the hired coaches, used by both official supporters clubs and those unofficially organised by private individuals or groups, are often met at various points away from the town by a police motorcyclist who will escort them to a special parking area close to the ground. The purpose of this is not only to ensure their safe journey to the venue but to take the opportunity of checking to see that no breach of the alcohol ban has taken place.

Another important factor in the police effort to prevent trouble arising is the co-operation with other forces in a mutual scheme designed to identify at an early stage those visiting fans who have been banned by the Courts from going to football matches any where in the country. Many of them believe that they may succeed into getting into a game away from home where they will not be known. Because of this, some forces have combined to work with each other on certain matches and will send officers known as 'spotters' who can easily pick out these offenders in the crowd. In return, we send 'spotters' to many of Watford's away matches.

In the weeks leading up to the match, two officers at Watford police station take on the task of gathering information about the fixture or cup tie so that plans can be drawn up to use all police staff to the best possible advantage. The football 'intelligence' officer will receive and distribute all relevant information and the football 'liaison and planning' officer has then to draw up the Operation order for deployment for a number of 'squads'. Any number of squads, consisting of police men and women, constables and sergeants, led by an inspector, will be utilised each match, dependant upon many factors. These include the estimated number of supporters, both home and away; the history and current behaviour of groups and individuals; the degree of rivalry known to exist between the two clubs; and the need to ensure successful segregation and crowd safety until the end of the match. Nowadays, in accordance with the assessed degree of risk, anything from 80 to 150 police officers will be deployed on a Second Division match. Many more could be involved in a high category cup tie against one of the more prestigious leading clubs in the First Division.

Who, in the 1881, when the club was first formed, could have imagined that a century later, it would be necessary to establish all these measures just to facilitate the playing of a game of soccer - even at Vicarage Road, the home of a widely acclaimed, friendly club like Watford!

The face of soccer is constantly changing and, with it, must change the approach to its policing. Whether Watford survives to remain in the Second Division at the end of this season or is relegated to the Third where, in 1920 it was one of its founder members, remains to be seen. Whatever happens, the commitment of the Hertfordshire Constabulary to the safety of all spectators and to the containment of the few hooligans, will continue.

(Our thanks to Ollie Philips of the Watford Observer, for supplying some of the clubs history.)

'Mencop' 1981 - 1991

By Police Constable Bill Wells

Mencop, was officially designated a Registered Charity in 1981. Prior to this, a small group of Police Officers, friends and their families had been raising money primarily for a holiday bungalow in Norfolk, This was the idea of Graham Russell, a serving officer in the Hertfordshire Constabulary, who was at the time the Chairman of both the Hertfordshire and St. Albans Societies for the Mentally Handicapped (Mencap).

After the opening of 'Russell House' in 1977, it was handed over to Mencap. Graham and his friends then took to raising money for various projects, including the Harpenden Short Stay Home 'Stairways'.

In 1980, following the assassination attempt on his life, it was proposed to take the Pope a greeting from the City of St. Albans. In this area, there is of course a link with the Vatican as the only English Pope, Nicholas Breakespeare, later in 1154, to become Pope Adrian IV until he died in 1159 was born in Abbots Langley. The visit was sponsored by British Leyland, who supplied a brand new coach, Shell UK who supplied the fuel and various local companies who took up advertising space on the coach. local schools, took up the idea and became involved in holding collections and their own fund-raising events. Sack loads of letters from the children were loaded on the coach to be delivered to the Pope. Several Police Officers, went on the coach and were given permission to wear their uniforms during a 'line up' in St. Peters Square. This was quite a sight, and the media were to give the occasion tremendous coverage. The Pope spoke to each officer, accepting various momentoes from them, and then came back to them, when a mentally handicapped boy was passed over the heads of the crowd to the officers. The Pope blessed the boy and thanked the officers for the work they were involved in for the mentally handicapped. Although none of the Police Officers were Roman Catholics, and only one of them had a mentally handicapped child, they were all very moved by this experience (there was not a dry eye amongst the officers or the surrounding crowd). The visit, was very successful financially, raising over £8,000 for the Adolescent Special Care Unit (A.S.C.U.) in St. Albans. On their return, there was a special service at St. Albans Abbey for the handicapped, to which the officers were invited to attend.

It was during this trip, that the officers decided to break out on their own and form their own charity. Sir Eric Cheadle who had been involved, suggested the name 'MENCOP' and so in 1981 'MENCOP was born, and became the charity it is now.

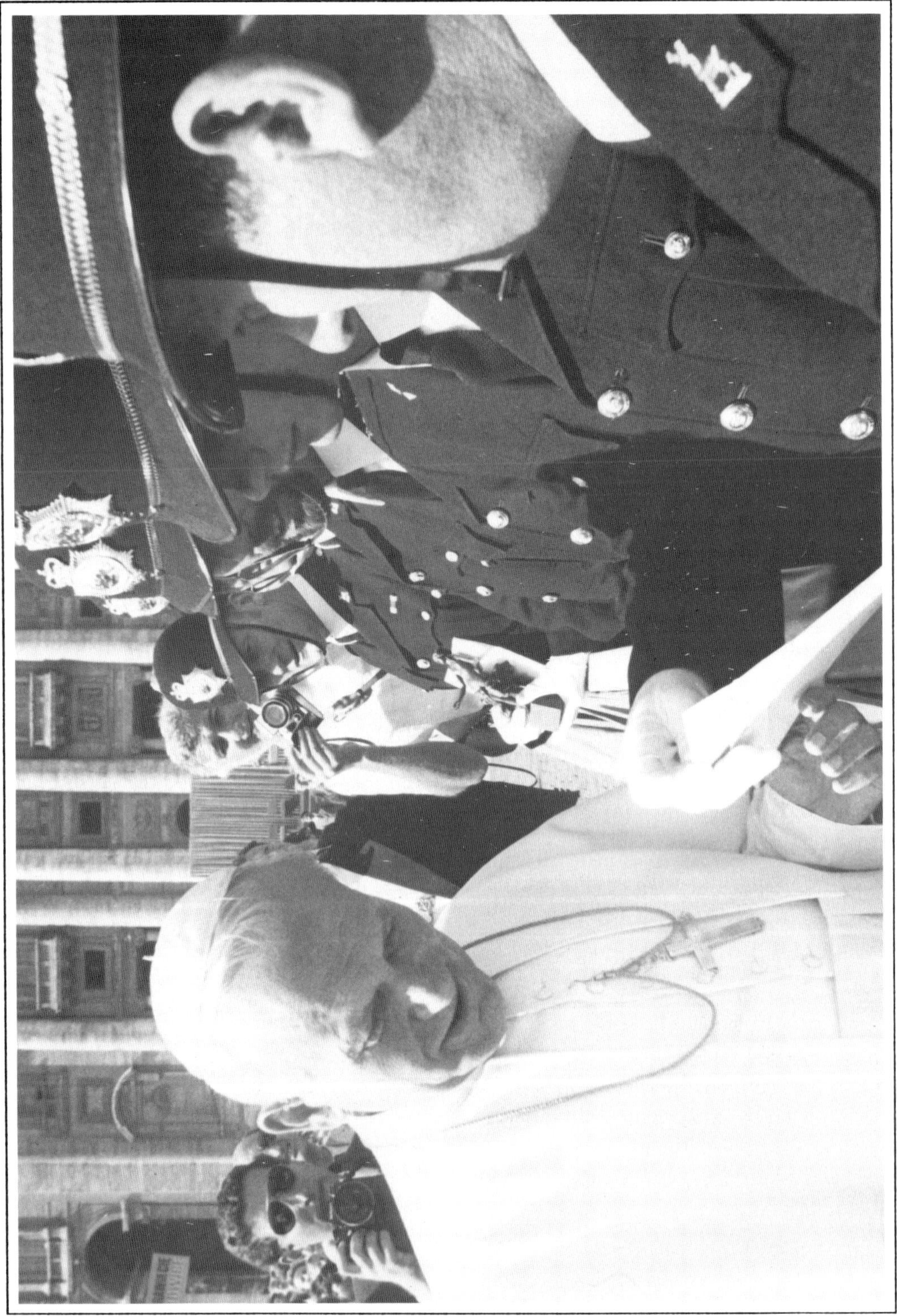

Shortly after returning from Rome the A.S.C.U. centre was completed and the officers decided that it would be appropriate if there was a book in the centre with details of all the persons who had made a donation. It was also felt appropriate that this book should have a foreword by the Prime Minister, Mrs Margaret Thatcher. So it was after many letters the officers arrived at the door of 10, Downing Street, in the middle of the Falklands War. In fact it was the very day of the Goose Green and Darwin Bay Battles, due to this the officers were informed that they might not be able to see the Prime Minister. They waited and after an hour and a half they were shown into the Premiers Office. She immediately switched off from the affairs of State and gave the officers her undivided attention. She wrote the entry in the book, posed for photographs and gave the officers an escorted tour of No.10. At the end of the visit, the officers presented her with a dark blue powder compact, bearing the Hertfordshire Constabulary crest.

In 1982, it was decided to take a Police Helmet to Boston, U.S.A. as a fund-raising event to celebrate the Boston Tea Party. The helmet to be taken, was no ordinary helmet, but a scale model measuring 8' in height and 12' long. The helmet was made at the St. Albans College of Art as a project by the students. The helmet appeared on the television programme "Record Breakers", being billed as the "Biggest British Bobbies Bonnet in the World". It was then transported to the States by an Air Freight Company, but getting it to the airport posed a few problems, finally solved by loading it onto a low loader lorry supplied by the Post Office. On arrival in America, the helmets sheer size still posed problems, they did not have any vehicles wide enough to get it to Boston. However, it finally arrived, where it is now on display in a "Giants Museum". Once again, the accompanying officers were given permission to wear their uniforms on official occasions, such as their visit to the Senate and when meeting members of the Kennedy family. On both of these trips, the officers paid for all their own expenses and all monies raised went to MENCOP.

In 1986, MENCOP organised a 'Holiday of a Lifetime' for a group of mentally handicapped children to visit 'Disney World in Florida. The trip left the officers exhausted and the children with a memory that they will never forget. This trip, was the start of MENCOP'S biggest project yet, another holiday home, this time a bungalow for Free holidays for any Mentally Handicapped person and their families or carers. In order to achieve this, it was necessary to raise over £40,000.

MENCOP achieved their aim and purchased a bungalow in Llanbedrog, North Wales in 1988. It was opened for holidays in 1989. Unfortunately, before it was finalised, Graham Russell one of the founding officers and first chairman of MENCOP died. The Bungalow was named "Graham House" in his memory. Monies collected in lieu of flowers at his funeral, totalled over £3,000 and this has been used to convert the garage at Graham House into a large playroom.

During the last 10 years, the officers have devised many ways in which to raise money from the public, both for their large schemes and for many smaller ones throughout the years. Some of these, have become Annual Events like the Christmas Sleigh Pull from Watford to Cell Barnes Hospital in St. Albans, during which the officers, their families and friends dress in pantomime costumes and haul the sleigh complete with a 'Snow Queen', collecting money all the way. On their arrival at Cell Barnes, Father Christmas delivers his goodies to all the

Margaret Thatcher

patients. Also during the Christmas period, a small group of dedicated Carol Singers entertain the public at local hotels. In Harpenden High Street, an Annual "Mile of Coins" is performed.

The Charity also organises an Annual 'Themed" Dinner and Dance, such as the '50th Anniversary of the Battle of Britain', which was held in a hangar at Leavesden Airport with over 700 diners present. Other dances have included a Twenties Night, a Haunt Ball, Arabian Nights and a Roman Night amongst others. This year, it was the 'MENCOP Showboat' a Mississippi Paddle Steamer complete with Roulette, Blackjack and croupiers. All our guests dress to the theme of the evening.

1991, will continue to be a busy year for MENCOP. Money will be needed to cover the general maintenance costs at 'Graham House', and the charity will continue their programme of supplying where possible, the needs of their local mentally handicapped friends. However the main project for the year will be to raise enough money to install double glazing at 'Graham House' which together with recently installed central heating will enable them to offer free holidays throughout the year.

MENCOP would like to take this opportunity to thank everyone, who has supported them over the last ten years, which enables them to carry on their work for the good of the local mental handicapped and thereby enhance the quality of their lives.

A visit to Mainz - Watford's twin town

By Special Commandant Peter Mould

Mention the German town of Mainz to anyone who has had the pleasure of walking through its cobblestoned precincts and visiting one of the many lively little wine-houses, and his memory will immediately conjure up a picture of a beautiful city, nestling amongst the lush vineyards and fairytale castles on the most picturesque stretch of the Rhine. Mention the same town to one of the many Watford Police Officers who has been privileged enough to have been a guest of his German colleagues, and his recollection will be further extended to include a spirit of unrivalled generosity and hospitality.

The foundation for this true brotherhood between Police Officers of both towns, was laid in 1979, when the leader of the Mainz Police Choir, Hans-Jurgen Rinner, wrote to Chief Superintendent Mick Webber asking if a visit to Watford was possible. The answer, was an immediate "Yes"; the task of liaising with Herr Rinner and making all the necessary arrangements was delegated to myself, since my mother was German by birth and I speak the language fluently.

The visit by 50 colleagues from Watford's twin town was a resounding success and initiated many personal friendships which have stood the test of time. The farewell speech by the President of the Rheinland-Pfalz Police, Herr Kaesehagen, included an invitation for a return visit by Watford Officers. Arrangements, were immediately put into hand to accept the offer. Several months of constant liaison between Hans Jurgen and myself finally came to fruition when, on a gloriously hot day in late spring the following year, the coach transporting us to our first view of Mainz was met at the German frontier town of Aachen by a marked patrol car and two motorcycle outriders. The tone of the visit was set when the patrol car driver, Kurt Haffner, opened the boot of his vehicle and unloaded twenty bottles of ice cool wine! After a suitable period for refreshments, we were escorted the 80 miles to Mainz in VIP style.

It was a holiday to remember! Nothing was too much trouble for our hosts and their 'entertainment fund' seemed inexhaustible. A programme for the week was drawn up and with renowned German precision, we were whisked off to a wine tasting session in a local vineyard, a steam boat cruise on the Rhine, a picnic on top of the famous Lorelei Rock and endless nights of singing and dancing. This new era of international hospitality soon spread throughout the region, and, so as not to be outdone, the local fire brigade invited us to an afternoon 'banquet' of coffee and cakes. The German Railworkers Union, fearing that they might

otherwise miss the opportunity to entertain us, arranged a massive outdoor evening barbecue for us at their Regional Headquarters on the banks of the Rhine. The Mayor of Mainz welcomed us, the President of the Police greeted us and everyone made us feel like visiting royalty. No-one, who took part in that pioneering visit will ever forget the experience.

Since that first embrace by our friends in Mainz, there have been many visits, both official and unofficial, by large and small groups. Sergeant Keith Gladden, Chief Inspector (then PC) Stephen Reid and I were honoured to be invited to the opening of the new Rheinland-Pfalz Headquarters in 1982. Together with other officers from Mainz's other twin town Valencia, we spent a couple of hours of uniformed foot patrol in the centre of Mainz, much to the amusement of the local populace, followed by a few hours on one of the many high powered Police Launches which operate on the Rhine. In 1985, Detective Sergeant Bren Hayden, PC Bill Wells and I were part of a multi-national delegation invited to take part in a ceremony to mark the opening of a hostel, set in beautiful woodland on the outskirts of Mainz, belonging to the International Police Association. This hostel, perhaps more than anything else, has been responsible for establishing firm friendships between Police Officers from several countries; addresses are forever being exchanged in the spacious bar, restaurant and TV lounge areas, and invitations to spend holidays with colleagues in all parts of the world proliferate.

In recent years, several Watford Officers and their families have been the guests of their pen-pals in Mainz, and vice-versa. Many of us can now find our way around Mainz's massive 10 storey Headquarters complex, complete with two firearms ranges, heli-pad, TV studio (linked into the national network for emergency broadcasts), underground nuclear shelter and extensive vehicle, radio and uniform workshops, better than we can around our own HQ. To a visitor from Watford, nowhere is 'out of bounds', and the President (Chief Constable) insists that you share a glass of wine with him in his palacial office before leaving; indeed, if you time your arrival correctly, you will be invited to have lunch as well. Some of us, have become quite expert on the Heckler and Koch machine gun, thanks to several visits to the firearms range under the tutelage of 'Willi'; indeed, he often comments that he sees some Watford officers more frequently than some of his own!

Mainz, is a wondrous city; once the only Holy See outside of Rome, it is rich in 2,000 years of history, combining old and new, commerce and leisure, tradition and innovation. Its inhabitants, work hard and play hard. The city is always pulsing with life, it is a University town, the sounds of the students singing in the taverns until late at night renews the youth in the oldest of us. The Rhine, flows slowly and gracefully by, adding colour and variety to a a city of spires and towers; barges transporting their cargoes between Switzerland and the North Sea fight quietly against the current, making slow headway in comparison to the pleasure steamers which thrash along, stopping at each little village between Mainz and Cologne. The call of the Lorelei, the maiden who sat high on a cliff in the middle of the Rhine and lured passing sailors to an untimely end is as loud today as ever it was. Whatever troubles and worries you may have melt slowly away as you drift down that mighty river, entranced by castles perched precariously above almost vertical vineyards and villages which seem to consist of lots of different pastel coloured Lego bricks, placed end to end along the river's shore. There is no rush and stress, no hurly burly here, just ordered peace and always with a foreign colleague, time for coffee and cakes!

The Victim Support Scheme

By Sue Tomson

The idea of offering help to the victims of crime was born in Bristol, and the research findings of that group, encouraged other areas to set up schemes. Bristol's findings, were that the emotional impact of the experience (of crime) was far more important than the physical pain or financial loss suffered. It also suggested, that even seemingly trivial offences could lead to major trauma. The main problems, facing the victims of crime initially seemed to be:

1. The shock and trauma of having a crime committed against them.

2. That there seemed to be a parallel between the experiences and reactions of victims of crime to those who were the victims of disasters, and that crisis intervention seemed to be relevant to their needs.

3. The official system, almost completely ignored the victim.

4. Relatives and friends felt the victim to be 'contaminated' by the criminal act.

5. No statutory or voluntary body was interested in them, except for the Criminal Injuries Compensation Board.

It was difficult to know where to start! In 1991, it is quite unusual to meet people who know nothing about Victim Support - there are over 400 schemes, 6,000 trained volunteers in the country who last year offered help to half a million people, a National Office, Royal Patronage and plenty of media coverage. However, in 1976 it was different. The Police felt Social Services should be supporting victims, they were concerned about confidentiality and certainly didn't want Police Officers to be on Management Committees. There was a suspicion that they were "do gooders". At this time, the Magistracy did not wish to be involved (giving support to victims would 'threaten the impartiality of the bench'), and it wasn't until 1983 that the Probation Service actively encouraged officers to become involved in order to promote community involvement in criminal justice problems.

In December 1975, the then Chief Constable of Hertfordshire Mr Ray Buxton once said "The impression I get is that a Victims Support Scheme is better suited to the more densely populated areas, but it may be that the idea could be tailored to the Hertfordshire scene".

Thanks to his encouragement, and the support of the local police the First Victim Support Scheme in Hertfordshire started in the the Three Rivers area in October 1977.

IN THE FIGHT AGAINST CRIME
WHO HAS TIME FOR THE VICTIMS?..

VICTIMS SUPPORT SCHEMES HELP VICTIMS OF CRIME

National Association of Victims Support Schemes

The scheme, was started by myself, a local Probation Officer and a Watford Magistrate. Initially, there were three major problems, finance, recruiting and selecting of volunteers and finally their training. Thanks to the local Magistrates Bench, Rotary and Round Table and some local churches, money began to trickle in.

It was our determination to have enough money in hand for at least one year i.e. £1,000, before launching the scheme. The original scheme in Bristol, had had to close down for a period because of lack of funds. Bristol's experience was of great value to us and to the other fourteen groups trying to get started in other parts of the country. Rereading the training programme shows how our early priorities have remained the same, namely the importance of listening, relating to the victim, a thorough knowledge of the local area and its varying resources (Citizens Advice Bureaux, Housing Department and other local agencies), and the importance of a good relationship with the Police coupled with a working knowledge of Police procedure.

The support and willingness to cooperate that was given by the officers of "C" Division, cannot be praised too highly. Despite early misgivings, every effort was made to adjust to new demands and I am sure that "C" Division's example meant that other Division's followed suit with less hassle. In this, Watford was the trail blazer for the County. Thanks to all those who were and are still involved.

What were the reactions of the victims? The overwhelming one was that of a gratitude that 'someone cared', and cared enough to visit the victim in their home. The major crimes, were burglary and theft, with other crimes like assaults and sexual offences being later additions. At that time, it was out of the question that Victim Support would consider giving help to the victims of rape, or families of murder victims, though now, as it is well known, volunteers who have undergone a special training for this work, are greatly welcomed and appreciated by these victims.

Volunteers, are the best advertisement for a scheme, and in the South West Herts Victim Support Scheme (as the scheme became known in 1985) which covers the whole of "C" Division and parts of the Metropolitan Police Area adjacent to "C" Division this has indeed been true. The regular meetings of the volunteers offers an opportunity for further training with the profesional input of the trainers and the sharing of their experiences thus enables a better standard of service to the victims of crime. In this, the support of the Hertfordshire Probation Service has always been welcomed and appreciated. Confidentiality was recognised, but so was the support and supervision of the volunteer and our codes of confidentiality allow information to be shared within the scheme.

What of the victims? One of the earliest victims, was a lonely old man, who was the victim of a burglary artifice (bogus callers to his house). He was tied up, left for dead while the thieves stole his entire savings from under his mattress. The help he received, had a ripple effect - his far flung family and his neighbour recognised victim support and he has since featured on a documentary on victims! This case, demonstrated the importance of victim support in finding out the needs of the victim and how best they might be met. In this particular case, the Scheme obtained an allowance for the neighbour, and arranged with the Social Services about other benefits that could be applied for and then at an appropriate moment withdrew.

Now that the demands are greater, with more categories of crime being referred, it is no longer possible for every victim of personal crime to be visited, but the 'outreach' aspect of Victim Support has been recognised, admired and even adopted by other countries (Israel, France and New Zealand for example). The early days were full of excitement, cooperation, and minor frustrations that haunt every new voluntary organisation. The National Association was formed in 1979, new schemes were springing up and the need for a more formal structure was recognised. With the advent of Home Office funding in 1987, coordinators in busy schemes were able to be paid, though throughout the organisation, fund raising is still a vital part of the work. The South West Herts Scheme. were able to employ two part time coordinators from 1989.

In 1987, the nine schemes in the County decided to form a Federation. Since 1988, again with the active cooperation of the Hertfordshire Constabulary who provided the facilities, I have been employed as part time County coordinator and have had the excitement and privilege of training new volunteers, keeping in close touch with the local coordinators and liaising through the federation meetings with the members of the various Management Committees.

On the 22nd February 1990, the Victim's Charter was published. The implications for all those involved in Criminal Justice are considerable and the Federation is actively encouraging inter-agency communication so that the victims of crime in Hertfordshire will be better served in the future.

Victims of Crime, are no longer the forgotten people of the Criminal Justice System, or as C.H. Rolph puts it: "Victim Support is here to stay, a vigorous new limb of a criminal justice system that badly needed it." The implications of servicing it though are immense and there will continue to be problems both financial and in terms of the correct personnel.

The continued support to the schemes of the Hertfordshire Constabulary is vitally important, and I am confident that this will continue.

ISBN 0 9517477 0 3

British Library Cataloguing in Publication Data.
A catalogue record of this book is available from the British Library.

CHAPTER THREE

Celtic Civilization

WHO were the bearers of a system of beliefs so extraordinarily tenacious?

The Spanish Franciscans who went to the newly conquered lands of Central and South America in the 15th Century expected to find the natives, members of a culture which practised human sacrifice on what can only be called a lavish scale, grim and blood-thirsty barbarians. Instead they found a people who were intelligent, good-humoured, courteous, and hospitable. At a distance, the Celts, too, would have been seen as the pathetic, half-brute creatures of heathen lands.

The similarities between the civilizations discovered and wantonly destroyed by the Conquistadores and that earlier one ravaged by the Romans are numerous and remarkable, and we know that, despite Tacitus' propagandist zeal in making the Celts and especially the Druids appear dark, sinister and sanguinary, their actual character was quite different. Cicero's encounter with Diviciacus makes this much plain.

Nor, by contrast were they the fey inhabitants of that ethereal half-world bequeathed to us by the romantics from Tennyson to Yeats. The real truth about the Celtic peoples is that they were a race of great originality, of artistic creativity and aggressive dynamism. They were, for example, among Europe's first iron users. Their artistic skill has led to their being called the most original creators north of the Alps. Their questing expansionism established them as masters of a vast province not only in Europe, but which stretched down into Asia Minor. The Greeks categorized them, with the Scythians and the Iberians, as one of the three great barbarian nations and with the rest of the ancient world viewed them with that terror later to be inspired by "the Mongol hordes".

In 390 BC the Romans, rather imprudently allowing themselves to become embroiled in a war between the Celts and Etruscans, found themselves the objective of a punitive expedition. Their attackers, advancing down the Italic peninsula, reached and sacked the Eternal City, putting to the sword those few patricians too proud to flee. Only a small enclave of refugees succeeded in holding out on a besieged Capitoline Hill, an occasion memorable for the famous incident in which the cries of the sacred geese gave warning of impending assault, saving the Temple of Jupiter from desecration. Nonetheless, as the price of their withdrawal, the besiegers demanded and received an extortionate ransom, which led to another famous incident: when the Romans complained that false scales were being used to weigh out the bullion, the Celtic commander threw his sword into the scale pan, thus increasing the weight, with the cry, *Vae victis*! — Woe to the vanquished!

A hundred and ten years after their attack on Rome another Celtic expeditionary force attempted to march on Delphi, where the Oracle itself was saved only by a sudden and unexpected onset of winter snow, thus vindicating its own prediction that it would be "saved by the white virgins". With this reversal in their fortunes, the Celtic commanders were forced to kill off their own wounded to secure a rapid escape.

In 225 BC, Rome was once more threatened and it took three armies to stay the onslaught at the Battle of Telamon, though not before one had been annihilated.

Where had it come from, this terrifying race which could defy even Rome?

About the middle of the Second Millennium BC, the tribes of pastoral and hunting nomads — the so-called Indo-Europeans — who inhabited an area round the Caspian Sea in south Russia began to spread eastwards and westwards. The westward thrust took them across the European Plain, down through the Balkans, into Greece and Italy and over the Mediterranean into Asia Minor, as well as northward into Scandinavia whose climate was at that time so temperate that wine-grapes were grown in what is now Norway. In all the places of their settlement, in admixture with the far more numerous existing populations, the Indo-Europeans provided the racial and linguistic matrix for most of the nations of Europe — including the Greeks and Romans.

But it was not until the 10th Century BC that a people recognizably Celtic began to emerge in an area roughly centring on what is now Bohemia. In a period between the 8th and 6th Centuries BC, they began fresh migrations which carried them into northern Italy, Spain, parts of Scandinavia, as well as France and Belgium, and later into the British Isles.

Their various migrations and their sojourn in their Bohemian homeland, "the cockpit of Europe", had brought them into contact with many other cultures, of which the Scythian particularly exerted a lasting influence upon them. The Greek, Polybius, who wrote a contemporary account of the Battle of Telamon, describes in detail the enemy tactics: the terrifying noise of their trumpets and war-chants and their use of two-wheeled and four-wheeled chariots, the manufacture and employment of which they must have learnt from the Scythians, one of the first races to domesticate the horse.

Also Scythian were their moustaches so thick it was said they served as strainers when they drank, and their odd custom of treating their hair with lime wash, which not only bleached it, but made it stand back from their heads like the mane of a horse — a fashion illustrated on some Celtic coinage.

Even in their manner of dress they imitated the Scythians: the breeches, obviously intended for horse-riding, but quite alien to the Mediterranean world of Polybius; their linen tunics reaching to the knees, and the cloaks they wore over them. These last, of purple, crimson or green dyed woven wool, or of tartan design, can only have been the predecessors of the plaids worn in Scotland and Ireland and the Welsh shawls.

With costume went another aspect of their appearance which enhanced an appearance already dauntingly weird to foreign eyes. They were, we are told, exceptionally tall. In part, this may have been by comparison with the slighter southern build, but one can scarcely ignore the evidence of their size from elsewhere. Giants figure repeatedly as the villains of Norse myth. Thor was said so to have hated them he killed them with his hammer on sight. The Celtic incursions into Scandinavia must have brought them into collision with existing inhabitants of the region. The stories of ensuing battles against tall enemies, passed orally from generation to generation, would gradually have become assimilated into legendary struggles between Norse heroes and giants.

A further association between Celts and giants is to be found in Diodorus of Sicily, who flourished about 40 BC. He attributed the foundation of Celtiberia, the Celtic region of Spain, now Galicia, to the mating of Hercules — whom Pythagoras characterizes as a giant — with a local princess.

As the physical appearance of the Celts so impressed observers by its strangeness, their environment, too, must have seemed quite unlike the bustling, teeming cities of Mediterranean and Aegean seaboards. In Gaul, where cities were found at all, they were usually sited near Greek or Roman settlements, and demonstrative, therefore, of a desire to emulate.

Overall the Celtic landscape was one largely of forest, dotted with isolated farmsteads, often enclosed behind high walls of stone or wood, like miniature fortresses, much like the farms in the Channel Islands today. The largest centres of population in Gaul, Britain or Ireland would have seemed scarcely more than villages to outsiders. In *The Conquest of Gaul*, Caesar describes the groups of hilltop dwellings, surrounded by their defensive palisades, which he calls *oppida*, and he mentions the difficulties facing an attacker trying to find means of scaling the formidable structure of steep walls and ramparts. Remains found by archaeologists, such as those at Mont Beurray in Burgundy, bear him out.

Behind this shield, the dry-stone houses, often circular in shape and with deep-pitched thatched roofs, stood round an open, central area, as has been found at Heuneberg in Austria. In the story of the naming of Cu Chulainn in the Irish *Cattle Raid of Cooley*, King Conchobhar of Ulster first encounters the boy demonstrating his prowess at a game like football "on the green" and one can suppose that, like those of English villages, such areas functioned not only as a playground, but also as places of assembly.

In the actual buildings, though mortar was not employed, for those points such as door lintels where movement had to be obviated, joints were constructed by a system of wooden pegs fitting into matching holes in the abutting stones. The Etruscans used a similar technique and Kendrick believes it to have been copied from them.

The internal decoration would obviously vary with the wealth of the owner. But a description, also in *The Cattle Raid*, tells us that Conchobhar's house had 150 inner rooms, panelled in red yew. The king's own room in the centre, was guarded "by screens of copper, with bars of silver and gold birds on the screens, and precious jewels in the birds' heads for eyes". The passage also describes some of the other rooms of Conchobhar's palace, including the armoury which "twinkled with the gold of sword-hilts and the gold and silver glimmering on the necks and coils of grey javelins, on shield-plates and shield-rims, and in the sets of goblets, cups and drinking horns". The length of the description and its detail is indicative of the interest in home decoration shown by the Celts.

Wherever they settled, the Celts brought the benefit of improved agriculture and animal husbandry. Thanks to their use of the iron plough they were able vastly to increase the productivity of the land, while as cattle- and particularly as horse-breeders, they pioneered many advances. A measure of this is the fact that almost all the words in Latin connected with horses and horse-management are Celtic loan-words.

For the cultivation of cereals, the plains of Gaul were obviously the more ideally suited, so that although some were grown in Britain and Ireland, these islands were principally given over to livestock rearing.

A thriving trade in farm-products was complemented by other exports, such as of metals, in the forms both of ingot and finished products, and of salt, for which there was a high demand in the ancient world. This prosperity enabled them to import a wide range of goods, among them many luxuries, especially wines from the Mediterranean vineyards. For these they had developed so inordinate a fondness that it inspired derisive comment by the classical writers, besides yielding unsurpassed opportunities to unscrupulous vintners, by whom it was said that the Celts would offer a slave for a jug of wine, a servant for a single swallow.

It also allowed them to indulge their taste for personal adornment by importing precious metals and gems. Their woollen cloaks were secured by a pin or brooch, often intricately wrought from gold or silver (though for the poor, we are told, a thorn had to suffice). Both sexes, who in general dressed similarly, wore rings, armlets and bracelets and had ornate buckles to their belts often, like Conchobhar's birds, studded with jewels. Articles of this kind have been found among grave goods, together with wrought and inlaid weapons. Indeed, a preoccupation with ornamentation and appearance was so prominent a feature of the Celtic character that it finds reflection in legend. In one of the early Irish stories, for example, Loegh, charioteer to the hero, Cu Chulainn, details the dress of another, approaching charioteer: " ... A crimson cloak round him with a golden brooch in it, and a hooded tunic with red embroidery on him. A convex shield with a rim of ornamented white bronze on it ...". In another story, that of Etain, the appearance of one of the characters is described in even more detail. We are told that an approaching horseman has a "long, flowing green cloak behind him, a shirt embroidered with red gold and a huge brooch of gold at his throat reaching to either shoulder".

In the production of these and other items they were by no means dependent on foreign craftsmen. They had themselves developed techniques for enamelling and their own artists possessed a brilliant creative originality. It was the discovery made at La Tène, a shallow area in Lake Neuchâtel in Switzerland, in 1858, which first made archaeologists aware that the Celts were by no means the artless barbarians as had once been supposed. The hoard included swords, spears, fibulae and tools, all testifying to enormous skill and confidence in the handling of metals. Other, though less dramatic, discoveries have come from river beds, lake bottoms, wells and shafts all over the Celtic world and there is no doubt much more to be found. Work similar to that discovered at La Tène was probably still being produced in Ireland as late as the 3rd and 4th Centuries AD. The designs, those patterns of intertwining tendrils which have come to be regarded as typical, sprang directly from the forms of nature, as observers of which the Celts have never been surpassed. Even their most modest work reflects not just the contours but the very essence of the living world, its shapes, motion and rhythms.

The talent of their craftsmen was matched in other spheres. Though literate, the Celts used writing principally for account keeping or for inscriptions such as on coins. The reason for this was that their concepts of history, law and practical knowledge were all believed to be of sacred origin. Their exposure to written form might accordingly lead to devaluation and sacrilege.

The practical effect was, however, that there was no written literature, though there was a brilliant and vigorous oral one. The trustees of this were the bards, who stood close to the nobility in the social hierarchy, "a nobility of art", in Markale's words, enjoying special privileges. The epics and eulogies which formed the bardic repertory were certainly designed to be sung to their own accompaniment and the harp has become an instrument closely associated with the Celts.

There are, as we shall see, good reasons for associating the Druids with this thriving creative life.

The manifest artistry of the Celts drew little response from their classical observers. Like Victorian travellers in Africa who saw in, say, a Benin bronze just the distortions of a pathetic primitivism, they could only contrast the fighting, feasting and fornicating barbarians of the Celtic lands with the home life of their own dear Royal Family where, admittedly, guests at banquets did not reject the charms of the ladies — for all that they are shown to us as Amazons — in favour of open sexual frolics on animal skins with their boy friends.

Blinded by xenophobia, the classical writers failed also to perceive that though different from their own world, Celtic society still displayed a cultural homogeneity which proclaimed it to be an organic entity, governed by customs, institutions and laws no less comprehensive than theirs.

Good manners, courtesy and particularly hospitality marked Celtic social life and extended to strangers whose primary needs of food, drink and shelter had to be satisfied before any inquiry was made about their presence or intentions, and, like so much else, this has survived down to the present day in the renowned hospitality of the Celtic peoples. Even those great feasts to which they were so addicted were far from being orgies of animal gluttony. Guests sat on hay or skins before a low table, their position being governed by an etiquette of precedence in which the visitor was always accorded a high place. Food served included roast or boiled meats, beef, mutton and especially pork, the "champion's portion" being allegedly a whole roast boar. The meat was accompanied by bread and there would be locally brewed beer and mead, as well as imported wine.

On such occasions they undoubtedly drank to excess, yet this over-indulgence must have been the exception for, because no doubt in a warrior society a fat man made a poor fighter, obesity was a punishable offence.

Among the peculiarly Celtic customs mentioned by Caesar and confirmed elsewhere is that of fosterage which continued down into Christian times. (King Arthur was fostered and we are told that Kai was his foster-brother.) Under the system as practised, the responsibility for the upbringing and education of a child was taken over by others and he did not return to the bosom of his own family until puberty.

Outside the purely traditional and customary, there was a strict legal code, largely as we shall see administered by the Druids, and transmitted orally. This, too, has survived in some measure. A class of itinerant jurists, the *brehons*, existed in Ireland down to Elizabethan times when, with an associated body of poets, it was among the first victims of the terror imposed by the Queen's Commissioners. In the Isle of Man, the unwritten "Breast Law", derived from the decisions of successive Deemsters, or local justices, is regarded as no less binding than the written law, which did not come into existence until 1423. In the Channel Islands those numerous precedents, so colourfully alluded to as "lost in the mists of time", must have been unwritten.

Among other things, Celtic law guaranteed the place of women, who could own property, even if married; could choose their own husbands; could divorce and were entitled to substantial damages at law if deserted or molested. Women played an important part in political life; could take their place in the battle line and could even ascend to the chieftaincy. In general, the role they play in Celtic life reminds one of that found in some Asiatic societies, particularly in Thailand and Tibet, where men and women share even manual labour and these surprising coincidences are ones which we shall find frequently recurring.

The survival of matrilineal descent in both Wales and Ireland whereby a man is described not as his father's, but as his mother's son, so that, for example, King Conchobhar is called 'Conchobhar mac Nessa', after his mother, no doubt arose originally from the ignorance of the male role in conception and from the loose nature of sexual ties.

Though Caesar was certainly exaggerating in his description of the depressed condition of the plebians, Celtic society was a slave-owning and aristocratic one, even though its leaders may have been men of shrewdness, capability and, above all, of taste.

The social base was the clan and the tribe, itself a grouping of several clans under a chieftain or king called a *rig*. The Celtic clan, called a *fine*, was rather different from those of Scotland and Ireland as they were later known. The foundation of the clan was a common ancestor, hence the prefix "Mac-", "son of . . .". This made possible a potentially infinite extension as sons married, begat and their sons did similarly. The *fine*, instead, was restricted to four generations, from father to great-grandson. Thereafter, there was a splitting with a compulsory sharing of commonly held property.

The head of the *fine* had his tribal counterpart — the *rig*. To an extent hereditary, in that he was always chosen from a single royal *fine*, there was no automatic succession from father to son. When a chieftain died, the choice of successor was a matter for deliberation by a tribal assembly at which all the *fine*s were represented, but in which — as we shall see — the Druids played the crucial role.

The *rig* or chieftain's domain was not defined territorially, but by its people, the *tuatha*, a Celtic word from which the name of the god, Toutatis or Teutatis (?God of the People) as well as the word Teutonic may be derived. The consolidation of the *fine*s which the *tuatha* represented was, no doubt, the first tentative step in the evolution towards nationhood, but as has happened elsewhere, the jealous rivalries which developed between tribes were such as successfully to prevent political unification. The Celts of Ireland, Britain and Gaul were, therefore, never anything but a loose confederation of tribes gathered within a given land area.

Sometimes, however, a tribe might itself split and part of it migrate, so that tribal names occur twice, often at places distant from one another on maps of the Celtic world. This would perhaps indicate that the division was the result of internal quarrels, possibly over succession, but it could also have occurred because a particular region was becoming over-populated in relation to its land-resources. The Atrebates, who had settled in an area of France round Arras which takes its name from them, are to be found, as well, in a region roughly corresponding to Berkshire and parts of Wiltshire in Britain. The Parisii, who gave their name to Paris, also established themselves in the East Riding of Yorkshire.

Choice of chieftain was by no means the only matter referred to the tribal assemblies all of which, as we know from Strabo, were governed by strict rules of discussion. Some would have taken place on the central green in the townships, but the more important ones, such as those held during the religious festivals, took place near the royal burial place. In most tribal societies, the link between its living and its dead is of supreme importance and in this the Celtic was no exception. Although it is of Norse origin, one is reminded of the annual meeting at Tynwald on the Isle of Man, held under the presidency of the Lieutenant-Governor as representative of the British monarch. It is significant that Tynwald Hill is itself actually a tumulus or burial mound.

Given the form of their society, it is not difficult to understand the need for such communal decision-making. Despite its essentially hierarchic nature, Celtic society did not possess the pyramidal structure of inter-connected allegiances to be found in feudal ones, where each class stood in utter dependence upon the next one above it. Here the social bond was the custom of *celsine* or cliency. The essence of this was that a *fine* or even an individual placed himself under another's protection, rendering in return agreed payments in kind, as well as armed service if it were required of him. No sacrifice of rights or liberties was involved and the *cele* or client could freely withdraw from the arrangement.

In origin *celsine* must have dated back to the times when land-winning expeditions were being mounted, but no doubt they would also have been entered into after natural disasters such as the failure of the harvest had afflicted a particular tribe or when, for example, inter-clan or inter-tribal feuds broke out. The last were probably common, for lacking the public administration of law through a permanent system of courts, the settlement of many grievances would have been an individual or clan matter, and we know that feuding persisted late into Scottish history. Faced with such external threats, the weaker party might well feel it prudent to place itself under the wing of a more powerful one.

In actual practice, *celsine* would probably have become a mutually dependent arrangement, for while the *cele* needed the protection of the stronger unit, his patron would measure his power as well his prestige and actual wealth by the number of his *cele*s. It is also significant that land tenure was by *fine* and not by individual so that each family with its holding represented a lesser domain within the larger one of the *tuatha*. (It is of course the reason why clan areas are to be found in Scotland and Ireland.) Because of this, the extent of tribal territory would also be decided by the number of *cele*s constituting it, each of whom was basically an independent unit[1].

[1] In this connexion, the Channel Islands afford an interesting parallel. The "parishes" into which Jersey and Guernsey are divided must once have corresponded with clan areas. In earlier times,

As a grouping of at least theoretically free entities, mutual agreement in all decisions would obviously be essential and there are good reasons for thinking that this was far from being a pure formality. Everyone in Celtic society was not only conscious of, but exercised his rights and freedoms as Strabo among others tells us. Indeed, it was as a result of this that the Celtic regions proved so resistant to feudalism and in many instances avoided it altogether.

Markale suggests that the tribal assembly was the supreme authority in Celtic society, implying that when they took place the chieftain's role was little more than that of chairman, which accords with our knowledge, for it is obvious that he did not enjoy the unquestioned dominance to be found elsewhere. This, of course, is most noteworthy in religious matters, for where, in other cultures, the chieftain or king was principal mediator with the gods on his people's behalf, in the case of the Celts this was the prerogative and perhaps the monopoly of the Druids.

In war, the chief delegated his powers of leadership to an elected war-chief. The leaders of expeditions against Rome and Delphi are nowhere mentioned as chieftains. In the cycle of Irish stories, the warrior-hero is Cu Chulainn, not the king, Conchobhar. In the Arthurian legends the king is repeatedly found, less as commander in battle (though in the first historical references Arthur is mentioned as a *dux bellorum* or war-leader), than as rewarder of heroes, and arbitrator in disputes.

There was good enough reason for this. In the case of both the march on Rome and that on Delphi a century later we have the same name given as that of the Celtic commander — Brennos or Brennius. The explanation once offered was that two men of the same name were involved, the later perhaps the descendant of the earlier. The truth is that Brennos is the name of a Celtic god, otherwise Brân or Brân Vendigeit — Brân the Blessed. What we have then is a military expedition under, as it were, divine patronage, in other words "a holy war". This raised it above the purely tribal conflicts, attracting to its banner warriors from the entire Celtic world. References to continental expeditions occur in both Irish myth and in the much later Geoffrey of Monmouth, who has two brothers Belinus (obviously Belenos) and Brennius attacking Rome. If command had been entrusted to a tribal chief there would have been the risk of intertribal rivalries breaking out during the actual campaign, as they sometimes did, anyway.

There was, however, a second link uniting *fine* and *tuatha*. This was the

major decisions were taken through *l'ouie de la paroisse* — a parish meeting. This continues today through what are called the Parish Assemblies, which all rate-paying householders are entitled to attend.

religious one. Whether *celsine* contracts actually incorporated a clause whereby the client invoked the gods of his patron we have no way of knowing. We can conclude, all the same, that even if the clan deities were not abandoned when it became a client the tribal ones, in origin probably those of the "royal" *fine*, were also venerated. We have evidence, for example, of the separate communities within a tribe being expected to provide victims for sacrifice. As we saw many tribes took their names from gods like the powerful Brigantes, who spread over much of Northern England.

By general consensus among the classical writers, the Celts were an extremely superstitious people. Since superstition was not a thing either Greek or Roman was totally free from, Celtic conduct, in their ordinary affairs, must have been such as to display a more than normal concern with the supernatural. Their divination and human sacrifice we know shocked and fascinated outside observers, but there were other surprising Celtic practices. Polybius, at the Battle of Telamon, was struck by the appearance in combat of naked *gestatae* or spear-throwers, and a practice so contrary to the instinct of self-preservation seems likely to have had a religious basis. Another custom was the wearing of the torc or neck-band of twisted metal, apparently common to all sectors of Celtic society, with only the costliness of the metal involved distinguishing the classes. Since torcs are presented on even the most rudimentary images of their gods, this too must have had a religious significance.

Strabo refers to Gaulish warriors returning from the fray, carrying hung from their saddles, the severed heads of those who had fallen at their hands. These grisly trophies were also to be found decorating the exteriors of houses and the same author mentions instances of heads being embalmed in cedar oil and shown off to guests.

For this custom there is a wealth of supportive archaeological and other evidence. Niches cut into door lintels must have been for the display of heads, and skulls with nails driven through them have been found. In surviving myth the decapitation of enemies is a recurrent motif, down to the Arthurian legends and beyond. In the 14th Century story of *Gawain and the Green Knight*, the hero is challenged to decapitate the Green Knight. If he succeeds, as Gawain does, he must meet his rival who obviously survives the blow in single combat a year later. The knight is plainly, if not a god, at least an Other World being and the entire story bears marked similarities with earlier pagan ones.

If religion and the worship of particular gods assisted the process of cementing the *fine* to the *tuatha*, it can also be shown that they actually impeded the progression from a tribal to a national identity. Nationhood would have involved the acceptance of a state pantheon. This would have meant that either new gods would have to come into being or that existing ones would have to be elevated to this new, greater role. It would also have meant the degradation of other deities.

The unwillingness of the Celtic tribes to cooperate in such a process is indicated by the very large number of deities which iconographers have identified, something approaching 400, of which the majority must have been local or exclusively tribal. But there were, besides, those gods associated with features of the landscape, especially rivers or other water sources. The demotion of these, or their supersession by others would, of course, have been to risk the anger of divine forces which as territorial deities were unhealthily close at hand for the tribes involved.

CHAPTER FOUR

Witnesses and Their Testimony

CELTIC religion is, as Caesar declares, the province of the Druids. Diogenes Laertius (AD 200-250) makes clear that Druidism was regarded as an ancient institution in the times of Aristotle, the 4th Century BC. This gains at least partial support from other information: one of the earliest references to the Celts occurs about the 5th Century BC. It records a meeting between Alexander the Great and a Celt, possibly a Druid. Certainly the brief interview contained one phrase with an unmistakably Druidic ring: Alexander asked his visitor what it was his people most feared? He was told, nothing "so long as the sky does not fall or the sea burst its limits".

Those words re-echo down the centuries. They occur twice in *The Cattle Raid of Cooley*. Once when things are going amiss, Sualdam seeks to put new heart into the Ulstermen: "Are the heavens rent?" he asks; "Is the sea bursting its bounds? Is the end of the world upon us?" Later, the warriors of Conchobhar assure him: "We will hold out until the earth gives under us, or until the heavens fall on us and make us give way."

In the 5th Century AD we find it being employed in only slightly altered form by the bards Taliesin and Myrddin. Thus, Myrddin: "Since the Battle of Arderydd, nothing can touch me — even if the sky falls and the sea overflows."

Yet, for all the antiquity of Druidism, for all the contacts between the Celts and other nations, for all the fascination they evoked, nowhere do we find a systematic account of their religion, and this stands in sharp contrast with the body of often explicit detail about Celtic life in general. The Druids, who took such pains to invest themselves and their teachings with mystery and secrecy, may perhaps have succeeded better than they knew: if ever they stood guardians of the founts of an Ancient Wisdom they certainly ensured its treasures were not passed on.

Obviously their reluctance to commit their teachings to writing is in a large measure to blame for this, forcing us to rely on enigmatic hints and on fragmentary and second-hand information as it is offered to us by the small band of alien observers of Celtic life.

Of these, two have contributed most to delineating the popular conception of the Druids.

In countless illustrations adorning books down the ages, their full-bearded figures are portrayed standing among the oaks of some forest glade, knife poised over human victim; or hacking mistletoe from amid the tree's branches with their golden sickles. These images and the white robes which have become the universal insignia of those "Druidic" brotherhoods, descending from the group round Iolo Morganwg's pebble *gorsedd*, owe their sanction to a single reference in the Elder Pliny's *Natural History*. This and a famous passage on sacrifice in Caesar's *The Conquest of Gaul* are the two best known accounts of Druidism in action.

Pliny we know to have been a keen observer — he was killed in AD 79 when he approached too close to Vesuvius to study its eruption. His *Natural History* was dedicated to Titus, later emperor, and dated two years before its author's death. Since it is made up of some thirty-seven books, production must have been spread over many years, but in AD 37, with Gaul firmly under Roman control, Tiberius issued his edict prohibiting the practices of Druidism. This would have made first-hand study of it extremely difficult so that his information probably came from other, earlier sources.

The book is actually a discursive account of the state of what we should now call "scientific knowledge" and, for the modern reader, it is its very digressions which are among its greatest attractions. They take the form of illustrative anecdotes, hence the description of mistletoe in what is actually a general account of the medicinal properties of herbs. It was, he tells us, held in the highest awe by the Gaulish Druids especially when found growing on an oak-tree, a comparatively rare occurrence. What gave it this special character was that oak itself was so venerated that groves of it were chosen as the centres of Druidic worship. In consequence, anything which grew on it was regarded as divinely sent, as further proof that the tree was "chosen by the god himself", though he neglects to state which god.

Besides the famous description of the mistletoe gathering, Pliny also tells us of two other herbs held in high esteem by the Druids, as well as how they were ritually gathered, and of a magic egg called *anguinem* — supposedly made from the secretion of snakes — said to "ensure success in lawsuits and a favourable reception with princes".

What he gives us, then, are some fascinating snapshots of specific activities, but it would take a good many such before we should have anything like "A Day in the Life of a Druid". Indeed, as we shall see, Pliny may actually have been responsible for distorting our image, because his information about what are special events has been interpreted by others as having general validity.

Set beside Pliny's close-ups, Caesar's viewpoint is panoramic and that he was contemporary with the matter he was describing gives it added attraction. As commander-in-chief of the Roman forces he travelled in Gaul and hence had unrivalled opportunities for obtaining information. Thus he is able to tell us about the structure of Celtic society; of the central role of the Druids in religious life; of the variety of their functions; of the importance of sacrifice; of their recruitment, training and organization; and he provides us with a list of the most important gods worshipped by the Gauls, though giving them under their Roman equivalents.

He has to be treated with scepticism, none the less. Firstly, he was pre-eminently an interested party. He was in Gaul as an invader and one of his intentions in writing *The Conquest* must certainly have been to justify himself in the eyes of the senate and people of Rome. Hence, he could be expected to paint the Gaulish Druids as superstitious primitives, given to such deplorable practices as human sacrifice. It was from this that he came to deliver them and bring the fruits of Rome's matchless civilization. It is, as we know, the oldest of imperialism's excuses, employed alike by the British in India and the French in North Africa.

Secondly, the observations made by enemies of one another, especially at the time of actual hostilities, are notoriously unreliable and coloured by the prejudices of the moment. Having come to Gaul with, among other objects, that of extirpating Druidism, it was hardly to be expected that Caesar would have been invited to be guest of honour at the public performance of its rituals.

Lastly, the two initial chapters of *The Conquest* were the kind of mandatory preface all works of this kind were expected to contain so that one cannot be sure whether its author was recording the result of personal research or merely providing his readers with what they expected of him — a description of the people and places in the narrative — without too meticulous consideration of the credentials of his information.

The classical writers actually possessed a source-book on the subject, unfortunately lost to us. This is the fifty-two volume *Histories* of the Syrian Greek, Posidonius, written at the end of the 2nd Century BC. Now Posidonius cannot himself be taken for a totally impartial witness. He was a Stoic philosopher, that is to say a member of that school which believed that truth was available only to those who lived the simple life, free from the enervating luxury and the influence of extraneous ideas which corrupted their own over-civilized society. In writing about the Druids he was simply using them to prove this thesis.

This bias duly discounted, however, Posidonius was an eminent scholar, employing methods of research which could be said to have pioneered those in use by historians today. There had been a Greek colony on the toe of Gaul, at Massilia, now Marseilles, since about the 7th Century BC. Not only did Gauls and Massiliots have long-standing trade relations, but the Greeks had been so emulated by their neighbours that one writer was moved to describe the nearest Gauls as more Greek than the Greeks. By conducting his inquiries here, as well as by travelling extensively through Gaul itself, Posidonius put together what must surely have been the most balanced and complete account of Celtic life, including its religion, ever produced.

Later writers borrowed from him freely, and it is thanks to this we know of the original work at all. Among them was Strabo (63 BC — AD 21), another Stoic, who had known Posidonius personally; a second was Diodorus of Sicily (circa 40 BC). In his descriptions, Strabo is careful to acknowledge his source. Diodorus, while he fails to do this, often reproduces him almost word for word. It is possible, therefore, to trace the influence of the earlier writer on both.

But what is germane to us is that Caesar has also used Posidonius. For example, the description of the man-shaped wicker colossi in which sacrificial victims were burnt is Strabo verbatim. In other passages, however, since we do not have the original work, it is impossible always to know where Caesar was plagiarizing, where using information of his own. Hence, three of his most important statements stand uncorroborated by other writers and are open to doubt and debate. The first of these is the description of the annual assembly organized by the Druids in the territory of the Carnutes, regarded as the centre of Gaul; the second is his declaration that the Gaulish Druids were subject to a single overriding authority, a kind of "Archdruid", as he has been called; and the third, the statement that the doctrines of Druidism originated in Britain. In assessing these it is necessary to consider other, circumstantial evidence.

With Strabo and Diodorus, Caesar is one of the tiny group of writers whose work is extant and who were alive at the time the Druids were openly practising. There are two others, one of whom is Cicero, contemporary and one-time friend of Caesar's. He claimed actually to have met a Druid in the shape of Divicacus, chief of the Aedui, who sought Rome's assistance against the Helvetii, thus precipitating the Gallic war. Some scholars argue that Cicero was mistaken and that Diviciacus was not a Druid. Error seems unlikely, however, unless the visitor purposely set out to deceive, and such a deception would have been pointless as it would quickly have been discovered if his embassy had succeeded.

What is plain is that the Roman orator and statesman was deeply impressed, perhaps a little too deeply for his judgment to be quite sound. He attributes to Diviciacus "that knowledge of nature which the Greeks call 'Physiologia' " by which he means natural science. But what was it he exalted by this name? Was it, as some scholars hold, little more than that nature- and herb-lore which Pliny shows the Druids to have possessed?

In any case, this kind of idealizing gets scant support from the only other eye-witness, Tacitus, who is the only one to give us any direct information about Druidism in Britain, but who saw it only from the point of view of the forces which had come to destroy it.

For him the Druids are ignorant savages who "deemed it indeed a duty to cover their altars with the blood of captives and to consult their deities through human entrails". This forms part of the passage in the *Annals* in which he describes the terrifying scene confronting the Roman troops attempting to take Anglesey: the "dense array of armed warriors"; the women in black, dashing between the ranks "like the Furies", hair dishevelled and waving brands; the Druids with uplifted hands "pouring forth dreadful imprecations". For all that he is a key observer, one must take into consideration his unconcealed prejudice. He fully accepted the pleas of Roman imperialism and was at pains to make clear to his readers what benefits the conquerors were conferring on "the poor, benighted heathen".

Outside this tiny band we are left with those writers who, on the whole, are merely recycling old facts and offering conclusions about the Druids which become more extravagantly idealized as the distance in time separates them, though, it is true, occasionally providing some new detail verifiable by the light of other data. Lucan, who lived from AD 39 to 65 and, therefore, at a time when at least some first hand witnesses were about, describes the Druids in his epic poem *Pharsalia* as having their abode in "the innermost groves of far-off forests". He may well have heard of the celebrated Druids' grove near the Greek colony of Massilia, always considered to be of great antiquity, and, of course, he corroborates Pliny. The Medieval Berne *Scholiasts* who annotated the *Pharsalia*, provide some additional information, including the names of some gods like Esus, Teutatis and Taranis, known from other sources and it is conceivable that they may have been working from some earlier now lost work, possibly Posidonius.

Valerius Maximus, who wrote a book of anecdotes principally intended to be of assistance to orators, and who lived in the times of Tiberius, himself responsible for the ban on Druidism, mentions the curious custom among the Gauls whereby money lent was made repayable beyond the grave. This links with Diodorus' statement about letters being sent to the dead.

Diogenes Laertius, already mentioned, wrote *The Lives and Opinions of the Eminent Philosophers* in Greek. The prologue begins: "There are some who say that the study of philosophy had its beginnings among the barbarians" and he summons in support the Magi of the Persians, the Chaldeans of the Babylonians and Assyrians, and an Indian caste he calls the "Gymnosophists". He then tells us that "among the Celts and Gauls there are people called Druids or Holy Ones". As his authority he cites the *Magicus*, a lost work by Aristotle, who had lived between 384-322 BC, and Sotion of Alexandria in the twenty-third book of his *Succession of the Philosophers*.

About 390 AD, Ammianus Marcellus wrote a continuation of the *Histories* of Tacitus, using Latin, though his native tongue was Greek. As his source in references to the Celts, he cites Timagenes, a Greek historian of the 1st Century BC and the author of a history of the Gauls also now lost. Ammianus, himself a meticulous and painstaking historian, says of Timagenes that he was "a true Greek in accuracy as well as language" and that he had collected out of the various books those facts long unknown. For his part, however, Ammianus merely recapitulates Strabo, though he does introduce the name of Pythagoras, inferring that he was the initiator of the Druidic doctrine of metempsychosis or transmigration of the soul. The Druids were, he informs us, "bound together in a fraternal organization, as the authority of Pythagoras determined". The mention of an organization might seem like confirmation of Caesar's statements about the annual Druidic convocation in the territory of the Carnutes and the existence of an Archdruid — one would expect such an organized body to have its annual general meeting and its chairman. But the suggestion that the Druids were mere disciples of Pythagoras is so fantastical that the entire passage becomes dubious.

Nevertheless, the Pythagorean link is one pursued by others. In the view of most contemporary scholars it had its origin in the coincidence that both Druids and Pythagoras believed in metempsychosis, though a writer before Ammianus explains it by declaring that the Greek mathematician's mentor was an Assyrian named Nazaratus and that he had himself studied the teachings of the Galatae and the Brahmins. The Brahmins are, of course, a caste of Hindu religious teachers, but

"Galatae" means simply "Gauls" so that one has to assume that what he really intended was that Pythagoras studied the teachings of the "Brahmins and Druids", which might well have been true. And the fact is that the Brahmins, also, believe in and teach metempsychosis.

Hippolytus, writing in his *Philosophoumena*, about the 3rd Century AD, asserts that philosophy, "a science of the highest utility", flourished among the ancient barbarians, and only from them arrived in Greece. His list of those he regards as the precursors of Greek philosophy include not only the Druids of the Gauls and "the Philosophers of the Kelts", a curious distinction, but most of those earlier listed by Diogenes.

Perhaps it was sheer patriotism which led later Greeks to reverse previous trends and restore Pythagoras as instructor of the Druids. For by the time of Cyril of Alexandria in the 4th Century AD, we have the Greek master's Thracian slave, Zalmoxis, as missionary to the Gauls. In any event, the association of Druids and Pythagoras is one which shows considerable persistence, a fact which, of itself, leads one to wonder if it can be totally without foundation. Can this possibly mean that Pythagorean mathematics had a Druidic base? Incredibly the idea is less far-fetched now than it once seemed.

There are four further references to the Druids which though of extremely late date speak of them as if they were still in existence. The *Historia Augusta* is a series of somewhat journalistic biographies of the Roman emperors from Hadrian to Numerianus, covering a period from AD 117 to 284. In the life of Numerianus, we are told that once, when Diocletian, then a young subaltern, was staying in Gaul, his hostess chided him with parsimony. He answered jestingly that he would be more generous once he became emperor — an office which he can at that time have had no hope of attaining. The woman told him not to mock, "For," she said, "when you have killed The Boar, you will indeed be emperor". From then on though he missed no opportunity of killing boars when hunting, he came no nearer to the purple. At last, he killed the prefect Arrius, surnamed The Boar, and was made emperor. What turns this anecdote of fortune-telling into a curiosity is that his hostess, presumably an innkeeper, is described as a "Druidess".

From the life of Aurelianus, also in the *Historia Augusta*, we are told that that emperor was in the habit of consulting "the Gaulish Druidesses" to find out if the imperial diadem would remain in his family's keeping.

And in a third story from the same source we learn that when the emperor, Severus, was on his way to engage the Germans who, in AD 235, were laying Gaul waste, a Druidess called out to him, "Go forward, but hope not for victory, nor put trust in thy soldiers". In fact he was assassinated by mutinous troops and hence won no victory.

The usual explanation of these late relics is that by this time Druidism had degenerated into mere fortune-telling, herbalism and folk-medicine. In any case, it is pointed out, there is no evidence of Druidesses among the earlier writers.

But there may be more to it than this and it is here that the two other sources are relevant. Decimus Magnus Ausonius was born in Bordeaux in AD 310, and subsequently became tutor to the son of the Emperor Valentinian. Before his elevation he had been teacher of rhetoric at the University of Bordeaux, as well as a somewhat idiosyncratic versifier who found his inspiration in such subjects as the months of the year, his own ancestry or, as in this case, his fellow-professors. Of one, whose name he gives as Phoebicius, he writes that he had been keeper of the temple of Belenos and came from the stock of the Druids of Armorica. In an early specimen of academic bitchiness, he adds that getting no profit from his sacerdotal appointment, Phoebicius used the good offices of his son to obtain a chair at the university. The fascinating point is, however, that here we have Druids mentioned some 350 years after the Roman conquest of Gaul and their supposed disappearance.

Since the classical sources are so niggardly of information regarding Druidism we must obviously try to fill the numerous gaps from elsewhere.

The obvious place is archaeology, but, in spite of all the jokes about finds labelled "Cult Object" which have later turned out to be some ordinary domestic utensil, religion is precisely the sphere which finds archaeologists at their most reticent. All too often the "Cult Object" is precisely equivalent to a domestic article. The chalice and paten of the Christian communion are ready examples: the one is goblet, the other a plate and they could as easily occupy a dining table as an altar. The cauldron of the Druids is a similar case, and not even the sacrificial knife necessarily has anything to distinguish it from the common or kitchen variety.

Under certain circumstances, to be sure, the archaeologist, coming on a hoard of objects, perhaps at the bottom of a lake, may be confident enough to pronounce it a votive deposit; or finding a building, declare it a temple.

But, then, did the Druids worship in temples? In general, almost certainly not. Their rites were conducted in the open, in oak groves. And although Diodorus of Sicily, Suetonius and Polybius all speak of "temples and sanctuaries", they may well have been writing in a more or less figurative sense. Certainly many of the buildings identified as Celtic temples or shrines are post-Roman. Nevertheless, in some cases traces of

presence of mistletoe could be taken as substantial proof of origin. Unfortunately, a great deal of doubt surrounds the entire discovery, including the identification of the foliage, and it cannot be taken at face value.

At Port St Mary in the Isle of Man is a four-foot high sandstone slab dating from about the 5th or 6th Centuries AD. Its inscription is in Ogham characters, a form of runic or linear script used principally in Ireland and confined to epigraphy (though Robert Graves suggests it was also a means of secret communication among the Druids). It has been read as: Dovaidona Maqi Droata, and this translated would mean: Dovadona, Son of the Druid.

This, in the broadest terms, is the sum of archaeological knowledge of the Druids. But there remain two admittedly more problematical sources: one, the so-called vernacular texts; the other, the existing survivals of customs whose origins can be traced back to pagan Celtic times, some of which we discussed in the second chapter of this book.

The texts comprise a series of stories originally without doubt transmitted orally and only at a very late date committed to writing. The older and probably, therefore, more reliable are the Irish ones whose written form dates from the 8th Century AD on; the Welsh stories were in the main transcribed only in Medieval times so that besides undergoing the corruption of time they were also subjected to other literary influences in particular French ones.

Professor Ross hints at a third repository of vernacular material, as yet unpublished, in the traditional oral literature of the Scottish Highlands. These are later still: indeed many did not achieve written form until our own times when folklorists were able to persuade the story-tellers to recite their repertories into the microphones of tape-recorders. Although they contain references to Celtic gods and known practices, these have become inextricably confused with later Christian legends and with events in Scottish history down the centuries.

Whether Irish, Welsh or Scottish, the stories are in epic form and, superficially, are the description of intertribal and dynastic quarrels, conquests and invasions, occasionally with a kernel of known history beneath the thick husk of legend.

At the same time, they are replete with creatures — bulls, boars, salmon, eagles, ravens — with supernatural powers whose existence we can trace back through the layers of Celtic prehistory, and with known customs and references to gods. Unrecognized as such by the Medieval scribes who wrote the stories down, however, these last now stand on terms of parity with the human characters and often play subsidiary roles. Thus, in *How Culhwch Won Olwen*, one of the earliest stories in which King Arthur figures, one character, Mabon ap Modron (the name means, Son, Son of Mother) is undoubtedly the deity, Maponos, whose name also means "Son" or "Divine Son". He is to be found on five dedications in the north of England and is recalled in two place-names, Lochmaben and Clochmabenstane in Dumfriesshire.

The "divine son" who is abducted and taken to the Other World, finally to be rescued, is a fundamental myth found in most agricultural societies and personifies the cycle of seedtime and harvest. In four of the dedications, which are Gallo-Roman, Maponos is equated with Apollo and one of these, a partially-defaced altar stone found at Ribchester, Lancashire, originally had four figures, of which two are of goddesses, interpreted as huntresses. In one of the best known versions of the "abducted divine son" myth, that of Adonis, the god is wounded in a boar-hunt. Mabon, who in the story has also been abducted, participates after his rescue, in a hunt for the supernatural boar, Twrc Trywth.

The Celtic god most often regarded as the equivalent of Apollo is the sun-god, Belenos. But if one follows the genealogy of the "divine son" further back one finds that he, too, was a sun-god, as in the case of the Egyptian Horus, son of Isis. Can it be, then, that Maponos is simply the sun-god Belenos designated by some other name, and that here we have the vestiges of a Celtic "abducted divine son" myth?

This is not, by any means, the only case of such hints' being left hanging tantalizingly in mid-air. In the Welsh *mabinogi* of *Pwyll Lord of Dyved*, there is another. In one incident in the story, Teirnon Twrvliant has a succession of foals stolen each May Eve (the Celtic festival of Beltain). Finally, he decides to keep watch over his mare and, as she delivers, a huge claw comes in through the window and grabs the new-born animal. Teirnon slices the claw from its arm with his sword and rushes outside, but all he finds is a babe in silk swaddling bands. The child turns out to be the stolen son of the queen, Rhiannon. Another thread is pursued, however, and so we never return to this intriguing theme to discover who is the owner of the giant claw. The story-teller is obviously unaware of much significant detail: that, for example, Rhiannon is the Welsh form of the great horse-goddess Epona, known right across the Celtic world. This must have been the connexion with foaling mares—a theme also abandoned.

For all this, the stories constantly reiterate important pagan Celtic themes. There is, for example, the struggle between an older man (often the father) and a younger man for a woman. The cost of the younger man's victory is, invariably, the sexual virility of the older one. This occurs in both the stories just mentioned and altogether no fewer than seven times in the Welsh *mabinogi* legends. Jeffrey Gantz, editor of the Penguin edition of them suggests it can be taken to represent spring, the woman, and summer, the young man, in conflict with a god governing winter.

There are in these stories too accounts of those visits to the Other World to wrest from its guardians some magical treasure beneficial or essential to humanity. This illustrates that movement between the two planes of existence always easily made in Celtic myth, especially during the season of Samain. Lastly, there is the notion of the violated or abducted queen, without doubt a mother-goddess whose absence spells disaster for her people and who must accordingly be rescued.

As leads in a search for the Druids, one cannot rely on the myths as we now have them to provide unsupported evidence though they often give useful confirmation and elucidation of data coming from other sources. And what is perhaps more important, they often evoke the atmosphere of the Celtic supernatural with that mysterious interlocking of the living and the dead through the tremendous powers latent in the natural environment.

The same caution also applies in assessing surviving and recently abandoned folk-customs; nonetheless they do give us some idea of the spread of pagan Celtic festivals and hence of the deities which these celebrated. The horned god is a case in point, since it seems a reasonable conjecture that customs like the Abbots Bromley stag-dance and the *Pardon* St Cornely must commemorate him.

But it can also suggest leads to be followed up. We know, for example, that both prophecy and herb-medicine are practised by latterday "wise men" and "wise women". This might well cause us to consider whether the Druids also practised these arts, as of course we know they did. Similarly, water-divining or "dowsing" is also associated with "wise" men and women, indeed the French word *sorcier* means, literally, "one who finds sources"—in other words, a water-diviner. This provokes the question: did the Druids practise it?

CHAPTER FIVE

An Ancestry Of Druidism

IN the descriptions of the Druids among those classical writers who can be taken as contemporary with them there is a singular omission. While most standard reference works speak of them as "priests of the Celts", none of the Posidonian sources so describes them.

Caesar says that they were "occupied about things divine, they carry out sacrifice—public and private, and interpret religious matters" (" . . . ulli rebus divinis intersunt, sacrificia publica ac privata procurant, religionem interpretantur"). Pliny writes of "magicians" and in so far as he defines this further it is as "diviners and physicians", the latter word chiming with his description of their practice of herbalism. Among the others: to Strabo they are "natural and moral philosophers"; to Diodorus "philosophers" versed in religious affairs; and to Diogenes Laertius, quoting Aristotle and Sotion, "philosophers", without qualification.

Since each of these writers was, in his own way, endeavouring to interpret the Druids to those presumed to be ignorant of them, it is surely a little strange that none made the one comparison likely to render them immediately understandable: that between the priests with whom their readers were familiar, and those of the Celts. In other contexts, alien sacerdotal bodies are quite freely, even wantonly, translated so. Titus Livy, for example, uses the expression *antistites templi* to describe a foreign priesthood; a Gallo-Roman inscription at Arles gives the feminine form, *anti stitia deae*, while another at Antibes records a *flaminica sacerdos* serving the goddess Thucolis, notwithstanding the fact that the *flamens* were a specifically Roman body. Even Caesar, who himself bore the sacerdotal title of *pontifex maximus* and who glosses Celtic gods with Roman ones, does not describe the Druids by any word approximating in meaning to "priest".

The most obvious explanation is that the Druids were so unlike what these writers understood a priest to be that the term appeared quite inappropriate. But it could have been that there was, in addition, a totally different body recognizably functioning as a priesthood as they understood it.

If this was the case, why do we know so little of it? The first part of the answer lies in the mental attitude of the observers themselves. Despite the admirable opportunities available to them, neither Greeks nor Romans showed any inclination towards the study of comparative religion. The fact was that they saw the beliefs of most of the subject peoples as only an unrefined version of their own—which to some extent they were. To be worthy of comment, the manifestations of a religion had to be both different and dramatic. Druidism succeeded in both respects.

The second part of the answer is that other religious leaders among the Celts are recorded, though by little more than intimation. Diogenes Laertius, for example, mentions "druidae" and "semnotheoi". The second word is totally mysterious and without any agreed interpretation, though the suffix "-theoi" means "gods".

There were in addition various bodies of priestesses, like those of the Cimbri described by Strabo. He mentions also a body of women practising on an offshore island of Gaul, which may be one of the Channel Islands. They were, he says, devoted to a Dionysian cult whose rituals included an annual rethatching of their temple in a single day. If, in the process, one of their number had the misfortune to stumble and drop her load she was set on by the rest and torn to pieces. The victim was, he assures us, always settled on in advance and a means found of tripping her.

Besides these, there are the accounts of tribal leaders performing sacrifice. One is Queen Boudicca offering women to her victory-goddess, Adraste, after her defeat of the Romans. The other is Queen Cartimandua, ruler of the Brigantes, who invokes the goddess Brigid or Brigantia.

More promising than such random and casual instances, however, is the Celtic title *gutuater*, found on four inscriptions and twice mentioned by Caesar. These two references occur in the Eighth Book of *The*

Conquest of Gaul, which was written not by Caesar but by his friend Hirtius. Here the word appears to be used as a proper name, but it is generally held that this was an error and that it actually refers to a man who held the rank of *gutuater*. As Kendrick points out, he was plainly not a Druid, since while both Caesar and Hirtius were obviously confused about what a *gutuater* was, they knew perfectly well what a Druid was and would, therefore, have so described him had he been one.

The word has been variously translated as "master" or "father of invocation" (of prayer) or just as "the Invoker". It may be, as some scholars hold, that the *gutuater* represented a grade of priesthood, in other words some kind of 'curate' Druid, but if this is so we have no mention of them as such. In any case, the various renderings of the word actually makes them sound more like priests than any of the definitions of the word Druid ("wise man", "wise man of the oak", "man of great wisdom" to quote a few). And invocation or prayer is nearer to a priestly function than most of those ascribed to the Druids, though one must bear in mind that Diogenes Laertius says they were called "Druids or Holy Ones".

But perhaps it is here—with definitions—that we should begin: if we can find an acceptable definition for the word "priest" we can then decide whether the Druids come within its ambit. In essence, it can, I think, be agreed that a priest is "one who acts as mediator between a community and its deities". The concept of deities itself represents, as we know, an advanced stage in cultural development. Gods have personalities, are capable of being pleased and displeased and so there stems from them the notions leading to the development of morality and religious ethics. Initially, however, what is likely to exercise their worshippers is less abstractions of this kind than the manifest power of the gods to harm or benefit mortals. For are they not masters of the elements; commanders of sun, moon, tides, seasons; lords of life and death? Accordingly, the only person equipped to mediate with them must be the most powerful of mortals—the tribal chief. And as the tribe is subsumed into nation, the king will succeed to the function.

The hypothesis is confirmed by the evidence. With the Egyptians, for instance, the pharoah was also high priest. A drawing of King Ay, predecessor of Tutankhamen, shows him in his ritual garb. If one takes the Hittites, first of the great Indo-European civilizations, for whom nationhood came late in their history, one finds a similar state of affairs, saving that beside the national deities there still remained a large pantheon of local, formerly tribal ones, and among the priest-king's duties was that of making an annual tour of their shrines to render tribute.

That the Celtic chieftain, at any rate in late time, fulfilled the sacerdotal role is obvious from the instances of Boudicca and Cartimandua.

The Egyptian word usually translated as "priest" means strictly

"Servants of the Gods" and we know they were restricted to the menial, quotidian tasks of the temple. The Roman pontifices, for all they were often patricians, were also originally appointed to carry out the more or less routine liturgical functions, the main ones belonging to the kings up till republican times whereafter they were largely secularized to become sinecures.

What emerges, therefore, is that on the whole priests as the ancient world understood them fulfilled a secondary rather than a primary religious function. But the classical sources are virtually unanimous in pronouncing the Druids supreme in Celtic religion. In any case, the order displays an independence and superiority which makes it inconceivable that they can have been mere royal appointees. The king was not, for example, permitted to speak until his Druids had first expressed their opinions. In *The Cattle Raid of Cooley*, we are told that, "in Ulster no man spoke before Conchobhar, and Conchobhar would not speak before the three Druids".

If the Celts had priests in the sense of secondary religious functionaries, like those of Egypt, Rome and elsewhere, we can declare with some confidence that they could not have been the Druids.

What then were they?

To my mind the most helpful guide towards a definition is the list of "barbarian philosophers" provided by Diogenes Laertius who brackets together Druids, the Persian Magi, the "Chaldeans" of the Babylonians and Assyrians, and the body he calls the "Gymnosophists" of the Hindus. Why of all the enormous numbers available did he alight on this four? The vital clue is the inclusion of the Persian Magi, for it is this which shows what unites the names on the list. All were magicians—indeed, the word itself comes from Magi as Aristotle whose *Magicus* provided Diogenes with one of his two sources knew.

And if we exclude the term "Chaldean" we find that they are also united in another way. Druids, Magi and "Gymnosophists" all existed among peoples derived from the same racial root-stock, the wandering tribes who were the original inhabitants of Southern Russia—the Indo-Europeans. Their migrations towards Europe, Iran and India could be said to represent the three thrusts of their first expansion, westward, southward and eastward.

And, as a matter of fact, the inclusion of the word "Chaldean" plainly arises from a misapprehension on the part of either Diogenes or his source. It was not the name of any sort of religious body; it was that of the founding race of the Babylonian empire, which, of course, absorbed the Assyrians. In other words, Babylon consisted of the Chaldeans and the Assyrians—Babylonians and Assyrians were not separate peoples as the text implies. The error arose because the priesthood of the Babylonians whose members could with some accuracy be called "magicians" was largely drawn from the Chaldeans, as was the ruling aristocracy of the empire. They were, inter alia, pioneers of astrology, astronomy and mathematics—the Greeks called them *mathematiki*. In late time, however, they became itinerant astrologers, and frequently turned up in Rome (though forbidden the city), where they were known as "Chaldeans"; thus the name became synonymous with the practices of astrology, fortune-telling and associated quasi-magical pursuits.

Though their relevance to Diogenes' list will shortly become clear, for the moment we can safely ignore them and consider whether it is possible that the migrating Indo-Europeans carried with them a system of ideas so similar that all qualified for inclusion in a list of what might be called "pioneer philosophers" drawn up a millennium later. But let us first be clear what was meant by "philosophy". To Greeks like Aristotle or Diogenes, as to 18th Century Europeans, it signified as much a preoccupation with the natural world as with pure metaphysical speculation. Newton was no less a philosopher in these terms than Hume, and was so described. And our own universities, after all, still make our postgraduate scientists Doctors of Philosophy. Astronomy, even under the guise of astrology, calendary, mathematics, herbalism, as well as those sheer speculations "about the heavenly bodies and their movements", to which, according to Caesar, the Druids were so much addicted, would all come under the heading of "Philosophy" to Aristotle or Diogenes.

As it happens one of the three bodies on the latter's list has survived. The Indo-European migrants who, about the beginning of the 15th Century BC, reached India were the "Aryan" invaders, founders of Hinduism. There are numerous startling resemblances between Hinduism and Druidism. Both practised cremation of the dead, carried out human sacrifice, had vast numbers of deities and taught metempsychosis. (The similarities actually go down to quite trifling detail: Buddha is normally depicted as sitting in the same cross-legged position the Celts are described as adopting and in which their gods are often shown.)

But there had emerged in Hinduism, as its intellectual leadership, the Brahmins: these must be Diogenes' "Gymnosophists". The late Myles Dillon, Professor of Celtic Studies at the University of Dublin, has drawn up a list of the similarities between Brahmins and Druids. He points out that, for example, they were highest caste of a four-caste system, with the knights or *Kshatriyas* coming next below them. Caesar declares that the Druids and the knights were the two most highly esteemed classes in Gaulish society. He does not actually give one or other precedence, though he describes the Druids first and begins the next section with the words "The second class is that of the Knights . . ."

The Brahmins, like the Druids, were communal lawgivers. Both recognized either forms of marriage. Of the Brahmins, Max Weber says that they occupied the positions of princely-chaplains, and acted as counsellors and as theological teachers. They were to be found as singers of epics extolling the heroic and deriding the unworthy. All were functions of the Druids.

Like Druidic doctrine, that of the Brahmins was originally transmitted by word of mouth. Weber points out that even when it came to be written down it still plainly exhibited that it had been fashioned for easy memorization and reproduction. Extensive use was made of plays on words, epigrams, aphorisms, verse and recurring refrains of the "This-is-the-house-that Jack-built" type.

Most importantly, both acted as advisers on ritual, placing great emphasis on its correct execution.

The similarities are such that one might suppose that Brahmins and Druids had been in contact, but as this is inconceivable, the only answer is that both developed out of an earlier, parent body.

We might suppose that they encountered this in their original Indo-European homelands, which must have been not only a racial nursery, but also the place where the stirrings of an apprehension of the supernatural occurred. According to Father William Schmidt who in 1931 produced his magnum opus, *The Origins of the Idea of God*, the first signs of this are those pre-hunt rituals whose aim is not merely to ensure mastery over the prey, but also to allay the anger of its "spirit". He gives a typical example from anthropology and describes a pygmy-artist drawing a representation of his quarry before pursuing it. Afterwards, having been successful, he puts blood and hair from the slaughtered animal on his picture, then rubs out the entirety as the rising sun touches it. The cave painters, such as those of Lascaux with their scenes of hunters and prey must certainly have had similar intentions.

This concern with the wrathful spirits of the dead forms not only an initial, but a constant manifestation of the notion of the supernatural among early peoples. Everything possesses a soul—not just such animate things as humans, animals, fish, plants, but also the apparently inanimate, stones, earth, water, wood. As an Eskimo told the Danish explorer Rasmussen in 1929, it was in this that the greatest threat to humanity lay. "All those we have to strike down . . . have souls, as we have," he pointed out, "souls that do not perish with the body and which therefore must be propitiated lest they revenge themselves on us for taking away their bodies."

What first changes is that stage at which the propitiatory rituals are carried out by each or any member of the group of hunters. It gives place to one wherein, the social units having increased in size and complexity, this becomes the responsibility of an expert. He is the shaman, able to throw himself into trances in which he can enter the Land of the Spirits, communicate with its inhabitants and hence on his return dictate the rituals necessary not merely to banish those which are malign causing illness or other misfortunes, but also with the help of his personal tutelary spirits to invoke the aid of others both powerful and well-disposed.

The word "shaman" is derived from the language of the Tungus peoples of Siberia, among whom he is still to be found practising, as he is among the nomadic herdsmen and hunters of northern Europe, the Arctic and the plains of north-east Asia. But under a score of different names he is to be found all over the world in rural communities living by hunting and fishing, with at best a little subsistence farming or nomadic pastoralism. His reputation, however, may well spread beyond the confines of his native village. The witch-doctor, the *obeahs* of the Caribbean, the Voodoo-priests of Haiti and West Africa, the Candomblés of Brazil, all have among their patrons and membership of their cult-groups sophisticated and often well-educated town-dwellers.

More than anyone, the shaman can claim to a vocation: that it is shamanism that chooses him, not he it. Impelled by some power he cannot resist, often a succession of dreams, he withdraws from the society of his fellows to live in the wild, where, fasting and meditating, he lays himself open as it were to the very forces immanent in his natural surroundings.

Soon he will become prey to terrible visitations. He may believe himself to be undergoing many incarnations in the space of a few nights, culminating in some dreadful act of symbolical self-immolation. At last he will reach stasis and his own ultimate reward—a total union with the Cosmos. As well as the spirits of the dead, he will have emerged from his trauma in touch with "all the spirits of earth and sky and sea" in the words of Rasmussen's informant who was himself a shaman. From now on all these will be his guides and helpers.

Thus reborn, his first companions will be other shamans who recognize him as one fit to share their secrets: those of animal and bird life; of cloud and climate; stars and their motions; herbs and their properties. But above all, he will learn the great myths which are the history of his people.

When he returns to the midst of his fellow men, probably under a new name as token of his regeneration, they will quickly recognize that he is a different person, the recipient of special wisdom. At one with nature and the elements, he may now choose for his habitat some remote place in the forest and it is here he will have to be sought for consultation.

The intimacy of his union with nature will be demonstrated by his very costume, so that when he wishes to commune with bird-spirits he will wear a dress of feathers; to reach animal-spirits he will wear skins or adorn himself with horns or antlers; when it is the spirits of tree or plant life he seeks he will don the green of foliage or the colours of flowers or fruit. He has become, one would say, a magician—the word the classical writers most frequently use in describing the Druids.

Certainly in shamanism we have a system of belief whose lineage stretches back perhaps 20,000 years. Something very close to it existed among the inhabitants of Scandinavia as early as Neolithic times. Its effect on the Druids is obvious and it is virtually certain that there were shamans among the Indo-Europeans before the great migrations.

On the other hand, if the Druids had developed out of what had been the common heritage of the Indo-Europeans, why should the practices of the Magi, the Brahmins and the Druids have excited the comment of Greek observers, themselves Indo-Europeans? And it is surely unlikely that they would have attributed the foundation of philosophy, of which the Greeks were so proud, to these quite alien bodies unless there was good reason for their doing so. How, in any case, does one account for the presence of the Babylonians on the list, since they were not Indo-Europeans?

The truth is that there may well have been another shamanic body, infinitely more highly developed than the normal run or, indeed, than most contemporary shamans as they have been encountered by anthropologists. We might call them the "super-shamans".

Their trail can be followed by the clear imprints they have left behind. One of these which Geoffrey Ashe pursues at length is the universality of the "sacred heptad", the number seven: seven days of the week; Seven Deadly Sins; seven planets; seven metals of alchemy; Seven Pillars of Wisdom; seven seas; the seven-tiered Ziggurat of Babylon; the seven-branched candelabra of the Jewish temple—and the list can be extended still further.

In almost every instance the choice of the number is arbitrary and can be explained only by attaching an occult significance to it. This is probably an association with astrology so that it represents either the seven planets or (as Geoffrey Ashe argues) the seven stars of the Great Bear. With astrology or astronomy must go mathematics, without which calendration, which is one of their practical fruits or, for that matter horoscope casting, is impossible. We can conclude, therefore, the super-shamans were also astronomers and mathematicians.

Eliade has pointed out another clue to his presence: the importance of the "Cosmic Centre". This has nothing to do with purely geometrical centres, but relates to the belief that there are special centres at which the powers of the supernatural are greatest. Typically they take the form of a mountain, like Mount Zion, or a tree, of which the Norse World Tree, Yggdrasil, is a good example. Both may take symbolical form. The Ziggurat was a symbolical mountain connecting heaven, earth and underworld, and the ascent of a symbolical tree formed and still forms part of the ritual of central and north Asiatic shamans.

With these and other clues we can trace the influence of the super-shaman on many of the world's great religions. Its ideas crossed the Bering Straits to reach those of the civilizations of Central and South America probably no later than 10,000 BC. It plainly influenced Babylon and the other Semitic religions. It underlies Chinese Taoism, as well as Tibetan Buddhism. And is it not significant that in his search for "enlightenment", Gautama Buddha, himself an Indo-European, chose the traditional shamanic way of withdrawal from society and solitary meditation in the wilderness?

If we return to Diogenes' list and look for connexions with the super-shamans we find that Magi, Brahmins, Babylonian priests and Druids were all astrologers, mathematicians and calendarists. The Babylonian priests were, indeed, pre-eminent in these fields, and are credited with the introduction of concepts still in use. Their calendar, counted among the world's first accurate ones, was based on the nineteen-year or Metonic cycle. A similar system was used by the Druids. The number seven repeatedly occurs in connexion with all four—the Ziggurat, for example, had seven-tiers.

And if we look at the Brahmins, about whom we are best informed, the coincidences are even more striking. Seven is their mystic number, occurring no fewer than 154 times in the *Rig Veda*, the sacred book of Hinduism. They were both astrologers and mathematicians and they showed a special preoccupation with the "Cosmic Centre" so that in the invocations which accompany the felling of the tree to be used as a sacrificial stake, it is addressed as the link between earth, air and heaven—a concept very similar to the Babylonian.

Their main function was that of ritual advisers. They are, as Weber says, "magicians who developed into a hierocratic caste of cultured men".

But perhaps, in passing, we should say something about this very concept of "magician". The word, as used by the classical writers, comes from the Greek "mageia", itself from the Persian word "Magi" and means simply "possessors of wisdom" (as in the Wise Men who visited the Christ-child in Bethlehem). As men of wisdom the Magi commanded the respect of virtually the entire ancient world, including that of the otherwise rather self-satisfied Hebrews. Their astrology had, for example, enabled them to predict that the star seen over Bethlehem portended an important birth. Through their founder, Zoroaster or Zarathustra, they taught what is virtually a montheistic religion of which the tenets were highly influential on others, notably Judaism and Christianity.

It was probably in this sense of wisdom and knowledge, rather than in the accepted later one with which we are familiar that the term "magician" was applied to all three bodies, including the Druids, though it undoubtedly also comprehended the occult skills they were thought to possess.

But, in any event, magic has been of inestimable benefit in the development of science, of which it is the true ancestor, so that mathematics develops from numerology; astronomy from astrology; medicine from magical herbalism; and chemistry from alchemy. But even to say that the "one develops out of the other" is imprecise. In reality they go hand in hand. One cannot, for example, practise numerology without a knowledge of mathematics or astrology without some knowledge of astronomy.

We can say that all four of the bodies listed by Diogenes had been influenced by the super-shamans and that the practices of this body probably included mathematics and astronomy, even if under the guises of numerology and astrology.

But what does not follow is that these contacts were all at first hand. In the case of the Druids it seems to me very probable they were not. They could well have encountered them at second hand. The most likely vehicle of transmission, therefore, would seem to be the Scythians. Originating perhaps in Iran or the Caspian Basin their migrations had brought them into contact with the early Celts in their original Bohemian homeland.

The Scythians practised a form of totemistic shamanism, that is to say they believed themselves to have descended from animal-spirits and they employed shamans to mediate with them. Among the numerous similarities with the Druids were their practices of sacrifice by drowning and their use of a magic wand. According to Markale, the Scythians preferred willow while the Druids chose yew or mountain-ash; in both cases, the wand was an essential tool of prophecy. Both decapitated fallen enemies and believed in metempsychosis, as is evident from their waggon and chariot burials with grave goods including food.

It would be difficult to deny the extent of Scythian influence on the Celts or their religion. On the other hand, the more esoteric reaches of Druidism, those aspects of it which so impressed outsiders, were, I believe, the result of quite different encounters, encounters with a system of beliefs both more potent and much nearer home and these will later be discussed.

CHAPTER SIX

Successors Of The Shamans

CELTIC society was, of course, much more highly developed than that in which shamans are usually found: hunting and pastoralism had given place to farming; metal was mined and worked; there was an external trade. We can hardly expect, in these circumstances, to find shamans as known to contemporary anthropology and the Druids on all fours with one another.

Nonetheless, it is a recognizably shamanistic viewpoint, one which sees human and natural environment as totally interpenetrated which gives Celticism its characteristic ambiance, its special flavour. A breathing vitality sometimes benign, often menacing, charges the landscape and especially those deep, looming forests which must have covered so much of Gaul and the British Isles. The feeling of it is present in their art, in the accurate rendering of leaves, birds or animals; it is present, too, in the Arthurian legends and the earlier myths. The strange giants and other creatures there encountered seem to grow out of woodland itself, to personify it. It is, we might say, the world of nature as apprehended in shamanistic terms, one which can never be seen as deserted because it is peopled by the very things which make it up—rocks, trees, fungi, fern, wild flowers, running stream or spring, even air

Heads played a crucial role in Celtic religion. The Celts often displayed sacred severed heads of fallen enemies outside their homes. They were also reproduced as stone heads as in the three examples here: (top left) from Heidelberg 400 B.C.; (far left middle) from Westmoreland; and (centre) from Bath, a watering place sacred to the Celts, a head of the god Belenos, whom the Greeks called Apollo. Among them (centre left) is the figure of Cernunnos, the horned stag god, a figure which survives in modern morris dancing. (Bottom far left) Druidic elements, such as birds, survived in Christian art, such as this eighth-century Irish crucifix, and (bottom middle) the Cross of Muiredach (tenth century) in Ireland. (Above) The Desborough Mirror, a fine example of Celtic art which has had widespread influence on European art.

necessary for it would have been essential to the correct execution of ritual. The state of the moon would have to be known, as in the case of the mistletoe-gathering ceremony which Pliny says took place on the sixth day of the new moon, or in deciding the proper day for the celebration of a festival. This would have been a particular problem for the Druids, since the system they used to synchronize solar and lunar time involved the introduction of intercalary months of thirty days at intervals of two-and-a-half and three years in alternation (as opposed to our own system of inserting an extra day every four years). One has to suppose, therefore, that celebration of festivals was determined by the positions of sun or moon rather than by assigning fixed days each year to them. A similarity is to be found in the 'Golden Number' used to calculate the moveable feast of Easter in Christianity, and this was also formerly used for calculating Christmas. Significantly enough, the Golden Number is itself based on lunar reckoning and on the nineteen-year Metonic cycle employed by the Druids. Druidic herbalism obviously extended to what we should now call veterinary practice. Not only does this lie very much within the province of the shaman, but Pliny tells us explicitly that among the virtues of mistletoe was that of giving fertility to barren animals.

Onc would, however, be wrong I think to suppose that Druidic skill limited itself to those activities we associate with simple rural life, for it may well have gone much further.

Though it was basically an agrarian society, the Celtic was at least nascently a technological and, above all, an heroic one and as such preoccupied not only with its warrior-heroes, but also with weaponry. Spears and swords make frequent appearance in legend and are found in votive deposits. The *Cattle Raid* provides a page-long list of them and the various heroes who had wielded them. They included Lamthapad, the sword of Conall Cernach whom Ross tentatively equates with Cernunnos. Nuada's sword was one of the most treasured possessions of that great family of gods called the *Tuatha De Danann*, the People of Dana. Lugh's spear, which also belonged to the *tuatha*, was of such a nature that 'the woman or man who held it could not be conquered in battle'. It was of a potency which made it necessary to keep it immersed in a cauldron of water when not in use or the town in which it was housed would have been burnt down. The spear mentioned in the Grail legend had similar properties: its merest scratch could be fatal. If the thrower uttered the magic word "*ibar*" as it left his hand, it never missed its mark; if he said "*athibar*", it came back to him. Arthur's right to the throne was determined by the drawing of the sword from the stone and he later received the magical Excalibur through Merlin. In an extant Manx ˌegend, Manannan mac Lir, the island's divine founder, possesses not only a swift horse, Enbarr, but also a death-dealing sword The Answerer.

All this emphasis on magical weapons suggests a connexion with the Druids, that, in other words, they were their suppliers—as Merlin supplied Arthur with Excalibur—an activity which may, indeed, have provided a source of income for them. This posits a knowledge of metallurgy and practical metal-working on their part and it seems to me extremely likely they possessed both.

It is not only agriculture and husbandry which mythology ascribes to divine founders: technology, too, comes from this source. For this reason, smith-gods are to be found in many metal-using cultures. With the Celts it was Goibniu, the Welsh Govannon, son of Don or Dana, and hence one of the *Tuatha De Danann*. In Irish poetry he is celebrated as the maker of sharp weapons. As we know from the practices of alchemy, the working of metals is closely allied with magic, the alchemists' seven metals corresponding with the seven planets which were supposed to exert their influence upon them.

We have analogies in many heroic societies; among them was that of the Zulus of South Africa. Shaka, their great king, had his spear specially wrought in a foundry, run under the auspices of witch-doctors, which lay in the forest.

Supernatural foundries in the depths of forests or mountain hideouts, are the very stuff of myth, and the small scale of operation implied is perfectly possible. Even in Roman times many foundries employed no more than two or three people. In parts of the Middle East today it is possible to see individual craftsmen working, sometimes with one assistant, sometimes alone, in their backstreet premises.

Moreover, during the manufacturing process one step in particular lends itself to quasi-magical practice. This is tempering, the crucial point at which the blade is given the surface hardness which allows it to take and hold its cutting edge. This involves heating the blade to the correct temperature, then plunging it in a liquid. Usually this is oil or water, depending on the type of surface required, but some smiths, especially those in the Middle East, preferred to use blood because it yields phosphorus.

As both Arabs and Celts are likely to have derived their knowledge of iron-working from the same source, it is probable that they also used blood. This would bring in somthing akin to sacrifice and hence involve the invocation of a deity. In a real sense, therefore, these would be magic weapons.

There is actual evidence that the Celts had two qualities of blade. Celtic swords were highly sought after, as were the Arab ones later. Certainly, those which have survived to come down to us and which would, one supposes, have belonged to the wealthier members of society, are of admirable quality. On the other hand, Polybius in his description of the Battle of Telamon speaks of blades so poor they required straighbers are certainly pregnant with mystery. There is, for example, the paradox of zero (said to have been discovered by the Brahmins) and the minus quantity; the contradictory characteristics of unity, both indivisible and divisible; or the staggering qualities of infinity. Or there is the strange behaviour of the square of three, itself a holy number to the Druids.[2] But numerology was something in which Pythagoras was himself profoundly interested.

This brings us to an even more surprising, if highly contentious point. Many of the stone circles are not circles at all, but egg-shaped ellipses, ovals wider at one end than the other. One way of producing such a shape is by means of two circles, a smaller and a greater, drawn in such a way that the smaller circle's circumference overlaps that of the greater. The two are then connected to each other by means of tangential lines. And this, according to B R Hallam, is what the Neolithic designers of the megaliths did. The objection is that this method does not produce a true ovoid; it produces one with two straight sides, whereas aerial photographs show the ellipses in question to consist of continuous curves. Professor A Thom has shown that one way of solving the problem is to base the design on calculations using the right-angled or Pythagorean triangle. The implication is that the most famous of his ideas, Pythagoras actually derived from shamanic sources.

And here one is reminded of all the legends connecting Pythagoras with various such sources, including the Druids. One of the earliest of these, and hence that nearest to his own lifetime, comes from Hecateus, for whom Pythagoras' instructor is supposed to have been a certain Abaris, who seems to have been taken for a British Druid, or at least, a shaman practising in Britain.

As an admonition to caution, one need only say that one is here in the realm of those legends which unfailingly attach themselves to the names of famous men and that Pythagoras himself hardly assisted the disentangling of fact from fantasy by omitting to leave any written account of his work behind him.[3]

There are, nonetheless, three indisputable facts: one, that most writers connect Pythagoras with a mysterious cult of shamanistic character; two, that among the descendants of what I have called 'the super-shamans', namely the Babylonic priests, the Brahmins and the Magi,

[2] Nine is the number into which, during mathematical operations, other numbers most often tend to resolve themselves. For example, take any three (or more) digits (say 345). Reverse their order (543). Take the lesser from the greater (543-345=198). Add the digits together (1+9+8=18). Add them together again (1+8=9).

[3] Even his association with the Euclidean Proposition, which has made him so hated by generations of schoolchildren, is apocryphal, for all that he was said to have sacrificed a hecatomb (a thousand oxen) in honour of the discovery that the square on the hypotenuse equalled the sum of the squares on the other two sides.

were outstanding mathematicians, like Pythagoras himself; three, that they held a number of beliefs, of which transmigration was one, in common. It could conceivably be argued that, in these circumstances, his failure to commit his work and observations to writing was precisely because those with whom he had been in contact had sworn him to secrecy. As we know, the Druids were unshakable in their determination not to put their doctrines into writing and so, for centuries, were the Brahmins.[4]

[4] The fact that writers are so confused as to who his instructor was, that Pythagoras is variously associated with Druids, Brahmins and the Babylonians (or, as the text says, Assyrians), shows how similar all three must have appeared to the Greek mind.

But who were the original invokers of the *Tuatha De Danann*? The generally accepted belief is that the pre-Celtic inhabitants of the British Isles were a people who had migrated from North Africa by way of the Atlantic seaboard of Europe, marking their progress by the building of the megaliths. For this, the myths themselves offer two interesting pieces of supportive evidence.

The first is the name of one of the central *Tuatha* deities, Lugh the Many Skilled. The Welsh form of his name, Lleu, means "lion" and that it was understood to mean this elsewhere is indicated by the name of the large French city Lyon, which derives from Lugdunum, "the fortress of Lugh". The use of "Y" to stand for the vowel-sound we today represent by "I" was no less common in Old French than in Old English, so that Lyon actually does mean "Lion". Lions are hardly creatures that the Indo-Europeans would have come into contact with and they would not, therefore, have taken one as a totem. On the other hand, they would certainly have been familiar enough to a people from North Africa.

The second piece of evidence is Diana/Artemis herself who, as we have already observed, undoubtedly had connexions with that general area. The Temple of Diana (actually, Artemis) at Ephesus was one of the Seven Wonders of the Ancient World and was still very much in use at the time of St. Paul.

But whether or not Dana/Ana is actually Diana, the fact remains that it is her offspring which figure most frequently and prominently in the myths. There are, to be sure, references in both those of Ireland and those of Wales which could be interpreted as hinting at the gods of the earlier phylum. In two of the Welsh stories, *Branwen Daughter of Llyr* and *How Culhwch Won Olwen* we have a Glinyeu ap Taran mentioned. There is also Beli the Great, son of Mynogan and Beli Adver, names certainly cognate with Belenos. Ross discusses a giant in the story of *The Lady of the Fountain* who, because of the power over animals he possesses, may be Cernunnos. Among the Irish stories, she suggests that he may lie concealed under the name of Conall Cernach in *The Driving-Off of Fraich's Cattle*. Here he displays power over serpents. This is congruous with the representation of Cernunnos on the Gundestrup Cauldron where he grasps a ram-headed serpent by the neck, but it also leads one to wonder whether St. Patrick's proverbial power over snakes may not, in fact, have had a pagan origin.

All these identifications have to be tentative, however, and the roles played in the stories are very subsidiary; sometimes they feature only as names in long lists. This is in contrast with the *Tuatha* deities: usually clearly labelled and playing key-roles. One must, naturally, take into account the confused state in which we have received the myths, though it would be very strange if the relegation of a group of important deities had been brought about by such inadvertence alone.

But we have, in addition, the evidence of the Christian festivals which were intended to supplant the earlier, pagan ones. Of these, two—the Feasts of Brigid and Lugh—both commemorate gods of the *Tuatha*, while almost all the myths surrounding Samain are associated with the same phylum of deities. The only exceptions are Beltain, the festival of Belenos, and the various, now purely local festivals traceable back to Cernunnos or, say, Epona, with the Padstow "Hobby-Horse" providing a good example. No surviving occasion can be traced to Esus, Teutatis or Taranis.

What was it about the life-style of the existing populations that so impressed the newly arrived Celts that they felt compelled to take over their gods? Undoubtedly it was the megaliths of which these aboriginals had been the builders, though even for them this had taken place in a past so remote that their constructors had ceased to be regarded as humans and had become gods.

Stories of the supernatural origins of the standing-stone are to be found wherever they occur. In the Channel Islands, particularly rich in them, the patois word, "*pouquelayé*", means "puck or fairy" and not only does island folklore ascribe their building to these supernatural creatures (who are by no means to be conceived of as the tiny beings of later tradition), it also regards the stones as their dwelling-place which mortals disturb at their peril. In Brittany, down to late times, the stones were the centres of cults, probably pre-Celtic in origin.

We know, too, that the Celts were fascinated by them, burying their dead in megalithic tombs, absorbing them into their mythology as the *sidhs* and depositing round them what, in Piggott's words "looks like more than picnic debris". (There are also, incidentally, indications that some of the shafts and enclosures associated wih Druidism in Britain pre-date those of the Continent, offering support for Caesar's statement that Britain was the birthplace of the order.)

Among the megaliths were to be found, of course, the great stone circles, including the most astonishing of all—Stonehenge. From the work of Professor Gerald Hawkins and others it is now recognized that this is an astronomical computer, using a base of nineteen years (actually, 19+19+18=56) to bring solar and lunar years into syncronization. From the Coligny calendar we also know this to have been the system employed by the Druids. It is, therefore, likely that they used Stonehenge (which would be consistent, anyway, with archaeological data from other henges where signs of Celtic use have been found) and they could only have learnt its complex operation under the tutelage of the existing priesthood.

We can now assert confidently that these Stone-Age people were on Posidonius, tells that the Celts believe that when they died "after a definite number of years they live a second life when the soul passes to another body". In other words, there is between one life and another a period of fallowness, analogous to winter.

The similarity of the uterus to a cauldron is hardly one which could have escaped Celtic notice, if only because a woman in the final stages of pregnancy looks very much as if she had a bowl inside her. There are, to be sure, the numerous rustic jokes on the subject to be found almost everywhere in which an expectant woman is described as carrying a cooking pot, pitcher or something similar under her skirts.

One might hazard, therefore, that the Druidic doctrine of transmigration could be restated somewhat along these lines:

> Plants grow, flower and fruit through the summer. But *sidh*-god of winter seizes the magic bowl of the sun which gives them life and takes it to his castle, whereupon everything withers and dies. However, in death the plant drops its seeds upon the earth. Here it would remain, a dead thing were it not for the sun-god's courage. While hunting he is led by the magic boar (note the beneficent, totemic animal) to the winter-god's castle, which he bravely enters and where aided by his great mother, he repossesses the golden bowl, though not without many perilous adventures. When it returns to its proper place in the sky, the seed is quickened into life and the plant lives again.
>
> It is the same with men. As their winter comes and with it, death, their seed also falls, to remain in the Underworld until it is, under some guise, devoured by a woman to enter the cauldron of resurrection in her belly.

As the explanation of birth, these ideas would obviously have been modified as the male role came to be understood. (As we know, at this stage the man sees his own and not the woman's, function as the all-important one. His is the seed; she the mere soil into which it is implanted. From this stems patrilinear descent and with it the dominance of the male.) However, the idea would no doubt have persisted in myth where it would be seen as an example of "miraculous-birth" imbuing the child involved with supernatural qualities.

But could we, perhaps, have here the rudiments of an answer to another problem; the reason for the Celtic practiçe of severing heads? The custom is well-attested not only in the classical descriptions of the Celts, but also archaeologically and in myth down to late times. Herodotus describes their being set up on high staves, "so that the head sticks up far above the house, often above the chimney". He was told that it served thereby as "guardian of the whole house".

Archaeology has unearthed skulls in votive deposits, niches for them in buildings, stone and wooden representations of heads (all with a most uncanny look of death about them), as well as sculptured masonry, like the pillar at Entremont, Bouches du Rhône, whose principal sculpture was disembodied heads. Professor Ross has gone so far as to suggest that the adornment of houses and other buildings with representations of the human head, as for example in gargoyles or overarches, is a survival of the practice.

It occurs in Scottish, Irish and Welsh myth—in the story of *Gereint and Enid*, for example, Gereint is about to behead an enemy but has his handed stayed. Among the numerous references in the Arthurian legend is that in Chrêtien de Troyes's version to *The Maiden of the Mule*, who demands from Lancelot the head of a recently slain enemy. When he gives it to her she evinces the greatest gratitude, promising to aid him whenever he is in need.

In folk custom there are the numerous curative wells, some of which, like *Tobar na Ceann* in the Outer Hebrides, actually have the word "head" in their names, while others have saints' names.

In former days many of these had a skull, said to be that of the saint, standing by them for use as a drinking vessel. This connects with references in both Herodotus and Livy to skulls used as goblets.

Herodotus tells us that the cranium was sawn off above the eyebrows, the interior cleaned and the exterior covered in calf-leather, if the owner were poor, or lined in gold if he were rich. Livy cites the example of the chief of the Boii, who, after capturing the Roman consul Postumius, had his skull gold-mounted and used it as a cup.

The examples of skulls dropped into wells and particularly their use for drinking water from curative wells, by associating them, in one way or another, with health or its restoration, also, of course, link them with the maintenance of life itself. But, like the seed head of a plant, standing at the plant's top, so the head and the skull tops the man. It is his "seed-head", the place where the potential for life resides. In the shamanic spirit flights, in the legends surrounding such ecstasy-cults as that of the Pythian Apollo, as well as in some found in Tibet and China, even in contemporary reports of so-called "out-of-the-body" experiences the spirit is said to leave and enter the body via the head.

By taking possession of an enemy's head, therefore, one can ensure that he is not reborn to seek revenge, but at the same time, because of its potential for life, it also has health-giving properties of its own.

There is still, however, one aspect of the teaching of transmigration which requires examination. This is the all important Druidic notion of equilibrium, another idea found in early Brahminism and even in

8
Druidic festivals still observed today. The 'Obby 'Oss festival in Cornwall in which the horse features prominently.

9
The festival dedicated to 'The Stag Men' in Staffordshire, a survival of the Druidic stag deity Cernunnos.

10
The Guy Fawkes bonfires are a direct descendant of the Druidic Samain, also surviving in the Scottish burning of the Straw Man.

11
Winston Churchill installed in the Albion Lodge of the Ancient Order of Druids on 15th August 1908.

12
The festival of the Bards of Kernow in Cornwall, in which men and women sustain the Druidic tradition of Bardic poetry.

magical form in which he must stand, as he performs the crowning act, that of conjuration.

Such ceremonials can be traced back in Europe as far as the 15th Century when, indeed, they enjoyed something of a scandalous vogue among the wealthy. In fact, what they demonstrate is a hodge-podge of borrowings from many sources. In the spells dog-Latin is mixed freely with dog-Hebrew and even, according to at least one writer, Basque. In the various signs and hieroglyphs as shown in the book's illustrations one can see the influences of Persian and possibly, as is claimed of them, Babylonic. Yet there is, all said and done, a strangely familiar ring about it all. One thinks of the almost obsessive Brahminic preoccupation with ritual detail so that a single stone of an altar misplaced by a hair's breadth can nullify the whole proceedings. But even more one can detect clear signs of the Druids. Pliny tells us that the British Druids invested their magic with such ceremony, "that it almost seems as though it was they who had imparted the cult to the Persians".

The nine days stipulated as the period of fasting recalls that it is the square of three, the sacred number of the Druids, as the wand of hazel-wood, one of the materials they most favoured, recalls that they, too, used such a one. Mercury is the Roman equivalent of Lugh who is himself a magician and is actually connected with the hazel in some contexts. The pentacle also has the nickname of the "Druid's foot" and occurs in Celtic myth down to the 15th Century when, in the story of Gawain and the Green Knight, it forms the pattern on the hero's shield.

As so much of Celtic belief has survived, can it be that its masters and ideologues have also survived in some form?

Kendrick asserts that the very name "Druid", like the possessors of it, perished in AD 62 on the fires they had lit for their own sacrificial victims and did not reappear until the 18th Century revival. He acknowledges, however, that the stone found in Man with the word translated as "Druid" upon it dates only from the 5th or 6th Century. He also refers to the use of the word in the Irish version of the *Historia Brittonum* where the magicians of Vortigern are so described, though he points out that this is a late rendering and the original term was "magicians".

The view of a total eclipse of Druidism looks very much less tenable now than when Kendrick was writing in the nineteen-twenties, for all that we must acknowledge the latterday Druids are much changed, emasculated we might fairly say. The course Vortigern's magicians advocated, that of sacrificing a child and burying its body in the foundations of his fortress to ensure its impregnability is undoubtedly Druidic. A body found during excavations at Aulnay-aux-Planches in France is probably that of a sacrificed infant. There is a child's grave at Wood Henge, and I am indebted to Geoffrey Ashe for pointing out another example at Silbury. The concept even managed to penetrate Christianity apparently, for when St Columba was building his first church on the Scottish Island of Iona one of his associates volunteered to be buried alive to make sure the edifice stood.

There is also the mystery of the Saxon massacre of the British chiefs by Hengist. Of this there are a number of variants. One, occurring in a poem by an unknown early Welsh poet, locates the event in a circle of stone, possibly Stonehenge, though of course there were other such circles. Here a festival is taking place which includes the free flow of wine and mead. From other sources it is possible to conclude that it took place early in May which would make it correspond with the feast of Beltain. As we know Stonehenge to be associated with solar observation and Belenos to be ruling god of the sun, celebrations there on the day of his festival are extremely probable. We have in addition the evidence of Hecateus mentioned in Chapter Eleven that there was a temple, dedicated to Apollo, in an island plainly identifiable as Britain.

It was, furthermore, a common tactic for the Saxons to swoop on their enemies during religious festivals. It is probable, too, that Vortigern, aging and traditionalist in outlook, not only sought Druidic advice, but also kept up the important festivals.

This would bring Druidism down to the 5th Century, but we know also that the early Celtic saints were exercised by the problem of ridding society of the last tenacious traces of paganism. "Christ is my Druid," proclaims St Columba, a cry hardly likely to have evoked much response if the order had been forgotten. We know, as in the case of the Channel Island saint, Sampson, that it was necessary to go to the lengths of bribing children to keep them from attending pagan festivals. A 10th Century law of King Edgar forbade "well-worshippings, necromancies and divinations; enchantments and man-worshippings, and all other vain practices which are carried out with various spells"—a list of observances possessing an unmistakably Druidic character. The prohibition on well-worshipping, at least, seems to have been peculiarly ineffective, since, under the auspices of the church it still continues in several places.

And what is to be made of the Merlin-Arthur duality? For all that he was a latecomer to the stories and whoever his prototype may have been he certainly seems to carry with him impeccable Druidic credentials. This is not a matter of chance or because magicians, however they may title themselves, are still magicians and very much alike. Merlin, throughout, occupies a position in relation to Arthur which largely parallels that of the great Druids like Cathbadh or Mac Roth in the Irish stories. He plays the traditional role of chooser of the king, making his choice manifest through a miraculous sign; he changes shape and imparts the gift of doing so to others, as in the case of Uther Pendragon's seduction of Ygraine; he prophesies; he provides magical weapons; the spirits he invokes come up from beneath the waters; he is under a *geas* which leads to his own humiliating destruction.

The list of parallels could well be amplified and their existence becomes the more astonishing when one considers that Geoffrey, in whose work Merlin first appears, was writing at least a thousand years after the fall of Anglesey had supposedly brought Druidism to its end. One cannot escape the impression that the authors or the sources from whom they had borrowed knew very well what Druidic magic was and that their readers can scarcely have been ignorant of it either. Indeed, such a conclusion seems to me the only strictly logical one, since if the people of Man were talking of herb-doctors like the 19th Century Teare Bellawhane as a "successor of the Druids", how much more must those living in the 12th Century have thought in such terms.

In so far as the word "Druid" could be said to have disappeared it was, surely, because of the fundamental changes the language was undergoing. There was the spread of Saxon influence while the tongue of the literate élite became Latin. This was followed by the arrival of the Normans and the spread of French. What had actually been lost, though only to the world of scholarship, was the Celtic language. Their separation from it is shown by the frequent mistakes made in translation, mistakes which, incidentally, have sometimes survived to our times.

One can safely assume that this was why the word "Druid" had become incomprehensible and had been replaced by another, familiar one.

But, in any case, words are lost surprisingly easily. The pages of the Oxford Dictionary are littered with those which are followed by the rubric "obs." for "obsolete". One example, though from a possible myriad, suffices. As late as the eighteen-eighties, the word "Kickshaw" meaning literally an elegant or fancy dish, but extended to figurative connotations, was in common usage, employed among others by Dickens. Who now knows it, let alone uses, it?

Nor is the statement that the word "Druid" disappeared strictly true. There is evidence that in at least three Celtic tongues it continued in use. In Manx Celtic, the word "Druaight" plainly has a connexion and "Droat", actually meaning "Druid" remained in use until the language itself disappeared. In Ireland as we have seen, it was still current in the 9th Century. In the early 18th Century, a Protestant minister in Skye wrote his *Description of the Western Islands of Scotland.* He uses the word "Druid" for the man who conducted a clan ceremony—that of giving the chieftain's son his arms; a precisely similar ritual was carried out by the Druids of pagan times. It is obvious from his use of the word that the author was following the practice of the people he is describing.

There are good reasons for believing that in Wales the word "bard" for a long time connoted "Druid" (or, of course, magician), as in Scotland for an equal period the word "Druid" may well have been applied to those who in many ways were carrying out bardic functions.

Roman influence did not extend to Scotland so that there was no reason why men should not continue to call themselves Druids there. In Wales, matters stood differently, for Druidism was under Roman proscription. By taking up their harps and calling themselves "bards" they were probably able to circumvent the letter of the occupiers' law. Such subterfuges are well known to all those who have suffered enemy occupation, as I can personally testify. Certainly, if Myrddin is the proto-Merlin, he was officially a bard, and though he prophesied he concealed his gift under an appearance of madness.

Taken all in all, one surely has to concede that one is confronted by something more than sheer chance survivals of Druidism, cases comparable, say, with that of the court mourning ordered at the death of Queen Anne which somehow managed to live on to become the wig and gown still worn by English judges and barristers. Unaided chance can hardly have been responsible in this case, for to have come down to us, the customs and practices described here had to outlive not only Christianization, but both Roman and Saxon invasions before that, a period covering in all some six centuries. And how little, by comparison, the ideas of either have taken root!

The Romans, whose declared purpose was to destroy Celtic religion through its ministers, the Druids, had so far to admit failure as to allow the gods of their subject peoples to stand side by side with their own. The early Christian missionaries make it clear that Celtic paganism was very much alive at the time of their arrival from about 600 AD. They refer, specifically, to Druids.

One can speculate as to the course of events without risking too great a divergence from the facts. Roman occupation undoubtedly drove the Druids underground. I pointed out in Chapter Twelve that they had probably already lost much of their political power and possibly a measure of their religious dominance, too. Since, however, the Romans were not replacing Celtic religion by any dynamically new system, it is unlikely that there was any large scale abandonment. On the contrary, persecution would probably have touched the Druids with a heroic glamour in most people's eyes. But they were besides and before all else magicians, and the mark of their craft is that it is concerned primarily with specific and individual problems such as were beyond the skill and beneath the dignity of priests ministering to a religion in the true sense. (Though we know, of course, that the later Christian fathers took over functions like teaching and care of the sick.) One would expect, therefore, that those particular problems would seek them out. But, there was, anyway, for the fugitive Druids the question of gaining a livelihood. Fees for their services, in money or kind, would be one means of survival.

The departure of the Romans even after three hundred years of their presence, would have made possible a return to that "true Celticism" for which, no doubt, many had romantically yearned. In this situation, Druidism might well have enjoyed something of a temporary resurgence. If this did not include the repossession of political power in the sense they had once enjoyed it, their purely practical knowledge as physicians, astronomers, calendarists, possibly as expert metal-workers, even as natural philosophers would have come into their own once more. No doubt, too, their magical advice was taken by rulers on more than the single occasion when Vortigern is thought to have followed it.

The next threat was, of course, the coming of Christianity, but we must be clear about its effects on Celtic paganism. The missionaries were few in number and their successes can only have been limited. Even in the areas where these were greatest, the changes brought about would have been less sweeping than they are usually imagined to have been.

Whenever one examines at close quarters the lives of ordinary men and women through the great epochs of history—the Reformation, the Renaissance, the French Revolution—one is always struck by two things. One is their apparent indifference to what is going on around them or, when directly affected, their capacity for adapting. The other, even more striking one, is the human ability to modify the most radical new ideas, so that even the profoundest of changes quickly acquires the patina of things familiar. To say that the traces of old habits and ways of thinking survive from one regime to its successor is totally to understate the process: more often it is the new ideas themselves which seem to become mere traces. Perhaps the innate conservatism of the human baulks at too great an upheaval threatening to deprive it of the consolation of the known and familiar.

So when Christianity replaced the Old Religion, the gods simply took on fresh names, those of saints, and in this guise were worshipped at festivals which had gone on for centuries perhaps even before Celtic times. Such practices as human sacrifice had been banned by the Romans; it had no doubt gone on in secret, but was probably declining anyway. And when it came to the things that really mattered like curing an outbreak of boils or a lame cow or discovering what the future might hold, the ordinary man and his wife knew exactly where to apply.

It may be going too far to suggest that a writer as late as Malory knew of and used as his prototype for Merlin surviving magical practitioners, though, since they were still to be found centuries later, they must have existed and in greater profusion in his day. It is certainly in Malory that Merlin achieves his fullest development, not only as a rounded character, but as a magician in an overtly Druidic sense.

Malory is himself a mystery, however. There are no fewer than four candidates for the authorship of *The Morte d'Arthur:* A Welshman; a Huntingdonshire country gentleman; a wilder Thomas Malory known to have lived at Newbold Revel in Warwickshire, and a man of the same name from Ripon, Yorkshire. What we know, from his own testimony, is that at the time of writing he was in prison for an unspecified act of "turbulency against the king". This sounds as if he might have played a minor rôle in some revolt (if it had been a major role his punishment would have been more serious than imprisonment), but, on the other hand, the Newbold Revel Thomas Malory is known to have practised burglary, abduction and rape and been brought to trial for these acts which, naturally, makes him the favoured candidate of many scholars. The difficulty here is a psychological one: how does one reconcile the vicious criminal with the *Morte d'Arthur* itself, which certainly contains more than its measure of violence, but mixes it with chivalric gallantry, compassion and piety?

It is tempting to identify him with the Welshman, and the equation has certainly been made. Unfortunately, however, he specifically describes himelf as one "of us Englysshemen", an obstacle which no amount of ingenious argument has wholly been able to overcome.

In one of the most recent books on the subject, *The Ill-Framed Knight* the Professor of English at Berkeley University, William Matthews, presses the claim of the Yorkshire Sir Thomas with great skill and literary elegance. The proposition is at least a beguiling one, since the *Morte d'Arthur* appeared in a period when the Wars of the Roses were first fomenting and when England was ruled by a Lancastrian monarch.

From what he tells us about himself Malory would have been in his impressionable teens when some very dramatic events were taking place in Wales. Owein Glendwr, who claimed descent from Llewellyn, last Prince of Wales, had launched a highly successful revolt against the English king, Henry IV.

One would expect sympathy for this to run most strongly in Wales, but in England, too, partisanship was considerable and national loyalty divided. Henry IV had gained the throne by usurpation from Richard II, son of the Black Prince. The basis of his claim was so insubstantial that once the throne was secured he made no real effort to justify it. Feeble, inept and treacherous as Richard had often shown himelf to be, he nevertheless commanded an appreciable and loyal following. This was not easily to be silenced: a session of the House of Lords shortly after Henry's accession broke up in disorder as peers partial to one contender or the other slung gauntlets across the chamber, and was saved from degenerating into an open brawl only by the king's personal intercession.

Glendwr was among Richard's most devoted supporters. He had actually been taken prisoner with him by Henry's forces and released only on the king's surety. He had retired to his Welsh estates, to be mulcted of property in England by members of Henry's party, an act which provided his immediate incitement to revolt.

It was rapidly to acquire a nationalist complexion, but that it had been an attempt to depose Henry is shown by the challenge thrown out by the insurgents, in accordance with the laws of chivalry, before one of the key battles. This declared Henry to be not only a usurper, but a "false and perjured knight"—echoes of the Round Table. At the end of its list of charges it closed: "For these reasons we do mortally defy thee and thy accomplices and adherents, as traitors, and subverters of the commonwealth and kingdom, and invaders, oppressors and usurpers of the rights of the true and direct heir of England and France; and we intend to prove it this day by force of arms with the aid of Almighty God". The battle ended, of course, in Glendwr's defeat, though not his extinction, for he was to continue his fight, sporadically, into the reign of Henry V. He is believed to have died about the time of the Battle of Agincourt, that is to say in 1415, at the home of his daughter in Herefordshire.

We have no direct evidence that Malory belonged to Henry's opponents save only that if he did not it is very strange that he should have chosen to write a book about a great Celtic heroic age and a running struggle against an ambitious conqueror. Furthermore, the circumstances in which Arthur lost his throne and ultimately his life very closely parallel those in which Richard lost his. Arthur was abroad fighting when Mordred seized the kingship; Richard was in Ireland attempting to quell a revolt when Henry seized his.

But the name of Owein Glendwr is important for another and most intriguing reason. Born at Merioneth in 1349, he was indeed the great grandson of Llewellyn, but had been educated in London at one of the Inns of Court. He had been called to the English Bar, but quickly came to the notice of the king and was made an esquire in his court. A brilliant figure in courtly life, he had married Margaret, the daughter of Sir David Hanmer, a King's Bench judge and at the age of thirty-eight was knighted.

But he was, as we also know, closely associated with magical practice. One may look with suspicion on theories like those of the late Margaret Murray which have a whole succession of English kings involved in witch-craft, fertility cults and even of complicity in their own ritual sacrifice (William Rufus, is of course, supposed to be the classical instance). This does not alter the fact that in this particular case, Owein was probably practising his craft as early as his London days and that his patrons included Richard II.

Certainly, in the time of his rebellion the English inability to bring about his final defeat was freely ascribed by both friend and foe to his occult skill. He was known to spend large sums on "bards" and, through them, claimed to be the realization of the prophecies of Merlin who had forecast that he was to destroy Henry "the moldwarp accursed of God's own wrath".

In one battle, the English troops claimed that they had been unsuccessful because their enemy had summoned up a heavy rainstorm, making the scaling of the mountains to reach his hideouts impossible. On several occasions they were stopped in their advance by spell-casters bawling their imprecations down at them, practices similar to those mentioned by both Strabo and Tacitus in connexion with the Druids.

What we see in Owein, therefore, is the continuation of a number of Druidic traditions. His claim to descent from Llewellyn is traced in the maternal line, for example, but more significant is the association of magician and warrior-chief, though now in merged form, which he obviously exemplifies. As the early Irish heroes have their Druids, Arthur his Merlin, so he partly fulfils the magical role himself. Plainly, as leader of the Welsh national revival, the main reason for his involvement in these practices was because it was what would have been expected of him. Nor could he have practised any other form of magic than that of his Celtic forebears, the Druids. Furthermore, if my equation of the later Welsh bards with some sort of survival of Druidism is correct, then we can see he was surrounding himself with those who were probably at least in part magicians.

Owein Glendwr has a second claim upon us: he is regarded as spiritual ancestor by many of the witchcraft cults now practising in Britain. To take the claims of these groups at face value would, of course, put far too great a strain on credulity. As Frank Smyth, author of a book on contemporary witchcraft points out, their milieu is suburbia, their membership drawn largely from the lower middle class whose roots are urban. Even in the case of the Manx witch covens, those running or patronising them are mostly newcomers to the island. They are besides a recent phenomenon. Frank Smyth says it is difficult to trace their beginnings back earlier than 1949.

This is a slight exaggeration. Modern magic and witchcraft in Britain have two immediate progenitors: Aleister Crowley, who rejoiced in the title of "The Beast 666" from the Apocalypse and Gerald Gardner, so-called "King of the British Witches". Crowley, born in 1875 and who died in 1947, was strictly speaking more black magician than witch, though his influence was considerable. His Order of the Golden Dawn, mentioned in Chapter One, evolved with a type of latterday Satanist possession-cult, practising its rites at a cult centre in Sicily though also associated with Stonehenge. Its activities were of a sufficiently erotic nature to attract that press publicity their founder's vanity craved, but in substance seemed to have comprised only a mishmash of quirky notions gathered from a plethora of unrelated sources.

Gardner, who died in 1964 at the age of 80, was a later arrival on the scene and had himself been influenced by Crowley's ideas. He was the author of three books on witchcraft which purported to give details of beliefs, practices and rites derived from Medieval sources, the period when witchcraft was at its height. In fact, the book is little more than a regurgitation of other, readily available contemporary works.

At his death his vacant throne fell to Alex Sanders, who claims descent in the maternal line from none other than Owein Glendwr himself.

Gardner states in one of his books that he was converted to witchcraft by an old lady who lived near his own home at Christchurch in the New Forest, a venue traditionally redolent with magic. She persuaded him that it was a pre-Christian survival, truly the Old Religion. Alex Sanders says he was initiated into it by his grandmother, while a child in Wales. Although Gardner was quite capable of fabrication, there is little reason to doubt this particular statement and certainly none at all for doubting Alex Sanders.

And they give the whole matter an entirely changed aspect, since instead of being nothing but a mumbo-jumbo mugged up from cranky literature, it is now given roots of some sort in folklore. We need not be greatly surprised if pre-Christian religions ideas survived among isolated rural communities: it is no stranger than the survival of pagan myth; of pagan festivals like the Helston Furry Dance or of such other pagan practices as well-visiting, prophecy and even herb-medicine. Indeed, Professor Ross has discovered an entire community in Northumberland which venerates the "old gods" while still professing and practising Christianity. Its members claim that they are of Celtic stock, a remnant who refused to flee during the various migrations.

Witches have existed almost as far back as our knowledge of humanity extends. They were to be found among the Hittites and the Akkadians. Solomon, as we know, had recourse to one. But what witchcraft almost certainly represents is a shamanistic religion in a state of degeneration. It is then that, having lost intellectual credibility and hence its hold on the mass of its followers, it falls back on its old skill – that of mastering the elements of nature by means of rituals.

Properly speaking, therefore, there are not one but many witchcrafts. The witches of the Hittites, the Hebrews, Greeks or Romans each represented the survival of an earlier religion, and like the modern witches, their practitioners would have been perfectly accurate to call theirs the "Old Religion". In so far as it is possible to find similarities between these various strange relics these were no doubt brought about by similarities in the underlying religions themselves.

In view of its roots one would expect the witchcraft of the Celtic world or of those lands formerly inhabited by Celts to display markedly the elements of Druidism, and one is hardly disappointed. Modern witchcraft contains, beside a mother-goddess—who when actually named is called "Diana"—a horned god. Outsiders might equate him with Satan; the witches knew better.

Witchcraft has, of course, its strongly magical, ritualistic complexion. It frequently practises its rites in the open—where the spirits of nature are most accessible—and at night. The English word "witch" is itself at least partially cognate with "Druid", coming from the Middle English "wicca" or "wise". The various knives, daggers and swords with which witches surround themselves during their ceremonials can only bring to mind those of the Druids, used no doubt for sacrificial purposes and for divination. Even the traditional cauldron, still to be found in many groups, has it origins in the magical cauldrons of abundance and resurrection which figure so prominently in the myths and which may be the prototype of the Grail.

The persistence of such traces through the centuries is wholly consistent with the nature of Druidism itself and with the experiences the Celtic peoples underwent. We know, for instance, how Judaism provided a centre of coalescene for the Jewish peoples through all centuries of exile and persecution, while at the same time the former religious divisions disappeared (at least until our own times). The Celts, though not as a whole exiled, witnessed a species of national extinction and experienced subjugation to foreign invaders. They were not permitted to retain even their own form of Christianity, but had to submit to an alien and uncongenial one. It is only to be expected, in such circumstances, that they should turn back to the only thing with which they could identify as one—Druidism. The appearance so easily gained when contemplating them in retrospect, that the Druids were in the process of imposing a single pantheon overriding the myriad of purely local deities may be due less to any deliberate actions on their part, than to the consolidation of Celtic national ideology under the stresses of conquest and occupation. In other words, as with the Jews, differences, which, in the Celtic case were tribal, sank of their own accord before the greater external threat.

But Druidism was not a religion in any clearly understood sense: it was a magical cult. Thus to establish his credentials as national leader a man had also to prove his magical skill. He must, like Glendwr, be a magician himself, or else he must operate in close collaboration with one, like Arthur. This need to emulate is itself a tribute to the prestige of the Druids.

As a matter of fact, magic provides its own survival-kit. In Rome, although the punishment for practising it was as harsh as in Medieval Europe, magicians and witches were still to be found and enjoyed enough patronage to gain a living. There has never been an age, least of all our own, when the magician in whatever guise did not do a roaring trade. And the Druids were unusually powerful magicians, possessed of real and formidable knowledge, as we have seen.

Once persecution of witches began, those of Celtic lineage, who represented an abnormally high proportion of the total, could claim that this was merely the extension to them of the repression their people had so long suffered; that they were victims not so much on account of their arcane practices as their nationality. The accusation is not without substance; the non-Celtic peoples had the strongest dislike of witchcraft. In a number of cases, the reaction to it among Celtic nations themselves was comparatively muted. Where, as happened in Brittany, harsher measures were taken they were often imposed by outsiders. By contrast, in Guernsey and particularly in Jersey, only a few miles from the Breton coast, but always autonomous, things were quite different. Although innumerable witches were brought to trial in the 17th Century, torture was never used to extract confessions (though they confessed just the same!). Few were sentenced to death, some were merely fined. One was actually put on probation, and this in a largely Calvinist society.

The part played by Druidic influences in maintaining Celtic national identity, was combined with another, equally important factor. As I M Lewis has conclusively demonstrated with scores of examples, ecstasy and possession cults invariably spring into existence among deprived minorities. In Protestant societies this will often take the form of "revivalist" sects springing up among the poorest sections of the community. In the monolithic church of the Middle Ages this would have been inconceivable heresy. Instead the discontented reverted to something earlier or, at any rate, what they could recapture of it. The 19th Century French historian, Jules Michelet, was among the first to draw attention to the phenomenon. He describes how the French peasantry turned away from Christianity with the coming of feudalism and the accompanying suppression of the popular Celtic church in favour of one which united in tyranny clergy and aristocracy. It was in their distress that the peasantry, in isolated places and late at night, began reviving the Old Religion whose deities were the real masters of the earth and its fruits. And they, too, had a horned god.

The 13th and 14th Centuries which saw the great resurgence of witchcraft were also periods of dire hardship among the peasants and often of open revolt. There can scarcely have been a time when some group or other was not undergoing deprivation and when, therefore, it would not turn to the one force which offered hope, whose reputation had been passed down from father to son or, more probably, from mother to daughter, so that its framework always remained. There are certainly indications that witchcraft was being extensively practised during the time of the Industrial Revolution and the eras that led up to it. There was certainly a revival of interest in Druidism.

The circle has gone its full revolution: as we began with the Druids of the Celtic revival so we find ourselves back in their midst. Have we discovered anything which might lead us to suppose they were some sort of heirs to an Ancient Wisdom? Pursuing his search for it, by way of the sacred number seven, Geoffrey Ashe found it concentrated in a region beyond the Altaic mountains of Mongolia and Southern Siberia. This is the region of "The Great Bear"—the Seven Stars—to which all the signs ultimately point. "If the Ancient Wisdom did makes its way into the various cultures," he says, "this Altaic zone is the most promising place to look for its cradle-land."

Here among the Buryat peoples shamanism is still to be found, its practices surrounded by mystery and high magic. It is here, for example, that, so its people claim, thought can be turned into visible forms. (Geoffrey Ashe draws attention to a very early and well documented "Flying Saucer" appearance in this region in 1927. The natives, quite unsurprised by it, immediately described it as a thought-form.)

One must, naturally, remember that one is considering this region as it was perhaps four thousand years ago and even the Ancient Wisdom can hardly have stood quite still in all this time. Geographically, however, it was ideally placed to reach out in all directions: eastwards to Tibet and China; northwards to the Siberian steppe and the Arctic; westward to the zones forming the homelands of the Indo-European peoples.

There is every likelihood that it was the insights of Altaic protoshamans which first revealed astronomy and mathematics to the world. Though, almost certainly, they took the forms of astrology and numerology, they still represented the first giant stride towards the concept of an ordered universe, the Cosmos of the Greeks and their successors.

But the risk of over-estimating the extent of Druidic knowledge is as great as that of underestimating it. One has always to reconcile it with such barbarities as the taking of auspices from the death throes of a stabbed man, with the selection of the king through "the bull dream", with the decapitation of enemies and the retention of their heads, with the whole emotive and elaborate ritual of the great festivals leading up to the moment of immolation of the human victim.

It would be absurd to deny that the Druids possessed real and valuable practical knowledge and complemented it, no doubt, with intelligence and native shrewdness, but it was also adulterated with much that was no more than vapid ritual and gibberish, accepted quite uncritically. The fact that they could be credited with actual knowledge and skill in some fields would no doubt have given them credibility in others. Their ability to predict astronomical events, for instance, their skill as hypnotists, as mathematicians, as herb-doctors, perhaps as water-diviners, would have tended to predispose not only those of their own times, but also those who came later, to accept their claims to prophecy or to the casting of effective spells.

This is hardly what one expects of heirs to the Ancient Wisdom, however. But then, what of the Ancient Wisdom? Perhaps, even when looking at things from an evolutionist point of view there is something of which account needs to be taken. The physical law that for every action there is a reaction, equal but opposite, must apply here too. By adopting the upright posture the primates freed their forepaws to be developed into tool- and weapon-holders. We can justly say, therefore, that this represented "an improved adaptation" in the classical Darwinian pattern. On the other hand it brought with it adversities previously unknown. In pregnancy, women had now to bear the weight of the developing embryo dangling vertically in their wombs, where, hitherto, it had lain comfortably slung beneath them. There came also a whole train of diseases of which haemorrhoids provide an apt if nasty illustration.

But in mental and cultural evolution there must have been similar losses. It is probably true that the invention of writing led to the deterioration of the memory, as the invention of printing led to fewer people learning the art of calligraphy and so to the decline of handwriting.

The gift of telepathic communication might afford an example of loss at an earlier stage. There is an abundance of examples of "primitive" peoples, such as the Australian aborigines, who retain the gift.

Many cultures make a clear distinction between ordinary dreams and visions, indicating that they place each in a separate category. This can hardly have been mere caprice, so that the distinction, surely, is this: that the vision provided some kind of revelation. Through its medium some great inductive leap was made. Almost certainly many of the numerous cases in which deities are said to be responsible for bringing this or that gift to humanity can, in the final analysis, be traced to a vision in which the deity made his appearance. In the past, the vision was trusted so implicitly that none hesitated to act upon it. Indeed, as Hadfield says, it was often regarded as more "real" than waking life. This made the visionary himself a respected member of the community, even one set above his fellows.

There is a third instance. Earlier I discussed the shamanistic practice of "spirit-flight" or ecstasy. It was probably employed by the Druids. Of course, one can easily dismiss all such phenomena as mere superstitious delusion, but this is to ignore something very similar to "spirit-flight" known to paranormal research workers. It is the so-called "astral projection" or "out-of-the-body" experience.

In two, now very well-known books, Sylvan Muldoon and Hereward Carrington have described the case-histories of scores of instances of "out-of-the-body" experiences drawn from all over the world and from something approaching a century in time. More are to be found in other works. Typically, the subject finds himself (as he believes) separated from his bodily self, able, indeed, to observe it as discrete entity still lying in bed, for example. In some cases, the physical bodies appear to be dead and have even been declared so by physicians. The subject has watched them as they struggled with resuscitation techniques and, after returning to his body, has even been able to describe in detail their actions and their conversations during the period he appeared to be dead.

In its liberated state, the spirit is often able to travel great distances and numerous instances of such journeys are recorded. In one, the subject (the Professor of English at an American university) visited the home of friends in Los Angeles while "physically" in hospital in New York.

These cases all show a remarkable similarity to the shaman's "spirit flight" in which his body remains behind "a mere husk". Stranger still, in two classical instances, those of the Dionysian and Apollonian cults, both of which involved ecstasy, the god is said to enter the subject by way of the head or the nape of the neck, a detail which also finds support among the Haitian and other Voodoo-cults. Exactly this detail is given by many of those who have had "out-of-the-body" experiences; the "spirit" is said to have left and re-entered the body through the sagittal suture in the crown of the head.

Taking the various instances given over these last few pages together, all activities associated with religious practice of "primitive" peoples, it is plain that if the existence of the phenomena described can be accepted as established they must have possessed very great mastery of certain types of mental process which we should call "paranormal".

To us, if we tried to explain them it would be as manifestations of the unconscious mind. Yet, for all that it is our own discovery, we are strangely suspicious of the unconscious. Perhaps Freud has succeeded in making it appear as some sort of internal monster, controlled only at great cost and no little risk.

But had the same kind of extreme caution and suspicion been shared by other generations, much would have been lost to us.

Let us take hypnotism, a technique practised by the shamans and, no doubt, by the Druids, and one which, in its manifestations, has a remarkably "magical" appearance. It was discarded, we know, for centuries as pure hocus-pocus connected with such heresies as witchcraft, and it was more or less by chance that it was revived in Paris as Franz Mesmer's "animal magnetism". Mesmer was a charlatan within the most precise definition of the term, reason enough to dismiss him and all his works without for a moment degrading science by a serious examination of it.

Fortunately, there were sufficient open-minded men at the Salpetriere to avoid just this trap. They proved it to be reproducible and so finally convinced even the most sceptical, though not without experiencing difficulty and mockery. Things could very easily have been otherwise: a touch more scepticism and the whole thing would have been dismissed or consigned to the class of not-quite-respectable paranormal phenomena. For the fact is that hypnotism only works in the degree in which the person undergoing it believes it to do so. If he lies on the hypnotist's couch convinced nothing is going to happen, it will not happen.

One cannot avoid the feeling that had Mesmer appeared on the scene a little later than he did, there might well have been no Charcot or Braid ready to concede that perhaps, perhaps there was something here which deserved to be seriously considered. At the very best, scientists would still be arguing as to whether the phenomena had been established.

Taking all things into consideration, one might conclude that what had been lost was less an Ancient Wisdom, than what we might call "an Ancient Skill", an ability to harness the forces of the mind. Of this we have some inkling in the great Yogi and Fakirs of Hinduism whose amazing abilities are only now and very tentatively at that, being taken seriously.

Can we attribute such skills to the Druids? The parallels with the Hindu Brahmins are so astonishing and so numerous that it seems not unlikely that at least in rudimentary form they did. Like so much else the phenomena connected with trance states have hardly begun to be investigated. There are, for example, the well-attested instances where, in this condition, body weight has been significantly altered. Under hypnosis, the subject having been told his strength has increased, will lift with ease a weight he could not so much as move in a normal state. Since we have strong evidence for supposing the Druids to have interested themselves in trance-states, it is scarcely conceivable they did not experiment along these lines. There is no doubt either that the Greek preoccupation with philosophy largely took the form of a desire to discover ways in which mind could conquer matter and such demonstrations of an apparent capability in this direction would help to account for the impression the Druids, with the Brahmins and Magi and, possibly, the Babylonic priests, produced on observers like Aristotle, Aristeas or Pythagoras.

It would also account for the later denunication of Druidism and the "magical" skills of its practitioners by the Church, which would have taken them to be derived from "the Powers of Darkness".

Select Bibliography

Anwyl, E, *Celtic Religion in pre-Christian Times*, London, 1906.
Ashe, Geoffrey, *The Ancient Wisdom*, London, 1977.
Bromwick, R, *Trioedd Ynys Prydein: The Welsh Triads*, Cardiff, 1961.
Cagnat, R, *Sacred Spring of Alesia*, quoted as note in Ant. Journal, II, 147, London, 1922.
Campbell, J G, *Superstitions of the Highlands and Islands of Scotland,* Glasgow, 1900.
Campbell, J G, *Witchcraft and Second Sight in the Highlands and Islands of Scotland*, Glasgow, 1902.
Carney, J (ed.), *Early Irish Poetry*, Cork, 1965.
Chadwick, Nora, *The Celts*, Harmondsworth, 1970.
Danielou, Alain, *Hindu Polytheism*, London, 1964.
Davidson, H R E, *Pagan Scandinavia*, London, 1967.
Dillon, M, and Chadwick, N, *The Celtic Realms*, London, 1967, 1972.
Dillon, M, *Early Irish Literature*, Chicago, 1948.
Dillon, M, *Irish Sagas*, Cork, 1970.
Dillon, M, *Serglige con Culainn*, Dublin, 1953.
Dillon, M, *Tain Bo Fraich* (The Driving-Off of Fraich's Cattle), Dublin, 1933.

Dunn, J, *Tain Bo Cualnge* (The Cattle Raid of Cooley), Dublin, 1914.
Dumezil, G, *Les Dieux des Indo-Europeens*, Paris, 1952.
Dumezil, G, *Mithra-Varuna,* Paris, 1940.
Duval, P-M, *Les Dieux de la Gaule,* Paris, 1957.
Duval, P-M, *Teutates, Esus, Taranis,* Etudes Celtiques 8; 1958–9, 41–58.
Eliade, M, *Images et Symboles,* Paris, 1961.
Eliade, M, *Le Chamanisme et les Techniques Archaiques de l'Extase,* Paris, 1964.
Evans-Pritchard, E E, *Theories of Primitive Religion,* Oxford, 1965.
Evans-Wentz, W Y, *The Tibetan Book of the Great Liberation,* Oxford, 1954.
Filip, J, *Celtic Civilisation and its Heritage* (trs), 1962.
Graves, Robert, *The White Goddess*, London, 1975.
Gwynn E, *The Metrical Dindshenchas,* RIA Todd Lecture Series, IX, pt. 2, 1906; X, 1913; XI, pt IV, 1924; VII, 1900, Dublin.
Hadingham, Evan, *Circles and Standing Stones,* London, 1975.
Hamel, A G van, *Aspects of Celtic Mythology*, Rhys Lecture, Proceedings of the British Academy, XX; 207–42, 1934.
Harrison, Michael, *The Roots of Witchcraft*, London, 1972.
Hawkins, G S, *Stonehenge Decoded*, London, 1966.
Jackson, K H, *The Oldest Irish Tradition*, Cambridge, 1964.
James, E D (ed.), *The Cult of the Mother-Goddess*, London, 1959.
Kendrick, T D, *The Druids: A Study of Celtic Prehistory*, London, 1966; first ed. 1927.
Killip, Margaret, *Folklore of the Isle of Man*, London, 1975.
Kinsella, Thomas, *The Tain*, London, 1969.
Lambrechts, Pierre, *Contributions à l'Etudes des Divinites Celtiques,* Bruges, 1942.
Lambrechts, Pierre, *L'Exaltation de la Tête dans Pensée et dans l'Art des Celtes,* Bruges, 1954.
Lambrechts, Pierre, *Note sur le Passage de Gregoire de Tours relatif à la Religion Gauloise,* Latomus, 1954.
Lambrechts, Pierre, *Note sur une statuette en bronze de Mercure,* L'Antiquite Classique X, 1941. Brussels, 1946.
L'Amy, John, *Jersey Folklore,* Jersey, 1927.
Lempriere, Raoul, *Customs, Ceremonies and Traditions of the Channel Islands,* London, 1976.
Lewis, I M, *Ecstatic Religion,* Harmondsworth, 1975.
Macculloch, J A, *The Religion of the Ancient Celts,* Edinburgh, 1911.
MacNeill, Maire, *The Festival of Lughnasa,* Oxford, 1962.
Markale, Jean, *Les Celtes,* Paris, 1969.
Markale, Jean, *Le Roi Arthur*, Paris, 1976.
Markale, Jean, *Women of the Celts,* Gordon & Cremonesi, London, 1975.
Marwick, Ernest W, *The Folklore of the Orkney and Shetland Islands,* London, 1975.

Matthews, William, *The Ill-Framed Knight*, Berkeley and Los Angeles, 1966.

Maudite, J A, *L'Epopée des Celtes,* Paris, 1973.

Neumann, Erich, *The Great Mother,* London, 1955.

O'Rahilly, T F, *Early Irish History and Mythology*, Dublin, 1946.

Paine, Lauran, *Witchcraft and the Mysteries*, New York and London, 1975.

Piggott, Stuart, *The Druids,* London, 1965.

Piggott, Stuart, *The Sources of Geoffrey of Monmouth,* Antiquity, XV; 269–86; 305–19, 1941.

Powell, T G E, *The Celts,* London, 1958.

Rasmussen, K, *The Intellectual Culture of the Igluk Eskimos,* Copenhagen, 1929.

Rees, Alwyn and Brinley, *Celtic Heritage*, London, 1961.

Rhys, John, *Lectures on the Origin and Growth of Religion as Illustrated by Celtic Heathendom*, Hibbert Lectures, 1888.

Ross, Professor Anne, *Folklore of the Scottish Highlands,* London, 1976.

Ross, Professor Anne, *Pagan Celtic Britain,* London, 1974.

Sen, K M, *Hinduism*, Harmondsworth, 1975.

Shirokogoroff, S M, *Psychological Complex of the Tungus,* London, 1935.

Sjoestedt, M L, *Dieux et Heros de Celtes*, trs M Dillon, Paris, 1940.

Sjoestedt, M L, *Le Siege de Druim Damghaire,* Revue Celtique, XLIII, 1–123, 1926.

Soustelle, Jacques, *The Daily Life of the Aztecs*, Paris, 1955; London, 1961.

Stenning, E H, *A Portrait of the Isle of Man,* London, 1958.

Stokes, W, *Adventure of St Columba's Clerics*, Revue Celtique, XXVI; 130–92, 1905.

Stokes, W, *The Battle of Allen,* Revue Celtique, XXIV, 41–70, 1903.

Stokes, W, *The Battle of Mag Mucrime*, Revue Celtique, XIII, 426–74, 1892.

Stokes, W, *The Birth and Life of St Moling*, Revue Celtique, XXVII, 1906.

Stokes, W, *The Bodeleian Amra Cholimb Chille,* Revue Celtique, XX, 30, 132, 1248, 400, 1899.

Stokes, W, *Bruiden Da Chola* (Da Chola's Hostel), Revue Celtique, XXI, 149–65, 312–27, 388–402. 1900.

Stokes, W, *Coir Annan Irische Texte*, Leipzig, 1897.

Stokes, W, *The Destruction of Da Derga's Hostel,* Revue Celtique, XXII, 9, 165, 282, 390, 1901.

Stokes, W, *Find and the Phantoms,* Revue Celtique, VII, 389–307, 1886.

Stokes, W (and Windisch, E ed.), *The Irish Ordeals*, Irische Texte, Leipzig, 1891.

Stokes, W, *Life of St Fechin of Fore,* Revue Celtique, XII, 318–53, 1891.

Stokes, W, *Lives of the Saints from the Book of Lismore,* Oxford, 1890.

Stokes, W, *Prose Tales in the Rennes Dindshenchas*, Revue Celtique, XV, 272–336, 418–84. 1894.

Stokes, W, *The Rennes Dindshenchas,* Revue Celtique, XVI, 31–83, 1895.
Stokes, W, *Sanas Cormaic,* Calcutta, 1868.
Stokes, W, *The Second Battle of Moytura*, Revue Celtique XII, 52–130, 1891.
Stokes, W, *The Siege of Howth*, Revue Celtique, VIII, 47–64, 1887.
Stokes, W, *The Violent Deaths of Goll and Garb*, Revue Celtique, XIV, 396–449, 1893.
Stokes, W, *The Voyage of Hui Iorra*, Revue Celtique, 22–69, 1893.
Stokes, W, *The Voyage of Mael Phin,* Revue Celtique, IX, 447–95, 1888.
Stokes, W, *The Voyage of Snedgus and MacRiagla,* Revue Celtique, IX, 14–25, 1888.
Turville-Petre, E O G, *Myth and Religion of the North,* London, 1964.
Vendryes, J, *La Religion des Celtes,* Paris, 1948.
Vries, J de, *La Religion des Celtes,* Paris, 1963.
Weber, Max, *The Religion of India,* London, 1958.
Wright, R P, *The Whitley Castle Altar to Apollo,* Journal of the Royal Society, XXXIII, 36–8, 1943.

Index